TABUU BREAKERS

18 Independent Films That Courted Controversy and Created a Legend

TABOO BREAKERS

**18 Independent Films That
Courted Controversy and Created a Legend**

CALUM WADDELL

First published in England in 2008 by
Telos Publishing Ltd
61 Elgar Avenue, Tolworth, Surrey, KT5 9JP, England
www.telos.co.uk

Telos Publishing Ltd values feedback. Please e-mail us with any comments you may have about this book to: feedback@telos.co.uk

ISBN: 978-1-84583-030-4 (paperback)

Taboo Breakers: 18 Independent Films That Courted Controversy And Created A Legend © 2008 Calum Waddell
Introduction © 2008 Tim Sullivan

The moral right of the author has been asserted.

Typesetting, layout and cover design by ATB Publishing and Arnold T Blumberg
www.atbpublishing.com

Printed by Biddles Ltd

1 2 3 4 5 6 7 8 9 10 11 12 13 14 15

British Library Cataloguing in Publication Data.
A catalogue record for this book is available from the British Library.

This book is sold subject to the condition that it shall not by way of trade or otherwise, be lent, resold, hired out or otherwise circulated without the publisher's prior written consent in any form of binding or cover other than that in which it is published and without a similar condition including this condition being imposed on the subsequent purchaser.

CONTENTS

Lifting the Lid: Foreword by Tim Sullivan 6
Introduction 8
Chapter 1: *Blood Feast* 10
Chapter 2: *Night of the Living Dead* 25
Chapter 3: *Behind the Green Door* 41
Chapter 4: *Fritz the Cat* 54
Chapter 5: *The Tenderness of Wolves* 67
Chapter 6: *Coffy* 78
Chapter 7: *The Texas Chain Saw Massacre* 89
Chapter 8: *Candy Tangerine Man* 107
Chapter 9: *Ilsa, She Wolf of the SS* 119
Chapter 10: *Halloween* 144
Chapter 11: *Cannibal Holocaust* 157
Chapter 12: *Maniac* 178
Chapter 13: *Nightmares in a Damaged Brain* 193
Chapter 14: *The Plague Dogs* 205
Chapter 15: *The Evil Dead* 216
Chapter 16: *House of 1000 Corpses* 231
Chapter 17: *Oldboy* 243
Chapter 18: *Hostel* 252
About the Author 267
Without Whom 268
Bibliography 269
Cast/Crew Index 271
Title Index 280

LIFTING the LID

Once upon a time not so long ago, in a world without internet, without High Def, without DVD, should one wish to open Pandora's Box, the task involved a great deal more than just switching a channel or clicking a mouse across a computer screen. It involved getting down and dirty, being sneaky and stealthy, journeying great distances for brief, yet eternal, rewards.

Being a genre fan coming of age in the late '70s and early '80s was a full time occupation. Horror films were, for the most part, on the same societal shelf as pornography. One could not sit comfortably in the same theatre where *Jaws* unspooled and later watch *Night Of The Living Dead*. Chances are, should one wish to go *Behind The Green Door*, one had to do so incognito, in one town over, with fake ID in tow. Or one needed an older brother, an older friend, a mentor of mayhem, someone already initiated who could sneak you on a train from New Jersey to New York, convincing mom and pop you were off to some museum, when instead you were off to 42nd Street and a tour of duty of its notorious grindhouse cinemas; celluloid shrines where one would gladly step over sleeping homeless, ignoring the stench of urine, just to catch a wondrous glimpse of unlikely bedfellows such as *Coffy* and Leatherface. The age of 17 meant a driver's license and maybe a car, but definitely a road map to the drive-in, where dusk to dawn shows allowed you to catch up on your history lessons with double bills of the past and the future. Yes, drive-ins; the holy ground where H G Lewis met Sam Raimi. Where *Blood Feast* met *The Evil Dead*.

Those days are gone, replaced by a cold and sanitised accessibility. Convenient, yes, but with the blessing of ubiquitous availability comes the curse of taking things for granted. In a world of cloned Big Macs, can one thing truly taste different from another? But back then, folks, they did. I know that Mr Roth will tell you that without Bill Lustig's *Maniac* there could never have been *Hostel*. And Mr Zombie will surely confess to the following equation: No *Nightmares In A Damaged Brain* equals no *House Of 1000 Corpses*. Could there be a *Snoop Dogg's Hood Of Horror* without the *Candy Tangerine Man*? Hell, no. *2001 Maniacs* without *Two Thousand Maniacs*? The answer is obvious.

And yet, how often are the legends of today not remembered as the fresh, wet, nascent pioneers of their times? Those which may seem passé were once, in fact, considered shocking and revolutionary. Some still maintain their effect. Some do not. But no matter what time and comparison have done to reduce or strengthen the impact of those independent films that dared go beyond Hollywood norms, pushing the envelope that inevitably broke the box office, these films remain the first to lift the lid and unleash the demons that enthralled, inspired, exploited and fed generations of filmgoers, fans and filmmakers alike.

The book you now hold in your hands is both a passport to the past and a glimpse into the future. Your older brother and guide is Mr Calum Waddell, a man who knows the joys of dark culture. Who knows the value of what came before. So relax. Rewind. Remember. If you were there, you know of what I speak. If not, Calum is here to educate. Take his hand without hesitation and together confront the groundbreaking and everlasting taboos of sweet Pandora.

Spread the Red, Tim Sullivan

Tim Sullivan is the writer/director of Driftwood (2006), 2001 Maniacs (2005) and its sequel 2001 Maniacs: Beverly Hellbillys (2008). He also wrote/produced Snoop Dogg's Hood of Horror (2006) and worked, early in his career, on the cult classic The Deadly Spawn (1983). His next movie will be Brothers of the Blood, a haunting vampire romance starring Thomas Dekker (The Sarah Connor Chronicles). In 2007 Avatar Press printed an acclaimed 2001 Maniacs comic book.

INTRODUCTION

I guess the easiest way to introduce *Taboo Breakers* is to explain why I decided to write it in the first place. The reason is actually quite simple: it was to fill a niche. Sure, there are lots of books out there specialising in strange cult movies and I should know because I own most of them. However, what is lacking from so many of these tomes is insight from the people who were there. It is all fine and well to read an author's opinion in regards to why *Night of the Living Dead* is a milestone or why *Blood Feast* caused such a stink, but wouldn't it be nice to hear from the people who created such notorious movies? In writing *Taboo Breakers* I have interviewed many great personalities and I thank them all for their time, it was a pleasure speaking to each one and revisiting these motion picture milestones in the sort of detail that I always hoped for. Of course, some of the people interviewed in this book gave me more time than others and, as a result, I do not apologise for the length and/or shortness of any of the chinwags detailed herein. Instead, what really matters is that a number of new gems are dug up, fresh information is revealed and 18 cult classics are given, what I hope is, a pretty in depth overview.

The reason for choosing '18' films really boils down to the fact that, living in the UK, you had to be of adult age before any film featuring sex, violence or excessively rude language became available to you. I guess I was lucky in that, as a child, I lived in a household that entertained my love of cinema and permitted me to watch everything from *The Godfather* and *One Flew Over the Cuckoo's Nest* to *Death Wish* and *Re-Animator*, all of which yours truly had digested before even sprouting a single pubic hair. However, when I was growing up (after the video nasty fiasco) many of the titles explored in this publication were unavailable to me. This was frustrating to an 11 year old child because, even at that early age, I was eager to see as many different films as possible and to become a fountain of knowledge on the topic of cinema in general. Yet I never knew if I would ever see *Nightmares in a Damaged Brain* or *The Texas Chain Saw Massacre* (both had been banned) and I had no idea if *Coffy* would ever become available again (it had been deleted). I even recall learning that the first film to win all four major Oscars was *It Happened One Night* and wondering if a video release might eventually arrive on the shelves of my local independently owned, pre-Blockbuster rental shop. Looking back, I probably wasted most of my teens as a budding cinéaste when, in reality, I should have tried a lot harder to de-pant the opposite sex. As the late, great Frank Sinatra once sang: 'Regrets? I have a few...'

DVD has solved most of the problems inherent in being a fan of 'alternative' cinema (or even golden age classics) although readers of this book can rest assured that *Candy Tangerine Man* remains tantalizingly 'lost', a complete print of *Nightmares in a Damaged Brain* has yet to surface and, 35 years on from their original release dates, *Behind the Green Door* and *The Tenderness of Wolves* have still to obtain a UK debut. Therefore, if this book is to do anything then hopefully it will alert some attention to some films that, during different times, stood out from the pack

INTRODUCTION

and, in certain instances, left an important mark on cinema in general. Sure, you might not be familiar with *Candy Tangerine Man* but maybe that chapter, combined with *Coffy*, will lead you on a wild discovery of the heyday of blaxploitation. Likewise, perhaps you picked up this book to read about *Hostel* or *Halloween*, but I will feel as if I have done my own little bit for the world of bizarre movies if you later decide to check out *Fritz the Cat* or *Oldboy*. Moreover, in each chapter are the names of numerous other essential taboo breaking pictures, and if you're any sort of buff at all you should make it your dying quest to track down and watch them all.

I guess I should also answer why there is a big gap between 1982's *The Evil Dead* and *The Plague Dogs* and 2003's *House of 1000 Corpses*, although the reason for this is quite straightforward. Basically the majors began to extend a grip that resulted in very few controversial, and genuinely innovative, independent pictures being released as the 1980s came to a close (1984's *Silent Night, Deadly Night* and 1990's *Leatherface: The Texas Chainsaw Massacre 3* are two rare examples of indie-shock that can hold claim to censorship problems and headlines – but it is debatable that either really broke new taboos). The other answer is that no one gave me John Woo's phone number to discuss *Hard Boiled* or *The Killer*, although the influence of Hong Kong's 'heroic bloodshed' genre is addressed in Chapter 17.

Certainly, it is a testament to the guile and vision of Hollywood independent Lion's Gate that pictures such as *House of 1000 Corpses* and *Hostel* have grabbed the attention of the general public and cemented themselves into pop culture as a whole. Although the taboos broken in these two movies are entirely reliant on the films that came before them (*Last House on the Left, The Texas Chain Saw Massacre, The Evil Dead* and so on) it is no doubt a good thing to have this book come full circle and end by paying tribute to the youthful new shockers that have adopted the *modus operandi* of their forefathers in fear. As to me, well, I've come too far to give up now and I'm extremely proud of what you are currently holding in your hands.

In closing: thank you for trusting me, and my judgment, and picking up this little labour of love …

Calum Waddell
March 2008

BLOOD FEAST

Released: 1963
Directed by: Herschell Gordon Lewis
Produced by: David Friedman
Written by: Allison Louise Downe (with uncredited input from Lewis and Friedman)
Cast: Thomas Wood (Detective Pete Thornton), Mal Arnold (Fuad Ramses), Connie Mason (Suzette Fremont), Lyn Bolton (Mrs Dorothy Freemont), Scott H Hall (Police Captain Frank), Toni Calvert (Trudy – kidnapped girl), Ashlyn Martin (Marcy – girl attacked on beach), Astrid Olson (Tongue-pull victim), Sandra Sinclair (Pat Tracey), Gene Courtier (Tony, Marcy's boyfriend), Louise Kamp (Janet Blake), Hal Rich (Hospital Doctor)

In a nutshell: The eccentric caterer Fuad Ramses is organizing an ancient Egyptian 'blood feast' in honour of the goddess Ishtar. In order to supply Ishtar with the needed human body parts Ramses prowls his neighbourhood at night looking for attractive young women to kill. When a kind-hearted local woman comes by Ramses' shop seeking his catering assistance he convinces her to let him prepare a special, Egyptian-themed buffet for her daughter Suzette's birthday. She agrees, but, unbeknownst to her, the 'feast' needs human elements. Meanwhile, Ramses' murder spree continues and attracts the interest of a strait-laced detective, who also becomes close with Suzette, and the two attend a presentation about the history of the Egyptian 'blood feast' (allowing for an additional gore sequence). Finally, on Suzette's birthday, Ramses arrives at her house and readies her for a virgin sacrifice, but the police arrive just in time and his murderous meal is brought to a stop.

Prologue: Hammer's 1957 classic *The Curse of Frankenstein* was the first colour horror movie to create controversy over on-screen graphic content. Although the picture now seems ridiculously tame its close-ups of bloody wounds and dead cadavers caused a stink back in the late fifties. However, the movie that really inspired *Blood Feast* was presented in good old black and white and without any of the fantasy/period elements that made the Hammer movie so comparatively inauspicious. Indeed, in the early 1960s the horror movie was undergoing renewed popularity following the success of Alfred Hitchcock's masterpiece *Psycho* (1960), which introduced a hitherto unheralded level of violence to a mainstream audience. Whilst Michael Powell can take some credit for having earlier made an acclaimed serial killer horror film set in modern times, with a very real human protagonist, in his 1959 classic *Peeping Tom*, the feature simply did not have the impact or profile that *Psycho* did.

Nevertheless, because the acts of realistic brutality in *Psycho* were recorded in monochrome it was obviously only going to be a short matter of time before an aspiring low budget filmmaker added colour to the equation. This is, ultimately, how *Blood Feast* was born.

Prior to this notorious splatter picture Herschell Gordon Lewis had worked with producer David Friedman on nine low budget features including *The Prime Time* (1960), *The Adventures of Lucky Pierre* (1961), *Living Venus* (1961), *Daughter of the Sun* (1962) and *Nature's Playmates* (1962). Before *Blood Feast* began filming the enterprising twosome had experienced a busy 1963 and turned out several delirious exploitation movies in the space of the year: *Bell, Bare and Beautiful*, *Boin-n-g*, *Goldilocks and the Three Bares* and *Scum of the Earth*. The latter title is credited as an early 'roughie' and marks the first time the director and producer attempted to 'exploit' violence rather than teased-at nudity or sex. Nevertheless, *Scum of the Earth* was not the big success that Lewis and Friedman had hoped for.

However, with the bottom dropping out of the market for softcore nudie-cuties, and looking to offer audiences something truly original, the pair had a brainstorming session over the sort of product that the major studios simply would not touch. In 1963 the depiction of hardcore sex could result in criminal prosecution so that was out, and thus Lewis is credited, by Friedman, as coming up with the idea for 'gore'[1]. *Blood Feast* also introduced *Playboy* pin-up Connie Mason to horror film audiences. Hugh Hefner's magazine was nearly ten years old in 1963 and although Mason was not the first centrefold to make a name for herself in B-cinema (Yvette Vickers and Mara Corday had both preceded her) few are as well remembered.

About: '*Blood Feast* is like a Walt Whitman poem. It is no good, but it's the first of its type, and therefore it deserves a certain position.' Herschell Gordon Lewis[2]

Whilst *Blood Feast*, famous for being the very first gore movie, carries considerable historical significance, the end product, as even its own director indicates with the above quote, is a complete stinker. Indeed, make no mistake about it, *Blood Feast* is a tedious, badly made, repetitive little offering with horrible acting, dreadful special effects, static camerawork and a flimsy storyline. Yet, even in spite of such glaring faults, the feature remains a genuinely messy viewing experience, with its sequences of animal innards being pulled from blood red

---

1 According to David Friedman in his book *A Youth in Babylon* (Prometheus Books, 1990)

2 Lewis is first quoted with this line in *The Amazing Herschell Gordon Lewis* (Krogh and McCarty, Fantaco, 1983)

body wounds still holding up as examples of a particularly nasty form of on-screen *Grand Guignol*. More than that, of course, these over the top sequences of gruesome excess created an entirely new screen genre, something that would eventually be known as the 'splatter movie'[3]. Unwittingly, *Blood Feast* is the movie that paves the way for *Night of the Living Dead*, even if its actual influence on a filmmaker such as George Romero is minimal at best[4].

Blood Feast's most obvious legacy comes from *Psycho*, and not just in terms of that film's remarkably powerful shower murder. Stripping the genre of any supernatural elements and setting its story slap, bang in the middle of contemporary America, Hitchcock's feature was an obvious influence on Lewis and Friedman. When, in 1963, the twosome opted to mix the full colour set pieces of *The Curse of Frankenstein* with the contemporary surroundings of *Psycho*, it was the shadow of Norman Bates that fell over the production. For instance, *Blood Feast* begins with an attractive blonde woman undressing to her white undergarments before finally stripping nude and taking a bath (this being 1963 anything salacious is covered by carefully placed bits of foam). Without even a solitary credit on screen, we are led to believe, for just a few brief seconds, that this young lady might actually be our heroine. However, as with the ill-fated Janet Leigh in *Psycho*, it isn't long before a ghoulish figure enters the frame and proceeds to murder her with a butcher's knife. The grisly attack culminates with her hand slowly sliding down the side of the bathtub, creating a line of blood in its wake. With that, the splatter movie is born.

This opening can be seen as *Blood Feast*'s answer to Hitchcock's shower sequence; only, without the old master's filmmaking expertise, Lewis simply plays a game of one-upmanship. Whilst Janet Leigh dies in monochrome, her arm grabbing the shower curtain as she falls to her death and a river of blood flushing down the plughole, Lewis actually depicts limbs being hacked off and his killer's knife covered with unidentifiable pieces of body tissue. Any build-up of suspense or any attempt to flesh out the character of the unfortunate actress is completely ignored in favour of closing-in on a gouged out eyeball and an amputated leg.

Later in the picture, when *Blood Feast* has one of its young, blonde actresses check into a motel room, it is almost as if Lewis and Friedman are saying, 'Oh sure, you know that a motel room spelt doom for Janet Leigh but just wait until you see what we have in store…' Fittingly, the film's maniac proceeds to barge open the door, force his way on top of the actress and, after a lengthy struggle, yanks her tongue clean out from her throat. Even by today's grisly standards, this is a really stomach churning moment, with the actress 'selling' the special effect by subsequently rolling her head to the side and letting a cupful of blood syrup ooze slowly from her mouth. In fact, it is actually this example of post-death nastiness, rather than the phoney depiction of a (sheep's) tongue pulled from the lady's screaming features, that gives the scene its genuine upchuck factor. Put simply, no movie previous to *Blood Feast* had come close to the sort of explicit on-screen violence that Lewis was suddenly

---

3 Critic John McCarty is credited with inventing the term 'splatter movie' in his book *Splatter Movies: Breaking the Last Taboo of the Screen* (St Martin's Press, 1984).

4 'As a production, the film fits into the anti-Hollywood tradition of independent gore established by Herschell Gordon Lewis's *Blood Feast*' writes Kim Newman of *Night of the Living Dead* in *Nightmare Movies* (Bloomsbury, 1988)

depicting[5].

Whilst *Psycho* may have invited some criticism of misogyny (naked girl, shots of her showering, eventual death), with *Blood Feast* there can be absolutely no mistaking the vile treatment of beautiful young women, who are introduced on-screen merely so that they can be horrifically slaughtered[6]. Certainly, each of the film's deaths belongs to a female (only one male is even brutalised, although he survives) and two of them are killed after stripping out of their clothes. In another scene, a young woman is tied, barebacked, to a wall and whipped until her spine is covered in blood, a sequence that was still removed from the film's British release as recently as 2001[7]. Indeed, the movie's poster revels in this sort of barbarity ('You'll recoil and shudder as you witness the slaughter and mutilation of nubile young girls in a weird and horrendous ancient rite', screams the original tagline). As politically incorrect nowadays as the racial stereotypes seen in *Gone with the Wind* (1939) it is, however, doubtful that Lewis was attempting to create any sort of thoughtful link between sex and violence. Rather, it seems more than likely that this mixture of breasts and blood came together in *Blood Feast* purely out of commercial interest[8]. Call it cynical (even reprehensible) if you want, but considering that the Lewis-Friedman partnership had previously engaged in nine movies that were largely sold on the promise of exposed female flesh, it is hardly surprising that *Blood Feast* should have its female victims undress before the gory 'money shot'. Perversely, however, this curiously innocent misogyny would be adapted into far more mean-spirited low budget movies such as *Bloodsucking Freaks* (1976, also known as *The Incredible Torture Show*) and *The Last House on Dead End Street* (1977) where the violence would be more sexual and the overriding tone umpteen times more sleazy than Lewis could ever hope to achieve.

Likewise, it was perhaps because *Blood Feast* was aimed at the male market (hence its 'nubile young girls' marketing blurb) that Friedman and Lewis would cast Connie Mason, a *Playboy* Playmate, in the movie's leading role. Although the cast of *Blood Feast* comes from the Ed Wood school of screen acting, there can be no denying that the picture's camp theatrics would be far less appealing if the performances were on a par with Elizabeth Taylor. In Connie Mason, Friedman and Lewis had something approaching a recognizable name back in 1963. In the early sixties, *Playboy* magazine had been going for nearly a decade and had yet to become an institution, and this was long before the publication would disintegrate under a bevy of silicone-enhanced models. A popular read among men, and then approaching the peak of its popularity,

---

5 British horror movie critic John Martin claims that Mario Bava, with his 1960 shocker *Mask of Satan* (aka *Black Sunday*), was 'the guy who kicked off the whole gore ball-game' (*Spaghetti Nightmares*, Fantasma Books, 1996). This is, of course, simply not true. Filmed in black and white, *Mask of Satan* is a gothic horror effort with little in the way of explicit bloodshed, and contains nothing even remotely comparable to *Blood Feast*. Indeed, compared to the shower sequence that highlights the same year's *Psycho*, Bava's masterwork appears positively restrained.

6 As the film critic Jonathan Ross once mentioned, 'I'm sure all the arguments about the tendency towards violence against women as entertainment not only apply to Lewis's films, but pretty much originated with them.' (Ross, *The Incredibly Strange Film Book*, Simon & Schuster, 1993)

7 *Blood Feast* was finally released uncut on DVD in Britain in 2005.

8 In his book *Profoundly Disturbing* (Plexus Publishing, 2003), critic Joe Bob Briggs notes that *Blood Feast*'s audience was comprised of 'almost entirely male clientele'.

it is entirely possible that the same male clientele that previously flocked to nudie-cuties such as Russ Meyer's *The Immoral Mr Teas* (1959) and the Lewis-Friedman softcore spin-off *The Adventures of Lucky Pierre* (1961), were also buying Hugh Hefner's publication. Although Mason subsequently became *Playboy*'s Playmate of the Year in 1964, it is still her two films with Lewis and Friedman, *Blood Feast* and 1964's *Two Thousand Maniacs*, that she is most famous for. Whilst Mason's acting in *Blood Feast* is not especially convincing, the camera does love her natural good looks, and although Lewis never enjoyed working with her[9], the actress adds a sexy, blue-eyed innocence to her character. Appearing alongside Mason is Lewis veteran Thomas Wood (a pseudonym for William Kerwin) and Mal Arnold (who hams it up as the film's slasher) and it has to be said that the actress is in the good company of other bad actors. In fact, it is not too much of a shock to find out that the performers would sometimes end up breaking into laughter when trying to act out sections of *Blood Feast*'s ludicrous plot[10]. However, it is perhaps because of the bad acting and dialogue – and stilted photography – that the movie is still such a celebrated cult item. In other words: the film's very faults perversely succeed in bolstering its charm.

In all, *Blood Feast* features four gore sequences. Alongside the two already described we are also 'treated' to a female having her brains bashed in after her boyfriend is knocked unconscious and another young woman being sacrificed in a flashback scene. In this grisly set piece, the most gratuitous in the entire picture (which is really saying something), the victim has her heart pulled out of her body. As with every special effect in *Blood Feast*, the gore is shown after-the-fact, mainly because this low budget production was without the complex squibs and carefully designed foam rubber body parts that future screen wizards such as Rob Bottin and Tom Savini would perfect. Nevertheless, the sight of a body without a leg attached or of a big gaping wound in a girl's chest, whilst her assailant holds a blood covered heart above her, carries a certain crude realism all of its own.

The big problem with *Blood Feast* is that, outside of these money-drawing moments of oozing gore, the movie has nowhere to go and offers the viewer little in the way of entertainment. For instance, in one sequence Mason and her young friends clown around in an indoor pool for a few moments in what is clearly just some 'filler', and whilst this sort of cheesecake may have thrilled male viewers in the early sixties, today it is just boring beyond belief. There are also times when the movie is attempting to be deliberately funny and, yet, doesn't hit the mark. 'Have you ever had an Egyptian feast?' asks *Blood Feast*'s wide-eyed maniac Fuad Ramses to a potential client whilst the soundtrack lets out a comical ringing sound, almost as if the viewer should be providing their own laugh track. Too obvious and overstated to be funny, 'humorous' moments such as this have not aged particularly well … although back when the feature first

---

9 'Herschell and I had only three really serious arguments in our long business association and friendship. One of them was about Connie Mason,' states David Friedman in his book *A Youth in Babylon* (Prometheus Books, 1990). Lewis, meanwhile, was still holding a grudge as late as 1987 when he stated, 'Connie Mason and I are probably well off assuming that we'll never see each other again.' (Pina, *Bloody Best of Fangoria*, Vol 7, 1987)

10 'We had a hard time concealing the laughter,' reveals Mal Arnold in an interview with author Christopher Wayne Curry (*A Taste of Blood*, Headpress, 1998).

came out they may well have given a horrified audience the sort of breathing space that they needed amongst the graphic mayhem.

Indeed, with the films that *Blood Feast* would ultimately inspire, if not directly influence, one also finds many of the same problems, namely that outside of the token splatter gags the 'story' consists of little more than introducing as many secondary characters (re: victims) as possible. Consequently, watching something such as the *Friday the 13th* series, one can see *Blood Feast* replicated on a bigger budget and under the tutelage of filmmakers with more technical skill. Nonetheless, just like *Blood Feast*, the 'storylines' to these movies almost always feature numerous attractive teenagers being brought onto the screen simply so that, a few minutes later, they can be chopped to bits by a silent serial killer. As a result, the more gruesome the demise the more memorable each *Friday the 13th* entry ultimately becomes (for instance, 1989's part eight – amusingly titled *Jason Takes Manhattan,* is probably most famous for being 'the one where the guy gets his head punched clean off'). Thus, just as Lewis would ultimately attempt to outdo himself with each subsequent feature that he would direct (culminating in such lousy blood baths as 1970's *The Wizard of Gore* and 1972's *The Gore Gore Girls*) so too would the slasher genre that he inadvertently helped to create become lost in an ever-decreasing circle of spilled blood.

As with pornography, the whole mentality behind the gore movie quickly amounted to little more than offering audiences something even more shocking than the last big hit. Thus, if *Friday the 13th* outdid *Halloween* in terms of gruesome violence, then subsequent shockers such as *The Burning* and *The Prowler* (both 1981) would go *even further*, and storyline, performances, dialogue or even suspense quickly seem disposable. By the time the horror genre recaptured some mainstream respectability with 1991's Oscar winner *The Silence of the Lambs*, filmmakers had clearly become tired of offering up a bevy of non-stop gruesome special effects. All the same, the fact that the grisly amateur splatter of *Blood Feast* prevailed through the work of John Waters, Andy Milligan and Ted V Mikels in the 1960s and '70s through to the more mainstream likes of *Friday the 13th* and *The Evil Dead* in the 1980s and even to 21st Century fare like the *Saw* movies, speaks volumes about the influence that Lewis has had.

That said, although *Blood Feast* was a success in drive-in and grindhouse cinemas throughout the USA[11], Lewis never really penetrated the mainstream. His films still aren't included for review in Leonard Maltin or Halliwell's annual *Movie & Video Guide*, and outside of their own, admittedly sizeable, cult following they have never the gained major recognition that they perhaps deserve. Thus, it seems doubtful that the crude bloodletting, bad photography and hokey dialogue of something such as *Blood Feast* really had much of an influence on the gritty social commentary of George Romero, the exploding squibs of Sam Peckinpah's violent westerns or the widescreen craftsmanship of John Carpenter. Nevertheless, whenever anyone

---

11 According to Joe Bob Briggs, *Blood Feast* returned $7 million on its lowly budget of $24,000. 'That's a terrific return,' says Briggs, 'but it's no blockbuster, even by the standards of the sixties. Unlike most cult movies you're not likely to find many film buffs who saw it during its first release. It wasn't that kind of movie. In cities, *Blood Feast* played grindhouses ... In less populous areas, it played drive-ins, often as a late second or third feature ...' (*Profoundly Disturbing*, Plexus Publishing, 2003)

working on a low budget, even today, opts to exploit a moment of graphic, unflinching spilt innards, Lewis can genuinely claim to have been there first. Whilst the relationship between something such as *Halloween* and *Blood Feast* is indeed a slim one from an aesthetic point of view, what is certain is that when John Carpenter looked to make a scary movie back in 1978, and knew that he had only a tiny amount of money to do so, his head was in the same place as Lewis and Friedman fifteen years before.

In this sense, *Blood Feast* is a triumph of low budget entrepreneurism, and the only question the film really begs is this: 'Why did it take so long for someone to cash in on something so obvious?'

What happened next?

The Lewis-Friedman relationship continued through two further pictures, 1964's *Two Thousand Maniacs* (also starring Connie Mason and William Kerwin and easily the best of the Godfather of Gore's *oeuvre*) and 1965's awful, and surprisingly restrained, *Color Me Blood Red*. After going their separate ways Lewis, as a journeyman filmmaker, churned out a variety of pictures including two children's films (1966's *Jimmy the Boy Wonder* and 1967's *The Magic of Mother Goose*). However, whenever a producer was brave enough to let Lewis loose with his money, the instigator of the splatter movie would make increasingly vicious little pictures, culminating in the horrific *Wizard of Gore* (1970 – which was remade in 2007) and the brutal stripper-slicing movie *The Gore Gore Girls* (1971).

Friedman's most famous post-*Blood Feast* horror production is probably 1967's *She Freak*. Although it is little more than a tedious, no-thrills remake of Tod Browning's classic *Freaks* (1932), *She Freak* is reportedly due for a remake from Tim Sullivan, who also remade *Two Thousand Maniacs* as *2001 Maniacs* in 2005. Friedman's most notorious credit is undoubtedly 1975's gruelling *Ilsa, She Wolf of the SS* (more on which can be found elsewhere in this book), although he continued to work in the area of mild erotica with flicks such as 1972's *The Erotic Adventures of Zorro*.

Friedman and Lewis reunited for 2002's ultra-low budget *Blood Feast 2: All U Can Eat*, which went straight-to-DVD in North America. It is no wonder either because, although it has some amusing moments of comedy and a cameo from John Waters, the movie is very heavy-handed, overly laboured and soon wears out its welcome.

The 'splatter movie', of course, in the wake of such big screen hits as the remake of *Dawn of the Dead* (2004), *The Devil's Rejects* (2005) and *Hostel* (2006) is alive and well. For direct descendants of the Lewis school of low budget, splatter movie filmmaking check out the aforementioned *Bloodsucking Freaks* (1976) as well as *The Undertaker and his Pals* (1966), *Multiple Maniacs* (1970), *Invasion of the Blood Farmers*, *The Corpse Grinders* (both 1972), *Blood Bath* (1976), *The Evil Dead* and *Basket Case* (both 1982).

Connie Mason interview

Connie Mason is one of a number of *Playboy* Playmates that went from the centre pages of the magazine onto the big screen. However, whereas the likes of Stella Stevens, Erika Eleniak and Pamela Anderson managed to obtain some degree of mainstream recognition, Mason's screen roles were altogether trashier. Nevertheless, that is perhaps part of the reason why she still demands a considerable cult following to this day. When asked to look back on her leading lady turns in *Blood Feast* and *Two Thousand Maniacs* the centrefold-turned actress is instantly enthusiastic. 'It was kind of a quirky, happy streak of luck because being in these two movies really led the way for me in a lot of ways in regards to my future career. I was living in Miami and I had done the centrefold for *Playboy* but it hadn't come out yet – it was going to come out in three months. So this fellow I knew, just a local fellow, he said that he was going to an audition and asked me to come with him. So I said okay – and I had never been to an audition or anything at that point – in fact I was working in the Miami *Playboy* Club as a Bunny and at that time the *Playboy* clubs had been the biggest things happening for several years. I was making $300 a night, which was a lot of money back then, and I was taken to this interview and David Friedman liked me so much that he decided to use me as the female lead in *Blood Feast*. Now I didn't know anything at that point – I mean part of it was that he knew the *Playboy* centrefold was coming out in three months so he knew that he could use that for publicity. So they did that and it turned out to be a great thing – and it was great to be a part of their films although it wasn't until the past few years that these have become such hot, cult movies.'

When Mason set foot on the set of *Blood Feast* she had never acted in her life. 'I had no performing background,' she laughs. 'I only fell in love with acting when I did *Blood Feast*. I remember the last scene when the guy comes to kill me. I knew they were all breaking for lunch and I knew that I was going to have to get some real feeling for what it would be like if somebody was trying to kill me. So I spent the hour really digging deep into my soul and my life experiences and trying to find out what would bring up my real feelings of fear and terror, you know? So anyway they came back from lunch to film that scene and it was that sequence that inspired me to take up acting – I thought it was wonderful to be in a business where you could use your real feelings.'

Mason also has good memories of *Blood Feast*'s famous producer/director duo. 'David Friedman was very, very adorable and warm and just as nice a person as you could meet, but Herschell was actually quite shy,' admits the actress. 'All I remember is seeing this man who wouldn't smile, and was always behind the camera! I was so delighted to see what a wonderful man he has turned out to be when I met him again some years ago. He was very friendly to me and very appreciative – very "wow, I never knew you would turn out like this," and he said, "if only I was a few years younger." (*laughs*). But then after these films he went into advertising and became very wealthy. Back then I would say that we were all just beginners.'

Of course, no discussion of *Blood Feast* can go by without focusing on the film's famously messy special effects – although this is something that Mason admits she never had the chance to witness. 'Whenever somebody was in a scene they would have their call sheet and I never went and witnessed what was going on,' maintains the actress. 'So I never saw all the blood and gore! However, it was certainly very well done – and two or three of the girls that were in that movie were friends of mine – one of them was on the beach and she got her head hacked if I remember. But I wasn't there to witness that – so I didn't have the reaction of "oh my God, what am I doing on this movie?" It was extremely realistic and they did do a good job with that.'

After filming wrapped on the movie, *Blood Feast* began to open around the United States – horrifying deviant moviegoers with the sort of on-screen violence that no one had ever seen before. 'I remember that I was in New York modelling and they opened it on 42nd Street,' recalls Mason. 'It opened in a lot of theatres and a lot of people were calling me. People out there were doing films and they wanted to see that so they could consider using me in their own projects. There were people that seemed to think that *Blood Feast* and *Two Thousand Maniacs* were very hot and special. I guess from my frame of work there was just a whole flurry of people being totally wowed and interested and wanting to attend screenings. Of course, they played at drive-ins too, which were very popular back then, but they were both really well received and got a lot of publicity and so I was really grateful to David because I think that he really pushed using me. I look back on both *Blood Feast* and *Two Thousand Maniacs* with the fondest of memories. I am really amazed that they have lasted, you know?'

Following her success in the world of low budget horror movies Mason left behind the sight of pulled-out tongues and bashed-in brains to return to modelling – although she didn't shun her thespian side entirely. 'I did do some films with Renée Taylor and Ray Bologna, they are very well known and they had written *Lovers and Other Strangers* on Broadway and *Made for Each Other*,' she confirms. 'But I was more emotionally prepared and stable by then – I could really focus on what I was doing by then. I was more prepared. However, I am still very happy when people still bring these old horror films up to me when I do a show. That is what made the cult following even more known to me – and just how much interest there was in these two movies. All these shows – Glamourcon, Chiller and *Fangoria* magazine – it is very startling and it always makes me smile. It makes me laugh and makes me feel happy to know that people remember or still think about them – think of them as fun or whatever their slant is on them, you know?'

David Friedman interview

For any fan of exploitation movies no introduction is needed for David Friedman – the initiator of the splatter picture and, arguably, the man who has broken more screen taboos than anybody in history. 'I guess I am one of the pioneers of exploitation films in the United States,' laughs Friedman proudly. 'I had a very good job with Paramount Pictures when I was starting out and as a matter of fact I was on my way to being promoted as the head of the exploitation department in New York. But the reason I left is because I had met Irwin Joseph and Kroger Babb and other people that had these birth of a baby pictures so I got involved for one reason – I saw an opportunity to make more money than I was making at Paramount and I had the chance to become a partner and part-owner of a company. So that is how I happened to get into exploitation movies and it just drifted from there on and as the climate became more liberal, so to speak, we went a bit further in each our films. The "birth of a baby" type of films had begun to wear a little thin because Russ Meyer had made a picture called *The Immoral Mr Teas* so there was a whole new market for nudie-cuties. With that there was also a whole new exhibition and distribution area and I immediately saw that this was going to be very profitable. Of course, this led to me meeting Herschell Gordon Lewis and making *Blood Feast* and I know more about Herschell than just about anybody (*laughs*). As it happens Herschell and I were partners for six very profitable and very pleasant years and we are still in constant touch. He lives in Florida and I live in Alabama and we still speak at least once a month and we meet about two or three times a year.'

The Lewis-Friedman partnership, of course, would go down in horror history thanks to *Blood Feast* and the twosome's later effort *Two Thousand Maniacs*. 'In all Herschell and I made about 13 films together before we went our separate ways,' continues Friedman. 'We both lived in Chicago at the time and most of the pictures were filmed in and around Miami – because it was an excuse to get out of the city in the winter (*laughs*). That is basically how we established the nudist colony and the nudie-cutie films and then one day we began to get a little tired. Not only were we making pictures for ourselves but we had become paid mercenaries and these exhibitors that had these cinemas were showing our X-rated or adult product and we thought we could make one of our own and get our money back right out of our own theatre. So it was a very nice chap in Chicago named Tom Dowd, one of my Irish drinking buddies, he commissioned us to make a couple for him and then one day Herschell and I were sitting around the office and thinking, "wow, this is getting to be a bore." So Herschell said, "well let's think of something that nobody else had done," and out of that conversation came a four lettered word – "gore!" Of course, the result was *Blood Feast*, which was the seminal slasher movie and the one thing for which both Herschell and I are the most… now I won't say famous, instead I will say infamous (*laughs*).'

After *Blood Feast* both Friedman and Lewis believed that they had found their niche in the highly competitive exploitation film industry – but their partnership did not last. 'After *Blood Feast* there was *Two Thousand Maniacs* and *Color Me Blood Red* but Herschell and I had a stupid argument during the filming of that last picture,' admits Friedman. 'That is when we went our separate ways. I went out to Hollywood and Herschell continued to make gore films and he very rightly got the title of The Godfather of Gore (*laughs*). So that was one phase and in Los Angeles I went back to making the roughies – the first one was called *The Defilers*, which some historians of this business say is the best roughie ever made. A roughie is a black and white film that combined both violence and sex, but the emphasis was always on the violence. Something like *The Defilers* did not get to play too many places in Europe because European censors are a little more intolerant of violence than to sex, as you might know, maybe very rightly – but violence has always been a part of American film right back to the Westerns. We could show those pictures back when we had state and local censorship, and you'd have very little problem – but if you showed a girl's breast … then oh no! I used to say it wasn't acceptable to show a girl's beautiful naked breasts but you could cut them off with a hacksaw (*laughs*).'

Indeed, *Blood Feast* prefigured an entire genre of gory horror pictures – whether inadvertently or otherwise. '*Blood Feast* established a whole different genre of film, it was the forerunner to *Friday the 13th*, *Halloween*, *The Texas Chain Saw Massacre*, Wes Craven, George Romero – they all followed suit a few years after *Blood Feast*,' states Friedman. 'But they all had one great advantage over Herschell and me – they had money! When we did *Blood Feast* it was over five days in Miami for $24,500 and that was shooting in 35mm, colour, and included the answer print and the trailer! All for $24,500! Now I sold out early in that thing, but from what I have been able to gather – and I'm not talking about grosses, the things you see in *Variety*, I'm talking about film rental receipts – that movie made back over $6 million. It is still selling on DVD today – it is a huge seller for a company called Something Weird Video. Of course, the young people nowadays find them very campy and they laugh at them – and that is fine because by today's standards they are hilarious because they are so bad! But there is still a market for them because you, as a producer or a director, cannot determine if something is going to be camp. It has to be discovered by an audience and that audience might not appear for five or ten years. Look at *The Rocky Horror Picture Show* – that is a perfect example of that. When that was first released it was just another picture and then it became a camp item and played midnight shows all over the country and gradually it turned into this sensational, money making phenomenon.'

One person that Friedman remembers fondly is Connie Mason – even though she and the director of *Blood Feast* did not get along quite so well. 'Herschell seriously didn't like her,' admits the producer. 'In fact, he just *hated* her … He only used Connie at my insistence. Now, all of these historians have said over the years that the only reason Connie Mason had a career was because of her relationship with Dave Friedman. Well as I said in my book, *A Youth in Babylon*, and as I will repeat again and again, of all of the willing and beautiful young wantons with whom I was associated with in the film business I can truly say that I have never had illicit, carnal relationships with one, and that one was Connie Mason (*laughs*). Now I had met Connie in a Playboy club and I said to her, "How would you like to do a movie?" and she said, "You're David Friedman aren't you? I wouldn't do those nudist camp pictures." I told her, "I'm not doing a nudist camp picture – it's a horror movie." She said, "Oh really?" and I said, "Oh really yes." Connie was working for *Playboy* at the time but she had been a model for Oleg Cassini and she was well known in the New York jet set club – she was a beautiful woman. I gave her a script, and I didn't even know if Connie could read (*laughs*)…'

Certainly, Friedman admits that his new find was unlikely to become the next Meryl Streep. 'Connie was never on time and she never knew her lines,' he laughs. 'Herschell's great remark was, "If the key in Connie's back ever ran down, she would just stand in place." In other words, he was saying that she was a wind up doll. But a funny thing happened – she became the Playmate of the Year in 1964, shortly after *Blood Feast* was released, and Hefner had to mention this. So, on the *Blood Feast* one-sheet, I had this picture of Connie and this caption – "You read about her in *Playboy*." So she was a very big plus because she was selling the picture. Now when we were going to start shooting *Two Thousand Maniacs* I said, "We have to use Connie again," and Herschell said, "You are insane!" I said, "I might be insane, but we need to use Connie." So we were down in this little town in Florida and Connie came out and this time, believe it or not, she had learned her lines. We were all staying in this little hotel in this little town, about thirty miles from Orlando, 100 miles from Tampa – and we were all prisoners, we couldn't go anywhere.'

Unlike with *Blood Feast*, however, Mason actually puts in a worthwhile performance in *Two Thousand Maniacs* – easily the best horror picture that Friedman and Lewis worked on. 'On *Two Thousand Maniacs* Connie wasn't all that bad,' admits Friedman. 'Now don't get me wrong, Connie couldn't act her way out a paper bag back then but at least she was on time and Herschell was more than pleased with her. But face it – none of the people in any of our pictures were John Gielgud or Laurence Olivier. We didn't hire girls because they could act like Barbara Stanwick, we hired them if they had great looking tits (*laughs*). But once in a while you'd come along one that could learn her lines and be convincing. If they had a good body and could remember their lines then we hired them – and Connie was good. So Herschell never particularly liked her … and that is the Connie Mason story. But I still like Connie and continue to speak to her quite often. She has aged very well, she is about 64 or 65 now and still has her long blonde hair – it is not as natural as it used to be – but she looks well …'

When *Blood Feast* originally opened, audiences were given a free sick bag, adding to the geek show theatrics of the picture. 'We had a meeting with my wife,' says Friedman. 'Now she was never very enthusiastic towards my films, she was a speech and drama teacher, but she came to a very early screening and there were only another couple of people there, including Herschell, and this was in Chicago. On the drive back home she was strangely silent and I asked her what she thought of it and she said one word: "Vomitious." So with that I went out the next day and ordered half a million vomit bags, the kind you see in airplanes, and I printed on them, "You may need this when you see *Blood Feast*." We handed these to people in theatres weeks before the picture even came out and we didn't just leave it up to the theatre employees – I had ambulances outside the theatres with stretchers and I hired a couple of pretty girls, put them in nurses uniforms … and when people came to see a show they saw the show before they even came in (*laughs*). But that was the whole secret of that. Of course, our big market was the South – there were hundreds and hundreds of drive-ins in the Charlotte, North Carolina territory. There were over four hundred drive-ins and this picture went from one to the other and those good ol' boys just loved that! (*Puts on a Southern accent*) "Did you see that? They cut her head off – hot damn!"'

Blood Feast would go on to play in California and New York, although Friedman insists that his biggest business came from the Deep South. 'It played in New York, up and down 42nd Street. Now 42nd Street has been cleaned up and there are some beautiful theatres … a lot of the grindhouses were torn down and now you see these beautiful; legitimate theatres. There are now 24 screen multiplex theatres in the same place where you used to have porno cinemas and places showing chop 'em up films. It is now very chic to go to 42nd Street. There was a market in New York of course but our great market was what the Hollywood people called the "fly over land" – they don't believe there is anything between Los Angeles and New York. But of course there are a lot of people in Kansas and Missouri and Nebraska and Iowa - and they all came out to see the pictures but, again, it was the South – and when it came to the nudie cuties and the nudist camp pictures, the South was always our great market. As Lord Byron noted in *Don Juan*, "What men call gallantry and the gods adultery, is much more common when the climate is sultry."'

As mentioned, Friedman and Lewis would go their separate ways after 1965's surprisingly tepid *Color Me Blood Red*. Looking back, Friedman admits that taking his own path had its benefits. 'It is a funny thing because after Herschell and I went our separate ways it was like I had struck oil out in Los Angeles,' he says. 'Everything I made was very, very profitable and, although I had gone back to doing nudie-cuties, it was a different kind of nudie-cutie because they had stories. But Herschell went on to make more blood films, *The Wizard of Gore*, *The Gruesome Twosome*, *A Taste of Blood* and so on and so on. He went into partnership with different distributors, and he did a picture right after we split up called *Moonshine Mountain*, with a distributor down in Charlotte, and that got all of its money back and made a nice profit just out of the South. That never played anywhere except in the South. After that he got interest from other distributors but none of them had the knack that we had as a team and Herschell was busy with his other business and that is the one thing about him – he is known for his one take movies! His great remark is, "The difference between take one and take sixteen is ten thousand feet of film." So he and I got together two or three years ago and made *Blood Feast 2*, which is a monstrosity.'

Unfortunately, the long-awaited *Blood Feast 2* was indeed something of a monstrosity, a shot-on-digital travesty that failed to recapture the barmy charm of the original film. 'I read the script for the sequel and I said, "This is nothing new, this is just *Son of Blood Feast*, there is nothing original in here and it is terrible."' says Friedman. 'But they wouldn't change anything ... Well it got made and everybody passed on it. I even showed it to Paramount (*laughs*). At any rate, there is this guy, an Italian fellow called John Sirabello, who has a company called Media Blasters and he gave producer (Jacky) Morgan enough money to get him off the hook – so he was able to pay SAG and pay the labs and everybody else is waiting for their share of the profits. Surprisingly, they made two versions of it, because Blockbuster would only take an R rated version. So I said to Morgan, "Now look, I have battled with the MPAA for years. If you want I'll come down there and go down to the MPAA with you and, believe me, I can keep more in than you will be able to." But he said, "That's alright, I know everybody at the MPAA." Well by the time the MPAA got through with it he had little more than the opening title and the end title. The R-rated version was just terrible, but Blockbuster stocks it, they have nothing to lose because they can return the copies and get credit.'

Herschell Gordon Lewis interview

Although Herschell Gordon Lewis is now known worldwide as 'The Godfather of Gore' the filmmaker admits that he had no idea how people would receive *Blood Feast* when it premiered back in 1963. 'I had no expectation that this film would be accepted at all,' laughs the director. 'In fact as we were cutting the film back in my little cutting room in Chicago I remember looking at the pieces and I said, "What have we done? Where can I ever show this movie?" I was thinking "maybe a midnight show at Halloween," but I had no idea of the groundswell movement that we were creating until we opened that movie and the response we got from audiences ... and some of these responses were a little on the strange side (*laughs*) ... but when I saw the business the movie was doing I knew that we tapped into something. I did not know, of course, that we were starting what might be considered a footnote to motion picture history. I am quite convinced that, by this time, somebody would have made a movie like that but we were the first ones to do it.'

Although *Blood Feast* offered viewers the sort of graphic gore that no filmmaker had ever dared to depict in the past, it is hard not to view the movie as a more gruesome low budget alternative to Hitchcock's *Psycho*. 'Of course *Psycho* is the one that had come closest to being graphically gory,' admits Lewis. 'But the difference between *Psycho* and *Blood Feast* is that *Psycho*, of course, was in black and white. Secondly, *Psycho* cut away, so we only saw the residue of the special effect and not the effect itself. Third, *Blood Feast* was the first movie in which anybody died with his or her eyes open. Now it is quite common in cinema, in fact, you see it on the television news, but at the time, to show somebody dying with their eyes open was considered quite a heresy. So we had no masters, except perhaps the *Grand Guignol* in Paris that had already gone out of business, but which was still quite a historical artefact. There were no predecessors at all and one of the crosses that we bore was that nobody had the type of makeup or effects that this called for. Now, of course, you can go into any magic store and get the kind of things that we couldn't believe would ever exist. So I guess we were architects of destiny in that regard. But the movie itself is camp and I cannot imagine anyone taking it seriously!'

However, people did, especially in the UK where *Blood Feast* became one of the original 'video nasties' in 1985 and was banned outright for almost two decades after that. 'For years I would go to the UK and apparently they would show this thing at a "film club" says Lewis. 'And what was a "film club?" It was a theatre which, for one night, became a "film club"' (*laughs*). Somebody told me that as recently as four of five months ago Australia banned *The Gore Gore Girls*, which has been showing there for 30 years. Now that makes no sense at all. How do you ban something that has already been out there for 30 years? All these things do is add somewhat to the cachet.'

Although there is no denying the importance of *Blood Feast*, the film is not as well made as the feature which Lewis made after it, 1964's *Two Thousand Maniacs*. The director is happy to explain why. '*Blood Feast* was purely experimental. We shot it with no money, no cast and no crew over four days and that is because we were unsure if anybody was going to show it. After we saw the business that it was doing, I said to Dave Friedman, "Well what if we made a good one? How simple is that?" So we went to a little town in Florida called Saint Cloud, which is now engulfed by the Disney Empire. *Blood Feast* was barely scripted but I wrote a full screenplay for *Two Thousand Maniacs* and we shot that with some degree of care. I felt that the acting level was at least five cuts above the acting level of *Blood Feast* and that the sense of impending doom was there too. So it was, quite intentionally, a better picture. That was also because a lot of the theatre owners were saying to us, "If you had a little less blood and a little more plot we might play your picture." Well it turns out they were lying! But we found that out after the fact (*laughs*).'

Lewis claims that *Two Thousand Maniacs* is the movie he is most proud of. 'Of all the movies that I made, *Two Thousand Maniacs* is my personal favourite. Of course, they remade it, and *The Wizard of Gore* has also been remade with quite a budget by some respected and well established Californian filmmakers.' For Lewis, seeing his work brought into the modern day is just part and parcel of his success. 'I have no knowledge of what they do with these films but I am delighted to see *The Wizard of Gore* being remade because it was actually a problem picture for us. We made it at a time when we did not have the financing to make the kind of movie that we wanted to make. It was the one in which they threw us out of a location because the person who was hooking up the electrical power started a fire and they said, "That's it, get it out of here." I had planned, in *The Wizard of Gore*, to have my ultimate effect: where we take a body and pull it to pieces and we bought a goat carcass for that purpose. We shot it in somebody's apartment and we had our own rug on the floor and a piece of plastic under that so that we wouldn't damage their carpet. But they threw us out and we never got the effect that we wanted. So it doesn't bother me at all that they are remaking that one, and now I hear that the same people who are remaking *The Wizard of Gore* also want to remake *She Devils on Wheels*.'

She Devils on Wheels is, according to Lewis, his answer to the critics who claimed that his early horror pictures, such as *Blood Feast*, were misogynistic. 'Yeah, my point has always been that *She Devils on Wheels* has women which are totally dominant,' he laughs. 'You see, the trick in making these movies, and this is especially true at the time I made those, is to appeal to the audience that goes to see these movies. At the time, the audience for these movies was predominantly masculine. Now when we get to my latest picture, *Grim Prairie Tales*, which I am working on now, we have no gender bias at all. We are equally obnoxious to both sexes.'

It took Lewis almost four decades to make a sequel to his original schlock hit. Unfortunately, *Blood Feast 2: All U Can Eat* (2002) quietly slipped into the straight-to-DVD market with very little fanfare … It is something that disappointed Lewis. 'I didn't understand that at all,' he says. 'I just did not understand it. My old partner Dave Friedman said something true to me about eight or ten months after we had looked at the finished video. He said, "by this time we would have played 2000 theatres and made our negative cost back." *(laughs)* I was not in control of that movie. It was not my script, it was not my crew and it was really not my decision. Jacky Morgan was the producer and I was really grateful for the chance to direct it but it wasn't what I would have made. I don't want to damn the movie but, as far as I know, the original negative has not been cut. It was released, I should say excreted, directly to video, and that was also confusing. I didn't even see an ad campaign, we put a campaign together before we were through shooting and I never saw it in action. But I don't want anybody to think that I am not happy to have made the movie, I just do not understand the exploitation of it.'

One thing Lewis is happy about, however, is the opportunity to point out his favourite gore effect from his vast *oeuvre* of hack 'em up movies. Perhaps unsurprisingly, it is the original centrepiece of his first blood-soaked endeavour that still wins him over all these years later. 'I guess the one that I would look at is the watershed tongue effect in *Blood Feast*,' he muses. 'However, I did like one of the effects in *Blood Feast 2*, which the special effects genius Joe Castro did. We had this girl who he rips the skin from the back of her head all the way across her face leaving nothing but raw flesh and it is quite a good effect. I have sat with audiences who scream at that moment *(laughs)*.'

NIGHT of the LIVING DEAD

Released: 1968
Directed by: George A Romero
Produced by: Karl Hardman and Russell Streiner
Written by: George Romero and John Russo
Cast: Duane Jones (Ben), Judith O'Dea (Barbra), Karl Hardman (Harry Cooper), Marilyn Eastman (Helen Cooper), Keith Wayne (Tom), Judith Ridley (Judy), Kyra Schon (Karen Cooper), Charles Craig (Newscaster), Bill Hinzman (Cemetery Zombie), George Kosana (Sheriff McClelland), Frank Doak (Scientist), Russell Streiner (Johnny)

In a nutshell: A bickering brother and sister, Johnny and Barbra, arrive at a cemetery in Pittsburgh one Sunday in order to place a wreath on their father's grave. Johnny begins to antagonise his sister but she is attacked by a strange, pale faced man who subsequently tries to bite her. Johnny wrestles the man from his sister, but he is knocked against a gravestone and killed in the resulting battle. Barbra takes the car and tries to drive to safety but, after crashing the vehicle, runs for refuge in a nearby farmhouse. There she meets Ben, a resourceful man of African-American descent. Barbra goes into shock whilst Ben starts to secure the house. Meanwhile, a number of zombies begin to gather outside. Finally some people emerge from the basement, including the confrontational Harry Cooper, whose young daughter has been bitten and is in a terminal state. Ben and Harry argue constantly, although they attempt to work together during a botched escape plan, whereby two lives are taken. As sunlight begins to emerge, the flesh eating ghouls pummel their way into the house, whilst Ben – the sole survivor – takes refuge in the basement. Outside, the local sheriff leads a group of men closer to the farmhouse, shooting their way through the living dead army ...

Prologue: The living dead had featured in horror cinema before Romero came along, notable examples including 1932's *White Zombie*, 1943's *I Walked with a Zombie* (which immediately spawned the same year's *Revenge of the Zombies*) and the 1966 Hammer effort *The Plague of the Zombies*. In none of these instances, however, were zombies given a threatening persona. They tended to be resurrected family members or humans used as hapless slaves. In the world of *Night of the Living Dead*, however, the living dead were seeking to tear out throats and munch on brains. Thus, Romero gave cinema the zombie as a genuine, contemporary threat, born out of the Cold War, military experimentation and with only the most base of survival instincts ... the need to eat. Although filmed in black and white, *Night of the Living Dead* featured the sort of graphic gore that mainstream crowds simply had not seen before. Whilst Herschell Gordon Lewis had graphically hacked off limbs in *Blood Feast*, he did not manage to reach the wide audience that Romero would and therefore, for most viewers, *Night of the Living Dead* was their sole introduction to 'splatter' cinema[12].

Before his *Night of the Living Dead* success, Romero produced and directed low budget television commercials in his local town of Pittsburgh. The crew and a great deal of the cast for his debut picture were simply his friends, although lead actor Duane Jones was discovered via an audition.

Although the movie may have its origins in Richard Matheson's novel *I Am Legend* (1954), *Night of the Living Dead* is an incredibly original and innovative piece of horror cinema. Prior to Romero, the horror film always had a clear 'survivor', the person that made it through the terrors, supernatural or otherwise, defeated the 'evil' and restored order as the end credits began. *Night of the Living Dead*, however, showed that a genre director does not need to work within conventions and that a horror film is all the more terrifying when the viewer is unaware of its outcome[13].

About: Looking at *Night of the Living Dead* today as a singular movie is difficult, simply because it shaped the horror genre for decades to come and can be more easily viewed as the beginning of a very personal series of films from its director. Indeed, the sequels, *Dawn of the Dead* (1979), *Day of the Dead* (1985) and *Land of the Dead* (2005), as well as the 'sort of' prequel *Diary of the Dead* (2008), play out a fiercely independent vision of America, using the

---

12 As critic Maitland McDonagh affirms, 'Lewis was an isolated, though indicative, case; Romero defined a trend.' (*Broken Mirrors/Broken Minds*, Sun Tavern, 1991

13 'In 1968, the year that popularised rebelliousness and nonconformity, *Night of the Living Dead* did its bit for the Age of Aquarius by ignoring decades of cinema convention.' (Kim Newman, *Nightmare Movies*, Bloomsbury, 1988)

living dead 'crisis' to comment on the politics of each given decade. Whilst *Night of the Living Dead* was not the first horror movie to be interpreted as reflecting political and social events, nothing that had come before it had attempted to be quite so intelligent and forthcoming with its 'message'. Thus, born at a time when the war in Vietnam was raging, tensions between the United States and its self-proclaimed 'enemies' (namely the communist states of Russia and Cuba) were ever present and such civil rights leaders as Martin Luther King and Malcolm X had been assassinated, Romero shows a country in chaos. It should come as little surprise, therefore, that his movie is deeply cynical and this is perhaps best represented in his cast of on-screen personalities: a ragtag bunch of characters that, during a time of disaster, completely fail to get along with one another. Thus, instead of bonding together in an attempt to solve the immediate problem at hand, Romero's characters make rash decisions, squabble and fight amongst themselves. In doing so, they become weakened, ignore the 'real' enemy and ultimately end up unprepared for the eventual onslaught of the 'living dead'. By the time *Night of the Living Dead* comes to an end every central character has been destroyed, and, at a time when the United States itself was senselessly bombing Indochina and engaged in Cold War bickering (and in the process become split from the inside – as seen with the Kent State shootings) Romero's faith in humanity appears to be at an all time low.

Night of the Living Dead opens with Barbra and Johnny driving to their father's grave. We know that the two are close because they have spent no less than 'three hours' on a Sunday to get there, all for their late dad. This is, of course, a picture of quaintness and dedication … the sort of nuclear family love-in that the post-Beaver Cleaver-era America still dearly wanted to believe in and which was becoming shattered in the wake of the many young men being drafted, sent to war and taken from their wives and parents. Of course, the initial closeness between Barbra and her brother is also quickly destroyed when Johnny begins to spook his sister; preying on her age-old fear of graveyards and finally taunting her with the classic line: 'They're coming to get you, Barbra.' Watching the film today, one can feel a genuine uneasiness as Johnny's cruelty unfolds and, yet, the acting remains campy enough for us to be lulled into a false sense of security. For all intents and purposes, this is 'just another B-movie'. But then, in a split second, *Night of the Living Dead* becomes an altogether different kind of beast. Indeed, despite displaying such expected 'scare' devices as the rumble of thunder on the soundtrack (a tried and tested device even back then) very little that Romero does from here on in is hackneyed. Instead his debut picture does absolutely everything to play against expected horror movie conventions.

Night of the Living Dead begins its descent into pure terror, the likes of which the silver screen has rarely experienced since, when a lone, rambling ghoul attacks Barbra and her brother attempts to fight him off, being killed in the process. Abruptly one of the movie's two introductory characters is gone and the viewer is left to assume that this is going to be a picture about Barbra. Certainly, this is how events proceed for several minutes as the young lady attempts to drive away from the scene of her brother's death, crashes her car and subsequently takes shelter in a nearby house. Once inside, Barbra notices the walking dead beginning to gather outside. She tries to use the phone (out of order) and finds a dead body on the first floor (the movie's first gruesome sight). Romero expertly frames Barbra's ensuing breakdown, with

TABOO BREAKERS

his tilted, forced, expressionist camera angles and rapid-fire editing giving the viewer one of the best visual depictions of madness since Polanski's *Repulsion* (1965). Finally, our 'heroine' is greeted by a tall black man called Ben who is in the process of securing the doors and windows. From this moment on, he becomes the real focus of *Night of the Living Dead*.

Not to state the obvious, but, with this being 1968, the colour of Ben's skin is impossible to ignore. For here is an African-American man taking the lead role; the 'hero' of the picture, the smartest person on screen and, eventually, the sole character for the audience to relate to. Although Romero may state that Jones was hired simply because he gave the best audition (see his interview in this chapter), the fact that so many reviewers of *Night of the Living Dead* have acknowledged the significance of his lead actor's ethnicity leads one to believe that the director was equally wise to this. Certainly, it should be noted that never once in the movie do any of the characters use any racial slurs, perhaps indicating that, yes, the part could have been written for a white person[14]. All the same, Jones would be the first black hero, leading an all-white cast in an action/horror movie role. Whilst one can certainly acknowledge the importance of Sidney Poitier's leading man turns in such titles as *The Defiant Ones* (1958), *Guess Who's Coming to Dinner* and *In the Heat of the Night* (both 1967), the great actor was, in each case, placed alongside a Hollywood A-lister. Furthermore, each story was based upon a black character's relationship with someone white whereas *Night of the Living Dead* is 100% colour blind. Ben's skin is neither here nor there – all that we are made aware of is that he is tougher and smarter than anyone else in the movie and acts as a hero when it is required of him. For many audiences in 1968, this was quite a striking thing to see on-screen.

However, it is primarily because of the colour of Ben's skin, as well as the fact that no one verbally acknowledges it, that *Night of the Living Dead* ultimately ends on such a painfully topical note. Had it been a white man shot dead at the end, it would no doubt still be a shock (the storyline heroes didn't die back then, and still rarely do) but in light of the assassinations of Malcolm X (in 1965) and Martin Luther King (1968), Romero's classic takes on an altogether more powerful resonance. Hence, the sight of a gun-toting, beer-bellied redneck sheriff, led by some white policemen with dogs, ordering a rogue rifleman to take aim at Jones, who is killed with a solitary shot, is a hugely important part of sixties celluloid. It is unmistakably reflective of a lynch mob, the sort that was assembled all too frequently in the Deep South of the time. Even the final line of the film: 'Good shot, okay he's dead, let's go get him, that's another one for the fire,' hints at something far more relevant and sinister. The fact that Jones' death is followed by a series of still photographs, depicting his casual handling and burning, indicates a further comment on the times for, as if the death of the leading man is not bad enough, we then see his cremation played out in still form. In these closing moments, it feels as though we are watching reality, the sort of photographs that many Americans were seeing on television and in the newspaper every day (be they of assassinated leaders, racial violence or, most commonly, dead military servicemen).

Indeed, the bloody paw print of the Vietnam War is all over Romero's movie, but never

---

14 Critic Jonathan Ross, for example, notes that the film features 'a problem-solving black hero, without making an issue out of his blackness.' (*The Incredibly Strange Film Book*, Simon & Schuster, 1993)

more so than in the feature's closing moments. Even before Ben is shot dead, we see a shaky, helicopter eye-view of the action below, which feels all the while like newsreel footage from a war zone. This, coupled with Romero's earlier device of 'interviewing' politicians during a television newscast about the crisis taking place, gives *Night of the Living Dead* a very special aura. The movie is, ultimately, incredibly media savvy and it knows how to place the audience in the middle of a fictional contemporary problem that they will recognise (be it through the metaphor of a landing helicopter, a wandering lynch mob or grainy television forecasts). As a result, although Romero has made a picture of obvious fantastical or supernatural content, it has a stark realism to it that few horror movies have been able to rival.

It is also possible to view the cast of *Night of the Living Dead* as representative of the Vietnam era itself. Jones, of course, is the black man who has long been denied the right to vote but, nevertheless, is expected to fight for his government (the Voting Rights Act of 1965 was still recent at the time of Romero's picture). Barbra is the middle class white girl, thrown into a mental breakdown after losing a loved one. Tom and Judy are the teens in love, their lives taken by the 'war' that exists outside of their barricaded house (both die only moments after exiting the comparative safety of indoors). Harry Cooper is the hardnosed conservative, the domineering personality who is always right and who fails to listen to the opinions or advice of anyone else. His wife is the helpless 'first lady' of the house, standing by her husband's side in silent agreement but professing her doubts more vocally behind closed doors. Their child is the ultimate innocent, a young, adolescent girl, ravaged by the horrors of this new 'invasion'. When she finally rises (as the 'living dead') and kills her mother it is the perfect visual scenario of the child gaining revenge over the adult world that has cheated her of growing into a woman.

For, let us not forget, that *Night of the Living Dead* is a product of a time when man was challenging new frontiers, and spending billions to do it. Whilst many celebrated, and continue to celebrate, the Apollo 11 landing on the moon in 1969 (and the many earlier attempts to perfect such a mission), there are others, such as this writer, who consider the entire scenario a depressing waste of money in a world where wars were, and still are, being waged and famine is ever present. Although made before Neil Armstrong took his 'one giant step for mankind', *Night of the Living Dead* is well aware of humanity's meddling in outer space, with the destruction of a fictional 'space probe' to Venus said to have caused radiation and being suggested as the reason for the dead rising. Naturally, this makes the zombie holocaust of the film's storyline a man-made disaster, as all wars are, and lends a notable cynicism towards science that Romero would continue to explore in his underrated *The Crazies* (1973) and *Day of the Dead*. With a social conscience that is second to none, it would be through such projects as these that Romero would prove himself, time and again, to be one of the most intelligent American filmmakers in history, regardless of genre.

Another thing that distinguishes a great deal of Romero's work, and which no doubt contributes to him being a fringe interest, is his reliance on graphic gore[15]. This is one element

---

15 Although the late Leslie Halliwell, whose cynicism towards the contemporary horror movie is well known, rated *Night of the Living Dead* highly, even he had to maintain that it opened the 'floodgates to admit every conceivable kind of cinematic nastiness.' (*The Dead That Walk*, Grafton, 1986)

of *Night of the Living Dead* that is difficult to ignore and, even in black and white, the movie remains a stomach churning experience. The aftermath of Tom and Judy's death is especially grim, as the zombies fight over their intestines and rip the flesh from their bones. There is an uncomfortable realism, and documentary feel, to this gruesome set piece and it makes the sequence all the more unpleasant to watch (especially since Romero manages to make his previously docile and slow moving ghouls suddenly appear animalistic and fierce). The second really nasty moment in *Night of the Living Dead* occurs when little Karen Cooper stabs her mother to death with a small garden shovel. This remains a very challenging sequence to watch, mainly because Romero captures a scenario that is unimaginably terrifying. Here, the mother is unwilling to do anything to harm her daughter and, thus, is secure in her painful fate, looking on in horror and sadness as her offspring slaughters her. Even taking into account his four decades as a genre director, Romero would never manage to film a scene as harrowing and repulsive as this again. In this moment alone, Romero distinguishes his work from the comic splatter of Herschell Gordon Lewis and the more flamboyant and stylish shocks of the European movement (then led by Mario Bava). Instead, the pure terror of this scene, and its unflinching matter-of-factness, introduce a very unique vision of horror filmmaking[16].

In a movie of consistent high points, and a story that is rich in detail and metaphor, the one aspect of *Night of the Living Dead* where Romero is not thinking ahead is with his treatment of the leading lady. Strangely, whereas the film still feels contemporary when watched today, there is something decidedly awkward about seeing Jones knock his co-star, Judith O'Dea, into unconsciousness. Especially since the arc of the scene is that 'she asked for it.' (Romero really allows the woman's hysteria to build up and grate.) There can be no denying Barbra's hysterical gibbering is annoying but it is also possible to identify with the poor woman who has, after all, just lost a loved one. It is slightly odd that *Night of the Living Dead* is the sole Romero picture that does not stand up to a feminist reading and, after the introduction of Jones, O'Dea's character feels left in the background, little more than a prop to the squabbling between Ben and Cooper that takes centre stage. Regardless of this, however, O'Dea's damaged Barbra is far more believable than the ridiculously butch one, played by Patricia Tallman, who takes the lead in Tom Savini's lacklustre 1990 remake.

Released independently and progressively establishing its reputation through word of mouth and critical accolades, *Night of the Living Dead* took some time to really make a global impact. However, alongside Hitchcock's *Psycho*, *Night of the Living Dead* is arguably the most influential and important horror film ever made and, despite the more mainstream acclaim that *Easy Rider*'s nihilistic finale obtained in 1969, the fact remains that Romero got there first. As a result, whenever a director turns the 'safety button' off and takes the viewer on an uncertain journey, killing the hero or unravelling a story of uncertain direction, you can be sure that it is Romero's shadow that is being cast over the proceedings.

---

16 Revisiting his experience of seeing *Night of the Living Dead* as a ten-year-old child, author Ptolemy Tompkins comments, 'With this film, I began to realise I had stumbled upon something genuinely adult, something which, as my mother put it, I was "not ready for".' (*Screen Violence*, Bloomsbury, 1996)

NIGHT OF THE LIVING DEAD

What happened next? Where to even start?

Due to the fact that *Night of the Living Dead* took some time to really establish its reputation, Romero never experienced the sort of overnight success that gave such contemporaries as John Carpenter (after *Halloween*) and Tobe Hooper (after *The Texas Chain Saw Massacre*) the key to bigger budgets and major studio projects. Instead, the filmmaker continued to blaze a truly renegade path with the low budget romance *There's Always Vanilla* (with *Night of the Living Dead* star Judith Ridley) and the slow-moving feminist parable *Season of the Witch* (aka *Jack's Wife*). Both films were shot in 1971 and remain largely unseen. Both projects are also rare examples of Romero's non-horror work. The director's return to terror came with 1973's enjoyable *The Crazies*, another very low budget feature and a warm-up for the similar themes of scientific irresponsibility that the director would explore in *Day of the Dead*. However, Romero's first certified post-*Night of the Living Dead* classic would be 1976's excellent vampire story *Martin*, a fascinating story of wasted youth and suburban melodrama.

Although a critical hit, *Martin* was not the mainstream success that its director may have hoped for and he ended up making his next movie, *Dawn of the Dead* (1979), on a shoestring budget of $500,000. This is especially impressive considering *Dawn of the Dead*'s epic running time (the director's cut is 139 minutes long). This classic follow-up to *Night of the Living Dead* remains one of Romero's finest achievements and one of the most impressive satires on modern day consumerism and military jingoism. Following up the lofty heights of *Dawn of the Dead* would be difficult for any director but, ever the independent, Romero chose to make *Knightriders* (1981), a brilliant, symbolically rich drama about a group of travellers (led by Ed Harris) who stage competitive, medieval tournaments on motorcycles. *Knightriders* was a flop upon its release, but is the best of his non-*Living Dead* pictures. Romero returned to horror with the big budget, all-star, anthology movie *Creepshow* (1982), a fun commercial hit based on the classic EC comics from the 1950s, but a surprisingly empty project.

The zombies returned in *Day of the Dead* (1985), an excellent commentary on Reagan-era America and one of the few mainstream movies to tackle the issue of vivisection. Although its pessimism may not have been what viewers wanted to see at the time (*Day of the Dead* under-performed theatrically), retrospection shows the film to be one of the most politically smart analogies of its decade. Following *Day of the Dead*, Romero went through a frustratingly unfocused stage, making the mediocre thriller *Monkey Shines* (1988), the threadbare *Two Evil Eyes* (1990, co-directed by Dario Argento), the lavish but underwhelming Stephen King adaptation *The Dark Half* (1993) and the awful *Bruiser* (2000). Unsurprisingly, it would be 2005's *Land of the Dead* that showed he could still cut it. A masterpiece of post-9/11 cinema, the film is a smart, thoughtful attempt to satirize the politics of Bush-era America. Although not a box office success, *Land of the Dead* led to *Diary of the Dead* (2008). Something of a let-down after its thrilling and underrated predecessor, Romero's fifth zombie offering is a little bit too sloppy and overstated (it also features, for the first time in his living dead saga, characters nearly impossible to sympathise with) but its fiercely anti-war leanings, and fleetingly sharp social commentary, show that he still has its heart in the right place. Moreover, *Diary of the Dead*'s final shot, a shocking scene of violent torture dished out at the hands of two gun-happy good ol' boys, hits almost as hard as any imagery in his previous work. It also makes one wish that he would dump the zombies and make a sensible, straightforward political satire outside of the horror genre.

Night of the Living Dead, as with all films of lasting influence, paved the way for an unstoppable tide of zombie-themed horror. Post *Night of the Living Dead* zombie features include Jorge Grau's sub-par 1974 offering *The Living Dead at the Manchester Morgue* (which remains acclaimed in some quarters), the passable Spanish *Tombs of the Blind Dead* series (which began in 1971) and grindhouse favourite *I Drink Your Blood* (1971). A number of Italian filmmakers got in on the act, including most famously the late Lucio Fulci, and their output tended to epitomise the genre of cash-starved, shambling, carnivorous undead movies. Fulci's best work was 1980's dozy cash-in *Zombi 2* (Romero's *Dawn of the Dead* was released as *Zombi* in Italy), also known as *Zombie Flesh-Eaters*. Although not in the same league as Romero, *Zombi 2* is certainly stylish and at least has some moments of wincing horror amongst its clumsy plot and ropey dialogue. This is more than can be said of other Italian living dead epics such as *Zombie Creeping Flesh* (1980), *Nightmare City* (1980) and *Zombi 3* (1988). Fulci himself would have less success with *City of the Living Dead* (1980) and *The Beyond* (1981) although both pictures have fleeting instances of absurd appeal, sporadically impressive art direction and a charmingly esoteric sense of logic.

1985's more irreverent *Return of the Living Dead* is a sort-of sequel to *Night of the Living Dead* and one of the best American horror films of its decade. John Russo's script, in particular, leavens the horror with some humour and the picture features some impressive undead special effects. With the exception of the Brian Yuzna directed *Return of the Living Dead III* (1993), the less said about the other sequels (which reached a fifth instalment in 2005) the better. One of the other interesting post-Romero living dead franchises is *Re-Animator*, begun in 1985 by Stuart Gordon, and spawning two disappointing sequels to date.

Night of the Living Dead itself would enter the public domain and eventually be remade in 1990 by special effects whiz Tom Savini (with Romero producing). The end result is a disjointed affair but still more interesting than the ludicrously testosterone fuelled *Dawn of the Dead* re-hash from 2004, which takes the gung-ho, pro-firearm, 'if it moves kill it' sensibility of the modern action picture seriously and fails to even acknowledge the left-leaning politics of Romero's original. Steve Miner's so-so *Day of the Dead* remake hit DVD in 2008 and, like the *Dawn of the Dead* redux, has little in common with its namesake.

In 1999 producer John Russo went back to the original *Night of the Living Dead* and added in several, newly filmed sequences. Predictably, the end result was a total disaster. The latest incarnation of Romero's hit property is the preposterous *Night of the Living Dead 3D* (2006), featuring popular B movie actor Sid Haig. In other words, even a bullet through the head won't stop more of these movies.

George Romero interview

'*Night of the Living Dead* was a rip off of *I Am Legend* except that they used vampires and I needed something else so I went with ghouls,' admits George Romero when asked about the genesis of his original horror classic. 'I never called them zombies to begin with – I didn't even think of them that way. I thought of them as ghouls or flesh-eaters. Our original title was *Night of the Flesh Eaters*. Zombies in those days were the guys in Haiti...'

NIGHT OF THE LIVING DEAD

For Romero, the success of *Night of the Living Dead* was both a blessing and a curse. Indeed the filmmaker admits that, despite his later career being trademarked by gory horror shockers such as *Creepshow* and, of course, the continuation of his zombie franchise (most recently with *Diary of the Dead*), he never envisaged a future in fear. 'Right after *Night of the Living Dead* I wanted to escape,' he laughs. 'After that first film I said, "I am always going to be labelled as a horror guy." I don't mind that but I didn't always want to have to do these films, so the second movie that I made, which no one has seen, was called *There's Always Vanilla*, which was a little romantic comedy. It actually opened theatrically and I did that because I just didn't want to do another *Night of the Living Dead* right away and then I did *Jack's Wife*, which had only little overtones of horror, and we were able to finance that for very little money: $100,000. I'm still very pleased with that movie. In fact, Ed Harris got me involved in a project a couple of years ago that I was just in love with. It was a historical thriller about the assassination of Trujillo in the Dominican Republic and I loved the script. Ed had committed to it and he got me involved in it. We were ready to shoot and we scouted for five weeks in Puerto Rico and we had Anthony Quinn as Trujillo and then the project blew up. That's just what happens.'

Nowadays, however, Romero knows exactly what an audience wants from one of his movies. 'I think that my audience expects meat,' he says. 'I think that, out of all of them, *Day of the Dead* probably had the most graphic effects and Tom Savini did a really good job with them. I think my fans expect a certain thing from me and I enjoy doing that sort of thing. I grew up on EC comic books and I don't cringe when I see gore scenes in other people's movies – in fact, I giggle (*laughs*).' All the same, the director bemoans the days when an independent horror flick could hit cinemas without a rating and still take in a tidy profit. 'If you released a film unrated back in the seventies or eighties then it was treated as if it was an X,' he reflects. 'That is what happened with *Night of the Living Dead*. But nowadays that has become the NC17, and you couldn't advertise films with that rating nationally in certain newspapers. So with *Day of the Dead* I was told, "Look, if you want to spend $6 million then you have to deliver an R, but, otherwise, you can take $3 million and you can do whatever you want with it." With *Land of the Dead* I had to deliver an R-rating and it wasn't such a problem. I shouldn't have been so afraid of it, but I do think that because it was Universal the MPAA was a little more lenient, whereas if it had been purely independent then they would have hit it harder.'

Although *Night of the Living Dead* is now recognised as a turning point for the horror film and a forward-thinking movie in terms of its representation of an African-American character, Romero admits to some regrets with the finished picture. 'With *Night of the Living Dead* I had Judith O'Dea running around. She broke her heel, fell down, did all these embarrassing things that women in horror movies did,' he says. 'So I apologised in the remake – the one Savini directed – when I wrote that script I made her strong and I have tried to stay with that. Back then, with *Night of the Living Dead*, I guess I just fell into that pattern. The woman was the weak one, catatonic, falling down, unable to do anything and I've felt bad about that ever since.'

Romero also denies that there was any great plan behind the casting of a black actor. 'Duane Jones was just the better actor among our friends,' he shrugs. 'The script wasn't written with any description of race and when we decided to use Duane we did talk about changing the script but we decided not to. And I'm now wondering if we should have. I mean, I think we might have missed a beat there. I think we should have acknowledged it, had some argument and addressed it somehow. But nonetheless what happened, happened. I used an African-American lead in the second film and when I did *Land of the Dead* I sort of switched allegiances and made the lead zombie, Big Daddy, an African-American in the hope that people might notice and say, "Hey look at this – this guy's okay.'"

Romero also gives an example in regards to how the *Night of the Living Dead* shoot took some unexpected on-set accidents and turned them into a positive. 'I remember that we borrowed a car which belonged to Russ Streiner's mother,' he explains. 'He was the guy who played Johnny, and we shot a couple of scenes with it and then his mother hit a tree with it, or something, and dented the door so we couldn't shoot it from that angle. But I thought, "Well maybe we can use this," and in the finished movie you see Judith drive down a hill and into a tree so we took advantage of that situation.'

Although the director is considered to be the undisputed innovator of the modern zombie picture, Romero admits that he never knew exactly what the wandering, pale faced, flesh-hungry creatures in *Night of the Living Dead* actually were. 'I think it was with *Dawn of the Dead* that I decided they were zombies,' he says. 'When *Night of the Living Dead* first started to get noticed as something more than a penny dreadful some people that wrote about it called them "zombies" and that woke me up and I said, "Well gee, maybe they are." And I got credit for sort of re-inventing the zombie and I didn't even realise I was doing it, so I don't know whether I deserve credit for that or not. In my mind they were ghouls. I mean, ghouls are really the forgotten monster, right? *The Mad Ghoul* and those old Universal flicks … I'm old enough that I saw the Universal films. I'm not that old to have seen them in the thirties, but I saw them re-released on the big screen. I was a Hispanic kid in the Bronx getting beaten up by the Italian guys and I remember black-outs during the end of the Second World War and I remember John Cameron Swayze telling me, personally, out of that little boob tube that the Russians had the bomb. That scared me. That was the stuff that scared me the most - the real life shit.'

After *Dawn of the Dead*, Romero also began to see his zombie franchise as documenting the political era of each respective decade. 'I had this concept,' he says. 'I made *Night of the Living Dead* in the sixties, *Dawn of the Dead* was the seventies, *Day of the Dead* was the eighties and I wanted to do the nineties. But I just missed it. However, I think of the films as reflective of the times they were released. They were little snap shots: "Here's what happening now." I'm not trying to answer questions but I love the idea that each one is a reflection of what was going on. That is important to me. Even when I wrote the first version of *Land of the Dead*, before 9/11, what it was about in my mind was ignoring the problem.' That said, the director admits that he almost didn't bother continuing *Night of the Living Dead* into a film series. 'I didn't want to do a sequel until, socially, I met the people that owned this shopping mall,' he reveals. 'I went on a tour of the place and this guy said, "There's all these rooms above the mall and there are all these civil defence supplies and you could live there for about a year." That is how I got the idea for *Dawn of the Dead*. This was the first of these big enclosed palaces in Pittsburgh and I thought, "This is just too good to pass up." Then by pure coincidence I got a call from Dario Argento asking me if I wanted to do a sequel to *Night of the Living Dead*. So I went to Rome and he stuck me in a little apartment, took me out for dinner once in a while, but he just kept saying, "You write, you write." Within four weeks we had the script. So that was how that happened.'

Dawn of the Dead was also, at least originally, intended to have a direct link to its predecessor. 'When I first started the script to *Dawn of the Dead*, I had written the sheriff from the first film into it as an ongoing guy and I was going to set it in a small town again but it was just too long. This was the seventies as well, so I was thinking, "Well what do I do? Do I keep the cars and the hairstyles from the sixties just to link it to *Night of the Living Dead*?" (*Laughs*) So I decided that *Dawn of the Dead* would be sort of like a continuing story, but in a different time and it doesn't really matter. That gave me the revelation that I could keep doing this forever and they don't ever have to connect. I could tell the same story but disregard real time, so that is how that happened.'

One thing that Romero denies any responsibility for is the inferior zombie films that followed his own classic, such as those directed by Italian splatter king Lucio Fulci and the likes of Bruno Mattei (*Zombie Creeping Flesh*) and Umberto Lenzi (*Nightmare City*). 'I don't feel as if I opened these gates or anything,' he says. 'I don't think my stuff should be blamed for all of that. My stuff was just in there at the right time, and it was a little more political and that made it a bit more noticeable.'

Romero's most recent visions, *Land of the Dead* and *Diary of the Dead*, are a long way removed from the skid-row production values of his earliest work. Consequently, the director now has the endless possibilities of digital technology at his feet, something that he considers a mixed blessing. 'As a filmmaker you have to appreciate that computers allow you to do things that you couldn't think of doing if it was a smaller project,' he says. 'But, for example, I don't like using CGI. I mean I'm a Ray Harryhausen fan, I much would have preferred if we could have done all the effects mechanically. There's a scene in Savini's *Day of the Dead* where he pulls the guy's head out. It's fabulous and seamless the way that he did it. But it's CGI, it's obviously CGI. Maybe general audiences don't recognise it as readily as we do in the industry, but it bothers me. I'd rather be amazing and be like a magician like David Copperfield: "Here it is, live and in person ... you figure it out" (*laughs*).'

Currently Romero's most famous work is also undergoing the remake treatment, something that the director admits surprise at. 'My ex-partner (Richard Rubinstein) remade *Dawn of the Dead* and I knew that he was doing it, but I wouldn't have done it,' he says. 'The *Night of the Living Dead* remake that I worked on was done to try and re-establish the copyright over the name as the film was at the time in the public domain, and I wanted to get the director, Tom Savini, a feature credit. I went to see the *Dawn of the Dead* remake, Richard asked me to go and look at it. I wasn't the first guy in line (*smiles*) and I don't think that they were thinking much past the commerciality of it ... But it was much better than I expected it was going to be. I think they did a pretty good job with it, but it was an action film – it was more of a video game than anything else – and my zombies don't run, man, they would snap their ankles if they tried to run! My joke is that my guys would take out library cards before they'd join a health club. I don't care though. Honestly, I don't care what they do (*laughs*). It is amazing to me that all of this stuff is being remade.'

One thing that Romero is sure about, however, is that such remakes do not damage his starkly original visions. 'The first question that Stephen King always gets asked about his books is, "What do you think about Hollywood ruining your stories?" and he always says, "What do you mean? They're not ruined. Here they are right now, on the shelf, right here. Nobody ruined them. They're not touched." And I guess that is really the way I feel. I don't really look too much at other horror films, I'm not a student that way, I mean I'm just kind of doing my own thing and I don't particularly care what goes on around it.'

So, will the day finally come when the legacy begun by *Night of the Living Dead* drives to a close? Will Romero ever decide to make the final instalment in his decades-long chain of zombie horror? 'If I was faced with the idea of having to end the series then I don't know how I would do that,' he laughs. 'You'd have to arrive at some sort of a balance: "If you stop eating us, we'll stop shooting you." I think that it goes both ways.'

Judith O'Dea interview

Actress Judith O'Dea may have made her feature film debut in one of the most famous titles of all time but *Night of the Living Dead* was still being developed by its creators George Romero and John Russo when she was given the chance to audition for the part of Barbra. 'I had worked with a number of the people who ended up on that film in the years prior to *Night of Living Dead*,' she says. 'Karl Hardman and Marilyn Eastman especially – I did a lot of commercial, and voiceover, work at Karl's studio. We struck up a good friendship there and I went off to Hollywood in 1967. I had hoped to break into the film business out there but then I got a call from Karl that said, 'We're going to make a movie, why don't you come back home and do an audition?' So I left Hollywood, went back to my home in Pittsburgh and auditioned – that is how I got the role. I remember that the picture started off, at least as I recall, as *Night of the Anubis* – there might have been other titles but that was the one they had when I became involved. Of course, it changed to *Night of the Living Dead* and one of the reasons for that is that I don't think the general public would understand the word "Anubis" (*laughs*). I think *Night of the Living Dead* is much, much better.'

However, the movie's groundbreaking depiction of graphic violence, pessimistic situations and its then-shocking use of an ethnic actor in the lead role was lost on O'Dea. After all – she never got to see the screenplay. 'I don't believe I got a script,' she laughs. 'I do recall getting a script before the actual film began but what happened to it I have no idea. But I don't remember any of these "groundbreaking" elements at all. One of the reasons is that I don't believe the fate of the characters was totally decided upon until the filming progressed. I didn't even think about my character dying because, to me, when I realised it was going to happen it was just a part of the film.'

Back in the late 1960s, George Romero was an unknown and unproven filmmaker, but O'Dea has nothing but fond memories of him – and his professional demeanour. 'George and I had met some years earlier at an audition,' she reveals. 'He wanted to make a feature and we didn't have much association after that until we made *Night of the Living Dead*. But when we made the film I was very impressed with him. I thought he was very intense about what he was doing. He wasn't hyperactively intense, he was just very focused, if you understand what I'm saying. He worked long, long hours – probably longer than anyone. In a way I suppose you could call him a workaholic because once he got involved he just wouldn't stop until he was finished. I was also extremely impressed with his creativity, his thoughts on how a scene should be shot and some of the unique characteristics that he would devise for a sequence. For example, there is a shot of Barbra – my character – touching a little beauty box. I touch the box and a little door opens. Well George shot that and cut to a close-up through the little door where, just for a second, you saw my eyes intensely watching until the little door closes. Things like that impressed me greatly – I think it made the film more special.'

O'Dea's co-star was the late Duane Jones, a black man headlining a movie in a decade of notorious racial conflict. 'I didn't think of it at all,' says the actress when asked about his casting. 'I don't see colour, I just see individual people and their talent and values. That is what makes a person for me. The fact that Duane was a black man ... I didn't give two shakes of a pole. Was he talented? That was all I thought about. We had to do this show together so how well would we work? Would there be difficulties with our acting styles? Duane was an extremely intelligent, quiet man, and terribly professional. If he wasn't shooting he would be reading. I would be off walking and he would be off reading. We had a great time. George and I never spoke about any political ramifications of Duane's casting. If he spoke of it with Duane or with anyone else then it was a conversation I wasn't privy to. As far as I can remember, and I was 23 at the time, we didn't ever talk about the political ramifications. We were making a film with a very low budget, which we hoped would make a bit of money so that we could then go on and make a bigger and better film. That was my understanding of it. I think the biggest conversation was over whether or not Duane should be killed at the end because, initially, I think they were going to leave him as the only survivor. However, they decided to go ahead and I think that it was a monumental decision. It is the keystone of what makes *Night of the Living Dead* a landmark horror film.'

Perhaps unsurprisingly, therefore, O'Dea admits to being bewildered about the more academic readings of *Night of the Living Dead*. 'I have to smile,' she says. 'It amazes me ... the older these films get the more people analyse them. People talk about what we were trying to do and what the meanings were. I would be very curious about what George says about all of this. But at least we've given people something to chew up (*laughs*). But we didn't build the film on politics. I think *Night of the Living Dead* just happened to happen at that time. George's creativity, and the way the film was edited, it just hit what was going on. In the end, it was just far different from what anyone had done before. There was no big deal made about the fact that Duane was a black man and I was a white woman, we were just two souls trying to survive. One of the things that I love about the film, is that it leaves a lasting thought in the mind: it really doesn't matter what colour you are. If you can help each other get through difficulties, then that is what is important.'

One thing that O'Dea can, however, relate to is seeing her on-screen character screaming for her life. Indeed, the actress admits to throwing herself into the fantastical terror of *Night of the Living Dead*. 'I am a woman of great imagination,' she explains. 'I was terrified when I was a child after I went to see the 3D version of *The House of Wax*. So it doesn't take that much to really frighten me, or at least it didn't take much then, I have changed a bit since the years have gone on. Death was also something that frightened me so I am very grateful that others find my performance believable.'

O'Dea also had the chance to sample some of the picture's macabre visions first hand. 'I was around the special effects and I really got a kick out of seeing how they did these things,' she reveals. 'For example, I watched them tape the explosives on people's bodies where they would try and represent a gun shot. I was fascinated by how that was done even though the effects in our film were rather juvenile when you compare them to what you see today. Still, it is interesting how they put it all together and made it look fairly genuine. There was one element which looked fake, and I don't think I have told this to anyone, and that was when some fingers were cut off with a knife ... you know, the hand that came through the window? You saw a real hand come in and then a close up of a very obviously fake hand (*laughs*). Now, the scene where I am attacked by the zombies was a pretty terrifying thing for me to film because even though you know what is coming, being pulled out by beings that want to destroy you, when you put your mind to it that is pretty scary. For me, there was no way out – that was the way I was going to leave this earth.'

The actress also offers her own reasons for the famous sequence in which Jones slaps the hysterical Barbra to the ground, knocking her unconscious. 'Looking at Duane's character, I think that he is going through his explanations,' she says. 'He has no idea what is going on and all he wants to do is survive but there is testosterone involved. Some males react ... well how do I want to say this? There is oestrogen and testosterone and they are two different animals, but good old Barbra had some testosterone of her own left at the end when she got up and fought.'

Over the years, Romero himself has said that he regrets the fact O'Dea's role called on her to be a typical damsel in distress. For instance, the actress runs around hysterically, loses her shoes, cries, takes a slap from her male co-star and, finally, disintegrates into a blubbering mess. However, the actress has her own take on Barbra. 'First of all, I actually did fall when I was running, and rather than shooting it again they kept it in the film. They also added a pick up shot where I kick off my other shoe so I could run with bare feet.

'I did not consider Barbra to be a weak character. This was just one human being's reaction to an extremely unbelievable terror that was happening. Of course what Barbra does is to retreat inside herself. I think that is the saving grace for her because, rather than going completely bonkers, she tries to make sense of it all and in her very quiet catatonic way she does this. I think she is trying to get a grip on the fact that she has just seen her brother killed. You don't just blithely react to a relative being killed and then go on to be Queen of the Amazon (*laughs*). I think the way she behaved and the way that George handled it was really very obvious. Some people might react totally differently, but the wonderfully strong thing about Barbra is that she finally reaches a point where, when Marilyn is being attacked at the door and the zombies are getting into the house, she gets to the point where she sees another human being under attack and she reacts to that. I think this is a tremendous strength of character for her because she is not going to allow that woman to be killed. Her own brother is dead and she is going to do whatever she can to help that individual and, in doing so, she saves Helen from being pulled outside. Instead, Barbra gets attacked. She shows her strength but she has to think about it, she has to retreat for a while but she ends up fighting.'

O'Dea's character became a more Sigourney Weaver-in-*Alien* type of character in Tom Savini's *Night of the Living Dead* remake. Having seen her successor in action, O'Dea offers some feedback. 'People ask me what I think about that film and I tell them that they are two different movies. One was made in the late sixties and the other was made in the early nineties. Women's lib, the women's movement and the strength of women asserting themselves all had become far greater by then and I can see why Tom Savini might change Barbra's character that way. It was more towards what they felt women, at that time, might do. The two films may have similar storylines but Patricia Tallman's character is so different that I don't even compare the two and take them each for what they are. However, when women become superheroes, and they go over the top with it, I think it loses the believability.'

One version of Romero's zombie masterwork that O'Dea has not seen, however, is the updated version to which John Russo added extra scenes. 'I did not see the version that John did,' explains O'Dea. 'I can only go by what I've heard, and that is, "Don't watch". I have heard that it really did not add anything to the film and I am upset that this happened and people were affected by it in that way. I also know that they released a colourised version and, in my mind, *Night of the Living Dead* – like *Casablanca* – should always be in black and white. Colourising does not make it better, it does not change the story … in fact in many ways I think it takes the edge off it, takes the weight from it.'

Asked about her experience of seeing *Night of the Living Dead* on the big screen for the first time, O'Dea has nothing but positive memories. 'The first time I saw it was at the premiere in Pittsburgh,' reflects the actress. 'We had a great get together and it was amazing and I was able to separate myself from myself on-screen (*laughs*). I really enjoyed the experience. Then as the years went by I just grew more and more amazed. It wasn't for quite a few years that I discovered people were seeing this film in a way that I never thought it would be seen. The general public is a tremendously powerful force and what it makes of something, whether it is a film or a happening, can be instrumental in creating change. The public really changed the course of that film. They have made *Night of the Living Dead* what it is today. I think that is why when I, Marilyn, Russ and John, whenever we get the chance to meet that public, we can only say, "Thank you." Thank you for embracing this film in the way you have and thank you for bringing our attention to the things we may not have thought about.'

O'Dea's family were not among those shocked at the violent on-screen shenanigans. In fact, her father even appeared in the movie. 'I always wanted to be in the theatre,' explains O'Dea, 'and so my getting involved in the film was fine with my parents. They were just keen that I had the opportunity to experience a different part of the entertainment world. Now my father and several of my friends are actually in the film. When the police and the helicopters go by the cottage … we were told that they needed extra people. My father was thrilled to be a part of it but as he also found out it can be extremely tiring. He is carrying a rifle, coming across the wide open countryside, trudging about a quarter of a mile whilst George is filming him. Then George says, "Cut! Everybody get back to their original positions!" I think they did that shot several times and by the end my father was literally dragging his rifle across the ground (*laughs*). But he did enjoy it. My parents also got some telephone calls from the general public and people would ask, "How could you let your daughter perform in such a violent, horrific, terrifying film?" So they had to deal with people's reactions but I don't know what they told them. I mean, it wasn't that they allowed me or didn't allow me. It was something I chose to do (*laughs*).'

After *Night of the Living Dead*, O'Dea largely disappeared from motion pictures. Considering her fine job in Romero's classic the inevitable question has to be: what on earth happened? 'Well life takes some interesting turns and mine certainly has,' she replies. 'Once again, I went back to do theatre. I went back to the stage. Because I was not what people classified as a beautiful woman, I was more of a character person. Maybe that is one of the reasons why I didn't get a lot of calls. Even though, for a while, I had an agent out in Los Angeles - but there was no real effort to get the actress from *Night of the Living Dead*. It is only in the last five or seven years where independent filmmakers, who have been influenced by *Night of the Living Dead*, have got in touch with me and asked me if I would be in their films. I am very grateful towards them.'

BEHIND the GREEN DOOR

Released: 1972
Directed by: Jim and Artie Mitchell (The Mitchell Brothers)
Produced by: Jim Mitchell
Written by: Jim Mitchell
Cast: Marilyn Chambers (Gloria Saunders), George S MacDonald (Barry), Johnny Keyes (Stud), Lisa Grant (Australian Lady), Yank Levine (Storyteller), Adrienne Mitchell (Waitress), Dana Fuller (Cook), Dale Meade (Hotel Clerk), Jim Mitchell (First Kidnapper), Art Mitchell (Second Kidnapper), Mike Bradford (Parking Lot Attendant), Tony Royale (Guard).

In a nutshell: A chef at a diner asks a pair of men to tell him the story of the 'Green Door'. One of the men volunteers and the focus of the film becomes an attractive young blonde girl called Gloria Saunders. Whilst holidaying, Gloria is kidnapped by two men and driven to a private member's club in the city of San Francisco. She is then calmed down backstage by an Australian lady who reassures her that, 'no one is going to hurt you.' Led on stage in front of a mixed sex audience, Gloria is stripped and 'ravished' by a group of women, a black man and then four males at once. As the 'ravishing' progresses, the onlookers begin to lose their inhibitions and make out with each other. Finally one of the male viewers leaps on stage and 'rescues' Gloria from the orgy. With this the story comes to an end and we are brought back into the diner. As one of the men leaves and drives away he begins to fantasise about making love to Gloria. In this moment he is revealed to be the person that carried her off stage and away from the 'Green Door' … but is it all just his fantasy?

Prologue: Art and Jim Mitchell, more commonly known as the Mitchell Brothers, had set up the O'Farrell Theatre in San Francisco in order to show their own pornographic short films with titles such as *Flesh Factory* and *Rampaging Nurses*. Risking the wrath of the local authorities, who would commonly raid showings and attempt to prosecute the brothers, the movies were nonetheless enormously successful in the Bay Area. As a result, Art and Jim decided to embark upon making a full length pornographic picture that could be released throughout the United States and which would 'show it all'.[17]

Prior to being cast as Gloria Saunders in *Behind the Green Door*, Marilyn Chambers had been a model and appeared briefly in the Barbra Streisand picture *The Owl and the Pussycat* (1970). She followed this up with a leading turn in Sean Cunningham's softcore offering *Together* (1971). Even back then there was evidence that Chambers was a wild one, with the director (who would go on to helm 1980's smash hit *Friday the 13th*) commenting, 'She was this crazy girl … she was coming to my backyard and taking off her clothes and doing naked diving on film for what reasons, God knows …'[18] Eventually Chambers moved from the East Coast to the West Coast, arriving in San Francisco and answering a casting call for *Behind the Green Door*. Initially refusing to take part in the movie, due to its graphic sexual content, Chambers relented in exchange for a percentage of the feature's box office revenue.

Although short hardcore porn loops were shot and exhibited through American sex shops, a full length feature depicting graphic lovemaking was a rare thing indeed in the early seventies, and anyone who would attempt to release such a title was almost certainly going to run the risk of obscenity prosecutions. 1970's *Mona*, which was made by the same team that later hit cult pay dirt with *Flesh Gordon* in 1974, is commonly identified as being the first porn feature but it failed to become a household name, suffering from terrible distribution. By the time *Behind the Green Door* had wrapped, however, 'porno chic' was beginning to take a hold of North America on the back of Gerard Damiano's *Deep Throat* (also 1972) which made an instant star out of its leading lady Linda Lovelace.

Suffering police raids and criminal prosecutions just as quickly as it collected box office receipts, *Deep Throat* showed that the commercial demand for hardcore fare was nothing less than phenomenal. However, *Deep Throat*'s cult began in the grindhouse cinemas of New York, whereas *Behind the Green Door* would be the first adult feature to gain a wide release across the USA.

---

17 'Jim's thinking was, look, if the police are going to storm in here for us showing soft-core porn, we might as well show it all,' states one O'Farrell 'insider' in *X-Rated* (McCumber, Pinnacle Books, 2000)

18 As told to the author in an interview for *Shock Cinema* (Issue 27, 2005)

About: Whenever anyone reflects upon the cinema of the 1970s there are three adult features that stand out as carrying a large degree of influence and importance, the 1972 films *Deep Throat* and *Behind the Green Door* and the strangely depressing *The Devil in Miss Jones* in 1973. During the brief time when mainstream American audiences actually paid to attend showings of pornographic features in cinemas, the chances are that it was one of these three movies they were going to see. Both *Deep Throat* and *Behind the Green Door* not only created two of the decade's most famous actresses (regardless of genre) in Linda Lovelace and Marilyn Chambers, but, because they were first, they effectively paved the way for the widespread theatrical distribution of such material.

By the time of *The Devil in Miss Jones*, the infamy of *Deep Throat*, coupled with the more arty aspirations of *Behind the Green Door*, meant that even critical acceptance towards the sex film was starting to emerge. 'With *The Devil in Miss Jones*, the hardcore porno feature approaches an art form, one that critics may have a tough time ignoring in the future,' stated a reviewer for the trade journal *Variety*, who went on to single out the picture's 'technical quality'[19]. Of course, it was all downhill from there, as continuing criminal convictions (and, in particular, the Miller vs California case[20]) forced adult films back into sleazy side-streets, grindhouse cinemas and, eventually, obscurity. However, for a fleeting moment, it really did seem as if the enormous financial success of these three titles would lead to an eventual crossover between big studio features and hardcore efforts, perhaps the ultimate in taboo breaking. In reality, it would take decades before explicit, hardcore copulation would once again grace the screens of mainstream cinemas (the most famous being Michael Winterbottom's mundane 2004 effort *9 Songs*), and, even then, the final result managed only fringe appeal.

Whilst academic studies on pornography tend to fall into either an outright acceptance and defence (Linda Williams, Camille Paglia) or a call for censorship (Andrea Dworkin, Catharine MacKinnon), few actually deem the movies themselves worthy of critical evaluation. Yet, as recently as 2000, esteemed British critic Derek Malcolm published a list of his top 100 movies in the *Guardian* newspaper, with at least one controversial choice. In a roll call that included no Spielberg and certainly no *Star Wars* (too lowbrow presumably), Malcolm nonetheless listed *Behind the Green Door* as one of his favourites, maintaining that, 'the film does have a charge that you can't deny, Chambers is certainly some sort of an actress, and the Mitchells could at least claim some imagination in making it.'[21] Perhaps most shocking of all is the revelation that Radley Metzger's hardcore features, which were directed under the pseudonym of Henry Paris and include the popular *The Opening of Misty Beethoven* (1976), are featured in the New York Museum of Modern Art[22].

---

19 As quoted in Lewis J, *Hollywood v Hard Core* (New York University Press, USA, 2000)

20 The Miller v California case came about when 'adult bookseller Marvin Miller' was 'busted for mailing dirty pamphlets.' The result of the case was that the Court handed 'states the right to decide their own obscenity laws.' This ruling basically ensured that many adult titles would not be granted a run in more conservative areas of America and, thus, the boom in porno chic came to an end. (Grahame-Smith, *The Big Book of Porn*, Quirk, 2005)

21 From web site: http://film.guardian.co.uk/Century_Of_Films/Story/0,,338341,00.html

22 As mentioned in Muller, E and Faris, D *Grindhouse: The Forbidden World of 'Adults Only' Cinema* (St Martin's Press, New York, 1996)

TABOO BREAKERS

Of course, all of this merely serves to indicate that pornography was not always the faceless, cheap and, often, nasty product of the present day; wherein silicone enhanced, bleach-blonde 'contract girls' bounce in amateur gonzo backyard productions all trying to attract the male punter's attention. The end result is merely ugly, with the female performers' own self abuse (increasingly large breast implants and so on) perhaps reflecting their on-screen role as nothing more than living, breathing Barbie dolls, obtaining a pay cheque by being pushed into increasing levels of sexual extremes[23]. Whilst the late Linda Lovelace did declare in her notorious autobiography from 1980 that she was beaten by her manager and husband Chuck Traynor in *Ordeal*, the fact remains that her film *Deep Throat* is almost quaint when viewed today. Whilst the sex is still very graphic and Lovelace's performance of the title act looks positively unpleasant (at least for her), the plot of *Deep Throat* carries a comical charm and the women at least look like natural, everyday people. Moreover, the performers, both and male and female, *appear* to be having fun in amongst all of the bumping and grinding, and the humorous soundtrack that accompanies the sex indicates that *Deep Throat* is not really meant to be taken seriously. Consequently, in not only *Deep Throat*, but also in his far superior follow-up feature *The Devil in Miss Jones*, director Damiano cast strangely unglamorous women, and as a result, watching Lovelace, and her successor Georgina Spelvin, have sex is distinctly un-erotic. Indeed, one presumes that the reason behind the success of *Deep Throat* is simply because a wide audience had yet to be exposed to such explicit sexual scenes, and the attractiveness of the on-screen performers simply did not matter.

This, however, is where *Behind the Green Door* genuinely stands out. Unlike *Deep Throat*, *Behind the Green Door* features an attractive leading lady in Marilyn Chambers (whose dashing, clean-cut looks are slightly reminiscent of Cybil Shepherd). From the moment that we glimpse her rusty blonde-haired visage on the screen it is clear that this is not the type of girl that you would expect to be placed in the midst of various explicit sexual situations. Moreover, whilst *Deep Throat* is crudely made and its sex sequences are badly edited and shot, *Behind the Green Door* actually one-upped its predecessor by displaying some filmmaking competency. This is not to say that the Mitchell Brothers showcase any great gift for storytelling, characterization or cinematography (which is mediocre throughout), but they do manage to frame everything reasonably well and the colourful costumes and sets demonstrate some imagination. As a result, *Behind the Green Door* is edited and paced just about as well as any low budget porn movie from the seventies could aspire to be.

Although studies of porno chic invariably focus on *Deep Throat*, and the obscenity trials that followed the movie's blockbuster takings, an argument could well be made that it was *Behind the Green Door* which actually inspired the majority of the hardcore movies that would follow. Indeed, from the far more inspired storytelling and set design of *The Devil in Miss Jones* and the aforementioned *The Opening of Misty Beethoven*; to the shattering of such timely 'taboos' as interracial sex and lesbian activity (neither of which played a part in *Deep Throat*), *Behind*

---

23 In 2004 Sky Television showed a multi-part documentary called *Porno Valley*, in which the Vivid 'contract girl' Mercedes was offered an updated contract, but only if she agreed to anal sex scenes. The performer, vocally uncomfortable with this stipulation, nonetheless signed.

the Green Door can be seen to have successfully predated and influenced the entire adult film genre. Furthermore, unlike *Deep Throat*, the Mitchell Brothers were less interested in climaxing each sex scene with a 'money shot' (whereupon semen is deposited on a female player's body). Instead, *Behind the Green Door* commonly focuses on the face of Chambers, in tight close up, as she approaches orgasm. In fact, only in one instance is male ejaculation the focal point of a sequence. In a genre that is mostly interested in graphic, gynaecological detail, this makes *Behind the Green Door* a decidedly unusual movie. In short, it appears to be far more interested in arousing the viewer through the sexual satisfaction of the female character than through the pleasure of the male performers. Hence, in at least two love scenes between Chambers and her co-stars, it is her facial expressions that are kept in shot, rather than, as might be expected, her naked body.

Ultimately, in the sole set piece where male bodily fluids are released, the images on-screen begin to morph and a psychedelic medley of bright primary colours overtake the screen. The result is simply not erotic. Whilst one can make an obvious accusation of male dominance in this instance, predominantly because three men climax over the face of the film's leading lady, the sequence's breakdown into slow motion and colourful LSD imagery seems to actually indicate that this is the height of Chambers' sexual experience. Her male co-stars are never in shot (aside from their genitals, obviously), instead it is the film's actress who is shown to obtain pleasure from an act that many of us would assume is the culmination of a male power trip. It is *Behind the Green Door*'s greatest failing, and yet also the film's most fascinating moment, the point in the story where special effects, however crude, are introduced to signify a woman's sexual awakening. Yet, that this 'awakening' comes on the back of the *male* orgasm, rather than the female orgasm, seriously belittles any feminist reading of the picture.[24]

In saying this, the fact remains that *Behind the Green Door* itself is, literally, open to be read as a male fantasy from beginning to end and this could indicate that all of the sex scenes are designed to be viewed from a masculine standpoint. For instance, it is strongly suggested that the 'Green Door' element of the movie is within the mind of the storyteller (Yank Levine) only. That the tale unfolds with both Levine and his friend (George S MacDonald) in a diner actually explaining the legend of the private member's club, and also making a brief appearance in the sequence before Chambers is kidnapped, furthers this notion. Finally, it is MacDonald himself that closes the movie, having, within the story, portrayed the part of the man that 'rescues' Chambers from the live sex performance. In the feature's final moments he drives out of the 'real' narrative and into another fake one, whereupon his own fantasy is shared with the viewers. In this context, every sex sequence in *Behind the Green Door*, including the group sex scene involving Chambers, can be concluded to be within the framework of an imagined male fantasy. Within this reading of the movie (which is the most logical considering that the film's main narrative comes to an end with the storytellers in the diner, the same men that began it), the kidnapping of Chambers and her subsequent acceptance and enjoyment of her sexual

---

24 Indicating the scene's orientation towards male fantasy, Chambers commented, 'What's a better turn-on than five different guys jerking off over a pretty girl's face and letting her lick the sperm from her lips and chin?' (McNeil, L & Osborne, J, *The Other Hollywood*, HarperCollins, New York, 2005)

awakening ultimately makes more sense.

However, it is still hard to ignore the fact that *Behind the Green Door*'s central female figure is not given any dialogue and is depicted purely as the focal point for sexual fulfilment. She is never permitted to speak up, to argue against her ordeal or to even express enjoyment through words. This can hardly be said to encourage a feminist reading of the movie (*The Devil in Miss Jones* is a rare example of an adult feature that can actually stand up to this challenge, by the end of the movie the male, rather than the female, is the object of subjectification) and only furthers the notion that the entire movie is a lengthy male fantasy. The question then arises over whether or not the Mitchell Brothers could have made this element more explicit to their viewers, perhaps through an on-screen voiceover at choice moments. Certainly, by making their feature so ambiguous, and with the sex being, at least initially, in a non-consensual form, *Behind the Green Door* is an example of a movie that contemporary political correctness has dated to the time in which it was made.

Subsequently, it is difficult to imagine many viewers, be they returning to the genesis of adult cinema or just curious about porno chic as a whole, believing that the picture represents anything in the way of female liberation, either sexual or otherwise. As a result, even more than *Deep Throat* (the focal point of that movie, as its title indicates, being male relief) *Behind the Green Door* opens itself up for criticism of pandering solely to the men in the audience. Certainly, this is justifiable, after all, the clientele for pornography is overwhelmingly masculine, but when the feature pays such attention to the on-screen pleasure of its leading lady, it does feel a tad schizophrenic in tone. On the one hand, the Mitchell Brothers seem to be hesitant to get in close and document too much in the way of penetration (of all the porno chic blockbusters, this is the tamest), and yet the storyline paints Chambers as nothing less than a body-for-hire. Someone dragged on stage and shagged senseless by all and sundry. For a sex film, then, *Behind the Green Door* is remarkably short on explicit detail, but as a movie for couples, or that might attract women, its focus on male domination is likely to be very off-putting.

However, perhaps the strangest quirk of *Behind the Green Door* is the part of America that it came from. As a movement, porno chic was predominantly based in New York, the city whose famed 42nd Street was the launch pad for many porno chic classics (in Scorsese's *Taxi Driver* one can even see Robert De Niro taking his date, Cybil Shepherd, to an adult theatre on The Deuce to see the SAG-approved *Sometime Sweet Susan*). Even with later 'classic' titles such as Metzger's *Barbara Broadcast* (1977), *Babylon Pink* (1979) and *Roommates* (1981) the landscape of the Big Apple looms large, not only in the setting and (at times) the accents, but because this was the adult film world's production and distribution base. Yet, *Behind the Green Door*, as with subsequent Mitchell Brothers ventures, was filmed and developed in San Francisco, making it unique within its own genre, and perhaps giving further credence to its filmmakers' individualist, renegade attitude. Whilst there is nothing in the way of California glamour hanging over the proceedings (the inherent grubbiness of the movie's 16mm stock is obvious from the very beginning), it is interesting to note that within just a few years the entire adult film industry would relocate to the 'Golden State', leaving New York behind. Currently the headquarters of the world's pornographic film trade, California's somewhat dubious legacy in this movement nevertheless begins with *Behind the Green Door*.

Strangely, for all that the adult movie world barks about libertarian attitudes towards virtually everything and whines about any censorship of their product (no doubt because it loses them money rather than through any heartfelt beliefs) the treatment given to the genre's early genesis is pathetic. To this day, titles such as *Deep Throat* and *Behind the Green Door* have only been given the most minimal, bare bones DVD releases, and with variable quality as well[25]. If ever one wanted the harsh reality of pornography then this is it, a cold, capitalist machine interested only in pick-pocketing as much money as possible, with the barest of effort given to actually respecting the stars or titles of yesteryear. Why bother when the punter's hand is more likely to reach into their pocket for the latest release featuring loud, passionless, dirty sex with bleach blonde plastic surgery victims? Indeed, any talk about pornography liberating *anyone* ultimately begins and ends with these cold, hard facts. Back in the seventies you had skilled filmmakers, such as The Mitchell Brothers, Damiano and Metzger, who were at the forefront of creating increasingly ambitious features that happened to highlight graphic intercourse. These people were misfits, deviants and, perhaps unintentionally, visionaries[26], and yet their memory is disregarded, their films thrown out in scratchy, obscure home video transfers as an afterthought in the modern human meat market that is pornography.

So, as films such as *Deep Throat* and *Behind the Green Door* won their court battles and managed to stay in cinemas, the modern porn business was born. This, of course, leads us to the present day and the industry in all its gory glory, with its ruined lives, Max Hardcore, Rob Black, 500 guy gang-bangs and obese fake breasts.

The question, then, has to be: was it really worth it?

What happened next? The Mitchell Brothers followed up the success of *Behind the Green Door* by re-teaming with Marilyn Chambers (and male stud Johnny Keyes) on *The Resurrection of Eve* (1973). The movie was critically well received but did not enter the popular vernacular as its predecessor had[27]. Not to be dissuaded, the twosome continued with two big budget porn flops – *Sodom & Gomorrah* (1975) and *The Autobiography of a Flea* (1976), the latter of which they only produced.

With the bottom dropping out of the short-lived popularity in porno chic, the brothers' intake of illegal drugs (especially cocaine) reached titanic proportions. Jim Mitchell managed to cool down, whilst Artie continued his life of excess, often violently harassing the nude dancers at the famous Mitchell Brothers' O'Farrell Theatre. On the evening of 27 February 1991, after receiving threatening phone calls from his brother, Jim visited Artie and his latest girlfriend at

---

[25] A new exception is the erstwhile horror movie company Media Blasters who have begun dabbling in adult cinema with 2-disc special editions of *The Devil in Miss Jones*, *Debbie Does Dallas* and Chambers' own *Insatiable*. Nevertheless, this really is the exception rather than the rule.

[26] The Mitchell Brothers most certainly were unintentional visionaries, when the mob attempted to pirate prints of *Behind the Green Door* the twosome did the unthinkable for smutty porn producers: they got into bed with the FBI. 'The big red-and-white FBI warning you see now at the beginning of videotapes is brought to you in part by the Mitchell Brothers.' (McCumber, *X-Rated*, Pinnacle Books, 2000)

[27] *Behind the Green Door* grossed over $30 million in the US (McCumber, *X-Rated*, Pinnacle Books, 2000)

their San Francisco home. Carrying a loaded rifle, Jim subsequently gunned his brother down after breaking into his house. Upon leaving the scene of carnage, Jim was arrested. Surprisingly, Jim Mitchell only spent three years in prison for killing his brother. Most perversely of all, four months after Artie's death, Jim, out of prison on bail, held a party on behalf of his dead sibling at the O'Farrell Theatre. This, frankly gob-smacking, modern day Cain and Abel story was immortalised by Emilio Estevez, who directed and starred (alongside his brother Charlie Sheen) in the superior television movie *Rated X* (2000). The brothers' legacy came to an end when Jim passed away from a heart attack on 12 July 2007.

Following *Behind the Green Door* Marilyn Chambers never quite moved into legitimate films as she had hoped, although she gained herself and the movie instant notoriety when her face appeared on the Ivory Snow soap box at the time of its release. As the model for a national brand (Ivory Snow was a Procter and Gamble product) every last item had to be withdrawn from shops, giving Chambers and the Mitchell Brothers the sort of publicity they could not afford to buy. After her turn in *The Resurrection of Eve*, Chambers was cast in the leading role in David Cronenberg's excellent horror shocker *Rabid* (1977). Although the movie is now regarded as a classic, it bombed upon release and the actress ended up back in porn, directed by Artie Mitchell in his rough short *Never a Tender Moment* (1979). In 1980 she made a last attempt to revive the fading interest in cinematic adult features by starring in *Insatiable*, which had high production values and a decent director (Godfrey Daniels, who would go on to produce the hit television shows *Hunter* and *Renegade*). The movie was a relatively big money maker and brought Chambers back to public recognition, eventually leading to another legitimate movie role in the low budget science fiction opus *Angel of H.E.A.T.* (1983). In the late nineties, the actress returned to hardcore (now in her late forties and sporting breast implants) with such titles as *Still Insatiable* (1999). Most recently, Chambers was the official candidate for United States Vice President on behalf of the Personal Choice Party, a fiercely libertarian (ie: pro-guns, anti-taxing anyone, save the world through capitalism etc) front that garnered only 1% of the vote in Utah.

As for hardcore pornography, well, it's pretty much everywhere these days, with Ron Jeremy developing into a reality television mainstay and Jenna Jameson becoming the most famous adult film star since Chambers herself (and starring in a legitimate horror movie, 2008's *Zombie Strippers*, opposite Robert 'Freddy Krueger' Englund). The 'golden age' didn't last long, however, as VHS soon drove features out of the theatres and into the home, effectively diluting production values and filmmaking skill in the process. Following on from *Behind the Green Door* was the incredibly successful *The Devil in Miss Jones*, after which pornography was largely pushed away from the mainstream due to a series of prosecutions in the United States. Nevertheless, the work of Radley Metzger has garnered a major cult following, as has 1976's sex-musical *Alice in Wonderland* (arguably the best pornographic feature ever made) and 1982's strangely moral *Café Flesh*. *Deep Throat*'s Damiano continued to obtain critical accolades, shooting his *Story of Joanna* (1975) in cinemascope, but he never repeated the success of his first two features again.

The last huge 'golden age' smash was 1978's *Debbie Does Dallas*, whose catchy title and attractive leading lady (Bambi Woods) made it possibly the most famous adult film to date (it has since been adapted into a stage musical). The Mitchell Brothers did a belated, 'safe sex-condoms only' sequel to *Behind the Green Door* in 1986, starring Artie's then-girlfriend Missy Manners, but it sank without a trace. The influence of the original is best seen in Stanley Kubrick's last film *Eyes Wide Shut* (1999), whose orgy sequence is almost certainly inspired by the Mitchell Brothers. Most recently, big studio efforts such as *Boogie Nights* (1997), *Wonderland* (2003) and *Inside Deep Throat* (2005) demonstrate that the days of 'porno chic' continue to spawn stories. Jackie Chan can even be caught watching *Behind the Green Door* in *The Cannonball Run* (1980).

Hardcore acts of sex can also be seen in mainstream cinema, such as the aforementioned *9 Songs*, *Intimacy* (2001), Catherine Breillat's *Anatomy of Hell* (2004) and, briefly, in Lars von Trier's ridiculously overrated *The Idiots* (1998).

Marilyn Chambers interview

Released in 1972 to tremendous box office, and even some mainstream critical acclaim, *Behind the Green Door* became one of the most popular adult films ever made. It also, of course, made a star out of Marilyn Chambers who, prior to hooking up with the Mitchell Brothers, had starred in an obscure softcore sex film called *Together*, which was written and directed by a young Sean Cunningham and featured Wes Craven on associate producer duties. Cineastes will, of course, know that Cunningham and Craven would later team up for 1972's *Last House on the Left* and the rest, as they say, is history. Consequently, *Together*, which is now considered lost, has its place in the legacy of cinema, if only as a footnote.

'I did that film a long time ago,' remembers Chambers of *Together*, 'We all grew up in the same town, West Port, Connecticut,' she adds, 'And I was actually going out with Sean's brother – I knew his family for years. So Sean was going to be making this film, I think I was seventeen at the time, and he was going to be making this film that was a "quote" documentary. This was back in the days of sex, drugs and rock and roll where everyone was trying to find themselves. So Sean asked me if I wanted to be in it and I said, "Sure." Now *Together* was one of Sean's first productions so he is probably embarrassed by it now, but what they did, which was a really good notion, and it really allowed the film to make a lot of money, is that they got with a chain of theatres, I can't remember the name of them, and they put advertisements on television for the movie. It got the most phenomenal publicity, so everybody knew about the movie and, of course, I wasn't called Marilyn Chambers back then (*note: she was Marilyn Briggs*) ... because we were supposed to be like "real" people. And what they did, which was kind of deceiving to the public, is that they had a showing at ten in the morning for all of the housewives and in that showing they would include a scene with this black man who had this really big, you know ...'

Incredibly, Chambers seems reluctant to say 'penis'. 'Well anyway,' she laughs 'the girl was sitting there and she was putting a flower on it and teasing it and the guy got a hard-on and it was like, "Wow" and, of course, it took up the whole screen so these housewives would go home and go, "Oh my God you have to go and see this movie and blah, blah, blah," and then people would go and see it and that scene wouldn't be in there. So it was a teaser, and in some showings they would take it out. So it was a pretty clever advertising scheme and a lot of people saw the movie as a result.'

Indeed, the actress admits that she has fond memories of her big screen debut, 'I knew the

Cunningham boys for years,' she says. 'They painted my house and, of course, I would run around with just my underwear on while they were painting the windows and they would almost fall off their ladders (*laughs*). I was very much a tease ... Sean was the older one and they were just kind of wild and crazy guys. They would have drinking parties over at their house and, you know, they had a swimming pool and my sister, who is about five years older than me, she knew Sean and Noel, his brother, and Kevin, and I went out with Kevin for a while. So they were crazy. Now, you know, Wes Craven ... I really don't remember Wes a lot, but I'm sure I've met him.'

Following *Together*, Chambers packed her bags and headed to New York, where she won a small part in the Barbra Streisand comedy *The Owl and the Pussycat*. 'That was after *Together* and I was still only 18,' she says. 'I didn't say anything but I was Robert Klein's girlfriend, "Barney's girl" was my credit on the movie. They forgot to put my name on the credits (*laughs*). I did get my SAG card and I did go on a publicity tour for *The Owl and the Pussycat* with Roz Kelly, who played a hooker in the movie. So we went and did all this publicity stuff and they didn't even put my name on the credits, which was ridiculous. I got the role because I had met this guy who was a male model and back then they weren't all gay or anything (*laughs*) - in fact he was my boyfriend. Well he said, "Hey, I'm playing George Segal's stand-in in this movie, would you like to come and see how a real movie is made?" I said, "Sure," and so I went to the set, they were shooting in Manhattan, and I was thrilled. Of course, I had my modelling portfolio with me and Ray Stark, the producer, saw me and they were casting ... he asked me what it was that I do and of course I said, "Oh I'm an actress." So he said, "We're casting for Barney's girl upstairs right now, would you like to try out?" and I said, "Well yeah," and so I went upstairs and he called me in his room – there's probably about twenty-five or thirty other women sitting out there – they talked to me, then I went outside and they came out and said, "Well you got the part, you ready to go?" Then they took me downstairs, took my clothes off, put me in bed, made me sign a contract and that was my introduction to film.'

Strangely, however, this flirtation with the mainstream did not lead to bigger things for Chambers. Instead, after a modelling gig for Procter and Gamble, on the Ivory Snow soap box, she headed to San Francisco and hooked up with Artie and Jim Mitchell. 'I shot the picture for the soap box probably when I was about 16, a senior in high school, something like that,' confirms Chambers, who looks remarkably mature on the final image, holding a small child and looking akin to a mother in her late twenties. 'However, it took them a couple of years to get the old picture off the box and the new picture on the box. And I kind of forgot about it, they told me about it and everything ... but in the interim I had done *Behind the Green Door* and when I remembered it I told Jim and Art Mitchell, "Oh by the way, I'm the mum holding the baby on the Ivory Snow soap box." And they went to the supermarket to see if it was there and it had come out the exact same week that *Behind the Green Door* came out. So the soap box logo of "99 44/100% pure as driven snow" and *Behind the Green Door*, you know, the controversy of the two was phenomenal. It was great. Procter and Gamble just freaked out and, of course, they bought out my contract after they had put my illustration on the box. It must have cost them a lot of money.'

Still, this controversy was good news for *Behind the Green Door*'s box office, which took off to great heights after it was revealed that the movie's starlet was the beauty on the packaging of a national soap powder. Back then, stunningly gorgeous women did not do pornography. 'Porno chic: that was what they called it,' says Chambers. 'It was a phenomenon. Back then you had to go to the movie theatre and stand in line to actually go see the movie. There was no VHS and DVDs or anything like that. You weren't anonymous by any means. So people like Johnny Carson and other celebrities were going to see the movies and it became this cool thing to do. It wasn't just these guys wanking away at the back of the theatres; it was the couples and the respectful businessmen going to see these films. It kind of brought a different flavour to things and made it a pop culture, cult kind of thing.'

Being a porn star is probably not what any parent envisages for their son or daughter, so it is no surprise to learn that Chambers' mother and father were less than thrilled with her appearance in *Behind the Green Door*. 'Oh they were horrified,' she insists. 'They were absolutely just ... "Yeuch!" My parents didn't speak to me for a couple of years. They just said, "Oh you've ruined our image." My dad was in the advertising business so all his buddies knew. There is actually a story ... I don't know if it is true, my dad and I really never discussed all the graphic things about my career although they knew I was famous and we kind of talked around it for all those years – they've both passed away now – but I heard a rumour that his friends had taken him to see *Behind the Green Door* and didn't tell him that I was in it. Apparently it blew his mind and he was so embarrassed. I mean I have a daughter so I can imagine what that must have been like. I didn't want to tell him, but then he found out and I had to tell him ... but, of course, I actually became the toast of the town. I was drinking the best champagne, staying at suites in the Plaza Hotel. I was treated like a queen and it was something else. I went to Cannes with it and I gave a speech in French. We went over there and it was a very good reception. They were totally blown away.'

The actress also feels that it was 'right time, right place' as far as the success of her debut adult picture goes. 'It was a first and it used different film techniques, like the famous polarization for the cum shot,' she says. 'It was kind of absurd and today it looks corny, but the thing about *Behind the Green Door* is that back then it was new. Also, it was, first of all, shot on 16mm and then brought up to 35mm. So it was very grainy and the quality of the film sucked but it was supposed to be like you are looking through a keyhole and you're a voyeur and you are seeing something that you're not supposed to see. So that was cool and (*pauses*) well, by today's standards it's really not so explicit. It's not from a gynaecologist's point of view, let's say, there's a lot of day shots of, like, pretty stuff and there's not a lot of insertion shots which, today would be considered hardly adult at all. But for its time it was very advanced. But, personally, I don't know if it would really be a big successful film if the Ivory Snow soap box had not come out that very same week. It was the controversy of these two. Success comes in many forms and reasons and mostly it's because you are in the right place at the right time with the right elements ... and the combination of everything makes it a hit. I think that was certainly the case for *Behind the Green Door*. Our society at the time was screaming for something like that ...'

Indeed, Chambers' biggest disappointment with *Behind the Green Door* was that it did not give her any dialogue. 'I like to think that I can act,' she states. 'I was told when we began *Behind the Green Door*, and this really disconcerted me, that I wouldn't be saying a thing. I thought,

"Well there goes my acting career and those acting classes. What do you mean I'm not going to be saying anything?" I uttered not one word in it which was (*pauses*) definitely a challenge. I really needed to know what was going on in my head, when I was giving head (*laughs*), but yes that was a very big challenge. I didn't know how it was going to come out but I guess it came out okay.'

In the fallout from *Behind the Green Door* the Mitchell Brothers became well known for their heavy partying, often at their own O'Farrell Theatre in San Francisco, and for battling the mafia, who had helped to fuel the explosion in popularity for pornographic features after funding *Deep Throat*. 'The Mitchell Brothers wouldn't let the mafia get involved,' says Chambers. 'They said to them, "Screw you, we're not paying you anything," and so they got busted a lot and they had a lot of problems but it meant that Jim Mitchell owned the rights to everything, he never sold himself out.' Asked about her memories of the brothers and Chambers is forthright. 'They were crazy,' she laughs. 'They were like my brothers, again, that was the time of sex, drugs and rock 'n' roll and there was a lot of sex, a lot of drugs and they were filmmakers, very preppy guys that grew up in California. The first time I met them they were wearing sweater vests. They had on these vests with a Brooke Brothers shirt and a tie on. So they were these all-American guys, clean cut, just trying to make a buck and they liked sex. They were very cool and what happened later was definitely a tragedy but that's what happens when the drugs and alcohol become out of hand.'

The Mitchell Brothers would follow *Behind the Green Door* with 1973's *The Resurrection of Eve*. The movie once again starred Marilyn Chambers but, oddly for an adult movie, did not feature any complete sex scenes and also mixed in homosexual sequences with the expected heterosexual groping. In the picture Chambers stars as a car wreck survivor who goes on a voyage of *Emmanuelle*-like sexual discovery after recovering from the accident. 'There is too much story and too much talking,' says Chambers of her follow-up flick. 'I've found that the best formula for adult films is sex, sex and more sex. The more people are talking you just want to say, "Oh please shut up." No one wants to see a big story – that was the whole thing – "Oh it's for women." Oh bullshit, it's for men. Men like sex on films and women can come along for the ride. You know, it was a good attempt but the Mitchell Brothers' attempts thereafter … they blew a lot of money on big productions when what people want to see is just vignettes of their favourite fantasies.'

The early lives of Chambers and the Mitchell Brothers would be documented in the acclaimed made-for-television movie *Rated X*, which starred real life brothers Charlie Sheen and Emilio Estevez, with the latter also directing. 'Yeah, I thought *Rated X* was pretty good,' says the actress. 'They had invited me to the opening night and I said, "Why didn't you guys consult me on this?" and they said, "Oh we never thought about it." They didn't want to pay me that was what! So, you know, it was pretty accurate. Tracy Hutson, who played me, she was pretty good – I would probably have chosen someone else but she was okay (*pauses*) yeah she was good. And it went a little over the top but I think it had to be when you're dealing with The Mitchell Brothers and all the drugs and stuff. There were plenty of drugs and alcohol and craziness but they drove it over the top a bit. However I thought the way they (Estevez and Sheen) portrayed their roles … it was uncanny. They were both very good.'

Following her popularity in the adult film industry, Chambers went on to appear in David

Cronenberg's early shocker *Rabid*, although her liaison with the mainstream did not last for long. 'I know, what happened?' bemoans Chambers. 'I had the intentions of doing more legitimate work,' she maintains. 'That was how I started out in this business – with the intention of being a mainstream actress. I hoped that *Behind the Green Door* would be a stepping stone to better things but essentially it blackballed me. There's a very big stigma attached, even today, to porn: once a porn star, always a porn star and people don't forget that. But with *Rabid*, David Cronenberg was talking a lot about acting. He was wonderful to work with, a very introspective, weird kind of guy. You know that was the one film we did together and that was it, and we never really spoke to each other afterwards or over the years and I always wondered why that was. I really wanted to do more films, but I just went to do a lot of other things and our paths never crossed again. When *Rabid* came out, it was panned as being real cheesy. It was seen as a really crappy horror movie. Of course, now it's a cult film, because people look back over the rest of David's work and see how he started. It was a fun film to make and I went on a big publicity tour with it and I thought it was going to do a lot better than it did. I was surprised that it didn't do well, because Roger Corman distributed it and he was the horror, or B-movie, king. But it just wasn't a big deal when it came out.'

FRITZ the CAT

Released: 1972
Directed by: Ralph Bakshi
Produced by: Steve Krantz
Written by: Ralph Bakshi
Stars: Skip Hinnant (Fritz), Rosetta LeNoire, John McCurry, Phil Seuling, Ralph Bakshi, Judy Engles (voices)

In a nutshell: It is the 1960s and Fritz is a disillusioned college student at New York University, looking to get high, get laid and find 'the revolution'. When a college party is invaded by two especially violent policemen a stoned Fritz takes one of the officer's guns and shoots the place up, too inebriated to really grip what he is doing. Later, on the run from the law, Fritz goes through a number of eye-opening experiences, including hiding out in a ghetto area, joyriding, interracial sex and, finally, hooking up with a pack of Neo-Nazis as they endeavour to blow up a power plant.

Prologue: *Fritz the Cat* started life as a comic book character drawn by counter-culture hero Robert Crumb. Fritz debuted in 1968, later attracting the interest of producer Steve Krantz and animator Ralph Bakshi, who had worked on such cartoon favourites as Mighty Mouse and Heckle and Jeckle for the Terrytoons studio. Bakshi had later moved to Paramount Pictures but left to make his first, independently financed, full length animated feature. Unlike anything before it, *Fritz the Cat* was aimed at an adult audience, an approach that had no commercial precedent.

Full length animation was popularised by Walt Disney with his 1937 production *Snow White and the Seven Dwarfs*, which at the time received much negative consensus among critics[28]. However, *Snow White* surprised many by becoming an instant success and the full length animated picture was born in its wake, with the Disney studio leading the way with successive masterpieces such as *Pinocchio* (1940) and *Fantasia* (1940). *Fritz the Cat*, however, plays out like a reaction against Disney animation: the characters are certainly 'cute', and the depiction of talking animals is just as anthropomorphic, but Bakshi's creations react, from the offset, in a way that is sexual, aggressive and often vulgar. Likewise, *Fritz the Cat* uses the animated format to address political and social issues, depict drug use and reflect the New York of the late sixties/early seventies. Nothing could be further from Disney's family orientated approach.

About: 'The 1960s, happy times, heavy times …'

Fritz the Cat is one of those rare movies that acts almost like a time machine. Just as with such classics as *La Dolce Vita* (1960) or *Easy Rider* (1969), Bakshi allows the viewer to be transported back to a period when the movie's politics and social issues were hugely relevant to the target audience and, as such, his stunning debut is very much a product of its era. However, it is a testament to Bakshi's filmmaking skills that *Fritz the Cat* still holds enough authority to function in this way, and, when watched today, the feature remains quite powerful; even if its once controversial content seems a tad quaint in the era of irreverent cartoon series such as *Family Guy* and *South Park*. This said, however, the politics of Bakshi's vehicle are far more upfront than his adult-orientated successors and his (brief) addressing of the Israel-Palestine conflict is a decidedly unusual trait for any American motion picture, past or present. Nevertheless, it is *Fritz the Cat*'s depictions of cartoon sex and foul language that leave the biggest impression and which, more than likely, created such controversy upon its initial release.

Bakshi's movie is, fundamentally, about looking for a revolution where none exists. It is about a character (Fritz) who dreams about being a part of something important and productive. Indeed, at a time when America was embroiled in the Vietnam War and black-white relations were still tense, Fritz rightly believes that there should be something counter-culture happening, such as a rising of the people to topple the government and the police. However, as a student by day with too much time on his hands, Fritz's real motivation soon becomes more apparent. Far from wishing to protest and 'rise up' in the name of any deep-felt political beliefs, the character instead sees a revolution as the perfect opportunity to score with women and to liven up his mundane existence. For Fritz, revolution is sexy (in much the same way that Che Guevera's visage now emblazons skinny t-shirts). Indeed, it is the hunt for sexual relations that is ultimately what drives the character through the movie, as he goes from one ill-thought out encounter to the next. In light of this, the director seems to be saying that the reason society remains stagnant is because many of the people involved in political gatherings, and protesting, are only interested in appearing 'sexy' and 'with it'. When Fritz mentions, 'my duty as a poet and as a writer is to get out there and see the world,' Bakshi depicts him treading over a tunnel filled

---

28 'United Artists executives exhibited little enthusiasm in the project, and influential figures throughout the film industry doubted the wisdom of the Disney experiment with a feature cartoon. Walt learned it was being called "Disney's Folly", and there were predictions that *Snow White* would sink him into bankruptcy.' (Thomas, B, *Walt Disney: An American Original*, Pocket Books, 1980)

with voluptuous breasts – aptly representing his mindset and indicating what he really wants. Finally, in the movie's climactic sequence, Fritz, desperate to just do *anything* outside of the norm, joins up with a small group of loathsome Neo-Nazis who are driven to blow up a power plant. In other words, the thrill of the quick fix, the hunger for excitement, has finally led to a very real, destructive climax.

Thankfully, the cat belatedly comes to his senses and exclaims, 'All you care about is a reason to hurt, a reason to destroy, to blow up! You don't know what a real revolution is.' Of course, the irony is that neither does Fritz. From his famous, baffling opening gambit of, 'My soul is tormented! I've been up and down the four corners of this big old world … and still my heart cries out, yes, cries out in this hungry, tortured, wrecked quest: "More!"' to his ignorant arrival in a black ghetto area, the character is blind to the world that surrounds him. Certainly, it is difficult to think of a more self-centred film character than Fritz, whose every speech is spoken with the desired effect of appearing more attractive to the opposite sex. Following his 'my soul is tormented' outburst (which he gives to three women) he takes the trio back to his friend's apartment and organises a gang-bang in the bathtub, complete with copious pot smoking. When more men join in Fritz begins to protest but finally becomes little more than a pawn, shoved aside by more free-wheeling students seeking sex and drugs (exactly the type of personality Fritz masquerades as but, when faced with a group of them, suddenly reacts to the contrary).

Bakshi, however, does not promote drug usage in his movie. Instead, he seems to despair at the marijuana generation. All this talk about getting something done and, yet, puffing on a drug that slows down your machinations, the filmmaker's opening set piece of a working class builder urinating from atop a city construction and onto the head of a student hippy speaks for itself. In fact, it is our introduction to three hard grafting, foul mouthed builders in the movie's prologue that sets up the tone of the feature so perfectly. For example, they complain about their children wasting their college money on dope and drink, highlighting a generational gap that Bakshi refrains from touching on again in his movie, which leads into the aforementioned set piece of one of the workmen pissing onto the head of a youthful, flower-power passer-by. From hereon in we are introduced to Bakshi's landscape, where African-American characters are drawn as crows and white males are cats or dogs (i.e. natural predators). 'As a cat, my kind has always brought suffering on your kind,' says Fritz to a crow in one of Bakshi's wonderfully symbolic moments.

The police are, perhaps inevitably, represented as pigs, although their dim-witted delivery, and heavy handed brutality, indicates that they are little more than 'livestock' themselves; serving a corrupt state and dishing out punishment to anyone that deviates from society's norm. Therefore, as you might be able to imagine, *Fritz the Cat* is nothing short of pessimistic, and it delivers a very doom laden soliloquy, indicating that war, greed and racial inequality are just as central to human nature as eating and sleeping. For example, when Fritz stands tall in Harlem and begins a left-leaning speech of, 'Revolt, revolt, come the revolution there's gonna be no more limousines, come the revolution there's going to be more strawberries and cream,' he inspires a riot. The result is not only police brutality but a depiction of the heavy carpet bombing that took place during the Vietnam War, when a number of aircraft fly through New

York and drop bombs on the troubled area (albeit only after a white police officer has been shot). What comes of this, of course, is a lot of dead and beaten bodies but no solution, something that is as true of the Vietnam conflict as it is of the current battle in Iraq. Furthermore, it is Fritz's liberal words, which suggest the possibility of a communist society, that ultimately result in the state sending out armed forces (again, this is another, eerie reflection of how Vietnam began). However, perhaps the most amusing thing about this segment (and let us not forget that *Fritz the Cat* is still largely played for laughs) is the sight of three very Disney-like characters hopelessly waving an American flag as the bombers fly past. Clearly, Bakshi saw an America that was losing its innocence and, perversely, the explicit vulgarity and cartoon violence of his debut feature proves to be a fine way in which to address this.

Bakshi also pays homage to his Terrytoon past by briefly showcasing a character that loosely resembles the classic Deputy Dawg. However, whereas that particular children's personality only hinted at a redneck sensibility, the director makes the link far more explicit by having the dippy hound mercilessly beat a truck full of chickens to death with a plank of wood. Presumably a personal dig at his former employer, and possibly such Southern stereotypes in their own right, this brief sequence is irrelevant to the movie's plot but, nonetheless, is successful in instigating laughter. Moreover, if there is one thing that Bakshi appears to love in *Fritz the Cat* (and in his later animated classic *Coonskin*) it is stereotypes, including the dedicated, indistinguishable rabbis (who break character only to celebrate the US support of more arms to Israel, and bear in mind that Bakshi is a Palestinian-born Jew) and a pair of trigger-happy, bigoted cops.

However, such caricatures are presented with the goal of inspiring thought, rather than just laughter. As mentioned, at its heart, *Fritz the Cat* reveals a very notable nihilism, largely based upon humankind's apparent inability to co-exist peacefully and deal with difference in a non-violent manner. From the rabbis applauding the news of more war in the Middle East to Fritz's ridiculously ignorant call of 'hey boy' in an all-black bar, Bakshi aptly demonstrates that far too many people seek confrontation, or at least fail to accept difference, and the result can only be continued separation and violence. Indeed, every major sequence in his movie ends with some form of brutality, and, amongst the general hilarity of cartoon characters exposing their genitals or swearing, it is hard not to feel affected by such a strong, intelligent voice. Ultimately this may be Bakshi's greatest coup, sucking us in with the foul language and animated sex before revealing a distinct social commentary, aptly conveyed through his cartoon personalities.

Consequently, although there can be little denying that *Fritz the Cat* is rich with metaphor and subtext, let us also not forget the actual *vibe* of the movie, which is so funky, cool and just plain outré that it becomes difficult not to fall in love with it. Take, for example, the sequence where Bakshi cuts for an interval by introducing a solitary, beautifully animated crow who clicks his fingers along with 'Bo Diddley', a classic soul tune that positively lights up the screen. Coming from the blaxploitation era, where features such as *Shaft* had proven that a soundtrack could be something special, *Fritz the Cat* sports a wonderful score, mixing Billie Holiday with original numbers from Ed Bogas. This, coupled with Bakshi's renegade approach to animation, makes every scene a joy to behold.

As for the artistry itself, *Fritz the Cat* features the sort of minimalist approach that would later become popular in the likes of *Beavis and Butthead* and *The Simpsons* on television. Whilst

TABOO BREAKERS

Fritz and the rest of the main characters are beautifully illustrated, Bakshi's backgrounds are much rougher around the edges, although his dimly lit paintings of the New York skyline are vivid and powerful. The movie also carries a curiously realistic death sequence whereupon a character is shot in the chest and his final gasps of air are represented as pool balls pumping through a black background. As the thud of his heart slows itself down to a crawl, so too do the balls become fewer and fewer … with the overall effect actually being quite painful to watch. Likewise, although it is hard to take the cartoon sex seriously, there is still something rather off-putting about seeing an animated cat have sex with an obese black woman. Yet, as bad taste as this may be, Bakshi never sinks to the degrading level of some of his successors, and, for all of the explicit sexual shenanigans, his movie never feels misogynistic. Rather, it is Fritz himself that comes out of his endless fucking looking like a schmuck. Unable to hold down a proper relationship and aimlessly moving from one woman to the next, one really feels for his 'girlfriend' Winston when she maintains, 'You can't cope with a mature woman.' Of course she is correct because, for someone who thinks he has the world all sorted out; Fritz doesn't have the emotional maturity to devote himself to anyone, rather, he is a product of boredom. 'You spend years and years with your head buried in these goddamn books while the world outside passes you by,' he sighs whilst in his college dormitory. Uninterested in his studies, and unable to find a meaningful long term pursuit, Fritz lives for 'the moment' even if, as we see at the end of the movie, it almost leads to his death, and the destruction of property.

And so we have *Fritz the Cat*. Inevitably, anything this groundbreaking is bound to look different when viewed all these years later, and the lurid appeal of the first X-rated cartoon has undoubtedly been softened. Still, as dated as it undoubtedly is, there is a stark independence to the feature that still rings true, the feeling that you really are watching a bold, brave labour of love by a hugely underrated auteur. Sure, it might not be the same watching it today as it was back in 1972, but *Fritz the Cat* still contains enough food for thought to warrant slipping the old puss a bowl of milk and curling up on the sofa for one of animation's dirtiest little gems. It is little wonder that after this Herculean achievement Bakshi felt that animation could conquer anything, from *Lord of the Rings* to *War and Peace*.[29]

What happened next? Bakshi mixed live action with animation in his follow-up feature, the 1974 masterwork *Heavy Traffic*, a quirky, fiercely imaginative (and very adult) trip through big city life via the eyes of a budding cartoonist. Coupled with *Fritz the Cat*, the two make for an interesting, and very personal, view of life in the Big Apple (Bakshi's sophomore effort is also based on a Robert Crumb comic strip). Bakshi followed up *Heavy Traffic* (which was not a commercial success) with his most unconventional offering to date, 1975's controversial *Coonskin*, a hard-hitting, racial satire on Disney's classic *Song of the South* (1946) and the blaxploitation genre as a whole. To this day, *Coonskin* remains something of a 'lost' movie with bootlegs frequently appearing on eBay whilst a legitimate DVD release has yet to appear.

---

29 'Bakshi became the Great White Hope of animation,' writes critic Leonard Maltin. 'In interview he talked about a brave new world of animation, and asked rhetorically why it wouldn't be possible to tackle any kind of subject matter in this medium, even *War and Peace*.' (*Of Mice and Magic*, Plume, 1987)

After his trilogy of adult films Bakshi went into production with two more family orientated fantasy features, 1977's *Wizards* and 1978's still unfinished *Lord of the Rings*. The latter caused controversy when Bakshi was criticised for rotoscoping (tracing over live action movements) although hindsight now shows his Middle Earth adaptation to be a solid and inventive journey[30]. Less remembered Bakshi works include his musical *American Pop* (1981) and the comic book epic *Fire and Ice* (1983), whilst his last full length feature stands as the commercially disastrous *Cool World* (1992), a muddled, part-animated noir featuring Brad Pitt. Some of his best, more contemporary work, can be seen in his 1987 *Mighty Mouse* television series.

Although Robert Crumb would kill Fritz in print (after vocally dismissing the movie) the world's most famous adult cartoon character would return to the big screen in 1974's awful R-rated sequel *The Nine Lives of Fritz the Cat*. Bakshi wisely decided to have nothing to do with it and the feature, which has Skip Hinnant once again lending his voice to Fritz, is surprisingly difficult to endure. *Nine Lives*' director Robert Taylor went on to work for Disney, although he also served as an animator on Bakshi's *Heavy Traffic* and *Wizards*.

Fritz the Cat didn't lead to an instant boom in adult animation, although a handful of productions quickly, and quietly, slipped out, most notably the Roger Corman-produced *Dirty Duck* (1975) and the rather more lewd *Once Upon a Girl* (1976). Later, more adult orientated, animated productions included *The Plague Dogs* (1980, see later chapter in this book), *When the Wind Blows* (1986) and *The Big Bang* (1987), the latter being the most Bakshi-inspired of the bunch. Of course, Bakshi's lineage also stretches to television and in the likes of *Beavis and Butthead*, *Family Guy*, *Ren and Stimpy* (in which Bakshi provided a vocal appearance) and *South Park* one can see the great animator's cutting edge comedy and lewdness being picked up by a new generation of cartoonists.

Ralph Bakshi interview

Ralph Bakshi is now an icon in the field of animation. However, when he is asked if he ever expected adults to line up for a full length X-rated cartoon the director admits that he neither knew nor cared – he was merely chasing his own vision. 'That is a good question to start with,' says Bakshi. 'And I'm very serious about this: I didn't care if there was an audience out there. I did not care (*laughs*). I had grown up with Disney and then I went to work for Terrytoons, which was all children's cartoons ... Everything was children's cartoons. Sometimes they would get a little risky, like Daffy Duck, which, compared to the other children's cartoons, was the highest point of outrageousness. I was a young man and bored out of my mind. I just couldn't stand what I was doing anymore because it didn't do anything for me. So when I did *Fritz the Cat* it was personal. I didn't care if there was an audience there or not.'

Certainly, although Bakshi didn't care about who would, or would not, watch his latest

---

30 There is some evidence to suggest that Bakshi's renegade status, and his success with independent productions such as *Fritz the Cat*, was what caused such critical disdain towards rotoscoping. For example, Disney never came under any fire for its re-use of old footage in 1973's *Robin Hood* where animators 'took a shortcut by tracing the dance movements from a famous scene in *Snow White*.' (Maltin, L, *The Disney Films*, Disney, 2000)

endeavour he does admit that others were not quite so blasé. 'Everyone fell apart over, "Is there an audience out there?"' laughs the artist. 'But animation was my medium and what I did from morning to night. So what do I care if there is an audience out there when someone is paying me to do something I love? It is that simple. It has always been that simple for me. I have always had trouble with Hollywood where they say, "You have to consider the audience." I can't consider the audience. I don't know what audiences like. I only know what I like. If I considered audiences then I wouldn't have done anything in *Fritz the Cat*. If you consider audiences you get some of the dumbest movies ever made. But you have to also consider the time, and this is very important, it was a time when we were protesting the Vietnam War. A time when we were trying to get integration so that black people could vote ... the whole country was in turmoil. Miles Davis was doing *Sketch of Spain* and all of this was stuff that I loved as a young man and none of it was safe. I knew a small minority would like the film. My friends in the block I grew up with would like it, my friends that I went for a drink with on Friday night ... I knew they would like it. So I didn't consider an audience for a second.'

Indeed, Bakshi's main motivation in making his first full length feature was in changing his own horizons and regaining his love of animation. To do this he decided to go all out with a project that would either make or break him. 'I was in the animation business and a lot of the directors that I met had never been part of a feature film,' he says. 'Unless you worked for Disney you were lucky to do one feature film in your whole life, and nobody ever did two or three. Nobody made features except Disney back in '67. So I thought, "This will be my last feature so what the hell ... I don't care if nobody shows up." I still don't – and that is where this whole conversation should go. I don't give a shit. When I was making the film I was having the best time of my life and wrestling with problems that I was never allowed to wrestle with. Now it is a little different because of cable and the world has changed but back then I had to ask myself, "Do you draw a penis or do you not draw a penis? Do you draw pants on the cat?" All of those millions and millions of details and I had nowhere to look for the answer. If you are going to kill someone in a picture then it has to be real, but how can it be real if you kill a crow in the middle of a black race riot? On the soundtrack I used Billie Holliday, rock 'n' roll and jazz, and that was the first time that had ever been done in a feature film. That was what I was listening to.'

One might expect that gaining the rights to a Billie Holliday song would cost serious cash, but Bakshi insists that nothing could be further from the truth. 'No one cared,' he insists. 'I got Billie Holliday for $100, I got the Rolling Stones ... what I am saying is that in those days no one used rock 'n' roll, believe me. Kid, I'm 68. It's a different world, no one used rock 'n' roll in animated features. When I went to buy the rights they gave me them for nothing, and it was the same right through until *American Pop*. If I had to buy the music to *American Pop* now it would probably cost ten times what the movie cost to make. I was getting major songs for $500. My friend is in the movie business just now and if you want a major hit in a movie these days it will cost you $100,000. I had 20 major hits in *American Pop* and the movie only cost $1.2 million, so you can figure it out for yourself.'

Fritz the Cat ran into some initial turmoil when the movie's original backers, Warner Brothers, dumped the picture after Bakshi gave them a preview of a completed sequence. Suffice to say, they were horrified. 'That is a funny story,' he recalls. 'Warner Brothers liked the idea of an adult cartoon. So I pitched it. I was young and I wore bell bottoms so what the fuck, they liked the way I looked, you know? They liked the idea and gave me $250,000 to show them what I meant. No one knew what I was talking about – I had this presentation of race riots in Harlem and stuff – and I go back to the studio in New York because $250,000 is a lot of money. I was happy. I was really fucking happy because this is it! No one gives you $250,000 unless they are serious. The picture only cost $1 million so that is a quarter of the film. But I wanted to make sure that everyone clearly understood what I was doing. I knew at that point I was going to go as far as I could go, because of Robert Crumb and because of my film. The first sequence I animated was Big Bertha and Fritz in the junk yard, where they are running from their friend's house to the junk yard, they end up in a bus, Fritz drops his pants and Bertha says, "You're not big enough." It was the whole illusion that white guys were afraid of black guys with bigger dicks ... I packed it up, this is a good five minutes, and I go back to Warner Brothers to screen the film and the room is full of executives. The lights go up, everyone looks at me and says, "You are out of your fucking mind," and then they all walk out (*laughs*). They cancelled the deal! That is a true story. So I was flying back to New York and when you hear what comes next you'll either think I'm the luckiest guy in the world or I'm lying. I think about it today and say, "God must have been watching me," and I'm not even religious (*laughs*). I took the plane from LA to New York and I took a cab to my office building, which was on Broadway, I get on the elevator and I had a film can in my hand, and you are not going to believe what you hear ... This short little man taps me on the shoulder and says, "What have you got in the film can?" I said, "The first adult cartoon I am afraid to say." He said, "Yeah? Is anyone distributing it?" So I told him, "Not anymore," and he says, "Come with me." Now it turns out this guy is Jerry Gross ...'

Jerry Gross was a major player in the exploitation film industry, using his company Cinemation to distribute such cult hits as *Sweet Sweetback's Baadasssss Song* and *I Drink Your Blood*. 'He says, "Let me see it,"' continues Bakshi. 'So I took it into his office and showed him it and he says, "We will make it." So by the time I got up to my place I had another deal and I didn't even do anything! So now this producer has me around his shoulder and he's hugging me again (*laughs*). Jerry Gross was the hottest independent producer in the country with a massive hit, *Sweet Sweetback*, under his belt. He had money in his office coming out of drawers. In those days the independent business was just getting started and it was a very big deal. That is a true fucking story.'

Nevertheless, in a perverse twist of fate, Warner Brothers ended up distributing *Fritz the Cat* in the US. 'Yeah, Warner ended up distributing *Fritz the Cat* on 16mm and then home video some years later,' explains Bakshi. 'But when the picture came out everyone blew it, all the major companies had turned me down, Warner was the only one brave enough to go through with it, and then they backed out. But when the movie came out the kids were lined up down to Mars. The audience was every fucking teenager in the world and how did we not know that? (*Laughs*) When the kids started lining up to see it I actually thought, "What is the mystery here?" If I was a kid I'd have been in that line! *You'd* be in that line ... it shows you how stupid you can be when you can't see the forest for the trees. How idiotic I was, Krantz was, Warner Brothers was, how could any of us not have known that every young person in America would go and see that film? How could they stay away? So that is what happened there. Then Warner Brothers bought another film from me. *Hey Good Lookin'*, I had another problem with that. I really should have learned from the first time around.'

Upon its release *Fritz the Cat* was given an X rating, but that didn't stop those under-18s from checking out the latest cult phenomenon. 'The people who were underage would sneak into the theatre,' says Bakshi. 'It became like what rock 'n' roll was when it started – if you are hip then you want to see it. That's the whole point. It was rock 'n' roll, it was Presley swinging his hips, it was something that your mother wouldn't want you to see. It was the first of a kind. That in itself was amazing. How do you do the first of anything? That was the first kind of movie like that on the planet, it left a watermark. So how could you not go and see it? And it was animation … it was a joke … people forgot about that, but it was a cat and crows running around. Everyone took what I was doing so seriously, they were terrified. I could maybe see it with *Heavy Traffic*, where I was doing humans, but these were animals! This is all after the fact, of course, none of this was apparent when I was making the film.'

Yet, even those who were attracted to *Fritz the Cat* because of the promised vulgarity and shocking on-screen images would have found it hard to ignore the political messages inherent in the picture. 'Well that is what people tell me,' laughs Bakshi. 'I don't want to be self-serving but I am shocked that most of my films are still being looked at and that this is what the young people today are saying. To be honest, I kept adding to the material and expressing how I felt about things back then. In other words, that was the personal part … I made personal films. When I said I didn't care about audiences, believe me, I was airing things that I wanted to get off my chest whether people agreed with it or not. I can make this really clear. Most filmmakers, and they can be good too, are liars. They don't really believe in what they say and they haven't thought it through. I have seen a lot of filmmakers come out of meetings and when guys have said to them, "How do you think the audience will react to this and this?" I would always say, "You are the director, what do you care? Why don't you just put in what you think is right?" So all of those guys, they have script meetings and studios are always trying to figure out what the audience wants and they have yet to define it. No one is trying to make a film anymore as much as they are trying to make a hit and make a lot of money. If that is what you want, then fine, I'm not going to argue, but you can't have it both ways. You can make films that are personal and that you want to make and hope that audiences feel what you want them to feel, I never said I didn't want people to line up outside. That just wasn't my motive to make the film. Instead, I was able to talk politically.'

Back in 1972, full length animated film had never been used to make an anti-war statement. Indeed, few motion pictures were making anti-war statements. 'You know, art has a way of transforming itself into something else,' maintains Bakshi. 'A great painting does, great music does … I was so much acting as an artist but without realising it. I was so uncaring about what audiences wanted to see, but wanted to tell them what was going to happen if they continued to do what they were doing. I was so tired of bullshit, where money would be poured into the ghetto and the leaders of the black revolutionary groups would drive around in Cadillacs … and the sellers of coke and drugs – I knew where these guys were but the cops didn't? It was such bullshit, you know? That is why I quit Hollywood … just look at it today. I am dead fucking serious, after World War 2 – I'm Jewish right – I was very, very naïve. Naïvety is probably what causes my films to be so honest. Look at the world today and you see the same genocide that you saw in World War 2. To say that nobody learned anything – what is wrong with us? Here in America people only care about money, only care about themselves… what sort of society do we live in? You want to ask me what I'm doing in New Mexico? I am hiding. It is beautiful here, I can look out at the sky and it's clear and there's deserts and everything. I don't want to get too much into it but the world has gotten worse, worse even than I imagined it could get, and I thought we were pretty fucked up back then. I said during the integration riots, I was so naïve, "I can't believe black people can't vote." That was news to me! I couldn't believe they were going to kill these white kids for trying to get black people to vote – what country am I living in?'

Bakshi's social conscience erupts throughout *Fritz the Cat*, with the artist making statements on the Israel/Palestine divide and expressing a sincere disgust towards America's involvement in Vietnam. 'I could not believe we were in Vietnam,' sighs the director. 'Young kids were getting their heads blown off, and for what? It was so insane and it has gotten worse. I don't believe we are in Iraq! So if there is anything political in my films, it has to do with me clearing up in my mind what I think is right and wrong. This is what is interesting. If you are a film director in a room with a bunch of studio execs and they say, "How do you feel the audience feels about racism?" Well if you think the audience is racist then you're not going to do an anti-racist film or joke, you'll keep it out of your movie. However, if you don't care then you're going to put in whatever is on your mind so that the shoe fits whoever wants to wear it. I think my strength was my freedom. I've written a couple of scripts and put them away because I don't like what they have to say about where we are going. So it is a question of not concerning yourself with anything but what is in your head. I just tried to be honest. I eventually quit the business because the battles were never-ending and it was making me sick. The way they'd try to corral me was that they'd sign anything I wanted to make, but then when I handed it in they would start to throw stuff out and start changing it. It was very, very hard and it finally caught up with me.'

As a result of its director's stark intelligence and sharp wit, *Fritz the Cat* stands up as one of the most interesting anti-war movies of the 1970s. 'I'm against war and I'm against the stupidity of war,' says Bakshi. 'This is what I've been saying to you. We have got to find other ways for everyone to be able to live the life they want to live. You can't push democracy on people through the use of a gun. The whole thing is insane. This is something that has always been very clear to me. As a young man, growing up in Brooklyn, which is a very congested neighbourhood with a lot of tenement houses and a lot of guys living there. There were hundreds and hundreds of guys on each block and hundreds of hundreds of apartments. Well I saw hundreds of my friends, the older boys, go to Korea and never come back. One or two did come back and you should have seen the look on their faces. They melted away into the crowd. I saw first hand the insanity of it all. Hundreds of these guys, running around playing ball and then suddenly they left, and never came back. Like when World War 2 ended, there were guys that got home from that, including my uncle, who were crazy. There are hundreds of stories that have never been told, but a lot of patriotic positionings. These men were destroyed because of what they had gone through and, yet, the minute the war ends, here we are fighting the Russians! What the fuck is the point of it all? Of course I know what it is now. It has to do with economics and who is going to end up with all of the money. Nothing is ever fought for the reasons I used to think they were fought for, which is pride or country. There is nothing very legitimate about any war on the planet. It all has to do with Empire. We are very quiet in America today because the Chinese, who are communists, are better capitalists than we are. So what are you going to say? We are trying to sell everything we can to them because now they are capitalist communists! Here I go again, I'm sorry ...'

Speaking to Bakshi, one begins to understand what an individual talent and independent mind he really is. It also becomes apparent that the politics inherent in his movies are no accident. 'I don't think the world is ever going to be perfect but I think people should be allowed to live the way they want,' he says. 'We can't force a so-called democracy, which is really capitalism, on people so I think we should just try and get along with each other. The world is insane right now, arms and missiles ... I don't like where it is going. The world has gone crazy and that is why I am in New Mexico. I'm not just talking about America, everyone is out of their mind. You can't get two people, for example the Palestinians and the Israelis, to sit down and say, "You take this half and build nice houses and we'll take the other half." Instead they are banging away at each other, and for what purpose? We have 65, 70 years to live ... just do the best with it! We are out of our fucking minds. A man can go to the moon and yet we have all these other things going on. There is something wrong with us.'

Bakshi's disappointment with the world surrounding him is evidenced through Fritz himself, a character looking for a revolution even when none exists. Yet, the glamour and the sexiness of the idea is what appeals to the fed-up feline rather than any inherent moral stance. 'Basically Fritz is full of shit,' confirms Bakshi. 'There were so many college kids marching and screaming out of boredom, just because everyone else was doing it, and then as soon as the trouble started they were gone. In other words, guys like Fritz learned to play guitar – everyone was into folk music in the sixties – but it was just so they could get laid. You know, I was always trying to expose the bullshit that we surround ourselves with. I mean, *Fritz the Cat* was an anti-bullshit situation. I think Billie Holliday was real, that's why I played her records, but Fritz was so full of shit. He was a con artist, all the way, and most of the kids in the revolution were that way. What happened was Nixon knew that, so when he ordered the killing at Kent State of the college students rioting, that was the end of the American Revolution. You saw real people dead because of what they were saying. Nobody spoke anymore. That is what Kent State was about. He knew that if he shot a couple of college kids there would be no more riots and that is exactly what happened. Nobody talked in America. How can National Guards shoot students, at college, on American soil? Well someone gave the order because that is what stops revolutions ... like with Malcolm X and Robert Kennedy and all the other guys that were assassinated. Now from that point, Kent State, to where we are today – the right wing has taken over America and we're living here today, right now.'

Finding out that Bakshi now lives in New Mexico is something of a shock considering that New York seemed as personal to the filmmaker in his twin hits of *Fritz the Cat* and *Heavy Traffic* as it does to Woody Allen or Martin Scorsese. All the same, the director says that he has no regrets about leaving the Big Apple. 'I grew up in New York, I stayed in New York and then New York changed,' explains Bakshi. 'I mean you can't go to the Lower East Side without seeing sushi parlours and boutiques. All the poor people have been thrown out. We're at the height of our Empire right now and New York has totally changed. Unless you are very, very rich there is no place to go anymore. I saw the best of New York in the forties, fifties and sixties ... but then it changed, turned into an ethical kind of richness. It lost it for me. My old neighbourhood used to have these wonderful old buildings where immigrants and ethnic groups lived but now they are all gone. It's all massage parlours, sushi parlours and apartments that you used to get for $40 a month on the Lower East Side now cost you $3 million, and if you think I'm kidding, I'm not! That is what happened to New York. New Mexico, however, is real. I ride around and the cowboys are rounding up cattle, it's cheap to live here, a handshake is still a handshake. This part of the country is isolated and it is very honest. I really appreciate that. If a man tells you he will do something here then he'll do it. You can't drive fifty miles in New York without it costing you $30. I used to go from one place to another but every time you cross a bridge it's $8 – that is the toll! I must have been across that bridge a million times! You can't live in New York if you don't have money and if you don't have money no one will talk to you because they think you're an asshole. Everyone is so into fame, fortune, and everyone wants to be a star. That is all we're about now. We're not about marching in the streets, we're not about trying to make things better in the world or asking what Bush is doing, we're about becoming rich and being a star. It's insane. There I go – but that's me. That's why I made my films. I have gotten older and gotten a little wiser and I've done a lot more reading, that's all.'

Another thing that Bakshi does not regret is passing on the chance to make the sequel to *Fritz the Cat*. 'I didn't want to do a sequel and I had nothing to do with *The Nine Lives*,' he says. 'In fact I never even saw it. I said all I wanted to say about *Fritz*. I was doing *Coonskin* at the time and, as far as I was concerned, that was a lot more important.'

Bakshi's *Coonskin* would be even more controversial than *Fritz the Cat*, although the director claims that this was never his intention. 'I didn't go after controversy, not really,' he laughs. 'I was simply getting up to bat, in baseball terminology, and swinging at the ball because I never thought I'd have another chance. In other words, I never thought there would be a picture after *Fritz the Cat*, I never thought there would be *Heavy Traffic*. Like I said earlier, and I mean this, I was just trying to say things that I thought were right, before they took it away from me. I knew that I would get smaller audiences than if I did something more commercial, I knew I was hurting myself as a film director – I knew that – I knew that they would never give me a lot of money to make films because they wanted PGs so people could bring their kids. So I did know that I was throwing money out of the window, I'm not dumb, I did know, but I didn't care. So I'm looking back and scratching my head and wondering if I should have done something just for the money (*laughs*). When I did *Lord of the Rings* it was the first picture where I knew it could break out, where money was concerned, and I absolutely love Tolkien. If it is something I love dearly, and can also give audiences something they will enjoy, then how can that be a bad move? It was also a good break away from my city films ...'

Another aspect of Bakshi's legacy that has caused controversy is his use of rotoscoping, something that resulted in some stark criticism for his ambitious animated take on *Lord of the Rings*. Yet, in today's age of CGI where the animated action can be generated from the recorded movements of real actors, such barbs seem decidedly ridiculous. 'CGI is the modern equivalent of rotoscoping,' says Bakshi. 'We didn't have CGI in my day and I couldn't do *Lord of the Rings* using traditional animation without losing my head. In effect I created my own CGI. It was criticised, absolutely, and now it is everywhere. When you go and see a Pixar or a Dreamworks film it is all rotoscope. They use a machine but it is the same process. They pump in live action and they scientifically plot the points. People always come after you in Hollywood.'

As adult-orientated animation, such as *Family Guy* and *South Park*, continues to break the mainstream, Bakshi is now seen as someone who was distinctly before his time. The often sophomore politics of *South Park* pale in comparison to the director's highly literate social conscience, yet the likes of *Coonskin* remain unreleased on DVD whilst *Fritz the Cat* and *Heavy Traffic* have garnered only the most minimal of home video releases. 'Of course that pisses me off,' says Bakshi sadly. 'Those are my films. Bad, good or indifferent those are the things that I leave behind so, yeah, it does piss me off. So, yeah, that is the way I've always been treated. "There's no need to work with Bakshi because it ain't gonna make money." The only reason to work with somebody or to do something for somebody is if it is economically viable. If it is not economically viable for you then nothing will happen. Countries will go down the drain, African countries will go down the drain because there is no oil there and working with Ralph Bakshi, economically, does not mean anything. You see? So they couldn't care less about the legacy of those films, they don't care about art. They don't care. That is why I left. The people in Hollywood don't care about the product they make, they only care about the money it brings in.'

The TENDERNESS of WOLVES

Released: 1973
Directed by: Ulli Lommel
Produced by: Rainer Werner Fassbinder, Michael Fengler
Written by: Kurt Raab
Stars: Kurt Raab (Fritz Haarmann), Jeff Roden (Hans Grans), Margit Carstensen (Frau Linder), Ingrid Caven (Dora), Wolfgang Schneck (Kommissar Braun), Brigitte Mira (Louise Engel), Barbara Bertram (Elli), Rainer Werner Fassbinder (Wittowski), Heinrich Giskes (Lungis), Friedrich Karl Praetorius (Kurt Fromm), Karl von Liebezeit (Herr Engel), Walter Kaltheuner (Schumacher)

In a nutshell: Given a job as a police informer, Fritz Haarmann prowls the rundown streets of post-war Germany offering refuge to homeless young men. Once the boys are taken back to his home, Haarmann kills them and sells their clothes on the black market. He also grinds the bodies into sausages and sells the meat as 'pork' to his neighbours. The residents of the dingy apartment complex that Haarmann lives in are suspicious of his activities, although one of his friends actually helps him to cover his tracks, but they are not interested in raising awareness to the police. Instead, they continue to buy his cut-price goods and seem to view him as little more than a reclusive deviant. Finally, however, the police are led to Haarmann's flat where they catch him in the middle of an attempted murder and arrest him.

Prologue: The biggest name to be associated with *The Tenderness of Wolves* (original German title: *Die Zärtlichkeit der Wölfe*) was undoubtedly the film's co-producer Rainer Werner Fassbinder, who, at the time, was the darling of the arthouse circuit and the pioneer of the German new wave movement. From his debut with 1969's outstanding *Love is Colder than Death*, Fassbinder was clearly a talent to watch and, surrounding himself with a group of creative film devotees, he would prove to be a highly proficient and resourceful director. By the time of *The Tenderness of Wolves*, Fassbinder had already overseen the production of over 15 movies, many of which starred his protégé Ulli Lommel. Actor Kurt Raab was also a Fassbinder regular, having appeared alongside Lommel in several features since *Love is Colder than Death*, however *The Tenderness of Wolves* marked his writing debut. Further members of the *The Tenderness of Wolves* cast and crew were also Fassbinder protégés, such as starlet Margit Carstensen, who had played the lead in 1972's *The Bitter Tears of Petra von Kant*, un-credited musician Peer Raben and co-producer Michael Fengler. *The Tenderness of Wolves* was not Lommel's first film as a director (1971's rarely seen sci-fi oddity *Haytabo* takes that honour) but it most certainly was his first widely-seen picture and the movie that, to date, has afforded him the most critical acclaim.[31]

Prior to *The Tenderness of Wolves* the most famous motion picture about a child-killer was Fritz Lang's *M*, which Lommel pays tribute to throughout his movie (it should be noted that *M* was, like *The Tenderness of Wolves*, also based on the true life crimes of Fritz Haarmann). Moreover, Raab's appearance and performance often mirrors that of the child-killer played by Peter Lorre in Lang's classic. Lommel's set design, rich gothic atmosphere and oft-forced camera angles, meanwhile, bring to mind such masterworks of German expressionism as Wiene's *Cabinet of Dr Caligari*, Murnau's *Nosferatu* (1922) and Dreyer's *Vampyr* (1932). However, his movie's more gory set pieces may owe just a touch to the burgeoning American splatter cinema of the time, something that Lommel would take further in his later movies, most notably in *The Boogeyman* (1981).

The movie's images of gay men kissing (not to mention lying in bed with one another) were not commonplace in European cinema at the time and, in this sense, Lommel was certainly a trailblazer. Prior to *The Tenderness of Wolves*, however, John Schlesinger's Oscar-winning masterpiece *Midnight Cowboy* (1969) depicted (off-screen) male-on-male fellatio, something that may well have won the picture its X-rating. Schlesinger's follow-up movie, *Sunday Bloody Sunday* (1971), also featured a homosexual relationship, whilst Europe's Dario Argento would depict positive gay characters in his 1971 sophomore effort *Cat o' Nine Tails* and the same year's follow-up *Four Flies on Grey Velvet*. Other famous depictions of homosexuality in mainstream cinema would include Robert Redford as a (likely) gay man in *Inside Daisy Clover* (1965, and which fell foul of studio-imposed censorship), Joe Dallesandro's street hustler in Paul Morrissey's *Trash* (1968) and Mick Jagger's bi-sexual starring role in *Performance* (1970). Lommel's mentor, Fassbinder, was of course, openly gay, although interestingly, his post-*Tenderness* releases, such as *In a Year of 13 Moons*

---

31 Reviewing the film on May 20th 1977 in *The New York Times*, esteemed critic Vincent Canby praised the movie commenting, 'It is beautifully and enthusiastically performed and it doesn't contain a single superfluous or redundant camera movement. Like Mr Fassbinder's own early films, *Tenderness of the Wolves* is cryptic, tough-talking and swaggering in the manner of someone who means to shock his elders. Like the early Warhol work, *Tenderness of the Wolves* seems to be sending up everyone and everything, but, unlike the Warhol movies, it takes filmmaking – the possibilities of the discipline – with complete seriousness, which becomes the redeeming factor in Fassbinder films, even when the subjects are off-putting.'

THE TENDERNESS OF WOLVES

(1978) and *Querelle* (1982), are more explicit about this than his earlier works.

About: There are only two acts of graphic violence in *The Tenderness of Wolves* and yet Lommel's feature, shot entirely in German, remains one of the most incredibly morbid meditations on a serial killer to date. This is largely due to the picture's unmistakably bleak post-World War 2 atmosphere of poverty and desperation, which permeates almost every scene, and its depiction of the criminal underworld, described as 'suffocating' by one critic, suits the film's dire aesthetics perfectly.[32] The fact that Lommel shot his movie on location, with an obvious eye for the most destitute districts and classic architecture to photograph, really adds to the maudlin feel and tone of the story and the surroundings become as pivotal to the on-screen narrative as the actors themselves. Indeed, one cannot help but feel that the real strength of *The Tenderness of Wolves* stems from its budgetary restraints for, without the use of glossy studio sets or lighting, the feature comes across as all the more authentic and the end result is so much more powerful. Even interior shots within Haarmann's unkempt apartment have a certain picturesque resonance thanks to the genuine crooked structure of the building. In a sense, therefore, *The Tenderness of Wolves* is an achievement that Lommel would never better during his 30-plus years in the film industry.

Beginning ominously with the sight of a man's shadow prowling the streets at night, *The Tenderness of Wolves* consistently hints that the director's native Germany has yet to escape from the barren darkness of World War 2. Indeed, it is difficult not to assume that the reason Haarmann's neighbours remain so quiet about his suspicious late night rendezvous with young boys is simply because they don't want any trouble, in a post-Nazi environment, with the law. The sole exception to this is Frau Linder, played by Fassbinder fixture Margit Carstensen, a nosey, yet endearing, busybody who keeps count of the number of people whom Haarmann takes up to his room but who never seem to come out again. Besides, what *is* in these big, carefully wrapped packages that her neighbour keeps wrestling down the stairs and throwing into the lake? Immersed in a very dark sense of humour, *The Tenderness of Wolves* is too arty to really cut the mustard as a nasty exploitation flick and yet, its impact would likely have been lessened with cut-rate splatter effects (the only sort this low budget feature could have afforded).

Hence, when something grisly *does* happen it becomes all the more shocking because we don't expect it. It takes 45 minutes (almost an eon in horror films) before we are greeted with the infamous sight of Haarmann biting a chunk of flesh from the neck of a young man but, because Lommel has so carefully manipulated the character as someone who is little more than a likeable eccentric, the gruesome act carries the air of a friend's betrayal. Sure, the film's consistent air of grime and the brooding nightfall setting, which beckons Haarmann's nocturnal romancing of young runaways, indicates an unsettling gothic horror, but the dialogue consistently points to the contrary. 'He works at the midnight mission, he is a good person,' intones one of Haarmann's neighbours when someone complains about the noise upstairs. 'He pays well,' says someone else, 'he is also helpful if you get into trouble with the cops.' Thus, *The Tenderness of Wolves*

---

32 As mentioned by Phil Hardy, *The Aurum Film Encyclopaedia: Horror*, Aurum Press, 1993

is about, to a great extent, false appearances. Haarmann represents the monster within, the beast that all serial killers hide behind their pleasant exterior, but he is also an apt metaphor for Germany herself; a country that has just slaughtered most of its young population in a senseless war and which unleashed a monster (National Socialism) under the banner of trust. This split personality (and note the almost-oxymoronic title, 'tenderness' and 'wolves' are not words generally put together in the same sentence), Haarmann's calm before the storm so to speak (and his ability to lure people into a false sense of security), is also reflective of what is about to come for Lommel's home country. Setting his *The Tenderness of Wolves* in the period before the East/West German split, Lommel's decision to have most of his film take place in gloom or moonlight may well hint at the period of darkness that was still to come.

What may have proven most shocking back in 1973 was Lommel's depiction of homosexuality. Two men becoming intimate on-screen was not commonplace back then (and, to be fair, still isn't) and it is interesting to note that even the Oscar-winning *Philadelphia* (1993) shied away from a single full-on kiss between a male couple. However, in *The Tenderness of Wolves* actor Kurt Raab kisses his lovers, holds them in bed and we also see some surprising full frontal male nudity, all taboos for their time. Of course, because Raab is also a prowler, a killer of gay men, it might be argued that Lommel's movie is hardly a positive depiction of homosexuality, predominantly because it focuses on such a ghoulish character. Yet this would be grossly unfair because Haarmann's sexuality is never judged in the film and the very 'tenderness' of the title can be seen to allude to the delicate seduction of the young runaways that Raab brings back to his abode.

Whilst at least one critic has mentioned that 'this is not a "getting-to-know-you" exercise'[33] one could argue that the feature's icy detachment from Haarmann's murders, alongside its detailing of his (brief) relationships, shows us that this not a man entirely without compassion. For instance, the killer's one real bond is with a sleazy pimp called Hans, who wants little to do with the paunchy, bald headed loner but who nevertheless entertains him long enough to encourage some hope in the monster. In one scene of genuine 'tenderness' we see Haarmann finally at ease when he embraces and kisses the man, yet when Hans proves uninterested in any sort of relationship the murders continue. As if to emphasise the hope that Hans provides to Haarmann, Lommel shoots a sequence where the two eat in a restaurant with bright, vivid light, rare evidence of blinding colour in a movie otherwise shrouded in darkness.

Yet the biggest contradiction of *The Tenderness of Wolves* is within the title itself. As we know, 'wolves' hunt in packs whilst Haarmann stalks the streets alone. As such, the name of the film could just as easily relate to the victims, for they are portrayed as the true innocents and are lured to their deaths at night. Indeed, like a pack of wolves themselves, the movie's desperate runaways flock to the dilapidated streets of Düsseldorf hoping to start a new life. Lommel portrays them as the fatalities of a country that cannot offer its youth anything, indeed, Germany is shown, in her immediate post-Nazi guise, as an entity that has yet to fully regain its humanity and warmth. Thus, the police nonchalantly come across dead bodies and, in their biggest blunder, they fail to question Haarmann when, at the start of the movie, he discards

---

33 As maintained by critic Stephen Thrower (*The Eyeball Compendium*, FAB Press, Surrey, 2003).

something under his feet (obviously trying to hide it) and remarks that 'it's nothing' to no further probing from the law. Even Fassbinder, in his inevitable cameo appearance, takes on two sides, being the man who brings Haarmann to justice despite having previously supported his black market trade. Hence, he is just another contradiction in a movie that is full of them, from its title to its on-screen characters.

However, there is one sequence that changes our relationship with Haarmann entirely. Whilst seeing his slaughter of young adult men is indeed difficult to stomach, our feelings towards the character are demonised even further when he kills an adolescent boy. In this scene we see Haarmann invite him up to his apartment only for the boy never to come out again. Lommel does not have to show us anything for us to understand that his serial murderer is a diabolical, repellent paedophile, a man who has completely lost his soul but who also seems to be crying out for help. Raab's remarkable performance demonstrates a real inner conflict, a silent, brooding individual who cannot quite grasp how he has managed to get away with this for so long. It is almost as if he wants the law to stop him. Hence, he accepts an invitation to work for the secret police, and does very little to cover up his killing spree (he even invites one neighbour to help him dispose of a body, which she begrudgingly agrees to do), still he gets away with murder after murder. Haarmann is, ultimately, symbolic of what happens when a post-war society faces an uncertain future and ends up relying on criminals for their food and clothes (Lommel's monster is also a black market operative).

In *The Tenderness of Wolves*, the characters cannot bear to think about anything except their own immediate future and this is largely why Haarmann remains on the loose. At the film's end, for instance, as the killer is finally led away, an inspector maintains that 'the confidence in the German police system has been shaken, gentlemen. Various parts of the military government are starting to believe that the German police are working hand in hand with shady elements from the Nazi period.' Thus, there is also a lot of anger in Lommel's horror opus, most notably towards the way his native country (where he lived until leaving for New York in the mid-'70s) was left in disarray following the horrific events of World War 2. He also seems to be saying that one monster is very easy to replace unless proper restoration and infrastructure are allowed to develop in a military-controlled, post-war environment.

The real Fritz Haarmann, as Lommel documents at the end of his movie with an on-screen text, was executed in 1925. Despite popular opinion at the time, Lommel's picture was never meant to be a re-telling of the story of Peter Kurten, the so-called Vampire of Düsseldorf[34] which Fritz Lang had also allegedly drawn influence from in order to make his masterpiece *M*. Instead it is the real Haarmann's bloody hand prints that inform the crimes of *The Tenderness of Wolves*, namely his killing of young male vagrants (and the resulting rumour, after his capture, that the pork he sold on the black market actually came from human bodies). The real change between the genuine Haarmann crimes and Lommel's feature is the time period, indicating that the

---

34 In his *New York Times* review, Canby assumes that *Tenderness of the Wolves* is based on Peter Kurten, a German serial killer who committed a series of sex crimes and murders on children and women in 1929. He was captured and tried for nine murders and seven attempted murders to which he eventually pleaded guilty. He was sentenced to death and was executed in Cologne in July 1932.

director perhaps felt it was more personal to his generation, and to himself, to set the monster's rampage after the fall of National Socialism. Nevertheless, it is unusual (for any filmmaker) to admit, during their final credits, that the story the audience has just witnessed is indeed set during a falsified time period. In a sense it immediately breaks any sense of verisimilitude that has been built up and, yet, it also points to a social conscience, a desire to let the viewers know that Haarmann did exist (albeit during another decade) and that what they have just watched is indeed 'only a movie'.

Watched today, *The Tenderness of Wolves* may not have the same impact that it once did, however its artistry is unmistakable and its beautiful photography and excellent central performance from Raab (not to discredit the rest of the cast but this is close to a one-man show) should allow it to endure as a cult classic for years to come. Although the film may never obtain the recognition it deserves outside of its own minor fan base, for connoisseurs of deviant cinema it is among the most cynical and interesting character studies that the arthouse has ever spat out. See *M* first though.

What happened next?

A success in Europe, *The Tenderness of Wolves* never made a mark in the all-important American market, although it has created something close to a cult reputation over the years. It also brought Lommel to the patronage of Andy Warhol, and the artist starred in 1979's rock 'n' roll oddity *Cocaine Cowboys* (alongside Jack Palance) and *Blank Generation*, 1980's pseudo documentary of punk rocker Richard Hell. The director then entered his most interesting period, kicking off with *The Boogeyman* (1980), one of the best *Halloween* spin-offs and Lommel's most popular horror film. 1983 saw four movies from the director: *Olivia* is an arty homage to such Hitchcock classics as *Marnie* and *Vertigo*, *Brainwaves* is an enjoyable horror opus with a bizarre ensemble cast of Vera Miles, Keir Dullea and Tony Curtis, and *The Devonsville Terror* is an above-average modern witch-finder parable starring Donald Pleasence. After this, however, his films received increasingly poor reception, including the disastrous, cheapskate *Boogeyman 2* (also 1983) and the muddled, nonsensical *Revenge of the Stolen Stars* (1985). After a lengthy period of obscurity Lommel returned to horror through producing a series of grimy, ultra low budget, shot-on-video titles such as *The Zodiac Killer* (2005), *Zombie Nation* (2006) and *The Raven* (2007). Suffice to say, trying to find a link from *The Tenderness of Wolves* to the filmmaker's latest efforts is not easy. At the time of writing he is pondering a possible *Boogeyman 3* and has just wrapped *Savannah's Ghost*, with David Carradine.

Of the cast of *The Tenderness of Wolves*, the briefly glimpsed Jürgen Prochnow would go on to have a superlative acting career, featuring most famously in *Das Boot* (1981), *The Keep* (1983), *Beverly Hills Cop II* (1987) and *Judge Dredd* (1995). Kurt Raab continued to work extensively in film and on television before passing away from AIDS in 1988.

The Tenderness of Wolves was the first foreign language movie to present such a careful study of a serial killer and whilst its influence is not great, it does predate such well known successors as the ultra-grisly *Man Bites Dog* (1992), Michael Haneke's superior *Funny Games* (1997) and *Antibodies* (2005). The arthouse aesthetic of Lommel's movie may not have directly inspired these efforts but, in watching them, one can see that they at least came from the same sort of mindset.

THE TENDERNESS OF WOLVES

Ulli Lommel interview

No discussion of Ulli Lommel can ignore the fact that his early career owes a huge debt to Fassbinder. 'I met Fassbinder in 1968 when I starred in *Love is Colder than Death*,' begins Lommel. 'It was during that production that I became a producer. You see, one day Fassbinder said, because I drove an English sports car at the time, "Can you bring your MG to the shoot tomorrow?" I said, "No problem," and he said, "Just one more thing – can you bring me the receipt from its purchase?" I asked why, and he said, "Because after we use the car in the film we need to sell it because we have run out of money." I said, "Well okay," and I brought the MG and they sold it so that they could finish the film and so I became a producer overnight. Five years later, Fassbinder asked me if I wanted to direct *The Tenderness of Wolves*, so we went to a small town near Düsseldorf and in three weeks we shot the movie. I had access to the entire Fassbinder team because all of us were working at a theatre at the same time doing his plays. I discovered a cameraman who, up until that point, had only been a gaffer. His name was Jürgen Jürges and I thought a great deal of him as a gaffer, but the only problem was that he stuttered a lot. When Fassbinder came to the first day of shooting Jürgen said, "C-c-c-could you p-p-p-please move there?" and Fassbinder said, "Who the fuck is this guy?" I said, "He's a very talented DP," and Fassbinder said, "Well what has he done?" and I said, "Nothing yet … but he's really talented," and Fassbinder replied, "We're going to be shooting until Christmas if this continues because he obviously cannot communicate anything to the crew!" But then afterwards he also used Jürgen for his films and today he is one of the best cameramen in Germany.'

Fassbinder's approval of *The Tenderness of Wolves* was important to Lommel, who was thrilled when his mentor gave the movie the thumbs up. 'Fassbinder loved it,' beams the director. 'He said to me that he thought it was better than most of his own movies and, as a result, when the movie was released in Germany, it came out as "Fassbinder Presents". It was the first movie to come out from this new distribution arm that Fassbinder had set up and the most commercially successful film he had ever been involved with. Before this, he had never made a big, successful movie, his work was always marginal, arthouse projects but *Tenderness* played wide in Germany and made a lot of money. I travelled around Germany, went from theatre to theatre and it was pretty unbelievable because the film was so controversial. I remember that we got hate mail, people letting out their aggressions on the movie – there was a lot of confrontational stuff – but I loved it. I loved the controversy. Fassbinder said to me, just a year or two before he died, 'Now I am worried because everybody seems to love my movies and this is foreboding, it is not a good sign.' I asked why and he said, "Because it points towards the end. I love it when people love me, when some hate me and when I am the centre of controversy but you become peaceful when everything finds its own weight." He was scared of that (*laughs*).'

Lommel set *The Tenderness of Wolves* after the horrors of World War 2. He admits to doing this so that he could add some post-conflict commentary to the story of Fritz Haarmann. 'World War 2 was a recent experience,' he explains. 'Plus, the Americans were working together with the German police, and we later found out that a lot of ex-Nazis were put in charge of Germany because the US trusted them more than they trusted the Communists or Socialists. So there was the chance to add some social commentary by setting the film during this period.' On-screen at least, the picture's most enduring discovery is that of Jürgen Prochnow, who appears in a small role in one of his earliest screen credits. For the director, casting the future star of *Das Boot* was just a lucky accident. 'Jürgen was doing a play with Fassbinder at a theatre which was nearby at the time,' he reveals. 'Fassbinder used a lot of theatre actors to do smaller parts. He would ask them to come in for just a few hours and that way we would have a great ensemble.'

Surprisingly for a film with such a notorious reputation, there are only two graphically violent scenes in *The Tenderness of Wolves*. Despite Lommel's later reputation for overseeing low budget bloodbaths, the filmmaker admits that he excersised restraint during the making of his powerful debut for a reason. 'We wanted the audience to identify with Haarmann first, and then let him commit the killings. In other words, we wanted to humanise him,' explains Lommel. 'We went as far as possible in 1973, and God knows many audience members left the theatre at the opening of the Berlin Film Festival in 1974, objecting to the violence, but objecting even more to the fact that I had succeeded in making them like this monster. But this is what I wanted. I wanted them to love him and I wanted them to feel that they are him. Then, when he commits his murders I wanted them to think, "Well I felt that could have been me up until now. Is it still me killing? Or is it no longer me?" I wanted them to have a conflict in their own hearts: that there is no difference between Haarmann and them, and that Haarmann exists in all of us. I think that is what makes some people sick to the stomach.'

This feedback may come as a shock to many viewers of *The Tenderness of Wolves*. After all, when Haarmann's gruesome reign of violence begins, the character becomes a truly repulsive presence and the idea of 'loving' such a monster is difficult to comprehend. 'Well that is the major conflict, and that is also when the major questioning ensues,' states Lommel. 'For some, I think that conflict is very uncomfortable, because they liked this character at first, but for others I think that it is exciting. I think that this movie opens doors to the innermost darkness of your soul and for those looking to open those doors, it is a great movie, but for other people it is terrifying. But, you know, just as his tenderness is explicit, and his gentleness is explicit, why shouldn't his killing also be explicit? I always have a problem when people feel that only one side of our emotions can be shown in an explicit way and once we get into some complex and difficult matters we have to stay on the surface and can't show much. I don't like this ...' Certainly, the picture's depiction of cannibalism was enough to turn it into a *cause célèbre* in its native Germany. 'It was the cannibalism which caused 900 people to stand up and storm out of the theatre at the Berlin Film Festival,' laughs Lommel. 'They probably had to throw up ... I actually heard that there was a huge line leading to the men's and women's bathrooms (*laughs*). I guess some of them must have had to pee in their pants. The cannibalism was maybe too much for them.'

As a result, *The Tenderness of Wolves* secured itself a notorious reputation in its native country. 'Germany had major problems with the movie for a long time,' says Lommel. 'The reviews were sometimes devastating and it was only a few, more enlightened, critics who liked it. In Germany at the time, society was so vulnerable after two World Wars that they could not deal with it. In other places, such as Paris and in London, I think they could cope but in Germany, even to this day, certain subject matters are hard to deal with and I can understand that. But the distributor tried to market it as a horror film and it really isn't one. It is more like a human love story and a drama and an excursion into the innermost areas of the human soul.'

Unlike Lommel's later, American horror pictures, *The Tenderness of Wolves* carries a gothic sensibility, perhaps indicating a debt to early German expressionist cinema. For the director, such dark aesthetics hinted at a more literal take on the film's title. 'We used very little light because we wanted to show that wolves strike at night,' states Lommel. 'Moreover, it is always difficult to turn a scene in daylight into something with atmosphere because it is so flat. So we tried to escape into the night and do as much of the film as we could there. Of course, Jürgen Jürges, the cameraman, did an incredible job. It is also a foreshadowing of what is to come for Germany, namely the East/West divide. There are more lies to come and more deceit.'

The Tenderness of Wolves also remains somewhat indebted to Fritz Lang's masterpiece *M*, although Lommel feels that this linkage is only really blatant in a couple of scenes. 'There is one sequence where Kurt Raab picks up a ball and gives it to the little girl … that was in homage to *M*,' reflects the director. 'The other thing was the bald hairdo (on Raab) but, other than that we didn't have much more in mind. But I love Fritz Lang, and I asked my director of photography to check out his films prior to shooting.' Despite the overwhelming morbidness of the feature, when *The Tenderness of Wolves* finally arrived in North America it was advertised by a trailer that played a 'comical' child's nursery song about Fritz Haarmann over scenes from the movie. Inevitably, Lommel was not happy. 'I wasn't very impressed by that trailer,' he maintains. 'I thought it trivialised things but that is what the distribution people decided to do and they do what they do (*laughs*). You can't stop them but I thought it was a bad way to advertise the movie. Whether it helped or not I have no idea.'

Looking back at *The Tenderness of Wolves*, still Lommel's best film, the director admits that it was a time in his professional life where everything just seemed to work out. 'It was unique in every way because all the pieces came together and it turned into a brilliant experience,' he smiles. 'I mean, I had the greatest team of actors and I was very lucky with the cameraman. Our idea to revive one era worked out really well. All the pieces just came together, we found all the perfect locations to do it, and it is really a once in a lifetime thing when all of these aspects come together. You are lucky if that happens once in your life. For some people they may have to come back to Earth 100 times before it happens (*laughs*), so I am happy that it at least happened once for me. You know, I feel blessed by the experience.' Nevertheless, Lommel admits that he is hoping that lightning might strike twice, as evidenced by his feeling that a remake of *The Tenderness of Wolves* is not out of the question. 'I have actually been thinking about that quite recently and, so far, what has made me uncomfortable about going there is that the original is such a beautiful movie,' he muses. 'All of the circumstances were so unique that I am afraid I will never be able to get it to work again. Lion's Gate recently came to me and said, "Why don't you do a remake and call it *The Butcher of Hanover*?" You know, they wanted me to film it in an industrial area of America or London and I have been thinking about this but I haven't made up my mind and what stops me from doing it is the unique and unforgettable experience of making the original movie and then growing out of it.'

Lommel's debut feature also allowed him to gain a short-lived period of critical acceptance within European arthouse circles. '*The Tenderness of Wolves* was the movie that took me by the hand and allowed me to travel through the world,' he says. 'I came to Paris where the film was a sensation. It played for a whole year in an arthouse theatre in Paris where they called it one of the greatest masterpieces ever! I was so embarrassed and totally blown away by it, but I met so many important people in the city because of it. I met Anna Corrina who loved the movie and we fell in love through that and I moved to Paris. I lived there for three years and then I moved to America, again because of *The Tnderness of Wolves*, because Andy Warhol and others loved it so much. It was a movie that really created a destiny for me … For example, I remember that I was invited to a film festival in Chicago, and also in Montreal, and *The Tenderness of Wolves* and *Adolf and Marlene* – the Hitler movie I made – were shown. The producers took me to New York to introduce me to Andy Warhol and he saw both of these movies and loved them. He took me out the next morning for breakfast with Jackie Kennedy because at that point, in the late seventies, he was into the whole "society" thing. I remember that he said to Jackie, "This is Ulli Lommel and he is the greatest living director." So I stayed two and a half years with Andy and this was at the time of Studio 54 and all of that. Everybody he would meet he would repeat that line to, very much to my embarrassment (*laughs*). But he just loved those movies so much. In fact, when I later cast him in two of my pictures his secretary came to me and said, "This is amazing because Andy doesn't want to be in anyone's movies unless he gets paid a lot of money and, even then, he only wants to show up for 90 seconds and not say a word." But in *Cocaine Cowboys*, for example, he plays a very empowered role. Somehow he was a total fan of mine and I also loved him very much. There was a very important moment for me when we both did a press conference and somebody asked him, "Andy what is it that makes you this enormous American icon?" and he said, "It's the Andy Warhol in you." That, to me, was really awesome.'

However, despite its European success, *The Tenderness of Wolves* struggled to make a mark in the United States. 'The theatre owners and distributors in America were scared to death,' sighs Lommel. 'They were scared that they would go to prison if they showed it! They thought that the MPAA would just confiscate the movie. There were some that even thought the gay community would protest it at the cinema. There were some cases in Germany where the gay community thought that it was against them, which is completely crazy! So the movie was so controversial in so many ways. Let me give you an example because as it so happens I just discovered these reviews that were written in East Germany which was, of course, the communist part of the country. It had been reviewed as the worst piece of trash, they said it violated every part of what the Communist Party believed in – which was supporting humanity – and they considered it vile and disgusting, the worst example of Western society (*laughs*). It amused me beyond belief to get these KGB files from East Germany and find that my movie was torn apart like this.'

After *The Tenderness of Wolves*, Lommel would continue his arty ambitions with his fictional biopic *Adolf and Marlene* before embarking on an off-Hollywood career with such mainstream works as his punk documentary *Blank Generation* and the *Halloween*-inspired *Boogeyman*. Looking back, the director admits that he does not entirely approve of the path that he followed. 'If I made *The Tenderness of Wolves* today I probably would have made different movies after that but back then this is where I was and what I wanted to do,' he says. 'So it is easy to say what I would do today, with all of my experience and knowledge since then. However, I am very proud of *Adolf and Marlene*. That movie is still shown at film festivals and I think it is an awesome movie. We showed it at a film festival in Germany two years ago –25 years ago they did not like it at all in Germany – but after this screening the critics came up to me and said, "Ulli this is such a masterpiece, it should be shown all over the world and blah, blah, blah …" I think that the Hitler film is a really amazing movie.'

Furthermore, Lommel feels that if someone were to discover his work through seeing *The Tenderness of Wolves* then there are other movies from his past that deserve appraisal. 'I would say people who enjoyed *The Tenderness of Wolves* should see a German film I made called *The Second Spring* with Kurt Jürgen,' he says. 'I did this in 1975 two years later. I also think people should check out the first *Boogeyman*, *Olivia* and *The Devonsville Terror*. I remember telling Andy Warhol that I wanted to do something completely different from *The Tenderness of Wolves* and that is why I went off and made *Boogeyman*. I had planned to make something that would scare people and I made this my main goal when I was directing that picture. When the movie premiered it was awesome because I would see the audience hide behind their chairs, so I knew this had really worked out. It was made for $350,000 and was the number one movie in America for four weeks. It was an amazing thing and, to this day, *Boogeyman* is the movie that gets my other projects made, whilst *The Tenderness of Wolves* gets me respect. These two movies go together like a husband and wife team.'

COFFY

Released: 1973
Directed by: Jack Hill
Produced by: Robert Papazian, Samuel Z Arkoff, Salvatore Billitteri
Written by: Jack Hill
Stars: Pam Grier (Coffy), Booker Bradshaw (Howard Brunswick), Robert DoQui (King George), William Elliot (Carter), Allan Arbus (Arturo), Sid Haig (Omar), Barry Cahill (McHenry), Lee de Broux (Nick), Ruben Moreno (Ranos), Lisa Farringer (Jeri), Carol Lawson (Priscilla), Linda Haynes (Meg)

In a nutshell: Coffy is a Los Angeles nurse by profession and a gun-toteing vigilante by choice. Her intention is to find, seduce and kill the drug pushers that caused her sister's addiction to heroin. Coffy's ex-boyfriend Carter, a cop, tells her that the police force is corrupt and that some of his fellow officers are accepting pay-offs from the local crime lords. When Carter, who refuses to be involved in anything illegal, is bludgeoned into a coma by some home intruders Coffy takes the law into her own hands and goes undercover as a prostitute for the well known pimp/crime lord King George. Her mission is to seek out and destroy the drug kings of the city, although the deadliest of all could well be the person closest to her ...

Prologue: Finding a more masculine, and frequently misogynistic, series of films than those created by the blaxploitation fad is no easy task, with the likes of *Sweet Sweetback's Baadasssss Song*, *Shaft* (both 1971) and *Superfly* (1972) presenting tough, sexually proficient African-American characters in gritty, urban plots. Perhaps as a result of this overabundance of testosterone, the idea of doing a female-led blaxploitation movie surfaced in the mind of producer Larry Gordon, who was working as the vice president of worldwide production at AIP in the early seventies. Gordon actually wanted to make *Cleopatra Jones* but, when that project became attractive to Warner Brothers and was taken out of his hands, he went looking for an alternative and *Coffy* would be it[35]. The project was then rushed into production in order to reach theatres before its rival, something it succeeded in doing by only one month. In doing so, *Coffy* became the first blaxploitation picture in which a female was the token 'badass', slaying the villains and not afraid to use her sexual prowess to solve a problem or to take revenge[36].

---

35 As detailed by Dan Scapperotti, 'Erotic Auteur Jack Hill', *Femme Fatales*, Volume 8, Number 14, 2000

Cast in the lead role of *Coffy* was Pam Grier, who was already beginning to attract a fan following after her turns in the sleazy grindhouse hits *The Big Doll House* (1971) and *The Big Bird Cage* (1972), both of which were directed by Jack Hill and featured regular supporting player Sid Haig. However, Grier's subsequent films, such as *Black Mama, White Mama* (1972), were far less popular.

Although a successful independent filmmaker, Hill had yet to achieve a crossover success, with Roger Corman producing his most interesting work, *The Winner*, in 1969 and financing his two 'Women in Prison' features. Although Hill would later become a cult hero, back in the early seventies his most celebrated work, 1968's *Spider Baby*, had barely seen a theatrical release, whilst his former UCLA classmate Francis Ford Coppola had gone on to box office riches with *The Godfather* (1972). Hill no doubt had to feel slightly sidelined, and *Coffy* would prove to be his most commercial offering to date.

About: *Coffy* was released after the short-lived blaxploitation genre was largely defined by the success of three very different movies. The first is now, unfortunately, largely forgotten, although its importance cannot be diminished. Directed by the late Ossie Davis, *Cotton Comes to Harlem* (1970) was the first step towards a new, bold black cinema wherein African-American actors played strong, dominant, forceful roles. As at least one reviewer of *Cotton Comes to Harlem* asserts, 'This was not the glorified Uncle Tom African-American society of Sidney Poitier or Bill Cosby; friendly representations of blacks which would not upset white America.'[37] True to form, Davis had a 'record opening in Chicago'[38] for his movie and paved the way for what was to come ...

Following up on his satirical *The Watermelon Man* (1970), actor/director Melvin Van Peebles' low budget, anti-establishment movie *Sweet Sweetback's Baadasssss Song* (1971) further succeeded in showing Hollywood that there was a sizeable black audience interested in seeing stories and characters that they could personally relate to. Successful beyond even the then-impressive standards that had been set by *Cotton Comes to Harlem*, *Sweet Sweetback's Baadasssss Song* was a *cause célèbre*, scoring an impressive $15 million at the US box office[39]. Whenever an independent movie grosses figures like that the majors are not slow to get in on the act and, sure enough, it was only a matter of months before Warner Brothers released the most famous blaxploitation picture in history: *Shaft*.

Whilst *Sweet Sweetback's Baadasssss Song* created a cult of its own through its crude, violent and (proudly) X-rated language and plot, *Shaft* was a far more mainstream-friendly effort, a straightforward detective story that merely cast black actors in the main roles. Nonetheless,

---

36 'It is important to keep in mind the real differences between studios such as American International Pictures and a studio such as Warner Brothers, which produced Tamara Dobson's *Cleopatra Jones* ... AIP employed tactics that might not appeal to mainstream studios. Thus, the black action heroine had more latitude than her mainstream counterpart ...' (Yvonne D Sims, *Women of Blaxploitation*, McFarland, 2006).

37 As quoted in Mikel Koven, *Blaxploitation Films*, Pocket Essentials, 2001

38 As quoted in Donald Bogle, *Toms, Coons, Mulattoes, Mammies & Bucks*, Continuum, 1992

39 Figures quoted in Koven, *Blaxploitation Films*, Pocket Essentials, 2001

with an electric soul score from Isaac Hayes, confident direction from Gordon Parks and a brilliant, charismatic lead performance from Richard Roundtree (who is, of course, on the 'right side' of the law and far from the renegade threat that Van Peebles is in his offering) *Shaft* was a sensation at the box office. Most importantly, it was a crossover hit, with white audiences also paying to see the feature.

When combined, the influence of these three movies ushered in a brief craze for product that featured black actors, soul soundtracks and which dealt with urban American themes. As a result, the next two years would prove to be ripe with blaxploitation product, including two inevitable sequels to the fad's biggest hit (1972's *Shaft's Big Score* and 1973's *Shaft in Africa*) and titles such as *Slaughter* and *Superfly* (both 1972). What all of these films have in common is that the African-American star is very much the leading man and, in truly heroic fashion, tends to be a real lady killer. Consequently, looking at many of these films today, one cannot help but see their over indulgent masculinity as a document of a time when the value of strong female characters was obviously of little interest to anyone (although, to be fair, the same can be said about the era's Bond girls, with exception given to *On Her Majesty's Secret Service* star Diana Rigg). To give an example, the very first time that we see star Ron O'Neal in 1972's *Superfly*, he is laid out in bed with a naked lady at his side. However, she is quickly discarded as he goes out to 'be with the boys'. In *Black Caesar* (1973), meanwhile, Fred Williamson overpowers and rapes his girlfriend when she refuses to sleep with him. Afterwards we cut to a completely different scene and the woman's emotions are never even dealt with.

Thus, upon its 1973 release, *Coffy* took a genre that was ripe with misogyny and provided it with a no-nonsense, dominant, sexy, street smart *femme fatale*. Above all this, however, Hill made his female lead *real*. As a result, in desperate situations Coffy never pulls out any fighting expertise or weaponry, instead she has to rely on her sexuality, her brains and her tongue. Whilst it is certainly true that *Cleopatra Jones* also presented audiences with a tough black woman its influence on the genre was not as vast as *Coffy*. This is largely because, despite an imposing presence in its statuesque leading lady Tamara Dobson, the movie disregarded any hint of realism or rugged vigilantism in favour of a mundane, cartoon-like, secret agent storyline. Indeed, *Cleopatra Jones* is pure fantasy, as illustrated from its opening sequence in Turkey and the frantic overacting by its cast (Shelley Winters, as the film's villain, is especially over the top). If *Shaft* was essentially a by-the-numbers action movie, only with black actors, then *Cleopatra Jones* is effectively a James Bond flick (complete with the token prologue and widescreen photography) only with a black, female lead. On the other hand, Grier's *Coffy* is a more believable and sympathetic character, and her story is rooted in the tough, drug-ridden streets of urban Los Angeles.

Coffy may also be viewed as the very antithesis of one of the genre's biggest hits, that being the aforementioned *Superfly*. A politically incorrect action/drama, the slow-moving plot of *Superfly* has Ron O'Neal's character, Priest, as a cocaine dealer (and addict) who seeks to make one last score, sell his wares, make a million dollars and retire from crime. That the movie glamorises O'Neal's behaviour is never in doubt. Cast as the hero, O'Neal can be seen snorting cocaine in *Superfly*, as part of his 'chic', no less than four separate times. Hence, when Grier goes to war with the street dealers in *Coffy*, it is difficult not to feel that the underworld celebrated in

Superfly is perhaps being destroyed in the process.

Straight from the beginning of *Coffy*, Hill makes sure that we know Grier means business. The film kicks off with an unapologetically brutal sequence wherein the actress shoots a drug pusher through the head and injects his smartass assistant with a needle full of smack, causing him to overdose. We learn that Coffy's 11 year old sister is a recovering heroin addict and Grier is intent on exterminating the lousy sellers that hooked her sibling up with the junk in the first place. 'Some junkies started leaning on her,' explains Grier to her ex-boyfriend Carter (William Elliot) as he drives her to the juvenile hall where her young sister now resides. To make matters worse, Coffy's other relatives also boast a dark track record, with her older sister hustling on the streets and her brother 'snorting coke and shooting up' (interestingly, although we never meet Coffy's other siblings, this bleak description of her brother fits the scenario that highlights Hill and Grier's follow-up film *Foxy Brown*).

By day Coffy works as a nurse, which leads to a nice juxtaposition as, at the start of the film, we see her mercilessly kill two people and then, following this, we cut to a life-saving operation taking place at a hospital with the title character present. This gives the viewer an interesting parallel, the idea that Grier is comfortable with taking lives and, yet, it is part of her livelihood to save them. Whilst Hill plays this for some humour value (Grier leaves the room when the operation proves to be too graphic), it also adds to the character's development, humanity and the audience's subsequent interpretation of her.

For example, in one scene, Coffy, who appears to be harbouring some degree of guilt about the film's opening murders, comes close to confessing her crimes to Carter, her ex-boyfriend and policeman. She also speaks, more than once, about being in 'a dream'. Thus, it is safe to conclude that this is not John Shaft gunning down some villains without a second thought, rather Grier's Coffy is a more realistic, conflicted personality. She seems to feel that it is her responsibility to rid the streets of drugs because the police refuse to do so, and it is a task that she does not appear to want, which makes her subsequent killing spree all the more interesting. For instance, never, in *Coffy*, is the actress shown to relish murdering anyone (she commits her first slaughter through tears in her eyes), and it is to the credit of both Grier and Hill that they are able to make such a conflicted, yet violent, personality appear believable and even sympathetic.

Whereas *Coffy* is initially about Grier's desire to avenge her family's drug dependency through killing the dealers ('Kill all of them?' asks Carter when Grier hints at her erstwhile pastime, 'Well why not?' replies the actress innocuously) the film soon starts to carry a revenge motif. Early in the picture we learn that the district's police force is becoming increasingly corrupt, with the cops taking big pay-offs from the dealers. When Carter turns down the chance to get in on a piece of the action, two men in balaclavas break into his apartment and smash his skull with a baseball bat. 'He may be able to go to the bathroom himself one day,' states one doctor when the beaten policeman is brought into hospital. In turn, it is this brutal act that causes Coffy's subsequent rampage through the Los Angeles drug scene and leads the viewer into the main bulk of the picture.

However, what is perhaps most curious about *Coffy* is the way the film depicts a society run by men as one of corruption, exploitation and incompetence. In her role as the film's sole leading female, Grier seeks to change this establishment, to bring down the men, so to speak, and to add some balance to the crooked infrastructure that exists at the top. Whether or not this qualifies *Coffy* as a feminist tract is debatable, of course, largely because, just as with pornography or slasher movies, the film's designated audience is obviously male, highlighted by the ample nudity that permeates the story (within only the first 15 minutes there have been two different scenes featuring exposed breasts). Interestingly, Grier's willingness to appear naked caused some anger in her blaxploitation counterpart Tamara Dobson who refused 'to appear in the same book much less the same page as Grier' and who also 'refused to participate in the same celebrity events' as the *Coffy* starlet[40]. However, Grier maintains, nudity or otherwise, these early blaxploitation movies (although she disowns the term) were hugely positive for black actors in that they 'got a lot of people in the unions (and) they gave me the biggest break of my career.'[41]

Nevertheless, one could also argue that Hill, as a journeyman director, knew what elements were required for the movie to succeed commercially (i.e. nudity and violence) but, at the same time, he at least attempted to deliver a social conscience and provoke some intelligent thought in amongst the mandatory bare breasts and bullet-ridden set pieces. Thus, when Coffy goes undercover as an expensive female escort for a character called King George (Robert DoQui) she finds it remarkably easy to shatter the macho trust that exists between him and his new business partner Vitroni (Allan Arbus). One simple lie about being a hired hand for George, after one of Vitroni's henchmen recognises her as Carter's ex-girlfriend, leads to the luckless pimp having a rope tied around his neck and being dragged to his doom, tied to a speeding car. It is a brutal sequence, although Hill sees to it that we don't feel *too* sympathetic towards the pimp's prolonged demise (in a previous snippet of his character development we are told that George doesn't think twice about beating a woman and once 'cut the face' of an escort).

Most powerful of all is *Coffy*'s finale wherein Grier discovers that her apparently reputable, politician boyfriend Brunswick (Booker Bradshaw) is actually involved with the trade in illegal drugs. Having ordered her killed (which obviously fails), Grier pays a late night visit to Brunswick's beach house in order to shoot him dead. However, Brunswick, every bit a politician, starts to negotiate, trying to talk Coffy around. 'As long as people are deprived of a decent life,' he begins, 'They are gonna want something to just plain feel good with.'

In a sense this explains the drugs trade as an inevitable part of the 'supply and demand' chain that a wealthy society creates, the predictable result of capitalism, whereby those left out to rot by the new economic revolution (perhaps through their creed or social class) opt to fund crime or become a part of it. The problem, as Hill appears to insinuate, begins and ends with politicians (in the film's case, this metaphor is made literal, and Brunswick's death closes the picture), who are unwilling to provide a good life for everyone. Instead, only a select minority get rich whereas the rest are left to fend for the scraps. Hence, for all of Coffy's exhausting, hard grafting as a nurse she is not rewarded with the sort of economic stability that the film's petty drug lords possess, yet one assists in healing people, whilst the other trades in death. Whether

---

40 As documented in Sims, *Women of Blaxploitation*, McFarland, 2006

41 As told to Joe Kane, *The Phantom of the Movies: Videoscope*, Three Rivers Press, 2000

or not Hill himself was promoting a more socialist agenda through this display of inequality is debatable, but his dislike of political jargon and a system that creates drug abuse is impossible to ignore.

Speaking to the media about why drug dealers and abusers exist, the campaigning Brunswick blames it on 'our power structure', a motive that is further emphasised when we find out that the police and the politicians devise the very hierarchy that allows the underground crime syndicates to exist. Indeed, money is the driving force for everyone in *Coffy*, except for the title character and her ex-boyfriend Carter. As a result, it is easy to view Grier as some kind of working class avenger, a hard grafting nurse trying to purge society of its wealthy crooks and restore some much needed moral order. Whilst her way of doing things is hardly admirable, it is also difficult not to view Grier as being stuck in the middle of an urban hell, with the streets around her filled with prostitution, drug abuse, battery and murder. The breaking point for her comes when these things are forced onto her doorstep and she is no longer able to ignore them. In other words, she becomes a product of the very society that she lives in.

Of course, with *Coffy* being a blaxploitation movie, some comment needs to be given to the film's race relations. Whilst Hill obviously draws on the messy legacy of the Ku Klux Klan when it comes to the death of George ('this is how we lynch niggers,' states Sid Haig in his perennial cameo as a mob heavy), allowing the audience to cathartically rise against the white trash murderer, other elements of *Coffy* are less emotionally exploitative. For instance, the film's foremost villain, Brunswick, is a handsome, charming black male, the sort that would not seem out of place playing a Fred Williamson-type of blaxploitation hero. We see him at the movie's end aligned with Vitroni and the other white drug lords, almost as if he is a 'traitor' to his race, siding with the very people that keep the ghettos supplied with drugs and, thus, maintain the status quo of having poor black people fund the white hierarchy.

Even so, Hill aims for a cheap response in having Brunswick's death take place after Grier finds him with a white lover in his house. Her decision to shoot him between the legs is obviously designed to provoke a positive response from the ethnic target market that *Coffy* was aimed at. It is a strange decision because, whilst one may argue that this plot device concludes Brunswick's alienation of the black community, *Coffy* has been free of such knee-jerk set pieces up until this point. In saying all that, the sequence still cannot help but encourage a laugh. Grier sells her anger so well that her decision to shoot her scumbag ex-boyfriend dead has a ring of poetic justice to it. Hill then ends the movie with Grier walking, alone, along the beach. The question being, where does she go from here? A fugitive without friends, she is as alone as Al Pacino's Michael Corleone at the close of *The Godfather*.

Another thing that should be addressed about *Coffy* is that it gave renowned African-American stuntman Bob Minor his first chance at performing the role of stunt coordinator. Minor, the first man of his colour to work in such a position, would go on to become a major name in his profession and work on such blockbusters as *Glory* (1989), *Ocean's Eleven* (2001) and *National Treasure* (2004), but he claims that it was his early work in the blaxploitation genre that really allowed him to rise to such prominence.

'At that time it was pretty hard to get into the film industry,' he says. 'I started out at this gym in Santa Monica where I paid $200 to start my training. I was at the gym three times a week and the training consisted of fighting, tumbling, a little boxing, jumping off things … That is how I got started. Then five months later I got my first interview for a movie, it was on *Beyond the Valley of the Dolls*, and from there I took off and have never stopped since. Jack Hill gave me my start as a stunt coordinator on *Coffy*. I met Jack in 1972 when he was working with Corman. I think at the time he was just getting ready to start with *Coffy* at AIP and he called me in for an interview. He told me that he had heard a lot of good things about me and asked me if I would accept the challenge of doing the film as the stunt coordinator. He also gave me a little part, as a limo driver, and that was a small plus. It was a very action orientated movie and I like to say, "Bob is my name and action is my game!" Trying to become a stunt coordinator at that time, as an African-American, was very difficult. We did not get that privilege and it was a fantastic opportunity. Black exploitation gave a lot of us the opportunity to work in the industry. When they started putting black people in films they quickly found out that they were money makers. Films like *Coffy* and Fred Williamson's *The Legend of Nigger Charley*, they were making a lot of money because black people had never seen themselves on the screen as a black hero, the guy with the gun wiping out the bad guys.'

Although *Coffy*, like almost every blaxploitation feature, has aged in regards to its soundtrack, fashion and language, the movie still holds up as an invigorating action picture. The things that make the film dated now carry an irresistible charm ('Coffy baby, sweet as a chocolate bar, Coffy baby, nobody knows who you are,' croons one of the songs on the Roy Ayers soundtrack) and Hill's knack of creating suspense still works well. As with the best Bond movies, he consistently places Grier in sticky situations, exploits the drama to saturation point and then, finally, has her wiggle her way out of certain doom whether with her street smarts or by luring her captors into a false sense of security with her ample sexuality. Furthermore, by showing that a strong, African-American female could not only dominate a movie, but also attract large audiences and go on to become an international star, Hill staked his claim, with *Coffy*, as a forward thinking, important filmmaker.

What happened next? Unlike the other female stars of the genre, which included Tamara Dobson and *T.N.T. Jackson*'s Jeannie Bell, Grier would endure as the sole female icon of the blaxploitation movement. Her follow-up feature *Foxy Brown* (1974), which was also directed by Hill, may not be as innovative as *Coffy* but it is arguably even more entertaining. The actress would go on to headline the likes of *Friday Foster* and *Sheba, Baby* (both 1975), but by the mid-seventies the genre was beginning to simmer out and Grier's contract with AIP was not renewed. Besides which, none of these imitators had the quality or impact of Hill's *Coffy* or *Foxy Brown*, arguably the two peaks of the blaxploitation craze. Rising criticism of the consistently violent genre also began to alienate even the core African-American audience.[42]

Following his double whammy of *Coffy* and *Foxy Brown*, Hill would continue to work as a

---

42 As Sims documents, to many viewers and critics of the time, 'The blaxploitation films only served to solidify the common perception that African-Americans were dangerous, prone to violence and sexually lustful.' (*Women of Blaxploitation*, McFarland, 2006). This is, of course, the equivalent of holding up James Bond pictures as evidence that British men are cold-hearted, violent misogynists.

journeyman director, putting his own unique stamp on any project that was given to him. First up was 1974's *The Swinging Cheerleaders*, a tremendously entertaining teen comedy, which was a huge success at the time. Sadly Hill's commercial viability was shattered when his girl-gang thriller *Switchblade Sisters* (1974), a masterpiece of low budget action, flopped and his last film to date would be the abysmal Roger Corman-produced fantasy *Sorceress* (1982). Those who enjoyed *Coffy* and want to learn more about Hill are strongly advised to skip this one and instead check out *Foxy Brown*, *Pit Stop*, *Spider Baby*, *The Swinging Cheerleaders* and *Switchblade Sisters*, which are among the finest exploitation pictures ever made.

Grier and Hill would both enjoy a career resurrection at the hands of *Pulp Fiction* director Quentin Tarantino, who would, in 2000, re-release *Switchblade Sisters* to the cinema, and also on American DVD. Grier would be cast as the lead in Tarantino's excellent *Jackie Brown* (1997), which Hill gets a 'special thanks' on, and briefly reunited with her *Coffy* co-star Sid Haig, who has a cameo in the movie. Following her *Jackie Brown* success, Grier would feature in John Carpenter's *Ghosts of Mars* (2001) and the Eddie Murphy comedy *The Adventures of Pluto Nash* (2002), however her biggest success would be in the television series *The L Word*.

Although his success was long-delayed, Sid Haig, who starred in many of Hill's projects dating back to his student film *The Host* (1960), would finally find stardom after appearing in *House of 1000 Corpses* (2003) and *The Devil's Rejects* (2005). Now a leading man of many horror movies, including *House of the Dead 2* (2005), *Night of the Living Dead 3D* (2006) and *Brotherhood of Blood* (2007), Haig attracts a sizeable cult following.

Although the blaxploitation genre enjoyed hits with *Coffy*, *Foxy Brown* and *Cleopatra Jones*, this was really the last gasp for the craze. Whilst enjoyable post-*Foxy Brown* titles are few and far between, nostalgia for the period has kicked in over the decades resulting in *Action Jackson*, the spoof *I'm Gonna Git You Sucka* (both 1988), *Tales from the Hood* (1995), *Original Gangstas* (1996) and the disastrous re-launch of the genre's most successful franchise with the 2000 version of *Shaft*. At the time of writing, rumours continue to abound that actress Halle Berry is due to star in an updated version of Hill's *Foxy Brown*.

Jack Hill interview

A veteran exploitation filmmaker by the time *Coffy* went into production, director Jack Hill never expected that his greatest legacy would lie in a pair of blaxploitation pictures. 'When I first heard they wanted me to do what was called "a black film" my heart sank,' admits Hill. 'I didn't really think I knew anything about the subject matter but, as so often happens, when I have a challenge like that and I desperately need the work I get into it and I find something real interesting in it and it all comes out of somewhere. I don't know where (*laughs*). But people have asked me how I knew so much about black people's lives and I don't know that I ever did.' Adding to the director's woes was the fact that a rival movie was about to go into competition at Warner Brothers featuring a much larger budget and such named stars as Shelley Winters. 'When I got the call from my agent to go and meet with Larry Gordon the first thing they told me was that *Cleopatra Jones* was being made over at Warner Brothers. Larry seemed to be quite bitter about it and he had the idea that we would do something similar and get it out right away. *Coffy* took us 18 days to shoot and the budget on it was just $500,000. They had a limit on what they called black films because they thought that at that price they could make a profit on any of them.'

Indeed, *Coffy* made it to the cinemas a month ahead of *Cleopatra Jones* and it was also a far more violent and gritty effort. 'Oh I don't know that *Coffy* was that much more violent,' defends Hill. 'But I remember seeing *Cleopatra Jones* and thinking that it was just a James Bond rip off and there was nothing much special about it. To me, *Cleopatra Jones* was more a comic book. It wasn't about real emotions and that is what I like to deal with. It did not really use the female character aspect. It was just another action movie to me, except with a woman instead of a man. I can tell you that *Cleopatra Jones* cost a lot more money to make than *Coffy*. It must have cost twice as much and they had to spend more money on advertising. I remember that both films came out in the same summer. I don't remember the exact release dates but I don't think it was ever important to AIP that we come out first.'

Nevertheless, according to Hill, *Coffy* would turn in a bigger profit than its more expensive rival. 'The gross of both pictures was pretty much the same but because of the cost of *Cleopatra Jones* my little net profit percentage was worth many, many times over what I was paid to make the movie,' he reveals. 'So I got paid pretty well. Larry Gordon made a big profit on *Coffy* but I heard that the producer of *Cleopatra Jones* didn't earn a quarter.' Surprisingly, then, Hill's movie fared less well when it came to foreign sales. 'I was aware that the studio did not count on too much gross from the overseas market,' he says. 'They didn't think that they would be interested in black films, although some of them did really well. The big problem was that some of them got banned because of the violence and in Sweden *Coffy* got banned (*laughs*). I received a copy from there a few years ago, when it had finally been released, and even then it had been heavily cut.'

Before embarking on *Coffy* the director refused to research the blaxploitation genre and, therefore, entered the project without knowing much about what urban audiences had been flocking to see. 'I don't think I had seen many of them,' says Hill of the genre. 'The only one I recall seeing was *Superfly*. I mean, I saw *Shaft* but that was a major studio movie and I never viewed that as an urban picture. I didn't really take much from it. For me, doing *Coffy* was just an opportunity to do something with Pam Grier and to do something with her personality that other directors were not doing with black women. I thought that she had a unique style that could work out well if it was done right. That is about all I can recall.' Hill states that he always knew Grier would be the perfect leading lady. In fact, he had launched her to cult stardom in his previous films *The Big Doll House* and *The Big Bird Cage*, two of the better 'women in prison' movies from the early seventies. 'She was just one of many actors in those films,' he says. 'They had an ensemble cast of several girls and I just put the word out among a number of agents that I was looking for actresses that had potential. In *The Big Doll House* the part was not written for a black girl at all, but I was reading black and Asian actresses and she had never done anything before, except for a walk-on part in a Russ Meyer movie, and it was so small. I watched the movie (*Beyond the Valley of the Dolls*) and I couldn't even see her. I thought that her presence and authority worked and so I took a chance with her. I think that when *Coffy* came around it was just beginning to be accepted, but I wasn't thinking that way. I wasn't looking for a black actress, just good people to work with.'

Having seen at least one example of the blaxploitation fad, Hill set out to do something very different with *Coffy*. 'I didn't approve of the glamorisation of drugs in *Superfly* and it was important for me to write a script that attacked that,' he says. 'I thought that people who deal with drugs should get what they deserve and the same for pimps. The only other thing I really wanted to get into the film was the Vietnam War and how people of colour were being exploited by the military. So there is one section where Booker Bradshaw gives a speech for a commercial that they are doing and he talks about black kids going out to South East Asia. It was just a little thing but I wanted to point out the hypocrisy of him speaking about that whilst being in with the same people responsible for doing that. It was a small dramatic irony. I had been out marching against the war myself so I wanted to get that in there. But I had not the slightest intuition that, for example, casting a black woman in the lead role of an action movie was unusual. Honestly, I was just doing the job I was hired to do and trying to make the best movie I could on that subject matter. Normally movies like *Coffy* would run for a summer and then they would be tossed out. Home video wasn't even being thought of back then so I had no idea it would later be seen as an important film.'

Another factor that Hill took into consideration when he began work on *Coffy* was the fact that criticism had begun to arise over the fact that many blaxploitation flicks were being helmed by distinctly white faces. 'When we started *Coffy* the studio was very conscious about criticism in the press about black exploitation films. I don't think the term blaxploitation had been coined yet,' says Hill. 'Basically they felt that they might be taking money from black audiences in the theatre but not putting black people behind the camera. So we tried to find some black technicians but there weren't any because you had to be in a union to work on this. However, Bob Minor was an exception and he hadn't been a stunt co-ordinator before, he had been a stuntman, so this was a big break for him.'

Since *Coffy* Pam Grier has spoken less and less about her blaxploitation pictures and now has no contact with Hill, the director who launched her. Asked about whether or not he feels the actress is not as thankful as she should be, the director pauses for thought. 'I don't think that thankful is the correct word,' he admits. 'It was my feeling – and this is hard for me to really back up, it is just a feeling – that she envied Tamara Dobson because she had been a fashion model. So Pam wanted to have a classier wardrobe. In *Foxy Brown* she picked her own clothes and that is the funny thing when you watch that movie today, it looks extremely dated and very seventies (*laughs*). In *Coffy* I deliberately tried to avoid anything that might date it whereas in *Foxy Brown* I thought that all of these outfits were distracting. In *Coffy* I tried to keep her wardrobe very simple and plain because if you have clothes on a woman which are flashy it draws your eyes and your attention away from the actress and the emotion on her face. But she was the star then and she got to pick her wardrobe. I thought it was unfortunate and the wrong way to go but it was a different kind of movie so what the hell ...'

Hill also insists that his leading lady had no problems with disrobing for the camera. 'No, when you have a body like that, most actresses don't mind showing it off. That was just accepted back then. I'm sure that helped to draw in the men of course (*laughs*). It wasn't even a plan as much as it was an understood requirement. She didn't object to any of that, she was very good and her first job in movies was working with Russ Meyer. I don't know if she took her clothes off back then but it was understood and she was fine with it.'

TABOO BREAKERS

After he finished his work on *Coffy*, Hill was given no access to the post-production process, including the editing and scoring of the movie. 'I had no input into the soundtrack,' he confirms. 'The thing about AIP is that they hated directors, they didn't want to pay you anything extra and after you finished shooting they just didn't want to see you around anymore. They saw directors as a nuisance. But I shot *Coffy* in such a way that they had to edit it in the way I wanted. But as far as the music is concerned; they wouldn't have listened to me even if I had made suggestions. Thankfully, as luck turned out, they made very good decisions because the soundtracks have become incredibly popular over the years and are still talked about.'

The director also has vivid memories about the first time he saw his blaxploitation debut on the big screen. 'It was almost a frightening experience,' he recalls.' I saw the opening at a theatre in a black neighbourhood in Pasadena and it was far beyond my wildest expectations in terms of audience participation. They were in the mood from the beginning and even standing up and talking to the picture, shouting in places, it was a little scary but I realised that I had achieved a certain catharsis. I was pleased with that.' Such a strong reaction led to the commissioning of an immediate follow-up to *Coffy*, although Hill's proposed title of *Burn Coffy Burn* was turned down and *Foxy Brown*, a new urban action fable, was the film which went into production. 'The sales department had the ultimate say in matters like that and they told us that sequels were not doing well,' says the director. 'Larry Gordon disagreed, he thought that we could have had a real franchise but the sales department said they didn't want to do a sequel so some genius came up with the title *Foxy Brown*, which I hated, but it was not for me to question such things. So we went ahead and did it and, oddly enough, it turned out to be a catch word for the genre. I have no idea why.'

The TEXAS CHAIN SAW MASSACRE

Released: 1974
Directed by: Tobe Hooper
Produced by: Tobe Hooper
Written by: Tobe Hooper/Kim Henkel
Cast: Marilyn Burns (Sally Hardesty), Allen Danzinger (Jerry), Paul A Partain (Franklin Hardesty), William Vail (Kirk), Teri McMinn (Pam), Edwin Neal (The Hitchhiker), Jim Siedow (Old Man), Gunnar Hansen (Leatherface), John Dugan (Grandpa), Robert Courtin (Window Washer), William Creamer (Bearded Man), John Larroquette (Narrator)

In a nutshell: Five youngsters travel across Texas. Sally Hardesty wants to find out if her late grandfather's place of rest has been vandalised following reports of grave robbing across the Lone Star State. After discovering that the grave is still intact, Sally decides to try and find her grandfather's old house, despite being warned against doing this by an old man at a petrol station. On the way, the group picks up a hitchhiker, who wastes little time in carving the arm of Sally's wheelchair bound brother Franklin with a knife. They manage to wrestle him out of the van, but the hitchhiker writes a strange symbol, in his own blood, on the side of the vehicle. Arriving at the rundown house of Sally's grandfather, the youths split up, with Teri and her boyfriend Kirk heading to a large house next door to see if there might be anyone around who can give them some petrol. When they don't return, Sally's friend Jerry goes searching for them. As night falls and Jerry fails to make a re-appearance, Sally and Franklin make their way to the ominous house next door. They are accosted by a hulking man with a chainsaw, who kills Franklin as his sister watches in horror. The man chases Sally through an area of dense woodland, before she makes it to the petrol station. However, the 'nice' old man in the station is part of a bizarre, cannibalistic family, and he beats Sally into unconsciousness, before tying her up and taking her back home. There she experiences a night of terror at the hands of Leatherface, the Hitchhiker, Grandpa and the station owner.

Prologue: Despite popular belief *The Texas Chain Saw Massacre* was not the first film directed by Tobe Hooper. His previous low budget feature film, entitled *Eggshells*, is now considered lost. Made in 1969, *Eggshells* was advertised with the tag line 'time and spaced fantasy'. Although it won the best picture award at the Atlanta Film Festival few people have actually seen *Eggshells*, whilst Hooper himself describes it as being 'about a common house. It's a real hippy from the hippy days. It was about troops coming back from Vietnam. It starts with disbursement, the troops assimilating back into society. In the common house live four or five people, two couples and one guy that you never see. In the basement, deep in the house, is this ante-chamber … something that was built into the house, and there is this embryonic, kryptonic, hyper-electric presence in the basement.'[43]

The Texas Chain Saw Massacre's cast and crew was made up of those just starting out in the business, although Kim Henkel had worked as a grip on 1971's *The Windsplitter* which also featured short acting performances from Hooper and Jim Siedow. *The Texas Chain Saw Massacre*'s co-editor, Sallye Richardson, is also credited as being the assistant director on *The Windsplitter*. Aiming to obtain a PG rating[44], Hooper purposely relied on the power of suggestion in *The Texas Chain Saw Massacre*, although it is a testament to the young filmmaker's ignorance towards the MPAA that he actually thought the level of graphic torment and violence in his movie would allow for a family friendly rating.

Prior to *The Texas Chain Saw Massacre*, George Romero's *Night of the Living Dead* had shown that a gritty and violent low budget horror movie could cross over to a larger audience and make a great deal of cash. Although not as commercially successful as Romero's zombie opus, Wes Craven's *Last House on the Left* (1972) began a movement that displayed man as the ultimate source of evil, something that Hooper's movie, which had no supernatural undertones, would continue. Craven also included a brutal chainsaw battle in the bloody climax to *Last House on the Left*, wherein screen villain David Hess meets a memorably nasty end. Perhaps anticipating *The Texas Chain Saw Massacre*'s filth-ridden psychopaths, a pair of murderous backwoods residents

---

43 As told to the author of this book in *The Dark Side* magazine (Issue 113, 2005)

44 '*The Texas Chain Saw Massacre* was going to be PG, though I was aware of how the material was problematical. Anyway, I developed a relationship with the MPAA to check on certain matters … I got what I thought were certain commitments to ensure the film would get a PG rating, so I was surprised when it got an R.' (Tobe Hooper, as told to Philip Nutman, *The Bloody Best of Fangoria*, Vol. 7, 1988)

were the aggresors in John Boorman's classic *Deliverance* (1972), a movie which has an almost unrivalled ability to throw the viewer into life or death dramatics – something that Hooper was surely paying attention to. Mention must also, of course, go to Ed Gein, the 'Wisconsin ghoul', whose habit of dressing in human skin inspired the Leatherface character and some of the more macabre set design in *The Texas Chain Saw Massacre*. He was also known to rob graves, which has some bearing on Edwin Neal's portrayal of the Hitchhiker role.

About: You wonder if Hooper and company really knew what they had in their hands when the director called 'cut' on the final day of shooting *The Texas Chain Saw Massacre* over three decades ago. For, in spite of its trashy title, the movie remains that rare example of a horror movie which has entered the popular lexicon and, as the years have passed, gone from being a byword for cinematic nastiness to achieving its much-deserved status as a genre classic. Indeed, as the contemporary likes of *Wolf Creek* (2005) and *Hostel* push the levels of graphic violence to increasingly bloody extremes, Hooper's power tool opus now seems quite tame, although, much like Hitchcock's *Psycho*, its ability to scare the viewer has never weakened. Ultimately, where *The Texas Chain Saw Massacre* excels is in whipping up a carnival of fear as the story progresses, and much of this has to do with the exceptional cinematography and camera trickery of Daniel Pearl (who, unsurprisingly, would go on to achieve a renowned Hollywood career). One need only look at the lengthy scene where Burns is forcibly restrained at the cannibal family's dinner table to see how invaluable Pearl's photography, coupled with a frantic editing job, is to the movie, capturing the on-screen terror in a believable, *ciné verité* manner that throws the viewer right into the thick of things. This, alongside the movie's relentlessly noisy soundtrack and Robert Burns' outstanding set design, builds up a scenario of almost unrivalled alienation and torment, for both the viewer and the film's unfortunate heroine.

Certainly, it is these closing moments that, no doubt, contributed to Hooper's film being dubbed 'the pornography of violence' by a sickened James Ferman, the one-time director of the British Board of Film Classification (who banned the movie outright for 25 years)[45]. Although Wes Craven's earlier *Last House on the Left* was, undeniably, more blatant with its sexual horrors and far more barbaric, that movie never reached the lofty artistic heights of *The Texas Chain Saw Massacre* and Craven never attracted such an instantly large audience. Even in spite of the success of 1973's *The Exorcist*, whose graphic makeup effects outdo anything in *The Texas Chain Saw Massacre*, it is safe to say that the average cinemagoer in 1974 had not experienced such long, drawn out sequences of psychological distress as those displayed by Hooper.

Hence, it is the *threat* of something heinous that makes this feature so horrifying rather than the actual display of anything particularly bloody[46]. For example, when Sally simpers to

---

45 Ferman is quoted as saying this in Tom Dewe Matthews' book *Censored* (Chatto, 1994)

46 The British ban remained from 1974 right up until 1999 because the examiners felt that the film's 'psychological torture' was the 'problem'. One examiner even notes that the film 'was rather unique because it did not have particularly outrageous visuals; but it was so well made it had this awful impact all the way through.' (as documented in *Censored*, Matthews, Chatto, 1994)

her attackers, led by Neal's particularly unpleasant Hitchhiker, 'I'll do anything you want' (and thanks to Burns' exceptional delivery of this line it is clear that she is offering herself sexually) her transition to complete helplessness is completed. Yet, what makes *The Texas Chain Saw Massacre*'s lengthy torment of its leading lady so utterly gut wrenching is because there is no ulterior motive for Sally's capture outside of murder. Leatherface and company have no interest in a sexual outing with their captive female (Burns' 'offering' is met only with childish laughter and mimicry) rather they see her as something of a toy, a farm animal that is there to be played with prior to its slaughter.

The issue of misogyny, therefore, is not quite as relevant to *The Texas Chain Saw Massacre* as one may initially think. Certainly, one has to acknowledge that the attractive Burns has her clothes torn to shreds (her bust concealed by only the flimsiest of rags) and is chased, beaten, captured and abused beyond what most on-screen females have ever had to endure. However, Hooper's killers are so well fleshed out that this is not just a cavalcade of faceless, slobbering males tormenting a beautiful blonde. Rather it is mentally disabled men, who have been denied a maternal figure, suddenly being faced with an attractive woman. As a result, each acts in a different, but totally believable, way as soon as Sally is captured. The Hitchhiker, for instance, displays a cruelty that is unsurpassable, prodding Sally, playing with her hair and ridiculing her hysterics. He dehumanises her, letting her pleas for mercy fall on deaf ears, utterly unable to relate to her terror and incapable of seeing her as anything except a potential lunch. Leatherface is slightly more curious, perhaps this is the first live woman that he has been exposed to for any length of time, although he is content to follow his brother's lead. Hansen, in his portrayal of the hulking character, effectively grasps the childish mentality of the man behind the mask, this is a figure who can communicate through only the most basic of means and who is treated with disdain by his older kin despite being the one who kills and cleans up the house. Siedow's 'Old Man' persona (given the name Drayton Sawyer in the sequel) shows some sort of civil reaction to his brothers' sustained mental torture of Sally ('that's enough' he finally hollers) but even he finally breaks into a perverse smirk as the humiliation continues. As with the rest of *The Texas Chain Saw Massacre*'s cast, Siedow does a tremendous job of simulating the actions of a totally deranged mind, on the one hand being appalled by the inhumanity that surrounds him and yet unable to stop himself from lapsing into a guilty enjoyment of it.

Therefore, whilst it is tempting to view the horrific acts that are conducted by three men towards a bound, crying woman as being representative of a greater misogyny on the part of the filmmaker, Hooper's careful manipulation of his characters' psychology, and his creation of a believable setting, makes the movie's violence strangely sexless. As mentioned, these are crimes, not of sexual arousal or desire, but of simplicity: *The Texas Chain Saw Massacre*'s male protagonists are reflective of a far greater, real life evil … the plague of disillusionment and unemployment.

Set during a time when American troops were still stationed in Vietnam (with the Indochina conflict finally coming to a bloody close), the hippy generation having gone unheard in their own 'war' against the steadfast Republican presidency, *The Texas Chain Saw Massacre* introduces the viewers to five young Americans. We can accept that they are 'liberal', or even 'hippy', youths through their appearance (Pam's revealing clothing, Sally's flared trousers, Jerry's unkempt, long hair). This, coupled with the film's opening narration ('It was all the more tragic in that they were young ... they could not have expected nor would they have wished to see as much of the mad and macabre as they were to see that day') suggests that Hooper wanted to at least acknowledge the Vietnam era. As a result, the story of youth-meets-sudden-violence carries an evocative edge.

It is also difficult to ignore the poverty that has befallen the house of Leatherface and his two brothers. The sole breadwinner, Siedow's 'Cook', owns an off-road gas station and also takes on the responsibility of looking after his two brothers who have an adolescent desire to 'rebel' (most hilariously in the scene where Leatherface is castigated for sawing into the door). The cuts of human meat, it is hinted, are sold by Siedow at his service station ... just another way for him to make a few extra bucks in lieu of the floundering family business. Whilst the script, by Hooper and Henkel, does not illustrate any real lack of faith in a free market economy, it is interesting that the director's sequel to *The Texas Chain Saw Massacre* uses Reagan-era capitalism as a point of satire[47].

Much has also been made, by some critics, of *The Texas Chain Saw Massacre*'s attempt to reflect the breakdown of the American family unit. Certainly, it is interesting to view Leatherface as a stand-in 'mother', cooking and cleaning, be-wigged and in female attire when his 'duties' call for it, but the idea that Hooper intentionally aimed to poke fun at the nuclear family stereotype is far less interesting than looking at *The Texas Chain Saw Massacre* as a Vietnam parable. No doubt the director felt the same way, hence the introduction of Bill Moseley's 'Chop Top' character in *The Texas Chainsaw Massacre 2*, a Vietnam veteran whose role is also used to spoof the box office attraction of the war movies during the mid-eighties (such as 1986's *Platoon*). In a sense, *The Texas Chain Saw Massacre* really does mirror the fear of the outside world that youngsters in early seventies America had to deal with, the notion that they could well be drafted and sent somewhere alien to die. As one critic put it, '*The Texas Chain Saw Massacre* was the first baby-boomer shocker, in which pampered but idealistic suburban children, distrustful of anyone older than thirty, are terrorised by the deformed adult world that dwells on the grungy side of the tracks.'[48] Hooper's 'adult world' is suitably war-torn. His villains are misfits, living in repulsive conditions and numb to death and violence. It is hard not to make at least some comparison between the entire field of dead, abandoned cars that Kirk and Pam pass *en route* to the Leatherface house and the photos of graves of dead America GIs that were being beamed in newscasts all over the world.

Of course, none of these themes should distract from the fact that *The Texas Chain Saw Massacre* is best represented by the fact that it is, simply, a straightforward and very scary little movie. With every shot Hooper shows immaculate craftsmanship, the director really does appear to be fully dedicated to creating the ultimate screen nightmare. Thus, every single act

---

47 Hooper himself has admitted that *The Texas Chain Saw Massacre* is a film that exhibited a mistrust of the government of the time. 'It was around the time of Watergate ... shortly after the gasoline crisis in the country and people were being put out of jobs ... The opening of the film states: "The story you are about to see is true." That was a lie. That was a response to being lied to by the government ...' (Bowen, *Rue Morgue*, Issue 42, 2004)

48 Briggs, *Profoundly Disturbing*, Plexus Publishing, 2003

of shocking violence is very well thought out. When Pam meets the film's most horrific death (hung on a meat hook while still alive), Hooper expertly films the scene without a drop a blood but, due to a very sharp edit, we can almost feel the pain of the actress as the hook penetrates her back even though we do not see this happen. Not since *Psycho*'s celebrated shower scene has the use of clever editing made so little feel like so much … and, just as Janet Leigh's final moments are extremely difficult to endure, so too does *The Texas Chain Saw Massacre*'s meat hook sequence still carry a gut punch like few other horror movies. Likewise, when we first see Leatherface he is a screen monster of almost unrivalled threat. His bludgeoning of Kirk is sudden, violent and without any sort of expression (thanks to his mask). Although cinematic slashers had used face masks before (most notably in Mario Bava's 1963 classic *Blood and Black Lace*) never had any of them covered their features with such a grisly monstrosity as that used by Hansen. Ironically, the cheap latex job that Hansen sports on his face in *The Texas Chain Saw Massacre* is umpteen times more effective than the lavish, intricate (and still very impressive) makeup job that Tom Savini produced for the sequel. Sometimes less is indeed more (and the same goes for John Dugan's Grandpa, who plays only a minor part in the original movie, but whose makeup boasts a convincing simulation of old age).

One of the other masterful elements of Hooper's debut horror feature is, of course, its title. The words 'chain saw' and 'massacre' together create, in the viewer's mind, something far more gruesome than that which the director could ever hope to conjure up on-screen. Indeed, as when the animatronic Shark broke down in *Jaws*, forcing Spielberg to use his imagination and, in turn, to create a cinematic classic of suspense through *not* seeing the threat, Hooper's low budget worked to his advantage. Unlike the bloodbath that he would opt for in *The Texas Chainsaw Massacre 2*, the original lacked the resources to create such explicit effects and, as a result, Hooper uses sound, quick cutaways and inventive camerawork in place of outright gore. However, with the title ringing in our ears from the outset we are already on full alert as to what *might* transpire, and even though only one character (Franklin) actually dies at the receiving end of the chainsaw, we are constantly expecting to see the very worst acts of bloodletting. As such, whenever the awful din of Leatherface's power tool kicks into action it is difficult not to cling to the edge of your seat in horrible anticipation. Although future shockers such as *The Toolbox Murders* (1978) and *Nail Gun Massacre* (1985) would use clever titles to lure the audience into a similar feeling of dread, the end result, due to the films simply not being very well made, was redundant.

Viewed today, *The Texas Chain Saw Massacre* is still one of the most expertly controlled horror movies ever made. That it was created by a largely inexperienced cast and crew, on a low budget and a tight shoot, simply beggars belief. Whilst Hooper deserves a lot of the credit for the film's success, there can also be no denying the brilliance of his young actors, with Hansen putting in an admirably expressive physical performance as Leatherface (this is not some faceless stuntman under a hockey mask, but an actor who has thought about and understands his character) and Burns screaming her way into screen history. As her wheelchair-bound brother Franklin, Paul Partain has an unrivalled ability to get under the viewer's skin, whilst Siedow and Neal exhibit a psychosis that is thoroughly terrifying.

As with *Night of the Living Dead*, evil lives on at the end of the film. Hooper clearly didn't want to offer his audience any respite but, then again, the times hardly necessitated a happy ending.

What happened next? The *Texas Chain Saw Massacre*'s influence on the modern horror genre is vast, and not always positive. Described as 'maniacs with cameras' by Stephen King[49], the film's direct descendants include such sadistic nonsense as the aforementioned *The Toolbox Murders* (which Hooper would, ironically, go on to remake), 1980's *Mother's Day* and 1983's *Pieces* ('You don't have to go to Texas to experience a chain saw massacre' screamed the advertisements). Much better examples of Hooper's influence are 1979's *Tourist Trap*, 1980's *Motel Hell* and 2003's *Wrong Turn*. Although he denies ever seeing *The Texas Chain Saw Massacre*, Jeff Lieberman's nightmarish 1980 effort *Just Before Dawn* nevertheless plays out a similar story.[50]

After completion Tobe Hooper sold his little independent shocker to up-and-coming distributors Bryanston Pictures. However Hooper and his actors never saw royalties for the movie, a scandal that was covered in David Gregory's in depth documentary *The Texas Chain Saw Massacre: The Shocking Truth* (2000).

Regardless of this, one would have thought that being a part of such a sensational hit film would have elevated *The Texas Chain Saw Massacre*'s cast and crew onto bigger, if not better, things. Sadly, only a few would stay near the top of the A-list, including cinematographer Daniel Pearl who would go on to photograph music videos for Michael Jackson, Madonna (including her *Truth or Dare* documentary), U2 and Britney Spears. He would also work on such features as *Full Moon High* (1981), *National Treasure* (2004) and the big budget remake of *The Texas Chain Saw Massacre* in 2003. His wife, Dorothy Pearl, credited as *The Texas Chain Saw Massacre*'s makeup artist, would enjoy a superlative Hollywood career, employed on such hits as *Ironweed* (1987), *Rob Roy* (1995) and *Miss Congeniality* (2000).

Set designer Robert Burns, who passed away in 2004, would go on to obtain a cult following of his own after *The Texas Chain Saw Massacre* , and find himself working on such subsequent genre classics as *The Hills Have Eyes* (1977), *The Howling* (1981) and *Re-Animator* (1985). Of *The Texas Chain Saw Massacre*'s cast, Edwin Neal (a popular voice artist for children's cartoons) would make his horror comeback as the lead baddie in 2005's low budget, straight-to-DVD effort *Satan's Playground*. Meanwhile, Gunnar Hansen's cult following enabled him to headline the spoof *Hollywood Chainsaw Hookers* (1988) and the inoffensive monster-insect flick *Mosquito* (1993).

The most enduring member of *The Texas Chain Saw Massacre* squad is, of course, Tobe Hooper himself. Although given a bigger budget and studio sets for his next feature, 1976's vastly underrated *Eaten Alive*, the finished product failed to find much popularity, enduring re-releases under a number of different titles (it was originally banned as a "video nasty" in the UK under the nom de plume of *Death Trap*). More successful was 1979's made-for-television

---

49 King, *Danse Macabre*, 1981, Warner Books

50 'To this day I have not seen *Texas Chain Saw Murders* (sic).' As explained to the author of this book in *The Dark Side* magazine (issue 119, 2005)

adaptation of Stephen King's *Salem's Lot*, a terrific project showing that Hooper's flair for suspense was still ripe for exploitation. Universal Studios obviously felt the same way, hiring the filmmaker for 1981's *The Funhouse*, a *Friday the 13th* era slasher flick that is well above average if not a classic.

Steven Spielberg's approval has launched many directors onto a top Hollywood career (such as Joe Dante and Robert Zemeckis) and it looked like a stroke of luck when the legendary filmmaker asked Hooper to helm 1982's *Poltergeist*. Of course, the resulting project, despite being a commercial juggernaut, would create a great deal of controversy when it was rumoured that Spielberg himself took over the reins of the movie, regardless of the lack of evidence to back this up. Nevertheless, his success with *Poltergeist* allowed the Cannon Company to offer Hooper a three-film contract and bigger budgets than ever before. Sadly, the deal spawned three box office flops: 1985's ridiculous and overdrawn sci-fi epic *Lifeforce*, the dreary 1986 remake of *Invaders from Mars* and the same year's *Texas Chainsaw Massacre 2*. After this, Hooper's name was never as bankable again and his career continued with lousy direct-to-video titles such as 1989's *Spontaneous Combustion*, 1993's *Night Terrors* and 2000's *Crocodile*. A return to form (and cinemas) came with 2004's accomplished *Toolbox Murders*, an in-name-only remake of a rightly forgotten about slasher movie. Sadly 2006's disastrous *Mortuary* saw Hooper's (somewhat resurrected) profile come to a standstill all over again.

As with any successful franchise, *The Texas Chain Saw Massacre* (spelt as the single word 'chainsaw' in the sequels and remake) would spawn its own follow-ups. Hooper's own sequel is a masterful satire and one of the most underrated terror follow-ups of all time, a brilliant, apt spoof of the free market economy, right-wing politics and the slasher genre as a whole. 1990's *Leatherface: Texas Chainsaw Massacre Part III* saw Jeff Burr take over the series but, saddled with a pitiful script from David Schow, the glossy, big studio-produced opus was a severe disappointment. Likewise with Kim Henkel's *Return of the Texas Chainsaw Massacre* (aka *The Texas Chainsaw Massacre: The Next Generation*), a nonsensical, low budget tragedy, which tries to link Leatherface to a supernatural cult and, inevitably, ends up just looking foolish. 2003's remake *The Texas Chainsaw Massacre* is a step back in the right direction, capturing the ferocity of Hooper's original and relentlessly pounding away at the viewer's emotions. 2006 saw the release of *The Texas Chainsaw Massacre: The Beginning*, directed by Jonathan Liebesman, which featured more gore than ever before but, perversely, seemed to have sacrificed all of the suspense that its low budget inspiration had mustered on just a fraction of the cost.

Kim Henkel interview

Having penned the story of *The Texas Chain Saw Massacre* with Tobe Hooper (following their collaboration on the director's previous effort *Eggshells*), Kim Henkel continues to be tied to Leatherface and company thanks to his part-ownership of one of the horror genre's most famous, and profitable, terror franchises. Indeed, Henkel boasts a co-producer credit on 2003's glossy remake and its, largely disappointing, 2006 prequel. Nevertheless, few will dispute that 1974's original cannibal caper remains far superior to any of the sequels and spin-offs that have followed in the 25 years since its arrival. Henkel can also take credit for perhaps the most memorable line of dialogue to infuse the original film – that being, of course, the 'look at what your brother did to the door' sequence, which adds a very dark sense of comedy to the film.

'Sure, that line was mine,' chuckles Henkel. 'To me, it was a central part of what was going on in the film and it just emerged in the scene. It is what I referred to, at the time, as moral schizophrenia. It was the notion that within the individual there could exist a moral code and also absolute depravity. The story to *The Texas Chain Saw Massacre* was, at least in part, inspired by a murder case that took place in the State of Texas a few years earlier. It came from some of the comments that I heard from one of the culprits.'

However, less anyone believe that Henkel is speaking about Ed Gein, the 'Wisconsin Ghoul', whose influence on the film has become synonymous with it, the writer actually goes on to talk about another notorious serial killer. 'This particular crime happened in Houston,' says Henkel. 'It was this guy called Elmer Wayne Henley. He was a young man who had murdered an older gentleman and, after the fact, it was revealed that there was a history of violent homosexual relationships where Elmer would recruit young men and then he, and an older friend, would brutalise and kill them. Soon everything came out. Elmer was captured and the police took him around the countryside. He was identifying places where the bodies had been dumped and this was a different time so I guess they let the press get close to him. Well this Elmer was a skinny looking, tow-headed, white trash-looking character and he was just 17 years old if I remember right. Well some reporter came up to him to ask how he felt about this and that and Elmer puffed up his skinny little chest and he said that he had done wrong and he intended to stand up like a man and take what was coming to him. It struck me at that moment that here we had a guy who had been out brutalising and murdering and yet here he was operating with some kind of bizarre moral code about taking his medicine like a man. It was the conjunction of those two kinds of seemingly incompatible sensibilities that informs *The Texas Chain Saw Massacre* and, in particular, that "look at what your brother did to the door" line. As I said earlier, I tend to refer to it as moral schizophrenia.'

Destined for controversy from the start, *The Texas Chain Saw Massacre* would find itself banned in many countries. When Hooper's film hit the UK – which, back in 1974, was still reeling from the outrage caused by such shockers as *Straw Dogs* and *A Clockwork Orange* – the newspapers and general public alike greeted the movie as some kind of societal ill. Outside of London, the picture was summarily banned from British cinemas and, when it was released on video, it became the target of such notorious moral crusaders as the late Mary Whitehouse. 'I was aware that it was banned in the UK but I believe it came out in the cinemas in London and then it was banned and then it was not banned anymore,' laughs Henkel. 'I started to lose track of everything. I just thought it was fucking crazy! It seems odd, to me, that people could get this upset about a horror film.'

Telling of a younger, hippy generation (all flares and long hair) who get killed by a backwards family comprised of ageing, adult males – *The Texas Chain Saw Massacre*'s horrors, and relentless assault on its youthful characters, has led some critics to view the movie as a product of its time. A time which included the ill-fated Vietnam War. 'Well Vietnam was specifically at the core of that,' admits Henkel. 'It seemed, to me, to be a question of "what are the limits of one's conduct when one's survival, existence and way of life are threatened? How far do you go? And what is permissible?" For example – do you strap dynamite to your body and walk into a central market? Or do you, in another case of desperation, violate another sort of taboo? For instance do you resort to cannibalism? What are the permissible perimeters of conduct when we are faced with extreme situations? *The Texas Chain Saw Massacre* attempted to address those questions. Here are some very primitive people but they are faced with a dilemma and it was all folded into the zeitgeist of those times and not just the Vietnam War. It was also what was happening today, but in its incipient stages. For instance, gas shortages were the result of the problems in the Middle East and, for the first time, Americans had to face the prospect that cheap fuel was not going to be a part of their lives again. There were all sorts of malaise that resulted from that and, oddly enough, other types of shortages began to occur at the same time. One of which was a meat shortage and people were turning to alternatives, some people were buying horse meat.'

Interestingly, the cast of *The Texas Chain Saw Massacre* has stated that they never believed the film had any deeper meaning. Henkel laughs long and hard at this. 'Well I would say that you should go and look at the film if you think that. These things are apparent! And why would you discuss any of this with the actors? What you are dealing with, in as far as actors go, is the film and the nature of their characters. We did not sit around discussing thematic concerns. You might as a friendly proposition but I do not think that the director necessarily needs to spend a large amount of time talking to their cast about that stuff. It does not make any difference what I intended or Tobe intended or anyone else intended, it is all up there on the screen and the film has to stand for itself. If what I have to say about it is borne out by what is on the screen then fine and if it is not then move away.'

In 1986 Hooper himself directed a sequel and then, in 1990, director Jeff Burr unleashed the troubled *Leatherface: The Texas Chainsaw Massacre Part III*. Henkel had no input into either film. 'I was one of the rights holders and that was it,' he says. 'It has been a long time since those two movies. I am not sure what the story was but I recall we licensed the rights to all and sundry over the course of time. Certainly, a lot of the sequels that have been made were unsuccessful and pretty terrible for the most part.' It was this feeling that led Henkel to sit on the director's chair for the first (and, to date, last) time for 1994's *Return of the Texas Chainsaw Massacre*, a picture that introduced the world to soon-to-be-stars Renée Zellweger and Matthew McConaughey.

'We decided, "well we have the rights back and we cannot do any worse than what these characters have done with this property"' recalls Henkel. 'So my movie was an effort to revitalise the series. That was my point of view going into it.'

Sadly, Henkel's low budget follow-up left a lot of viewers confused and disappointed, largely because it removed the cannibalism aspect from Leatherface and his maniacal family and replaced it with a strange, oddball hierarchy that indicated that the clan was being manipulated by otherworldly beings. 'Over the years I wanted to evolve something that had to do with the underpinnings of this strange family,' says Henkel. 'My movie asked the question, "what are the underpinnings of this? What is going on here?" To me, the story was a way of replicating societal ills ... and I am not so sure how much I want to say about it because what I intended to do is one thing and what you get from the movie is another. I do not think it is valuable for me to explain where I was coming from because I think the material has to provide you with that understanding or else it is not there (*laughs*). A couple of superficial things though – I wanted to move the series past the notion that this was merely the solitary act of a few atavistic types because I felt the original was taken a little bit too narrowly. It was looked upon in the same way as *Deliverance* – the inbred appellation and the backwoods mentality. That was never my intention. There are all sorts of things that are in there which I was playing with in that regard. I would also say that violence is not an individual impulse. It is a larger cultural impulse. Certainly systematic violence comes from the individual – people have moments of impulsive or self-serving violence – but a larger violence comes from cultural consideration. There is a bit of that in there too.'

One thing Henkel is insistent about is that he never intends to call 'action' ever again. 'I am not particularly interested in directing again,' he says. 'I am a very solitary person, quite frankly, and it is only for that reason that I say that. For me, dealing with the directorial process is an awful experience. I enjoy working with actors, I like that aspect of directing, but the rest of it is not much fun for me.'

After a career that has largely been spent working in the independent sector, Henkel insists that remaining true to his roots (he most recently produced a low budget, Texas-lensed horror flick called *The Wild Man of the Navidad*) is essential. 'I have worked in Hollywood before but it was principally as a writer so it was different from going through the entirety of the filmmaking process,' he says. 'However, you still get a sense of how the industry works. It is just like any other major business. The artist recedes into the background whilst those who have power based on money take over and they involve themselves in the creative process. Their perspective is that of someone whose primary purpose is to create cash flow, which is detrimental to the approach of an artist. When you are involved in such a major industry, and in the mainstream of it, those things inevitably impact the process. Independents, to some degree, are free from that.

'I did live in LA, and I liked LA fine, but a lot of the time I was terribly broke and not getting a lot of work.'

Edwin Neal interview

Edwin Neal portrayed the ghoulish Hitchhiker in *The Texas Chain Saw Massacre*. Essaying a believable sense of moral depravity and insanity, the actor's appearance in Tobe Hooper's influential horror masterpiece is hard to forget. 'Tobe was under many constraints during the making of *The Texas Chain Saw Massacre*,' says Neal. 'He was totally consumed by the technical side of things because everything was a compromise. We did not have the lenses we needed because we were shooting in 16mm and then blowing up to 35mm, right? So we needed lots more lenses but we couldn't afford them! So everything became a compromise but, nowadays, you can do anything you want on $1000. I never had any conversations with Tobe at all about the characters. Gunnar Hansen came up with his character and I came up with mine. It was all going so well that Tobe hardly said two words to us during the entire filming process.'

Regardless of who was most responsible for the unhinged performances of *The Texas Chain Saw Massacre*'s macabre family of backwoods cannibals one thing is for certain: it has kept Neal popular with horror fans for over three decades. 'I think that the film's followers enjoy the Hitchhiker because he is such a fun character,' laughs the actor. 'Back in 1974 no one had seen anyone like that before. You have to remember that there have been a lot of Jason and Freddy films and everyone since then, but at the time we did *The Texas Chain Saw Massacre* there had been no one like that … a lot of people think that the Hitchhiker is a lot more interesting than Jason, because Jason never says anything, he just ambles about. The Hitchhiker can run, he can chase you, he's fast, and look at that wonderful scene where I'm killing Marilyn at the end of the film. I could have easily killed her but I don't. Instead I just run behind her and criss-cross, slashing her back 100 times because I want her to die slowly. I could have killed her at any time, but then, of course, I get run over by the truck. But people always thought that was just terrifying because when people toy with other people it is so much more terrifying than if they just whack them.' One such scene where Neal 'toys' with a victim is during Hooper's climactic chase, where actress Marilyn Burns is within the Hitchhiker's grasp but, true to the character's masochistic leanings, he instead tortures her with a switchblade instead of slaughtering her there and then. 'Exactly … now that is scary,' states the actor. 'Because you think, "My God, he can kill her any time he wants," but instead he's just, "Doo doo doo," and then slice and then, "Doo doo doo," another slice …'

All the same, there is a very dark humour in *The Texas Chain Saw Massacre*, which becomes all the more evident on subsequent viewings of the classic. This pitch black comedy is something that Neal acknowledges. 'Yes it is there, although you walk a thin line doing that in a horror movie. But I think that if there is at least some humour then it is all the better.' The actor then cites an example. 'There is a wonderful part in the film where there is this six foot four, 300 pound man, Leatherface, and he is chasing the little elfin, Marilyn Burns. Well she dashes up to the house, does a sharp turn and he comes running after, wants to make the sharp turn but he can't … so he goes running by the opening and has to come back. It is like a cartoon (*laughs*). The Hitchhiker does the same kind of stuff. Like he jumps off the van and makes a sacred mark on the side of the van, but if they even asked him what he meant he would say, "Well I don't know." For him it is just some sort of sacred mark. But when you stop to think about it, this guy has an IQ of 87, what does he know about sacred marks? He's just fucking around, you know?'

Sadly, the original cast of *The Texas Chain Saw Massacre*, with the exception of Jim Siedow, would fail to appear in any of the film's sequels. Neal, however, says that he has few regrets. 'No, I would not want to be in the other ones because look at the sequels,' he laughs. 'If they were good then the answer would have been yes. I use the line that all the critics have asked to borrow and I always say that they can because it is a wonderful line … they keep asking me what I thought about the latest remake. Well I always say, "Oh you mean the 90210, CGI version?" I think that just about covers it.' Certainly, the actor does not mince words about 2003's lavish remake. 'Why in the world would I want to be in that piece of shit?' he asks. 'When they explain the psychology behind Leatherface? How would you like to see two doctors explaining Dracula or something? It is just stupid, you know? So, no, sorry, I've been grateful to my agent that he never put me in them. On the second one they came and wanted me for that one. That was the only one that they wanted me to be in. We gave them a price which was three and a half times scale, which isn't a lot of money but we didn't want to price ourselves out of it. We wanted to keep it low. So they came back and said, "Well Ed is definitely worth that, it isn't a lot of money, but we don't want to take that much out of the coke budget." So my agent said, "Well then that's fine, we really have to go."'

THE TEXAS CHAIN SAW MASSACRE

With Neal out of the equation for *The Texas Chainsaw Massacre 2*, Bill Moseley took over his role, with the Hitchhiker's lines replaced by those of the character Chop Top, an equally excitable copy of the original villain. 'I love Bill to death,' says Neal. 'My character was supposed to have been run over by the truck – as you see in part one – but then, for the sequel, he had been put back together again. I think that the Matthew McConaughy role (in the fourth film) is the same thing. But, yeah, Bill is a fantastic actor. We have done a lot of shows together but never a film, and we're just dreaming that some day we will.'

The common consensus among film buffs and critics is that *The Texas Chain Saw Massacre* remains Hooper's best work in a decidedly uneven career that takes in the highs of *Salem's Lot* and *Poltergeist* but also the lows of *Spontaneous Combustion* and *Crocodile*. Neal has no love for the director though. 'All I have got to ask people is this: if he was this wonderful, fantastic director who moulded these young actors and did such a fucking fantastic job then how come he never did it again?' laughs Neal. 'The answer is that Tobe never directed Gunnar or I, we did all of our own characters, we did everything, the voice, the movements, he came up with a couple of the makeup ideas but that is about it. He said two sentences to me during the entire filming process. Two sentences! He said, "Hey Ed, do you know who Strother Martin is?" Now Strother Martin is one of the great character actors of all time. He is the one with the little porkpie hat in *The Wild Bunch*. Now he was so cool that on his W2 form, his tax form, he wrote down – for years and years – as his occupation: prairie scum, instead of actor (*laughs*). To him he was doing the same character over and over, so he was just "prairie scum". So the only thing Tobe would say to me was, "Ed, do some more of that Strother Martin stuff." That was it. That was all he said to me during the entire filming process. But now you go to these big meetings and everything, where they have speaking arrangements, and you listen to this guy and he's all, "Oh it was very difficult getting these good performances out of these young, inexperienced actors." Young, inexperienced actors? Get the fuck out of here – I'd done 187 stage shows by then.'

Unfortunately, due to the ill feelings between Neal and Hooper, the chances of a *Texas Chain Saw Massacre* reunion remain increasingly unlikely. 'A lot of people don't know,' admits the actor. 'The people that book the conventions, they sometimes say, "We're going to have a reunion and we're going to have you and Gunnar and Marilyn and Tobe." And Marilyn, Gunnar and I always look at each other and say, "Well Tobe won't be there." They say, "Oh he's already booked," and we say, "Well did you tell him who was coming?" "Oh we're sending him the list." "Well after you send him the list he will go to Istanbul to do a commercial." Sure enough they go, "Oh no – we've got it worked out, don't be silly." Then two days later, "We've just heard from Tobe's agent and he's not going to be able to make it because he has a prior commitment." Well what did you know?.'

Despite being burned on his debut feature film, Neal still looks back on his movie career fondly. 'I have had a lot of fun and met a lot of wonderful people,' he says. 'I still work in a lot of films and a lot of these young directors cast me because they know me from *The Texas Chain Saw Massacre*. That stupid little movie has taken me all around the world. I have gotten to meet wonderful people and do things that I wouldn't have been able to do otherwise so I'm really grateful. I don't get pissed off about *The Texas Chain Saw Massacre* any more because, to me, it is just funny now ... it is funny because I know the back story behind what we were doing at the time. Now the funniest thing to do, and what people do now because they've already seen it nine times, is that they invite me over and I have to do the *Mystery Science Theatre* thing. They have seen it so many times they can watch it and listen at the same time, so they get told the funny shit that was going on at the time, like a little travelogue. It is very funny.'

One of Neal's post-*Texas Chain Saw Massacre* roles was in the badly-received *Future Kill*, which reunited him with Marilyn Burns. 'That was primarily done as a favour to a group of friends of mine and, without wanting to be too egotistical, I had a great time,' says the actor. 'Here was a group of friends that I had known for years and years, just trying to make their movie – it was a first time director – and they were figuring it out as they went. I ended up doing the final edit on the film because the financier made me do it. I didn't want to do it, it was too much like a job, but it was a lot of fun and it gave me one of the greatest moments of my life and I've had a lot of great moments. It took me to Zurich, Switzerland and I got to spend two weeks with H R Giger, one of the greatest living artists. I was supposed to be there two days and I stayed two weeks. He did the limited one sheet poster for us. It is now a very famous piece of art and it was chosen as the 2005 cover for the H R Giger calendar. I have been in one of the greatest movies of all time and I've been drawn by H R Giger, I'm done! I mean the only thing I can do to even remotely compare to this is to cure cancer – I'd love to do that.'

Following his turn as The Hitchhiker, Neal also went on to have a long career in stand up comedy, something that, the actor admits, still surprises his horror fans. 'Sometimes when people meet me at a convention, and I'm signing their autograph, I am told, "I never dreamed that you would ever be this funny," he laughs. 'Well funny is where I make most of my money because I make silly commercials and I dub Japanese anime. I was with a comedy group called Esther's Follies for years. It was so intense - we were doing three or four shows a night. Now if you do fart jokes and mother-in-law jokes, six shows a week for three and a half years then all of a sudden nothing is funny. You do, "Someone please take my wife," one more time and you just want to throw up (*laughs*). They tried to hire us for *Saturday Night Live* but we were too raunchy. So they would send someone to see the show, they would laugh their ass off and then we'd have to say to them, "Nothing we did tonight, we could do on television," and they'd go, "Oh yeah." So I never had any desire to go on *Saturday Night Live*, I thought about it once in a while but I'm too laid back. A lot of native Texans are laid back, but we just don't get too excited by stuff. I would have moved to LA years ago if I wanted that kind of existence but I don't and never did.'

Gunnar Hansen interview

Gunnar Hansen remains perhaps the most well known name to have donned the mask of Leatherface, such was the almost instant notoriety that *The Texas Chain Saw Massacre* attracted upon its initial release. Indeed, nowadays the actor even has to be careful about who can access his private details, such was the influx of fans phoning his house and making power tool noises down the phone. 'Now my phone number is unlisted,' laughs Hansen. 'The calls did not happen a lot, but there were enough of them to be annoying, and this was before I came back and did *Hollywood Chainsaw Hookers*, before I was even publicly visible. After that, people were more interested. I had a woman call me in Texas once, and she asked if she could come and visit and party. I said, "No," and she said she was married but her husband was boring and wouldn't do anything! So I said, "Definitely no!"'

Another thing that Hansen is adamant about is the academic readings that *The Texas Chain Saw Massacre* has attracted. 'Well none of that was intended by the director or the writer,' he states. 'As a former academic myself, if your own reading is consistent with what is in the film then fine. One critic said that it was about the confrontation between the college educated and the reality of poor white Southern living. I don't think that it was a conscious decision, but it's a great idea … In fact I am working on a novel just now, and it has several references to coffee in it. I'm going to see if the academics will start writing about the use of coffee and smell. I was writing and I thought, "This is my second reference to coffee," so I decided to do it more. You have got to leave these gifts for scholars to keep their careers going.'

As with Edwin Neal, Hansen did not reap the financial rewards of starring in a picture that grossed tens of millions of dollars. In fact, he never even got to keep the film's notorious Leatherface mask. 'No, I never had any of those things,' shrugs the performer. 'I was just the actor. There were three different faces. The first face was the killing mask, which was worn up until Sally comes to the house. That belongs to a friend of mine now. The second mask was an old lady mask. Tobe Hooper may have it … he said that he had a mask from the film when he was giving a talk last year. I imagine that it would be that one. The pretty woman mask – someone else has that. If it wasn't worth so much he said he'd give it to me.' Hansen also has no idea how the film's paltry pay slips affected Tobe Hooper. 'I have no idea about that,' he says. 'Tobe was a major shareholder of the company but the real theft occurred at the distributor level. I don't know what Tobe made … he owned a significant part of the movie. The shares were worth less than I was led to believe, it is common knowledge now that my first royalty check was for $45, a whopping £25!'

Understandably, then, Hansen at least wanted some financial incentive to rev up the old chain saw once more. 'The only movie Tobe offered me after *The Texas Chain Saw Massacre* was *The Texas Chainsaw Massacre 2*,' says the actor. 'I think everyone except John Dugan, who played Grandpa, was contacted for the sequel. In an article, the producers of the sequel said that they wanted John but couldn't find him. I doubt that this was true because John has said that he phoned Tobe Hooper at home and wrote him two letters. In the documentary, *The Texas Chain Saw Massacre: The Shocking Truth*, Tobe is on camera saying that he wanted Gunnar, but he couldn't find him, which is a lie.' Still, one actor from the original film did return for the sequel, although Hansen believes that he was also short-changed. 'I think Jim Siedow, financially, received the same treatment,' claims the actor. 'I think he also received scale. It was only me who received the second phone call, and I said, "Yes, I'd like to be in the sequel, but you will have to pay me more." So they pretended to negotiate with me, while they went looking for someone else, and then they told me to get lost. I think Ed was lined up for it too – I always felt that Chop Top was supposed to be the Hitchhiker rebuilt. Clearly, that was the character that Ed was supposed to play. I'd always assumed that they'd changed the part slightly, made it out to be Ed's twin brother.'

Amazingly, Hansen was also forced to turn down an appearance in the two follow-ups that came after Hooper's original sequel. 'Yes, I was offered part three as well,' he sighs. 'I read the script and I discussed with the director, Jeff Burr, about fixing it because it was awful. He called me at home and told me that the studio said, "We don't have the budget to pay you any more than scale." I had no problem with that because he was straightforward. But for the fourth film they only offered me $600 dollars a week, which is a fraction of what I charge for a day. So I told (the director) Kim (Henkel) where he could go.'

When asked his opinions of the sequels, the actor does not mince his words. 'I have seen them all, and each one is worse than the other. Number four was particularly awful. I think that the guy in the limousine (in that movie) was supposed to represent Tobe Hooper, saying, "I'm sorry I ever did this." It was a poor ending. It changed the whole idea of the series. In the first one you're led to believe that there are people out there who are like that. It ruined the integrity of the film. I have only seen a pirate copy of part two – seeing as it was stolen I watched it because there was no money going to the producers and I didn't think much of it either. I think that it would have been OK were it not for it being a sequel to the original. The Leatherface in *The Texas Chainsaw Massacre 2* is nothing like the original. In *The Texas Chainsaw Massacre 2* he is thinking, "Should I have sex with this girl?" whereas in the first he's thinking, "Mmm, lunch!"'

Hansen does have one regret about his acting career, however, and that is turning down a role in another certified genre classic. 'I turned down *The Hills Have Eyes*,' he says. 'Right after *The Texas Chain Saw Massacre*, there was a film being shot in Texas called *The Great Waldo Pepper* with Robert Redford. I got offered that movie. I also got a call from the producers of *The Hills Have Eyes* and I said to them, "I don't do movies." Stupidly. The reason they called me was because Bob Burns was the art director on *The Hills Have Eyes*. So Bob Burns reads the script and says, "I have just the guy for that part." But even though *The Texas Chain Saw Massacre* was popular right away it took a while for the whole Leatherface cult to develop.'

One film that the actor did embark on following his stint as Leatherface was a little-known oddity called *The Demon Lover*. The mere mention of the title makes the actor cringe. 'That was a very bad movie,' says Hansen. 'On the first day, the director expected me to shoot a scene without any rehearsal. I said, "I'm not doing it. I refuse to do it without rehearsing." The director told me I had to because they were running out of light. I told him to get some more lights!'

The actor returned to the big screen a decade later, however, for the cult favourite *Hollywood Chainsaw Hookers*, re-igniting his popularity. 'That got a theatrical release in New York and LA, and some midnight showings elsewhere,' smiles the actor. 'It is not very well made, but it's a whole lotta fun and spending a few days hanging around naked women was tough (*laughs*). Especially Michelle Bauer, because once she was naked on camera she would spend the rest of the day without anything on … at least until her husband turned up!'

Robert A Burns interview

(*Interview quotes courtesy of Iain Robert Smith, this was one of Burns' last interviews before his death*)

As the art director on *The Texas Chain Saw Massacre* Robert A Burns turned an old country house into a macabre vision of poverty, rot and madness. With the whereabouts of Leatherface and his cannibalistic family littered with bones, skulls and flesh, Burns whipped up such a repulsive on-screen vision, so much so that the viewer can almost smell the rotten odour. Surprisingly then, in light of this lofty achievement, Burns reveals that he never studied art at university, opting instead to try his luck in front of the camera. 'Ever since I was a kid I played with arts and crafts assuming I would get a degree in art and become a commercial artist,' says Burns. 'Instead I got a degree in acting and became a commercial artist. Along with other commercial art, I made props, sets, and special effects for some TV and film projects.' However, it was the artist's friendship with a young filmmaker from Austin that secured his future career path. 'Tobe Hooper and I had been friends for several years before *The Texas Chain Saw Massacre*, and I had worked with him on two previous film projects,' states Burns. 'So when the time came for *The Texas Chain Saw Massacre* I was the logical choice to design it.'

For Burns, the trick with his art design and direction is to draw audiences into a world that they can believe in. However, the artist admits that the first obstacle in getting people to believe in such a vision is to make the various complexities of his set design look as natural possible. 'If the work doesn't stand out to the audience, it doesn't stand out to producers,' says Burns. 'An excellent example is the set designs of *The Texas Chain Saw Massacre* and *Re-Animator*. The sets in *The Texas Chain Saw Massacre* stood out because they looked convincingly like where maniacs would live rather than an art director's idea of such. Of course everyone knew we didn't actually find a maniac family's house, so they knew the work was created. The main set for *Re-Animator* was the basement of the hospital. Because of the twin requirements of speed of shooting and the many special effects scenes, the sets were quite extraordinary in their design. However, I was extremely pleased that no one knew they were sets. The double-edged blade was that *The Texas Chain Saw Massacre* led to a lot more work because producers wanted sets that reflected a similar theme. Whereas the set in *Re-Animator* convinced even producers that it was a hospital so it didn't lead to any other set work of that type … although several producers called Brian Yuzna to find out where the hospital was located because they wanted the look for their films!'

The Texas Chain Saw Massacre remains well known for keeping most of its visceral nastiness off the screen, something that Burns believes was a wise decision. 'I absolutely believe in this. Almost any graphic special effect calls attention to itself, even if only subliminally, because we know the filmmakers didn't really cause the mayhem and deep down we know it is fake. An excellent example is the scene in *The Texas Chain Saw Massacre* where the girl gets hung on the meat hook. Originally Tobe wanted me to make an effect of the hook coming out the front of her with blood spurting, but I convinced him it would be much more powerful without it. The scene still has the impact to drive audiences from the theatre thirty years later and there is not a single drop of blood in it. There is not the subliminal, "It's only a movie effect," to buffer the impact.'

For *The Texas Chain Saw Massacre*, Burns spent a lot of time creating body parts, tanned human skin and working with animal bones. Not that this ghoulish endeavour had much effect on the artist. 'Absolutely no effect … I was this disturbed to begin with,' he laughs. 'Seriously, this is rather like people asking actors if their love scenes were real,' continues Burns. 'There are so many things to think about and so many problems to solve that the end product is far removed from the emotion involved in creating it. On-screen blood is not human plasma; it is corn syrup and food colouring, with an additive or two as needed. There are infinite variations to take into consideration such as colour and the type of background the blood is to appear on, whether it is to be in someone's mouth or not, what the lighting is to be, how long the blood has supposed to have been exposed to the air, how small and long the tubing is that it needs to pass through for an effect. If a maniac is supposed to have done something horrible or lived in squalor, it is a technical challenge to try to create the believable event or place in front of the camera using materials that are appropriate to the situation. I sometimes refer to it as peculiar engineering.'

The Texas Chain Saw Massacre, with its focus on unemployment and a disillusioned, poverty-stricken family unit (being put out of business by the mechanics of new technology), has been seen by some as a social comment on the time it was made. 'Actually, Adam Simon and his crew interviewed me for that documentary *The American Nightmare*,' says Burns. 'I enjoyed the experience and Adam is a very nice guy, but I did not agree with his premise, which he came with beforehand, so I didn't end up in the film. I think all that pontificating was a splendid exercise in hind-sight and self aggrandisement. When Tobe came to me with *The Texas Chain Saw Massacre* he said he just wanted to crank out a quickie that could turn a buck. When I read the script I thought, "Oh, another one of these … A handful of less than brilliant kids go off to be killed by the monsters." Nothing that hadn't been cranked out for years, but because it was shot in 1973, it encompassed much of the culture of the time, but nothing more thoughtful than that.'

One might suspect that there is a sense of camaraderie and an 'all in it together' atmosphere on low-budget film sets, but Burns argues to the contrary. 'In spite of what one reads in the trades, there can be a surprising lack of camaraderie in most films. With so many egos involved, instead of trying to enhance each others' work, cast and crew departments too often compete with each other, usually to the detriment of the final product. Much of the camaraderie comes from hindsight. That said, *Re-Animator* had a good bit of camaraderie. Strangely enough, probably the film I worked on with the closest people was *Microwave Massacre*. It was done with no budget, but a great deal of fun and I think this is one reason it is still such a cult classic – the fun came through in the final product.'

When asked about his favourite moviemaking experience the artist, perhaps unexpectedly, does not opt for the Tobe Hooper classic. 'I would have to say that it is a toss-up between *Re-Animator* and *The Howling*,' he says. 'Stuart and Brian (Yuzna) had never even been around the making of a film before *Re-Animator*, so when they hired me they trusted me completely, even when it came time for trying things I had never done before. *The Howling* was a tremendous amount of work for very little money. Joe and Mike (Finnell) had been around films for years, but they also trusted my vision, even when it conflicted with an actress's ideas of what her house would look like, or if it might cost a few bucks more.'

CANDY TANGERINE MAN

Released: 1975
Directed by: Matt Cimber
Produced by: Matt Cimber
Written by: George Theakos
Cast: John Daniels (The Baron/Ron Lewis), Marva Farmer (Bella), Tom Hankerson (Dusty), Eli Haines (Maurice), Meri McDonald (Sugar Delight), Joann Brudo (Mama), George 'Buck' Flower (Asst Vice Detective), Edward Roehm[51] (Vice Detective), Barbara Bourbon (Working Girl/Victim), Tracy King (African-American Hooker)

In a nutshell: For five days every week The Baron is a pimp on the Sunset Strip in Los Angeles, driving around in his luxurious tangerine Rolls Royce and commanding a whole bevy of prostitutes. Every weekend, however, he sheds his pimp outfit for a suit and briefcase, wherein he returns home to his wife and two small children as Ron Lewis, committed father and husband and supposed computer operative. Back on the streets, The Baron's arch-rival is Dusty, an African-American man with an annoying laugh and a mean streak a mile wide. When

---

51 Pseudonym for Richard Kennedy.

TABOO BREAKERS

The Baron upsets him he has more to deal with than just a corrupt and racist police force, he also has a mob of heavies mutilating his 'workers' and looking to kill him. In the meantime, The Baron comes upon $250,000 worth of bonds, which could well be his way out of the pimping lifestyle …

Prologue: *Candy Tangerine Man* was released towards the end of the blaxploitation boom, whereupon the market had already become saturated and audience interest was beginning to wane. With the sequels *Shaft's Big Score* and *Shaft in Africa*, a badly received follow-up to *Superfly* (1973's *Superfly TNT*) as well as the flop *Cleopatra Jones and the Casino of Gold* (1975) and Pam Grier's *Foxy Brown* being little more than a continuation of *Coffy*, consumers of the genre were being spoiled for choice. *Candy Tangerine Man* was Matt Cimber's second blaxploitation offering, after 1974's explosive *The Black Six*, and followed 1973's *The Mack* in its use of genuine street prostitutes and hustlers in bit parts and background scenes.

Prior to *Candy Tangerine Man* Cimber was perhaps most famous for his short-lived marriage to the late screen icon Jayne Mansfield (they were divorced after less than two years as man and wife). His most notorious work had been in the sexploitation arena (including 1969's *Man and Wife* and 1970's *He and She*) which, prior to the onslaught of *Deep Throat* and hardcore pornography, was considered quite risqué with its full frontal depictions of naked bodies. As with *The Black Six*, *Candy Tangerine Man* was written by George Theakos.

The stars of *Candy Tangerine Man* were all unknowns, including lead player John Daniels whose background was largely in small, supporting roles, mainly in television (he had also appeared in Don Edmonds' 1974 effort *Tender Loving Care*). Character actor George 'Buck' Flower, who also appeared in *Tender Loving Care*, appears alongside future B-movie mainstay Richard Kennedy (billed as Edward Roehm) as a racist policeman. However, without any recognizable faces, the real star of *Candy Tangerine Man* is the carnage.

About: As the blaxploitation boom began to wear out its welcome with sub-par sequels and lame, low budget cash-ins, two interesting, and more cynical, voices began to surface through the quagmire. The first was Larry Cohen, who began his career with three blaxploitation efforts, namely 1972's interesting slice of class commentary *Bone*, the outstanding *Black Caesar* (1973) and the same year's superior, but rushed, follow-up *Hell up in Harlem*. A much underrated director (Cohen would achieve his greatest success as the writer of such blockbusters as 2002's *Phonebooth*) the likes of *Black Caesar* demonstrate an individual style and voice that would quickly become synonymous with the filmmaker's best work.

Although Matt Cimber would not achieve the sort of Hollywood heights that Cohen would go on to, his blaxploitation work is at least as good, with *The Black Six* and *Candy Tangerine Man* showcasing a sleazy and violent streak but also a strangely apt inner criticism towards the genre as a whole. Featuring ludicrous ethnic characterization, it soon becomes evident that Cimber is seeking to draw attention to how the stereotypes of the genre may have inadvertently damaged the very race-relations that the first black filmmakers set out to address. For instance, upon seeing The Baron in his full working regalia, two middle class white women exclaim 'he looks like one of those fellows we saw in that flick last week. He's a pimp or something.' That such hits as *Superfly* and *The Mack* were, evidently, crossing over to a white audience and giving some people their first cinematic interaction with R-rated black characters appears to have bothered Cimber and writer George Theakos and *Candy Tangerine Man* is the result. Effectively a spoof of the 'macho', jive talkin', street smart African-American, as popularised in *Superfly*, *Truck Turner* (1974) and, to a lesser degree, *Shaft*, The Baron is, in actual fact, a family man who wants to blend into middle class suburbia but who is, nevertheless, pigeonholed into working on the streets to support his family. Trailed by two redneck, racist cops (themselves so over the top as to be ridiculous stereotypes) The Baron still possesses the muscle, the urban lingo and the hard fists of John Shaft but Cimber plays a lot of his movie for laughs, clearly inviting the audience to comprehend how preposterous the genre has become[52].

Of course, the biggest issue with the work of Cimber, and indeed Cohen, is that they are white. Here are two Caucasian directors working within a genre that began with such deeply personal work as *Sweet Sweetback's Baadasssss Song* and which also manifested itself into a launching pad for gifted African-American filmmakers such as Ossie Davis and Gordon Parks. Yet, by the mid-seventies it was white faces calling the shots, Cimber, Cohen and Jack Hill being amongst the most prolific[53]. As such, it is difficult to accept the likes of *Candy Tangerine Man* as carrying the sort of rage/street-grit that informed the likes of *Sweet Sweetback's Baadasssss Song* and even *Superfly*, however, with that said, Cimber's film is far more enjoyable than either and its stunts and violent set pieces are as eye opening as anything the earlier films could present. Certainly, after the stark seriousness of *Across 110th Street* (1972, and perhaps the most thoughtful blaxploitation film ever made), the brutality of *Coffy* and *Foxy Brown*, and the inherent political message of *Sweet Sweetback's Baadasssss Song*, it seems as if there was little else for the genre to do other than to lampoon itself, which *Candy Tangerine Man* does perfectly[54].

Indeed, much like a better episode of *South Park*, Cimber goes so over the top with The Baron that we finally start to become numb to the stupidity of the whole set-up (a pimp driving a tangerine Rolls Royce whilst living a family life at weekends and out-smarting the LAPD) and begin to get involved in the characters and plot. In this sense, Cimber has a lot in common with Jack Hill, another director whose work frequently overcomes budgetary issues, and acting limitations, to grab the viewer by the throat and reel them into the plot via some vivid characterization and interesting, thoughtful social commentary. From the opening scene, *Candy Tangerine Man* offers the audience the chance to laugh *with* its satire (when The Baron unzips himself in front of a white prostitute, the girl screams 'Oh my God!') before the story

---

52 'Parts of *Candy Tangerine Man* are as cartoonish as *Batman*,' note Landis and Clifford in *Sleazoid Express* (Fireside Books, New York, 2002)

53 'As African-Americans put down their money to consume these images, the profits went into the pockets of whites. The fact that most of the profits from these films ended up in the hands of whites was a further justification to label the films exploitative.' (Sims, *Women of Blaxploitation*, McFarland, 2006)

54 'It's easy to understand why some self-righteous whiners complained about these films. But looking back at them now, they only seem to be an aberration of the times,' notes Steve Puchalski (*Slimetime*, Critical Vision, 1996)

kicks into gear and the laughter takes a backseat to an unexpectedly smart, and very well-paced, story.

Nevertheless, this initial sequence does jar somewhat with what we are expected to accept The Baron as, that being a dedicated husband and father whose (secretive) pimp work is solely a means to an end. Thus, never again after the prologue airs, are we shown the title character ever looking sexually at another woman and, therefore, it should be stated that Cimber's opening sequence is not ideal. It is definitely out of sync with the rest of the feature, wherein we get to look at The Baron as a loving family man, and even the character's initial dialogue (which includes labelling one woman as a 'sweet little moneymaking bitch') conflicts greatly with the film that *Candy Tangerine Man* becomes. Again, Cimber is attempting to satirize the genre but, at least momentarily, this does become a little clumsy, especially when his attempts at comedy (for example the stereotyping of a black male as being 'well hung') clash with the actual premise of the movie and our relationship with the characters. As a result, it becomes hard to accept The Baron as a great husband and parent when our first sight of him is relaxing in bed with another woman. Even if this set-up is used for the purpose of comedy (and it is hard to argue otherwise) it simply doesn't work in the grander scheme of things and would, ultimately, have been better off left on the cutting room floor.

This aside, however, when *Candy Tangerine Man* finally kicks itself into gear it transforms into a far more inviting movie. For his first leading role actor John Daniels does a fine job, especially when his character begins to develop outside of the jive talking, ultra-cool, sexist wretch that is initially introduced to us. The first indication of the character's humanity is when he wins a pool game with a rival pimp called Dusty (brilliantly played by Tom Hankerson in his only film credit) for the ownership of a girl that The Baron realises is underage. He beats his opposition in the contest and then tells the young lady to board a bus, 'I don't know where it's going, but you're going to be on it', giving her some money and telling her to leave the street life. Amusingly, before he drops the girl off at the station, we see him shoot some of his rivals with guns rigged into the headlights of his Rolls Royce. This James Bond-inspired gag is certainly amusing and, once again, reminds us that the movie's presentation of a 'super-pimp' is not meant to be taken seriously. However, when, at the movie's end, The Baron retrieves the $250,000 that was stolen from him by one of his working girls, it leaves the audience with mixed feelings.

On the one hand, the 'hero' has won and can now retire back to the California suburbs with his wife and children, but, there is a price to pay. In this case it is in the shape of a black working girl called Bella, who has been sliced up by one of her tricks and sees the money as her own way out of a horrible existence. The Baron gives her an apology as he takes the case of cash that she has run away with, but Bella will have none of it. 'Sorry?' she asks him. 'All you've ever been is sorry. Sorry you started me hoeing … and now I hate myself and that's the worst part.' As The Baron throws her some cash and makes off (Daniels showing enough emotion in the scene to let us know that he hates what he has done to this girl) we don't really view him as a 'heroic' character in the John Shaft, or even the Superfly, mould. Instead, we can see that, as with so many who achieve their goals in the modern free market system, The Baron has exploited others for his own financial gain and when it comes time to take the big pay-off, his workers are left without

CANDY TANGERINE MAN

any security at all.

In a sense, Cimber could well be indicating the very harsh brutality of big business and, when read in this manner, *Candy Tangerine Man* perfectly demonstrates that the hierarchy of the street is really not so different from that which exists in corporations around the world (the sole exception seems to be that the 'street' is controlled by those of a different skin colour). The blaxploitation genre always had a certain anti-authoritian slant, perhaps best exemplified by *Sweet Sweetback's Baadasssss Song* and *Superfly*, but Cimber's work, as with that of Cohen and Jack Hill, typically depicts the self-destruction of crime lords and those involved with them. Whilst *Candy Tangerine Man* dubiously separates the 'good' pimp from the 'bad' pimp in an attempt to send-up the genre, the movie still reveals the corruption of the local police force (who are cohorts of Dusty and his men) and The Baron's own attempt to escape from a lifestyle that he, ultimately, wants nothing to do with. The flipside of this is the character's willingness to exploit anyone for his own personal gain and financial security.

Indeed, whereas characters such as Cleopatra Jones and Foxy Brown fought to make things better for the black community, The Baron is perhaps most comparable to Fred Williamson's Tommy Gibbs in the aforementioned *Black Caesar*. Whilst The Baron is nowhere near as ruthless or psychotic as Gibbs he is, at the end of the day, still only out for himself. Perhaps the main reason that The Baron does not come across as completely repulsive, aside from John Daniels' likeable performance, is due to the scenes where he is depicted as Ron Lewis, the father of two small children. Knowing, as we do, that his wife wants to see him more and that he intends to obtain security for his own family life, the end to *Candy Tangerine Man* is predictable but it is still very difficult to feel that anything positive has been achieved from the character's time on the streets.

As if to point this out, Cimber has a coda where a new Baron drives by, in the same Rolls Royce, and speaks to one of the working girls about delivering her money on time. As with any corrupt hierarchy: when one leader falls another one is ready to take over and, in this sense, life on the streets is not so different from living under a dictatorship.

Even before *Candy Tangerine Man* the blaxploitation genre had become increasingly violent. The fad certainly reached some kind of bad taste apex when Pam Grier handed a man's pickled genitals to his lover at the close of *Foxy Brown*, whilst other efforts such as 1973's *Detroit 9000* and 1974's *The Klansman* contained enough visceral, slam-bang brutality to jolt even the most jaded of viewer. Obviously not to be outdone, Cimber splashes the screen bright red with *Candy Tangerine Man* including, most horrifically, a scene where a woman has her breast sliced with a knife. Violence against women (especially 'sexual violence') still remains an issue whereby Britain's classification board will remove offending sequences and the original UK release of *Candy Tangerine Man* suffered greatly[55].

It should certainly be noted that Cimber walks a very fine line here, and it is disturbing to see a screaming female have her chest squeezed and then cut by a grinning male attacker (thankfully most of this attack transpires off-screen). Whilst the moment in question is executed

---

55 As noted on the BBFC's web site, *Candy Tangerine Man* lost 4 minutes and 18 seconds to the censor: http://www.bbfc.co.uk/website/Classified.nsf/0/00363A912047A9368025660B002C0E44?OpenDocument

with more tact than the close-up nastiness of something such as 1982's reprehensible *The New York Ripper* (wherein a nude, bound lady has her nipple slowly sliced in half with a straight razor) and never enters into that feature's domain of pornographic distaste, it is still difficult to defend. More troubling is the fact that the actress playing the victim, Barbara Bourbon, was a porn star, perhaps indicating that she was probably unlikely to 'stand up' against such violent treatment after being cast in a 'legit' movie. Indeed, the sole justification behind showing the knife slice the woman's chest, before the moment of cut-off, is, one presumes, to set up the revenge scenario that follows shortly afterwards where The Baron forces the culprit's hand into a grinder (he is later seen with a hook in place of his bloody stump). Amazingly, this scene of on-screen misogyny (and the subsequent hand grinding) is actually outdone in the bad taste stakes by Cimber's sleaze crescendo when one of The Baron's working girls talks a rich businessman into signing some bonds by fulfilling his fantasy of being urinated on. Potential viewers will no doubt be relieved to find out that this watery scenario is left entirely to our imagination, although the inevitable sound effects lets us in on exactly what is transpiring. This could well be the very nadir of the genre's slump into outright crassness, although this kinky little interlude only adds to the sordid feel that Cimber's picture carries with it.

However, this sort of gross-out silliness aside, *Candy Tangerine Man* really is one of the blaxploitation genre's finest achievements and, when taken as pure entertainment, stakes a claim as one of the finest low budget action flicks ever created. Its mixture of satire with social commentary and street-grit is very well done and the theme song from the group Smoke is up there with the best scores of the time ('Nobody knows his double life/two small children and a wife' croons Barry White over the opening credits). The concept of a 'good' pimp, viewed as a reaction to *Superfly* or *The Mack*, is surprisingly well executed and the movie, as preposterous as it is, remains one of the grittiest examples of the trend. *Candy Tangerine Man* also features some razor-sharp dialogue that can hardly go ignored. Take, for instance, the scene where The Baron is dubbed a 'motherfucker' and responds with, 'The only mother I ever fucked was yours, and she was a lousy lay.'

They don't make them like this anymore.

What happened next? Cimber and Theakos would return with their third blaxploitation effort *Lady Cocoa* (1975), an above average entry into the black *femme fatale* division of the genre that Jack Hill had already conquered with *Coffy* and *Foxy Brown*. Following this Cimber would direct one of his most notorious movies, 1976's *The Witch Who Came From the Sea*, a grim and disturbing tale of a woman (excellently played by Millie Perkins) who, after being sexually abused as a child, carries the scars with her into adulthood and embarks on a series of murders. The feature was banned in the UK as a 'video nasty', although its arty ambitions could not be more removed from the tawdry exploitation that the 'nasty' title might suggest. The filmmaker's most notorious work is undoubtedly 1982's *Butterfly*, which, despite being well received at the Cannes Film Festival, ended up as one of the biggest flops of the decade. Cimber recovered, however, and made two of his most entertaining projects, 1983's fantasy adventure *Hundra* and 1984's *Indiana Jones* inspired *Yellow Hair and the Fortress of Gold*, both starring Laurene Landon. The director is currently slated to return with *Miriam*, a true-life story about a

Lithuanian woman who survived the horrors of World War 2. There is sure to come a day when Cimber is, rightfully, placed within the hierarchy of low budget, independent filmmakers - a director whose pictures are almost always eminently enjoyable.

Candy Tangerine Man has so far escaped a DVD release and quietly disappeared during the days of VHS. Although the movie's mixture of brutal violence and satire did not lead to a renaissance of the genre, which by the time of *Candy Tangerine Man* was on its last legs, its more comedic take on the trend can be seen to have anticipated the preposterous likes of *The Human Tornado* (1976) and *Disco Godfather* (1980). Of the movie's stars, leading man John Daniels would go on to feature in *Black Shampoo* (1976) and *Bare Knuckles* (1977), whilst George 'Buck' Flower and Richard Kennedy would go on to work in the schlock-heavy B-movie world of the seventies and eighties.

Matt Cimber interview

Despite a career that takes in working with such screen legends as Jayne Mansfield and Orson Welles, director Matt Cimber admits that *Candy Tangerine Man* has a special place in his heart. 'It is my favourite of all my films, although I haven't seen the picture for years,' he begins. 'Samuel L Jackson has said it was his favourite film of all time and I have had two major companies calling me up about a remake. I don't know how it would fit today because of what the premise was when I first made it, you know what I'm saying? I had a different image of it back then. On the set of *Miriam*, Quentin Tarantino came by and he was telling me how much he loved the film but he told me that his appreciation was nothing compared to the way that Sam Jackson felt about it. That was very interesting and then Sam went on television and said that (he loved it).' The movie also has an unforgettable, and strangely evocative, title. 'I guess that comes from his car,' says Cimber. 'It was a candy-apple colour, which turned out to be tangerine looking. I had bought the car for $2500 from a UCLA student and I painted it. We also put the machine guns in, which is another part of the satire, totally crazy (*laughs*). It was a mad dream, we were working 14 to 16 hours a day and almost every scene I re-wrote according to the location.'

Whilst the blaxploitation genre originally took off under the auspices of African-American filmmakers, it soon became white directors, such as Cimber, who were calling the shots. Whilst he acknowledges this fact, Cimber also claims that his films were, in their own way, forward-thinking. 'Gene Washington is a footballer who played very prominently in America,' he says. 'He was a Stanford graduate who was an All-American and he played football for the 49'ers. I cast him in *The Black Six* and *Lady Cocoa* and now he is one of the most important people in national football because he represents the player's union, which is a very powerful entity. Well he went on television a while ago too and they were talking about *The Black Six* and he said "the interesting thing about *The Black Six* is that it took a white man to make the movie and make black heroes pure. They didn't have to be street people – they were just pure people." I took *The Black Six* from *The Charge of the Light Brigade*, a very famous poem, and I applied it to six guys coming back from Vietnam. The thing that is interesting is that Gene said, "It showed the first and only pure good guy that did good deeds. Every other image of a black man was that he was a badass."'

Not that *The Black Six* demands the same fondness from Cimber that *Candy Tangerine Man* does. 'That film is very dear to my heart,' he smiles. 'I mean … how do you make a hero out of a pimp? And the reason I did it was because it was my answer to the black movement in America. Here is a black pimp and he's really a good guy with a nice wife and family living in the country. My film is only there to make the point that there are so few opportunities for black people in America that he took the only one he could to make a living. And the Superman thing, of him changing clothes, was that if he had been educated he'd be a great accountant or lawyer but life never gave him that opportunity so he's going to do what he can to survive. So that was it, but then of course I got into the whole culture and what makes *The Candy Tangerine Man* so strange is the ambience … that is what makes the picture, not just the hero himself. I shot it in ten days and I used the actual hookers of the street …'

That, of course, must be a story in itself. 'Yeah, we used real street people,' laughs Cimber. 'In fact there are only a few key roles that were played by actors but we got some incredible performances. They were really good, and they were real hookers. We went through a lot of nonsense trying to get some of their pimps on the Sunset Strip to allow them to be in a movie (*laughs*). The two cops were certainly actors and the man playing the "Candy Tangerine Man" was a real actor … That part was played by John Daniels who was a nightclub owner at the time and I'm going to tell you something interesting: I went to the cinema one night and I saw this black actor playing a small part as a preacher and I was listening to this guy and thinking, "Now this is a good actor but his voice sounds very familiar." Well it turns out it was Samuel Jackson and years later when he said he was taken by *Candy Tangerine Man*, that is when I realised that John Daniels has the same kind of delivery that Jackson has. That is quite possibly where he got it from, although I'm not saying that it is for certain, but if you listen to the dialogue delivered by John Daniels and then, twenty years later, you listen to the dialogue delivered by Sam Jackson in *Pulp Fiction* you can say, 'Wow, wait a minute' … there is definitely a comparison there.'

When asked about how he got involved in directing blaxploitation pictures, Cimber explains that it was through the small screen. 'It all began with the incredible impact of televised football,' recalls the filmmaker. 'Now this is going to seem strange, but television is really what made American football, it is considered the best sport to adapt to television and they started to create these very colourful characters. Like, for instance, you had a guy named "Mean" Joe Greene and you had another guy who was the linebacker for the Kansas City Chiefs, I forget his name, but he was this rough, tough character. You also had this very sleek running back for the Miami Dolphins and his name was Mercury Morris so you had these characters and then you had Gene Washington, who was this high collar university graduate. So people were talking about these people so what I decided to do was to put a screenplay together based on the poem *The Charge of the Light Brigade* that would star these fellows. The film became *The Black Six* and it was about these men coming back from Vietnam and saying, "We have seen enough, we've done our bit for the country, we don't want to see any more violence. We just want to get on our motorcycles and travel through beautiful America." Well, unfortunately, in the late sixties/early seventies there was no peace. There was a lot of conflict between the black man and the white man and the idea of *The Black Six* was: can you turn your back on your responsibilities? So when the lead character's brother is killed he knows he has to go back and fight. There were a lot of black pictures that were coming out and I knew that I was going to be very limited with budget and so on, because in those days these films were not considered to be crossover pictures. They rarely went into white areas. So after I finished the picture the UA theatre chain said, "Let's put this into New York." There was a banner on the Loew's Theatre on Broadway and it was six storeys high and it was pouring down with rain and every major film had opened across Broadway. However, the only film that had a line all the way along the block was *The Black Six*, it was amazing. The impact it had was amazing.'

After experiencing such success it is unsurprising that Cimber decided to stick with the genre for a while longer. This is, of course, how *Candy Tangerine Man* came about. 'I lived in Los Angeles and we had these very colourful pimps on the Sunset Strip, with their colourful cars – big white Cadillac convertibles – and they were really picturesque. So I decided one day that while we condemn the pimps, all they really are is another protection society. They are in the protection business. So I started to ask questions and hear stories. I knew this nightclub owner on Sunset Boulevard where there were a lot of strippers and he was a nice old guy. A lot of the pimps, and the better looking women, worked the clubs, and in the film you see that. For example, the girl who is involved with the banker in the movie, and who pees on him, she was actually one of the hottest dancers on the entire strip. She had a pimp and he would pawn her off at night to men with lots of money. So I thought, "You know what? I want to do a satire." Everybody says how despicable pimps are but we didn't let black kids go to schools in certain areas. These guys were doing what they had to do to make a living. So with *Candy Tangerine Man* it is a guy who has another aspiration. He is leading a double life. But he never got the education to work with computers, although he would love to have that life. So I wanted to create a character that was a satire on our social system and the social system of what was happening in that street world.'

There is, however, a question over whether or not Cimber glamorised his title character who, let us not forget, is still a violent street-cat and involved in the exploitation of women. 'I was accused of glamorising him,' admits the filmmaker. 'Although he didn't think his life was so glamorous, he just wanted to have enough money to live in the Valley with his wife and two children (*laughs*). But you see the dangers of it. Like showing a soldier going into battle and having his arm blown off. Certainly anything that deals with women – where you show a man with a lot of females – that is a male dream and perhaps that could be said to be aspirational. However, that was never my intention. I mean … take the pool room scene where they play for the little Indian girl. He wins and he lets her go. So there is another instinct in him, we had to redeem his character. But the guy who he is shooting pool with is totally different and I don't think we made him look so attractive. People still tell me that when he puts the guy's hand in the sink, turns on the grinder and then in the very next scene he has a hook … that wasn't very clever because someone might go and try that. I can't help that (*laughs*). Anybody who wants to put someone's hand into the waste disposal and cut it off. Well they must be pretty crazy anyway.'

Although *The Black Six* and *Candy Tangerine Man* are well-remembered by blaxploitation buffs today, both came at the tail-end of the genre. Therefore, is it safe to assume that Cimber had sat through such previous hits as *Shaft*, *Superfly* and *Coffy*? 'I saw *Shaft* but I never saw *Superfly* or *Coffy*,' he replies. 'I will tell you what happened. I think *Shaft* was made by MGM and they called me because they were very, very into the idea of a dual programme after the first run. They asked me, "Would you consider a double run? Would you consider putting *Candy Tangerine Man* on the same bill as *Shaft*?" This was a popular thing to do in these days. So I said, "Okay" and they said, "Well here is how it goes. We'll take 85% and you can get 15%." Now that didn't seem quite right to me so I called some of the theatres. I said to them, "I know that *Shaft* did big numbers and there was certainly crossover, but what do you think?" They all said, "Matt, whenever *Candy Tangerine Man* went against *Shaft* in the big cities, like in Atlanta, you almost equalled its grosses." So I went back to MGM and said, "Guys, you gotta up the ante here." I mean, I was thinking to myself, "Out of all of the black pictures that they can get – why are they coming after *Candy Tangerine Man*?" I'll tell you why: they were studying the numbers, so there you go. I turned them down.'

Indeed, Cimber maintains that *Candy Tangerine Man* was among the genre's most successful outings when it first hit cinemas. '*Candy Tangerine Man* was listed, by *Variety*, as one of the 100 highest grossing films made for under $1 million,' he says. 'It was way up there and we cost nothing even close to $1 million to make. I will tell you how I sold the picture. First of all, it was very difficult to sell it in Europe. You would be told, "Oh they don't want black pictures." It wasn't until the late seventies that these films started breaking through. So what I did was I made 50 prints of the picture, and nobody had ever done this before, and I said, "Okay, what will you give me for New York? You can play it wherever you want in the city." I think I got $120,000 for two weeks. You know, it was a good deal because the picture never cost a lot to make. I asked what they would give me for Chicago and I think I got $100,000 for Chicago, I got $80,000 for Detroit and it went on and on. New Orleans, Atlanta, Minneapolis, San Francisco, Los Angeles and so on … They played it in all the black areas. When I went to New York for the opening, they raffled off the car. When you bought a ticket all around the country, your ticket had a number and one of them would win you the car. When I went to Chicago there is a downtown area called The Loop and that is where they built the big old RKO theatres. What happened was I went to Chicago, at 9am on a Saturday morning, to a downtown theatre with 900 seats in the auditorium and also a balcony. That performance was sold out. It was unbelievable. I had never really gone into a theatre that was filled with just African-Americans and I stood in the back and they were yelling at the screen. I never saw any audience enjoy a movie so much in my entire life. If you ever try and talk to the screen in a theatre full of white people you get told, "Shut up!" but here it was this wonderful atmosphere. They were altogether in this experience. It was fantastic.'

Perhaps what makes *Candy Tangerine Man* so memorable is its central concept of a pimp with a conscience. A man who wishes to escape from what society stereotypes him as and become a loving and faithful husband and father. It is an interesting idea because it feels as if Cimber is asking his viewers to look at the genre as a whole and its depiction of black characters. 'That's a great analysis and, yes, you are completely right,' replies the director. 'That is exactly why I refer to it as a satire. This guy is like Superman, he is living two lives. He goes home and cuts the grass (*laughs*). We wanted you to say, "Well hold on, this guy could be like this all the time if you just gave him the chance." Every moment on *Candy Tangerine Man* was great because it was a different experience working with real people from the street.'

Cimber's favourite moment in the film is one of the more controversial. 'The scene in the club where the girl has to urinate on the guy – that was funny,' he laughs. 'The girl we used was a well known stripper and she thought that there had to be some other way to do the scene. She said, "Are you kidding? You really want me to do this?" Well it was in the script and it was essential that we had realism. She was very quirky about it and the guy who was playing the scene with her said, "Don't worry honey, we're all professionals. Any way you want to do it is fine with me." I would say that was definitely the quirkiest scene.'

Another facet of the blaxploitation genre was that the films usually had a scorching soul soundtrack, with the likes of *Across 110th Street*, *Shaft* and *Superfly* having, perhaps, the best remembered musical scores. That said, *Candy Tangerine Man* more than holds it own thanks to the input from Barry White's old band, Smoke. 'Barry saw *Candy Tangerine Man* and said, "I want to do the music to this film,"' recalls Cimber. 'I thought the music was fantastic and Smoke was a pretty well known group at the time, but I had to tell Barry that I couldn't pay him a lot of money. He told me, "Don't worry about the money, I like your film." He loved the duality of the character and he gave us a fabulous score. And with post-production that film was made for under $200,000.' Although not credited with the script to *Candy Tangerine Man*, Cimber admits that he was hands-on with the film's story. 'I always have input,' he says. 'Usually I let whomever I am writing with just give me some plot ideas. George (Theakos) was very good, very patient with me, because sometimes I would re-write an entire scene in the morning before we shot it.'

Candy Tangerine Man also gives a meatier than usual role to the late George 'Buck' Flower, an actor who was something of a mainstay in the exploitation films of the seventies and who appeared in several of Cimber's pictures. In *Candy Tangerine Man* the low budget veteran features as a racist policeman. 'I used to say, "Buck you are a terrible actor … but you have a great look,"' laughs the director. 'And he was a very chameleon like person because he could change the look of a bum unlike anyone else. He never got elegant (*laughs*). He had this incredible look and one film that he was very good in, and he played it straight, was *The Witch Who Came From the Sea*, where he played a detective. When I re-saw the picture recently, I thought he did a very nice job. It was the one film that Buck did where he had a few lines and he wasn't sitting on a bench (*laughs*).'

After *Candy Tangerine Man* Cimber made his third and final blaxploitation picture, *Lady Cocoa*, an attempt to follow in the footsteps of the Pam Grier hits *Coffy* and *Foxy Brown*. Unfortunately, the movie bombed. '*Pop Goes the Weasel* was the original title for *Lady Cocoa*,' says Cimber. 'What happened was that I was friendly with Sammy Davis Jr and his manager. Sammy was Lola Falana's manager, and he had put a lot of money into her career. She was the first black girl to headline, on a big salary, in Las Vegas. Lola was a showstopper and I was hoping that I would not only grab the black market but that she would also carry over to the white market, through her huge television exposure and because of her Las Vegas appearances which got a lot of publicity. She was big time and we cast her in the lead of *Lady Cocoa*. But it didn't happen, it didn't cross over …' One reason might be that *Cleopatra Jones* and the Pam Grier movies had exhausted the idea of a female-led blaxploitation picture. 'Yeah, except those were lead characters that became the heavyweights. In our film the character wasn't a badass,' states Cimber. 'All Lola wanted in *Lady Cocoa* was some time out of jail and yet this guy is going to have her killed.'

TABOO BREAKERS

Cimber's early films, which include *Candy Tangerine Man* and *The Witch Who Came from the Sea*, were also criticised for their violence, with the latter title even earning a ban in the UK. For Cimber, breaking taboos was just part of being a renegade filmmaker. 'That was part of what we were in the sixties and seventies,' he says. 'It was something that Hollywood – all of the majors – totally ignored, they would never think of that kind of film. But today the exploitation of the sixties and seventies is now the fare of the majors! We were the outcasts back then and now that is all they want in the studios because they realise that is what the public wants. There are so many things that change and not just the violence – when I made *The Witch Who Came From the Sea*, for example, the public at the time still thought that Rock Hudson wanted to sleep with Doris Day. There wasn't the exposure that there is today so the violence was accepted. The one that I loved the best was *The Wild Bunch*. Now I worked with Sam Peckinpah, I helped him with a screenplay of his called *Bring me the Head of Alfredo Garcia* and he was a crazy man. But *The Wild Bunch* was, to me, a brilliant film and it brought a whole new look to motion pictures. So there were some major films being made that started that movement. Sam loved the independent filmmaker, that's why he liked me, he loved the guys that didn't follow the rules as he was one of them too.'

Candy Tangerine Man is now considered a lost film. Cimber has been trying to untangle this mystery and to find a good quality print of his blaxploitation masterpiece. 'I had gone to Europe and the company that owned it, Movie Land, went under and I never got any written notice,' he sighs. 'I also got divorced and so I don't know if my ex-wife ever got any written notice and we can't find a negative. It is that simple and it is a terrible thing. At the time UCLA used to ask for donations, and this was such a rip-off, because they would keep all the films in storage. I gave them a print of every one of my films and they told me that it would be kept for posterity in their massive library. So they used this idea to raise lots of money and I think they were just knocking back salaries because when they went in to look at *The Witch Who Came From the Sea* and *Candy Tangerine Man* the prints were all messed up. I have been searching all over the world for a good print of the film. You have no idea what trauma this has caused.'

ILSA, SHE WOLF of the SS

Released: 1975
Directed by: Don Edmonds
Produced by: David Friedman (as Herman Traeger)
Written by: Don Edmonds and Ivan Reitman (Uncredited)
Cast: Dyanne Thorne (Ilsa), Gregory Knoph (Wolfe), Tony Mumolo (Mario), Maria Marx (Anna), Nicolle Riddell (Kata), Jo Jo Deville (Ingrid), Sandy Richman (Maigret), George 'Buck' Flower (Binz), Rodina Keeler (Gretchen), Richard Kennedy (Nazi General), Lance Marshall (Richter), John F Goff (Nazi Camp Guard)

In a nutshell: Ilsa is the concentration camp commandant at Medical Camp 9. She carries out gruesome experiments on a group of women whilst bedding the male prisoners. The men that cannot sexually satisfy her are castrated. Ilsa's grand plan is to show that women can endure more pain than men, and she discovers the perfect candidate for a number of painful experiments in a female prisoner called Anna. Over the course of the movie, Ilsa electrocutes and mutilates Anna several times, but she refuses to die. Meanwhile, a rugged American prisoner called Wolfe manages to satisfy Ilsa in bed night after night, and one afternoon she allows him to tie her up. It is a terrible mistake on her part, and as a result of her being incapacitated, Wolfe and the many prisoners make their escape as the Allies also begin to move towards the dreaded medical camp ...

Prologue: Don Edmonds had been an actor in theatre, television and film, with his early performing credits including *Gidget Goes Hawaiian* (1961), *The Interns* (1962) and the short lived television show *Broadside* (1964). He had moved into directing with such low budget, drive-in projects as *Wild Honey* (1971) and *Tender Loving Care* (1974).

Star Dyanne Thorne had been a showgirl in Las Vegas, and appeared in softcore fare such as *The Erotic Adventures of Pinocchio* (1971) and *Wham Bam Thank You Spaceman* (1975) before producer David Friedman brought her in for the leading role in *Ilsa, She Wolf of the SS*. Having been an early player in the 'roughie' genre (as seen with his production of *Scum of the Earth*) and also pioneering the splatter movie with director Herschell Gordon Lewis, Friedman was perhaps the ideal person to be involved in something as grisly as *Ilsa, She Wolf of the SS*; whose influences certainly stem from the 'roughie' and the graphic gore of *Blood Feast* and its ilk.

With the sleazy Canadian effort *Love Camp 7* (1968) having proven that there was some commercial potential in a concentration camp setting playing host to sex and sadomasochism, a follow-up was perhaps inevitable. What is surprising is that it took so long for a producer to exploit the same themes that made *Love Camp 7* popular among grindhouse crowds. However, 1974's *The Night Porter* showed that even mainstream audiences would buy tickets to a (serious) sexploitation movie set during World War 2. This, accompanied by the growing success of 'Women in Prison' movies (perhaps best personified by Jess Franco's tawdry 1969 effort *99 Women* and Jack Hill's hugely successful *The Big Doll House* in 1971), meant that someone, eventually, was going to take the genre to its most extreme conclusion ... *Ilsa, She Wolf of the SS* was the result.

About: Before showing the audience anything, *Ilsa, She Wolf of the SS* plays out an on-screen scroll that warns the viewer: 'The film that you are about to see is based on documented fact ... We dedicate this film in the hope that these heinous crimes will never occur again.' After that, you're straight into the thick of things ... Indeed, there are only a handful of films that, within five minutes of their start, leave you wondering who on earth would want to make such a thing, and, more to the point, why you are watching it, but *Ilsa, She Wolf of the SS* is just such a proposition. The title of the picture has only just appeared on the screen and we are shown a man, chained down to a makeshift operating table, having his testicles cut off by two bloodstained female doctors. Then he passes out, only to be awoken with a pail of cold water. 'Once a prisoner has slept with me, he will never sleep with a woman again. If he lives, he will know only the pain of the knife,' barks Dyanne Thorne's Ilsa in her forced German accent.

Ilsa, She Wolf of the SS is a feature that still carries the ability to offend virtually anyone foolhardy enough to sit in front of it for the duration of its running time (and, yes, yours truly is included in that list). Using a concentration camp setting to graphically exploit the very real medical horrors that took place under the Third Reich is sick enough, but to combine this with ample softcore sex, nude female flesh and perverse torture scenes is tasteless in the extreme. Arguably most shocking of all is a sequence where a spread-eagled young lady has her genitals mutilated, not hidden from the camera in any way, rather displayed in all of its obnoxious, full colour glory. It is simply mind boggling that anyone would have such insensitivity as to actually showcase such a degrading act, well aware that people who had suffered in World War 2 could feasibly stumble across the picture. Yet this is *Ilsa, She Wolf of the SS*, a big 'fuck you' to anyone that might think filmmakers have a social responsibility, or indeed, any responsibility at all, when it comes to the documentation of history or the treatment of blatantly sensitive subjects.

However, in saying this, it is very difficult to conclude that *Ilsa, She Wolf of the SS* glamorises the Third Reich. Indeed, when the movie finishes, it is impossible to imagine anyone not being disgusted by the medical experiments that have been graphically highlighted, made all the more horrific due to the sense of despair and torment that hangs over the proceedings. Certainly, whilst the softcore bumping and grinding is plentiful, when the movie jumps from such playful, nudie-cutie shenanigans to a moment of very gruesome excess the tone changes in a heartbeat. Regardless of how bogus the Nazi tortures that scriptwriters Edmonds and Reitman have come up with may actually be (and one sincerely doubts that electric dildos were ever used on female prisoners), the sheer desperation and lingering terror of Medical Camp 9 is genuinely difficult to forget. Consequently, this is what remains in the mind long after the movie's end credits have concluded. The straight sex, ridiculous dialogue and surprisingly well staged breakout sequence that finishes the film are not the things that make an exploitation picture such as this legendary, oh no, instead *Ilsa, She Wolf of the SS*'s real claim to fame is with its ability to push even the strongest of stomachs to the limit. Perversely, it is through doing this that the film ultimately manages to make the Third Reich appear as disgusting as possible and, in this sense, Edmonds even manages to anticipate Pasolini's notorious *Salo* (1975). Whereas one could charge *Ilsa, She Wolf of the SS* with trivializing the Holocaust for profit, the fact remains that anyone watching this warped little torture flick is likely to be left feeling horrified and nauseous by the actions of Thorne and her despicable honchos[56].

Nevertheless, this does not excuse the fact that the film's most grim and drawn-out acts of violence are taken out on women, opening the movie wide up for criticism of blatant, unapologetic misogyny. However, taken as part of the boom in 'Women in Prison' (or WIP) pictures that flooded seventies grindhouses, this on-screen excess may be a tad more understandable, if not exactly excusable. Certainly, in the early to mid seventies the market for female dominatrix figures torturing naked, submissive ladies seemed to have hit a nerve with a certain kinky clientele, and this trend spawned a number of pictures that would help to launch the careers of such vital directors as future Oscar winner Jonathan Demme and blaxploitation pioneer Jack Hill. Thus, it is worth paying a little more attention to the WIP genre and to investigate how the genre would finally lead to *Ilsa, She Wolf of the SS*'s bloody emergence.

Indeed, the rise and fall of the WIP movies is a strange footnote in the history of exploitation cinema, primarily because finding a stellar example of the genre is nigh on impossible. Films

---

56 'Ilsa, one of the most barbaric and depraved Nazis in film history, is exactly the image of National Socialism that a Nazi hunter would love,' states critic Joe Bob Briggs in *Profoundly Disturbing* (Plexus Publishing, London, 2003)

depicting attractive young women locked up in a brutal prison setting had been around since the 1920s, although the genre really began to take off in the fifties with titles such as *Caged* (1950), *Untamed Youth* and *Reform School Girl* (both 1957). However, it was 1968's trendsetter *Love Camp 7*, an abysmal and sadistic fantasy that drew some influence from the *Olga* movies of the early sixties, that began to push the genre to more violent, and sexually explicit, limits. Following on from this was Jess Franco's *99 Women* (1969), an altogether different slice of schlock from *Love Camp 7* and a movie that would effectively kick-start the proliferation of WIP movies. An adventure yarn set in an unidentified, tropical locale, *99 Women*'s story focuses on an attractive female convict and her attempts to escape from incarceration. Something of a surprise considering Franco's ultra-sleazy track record, *99 Women* is remarkably dull and subdued, although later releases of the picture would include some clumsily inserted hardcore footage (presumably in an attempt to spice things up). Even so, *99 Women* did feature a sadistic, authoritarian female prison guard (played by Oscar winner Mercedes McCambridge) and this is really where the genesis of *Ilsa, She Wolf of the SS* comes from.

Despite being a chore to sit through when viewed today, *99 Women* was a big hit upon its initial release, and the spin-offs were quick to emerge. Influential in its own right was Jack Hill's *The Big Doll House* (1971), which took the tropical setting of the Franco effort and introduced an even kinkier female prison matron, this time played by Kathryn Loder. Unlike McCambridge, the attractive Loder actually boasted sex appeal, and in scenes where she domineers over the, often topless, female inmates there can be little doubt that Hill, and producer Roger Corman, were hoping to appeal to fetishists and viewers of a kinky mindset[57]. Obviously spotting a cash cow, Corman would go on to produce a number of WIP efforts following his triumph with *The Big Doll House*, including *Women in Cages* (1971) *The Hot Box* (1972) and Jonathan Demme's *Caged Heat* (1974). Ultimately, the WIP genre would prove commercially proficient enough to spawn a Hong Kong spin-off in the shape of the Shaw Brothers' production of *Bamboo House of Dolls* (1974) as well as a Japanese series of caged ladies films beginning with *Female Prisoner #701: Scorpion* in 1972.

This, of course, is where *Ilsa, She Wolf of the SS* makes an entrance. As with many exploitation pictures, it is often the fortunes of a bigger, more mainstream picture that provides the catalyst for a low budget offspring. Hence, it would appear that *Ilsa, She Wolf of the SS*'s sudden, rushed production was inspired by the success of 1974's *The Night Porter*, with that film's appeal to a wide audience no doubt reawakening Canada's Cinepix to the commercial potential in revisiting the setting and themes of *Love Camp 7* (which they had distributed). This, coupled with the booming business of the WIP films released by Corman, makes the film a cynical attempt to cross-pollinate the historical realism, and Nazi fetishism, of *The Night Porter* with the dominatrix torture highlighted in the likes of *The Big Doll House*.

Certainly, no one can blame director Edmonds, and the rest of the unknown cast and crew,

---

57 Aptly put by Bev Zalcock in his book *Renegade Sisters*: 'Roger Corman, who owned and ran New World Pictures, was not slow to pick up on the potential of the WIP film, and throughout the '70s his Philippines-based productions churned out a run of cheaply made movies containing lashings of sex, violence, nudity, sadism and excess, feeding male fantasies of highly sexed, wanton women.' (Headpress Publishing, London 1998).

for wishing to make some money and get their start in the film industry, but *Ilsa, She Wolf of the SS* still carries a very male, fetishist outlook, with the camera obsessively recording pained female faces and scarred naked flesh. In other words, it does nothing to subvert its genre. Instead it merely adds further nastiness to an already unpleasant series of movies. Indeed, if *Behind the Green Door* eroticised the expression of a woman in the midst of sexual satisfaction then *Ilsa, She Wolf of the SS* is the exact opposite. It invites the audience to gaze at the faces of hapless prisoners as they are hanged, electrocuted and, in a particularly sickening moment, boiled alive. In each of these sequences, Edmonds focuses predominantly on the faces of his actresses, each of whom is undressed, leading one to question whether he wants the audience to empathise with their pain or to simply enjoy their agony in the most revolting, sadomasochistic manner possible.

The key to this question is probably in the scene where a naked prisoner is presented at a Nazi luncheon, hosted by Ilsa. The woman is shown standing on a block of ice, and with a noose around her neck. Thus, as the ice melts she will hang. Any question over Edmonds' intention with this sequence is made clear when he cuts away to the Nazi guests watching the woman struggle and, finally, gazing without pity at her death throes. If ever anyone was to be aroused by watching such a vile set piece (and, as aforementioned, the brutal and complacent kinkiness of the WIP genre was obviously exciting some audiences at the time) then Edmonds appears to have cleverly predicted it. Thus, in a sense, he turns his own camera on the viewers and, in equating them to the on-screen Third Reich voyeurs; he asks his audience, 'Why are you sitting here gazing at this naked woman choking to death? Are you no better than the very sadists that inspired this movie?'

As a result, one gets the impression during *Ilsa, She Wolf of the SS* that Edmonds is remarkably unsure of what he is creating. An imaginative filmmaker, he uses the sets from the *Hogan's Heroes* television show to create a believable atmosphere (this *does* look like a concentration camp) and his technical abilities often shine through. Yet, even in spite of the aforementioned 'ice block' scene, never again does he attempt to place himself above the material. Instead, every gruesome act is lingered on and no attempt is made to turn the movie into a farce (although whether or not intentional absurdity may have made *Ilsa, She Wolf of the SS* any more acceptable is debatable). Certainly, there are lines that evoke laughter, but the performers never say them with the sort of 'nudge nudge, wink wink' delivery that may indicate the comedy is on purpose. 'When I reached puberty I discovered something about myself that set me apart from all the rest of the guys,' boasts Wolfe, who can make love to Ilsa all night without climaxing. 'I could hold back for as long as I want … I guess you could call me a freak of nature, a sort of human machine.' Yet, with these lines delivered by the actor (Gregory Knoph) as if his soul depends on it, one has to conclude that any humour in *Ilsa, She Wolf of the SS* is probably unintentional[58].

Nonetheless, Edmonds stages many sequences with an inventive spark, most notably in the finale where the prisoners engage in a shootout with the Nazis and flee from Medical Camp 9.

---

58 Indeed, Bill Landis and Michelle Clifford echo this sentiment in their book *Sleazoid Express*, '*Ilsa, She Wolf of the SS* works because it is played straight, even if the actors occasionally speak with bad accents.' (Fireside Books, New York, 2002)

TABOO BREAKERS

This is a very well executed breakout sequence, with the director even adding a short moment of slow motion to the proceedings, giving *Ilsa, She Wolf of the SS* a brief, but nonetheless notable, feel of Hollywood legitimacy. It is really during these final moments that the promise of a low budget *Great Escape* comes to fruition, making one wonder if Edmonds could have crafted a far more enjoyable low budget picture if the producers had just dumped the Nazi/torture angle, although whether we would still be talking about *Ilsa, She Wolf of the SS* today if this were the case is anyone's guess. Even so, the *Great Escape*-type music that appears over the soundtrack when the manly characters of Wolfe and Mario talk appears to support the theory that *Ilsa, She Wolf of the SS* is as rooted in the World War 2 escape dramas of yesteryear, as it is in the WIP genre.

As a result of this, two plots run simultaneously in the movie, the first featuring Wolfe, the imprisoned American, and his attempt to organise a jailbreak from the camp. In order to do this, he must convince Ilsa that he is in love with her and lure her into a false sense of security, climaxing in her allowing him the 'reward' of tying her to the bedposts. This is the storyline that actually drives the narrative, and although it is far from groundbreaking, it serves its purpose and gives the film reason enough to reveal its secondary story. This is where the medical camp torture comes in, initially carried out on behalf of the Third Reich but finally enacted out by Ilsa so that she can prove women are more able to withstand excruciating pain than men. When she proudly shows a visiting Nazi general the battered, bloody body of Anna, a sympathetic prisoner who stands her ground, he remarks with disdain, 'You must not waste Germany's time on your own personal projects.' Here, and only here, are we given the impression that Ilsa might even be too insane for Nazi Germany.

It is within these torture scenes that *Ilsa, She Wolf of the SS* cements its reputation. There is already a high sleaze factor in watching naked women being abused, but the historical setting obviously makes this all the more uncomfortable. Couple this with genuinely graphic scenes of violence and you have a movie that really does dare you to keep watching. The sexual element of the horror is also particularly unpleasant. For instance, poor Anna is gang-raped, electrocuted and has a burning hot pole inserted in her most private of areas (this at least takes place off screen … but Edmonds makes sure that we know full well what is happening). A scene where a man and woman are bent over and whipped seems to go on forever and carries an obvious sadomasochistic element. Moreover, a sequence where a line-up of nude females have an electric dildo forced inside them (complete with a truly disgusting sound effect) pushes bad taste to its limits. Here we can see Edmonds utilizing the horrors of the Holocaust simply to play games of sexual perversity on-screen. Perhaps aware of the obviously heinous nature of this, the director wisely makes sure that the word 'Jew' is never uttered during the movie, although in the long and short of things it really does not make a lot of difference: *Ilsa, She Wolf of the SS* is still one of the most horrific features ever made. Most frustrating is the film's final pay-off, where the mutilated Anna finds Ilsa tied up in her bedroom but, before being able to kill her, drops dead … leaving the Nazi guards to shoot the title character in an all too quick manner. Even here, the viewer is refused the spectacle of the villain receiving her just deserts at the hands of her victims.

Attention must also be paid to Dyanne Thorne, the actress who has commanded a considerable cult following through playing Ilsa and who, at the very least, gives the character some authority and presence. Although a surprising choice for someone who has to play a role that requires ample amounts of nudity and some degree of sex appeal (Thorne was not a twenty-something waif when given the part), she managed to pull the role off with enough aplomb to even catch the eyes of *Playboy* magazine[59]. Stern and vicious throughout the movie, only once is Thorne allowed to be disgusted by the excess that surrounds her … and that is when her superior, played by Richard Kennedy, invites her to urinate on him[60]. Edmonds makes sure we hear the sound of this 'release', but we never actually see anything (*Ilsa, She Wolf of the SS* draws the line at depicting anything sexually hardcore, which is one of the few barriers it does put up), however it is yet another example of the film pulling out all the stops to either offend or titillate, presumably depending on the viewer's mindset. Regardless, Thorne is a rare example, in seventies cinema, of a female character who is permitted to be more monstrous than any male counterpart can dream of being. Truly, Thorne's Ilsa has no predecessors when it comes to being overwhelmingly terrifying.

Unsurprisingly, *Ilsa, She Wolf of the SS* was almost instantly notorious, and profitable, when it was released, although it would be banned in many countries. Since its release, much has been made about the film's loose ties to the real life Ilse Koch, the notorious wife of Karl Koch, commander of the Buchenwald concentration camp during World War 2. A perverse and sadistic woman, Ilse was most famous for collecting human skin from dead inmates, torturing female prisoners and indulging in late night orgies. She finally hung herself in prison for the crimes she committed under the Third Reich, at the age of sixty. However, Thorne has mentioned that the character she and Edmonds created, whilst influenced by Ilse, bore little similarity to the real thing[61]. Regardless of this, knowing that a female commander carried out vicious crimes against humanity under Hitler's Germany adds an increased air of horror to the film.

Certainly, by treating the most sensitive of subjects as a platform to showcase gore galore, sexual torture and Nazi fetishism, Edmonds, along with distributors/financiers Cinepix, managed to reveal a niche in the market. Even by the grindhouse standards of the time, *Ilsa, She Wolf of the SS* was extremely brutal, but, put into its correct historical context, it is possible to view the movie as the start of a whole new exploitation fad in nasty Nazis and even more sexually extreme WIP flicks. One of the most heinous and unapologetically gruesome features of its time, *Ilsa, She Wolf of the SS* is also well made, features an unforgettable turn from Thorne and boasts plenty of impressive special effects. Watching it today, it still feels like an outlaw

---

59 '*Playboy* found the movie vulgar, but true to their hypocritical philosophy, the magazine's *Sex in Cinema* pocket book series printed a still from the film,' state Bill Landis and Michelle Clifford (*Sleazoid Express*, Fireside Books, New York, 2002)

60 Oddly enough it was Thorne's willingness to do this scene that got her the role. According to Briggs' book *Profoundly Disturbing*, originally Phyllis Davis, from Russ Meyer's *Beyond the Valley of the Dolls*, had been cast as Ilsa but she refused to act out the offending 'urination' sequence. (Plexus Publishing, London, 2003)

61 'There was no character in that script. Don and I created that character together. She may have been inspired by Ilse Koch, but she had nothing to do with our Ilsa. We created a fictitious character.' (Dyanne Thorne interviewed by Steve Swires, *The Dark Side*, Issue 86, 2000)

movie, made on the fringe of society and, yet, somehow gaining acceptance from an audience of unapologetic thrill seekers that either want the most extreme ride possible or just want to see how far cinematic violence can be pushed. It is because of this that *Ilsa, She Wolf of the SS*'s cult reputation was virtually solidified for decades more to come.

What happened next? Pasolini released *Salo* in 1975 and, despite being even more debased, sexually cruel and vulgar than *Ilsa, She Wolf of the SS*, it somehow managed to attract some degree of critical respect[62]. Currently, one can buy *Salo* uncut in the UK whilst *Ilsa, She Wolf of the SS* still languishes in limbo as a banned movie. *Ilsa, She Wolf of the SS*'s biggest influence would be in Italy, where, strangely for a country that had been involved with the Third Reich, a flurry of rip-offs followed, including *Salon Kitty* (1976), *SS Experiment Camp* (1976), *The Beast in Heat* (1977) and *Women's Camp 119* (1977). The WIP genre continued to new extremes under the tutelage of one of its innovators, Spain's Jess Franco, who directed the likes of *Barbed Wire Dolls* (1975) and *Sadomania* (1981), both of which are about as far as the trend can go, short of hardcore (the latter features a simulated rape by an Alsatian dog).

Meanwhile, Don Edmonds directed the first of the sequels, *Ilsa, Harem Keeper of the Oil Sheiks* in 1976. A far more enjoyable 'R-rated' effort than *Ilsa, She Wolf of the SS*, the movie finds Thorne (whose character died at the end of the first film) lording over a female white slavery ring in the Middle East. Preposterous, and without the baggage of the concentration camp setting, the movie is played for laughs and manages to be thoroughly entertaining. Edmonds finally moved on with his best film, 1977's *Bare Knuckles*, and entered the mainstream when he acted as a producer on such hits as *Midnight Crossing* (1987) and *True Romance* (1993). Ironically, he is now trying to revive the *Ilsa* franchise with a new movie.

Actress Thorne continued to capitalise on her infamy with 1977's *Greta, The Mad Butcher*, in which she teamed up with Jess Franco. Even more sexually explicit than her *Ilsa* movies, the film would, nevertheless, be renamed *Ilsa, The Wicked Warden* upon its re-release. Her final appearance as Ilsa would be 1977's *Ilsa, The Tigress of Siberia*, a tame but enjoyable romp which finds her running a torture camp in Siberia, under Stalin. Of course, the idea of Ilsa, who began life as a Nazi henchwoman, managing to defect to the Middle East and then to Stalin's Russia is totally insane. A fifth movie called *Ilsa Meets Bruce Lee in the Devil's Triangle* was announced, but never made.

Ilsa, She Wolf of the SS's biggest success story was scriptwriter Ivan Reitman (whom both Edmonds and Friedman insist penned the movie and who is credited as a producer on *Ilsa, The Tigress of Siberia*). After his schlock filled beginnings, which included also writing/directing 1973's *Cannibal Girls* and producing David Cronenberg's early work (such as *Shivers* and *Rabid*), Reitman was given the chance to direct *Meatballs* for Cinepix, the lame Bill Murray comedy that, nevertheless, proved to be a huge hit in 1979. Reitman then proceeded to direct some of the biggest blockbusters of the eighties (including *Stripes* and both *Ghostbusters* movies) and

---

62 In his book *Censored*, author Tom Dewe Matthews notes that British Classification Board President James Ferman believed, back in 1975, that *Salo* was a 'remarkable picture' and subsequently passed it without cuts. (Chatto and Windus, London, 1994).

produced a fair number of recent hits too (successes include 2000's *Road Trip* and 2003's *Old School*).

David Friedman interview

Although he had already achieved a huge level of screen infamy thanks to the likes of *Blood Feast* and *Two Thousand Maniacs*, producer David Friedman's most shocking production remains *Ilsa, She Wolf of the SS*, a movie that he did not even put his name on. 'That was the one time that I worked as a paid mercenary for some Canadians,' reflects the producer of his time on the notorious Nazi-ploitation effort. 'John Dunning and Andre Lake ran this company called Cinepix, which was a pretty big Canadian firm. So they had called Bob Cresse, with whom I made a picture years before called *Love Camp 7*, and wanted to know if he could produce this picture for them and he said, "I'm too sick," and they said, "Well do you think Friedman would do it?" and so Bob asked me and I said, "I don't need the money that much," but, well, they won and so I flew up to Montreal and, well, I'll tell you a deep dark secret about that: it was written by a very well known Canadian director called Ivan Reitman, the guy that made *Ghostbusters*.'

Not something that Reitman chooses to advertise on his CV anymore of course! 'Well he wrote that thing,' insists Friedman. 'He doesn't claim it, and if you mention it he will deny it, but Don told me he was sitting there with Ivan for three or four days pouring over that script. So at any rate, they came back to me with the script and it was like *The Encyclopaedia Britannia*, and this was a $150,000 picture in which they had to pay my salary and Don's salary and everything else. This was when Ivan was a young Canadian filmmaker working for Cinepix.'

From this point onward, Friedman's experience on *Ilsa, She Wolf of the SS* became a nightmare. 'Now these guys from Cinepix couldn't even get a phone installed in the United States,' he says. 'They had to use my tax forms, my labour, all of the paper work and I had just done a picture out of the old Hitchcock Laird studios, the old Selznick lot where *Gone with the Wind* was made. I shot *The Erotic Adventures of Zorro* out there and I shot *Johnny Firecloud* out there and they liked me and the old *Hogan's Heroes* set was out on the back lot. It had been sold as property for condominiums and I said, "Can I tear that thing down?" and they said, "Sure, we don't care," and I get them into this studio and Don pretty much cast it except for Dyanne Thorne. I met her back in her burlesque days where she had been one of the Pussycat girls, she had been with the Pussycat theatre chain and I was one of the founders ... so we started to shoot and these guys (Cinepix) are playing a money game. The money is coming from Luxembourg to Panama to Nova Scotia and on the second day I needed about $7000 and I call the Bank of America and they say, "Your money didn't come in," and I had to ask them to cover me for a day. Well, (Cinepix) said to me, "Can you lend us $50,000 for the week?" and I said, "Hey, I'm working for you, I'm not your partner," and the next morning the money wasn't there. So I called them and said, "I'm closing this thing down and I'm reporting you to the California labour board and everything else and you'll never be able to set foot in the United States again." They said, "Oh no, no, no," and sure enough by the afternoon they had managed to get $25,000 to me. It was a miserable experience. I remember saying, "You've got a scene at the end where the Allied Army attacks with 5000 men and they liberate it." He said, "Well what are you going to do?" I said, "I'm going to set some firecrackers off and have somebody come running into the camp and tell them that the Allies have arrived," *(laughs)*. But at any rate we finished it and we put together the assembly that is basically everything that you shot in sequence. I sent it up to Canada and I got this letter back, "On reel one, at 26 feet, 14 frames, cut to 28 frames," or something. Yet this is an assembly, this isn't a first cut! And all the paper work is going between the United States and Canada, through customs, so finally I just packaged it all up and said, "Why don't you guys just finish it all up?" and I said, "By the way, take my name off it."'

Not that this was the end of Friedman's involvement with the troubled Canadian production. 'So the picture came out and there was no way in the world they were going to submit it to the MPAA,' laughs the producer. 'So they said to me, "David, can you get us an R?" I said, "Sure … we'll start with the opening titles and end with the credits," but the picture killed them in Europe. I mean, in France alone they must have taken in $2 or $3million. It never played in Germany but it played Spain and Italy. The only places they played in the United States were a few spots where they would show an X-rated film. But somehow they managed to get it through to French Canada and they had a French dubbed version.'

Friedman also mentions that, although the film caused some controversy in the United States, he never thought that audiences would take it too seriously. 'In the United States there were things that none of us would ever do, like kill animals or whatever,' he says. 'But in so far as *Ilsa* goes … *Ilsa* to me, with the possible exception of *Make Them Die Slowly*, is the strongest thing that I have ever seen in so far as mutilation but there again American audiences just said, "Hey it's just a movie." Unfortunately, a lot of these would-be censors think it is for real. Of course, for years there was a rumour spread around by the Citizens of Decency, which is a league that was eventually put out of business by the IRS when it was found out that they were gathering money under false pretences. They spread the rumour around that it was a snuff film. You know, that we were actually murdering people! They would say that all these films that came from South America were snuff … Now Roberta Findlay and her husband did go down to Panama, or one of these banana republics, and made a shoot 'em up movie down there. Then this guy called Alan Shackleton got his hands on it and he renamed it *Snuff*. But it never went anywhere. I think Americans are a little bit too hip to that, they just look at it and think, "Wow what a great effect."'

About the only taboo that *Ilsa, She Wolf of the SS* does not break is the use of hardcore sex. Presumably, then, the producers were at least drawing the line somewhere. 'Hardcore, to be very honest with you, is something that I never particularly liked,' reflects the producer. 'I mean, I believe that every American has the right to read or see whatever he pleases without any interference from priests, politicians or policemen. But to me hardcore was bad show business because I came from the carnival where it was all about the tease. "Oh boy, we never saw it but next week we are really going to see it …" but with hardcore you get the *denouement* the moment the curtain rises, so what else is there to do? So very few of us that were involved with the exploitation/softcore business drifted into hardcore. Suddenly they were a whole new bunch of people making these films, many of them looked like clerks in a dirty book store, but it just wasn't any fun. I made four of them. I made one called *Matinee Idol*, which is pretty good. One reviewer said, "This looks as if it was made in a studio," which it was, "and it has a plot and a sub plot and it has an original music score! But these pictures should not be made in studios, they should be made in motel rooms. These pictures shouldn't have any reason other to give the customer an erection." I read this review and thought, "Well maybe this guy is right. Screw it, I quit!" Of course, it went on, and today here in the United States something like 15,000 hardcore feature titles get released every year. A lot of people have made a lot of money, God bless them, but it just wasn't something that I particularly liked because it wasn't fun anymore.'

The producer also mentions that he has great memories of Ilsa herself. 'Dyanne Thorne is a lovely, lovely lady whom I have known for 25 or 30 years. She was in burlesque shows, she was what we called a talking woman in burlesque, which means that she wasn't the stripper, she has lines to read and it is all in little skits. She was one of the best at that and she was a model. I think she did several nudie-cuties, I think she may have done one for Don as a matter of fact. When we had the Pussycat theatres we hired a lot of models and Dyanne was one of these girls.'

Although Friedman decided not to get involved with the *Ilsa* sequels, he does have at least one memory from the shooting of the first follow-up. 'The funny thing is that they called me and wanted to make another one, *Ilsa, Harem Keeper of the Oil Sheiks*,' he says. 'I told them I was too busy but Don agreed to direct it. The filmmaker Radley Metzger was out in LA visiting with me at the time and he had never been on the set of a Hollywood studio film because all of his work had been done in New York and in Europe. So I said to him, "Well let's go out to the old Selznick lot where *Duel in the Sun* was made." Don then says to me, "Oh boy I want to meet Radley Metzger, I really admire what he's done," and I said, "Well finish up what you're shooting and we'll go and do lunch." So he was shooting this scene of a slave auction. They auctioned one actress off for more than the other and the girl who got auctioned off for less comes up to Don at the end of the shoot and says, "Hey how come they paid less for me in that scene?" Don was so tense he turned around and slugged this kid and she fell down on the floor, knocked out cold. I said, "Come on Don, let's get out of here before the cops come!"'

Don Edmonds interview

Despite a career that takes in producing duties on Tony Scott's modern classic *True Romance*, and such low budget gems as *Bare Knuckles*, Don Edmonds will forever be known as the man who directed *Ilsa, She Wolf of the SS*. Not that he minds of course ... 'David Friedman never put his name on it but I never denied it,' laughs the filmmaker. 'You know, when you make a movie and you're starting out ... I was just a guy out there in the street, trying to make the rent, *literally* trying to make the rent! And it was thrilling. Someone wanted me to direct a picture? "Well, sure!" "What's the picture about?" "I don't know, do you care?" "No." "Are you paying?" "Yes." "Well then, let's go, let's do it!" But when people ask me, "What was your motivation?" Well because I wanted to keep the lights on in my house (*laughs*). Come on! It was the early seventies, and I'm just a guy around Hollywood trying to make it. And you want me to direct your movie? I'd love to. I got to tell you, at that point in time when that thing came out, now I'm being honest with you, put it in your story, I don't care, I was flat broke man. Holes in my shoes. You wanted me to direct a picture, at that time, about a dog pissing on a flat rock with different camera angles, I'd have done it, what, are you kidding? It makes no difference to me. If they pay money then I'd go, "Yeah let's do it." I take responsibility for what I did. I was working with people that couldn't even get an interview for studio pictures.'

Considering Edmonds' honesty it might come as no surprise that he admits *Ilsa, She Wolf of the SS* was not the greatest of 'breakout' projects for a young director. 'The script was terrible,' he sighs. 'I told the producers that. I said, "This is the worst piece of shit I've ever read." They said, "We have got a lot of money to make it though," and I said, "Well maybe I can find the socially redeeming value in it." What a whore, but fuck it, I don't care. It was made to make money – just to make a few bucks. We kicked the shit out the Nazis, so what do we care? Just get some fool down in Hollywood, he'll direct it, some fool will do it (*laughs*).' The opening scroll at the beginning of *Ilsa, She Wolf of the SS* tells viewers that what is being shown is to remind people of the horrors of the Holocaust but, according to Edmonds, this was not his idea. 'I told them to take it off,' he says. 'You see that thing come up on the screen with the drum rolls and that German thing, and you just go, "What a bunch of shit," and you cut to this guy getting his balls cut off. I mean, come on! Get real. You know, I don't have a long history to the beginnings of that film, it came to me as a completed script and they asked me if I wanted to direct it. I said, "Yes," and they said, "Then show up here," so I did and that was it. It is only in hindsight that you look at all the where and the why, but all that was, was another in a string of pictures.'

Edmonds can, however, pinpoint where the producers of *Ilsa, She Wolf of the SS* got their motivation from. 'There was a film called *Love Camp 7* and that was the genesis of it all,' he says. 'That film went to Canada and it did very well. So these guys wanted to make another picture because it was a profit-making venture for them. Were they thinking that some kid down in LA was going to come up with something too heavy? I don't think they knew I was going to be able to do that. I made that film in nine days! I had a crew of nine and a cameraman that had never shot a movie before. You know, we were floundering around in there …' Nevertheless, Edmonds does admit that he trod carefully around some aspects of the movie's horrifying subject matter. 'The word Jew is never mentioned in the picture,' he says. 'It was just never there. It was not supposed to be the Jews, it wasn't about "the oven". It was about an individual in a camp that was outside of wherever. It doesn't mention Buchenwald; it just doesn't say those things. It is a cross section of Nazis and their abhorrent behaviour and some of the things that they did are not even in that movie but they really did them. So I don't think it trivialised anything. I think it showed what they did. I believe the Nazis were disgusting individuals. When you look at it from that standpoint … But there are people out there that will always take a negative and turn it into a positive. If you go to the internet and type in "Nazi" then I'm sure you will get thousands of web sites that glorify it.'

Edmonds also admits that he never really considered that a person who survived the Holocaust might see his picture and take offence. 'I know you'd like me to say yes and to say that I have all this moral conscience about it,' states the filmmaker. 'For me to say, "Oh yes there's this deep psychological thing of why I did it," because it makes really good copy. But the fact of it is this. The guy who hired me, John Dunning, said to me, "I really want to see this on the screen." I said, "You're going to see it babe, oh you're going to see it." He said, "I want you to put the cameras right in it," and I said, "Don't worry about that, I'll put the camera right where it's supposed to be." And that was my mandate. Look, we're talking with *Ilsa, She Wolf of the SS* about a film that over thirty or so years has become this social phenomenon, but it didn't start out this way. Okay? A bunch of people came in to work on it – and why? Because we were all at the beginnings of our career and we all wanted to work, and that's why we did it. We did what was on the page. I didn't write it but I directed it.

There was this woman from Claremont College and she wrote a Doctorate on *Ilsa, She Wolf of the SS*! A very serious paper on the social implications of *Ilsa, She Wolf of the SS*! She mailed it to me about two weeks ago and I'm reading this thing and thinking, "My God, who did this?" Now I know you'd like me to say, "Yes I had that on my mind the whole time and I knew it was going to be a film with social implications and the public was going to damn it! I did it with great gusto because I knew the world was going to come apart if they saw my movie." But I'd be lying to you, man! It didn't happen that way. It was a nine day quickie for fifty grand and maybe another fifty grand in the post-production of it. Nine days! Now you want me, at nine days, making that size of movie with a crew of nine people to be thinking about social implications? I'm just thinking, "Can we finish this with some raw stock left? Put it over here, shoot it. Cut! Can you see it?" "Yes." "Can you hear it?" "Yes." "Print it." Social implications, *really* …'

Not that Edmonds did not look at what he was shooting and fail to understand what kind of picture he was about to inflict on the world. 'Don't get me wrong, I'm a very smart guy and I knew what I was making,' he laughs. 'I would make some shot, look at it and shout, "Cut." Then I'd say, "Damn Don, what did you just make man?" Now you got to remember that this is 1972 … I'm looking at the maggots coming out of her arm and I'm going, "Cut, yeah print it," and then thinking, "What did you just make there?" But yeah, I knew about women's liberation and all the aspects of that which, over the last thirty years have become very prominent. You know, go back and do your history and your homework and you see that women were just beginning to burn their bras when we made *Ilsa*! But I knew that I wanted a strong woman because she had to lead the movie. You know, a real ball buster so I wasn't going to have a wimp, I'd give her a couple of moments where she gets a little soft, and shows there's another element to her but the whole character of Ilsa is about strength.'

Ilsa was shot on the sets of *Hogan's Heroes*, although Edmonds admits that he does not know if the show's producers were aware of it. 'I honestly don't know,' he says. 'You know the studio was kind of shut down at that point in time and when we went on the back lot, looking for locations to shoot the picture we were prepared to shoot it anywhere that looked like the army. So what happened was that we found it, and it was just sitting there, man. It had been sitting there for about four years. I mean, weeds were growing in it, and we went to the people and asked to use the set. We used the exteriors and we were so cheap we used the interiors too … and then we had to build a couple of sets so we rented a soundstage for a couple of weeks. The dungeons and stuff, we had to build that … but that was it. Like it or don't like it, we had so little money that we were out there and the lunch truck would come up to do lunch for the extras and we would have to charge them. (*Don speaks with disgust*) What a cheap bunch of shits we were, man. "Yeah, that'll cost you a dollar twenty-five." "Hell we're only making nine bucks!" "OK, then we'll give you a discount of thirty five cents." Charging extras to eat, it was cruel. We were all working twenty-hour days.'

In reflection, Edmonds wishes his film could have been blessed with higher production values. 'Well now, more money would have been fantastic,' he beams. 'Of course the film would have been different with a bigger budget. The actors would have been better and the production values would have been greater, it would also have had much more scope. We could have slowed down and we could have had more film stock and equipment to accomplish what we knew we *could* do, but couldn't *afford* to do. We did the very best we could with the material and resources we had, we stretched out every inch of available help and we worked like dogs and finished on exact time, not another inch of film was ever shot to make the feature. What I shot was what they used. But it would have been an absolute joy if we had more money, and I had a lot of ideas of things I wanted to do that just couldn't get done because of money restrictions. So we made do with what we had. Old equipment, an old small lamp package, extras doing acting parts, not enough location money to make the sets we wanted, not as big an extra crowd as I'd have liked, bad food and over all just not enough time. Money buys these things, so yes I'd have loved if we had more bucks to make it, but it is what it is and I can't go back and improve it now …'

Amazingly, Edmonds claims that actress Dyanne Thorne, who has since become equally synonymous with the character of Ilsa, was not his first choice for the role. 'There was a girl named Phyllis Davis who we cast in the picture,' he reveals. 'A very different character, much sweeter, she had done some soft-core stuff, not much … she was a beautiful girl. But Phyllis was dark haired, and at the last moment, literally, we were all set up and ready to do it, she dropped out. We had this rush call for casting: "Blonde, big tits, can walk and chew gum at the same time and can maybe do a little dialogue." We'll work around the rest of it. Julia Roberts and Meryl Streep don't work in these kinds of pictures (*laughs*) so your casting call is not too long. David had worked with Dyanne on something else, and he called her up and asked if she wanted to come in for a casting. There were maybe about fifteen girls that were blonde and busty and didn't trip over the cables so we asked them in. Now you got to understand, when you're paying fifty dollars a day and you're guaranteeing they're going to work an eighteen hour day, and you're going to damn near kill them, then their desire to be in your movie is not that great. Especially when you're going to cut the balls off guys and do a picture with whips and chains, which nobody had ever done before. But that day she walked in the door. She'd been in Dave's picture so she came over to see what was going on and the truth of it is she brought something to it. She brought a certain command. She had big boobs and blonde hair and all this stuff, but there was also something very commanding about her and it worked, it really worked. And she was sensitive, I mean everybody was sensitive about doing the film, but she was a spiritual woman. She is a minister now, she can marry you. She had her moments of doubts and we offered her X amount of money, which she needed, and figuring nobody was ever going to see this movie she did it. That's how she came to be, I didn't know her before but I got along fine with Dyanne. The film hurt her and it also made her. We still stay in touch. She makes good money on the convention circuit but she has taken a lot of heat from these pictures though. We were just two professionals making a film, it was just a job, but we never expected the ramifications of the film.'

Edmonds also admits that Thorne never had a problem with the movie's explicit violence and softcore sex scenes. 'She was fine with it,' he says. 'I told her what I was going to do and what I wouldn't do. I would do that with anyone who is going to work with me. Before I roll the camera I'm going to tell you what's going to happen and what's not going to happen and I make an agreement with that girl or guy and I don't break it. No, that would be dirty … I'm very good

… at this but I'm also very truthful.'

Edmonds is aware that his film had an international impact. 'It had social implications and it put countries against each other …' The film even caused at least one minor incident between Belgium, where the movie played theatrically, and Germany. 'From what I know, Belgium played it on the border between them and Germany for a year, and the German government told them to get it out of there,' laughs Edmonds. 'So Belgium, in essence, told them to go fuck themselves. It never went to Germany, unless they're buying it on the internet. But honestly … you are asking too much of the filmmaker by asking them to put in a political message, it is hard enough just to get the damn thing made.'

All the same, Edmonds maintains a little pride at the fact his low budget, grimy little project is still being spoken about over 30 years later. 'It has stood the test of time and that is what all films are about,' he smiles. 'Can they stand the test of time? If you look at it now you get the same impact as you did when you saw it thirty years ago. That is a mean trick. It's a well made movie but the point is that from a practical filmmaking standpoint we had nothing to work with. A film is 10,000 feet long once it is printed and in the theatre. When you make a film you don't make it 10,000 feet long, you make it 150,000 or 200,000 feet long and you cut it back, right? You got a lot of waste, a lot of extra takes and stuff there. Well we shot that film on 25,000 feet of stock. That means I got one-for-one, whatever I shot I put it in, that's it. I shot that film for a little over $50,000. That is nothing. So what I am saying to you is that we had nothing to work with. The actors were making $25 to $50 a day. I was taking actresses, and that is a laugh in itself because all these girls had done was spread their legs for still photographs, and I'm giving them parts and making them work. I was looking at that picture and thinking, "This is gonna shock the shit out of somebody." Everybody wants me to come out thirty years later and take it all back, but, no, I did it.'

Asked about whether or not he thinks *Ilsa, She Wolf of the SS*, in light of its sexual tortures towards women, is a misogynistic movie and Edmonds immediately answers in the positive. 'Yup, I do. You put enough S and M in it and then people say it's misogynistic, well I'd say that is right. But in 2006 I would say there is more misogyny, more S and M, more bondage … and it is coming over the internet every four seconds. You don't believe me, go check out some of the sites. Go to Yahoo and type in sadomasochism and see how many sites come up … But what people do in their lives is not my business, I'm not the arbiter of good taste, I refuse to even go there.'

Indeed, *Ilsa*'s continued fame and notoriety takes Edmonds by surprise. 'I know that Quentin Tarantino and Rob Zombie like it,' he says – noting that Zombie also paid homage to *Ilsa, She Wolf of the SS* with his *Werewolf Women of the SS* trailer for *Grindhouse* (2007). 'It has been a revelation because you have to know that I walked away from this whole thing for a long time. And what built behind it, I wasn't out there promoting it, in fact, I didn't even have it on my résumé. If you nailed me then I'd admit I did it, but I wasn't out there going, "Yeah I did *Ilsa, She Wolf of the SS*." I didn't for decades. It built on its own. The first time I met Quentin Tarantino, I was a producer on *True Romance* which he wrote. I said, "I don't know who this guy is, but this is a writer for the year 2000. This is a brilliant writer." Well Quentin is really a dynamic individual – he comes flying into this restaurant, this big tall kid, and I'm sitting next to him and he's talking and talking and talking and finally he turns around to me and says, "Hey, what did you say your name was again?" I said, "Don Edmonds" and he turned away, did a double take and then he went very still. He said, "Excuse me, are you *the* Don Edmonds? Did you do this picture called *Ilsa, She Wolf of the SS*?" I told him that I did and he said, "Oh my God that picture has been such an influence …" So is that picture known? You bet. And is it known by big time filmmakers? Oh yeah. How did that dinky two dollar movie get to be known? I have no idea. But I didn't make the audience. I didn't go on television and beg them to see the movie. They found it on their own and they've been finding it for thirty years.'

Edmonds also admits that, despite the statuesque Thorne in the lead role, and the copious close-ups of her chest, Russ Meyer was not an influence on him. 'Russ Meyer was doing his thing,' maintains the director. 'I had influences, but I came out of German theatre and I came out of Columbia Studios and Universal Pictures to make these little low budget things. And I had a lot of professionalism. You know, I think this is what I've always brought to the game. And I brought it into this low budget field. I knew how to make a movie, I'd made a lot of them. I'd just been at the other side of the camera. You bring what you have to the job that you do, at least this is how I do it.'

When *Ilsa, She Wolf of the SS* was wrapped, Edmonds was not given any control over the editing of his bad taste epic. 'The dailies went back up to Canada and they cut it up there,' he says. 'But the truth of it is that they didn't have very much. You take a 10,000 foot picture, 25,000 is stock, 5000 feet of it is going to be slates and the other 10,000 is going to be waste: false starts, wrong takes, the action didn't happen correctly; the squibs didn't go off on time or whatever. Once you get the usable footage out of that 25,000 feet of stock, you pretty much have what I shot. There weren't a lot of choices for them to make. You have to remember that Steven Spielberg shoots 1.5 million feet of film. You see where I'm going with this? I didn't have that sort of luxury.'

When asked about Ivan Reitman's involvement, Edmonds has no idea why he didn't wish to be credited. 'Do I know why he never put his name on it? It was not a picture that was in the mainstream of thinking and it was such a scathing film … maybe he just didn't want to be credited on it. That is just a guess because I really don't know. But it was Cinepix's movie. If they wanted to put their name on the front and call it, "John Dunning Presents …" then they could have done.' Edmonds confirms, however, that he worked with Reitman on the script and shot everything that he wrote. 'I wrote with him a bit. I went to Canada to do that. We whacked around with it for a while.'

Ilsa, She Wolf of the SS was released to American cinemas after the Vietnam War, which was a time that spawned a whole new wave of violently thematic material, such as *Last House on the Left* and *The Texas Chain Saw Massacre*. These films come from a point in history where the cinema screen was becoming increasingly less conservative, perhaps because, in light of the very real horrors that people had been seeing on the news, cinematic carnage was now being viewed as cathartic: a way to escape the everyday terror of real life. Edmonds admits that, whilst he never had any social intentions with *Ilsa, She Wolf of the SS*, this may just be a fair assumption. 'I don't doubt that films like *Ilsa, She Wolf of the SS* blew the doors open on making films that were much more pungent,' he says. 'I understand that and I knew that at the time.

ILSA, SHE WOLF OF THE SS

I was the guy who was in *Gidget Goes Hawaiian*, you understand? I was in all these little silly drive-in comedies and that is how I started in show business. I'm a very funny guy, as you know, and I got to tell you, you look at these films now and you will go, "What in the world is this?" Well it was a world where dad came in with his suit and tie on and sat down at 6pm with mom and son and daughter and she cooked and cleaned and they fed the scraps to Spot the dog. Well that is not the way the world is now. This is a violent, back-stabbing world. I didn't make it that way, politicians, strong opinions and religion made it that way. I didn't make anything. I'm just a reflector of it. I didn't make Ilse Koch, all I did was reflect her. I put big tits and blonde hair on her and that is called theatrical licence.' It also gave birth to one of low budget cinema's most frightening femmes. 'I knew that the audience was going to have a reaction towards her,' laughs Edmonds. 'But how can you predict anything like that? How can you predict that of a two dollar movie that you make in nine days on the back lot of an old studio using the *Hogan's Heroes* sets? Using girls that have never even seen a camera and you're giving them acting parts, squibbing them up and throwing them into walls, putting electric dildos in them, how do you figure that you are not going to get a reaction? That part I could figure out. What it was? There was no way I could predict what it was. In 1974 I had never heard the term DVD, I had never heard the word videotape, now you can play the film on your damn telephone, but I didn't know that then. Who would? So what I'm trying to say to you is that I never understood, at that point in time, that this film would have so many media outlets and that people would pick it up and talk about it as if it was *Catcher in the Rye*, which they do. It has had its own social impact and I'm the guy that did it, but how in the world anybody would predict that … I mean, how was I to know that it would go up to Canada, which was the country that funded the damn thing, only for them to find out they couldn't play it there?'

Ilsa, She Wolf of the SS was also banned in the UK. 'I take pride in that dude!' laughs Edmonds, who goes on to state that it almost immediately made a name for itself in America. 'It should have been a videotape,' he mentions. 'I didn't know it was going to even book. That wasn't my job! I was the director of the movie! It played in the Apollo Theatre in New York, it opened there. Now the Apollo was on 42nd Street before they cleaned up 42nd Street. This was when you had to kick the drunks and the junkies out of the way just to get in the door. There used to be a television monitor outside that would run a continual loop of this thing. In the newspaper there was no advertising, you know when you look at *The Times* you usually see that *Gone with the Wind* is playing at two and six and that's all it is, just this long list of films. Well we had *Ilsa, She Wolf of the SS* listed at twelve, two, four, six and eight. By the second week you couldn't get in there. The Apollo Theatre was where guys went in to stroke their puds and sleep. You know, the drunks and the junkies are in that theatre puking on the floor. They added screenings and then they added an all-nighter so that you could now see *Ilsa, She Wolf of the SS* at the Apollo Theatre twenty-four hours a day. The third week, Vincent Canby, one of the great reviewers of our day, he was the main reviewer of *The New York Times*. That's *The New York Times*, you hear me? He goes to 42nd Street, goes down to the Apollo Theatre and he sits through *Ilsa, She Wolf of the SS*. He came back out and wrote a two column review that ran in the Sunday *New York Times* and he hated it! He thought it was the worst film of the decade, and the funniest! Then he went into all the social implications, which was the first time I ever had any idea that anybody was taking this film seriously. I have still got the review, I'm stunned. Vincent Canby, man, he reviews all the big films, what incentive could he have had to go down to 42nd Street and sit next to some guy stroking his dick? I couldn't believe this was happening. Then by the third week it figured in the top fifty grosses of pictures around the United States in *Variety*.'

After that *Ilsa, She Wolf of the SS* began to travel across the US. 'It played wherever it could get a booking,' says Edmonds. 'Some States would play it and some States wanted nothing to do with it. As far as I know it went to video. Now you got to know that for thirty years, after I made *Ilsa, The Harem Keeper*, I thought, "Don you got to walk away from this or you ain't ever gonna have a career," because I wanted to do other pictures but most films today don't last for a week! They don't make it from Wednesday to Wednesday! I mean $50 million films too. But *Ilsa, She Wolf of the SS* has legs and it was a breakout picture. I remember shooting it and thinking, "Nobody has ever seen anything like this before." They wanted to open the picture in Rhode Island and this is where the religious right are, it's really strict. So some goof rents the theatre in Providence, Rhode Island. He gets out, you know these Nazi convertibles, the old Mercedes Benz that Hitler used to ride around in, well they found one. He gets some chick that is blonde and has got big tits and he puts up on the marquee, "*Ilsa, She Wolf of the SS*, opening Wednesday." They get the girl in the car with a sign on the side that says, "Come see *Ilsa*" and the details of the theatre. They drive her right down the main drag of Providence, Rhode Island to sell this movie. The people stoned her! The driver drives back to the theatre and then, like the villagers in *Frankenstein*, they're following them and throwing rocks (*laughs*). The poor girl and the driver run inside the theatre, the crowd runs in too, they tore down the marquee, tore up all the seats and tore down the screens (*laughs*). The picture has never played in Providence, Rhode Island. They weren't having it, man! That's a true story – you know the stories that go on about this shit are unreal ...'

Although Edmonds would go on to direct a whole slew of other projects, the filmmaker admits that the gruelling on-screen horrors of *Ilsa, She Wolf of the SS* did his career no favours. 'I made *Bare Knuckles* after *Ilsa, She Wolf of the SS* but I was still hurt,' he states. 'When you go to directors, there's always this need to have this centre, "I will only direct." But there are lots of things in the world I like to do. Directing I love to do, but there's other stuff I like to do, some things that don't even involve movies at all. I like life. And, hell, I'll drift off for a couple of years. I mean, why not? I have spent my whole life in the movie business.' Nevertheless, Edmonds did return for the sequel: *Ilsa, Harem Keeper of the Oil Sheiks*. 'They wanted to make it lighter,' he says. 'They wanted to put a little more humour into it. And they asked me if I would make the next one and I said, "Yeah." I mean, I'm already painted with the black brush, so go ahead. I went and did the sequel and it played quite successfully. I don't know that it did the numbers of the first film, you'd have to take that up with the Canadians, but it did very well. But by that time, a year and a half later, Dyanne was established and I knew the ramifications of her, I knew what she would do and by that time I had Dean Cundy working for me and I had Michael Riva, I had a good group of good people. So we just smoked some dope and went and made the damn thing.'

The follow-up, however, was nowhere near as nasty as its notorious predecessor. 'No it wasn't' agrees Edmonds. 'And I had to find some of the same people things to do. For example, I had to find something for Buck Flower, he played a beggar … It was just going over ground that I'd already been over. We made it in square, right wing, Glendale California. Now Glendale is the most right-wing city around here. They don't like *nothing*, in fact, they won't even let people shoot in Glendale a lot of the time. If you come in with a picture and they read your script and don't like it then they won't let you shoot in Glendale. So we're looking around, now there's a scene, we needed to have this big fight at the end, but we couldn't find a place that looked Arabic. And we found a nunnery. A fucking nunnery, man! Now we had to find a building that was like the Sharif's tower, now in Southern California, that's a little hard to do. So one of the guys says, "I know a place, it's in Glendale," and we all go, "Sheesh." "Well where is it?" "Glendale public library." I said, "You got to be kidding!" So we go over and look at it, and there it is, it's perfect. The guy says, "Do we go and get a permit?" and I said, "Don't even think about it, we're not going to get a permit." But we needed this place, so what happens in the picture is the Sharif comes down the stairs and meets the Henry Kissinger character who drives up in the limo and they shake hands and they go into what is supposed to be the Sharif's palace. Now we got to have this shot, *got to have it*. So on a Sunday morning, in square, dumb Glendale, I come down there with Richard Kennedy and this doofus as the Sharif and I pull up two jeeps with fifty calibre machine guns and I'm going to shoot this scene. We're driving up and all of a sudden the water sprinklers come on in this big lawn that's in front of the building. And I see this gardener, and this poor guy is just out there on a Sunday morning doing his thing, and I say, "Sir, didn't you get the word?" He goes, "What?" And I said, "We were supposed to shoot here this morning and you've got the water on. I demand you turn it off." He goes, "Oh I'm sorry," and he turns the water off. I say, "Now can you get out of the shot because you're bothering us?" So he gets out of the shot, people aren't even up yet. I say, "Shoot it," (*laughs*). In comes the limo, we do our thing and we get out of there by eight o clock.'

However, although Dyanne Thorne returned for a third *Ilsa* movie Edmonds decided that he had had enough of the exploitation franchise which he had created. 'Time had run out,' he admits. 'The third one was done in Canada and I just went on to other things. I went on to make a lot of other pictures and I knew it was time to go. I've never watched *The Tigress of Siberia* or *The Wicked Warden*. I know that must seem strange to you but I just never had any interest in looking at rip-offs of what I originally made. Maybe it is either ego or boredom that's kept me from sitting down and actually watching them but as to this date I haven't.' Edmonds also states that he was not involved with the wonderfully titled, but never made, *Ilsa Meets Bruce Lee in the Devil's Triangle*. 'No, that was not me,' he says. 'I think someone just must have made the title up, although there might have been a script. *Ilsa* is not my title – someone else must own it.'

Looking back at his days of toiling away in grindhouse cinema, Edmonds admits that he has a lot of fond memories. Especially since his work launched so many major Hollywood players. 'I was always able to get with one or two good people,' he reflects. 'I have been very fortunate to hook up with people who are just beginning their careers, and they go on to do wonderful things. You know, Dean Cundy was with me back then and Michael Riva, the late Debra Hill, people who have gone on to monster careers with Oscar nominations. Serious stuff, but when we were together they were just out of UCLA. Dean Cundy, who is a terrific guy, he did *Apollo 13*, the *Back to the Future* movies and Debra Hill, who started with me, was the one who produced *Halloween*. She was with me on *Southern Double Cross* and *Bare Knuckles*. If you look at the crew on *Bare Knuckles* and the crew on *Halloween*, except for maybe the craft service guy, it's the same crew. She just took my crew and went over and made *Halloween* with John Carpenter. And I had assembled these guys over two or three pictures. I think that's something you do in the movie business, you work with somebody and they're either good or they're not good. You know next time if you don't want to use them or if you feel, "Yeah I'd go down the barrel of a cannon with this guy or this girl." That's how I formed my group and Debra took them all.'

Now, Edmonds is positioning himself for a return to the *Ilsa* fold with a new movie: *Ilana*. 'I wrote a script that I like a lot,' he confirms. 'What I want to do at this time in my life is to make pictures that have a market and to be able to utilise now, if possible, the technology that I didn't have then. Back then we had a camera that was so loud that it could be heard on the soundtrack. It was this old, old camera – but it was still a camera and it was 35mm too. Every piece of equipment was so old, and the lamps, they had to fix the plugs and things. It was weird making movies that way but now, today, the technology is so terrific and I love it so much. Computers, I can use them now, they're wonderful!'

If *Ilana* happens, then the news is that *Ilsa*'s creator has not mellowed with age. 'People come up to me and say, "Oh man, I can't wait to see a new film – you're not going to cheat us though are you Don?" I say, "No, no I'm not." Now, what they edit out, I don't know, but that doesn't mean a thing because I'll just give you a director's cut. Oh yeah … I don't give a shit. If you're going to make this kind of movie then give it to them. I'm making this film for a core audience that want to see blood, that want to see me ripping a hole in your chest with my fist and jerking your heart out, with the ensuing blood and arterial sprays! So that's what they want? Well guess what, that's what they're going to get … You're dealing with a niche audience that wants a picture just the way they want it. These days there are people out there trying to fulfil that audience, but they just don't do it as good as me.'

Dyanne Thorne interview

Dyanne Thorne hit grindhouse paydirt with her unforgettable performance in *Ilsa, She Wolf of the SS*. Speaking to the actress today, however, and one finds a sweet, intelligent and gentle soul, far removed from her most famous screen role. 'The stage had always been my field,' begins the actress. 'Coming out of New York I had done many, many plays there and moved into the area of doing more comedic work. I was a comedic sketch artist and I was even at Caesar's Palace in Las Vegas with Tim Conway from *The Carol Burnett Show* so I had lots of experience in that area. I had done some film work, but again you don't look at something and decide, right then, if it will be successful or not successful. When you have an agent, someone who guides you in that area, you can be really picky and choosey but, quite honestly: all the work that I have done has come through auditioning and getting the job. It has not come as a result of having an agent, although it was an agent that hooked me up with *Ilsa, She Wolf of the SS*, but the day after I signed the contract that agent retired and moved to Florida. Then after that there wasn't an agent in the world that *wanted* to represent me except, of course, for someone that also retired the month after they agreed to handle me. I had no idea that *Ilsa, She Wolf of the SS* was going to be what it is. I didn't judge it, it was not pornographic when I read it, it was meant to be very dramatic, very bizarre if you will, sensational … it gave me a chance, and I was not 19 anymore, to be a leading lady in something that was not comedy and was the antithesis of what I might have had an opportunity to do. At that time I had been part of a Cannes film festival winner for best short subject, but those things had just been an opportunity to work as an actress. That is also what the film was, no more than that. They were going to pay me to be a leading lady and I was going to play someone who was quite heinous. It was not a real person and it was never meant to glorify anything or to make a personal statement, it was simply my opportunity as a character actress, because that is always how I see myself. It took off and I don't know what else I can say about that …'

Surprisingly, Thorne was not aware from the start how shocking *Ilsa, She Wolf of the SS* was going to be. 'The only time I became suspicious was when I realised that Don Edmonds and myself were the sole people using our own names and that everyone else was going under something fictitious. Now when I was holding a Screen Agent's Guild contract I didn't expect that from people. It's funny because in *The Erotic Adventures of Pinocchio* I played the Fairy Godmother but nobody thought that I was a real Fairy Godmother, but when I did *Ilsa, She Wolf of the SS* all of a sudden people thought I was this character. I don't know. Life is funny …'

Of course, back in the early 1970s a leading role for a woman was really difficult to get and the film gave Thorne the chance to genuinely own a movie. 'Absolutely,' she replies. 'And in the past I had turned down roles because I thought, "I'm not prepared to do that sort of thing." When they showed me *Ilsa, She Wolf of the SS* … putting a costume on any actor makes it so much easier to be the character. So in answer to that, yes it was a good opportunity. You know, in *Point of Terror* I murdered my husband, in *Blood Sabbath* I murdered everyone around me, in *The Swinging Barmaids* they killed me (*laughs*). When I did a role in *Star Trek* it didn't mean anything because I was just a pretty girl. I had done a small role in a film that starred Omar Shariff that they shot at Caesar's Palace, and even that ended up getting cut out, it was just another pretty girl part. All of these roles … if you didn't get killed you would kill somebody or be cut from the final print, but in *Ilsa, She Wolf of the SS* there was a lot more happening. It was like a monologue and I even said to Don, "She can't just be talking all the time," and we gave up half the dialogue just so that there would be something else coming up.'

Thorne also has nothing bad to say about her director. 'I think Don Edmonds did a superb job of rising to the occasion,' she enthuses. 'We didn't try and copy anyone, and someone asked me once, "What actress did you admire most?" I thought about it and named some wonderful actresses but the point is that I never tried to be anyone else. I just tried to create my own character. This character was heinous, but she died at the end of every single one of them (*laughs*). We never glorified her, she always got her comeuppance. We never said, "If you act like a bad girl you'll escape." Oh no, you're going to suffer for it, but along the way what fun to be so mean! But, yes, Don was amazing. A bit aloof and a bit full of himself but I think that was his protective covering to get the respect that he felt was due to him, so he conducted himself in a way where you just respected what he did. Either that or you suffered the consequences (*laughs*). I had a wonderful relationship with him and have no complaints whatsoever. I admired him and trusted him and it was a great disappointment to me that I didn't know how to manipulate in a way that would have allowed Don to do *Tigress*, or that would have protected me from doing something like *Greta*. He would have known how to handle these films, especially *Tigress*, in a way that would have made them every bit as valuable as the others.'

It is unlikely that anyone who sees *Ilsa, She Wolf of the SS* would say that it glamorises the Third Reich, mainly because Thorne's character is so repulsive, and the on-screen experiments are utterly vile. In its own twisted way, therefore, the movie shows the Nazi reign exactly as it should be: horrible, barbaric individuals ... 'Yes, and you know, I think we like burying our heads,' answers Thorne. 'I don't want to get philosophical here, but I sometimes think that seeing scenes like this reminds us that there are monsters and sociopaths out there. There are people who are not rightly motivated. Of course, my motivation with doing the film was not to deal with that, but looking at it later I have a better understanding. One person wrote to me later and said it was New Year's Eve and he was very low and he was going to go to the movie and go home and kill himself. He said, "When I saw the movie and realised how other people had suffered through life. I looked at mine and thought that I better get my act together." He then explained that it was a year later and his life was back on track. So you never know how people are affected by something.'

Now, over 30 years later, and Thorne admits that she is shocked her Nazi dominatrix still captures the imagination of exploitation film fans. 'It not only surprises me, it shocks me and, at one time, maybe even horrified me,' she laughs. 'It was one of these things where, as an actress, you enjoy doing the role and then on-screen it is even more horrible than it was in the script. Some things were improvised and they were quite shocking to me. I thought that it would just be buried and go away, and the first screening we had I invited some of my friends and two of them never spoke to me again, one berated me for doing it and another said, "Be aware that this is the end of your career. You will need to look for something else to do." So I went back to the stage and I have never been out of work as an actress, but aside from working with John Ritter in *Real Men*, which brought me out for a little role, I never tried to seek work in television or film again. I saw my career as going in a totally different direction and I don't regret it. My life took a turn that I'm totally happy with. It is very interesting that these films took on a life of their own. It is amazing because you have to realise that this film's biggest popularity was in the eighties and that was the last century! So I am quite moved by it because, honestly, I look at the big stars in the mainstream and they can't go anywhere without a bodyguard, they cannot just be themselves and I have met the most amazing people. I get these wonderful letters, "Do you have a piece of your clothing or wig you can post to me?" it is just the sweetest thing. I have made very good friends, and I don't know why, with the punk and rock stars. They really took an interest and I have formed some really fine friendships, without naming them, and they are quite famous. I even married a couple of them, and I never would have crossed paths with these people otherwise or imagined getting along so well with them. A part of an actor is, I guess, a little bit of everybody. I have been able to connect with people who have become fans, and I don't think that would be the same for a fan of someone like Michelle Pfeiffer, whom I very much admire, and there is not one fan that has contacted me that I would give up.'

Of course, Thorne would go on to reprise her most famous role in a series of sequels including *Ilsa, The Tigress of Siberia* – the softest of the short-lived franchise and the only one not to be directed by Don Edmonds. 'I regretted that Don was not there all the way along,' says Thorne. 'This is not to say anything bad about the other director but we had really low rapport and it just wasn't the same. But after the first I never even thought that there would be another one. I mean, I die at the end of all of these films! I think that the justification of it was to show that she was a larger than life character. I think it is healthier to be … I don't want to say tongue in cheek because every one of these films was based on a real life experience …'

Indeed, the original *Ilsa, She Wolf of the SS* is inspired by the horrific true-life Nazi Ilse Koch. 'Yes, Ilse Koch was the inspiration,' replies Thorne. 'And the other one, *Greta* was based on a true story too. But that was never supposed to be what it is, it turned into a totally different kind of film. I was being farmed out to Europe for that, which was nice, but little did I know what it would end up like! It was, however, based on a real sanatorium in Palomar where they were taking people who were not mentally stable and torturing them. They were doing all kinds of horrible studies on these people. I even got to meet one of the women who was involved with the person they were trying to get out, which is the story of the film, but it could have been done better and could have been written better. But in the beginning the allure was that this did happen, and it happened with people such as this Ilse Koch, who was a total sociopath. By the time we get to *Oil Sheiks*, and Don will explain this too, it was made during a time when college girls were disappearing and ending up in the harems of sheiks. A year later I actually met a girl who had escaped. She was an American student, and she had gotten away when they took her on a shopping tour to India. She got back to the United States. It was the same thing with *Tigress*, it was based on this woman who was a little bit like Heidi Fleiss and she had a ring of power, if you will.'

Thorne's fourth turn as a busty dominatrix, entitled *Greta, the Mad Butcher*, was re-released as *Ilsa, the Wicked Warden*, something that still bothers the actress to this day. 'When I saw it, it was disappointing and I love Jess Franco, please don't misunderstand me,' she says. 'I didn't know that this would just be a sensational film. I thought that he, too, was looking to make something that would go on a different stream but Erwin C Dietrich, the producer, apparently already had a reputation for doing films that were … Well, I think *Greta* was a step up for him. But, no matter what it is, everything was what it was and I met wonderful people and had the pleasure of travelling Europe. I got to express myself as an actress, through horrific characters, and very few girls get to that (*laughs*). Then I came home and worked in comedies and shows and musicals … so it never put me out of work, it only changed my focus.'

All the same, *Ilsa Meets Bruce Lee in the Devil's Triangle* was announced and there is even a poster in existence. Thorne reveals that she was to be involved in this harebrained production. 'The idea was that it was a fellow, who had changed his name to Bruce Lee and was equally proficient in martial arts,' she laughs. 'But, for whatever reason, after the *Greta* film came out, and even after *Ilsa, She Wolf of the SS* had a revival in its popularity, the backers in Canada, which is where most of the money came from, got very turned off. So, we were set to go ahead with it and it would have been quite interesting. I had actually taken up some martial arts stuff and I was saying to them, "We need to get back to Don Edmonds, look what happened with the others." Well that raised the budget again and, then, behind the scenes it just never happened. I would have been doing a little bit of everything – including karate – and they would have used stand-ins. But I'm a physical girl anyway, I enjoy sports and all that sort of thing, so it would have been a fun thing to do. If it isn't fun what is the point?'

Nowadays Thorne is a minister who marries people in Las Vegas. However, to this day, no one has ever asked to take their vows whilst Ilsa lords over them. 'I misled someone recently by telling them I married someone as Ilsa,' she laughs. 'They had contacted me because they had found out I was Ilsa and that I could do it, but the ceremony was done in a totally respectful way. I think they just wanted to say that Ilsa married them, but did I wear boots and a costume? No (*laughs*).'

Howard Maurer interview
(Note: Howard Maurer is Thorne's husband and acted as her agent for the Ilsa *films, whilst also playing background roles in each sequel)*

Howard Maurer never set out to become associated with a series of Nazi dominatrix horror flicks but this is exactly what fate had in store for him. 'I was involved with composing music, primarily, and when I met Dyanne she was just about to do the first *Ilsa*,' explains the actor. 'Somehow, I cannot even tell you, but perhaps by osmosis I did wind up acting in the second *Ilsa* with her and I enjoyed it so much I started doing acting lessons. I remember my mom said to me, "We tried to get you to take acting lessons years ago and you refused. So how come you are taking them now?" I told her, "Well, I just wanted to find another profession that I could be out of work in (*laughs*)." Music was starting to slow down at the time, and I started taking the acting lessons and somehow I ended up in quite a few films and TV shows. How I did that I have no idea. It might just be luck, the first time I went looking for an agent I got one, which has always been the hardest part of this game. So I've bounced back and forth between music and acting.'

Not that Maurer has any regrets about performing in the first *Ilsa* sequel and its subsequent follow-ups. 'My impression of these films is that they are fun,' he laughs. 'They are just fun, a big romp. If anybody, and there are some, takes these movies seriously then I think they need help. Every now and then, and more often now than then, I will see a film with pointless violence. Or explicit sexual content for no reason … Yet these go on and on, they play on television, and the *Ilsa* films are nothing compared to some of these. They just made everybody laugh, although my mother didn't find them funny (*laughs*).'

Maurer played a sheik in *Ilsa, Harem Keeper of the Oil Sheiks* and has good memories of Don Edmonds. 'Don was very calm, he was a young fellow then,' he says. 'Don is a great guy, I love him and he's terrific, always has a lot of passion going on. There was one time when Dyanne worked 22 and a half hours, without a break, on *Harem Keeper*. I only found out after the film wrapped. Nobody told me, I wasn't important enough yet, but I can tell you that I would have done some punching if I'd known about it (*laughs*). I tell you what it was, it was fun. I will tell you something else, Don had just gotten a brand new convertible Mercedes, *brand new*, and we were in the desert. We had a sandstorm and his paint job was ruined. It was unbelievable! I had a wonderful time.'

The actor also remembers that the first sequel did fine box office when it was released. 'Right from the beginning it did great. Within a couple of weeks the producers were back at Dyanne negotiating for another one. They never expected what happened to happen. I mean, it was on the front page of *The Washington Post*, it was all over the place, and all these years later I've lost count of how many calls she gets every week. The first film she negotiated herself because she never had an agent and nobody wanted to know about it. When they came at us for the second film, we called some of the agents in Los Angeles and nobody would touch her. So I negotiated it for her. We did very well, and by the time the second one was in the can all these agents that had turned her down started calling. By then it was too late. There was money to be made and we didn't want to know about them. So that is pretty much how it went and it just boggles my mind when we get calls from all over the world. It is a long time and these films still hold up.'

Maurer followed up the first *Ilsa* sequel by playing one of his wife's henchmen in *Ilsa, The Tigress of Siberia*. 'We were in the snow, on horses and I fell on my ass about one hundred times on that film,' laughs the actor. 'Here's what happened, we were on snow that was melting, and as we were shooting, the horses didn't want to do anything. In any event, what I remember most vividly in my mind was the producer asking Dyanne if she could ride and she said, "Yes," because she happens to be a very fine horsewoman. He said, "Well what is going to happen is, and we'll only have one shot at it, you are going to ride out from this camp as it burns down. Now, your two henchmen are very good so I need to know that you can ride with them." I was up with the producer somewhere watching this scene through binoculars and he was very nervous about the shot, because it was the most expensive in the film. I remember that he kept asking me, over and over, if she really could ride a horse (*laughs*). He was a very quiet, almost eloquent, guy. Well I remember that the camp blew up and Dyanne went riding out of there, fast as anything, on the back of a horse, but the two other guys couldn't keep up with her. Well this producer lost his cool and started screaming, "Yes! Yes!" He was excited and he started yelling for her. After it was over we threw a party because it was so good. Well here's the kicker, the director screwed it up, he shot it all wrong and they couldn't match it to anything so it never got used. The director, David Le Fluer, he would be, "So we need to shoot. Well, first we will have some wine and then we will shoot." (*laughs*).'

Regardless of how troubled the third *Ilsa* film was, Maurer and his wife returned to work on *Greta, The Mad Butcher*. 'That was the third one and we had a lot of laughs on it, but I was most impressed with Jess Franco,' says Maurer. 'Impressed really isn't the word, I was spellbound. He directed that film in seven languages simultaneously. He had people that spoke seven languages, including the crew, and he just fired off directions in different languages. It knocked my socks off. We had no idea what anybody else was saying. Not a clue. But Jess did something that just broke me up, we used to go for lunch with him every day. We never waited for a food wagon to come by, we would go and have a proper lunch … crab and wine, it was great (*laughs*). But the thing I'm proudest of when it comes to these films is meeting Dyanne, and that's the truth.' Clearly, the couple that slays together stays together!

HALLOWEEN

Released: 1978
Directed by: John Carpenter
Produced by: Moustapha Akkad, Debra Hill, Irwin Yablans
Written by: John Carpenter, Debra Hill
Cast: Donald Pleasence (Dr Loomis), Jamie Lee Curtis (Laurie Strode), Nancy Keyes (Annie Brackett), P J Soles (Lynda), Charles Cyphers (Sheriff Brackett), Kyle Richards (Lindsey Wallace), Brian Andrews (Tommy Doyle), John Michael Graham (Bob Simms), Nancy Stephens (Marion Chambers), Arthur Malet (Graveyard Keeper), Nick Castle (The Shape/Michael Myers)

In a nutshell: On Halloween night, 1963, ten year old Michael Myers stabs his older sister Judith to death after she has sex with her boyfriend. On 30 October 1978, Myers escapes from incarceration at a mental hospital, steals a car and drives back to Haddonfield, Illinois. Shortly after Myers' escape, a local schoolgirl, the virginal Laurie Strode, swears that she is being followed around by a masked man, but she is the only person that even notices this mysterious figure. Her friends don't believe her and the masked figure seems to come and go at random. However, on Halloween night, Myers begins to stalk and kill the student's friends, slaughtering three of them in violent, random murders, before setting his sights on Laurie herself, who is babysitting two young children. Meanwhile, Doctor Sam Loomis, Myers long-time psychiatrist, works closely with the Haddonfield police, and in particular the town's sheriff, to locate the lunatic.

Prologue: John Carpenter began his career with a short Western, *The Resurrection of Bronco Billy*, 'the story of a student who dreams of being a cowboy'[63], whilst still at film school in California. It won the Academy Award for best short film in 1970. In 1974 Carpenter made his feature length debut with the low budget, but hugely imaginative, sci-fi spoof *Dark Star*, a popular oddity at drive-in cinemas of the time. However, the director's first real break came with the European success of 1976's action masterpiece *Assault on Precinct 13*, which tells of a late-night gang raid on an isolated police station. An exercise in budgetary restraint, the remarkably simplistic story makes for one of the most suspenseful motion pictures in history. This was also the movie that brought Carpenter to the attention of producer Moustapha Akkad and the rest, as they say, is history.

---

63 As detailed in Boulenger, G, *John Carpenter: The Prince of Darkness*, Silman-James Press, California, 1993)

Perhaps the most immediately striking thing about *Halloween* is its stylish use of widescreen cinematography. Nevertheless this was not unique for the horror genre, just unusual for a film of *Halloween*'s low budget. Earlier movies which had shot their action in cinemascope include 1963's *The Haunting* and such Hammer efforts as *Dracula, Prince of Darkness* (1966). These were followed by Italy's Dario Argento, who produced several of his *giallo* thrillers in the scope ratio, including his 1971 debut *The Bird with the Crystal Plumage* and, eventually, his terror classic *Suspiria* (1976). By the time of *Halloween* the trend had caught some fire in Hollywood with blockbusters such as *Jaws*, *The Towering Inferno* (both 1975) and *The Omen* (1976) using the wide 'epic' look to suitably startling (and at times horrifying) effect. Carpenter had also filmed his action shocker *Assault on Precinct 13* in widescreen, giving the low budget feature a polished, 'Hollywood' feel.

Thus, a large part of *Halloween*'s success is undoubtedly down to the camerawork of future Oscar winner Dean Cundy, whose pre-Carpenter work had not really given him the chance to shine (although Matt Cimber gave Cundy the chance to shoot his controverisial shocker *The Witch Who Came From the Sea* in widescreen). For casting, Carpenter brought in the English screen veteran Donald Pleasence, no stranger to horror films having appeared in such Brit-classics as *Death Line* (1972) and *From Beyond the Grave* (1973). Leading lady Jamie Lee Curtis was then an unknown, jobbing actress, with only television work on her CV, whilst co-star P J Soles had made a minor splash thanks to her supporting turn in Brian De Palma's *Carrie* (1976).

Halloween's biggest debt is undoubtedly to Bob Clark's *Black Christmas* (1974), which also used first-person camera angles to represent a psychopath's point of view and which tells of young female students being stalked by a mysterious killer. Clark himself has gone on record as saying that the basic idea for *Halloween* actually came from him.[64] The audio score to *Halloween*, whilst far more effective and memorable than the one heard in Argento's *Deep Red* (1975), sounds similar enough to make comparison between the two soundtracks inescapable.

About: In light of the huge influence that *Halloween* had it is now extremely difficult to look at Carpenter's original film as a stand-alone movie, which is a great shame because in comparison to every one of its rivals (from *Friday the 13th* to *Prom Night*) it is in a class of its own. On account of its 'he's-not-quite-dead-yet' finale alone, whereupon the indestructible Michael Myers keeps rising from the dead, *Halloween* went on to inspire such inferior big studio products as *Fatal Attraction* (1987) and *The Hand That Rocks the Cradle* (1992), both of which shed their A-list ambitions in the final reel and degenerate into slasher movie clichés. However, when *Halloween* came along the stalk and slash genre was still very much in its infancy, with *Black Christmas* receiving little notice and Argento's *Deep Red*, a hybrid between the Italian *giallo* movement and a new level of serial stalker violence, going widely unseen in its dubbed, and shortened,

---

[64] Bob Clark explains: 'John loved *Black Christmas* and he asked me, "Are you ever going to do a sequel to it?" And I said, "John, I won't be doing another horror film if I can help it ... However, if I did, and I have thought about it, it would be a year later. They would have caught the killer but he would be in an asylum, he would escape and he would go back to the college campus and I would call it *Halloween*."' (Waddell, C, *Minds of Fear*, Midnight Marquee, Maryland, 2005)

American release as *The Hatchet Murders*. As a result, Carpenter's movie created a sensation because it did something that few other films in the genre had managed: *Halloween* really was as terrifying as its posters and trailers claimed. Moreover, it didn't feature the level of brutality, or violence-against-women nastiness, which typified previous independent shockers such as *Last House on the Left* and *The Texas Chain Saw Massacre*. In other words, *Halloween* was the sort of horror film that both sexes could enjoy.

Nevertheless, although Carpenter's flick is remarkably tame when compared to the early work of Craven and Hooper, there is still a level of sexism inherent in *Halloween*'s storyline that is difficult to ignore. For instance, although the director should receive due credit for his casting of Jamie Lee Curtis in the lead role (she is far from a typical screen beauty, and her 'girl next door' looks ultimately make her more believable than the numerous busty bombshell scream queens that would follow in her wake), she is held up as a ridiculously wholesome 'good girl' throughout the movie. Unlike her friends, Annie and Lynda, Curtis's Laurie Strode does not have sex, she is too shy to speak to boys and she is never seen smoking dope. However, it is her dire lack of success with the opposite sex that her friends tease her about the most. When, for instance, she briefly glimpses Myers (credited only as The Shape in the end credits) behind a hedge and best pal Annie goes to see if, indeed, there is someone present, she comes back empty handed and taunts 'poor Laurie, scared another one away'. In the rare instance when we hear Laurie swear it is only to say 'shit ... I forgot my chemistry book' and when Annie asks her secret crush to go out on a date with her, the poor girl is mortified and quickly asks her friend to call him and say it was all just a joke. Although Carpenter never spells out that Laurie is a virgin; it is easy to assume that she is and, when her promiscuous friends begin to die at the hand of Myers, there is a definite sexual resonance to their deaths. This can largely be attributed to Carpenter's desire to have the audience become complicit in the actual murders, his camera taking on the killer's point of view (which is masculine) and, therefore, allowing *us* to hold the knife that slashes away at the semi-naked Judith Myers in the movie's shocking opening.[65]

Certainly there can be no denying that the deaths of the actresses in *Halloween* are far more voyeuristic and perverse in nature than the film's solitary on-screen demise of a male. For instance, take the sequence where Myers spies on Annie getting undressed and eventually strangles her (all the while making a loud 'grunting' sound) before finally cutting her throat. During her ordeal, Annie is clad only in her underwear and her long, bare legs kick at the door of her car, which she is locked in. This adds an overwhelming feel of sexual dominance to the set piece (between Myers' grunting and the sight of Annie's legs the perverse symbolism does seem unmistakable). Following this, Myers kills Lynda after she has intercourse with her boyfriend (who is quickly slaughtered too). In the case of Lynda, the masked killer strangles her whilst she is topless, and after staring at her exposed breasts.

Thus, *Halloween*'s young female victims are all killed after the murderer views their nude bodies and at a point when they are in some form of undress. Whilst this could simply be

---

[65] In reference to *Halloween*, feminist critic Carol Clover states: 'That this first-person assaultive gaze is a gendered gaze, figured explicitly or inexplicitly in phallic terms, is also clear. Slasher films draw the equation repeatedly and unequivocally: when men cannot perform sexually, they stare and kill instead.' (*Men Women and Chainsaws*, BFI, London, 1996)

because Carpenter and co-writer Hill wanted the fatalities to occur when each person was at their most vulnerable (much like Janet Leigh's shower death in *Psycho*) it is unmistakable that the build-up to these murders has a sexual tone. Between Myers' grunting and his voyeuristic spying on each woman undressing it does equate the character's murders with a 'sexual release', which ultimately takes the form of bloody violence rather than masturbation or intercourse[66]. As if to assert this theory, Carpenter has the ten year old Myers view his older sister semi-nude and in a post-coital state of relaxation. When the child savages the girl with a knife it appears, for all the world, to be the work of a sexually repressed personality, taking out his longings in the most vile, murderous manner (naturally, when the killer is unmasked and revealed to be a child it is nothing short of horrifying).

In saying all of this, it is difficult to assert that Carpenter lets Laurie live merely because she dresses conservatively and doesn't have an active sex life. However, it is telling that she doesn't take her clothes off on camera, perhaps to maintain the character's air of purity, and that Myers' stalking of her has absolutely no sexual connotations[67]. Furthermore, and this is blatantly obvious, the main differentiation between Laurie and her two friends Annie and Lynda, is down to the fact that Curtis's character has very little overt sexuality and is not visibly functional in that department.

None of this, however, is to say that Carpenter, or indeed Hill, bless their movie with a misogynistic viewpoint (although the director's most famous work is typified by an overriding air of sweaty masculinity, for example: *Assault on Precinct 13*, *Escape from New York*, *The Thing*, *Vampires*), only that their screen killer more than likely holds such a point of view. Although Myers' bright white mask effectively helps to make the character sexless, his spying on naked, young females and apparent confusion when Lynda flashes her boobs at him indicates that his sexuality may be just as confused and repressed as an adult as it was when he was a child, slicing up his sister after she makes love to her boyfriend. Moreover, it is interesting that, at the close of *Halloween*, when Myers has his mask knocked off, revealing him to be nothing more than a normal-looking, twenty-something man, he struggles to get it back on again. In his mask, which as aforementioned makes his features weirdly androgynous, Myers has his identity. Without it he is as ordinary, and masculine, as any other male in his age group. Therefore, what would later become the ultimate cliché of the slasher film (the first person point of view) is used in *Halloween* as a way of allowing the audience to understand the monster's mentality. It is the ultimate difference between Carpenter's skilfully manipulative camera trickery and characterization and the numerous stalk 'n' slash kill orgies that followed in his wake. Yet, by

---

66 Making this link as clear as possible, the director of 1981's slasher spoof *Student Bodies* has his killer (once again the camera takes on the killer's vision) prowl and stalk the girls' locker rooms. Finally, however, he breaks down and begins to masturbate, a 'joke' that makes *explicit* what the genre only really makes *implicit*.

67 Carpenter went back to shoot some new scenes for the television debut of *Halloween* in America. These fresh additions suddenly added in the 'twist' that Myers and Laurie were indeed related. However, this was done to coincide with the cinema release of *Halloween II*, the sequel that developed this rather ridiculous turn of events ... Carpenter himself admits (of the television cut) 'I shot some bullshit connecting stall scenes to pad out the movie to whatever time NBC needed.' (Boulenger, *John Carpenter: The Prince of Darkness*, Silman-James Press, California, 1993)

blurring the line between spectator and conspirator, *Halloween* becomes all the more perverse (and interesting) as proven by the amount that has been written about the movie over the subsequent decades.

Of course, discussing the Myers persona, whose screen time is brief but whose presence is all over the story, remains interesting largely because Carpenter gives us more than just a random, bloodthirsty lunatic to watch. Indeed, rather than being tasteless, blessing his killer with some form of sexual repression/misogyny, and an actual, scary back-story, allows for Myers to be more three dimensional as a character. As opposed to the sequels, which would become more and more supernatural in tone, in the original *Halloween* 'the Shape' is presented to us only as a masked psychopath hungry to claim new victims, and the only hint that he might actually be made of something other than just flesh and blood comes at the very end of the film. The idea of a masked, escaped madman, who has been incarcerated since committing a childhood murder, senselessly killing young women, is decidedly more frightening, perhaps because of its randomness, than a murderer predominantly aiming his wrath at his younger sister. Indeed, the later link between Laurie and Myers, which flourishes in the sequels, doesn't really progress the *Halloween* story, or make much sense. For instance, why would the maniac take so much time stalking and slaughtering Laurie's friends, in *Halloween*, if all that he really wanted was to get to her? Whilst Carpenter cannot be blamed for the Myers sequels that followed 1981's risible *Halloween II*, he has to shoulder some of the responsibility for introducing the unconvincing idea – in the film's first sequel – that Michael Myers, rather than being a random 'bogeyman', is actually stalking his long-lost sister. Ironic as it is, the fact remains that as soon as the Myers-Laurie 'twist' is introduced in the extended, American television version of *Halloween* (now viewable on the film's DVD) the movie loses at least some of what makes it so relentlessly scary: the all-too believable idea of a small town invaded by an emotionless, and motiveless, psychopath.

Yet, in spite of a killer brandishing a large butcher's knife, Carpenter's 'taboo breaking' is largely confined to making a low budget, independent feature that would change Hollywood, kick-off a succession of rip-offs and show the big studios (and independent filmmakers) that less can be more. Ultimately, the road to such low budget wonders as *The Blair Witch Project* (1999) and *Cabin Fever* (2003), movies that sprang from nowhere only to create a huge, marketable buzz, begins with *Halloween*. On-screen, however, Carpenter breaks one long held no-no when Myers kills a dog; an act which indicates that the maestro does not want us to like his killer, instead, he only wants us to fear him and in this first incarnation the character is genuinely chilling. Of course, this is a massive change from the later, more marketable Myers, who would spawn collectible figures and Halloween costumes for kids.

Although this critique has singled out the Myers character and his, much hinted at, repressed sexuality, it should be noted that *Halloween* is far from the misogynistic gore-fest that many other horror releases of the time were. Certainly, in comparison to other fare from 1978, such as the amateurish bloodbath *The Toolbox Murders* and the vulgar rape/revenge title *I Spit on Your Grave*, it is easy to see why *Halloween* was such a phenomenon. Unlike these other titles, which would make for terrible date movies (both pictures feature rape, *The Toolbox Murders* also has a nude, masturbating woman being nail-gunned by a home invader), Carpenter's film at least has a strong female heroine and believable screen teenagers. In terms of personalities, it is really Curtis, Keyes and Soles who win out, with *Halloween* giving each young actress a chance to shine[68]. As far as bringing screen teenagers to life, Carpenter's film is one of the best and treats its young cast to far better dialogue than the horror genre generally offered at the time.

As with *Black Christmas* and *The Texas Chain Saw Massacre* before it, *Halloween* benefits from a tremendous cast, from the main players right down to the supporting cast. Of course, Jamie Lee Curtis pulls off Laurie Strode's doe-eyed innocence and vulnerability perfectly but she is complimented by the flirtatious P J Soles and the near-forgotten Nancy Keyes. Taking top billing is Donald Pleasence, although his screen time is minimal (ironically by the time of *Halloween II*, where Curtis had become the bigger star, the two would swap roles, with Pleasence moving into the series' lead). Nevertheless, the British actor does a tremendous job as Loomis and few can forget his now-classic monologue whereby he concludes, to Charles Cyphers' Sheriff Bracket, 'I spent eight years trying to reach him, and then another seven trying to keep him locked up because I realised that what was living behind that boy's eyes was purely and simply … evil.' Throughout his career Carpenter, even with his weakest work, had made a point of utilizing a first class, ensemble cast, and, in this regard, *Halloween* is up there with the best of the director's output.

Finally, comment must be made on the Carpenter/Cundy relationship, which began with *Halloween* and which would continue with such classics as *The Fog* (1980) and *The Thing* (1982). Despite a low budget, the two create an electrifying opening, filmed using steadicam, whilst the director uses the widescreen composition to build up some incredibly effective scares. The moment where Laurie (in the foreground) recovers from her battle with the 'dead' Myers, just as he rises (in the background) is composed so brilliantly, and lit with such care, that it takes *Halloween* into an area of art that few horror pictures ever get a sniff at. Even if Fellini or Welles had embarked on a scary movie, one hesitates to say that it would be as good as *Halloween*. All these years later, Carpenter's seminal slasher picture really is still *that good*.

What happened next? As with any hit independent feature film, the majors quickly got into the act. Paramount Pictures tried to buy up the distribution rights to another Jamie Lee Curtis stalker opus, Paul Lynch's awful 1980 effort *Prom Night*[69], but when that failed they picked up Sean Cunningham's low budget *Friday the 13th*. With that, the slasher boom was underway. Unlike *Halloween*, *Friday the 13th* was a lot more liberal with its use of gore and nudity. Although it was critically panned, *Friday the 13th* was the second top grossing movie of the 1980 summer season[70] and, despite its reputation for being explicitly bloody, the film now looks remarkably quaint. It may not be as expertly directed, or well told, as *Halloween* but *Friday the 13th* does benefit from some great jumps, a decent cast (including Kevin Bacon in one of his earliest roles) and, thanks to its wilderness setting, a genuine feeling of claustrophobia and alienation. What

---

68 Critic Kim Newman rightly labels *Halloween*'s three actresses as 'among the most convincing teens in the cinema' (*Nightmare Movies*, Bloomsbury, London, 1988)

69 As documented in 2006's documentary *Going to Pieces: The Rise and Fall of the Slasher Film*.

70 As noted in Morse, L A, *Video Trash and Treasures*, HarperCollins, 1989)

followed, however, is another story altogether ...

The general thinking of many filmmakers must have been that if *Halloween* had been a hit, and *Friday the 13th* had upped Carpenter's level of violence and also smashed the box office then, surely, going even further in the sex and splatter stakes would guarantee bigger grosses. The result was a series of boring, cynical, misogynistic clunkers, among them *The Prowler* (1981), *The Mutilator* and *Pieces* (both 1983), which consist of long, plodding sections of dialogue enlivened only by the odd moment of gory excess (the nastiest of which is directed towards women). Although too badly made to be really offensive, 1983's *Pieces* actually stoops low enough to have a topless female urinate in fear prior to being sliced in half. Even the more interesting variants on the theme (such as 1981's atmospheric *My Bloody Valentine*, the quirky *April Fool's Day* – both of which were remade in 2008 - and the entertainingly hokey *Silent Night, Deadly Night* from 1984) can only do so much within the confines of a 'madman on the loose' script. The slasher genre finally regained the quality of *Halloween* when, in 1996, Wes Craven unleashed *Scream*, a smart, scary and well-acted update on the familiar formula which ushered in a new era of sub-par films, namely *I Know What You Did Last Summer* (1997), *Urban Legend* (1998) and the abysmal spoof *Scary Movie* (2000) and several, equally abysmal sequels.

The *Halloween* series itself fared little better than most of its rip-offs. *Halloween II* reunited the producers as well as Pleasence and Curtis and cinematographer Cundy. Directed by Rick Rosenthal (and an uncredited Carpenter who added in extra gore effects) the movie is a bit of a mess, but benefits from strong continuity with the first film and a few moments of well-realised suspense. The Myers-less *Halloween III: Season of the Witch* (1982) is a great diversion from the slasher story and one of the most underrated horror pictures of its decade. 1988's *Halloween 4: The Return of Michael Myers* does what it says on the box but, without any of the original cast or crew returning (apart from Pleasence and producer Moustapha Akkad), it lacks Carpenter's touch. *Halloween 5: The Revenge of Michael Myers* is pretty bad, some outstanding cinematography excepted, and 1995's nonsensical *Halloween: The Curse of Michael Myers* is a new low for any commercial horror feature. The returning Jamie Lee Curtis, and a bigger budget, enabled 1998's *Halloween: H20* to be the best of the sequels and the only one to really honour the brilliance of the original. Sadly, 2002's abysmal *Halloween Resurrection* made such a mess of things that the franchise has had to start all over again, with a Rob Zombie-directed *Halloween* remake (2007).

Of *Halloween*'s alumni, director Carpenter has had an uneven career, although even his failures boast dazzling widescreen photography and a stylish touch. The best of his post-*Halloween* work includes *The Fog, Escape from New York, The Thing, Christine* (1983), *Big Trouble in Little China* (1986) and the underrated *Escape from LA* (1996). Producer Akkad went on to milk his cash cow until the day he died during a 2005 terrorist attack in Amman, Jordan. His colleague Irwin Yablans would produce such *Halloween* variants as the enjoyable backwoods opus *Tourist Trap* (1979), *Fade to Black* (1980) and the Linda Blair farce *Hell Night* (1981). Debra Hill, who passed away in March 2005, would work alongside Carpenter on *The Fog* and *Escape from New York*, and also produce David Cronenberg's *The Dead Zone* (1983) and Terry Gilliam's *The Fisher King* (1991). Dean Cundy would be nominated for an Academy Award in the cinematography category for his work on 1988's *Who Framed Roger Rabbit*, whilst his other credits behind the camera include *Jurassic Park* (1993) and *Apollo 13* (1995). Of the film's stars, Pleasence would continue in the Doctor Loomis role until his death in 1995, whilst also appearing in Carpenter's *Escape from New York* and the disappointing *Prince of Darkness* (1987). Jamie Lee Curtis would be launched into the A-list courtesy of John Landis who cast her in his excellent comedy *Trading Places* (1983). She followed this up with leading roles in the blockbusters *A Fish Called Wanda* (1988), *My Girl* (1991) and *True Lies* (1994). Of her co-stars, only P J Soles would briefly crack the mainstream, winning prominent roles in the hits *Private Benjamin* (1980) and *Stripes* (1981) before quietly disappearing. Michael Myers himself, Nick Castle, would go on to success as a director, helming such projects as *The Last Starfighter* (1984), *The Boy Who Could Fly* (1986) and *Dennis the Menace* (1993).

PJ Soles interview

Supporting Jamie Lee Curtis in *Halloween*, PJ Soles had already started to make a name for herself in the fear film thanks to her unforgettable turn as Norma Watson in Brian De Palma's *Carrie*. Suffice to say, the actress could not have been any more enthusiastic about her role in *Halloween* and looks back on the film with fond memories. '*Halloween* was great because there was no blood or anything,' begins Soles. 'It was like *Psycho* with the shower scene where, as we've all been told a thousand times, you don't see the knife or anything.' Then, of course, *Halloween* spawned a series of sequels which did not skimp on the gore. 'I know, and that is why I could not watch the other films,' continues the actress. 'Plus there was the fact that I wasn't in them of course, but the beauty in the original was the music and the thrills … but without having the actual gore, you know?'

Another thing that the *Halloween* sequels suffered from was a series of less talented filmmakers behind the camera. Despite its low budget origins Carpenter's thrilling original remains most notable for its director's technical expertise and his use of cinemascope to produce a number of high-tension shock sequences. 'I remember that the steadicam was very impressive,' recalls Soles. 'That was constantly around the three of us (Soles, Curtis and Keyes), especially when we were walking down the street, coming out of the school yard … just most of the time when the three of us were walking together. Even when I was coming out of the van and going into the house, it was all steadicam because that was the trend. We were just so amazed over how it worked, it was so weird and that was pretty cool. But in terms of Cinemascope and all of that, up until I saw the film at the very first cast and crew screening I had no idea. John was the wizard music writer/composer and, to me, that was 50% of the movie. Those simple notes were so perfect. When you were working with him you really did get the impression of working with this wonder boy genius. He really had that vibe, you know? It was so great, he was such an artist and so gentle.'

This 'gentle' genre filmmaker was also, according to Soles, a very different personality from De Palma. 'The only way to compare them is to say that they both clearly knew their objective and had a vision,' says the actress. 'They both worked hard to carry that out and they were both very creative. But as people they were completely different. I don't know about age or anything like that, but I think they had both cut around about the same number of movies before each of these films: *Carrie* and *Halloween*. Brian is completely silent and sits on his director's chair with a smirk of delight, watching actors play out their parts with this demonic glee on his face, and he doesn't usually say anything afterwards such as, "That was good," or anything. It was just, "Cut" and then some muttering so you felt quite distant from him. But John was very collaborative and very good with you. Right after we shot our scenes he would give you immediate feedback and tell you if he wanted anything changed. John would usually only do one or two takes but Brian liked to run it up to about eight takes but then Brian had a bigger budget on *Carrie*. We are comparing $1 million to $300,000, which is impossible to comprehend nowadays.'

Despite the success of *Carrie*, which also helped to launch a young John Travolta into stardom, Soles says that she is unsure if she got her role in *Halloween* because of the De Palma picture. Indeed, she auditioned for the Carpenter movie. 'I did an audition, however, I have heard that John Carpenter has said that after he saw *Carrie* he wrote the part of Lynda with me in mind. I am very flattered by that but he certainly didn't tell me this at the audition. Although after I read the scene he did tell me that I had the part if I wanted it, which is really stunning, you never usually get that ... Usually you have to wait weeks and keep calling your agent. But he actually told me on the day and said, "You're the only one that says 'totally' the right way." To this day I don't see how anybody could have read it differently but I'm glad. I also got to stick around and help him pick out the guy that would play my boyfriend so that was fun.'

Although Soles shares no screen time with Donald Pleasence in *Halloween*, the actress remains thankful for at least having had the chance to socialise with the late British performer, however briefly. 'I did get to speak to Donald, in fact we usually had lunch together,' she says. 'It was such a short shooting schedule, like 21 days, and they had everyone come to the set every day because they never knew when they would finish one scene and move onto the next. So we all hung out together all the time and, some days, you wouldn't necessarily be working together but you would be watching scenes unfold and he, for the most part, probably just thought that we were three giggling girls ... sitting there eating our lunch, probably just eating salad or something (*laughs*). He didn't have much dialogue with us but I remember reading bits here and there and we didn't really know that much about him. Now of course I know he did so much before *Halloween* and we could have asked him so many questions. If only we had IMDb back then (*laughs*). Unfortunately we didn't know that much about him except that he was this weird guy from England ...'

In *Halloween* Soles is the only female cast member asked to bare her breasts, a fate that she had avoided in *Carrie*, where almost every other on-screen actress strips during De Palma's iconic title sequence. 'It is funny because in *Carrie*, with the opening shot in the shower, that was my first movie and I was the only one that kept my towel on,' laughs Soles. 'It was because I knew my parents would be watching and I wasn't quite ready. Nancy Allen was like, "Wow, I love Brian DePalma, I'm going to show him everything," and I think Amy Irving was of the same mind but I was just thinking, "Oh this is creepy." So I think I stood out because I had the towel on and the red baseball cap and I went for more of a tomboy look. But in *Halloween* when it came time to shoot that scene, John said, "You know we'd like to show something," although he was more uncomfortable asking me. I just said, "Well okay I'll think of something," because he didn't really know what he wanted. I think maybe he just wanted a little wrestling around or something before I tell my boyfriend to go and get a beer. But as it turned out we came up with the idea of me pulling the sheets down and flashing him. That seemed to work because the biggest point of that scene was that the Shape had come up the stairs and I was unable to communicate with him. So I was trying to do anything to get him to talk to me.'

The scene in which Soles reveals her breasts has become well-known enough to warrant an in-joke in Wes Craven's genre send-up *Scream* ('I thought that was funny' admits Soles), however the actress is then killed whilst in a state of semi-undress. Asked about whether or not she felt her death scene in *Halloween* was misogynistic Soles says that she did speak to Carpenter about her demise during the filming and insisted on covering up. 'I think that we talked about it, and I told John that I would feel a little more comfortable if I could put my shirt on when I was killed, but maybe leave it open. Originally he wanted me to just slip out of the bed topless and talk on the phone,' she adds. 'But, you know, I don't think it was gratuitous because I had just been in bed with my boyfriend and in all of the rehearsals I always had my bath robe on which is why I see so many foreign posters of me being strangled but with my bath robe on. I guess they took those shots and someone got them (*laughs*)! So, you know … it was okay.' Of course, some academic readings of *Halloween* have indicated a sexist sub-text in the movie, with only the virginal Jamie Lee Curtis going untouched whilst, by contrast, her sexually active friends are slaughtered. 'I guess that will always be a topic of discussion but I don't think that John intended that,' claims Soles. 'I think that we were just easy targets, the girls were picked off during delicate moments (*laughs*) but I don't think there is any underlying thing … no huge psychological theory that you can ascribe.'

Soles also recalls the first time she got to see the completed slasher movie on the big screen. 'It was a cast and crew screening. I don't remember where they showed it but I remember it was one of the shortest films I had ever seen. I thought, "Wow, that was quick!" I just loved the music and the very beginning. I loved the titles with the pumpkin, I thought that was brilliant. Everything that John and Debra Hill did was so simple and yet so perfect, it was the sign of a true artist. Like when you write a hit song it is usually the simple ones that turn out to be hits and I thought it was the same with this, it was just really cool. Then watching the movie unfold … of course Donald Pleasence – he just held it all together with that stare and those big egg eyes (*laughs*), that was creepier than Michael Myers! I was impressed and very excited. I thought it was a very cool movie.'

More recently, the actress had the chance to look back at the entire Michael Myers franchise when she narrated the documentary *Halloween: 25 Years of Terror*. 'Doing that was really, really special,' she states. 'I had never narrated before but I found that I got into the right persona. I am constantly amazed about how this has grown and grown and moved into being this huge phenomenon. Whenever I have gone to a convention the fans line up to take pictures. They are just always so nice and have such affection, especially for the first one. They always say, "You know after the first one they tried to make it work and blah, blah, blah but you guys were in the best one." So I have a lot of pride in that.'

Amazingly, Soles retained her youthful looks long enough to play teenagers right up until her late twenties. Not just in *Carrie* and *Halloween* but also in the cult classic *Rock 'n' Roll High School* (1979). 'I did *Carrie* when I was 25, *Halloween* when I was 27 and *Rock 'n' Roll High School* when I was 28,' laughs the actress. 'I remember thinking, "Wow, this has to be my last teenaged role," (*laughs*). It wasn't difficult to play a teen because my father is from Rotterdam, Holland and has a youthful face so I have good, young Dutch genes I guess (*laughs*). Maybe I looked younger. I was born in Germany but I grew up in Morocco and Venezuela and I went to high school in Brussels so I never got to have the American experience. There were a couple of Americans in my international school but getting to play these parts, for me, was being able to finally be the American teenager that I always wanted to be. As a child I ordered all my clothes from the Sears catalogue and I didn't get to move to the US until I was 18, where I went to college and I lived in New York City and that was a chance to be the person that I always thought I should have been because my mom was back in New Jersey.'

Following *Rock 'n' Roll High School* the actress finally called it quits on playing characters ten years her junior and moved onto more mature parts in the likes of *Private Benjamin* and *Stripes*. 'I did feel after doing *Rock 'n' Roll High School* that I probably couldn't fake it any longer,' laughs the actress. 'The character of Riff (Randell) in *Rock 'n' Roll High School* had so much energy and was so youthful. But everyone else on that movie was in their mid-twenties. Nowadays they tend to cast people that are a lot closer to the actual character's age. Then again, kids are a lot more mature nowadays, there is more media and they are more interview savvy. People are exposed to films 24/7. Now, when I watch "candid" interviews on VH1 or *The Tonight Show* and they stop people on the street nobody is shy or nervous anymore. They are familiar with movie cameras and the media. I would say that it was *Carrie* that got me noticed and if you were one of the teens in *Carrie* then everybody wanted to see you at the next round of casting auditions. I got a couple of TV shows and guest appearances because of *Carrie*, but *Halloween* certainly enabled me to audition for *Rock 'n' Roll High School* because that was pretty stiff competition. The last four girls that were considered for Riff, I think Rosanna Arquette was one of them so you were really neck and neck. It was not easy.'

After the twin hits of *Stripes* and *Private Benjamin* Soles disappeared from the A-list but the performer admits that this was entirely her own choosing. 'I had a family, I had been married to Dennis Quaid and then we got separated and went through a divorce and I met the pilot that had flown in the movie *The Right Stuff*,' she says. 'He always said to me, "If you ever get divorced from this guy, give me a call and I'll take you for a P51 Mustang ride." I thought, "Okay," and we just sparked and we got married and now my son is in the Coast Guards and my daughter is about to start college but during the time when they were younger – my son was born in 1983 – they weren't really making a big deal out of actresses who got married and had kids. There was no nursery and no "Bring the baby to the set and we'll help you to take care of it," instead it was a secret and you kind of went about your business. I found it really hard to go away and do a movie for three months. I did *Sweet Dreams* and I had to fly to Virginia in the middle of nursing but I just thought, "Well okay I'll leave my son at home for three days with my husband," and, boy, I didn't realise that when you are nursing you can't leave the baby at home. It worked for the part though. I had to keep telling Ed Harris, "Don't touch my chest. It is like a rock (*laughs*)."'

John Carpenter & Irwin Yablans interview

'I think it is immortal. It will last forever and it is almost as if they have a responsibility to keep the quality going and to make sure the series lives on.' Clearly, Irwin Yablans, the man who served as an executive producer on the original *Halloween* and its first two sequels, is glad to see the legacy of John Carpenter's original slasher classic live on. 'I have very little say in the creative aspect of it any longer,' he admits. 'But my whole theory from the very beginning was the purity of the horror ... my inspiration on *Halloween* was people like Hitchcock and I'm old enough to remember the radio, listening to shows on that before television came along. So the whole idea was the suspense, keeping people off balance and the horror of the mind, if you will. That is still where I like to go and I prefer that to visual mayhem. I like to see as little as possible.'

John Carpenter agrees. 'I'd say the first modern horror film is *Psycho*. That took horror out of the gothic and the supernatural and showed us true horror in a modern setting,' he says. 'There's a lot of intelligence in *Psycho* and I'd say that's the start of modern horror and we were all influenced by that. These other (slasher) movies were just Xeroxes. They took the formula and just copied it.' All the same, despite not being involved with the *Halloween* series since part three ('I like that film a lot and I liked it at the time' he says) Carpenter admits that he was once interested in returning to the Michael Myers legacy. 'At one point there was this bidding war between New Line and Miramax for the rights to the *Halloween* sequels and I had the idea of sending him (Michael Myers) into space,' reflects the filmmaker. 'It was just as something that you could do to change the series. Unfortunately, then *Jason X* came along and now I don't think we can do that ... But I have no idea about these films anymore. I just don't really know what they are doing with them. They keep asking me to work on the next sequel but it doesn't interest me.' (note: *this interview took place before the Rob Zombie remake*).

In the opinion of Yablans, the *Halloween* series is unlikely to stop any time soon. The reason being simple: money. 'I think that there will be as many instalments as are profitable because that, ultimately, is the business of making movies,' he laughs. 'If they are profitable and people still come to see them then it is almost a self-fulfilling engine. Especially now, now it is like an institution and people are demanding another one, especially the hardcore fans. The hardcore fans alone will guarantee success.' Nevertheless, the producer admits that when the *Halloween* rip-offs began to be unleashed back in the late seventies he was less than impressed. '*Halloween* is the original and the blueprint upon which all of those others are measured,' he says. 'Remember that those others are all copies. Even I was amazed at the number of imitators. I almost didn't want to make a sequel because I thought other people had done it. We made the sequel out of self-defence because everyone was stealing from us frame for frame. There was a movie called *Terror Train* that literally dissected our film! They took our star – Jamie Lee Curtis – and re-shot *Halloween* frame for frame! So as a matter of self-defence we had to make the sequel.'

Unsurprisingly, then, Yablans still holds up *Halloween* as a career highlight. 'I'm especially proud of *Halloween* and everything else pales by comparison,' he says. 'There was a huge amount of freshness and passion that the first one was created with and also the innocence that we approached it with. We had no money and no support and the industry didn't even know we existed. We made it out of our back pockets and I distributed it myself, with very little help and against all odds. It is quite a story and that was a holy grail for me. Nothing ever approaches that. When the audience responded to that first one they – and we – knew something that the establishment, the critics and the powers that be didn't know. We taught them a few things and as a result the industry was changed.'

TABOO BREAKERS

However, *Halloween* has been accused, at least in terms of its soundtrack, of taking its cue from Dario Argento's twin terror masterworks of *Deep Red* and *Suspiria*. Carpenter denies any link between his slasher classic and Argento's Italian shockers. 'There was no overt influence, except perhaps in my unconscious,' he claims. 'I don't think they had any influence at all ... But *Suspiria* was very inventive and has one of my favourite scores of all time. It has sitars and voices and it's very strange stuff, very impressive ...'

It is commonly said that there are two taboos which should not be broken on screen. One is the killing of a child and the other is the killing of an animal, but Carpenter has done both: a child being shot in *Assault on Precinct 13* and a dog being strangled by Michael Myers in *Halloween*. Perhaps this is what makes the director's early works so unnerving. There is a feeling that anything goes (and this is especially true in *Halloween* when we see that the opening murder is committed by a child!). 'Yeah I've done both,' replies Carpenter. 'It is obviously very shocking for the audience *(laughs)*. I think killing the child was a lot more shocking than killing the animal though. However, I remember a couple of movies that also had kids being killed – *The Lord of the Flies*, the original black and white version, did that – and I thought it was very good. And more recently there was *Battle Royale*. That had kids killing each other and it was done very well, it was shocking. So you can still see that being done on screen.'

A lot of horror directors tend to be forever trapped within the genre, but after *Halloween* Carpenter managed to make movies such as *Elvis*, *Escape from New York* and *Starman* (which came directly after *The Thing*). Looking back, the filmmaker admits that he was fortunate to be able to escape having to make the same kind of thing over and over again. 'With *Starman* I just got lucky, it was offered to me by Columbia/Tri-Star at the time. They approached me, and wanted me to direct it. I didn't have to search for that movie. But when you make a successful horror film you get generalised pretty fast. One of the most famous horror directors was James Whale, who did *Frankenstein*, *The Bride of Frankenstein* and *The Invisible Man*. He was a terrific director, and he did other films but they were never as successful as the horror films he made.'

CANNIBAL HOLOCAUST

Released: 1980
Directed by: Ruggero Deodato
Produced by: Franco Di Nunzio, Franco Palaggi
Written by: Gianfranco Clerici
Cast: Robert Kerman (Professor Harold Monroe), Carl Gabriel Yorke (Alan Yates), Francesca Ciardi (Faye Daniels), Perry Pirkanen (Jack Anders), Luca Barbareschi (Mark Tomasso), Ricardo Fuentes (Felipe Ocanya), Salvatore Basile (Chaco), Paolo Paoloni (Chief NY Executive), Lionello Pio Di Savoia (Asst TV Executive), Luigina Rocchi (Lady TV Executive)

In a nutshell: A leading expert in the field of anthropology, Professor Harold Monroe, is sent from New York to the Amazon in order to find out what became of four American documentary filmmakers and their guide. The award winning crew had gone out in search of a genuine cannibal tribe, called the Yamamomos, but then failed to return to the States. Once in the Amazon, Monroe is accompanied by two local guides as he goes in search of the Yamamomo village. After his small group intervenes in a fight between the Yamamomos and a rival pack of Indians he manages to gain their trust, although the group remains very wary. Finally, Monroe discovers that the cannibal clan has kept the American documentary team's film cans as part of a ghastly shrine that encompasses the crew's rotting, skeletal remains. Once he has returned to New York, Monroe and some television executives go about investigating the footage and discover that the Americans created havoc in the jungle, dishing out rape and genocide, before they finally met their doom at the hands of the very natives that they intended to exploit ...

Prologue: Umberto Lenzi's 1972 venture *The Man from Deep River* (aka *Deep River Savages*) is rightly regarded as representing the beginnings of the Italian cannibal movie cycle, even if cannibalism features only briefly in the actual plot. Set in the exotic jungles of Thailand, the

TABOO BREAKERS

film features a British man (played by Ivan Rassimov) who falls foul of a primitive tribe. The picture's alien surroundings, coupled with scenes of genuine animal butchery and explicit (but faked) gore essentially laid down the ground rules for future titles in the genre. Lenzi passed on directing a follow-up to *The Man from Deep River* and the job went to Ruggero Deodato, a protégé of Roberto Rossellini. The result was 1977's *The Last Cannibal World* (aka *Jungle Holocaust*), which finds Italian actor Massimo Foschi captured by a flesh-eating tribe after he is left stranded in the Malaysian rainforest following a plane crash.

After *The Last Cannibal World* Deodato would go on to make a love story (1978's *Last Feelings*) and cash-in on the success of *Airport* with 1979's *The Concorde Affair*. Following these two subdued, mainstream efforts, he would return to the jungle with *Cannibal Holocaust*, casting veteran New York porn actor Robert Kerman (aka Robert Bolla) in the lead role. At the time, Kerman had been in such popular adult titles as *Joy* (1977) and *Debbie Does Dallas*, although *Cannibal Holocaust* marked his first time in the lead role of a 'legitimate' movie[71]. As at least one critic has noted, the Italian cannibal genre is 'one of those rare instances where an Italian cycle is not indebted to some Hollywood box office success. If anything, it pays its dues to that other Italian cinematic tradition: the mondo film.'[72] Certainly, the movement's reliance on fabricated realities and documentary style animal slaughter does lend itself to the stomach churning trend that began with *Mondo Cane* (1962) although the bewigged, barbaric, primitive screen savages which are seen in *Cannibal Holocaust* are almost entirely of the genre's own creation. Another possible influence on Deodato's film could be the more self-reflective *The Wild Eye* (1967).

Prior to *Cannibal Holocaust* came another couple of Italian flesh-munching epics, namely Joe D'Amato's wonderfully titled *Emmanuelle and the Last Cannibals* and 1978's *Prisoner of the Cannibal God* (aka *Mountain of the Cannibal God*), a relatively big budget offering directed by Sergio Martino, which starred such marquee names as Ursula Andress and Stacy Keach. This was about as prestigious as the genre would get, although it remains a strange sight indeed to see Andress and Keach appear in a film that features simulated bestiality, a healthy dose of animal cruelty and a native having his penis cut off. Furthermore, very much in the Deodato/Lenzi tradition, Martino highlights the 'wild' jungle from the start of his movie. Thus, as the titles roll a series of gritty animal vs animal fights take place (sadly, in each instance the 'weaker' creature has clearly been flung from off-set into the mouth of the more dominant species, hence, a tortoise ends up flying into the jaws of a crocodile and so on).

Nevertheless, with higher than usual production values, *Prisoner of the Cannibal God* certainly indicates that the trend for these movies was catching fire with audiences and impressing financiers enough to want more of them. As such, at the point of *Cannibal Holocaust* the genre began to spawn rip-offs from other countries. For instance, an Indonesian oddity called *Savage Terror* popped up in 1979, once again featuring animal violence and a story of

---

71 Nevertheless, bearing witness to the movie's animal cruelty, Kerman would be more horrified by *Cannibal Holocaust* than any of his adult work and ended up cursing the movie. 'It says something when a director can drive an actor who's been desensitised from years in the sex industry to prayers of destruction. The stench of Deodato's immorality must have been overwhelming,' writes Landis and Clifford (*Sleazoid Express*, Fireside Books, New York, 2002)

72 As noted in *Killing for Culture* (Kerekes and Slater, Creation Books, London, 1994)

Westerners being captured by a stone-age tribe. Never one to miss out on a cheap cash-in, Spain's Jess Franco churned out *Cannibals* in 1979, although, as with *Emmanuelle and the Last Cannibals*, this offering avoids the temptation to kill any live animals on camera. Obviously a new spin on the 'civilized man, or woman, meets backwards, flesh-hungry tribe' was needed and *Cannibal Holocaust* actually did something original within its narrative: a lengthy showcase of *cinema verité* that has kept the movie infamous to this very day.

About: By the time *Cannibal Holocaust* arrived, the genre that Lenzi and Deodato had innovated was already beginning to seem blasé. Joe D'Amato's ridiculous *Emmanuelle and the Last Cannibals*, which starred perennial exploitation sex siren Laura Gemser, played out a softcore jungle romp, albeit with its fair share of gore and misogyny. Although the film is largely uninspired, even taking a scene where natives line up to copulate with a tribal widow from *The Man from Deep River*, it does seem to have had some kind of influence on the making of *Cannibal Holocaust*. Certainly, D'Amato's film pillages the use of a pre-title disclaimer ('This is a true story as reported by Jennifer O'Sullivan') from the cannibal epics that preceded it, but it is the movie's opening, which pans around the crowded streets of New York, that seems to have at least carried some inspiration for Deodato. By visually comparing the modernism of the Big Apple with the primitive way of life in the South American rainforest, D'Amato invites the viewer to conclude which 'jungle' is the more fierce ... an idea that Deodato certainly toys with in *Cannibal Holocaust* (and which Lenzi would make more explicit in his 1981 effort *Cannibal Ferox*). Indeed, the immediate openings of both *Emmanuelle and the Last Cannibals* and *Cannibal Holocaust* are extremely similar - indicating that even at this early stage the genre was beginning to run out of ideas.

In a sense, *Cannibal Holocaust* is the most frustrating film discussed within this book; simply because it has all the trappings of a very effective low budget shocker and yet manages to throw its potential to the wayside relatively early on. A competent filmmaker, Deodato nevertheless falls back on such shock tactics as graphic sexual torture and real animal slaughter to get a rise from his audience and it is difficult to admire a movie that uses such blatantly obvious nastiness to grab the viewers' attention. With *The Last Cannibal World*, Deodato proved that he could create a genuinely compelling atmosphere of alienation, trepidation and suspense, all within an environment that is as foreign to the viewer as it is atmospheric and scenic. This feeling, to some extent, is imported through to *Cannibal Holocaust*, and our first glimpse of the film's jungle setting is wonderful, with monkeys swinging from the trees and a cacophony of bird sounds, bright sunshine, and vast rainforest immediately disconcerting the viewer and the movie's actors. It is a very easy picture to get lost in, which makes it all the more annoying when the entire thing finally becomes a total mess, a complete car wreck of a movie that makes little sense, has conflicting morals and seems intent on stretching the viewer's acceptance of graphic violence to breaking point. Yet, even in spite of the film's unmistakable clumsiness, here is a feature that remains acclaimed in many quarters[73], a bizarre state of affairs when *Cannibal Holocaust* represents the sort of right-wing fantasy that every liberal critic should be thoroughly

---

73 For instance, Kim Newman dubs it as being 'very impressive' in his *Nightmare Movies* (Bloomsbury, London, 1988).

appalled by.

First of all, let us start at the end of *Cannibal Holocaust*. After Deodato's fictional film crew has been revealed to the audience, through the recovered footage that has been salvaged by Robert Kerman's Harold Monroe character, and displayed in all their obnoxious glory, we are rewarded with a pay-off line. Kerman, having endured the sight of the documentary team slaughtering the natives, raping women and then being captured and devoured, leaves the television studio that was going to screen their material and utters the line, 'I wonder who the real cannibals are?' The problem here is that for us to accept the American men (the movie's sole female character, Faye, largely keeps her distance from the violence) as being 'worse' than the natives we would have to be given sympathetic tribesmen to rally behind. However, from the very start of *Cannibal Holocaust* we are left in no doubt that the movie's fictional jungle dwellers are a vicious, misanthropic bunch, capable of the most heinous acts of brutality in their own right.

For example, the very first act of human-on-human violence that Deodato depicts is a 'tribal punishment for adultery' in which a woman is raped with a giant stone dildo and then bludgeoned to death with a rock. The sequence goes on for far too long, drawing its apparent obsession with female distress out to ridiculous proportions, and yet this is only the tip of the iceberg. Later in the movie we see a pregnant native delivering her newborn. The baby is then buried in mud (without any explanation) and then the woman is beaten to death (again without any explanation). As the Americans film this act, some of the local Indian women 'shoo' them away, perhaps indicating that this ritual should remain private, but the revolting nature of the scene means that it is impossible to relate to anyone on the screen.

Certainly, the American documentary team, with the exception of Faye, is dislikeable, cocky and prone to acts of horrible savagery. However, *Cannibal Holocaust*'s most recognisable image, the notorious sight of a woman impaled on a pole, is done at the hands of the natives … the very people that we are, presumably, supposed to view as the victims of the 'invading' white people. Thus, if Deodato wanted to make us ponder upon whom the 'real cannibals' are (and the literal answer to this is obvious seeing as how the Americans never eat human flesh – 'I wonder who the real savages are?' would have made more sense) he really needed the narrative to take on a different standpoint. What would have made *Cannibal Holocaust* a much more logical film is if the American documentary team was seen to attack a group of people who live in peace with each other and with nature. It is this set-up that makes the climax of Roland Joffe's similarly jungle-set *The Mission* (1986) so much more powerful than anything *Cannibal Holocaust* can dream of conjuring up. Indeed, it is by depicting the natives as a group of barbaric half-wits that the movie ultimately falls prey to the criticism of racism, a thoroughly conservative impression of what the poor, un-modernised 'third world' is all about: rape, savagery, cannibalism, hunting monkeys with blow darts … it's all here folks, step right up and pay your entrance fee. In this sense, *Cannibal Holocaust* is nothing more than a tacky carnival attraction, with the geek show animal cruelty merely completing the equation.

Make no mistake about it; this is the biggest failing of the film. We see a violent group of filmmakers enter into a foreign environment and attempt to take control over those people that they view as being 'savages'. Yet, the difficulty here is that Deodato shows his native men and women as being exactly that, engaged in tribal wars, committing rape, burying babies in mud, impaling people on poles … it is, ultimately, hard to feel that these people should be left

Ferra

NOTHING SO
APPALLING
IN THE
ANNALS
OF
HORROR!
BLOOD FEAST

GIT BACK JACK—GIVE HIM NO JIVE...
HE IS THE BAAAD'EST CAT IN '75
R RESTRICTED
A MATT CIMBER PRODUCTION
THE CANDY TANGERINE MAN
STARRING TOM HANKERSON and introducing JOHN DANIELS as "THE BARON"
FEATURING THE ACTUAL HOOKERS and BLADES of the SUNSET STRIP—HOLLYWOOD
WRITTEN BY: GEORGE THEAKOS MUSIC BY: SMOKE DIRECTED BY: MATT CIMBER

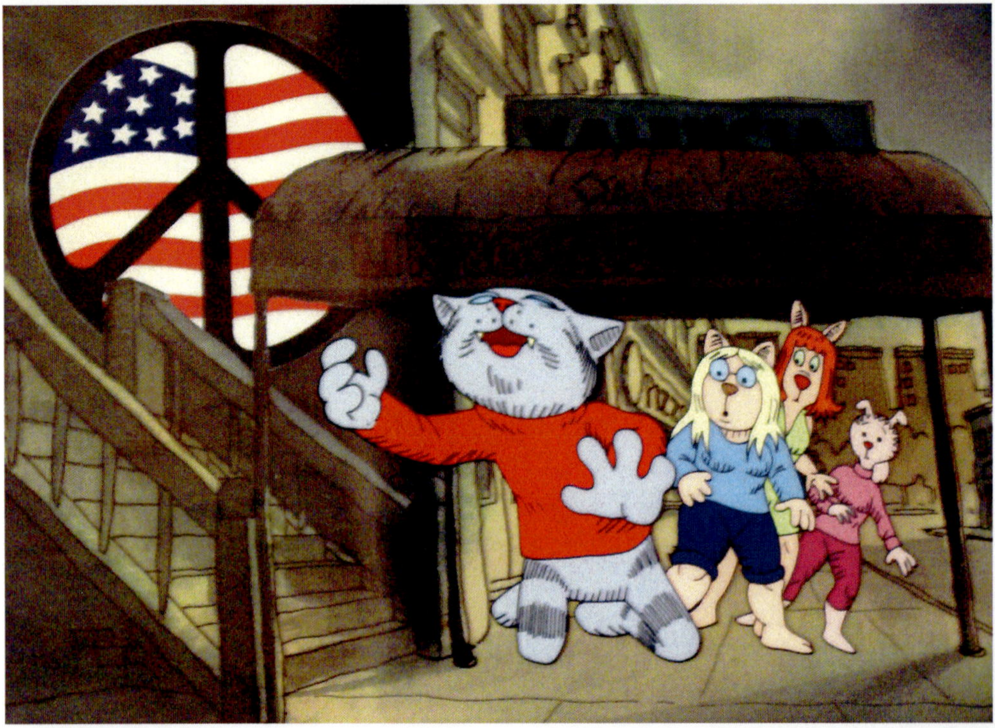

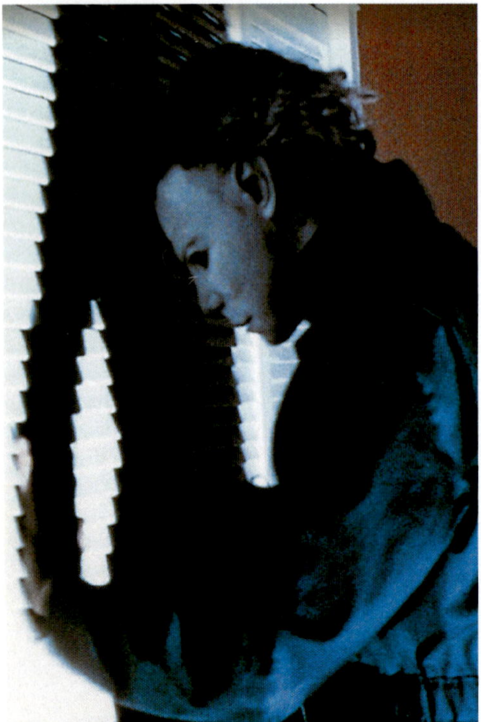

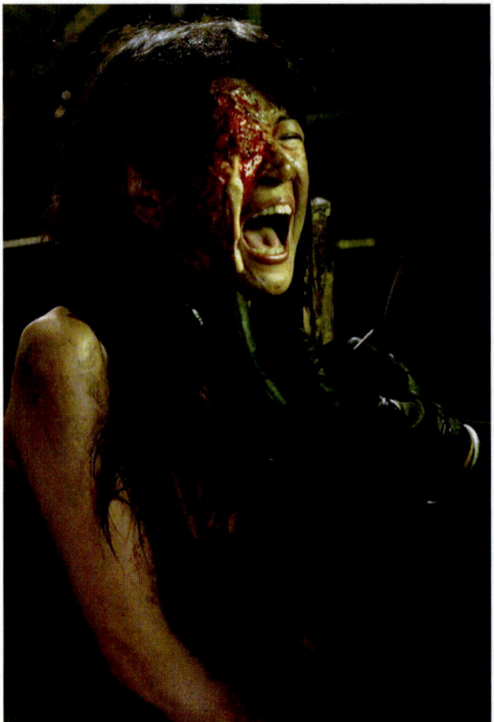

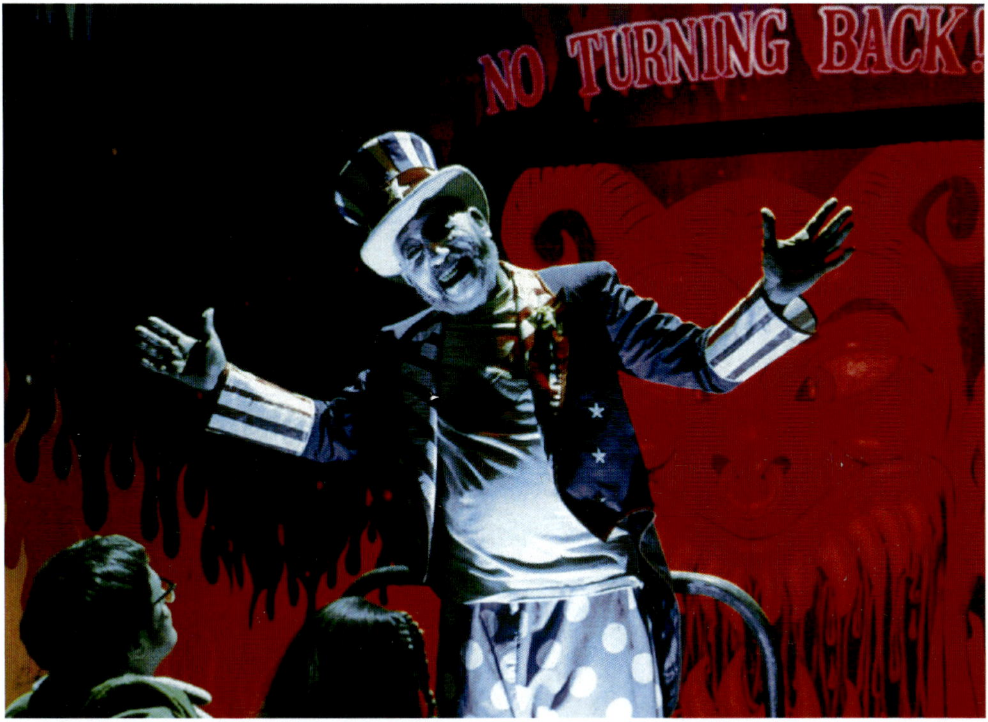
NO TURNING BACK!

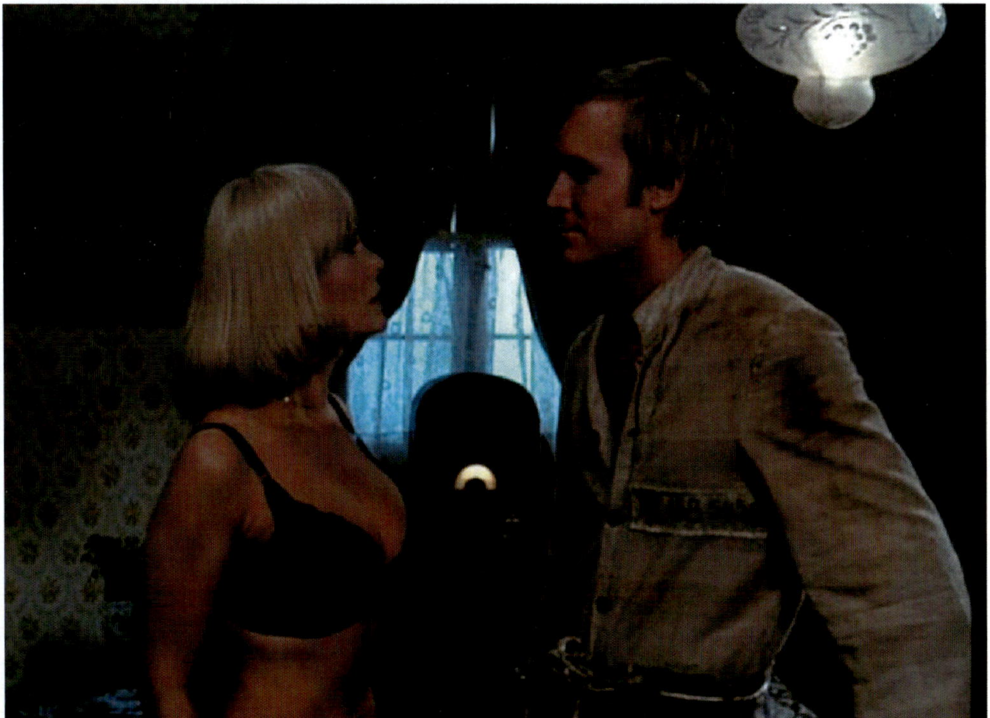

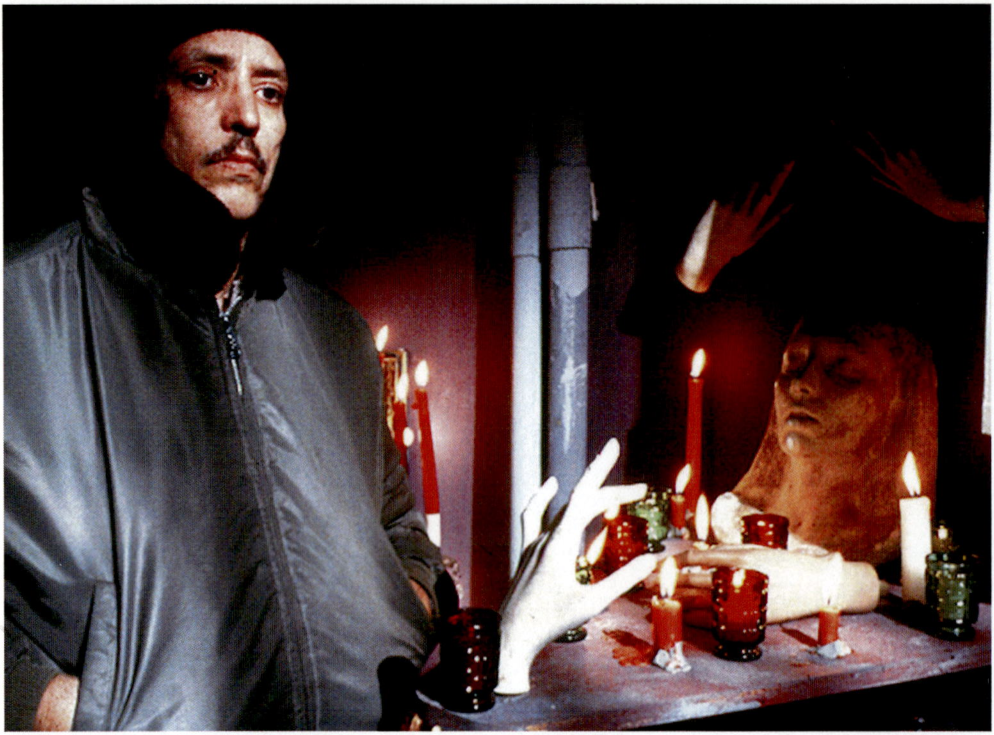

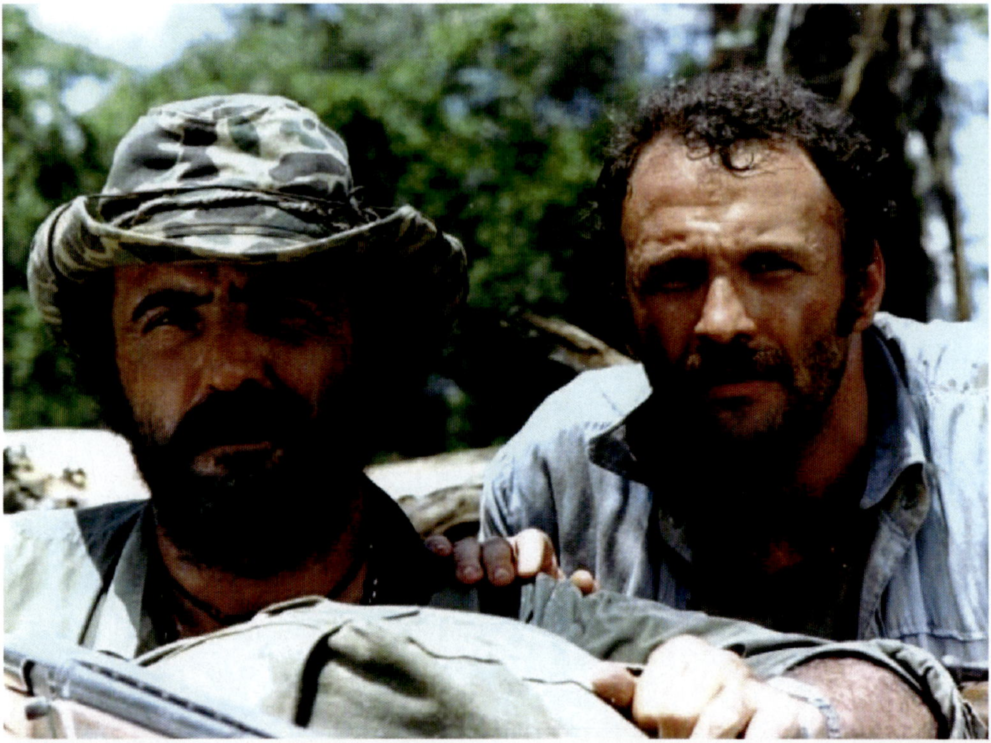

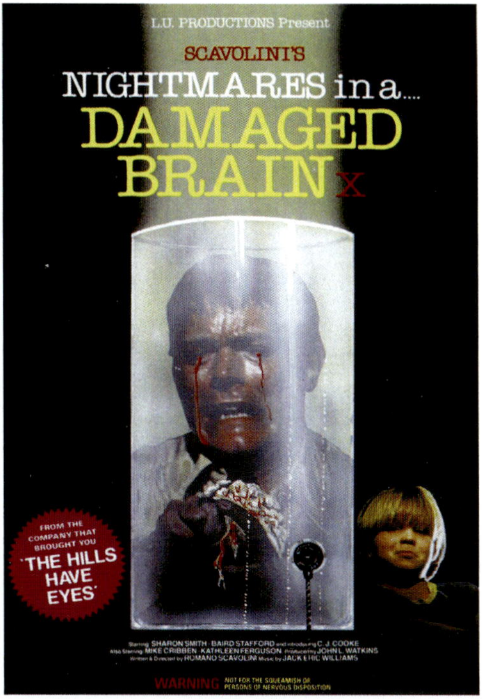
L.U. PRODUCTIONS Present
SCAVOLINI'S
NIGHTMARES in a....
DAMAGED BRAIN
X
FROM THE COMPANY THAT BROUGHT YOU 'THE HILLS HAVE EYES'
Starring SHARON SMITH · BAIRD STAFFORD and introducing C. J. COOKE
Also Starring MIKE CRIBBEN · KATHLEEN FERGUSON Produced by JOHN L. WATKINS
Written & Directed by ROMANO SCAVOLINI Music by JACK ERIC WILLIAMS
WARNING NOT FOR THE SQUEAMISH OR PERSONS OF NERVOUS DISPOSITION

THEY WON'T STAY DEAD...
GEORGE A. ROMERO'S
NIGHT OF THE LIVING DEAD
18
SPECIAL COLLECTOR'S EDITION
EXTENSIVELY RESTORED & REMASTERED

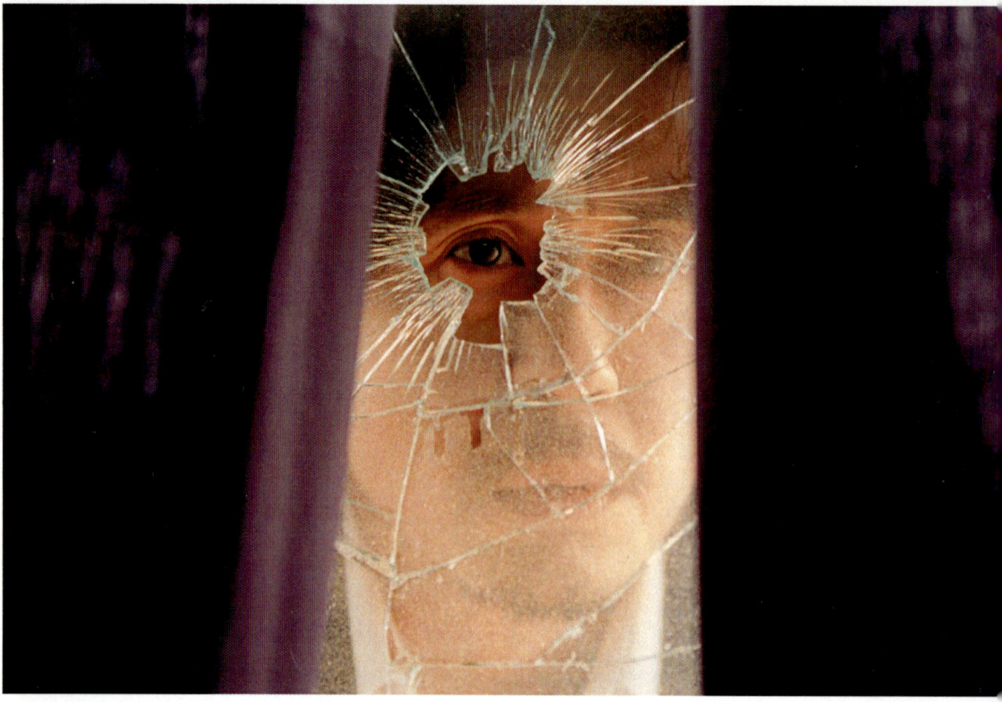

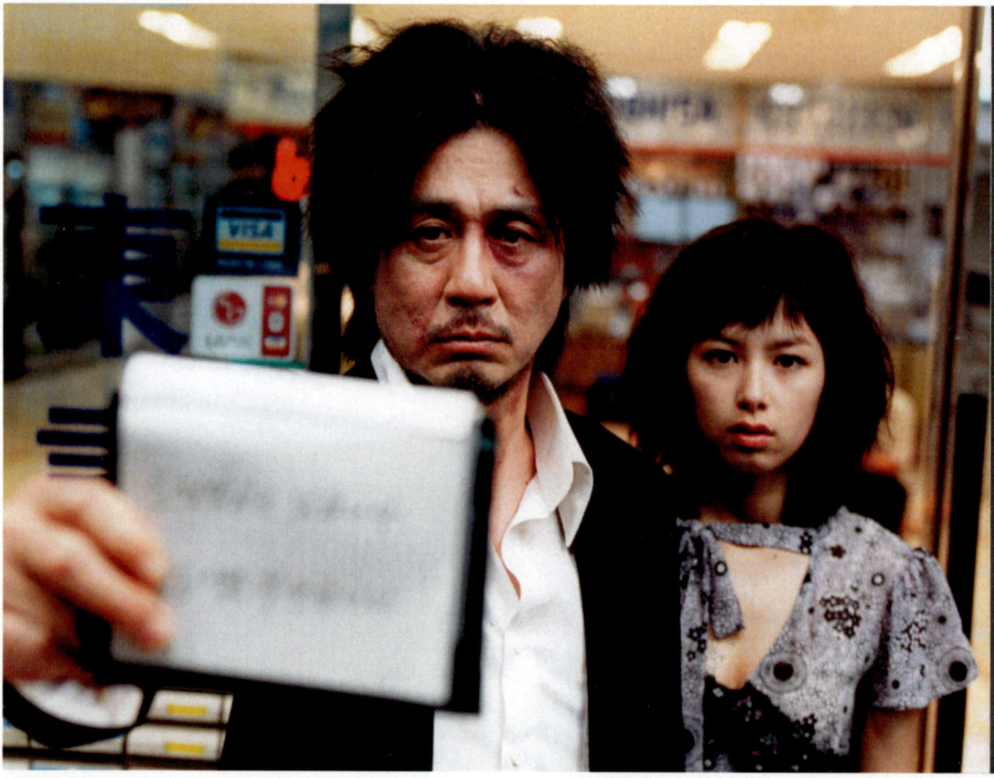
VISA

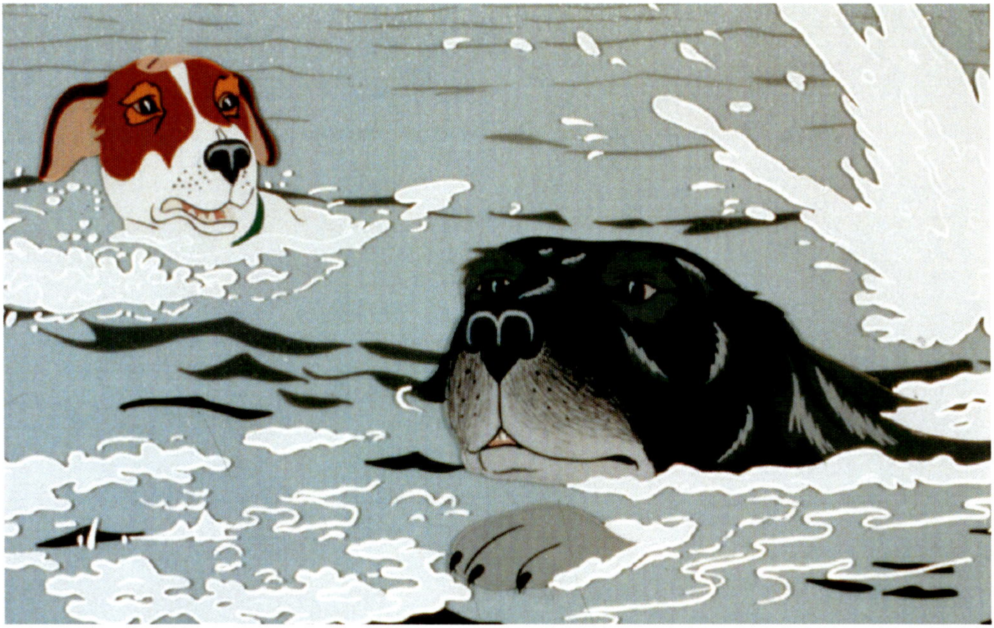

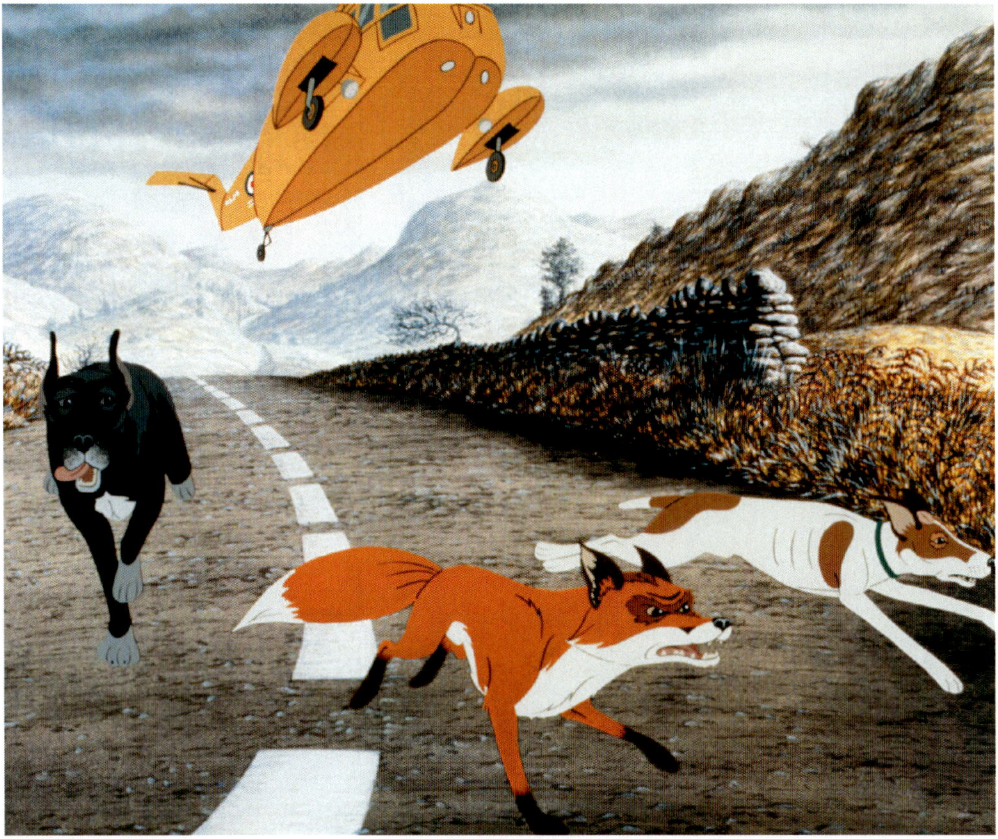

What happened is true.
Now the motion picture that's just as real!
America's most bizarre and brutal crimes!...
THE TEXAS CHAINSAW MASSACRE

to continue their violent existence and human rights abuse, without someone from the outside world making an attempt to stop it. Of course, this is not to say that they deserve the sort of 'interruption' that the white people dish out, but the movie clearly wants us to take the view of the native people as the 'innocents' being exploited by the capitalist Americans ('We're going to win an Oscar for this,' shouts one of the documentary filmmakers during the final slaughter). Yet, considering Deodato's apparent obsession with piling one act of graphic bloodletting on top of another, this scenario does not work, instead, the line between 'good' and 'bad' people is totally broken down and *Cannibal Holocaust* eventually just becomes a film about gross, unnecessary violence. Who is committing the murder and sexual torture eventually becomes neither here nor there, as long as Deodato has a chance to show it.

The cannibal genre is also notorious for the use, and abuse, of live animals. Although a handful of movies avoided this practice (including 1981's Spanish effort *Cannibal Terror* and 1980's bizarre zombie/cannibal cross-pollination *Zombi Holocaust*) it is a sorry state of affairs that this type of thing was part and parcel of these features. As yet, no one, not even the filmmakers themselves (who typically blame 'the producers'), has come up with a reasonable explanation as to why audiences needed to see a turtle decapitated and then gutted in order to make people feel that they had received their money's worth. More amusingly, some of the directors have even tried to completely wash their hands of these scenes[74]. Blame has been put on foreign markets, and especially the Asian market, but this seems like nothing more than a get out clause … a way of demonising an 'alien' culture for the inherent, and unacceptable, transgressions that have been staged in the name of entertainment. Yet, in trailers for *Cannibal Holocaust*, regardless of which country they are intended for, the element of animal violence is totally ignored, demonstrating that any so-called 'demand' for these scenes was probably fictional and done merely for reasons of verisimilitude. Not that Deodato was alone in such trickery. Indeed, fellow Italian Michelangelo Antonioni included some genuine, and painfully prolonged, news footage of a human execution in his 1975 classic *The Passenger* in much the same way that *Cannibal Holocaust* also showcases unfaked recordings of political uprising and human executions (in the movie's narrative this material is used as an example of the film crew's previous documentary). In both cases, the feeling that human death is being used for mere shock tactics is difficult to escape and even harder to defend.

The cannibal genre was in many ways indebted to the cycle of mondo documentaries (or shockumentaries as they are commonly referred to) that began in Italy with *Mondo Cane*. A travelogue of rituals from other countries, and some comical asides, *Mondo Cane* nevertheless features a great deal of footage that highlights the mistreatment of animals, something that the film's director, Gualtiero Jacopetti, would insist reflected his own stance against hunting and mankind's cruelty towards wildlife[75]. Whilst the scenes of harrowing big game hunting that

---

[74] 'I don't want people to think that I torture animals,' explained *Cannibal Ferox/Man from Deep River* director Umberto Lenzi to critic Loris Curci in a 1992 interview. 'Most of what you see in (these films) is special effects and if you look carefully, it shows,' he added of the unmistakably genuine deaths that meet the animals in his cannibal work (*Gorezone*, Issue 25, 1992).

[75] As detailed in the documentary *The Godfathers of Mondo* (2003)

dominate Jacopetti's subsequent epic *Africa Addio* (1966 aka *Africa, Blood and Guts*) could be taken to indicate a genuine concern for such issues, it was not long before mondo features would stage their own bouts of animal cruelty in an attempt to heighten the reality of their narratives. Indeed, starved of genuine atrocities to capture on film, such titles as *Savage Man, Savage Beast* (1974) and *Brutes and Savages* (1975) would simply fabricate scenes of human mortality, whilst upping the content of actual animal abuse in order to lend credence to such fakery. Deodato, with his prime focus on a 'found' documentary purporting to be real, kosher footage of people actually losing their lives, learns his tricks from the world of mondo filmmaking. Hence, as has been noted elsewhere, '*Cannibal Holocaust* manages to anaesthetise rational thought with the shock of real live animals being killed: *If this is real, what else might be real?*'[76]

The mondo documentary, with all its accusations of fraud, is, perversely, what Deodato seems to be critiquing in *Cannibal Holocaust* and this is what ultimately proves to be his downfall. As with the 'shockumentary' tradition, Deodato fails to practice what he preaches, condemning the horrors on-screen through his film's mock 'voice of reason' (Kerman's Professor Harold Monroe) and yet having no hesitation in executing such acts and showing them to the audience[77]. For example, it is doubtful that anyone could possibly benefit from seeing a long, drawn out sequence of a turtle being disembowelled, but by carrying this out the director makes the viewer uneasy and certainly increases the realism of the fictional 'documentary' footage. Furthermore, it is through staging such a vile set piece (let us not forget that giant turtles are endangered) that Deodato and his crew show themselves to be every bit the environmental terrorists that they castigate their storyline characters for being. In reality, it is the people making *Cannibal Holocaust*, working in a capitalist, profit driven industry, who have arrived on foreign soil and succeeded in pillaging the area's resources for their own gain. Not only are the local people cast in degrading roles as flesh chewing savages, but animals are captured and killed, their agony recorded for the film's viewers to … well, to what? This is, arguably, the problem with these movies as a whole, *what on earth does the director want us to feel?*

Even in the seventies, animal cruelty was a rare thing to see on-screen, and if *Bambi* (1942) could bring audiences to tears then why anyone thought people would react with an emotion other than disgust and/or anger at viewing real creatures being hacked apart is anyone's guess. Indeed, 1981's *The Animals Film*, a harrowing documentary narrated by Julie Christie, even showed viewers the horrors of endangered turtles being killed to make soup – and this was only one year after Deodato's movie, indicating that, under different circumstances, this sort of abuse was being used to educate, rather than thrill or merely disgust, audiences. Subsequently, even those reviewers that do profess admiration for the likes of *Cannibal Holocaust* tend to immediately follow themselves up with a cry of disgust aimed towards the real scenes of wildlife vivisection. In saying this, it would be hard to argue about the capturing of native luncheons on camera, as may have been the case with Deodato's superior *The Last Cannibal World* (although

---

[76] As noted in *Killing for Culture* (Kerekes and Slater, Creation Books, London, 1994)

[77] '*Cannibal Holocaust* is the bastard son of the mondo genre,' writes Fenton, Castoldi and Grainger in *Cannibal Holocaust and the Savage Cinema of Ruggero Deodato*. 'The most pertinent argument pitched against *Cannibal Holocaust* is that it is guilty of the transgressions which it seeks to condemn.' (FAB Press, Surrey, 1999)

the director denies shooting the few scenes of this nature that appear in that movie). Instead, what makes *Cannibal Holocaust* problematic is in having the film's actors indulge in these acts, although becoming overly uppity about this perhaps says a great deal about us and about our culture. Whilst most people have little difficulty with buying packaged meat from a supermarket, the reality of how this got there (or what animals suffered in a laboratory for our cosmetics and washing powder) crosses the minds of very few. Yet, when we really do get to see an animal dying, as is the case in *Cannibal Holocaust*, the reality of the act is bloody and disturbing. This is not a defence of the movie, but *Cannibal Holocaust* ironically stands the test of time as a reminder that the death of any sentient being is far from pretty.

The truth of *Cannibal Holocaust* is that Deodato has made a film of fleetingly impressive moments, and only on one occasion does he manage to get absolutely everything correct. Thankfully, for him, the moment in question is a powerful one. The sequence involves the documentary team entering a small village full of peaceful natives and summarily leading the Indians into their straw huts and setting them on fire in order to simulate a tribal war ('it will be just like in Cambodia'). At this point the director perfectly highlights the inhumanity of his actors, with even Faye, an innocent bystander up until this point, compelled to let out a whoop of 'get these suckers'. The sight of the women and children, weeping as they burn alive, is far more powerful than any of the explicit gore or animal slaughter that has preceded it. Yet, without spilling a drop of blood, Deodato, in this sole scenario, creates a moment of gut wrenching horror. The reason for this is simple and comes right back to the criticism of *Cannibal Holocaust* that began this chapter. Here, and only here, does the director actually give us blatantly 'bad' characters infringing upon the peaceful lives of the 'good' natives, a premise so simple, and so well executed in this moment of genocide, that it is a crime the film fails to build on it. Instead, in *Cannibal Holocaust*, virtually everyone is inhumanly violent, save for Monroe himself, and, under such circumstances, it is understandable why the picture may fail to raise any audience involvement with its many on-screen terrors.

If *Cannibal Holocaust* does have another incredible trick up its sleeve then it is its soundtrack, composed by Academy Award winner Riz Ortolani. A beautiful, romantic and epic sounding score leads the film's opening credits and re-appears at choice moments throughout the movie. Totally inappropriate for such a gruesome picture, Ortolani, nevertheless, outdoes himself with one of the most memorable motion picture themes in history. This, alongside the odd, fleeting moment of cinematic brilliance (including the aforementioned sequence of genocide, Deodato's effective use of natural light and the final 'twist', whereupon it turns out that Faye's fiancée has actually filmed her rape and murder) make *Cannibal Holocaust* a frustrating example of a movie that could have been fantastic. As it stands, however, it is nothing more than a testament of how far graphic violence can be pushed, particularly at the expense of women (the character of Faye is rewarded for her pacifism by being granted the most prolonged death out of all the documentary team). It is also remarkably clumsy in its final assault, with one of the on-screen filmmakers (Mark) actually vanishing from the action but with no indication of where he has gone.

Inevitably, with all of the violence documented in *Cannibal Holocaust*, and in particular its taboo use of animal cruelty, the result was a heap of controversy across the world. It barely gained any release in North America, premiering in New York's then-sleazy 42nd Street for a brief run.[78] Although claims that the movie was, at the time, the biggest grossing feature in Japan have yet to be proven with actual data (this seems like the stuff of cult legend), there is no denying that the feature, especially on VHS, was a grand success, with generation after generation of thrill seekers wanting to see the ultimate video nasty. Meanwhile, the director's previous venture into the 'green inferno', *The Last Cannibal World*, has gone largely unseen, despite being the better movie of the two. Largely on account of the excess of *Cannibal Holocaust*, Deodato's name is forever associated with the contemporary horror film, even if his best known feature is actually more reminiscent of a brutal jungle adventure (not once in the movie, for example, does the director set up a solitary moment where the viewer is 'jolted' by a sudden sound or on-screen intrusion).

What happened next? Deodato faced prosecution in Italy for first degree murder when it was rumoured that he actually killed his actors. When this was proven to be untrue, he was handed a suspended sentence for cruelty towards animals (presumably this had to do with the slaughter of an endangered species, the large turtle, as on-camera vivisection was already part and parcel of this genre). A cut version of *Cannibal Holocaust* became one of Britain's most famous 'video nasties' in the early eighties and the movie still cannot be viewed in its complete form in the country. Deodato's next film, the incredibly violent New York thriller *House on the Edge of the Park* also ended up banned as a 'video nasty' in the UK[79]. The director's last attempt at hyper-violent material is also his best work to date, 1985's *Cut and Run*, a fast-moving action thriller set in the Amazon that stars Michael Berryman and Karen Black. Following this, the director settled into a surprisingly mainstream career, with films such as the Cannon produced fantasy *The Barbarians* (1987), the *Friday the 13th* rip-off *Body Count* (1987) and the Michael York/Donald Pleasence detective shocker *Phantom of Death*. Today he works in Italian television, a humble and likeable gentleman who is hard to associate with his early days of cinematic brutality. Deodato still hopes to make *Cannibal Metropolitana*, an urban based 'sequel' to *Cannibal Holocaust*, but without any cruelty towards animals (a facet of his cannibal work that he now regrets).

Of the *Holocaust* actors, Robert Kerman, one of the most famous male faces of porno chic, gained a short career in Italian cannibal films. He followed up *Cannibal Holocaust* with *Eaten Alive* (1980) and *Cannibal Ferox* (1981) before falling back into appearing in such famous adult titles as *Amanda by Night* (1981). In the late eighties he managed to grab some supporting parts in television shows that included *Hill Street Blues* and *Cagney and Lacey*, but Kerman never quite made the leap into legitimacy. The rediscovery of *Cannibal Holocaust* in America by the Grindhouse DVD Company, headed by Hollywood editor Bob Murawski, led to the actor appearing in the blockbuster *Spider-Man* (2002) in a brief role. A convincing character actor, Kerman's career is one of the most bizarre footnotes in exploitation movie history. His

---

78 As mentioned by Landis and Clifford in *Sleazoid Express* (Fireside Books, New York, 2002)

79 'It's as though Deodato went progressively more berserk with each film, creating spectacles for their own sake, without regard for any living thing,' writes Landis and Clifford in *Sleazoid Express* (Fireside Books, New York, 2002)

Holocaust co-star Carl Gabriel Yorke has also kept working in front of the camera, largely in supporting roles in such features as *Apollo 13* (1995) and *Idle Hands* (1999). In Italy, meanwhile, Luca Barbareschi has worked continually in indigenous television and movie productions, even appearing, briefly, in Deodato's subsequent *Cut and Run*.

As for the cannibal genre itself, it was left to Deodato's rival Umberto Lenzi to turn things up a notch. His 1980 effort *Eaten Alive* – an attempt at cynically exploiting the Jim Jones tragedy – recycled footage of faked gore and real animal cruelty from *The Man from Deep River*, *The Last Cannibal World* and *Prisoner of the Cannibal God* and wove a new story into these stock sequences. The result was banal, a hodgepodge of excess that moves along at a snail's pace. 1981's *Cannibal Ferox* claimed to be 'banned in 31 countries' and seems to be an attempt to outdo even *Cannibal Holocaust* in the violence stakes. With more animal cruelty than ever before (a turtle is hacked up, a muskrat tied to a pole and fed to an anaconda, a pig stabbed, an alligator gutted ... you get the idea) and a scene where a woman has spikes rammed into her bare breasts, the feature is a horribly dislikeable viewing experience. After *Ferox*, the genre fizzled out, re-appearing only briefly in the far more tame visage of such mundane efforts as *Massacre in Dinosaur Valley* (1985) and *The Green Inferno* (1988 aka *Cannibal Holocaust 2*).

Cannibal Holocaust's most curious legacy is as the possible catalyst that inspired 1999's classic *The Blair Witch Project*. A movie about similarly 'found footage' the two films have little else in common, although a selection of critics have, unconvincingly, tried to draw a link between them. Not only does *The Blair Witch Project* not feature a wraparound narrative, it relies completely on imagination and suspense, as opposed to graphic gore and nudity, and is suitably terrifying. More recently Deodato's movie has been remade, in everything but name, as *Welcome to the Jungle* – a direct-to-DVD offering from 2007 in which a two man-two woman documentary crew gets lost and stalked in the wild jungles of New Guinea. Although far less gruesome than *Cannibal Holocaust*, and not without its faults, the low budget effort is considerably more palatable than its inspiration and surprisingly scary. Amazingly, *Welcome to the Jungle* was produced by Gale Anne Hurd – the producer of such major blockbusters as *Armageddon* (1998), *Hulk* (2003) and *Aeon Flux* (2005). In influencing such Hollywood royalty it would seem, on the surface at least, that Deodato has had the last laugh ...

Ruggero Deodato interview

Ruggero Deodato had a privileged start in cinema – learning his trade under the tutelage of Roberto Rosellini and such influential B-movie directors as Antonio Margheriti, Sergio Corbucci and Riccardo Freda. Asked about his beginnings and the filmmaker remains humbled by his luck. 'I started out with Rosellini and when people ask me, "Why did you become a director?" I say, "Because of Rosellini." I knew him and I knew his family. I knew Ingrid Bergman. In my young days I would spend time with his family in their summer villa, close to Rome. Then, one day, Rosellini said to me, "I would like you to be my assistant." My father was a very political man and he approved, he said, "Yes you should go into cinema." With Rosellini I shot six movies, they were nice movies, and one, called *Viva l'Italia*, I like very much ... My first film with him was *Il Generale della Rovere* and later (in 1960) I shot *Era notte a Roma*, which starred Peter Baldwin. This is the story about the resistance in Rome during the last war.

TABOO BREAKERS

The last one I worked on was *Anima nera* (1962), which starred Vittorio Gassman. After three movies I became his first assistant director. But with Rosellini it was not possible to learn many technical skills ... because he was very much an artist, naturalistic but not technical. After him, I worked with (Carlo Ludovico) Bragaglia, and he gave me a lot of technical training. After this, I shot several movies as an assistant director, always with a big Italian director such as Margheriti, Corbucci or Freda.' Inevitably, the young filmmaker eventually opted to follow his own path. 'When I started to direct movies myself, I started with comedies,' states Deodato. 'But then a producer asked me if I wanted to shoot a film in Malaysia called *The Last Cannibal World*.' It was history in the making. 'I saw, in National Geographic, pictures of a tribe and they might be cannibals ... it was a very lucky thing because this convinced me to say yes,' laughs the filmmaker. 'So I went to Kuala Lumpur with my assistant director and I remember the (national) park was not good for a cannibal movie. So we found a pilot, an Indian pilot, and we went to a location in a real jungle (*laughs*). It was the pilot, the assistant director and myself. We went to the real, green jungle and after two hours we found a place to land. It was incredible. The indios, the river, the big trees ... all incredible ... When we began shooting, it took seven hours for us to arrive each day ... we didn't go by plane but by canoe. The crew wanted to kill me (*laughs*) but after a week, everyone was happy because after 5pm there was silence in the jungle. You could only hear animals. The film did very well, it played in eight theatres in New York and after this everyone in the world called me asking, "We want another cannibal film," and this is how *Cannibal Holocaust* was born. I was afraid because, even with *The Last Cannibal World* I had problems with the animal scenes and the story...'

Indeed, although the quota of nasty on-screen deeds in *The Last Cannibal World* pales in comparison to *Cannibal Holocaust* the feature remains a rough ride to endure, with unsimulated animal snuff sequences, graphic human mutilation and, of course, some explicit flesh-eating. 'I am not a violent man, but by this time in my career I had shot a lot of movies,' begins Deodato. 'In fact, I have shot everything. In Italy, normally the director has only one road, you know? Only comedy or violence or political films ... but for me, no, it is different. I have shot everything, just like Spielberg (*laughs*). Like an American director I will shoot everything, and I like this more because I have done violent stories, love stories, comedies, commercials ... I have made many commercials.' Surprisingly, Deodato insists that the tribe he filmed in *Last Cannibal World* actually consisted of natives who would consume human flesh. 'It is a real Cannibal tribe,' he says. 'In *The Last Cannibal World* I shot with one family, one group. The cannibals were *really* cannibals. This was in Malaysia. We shot (some of the film) in the Philippines, in Mindanao the island, and that was fine, but in Malaysia they were really cannibals. I had the ranger with me, with a rifle, to protect me. But this was only in *The Last Cannibal World* – in *Cannibal Holocaust*, no, they were normal Indios.'

With its gruesome moments of animal death, rape and a final reel that amounts to an almost non-stop cavalcade of gore and humiliation, it is unsurprising that *Cannibal Holocaust* would meet with controversy worldwide. 'I had many problems with this movie,' sighs Deodato. 'In Italy, after ten days the courts banned it. At the box office it was taking millions and millions of lira, it was fantastic, but after ten days it was gone. I was prosecuted and the tribunal said, "You killed the actors," I told them I did not and we went to see the movie together. The jury had two women on it and they screamed through the film! The prosecutor blocked the movie and I got a conditional (sentence) for the animals. The movie sold around the world but it cost me a fortune. When I was shooting the movie in the Amazon, I was sending the rushes to Rome for MIFED, the famous film market. Every country looked at it and said, "Ah, I will buy it." United Artists arrived and said, "We will buy it for the whole world." One Frenchman, he said, "We have $400,000 to buy it," and United Artists says, "No. For France it will cost you many millions of dollars." In France the movie would do very, very well, also in Spain and in Japan it was second only to *E.T.* at the box office. CBS Fox bought it for Japan and we made this film for nothing ... we only had $100,000!'

As a non-union production, Deodato had to rely on no-name actors for his production, although he found a reliable squad of thespians in Rome and also in New York. 'The idea behind *Cannibal Holocaust* was to go to the Actor's Studio in New York and find four young people,' explains the filmmaker. 'I needed two young Italians, I needed them for the nationality of the film, and two Americans ... and in their contract it said, "You will have to disappear for one year." This is because in the film they die. It was their first movie and they said, "Okay." Then I had the tribunal in Milan and they said, "You killed the men,". So I had to call one of the Italian actors who worked with me, Luca Barbareschi, I said, "Luca, you need to come to Milan and I need to present you at the tribunal because you are still alive (*laughs*)." The idea was fantastic but not for me ... the young people who shot *The Blair Witch Project*, when they did this the internet had arrived and it was fantastic, but for me, no. It only caused me trouble.' Deodato's leading man, however, was a little more familiar, having starred in numerous adult titles. 'Robert Kerman worked with me before on my movie *Concorde Affair*,' says the director. 'But it was just a little role. I was shooting in New York, in an airport, and (after that) I knew him so when I came back to New York to cast for *Cannibal Holocaust* I remembered him and I put him in the movie. Don't talk about his porno films because I did not know about this before ... Really, I did not know about this. People still want to talk to me about that (*laughs*).'

The most controversial aspect of *Cannibal Holocaust* was the use of live animals. Especially gruelling is the sequence where a live turtle is beheaded, quartered, gutted and then cooked. Asked about this today Deodato grimaces and apologises, admitting that it was a different time and not something that he would do today. 'Normally, the tribes found the animals in the trees,' he says. 'The tribe will normally eat monkeys. They shoot the monkeys from the trees ... So the tribe gave me the animals, they gave me the turtle, gave me the monkey. Only the little pig was normal. The pig ... we killed that ourselves. My team killed the pig so that, for the first time, we could eat pork because every day it was fish, fish, fish. I shot this scene for the movie, but it was for us. The American actors had problems with it. One particularly, the blonde guy (Perry Pirkanen), he had some comments, but I don't remember. Now, if it was possible to turn back time, then I would not shoot any scenes with the animals because it was stupid to do that. But before the film, the marketing people all around the world wanted the animals, especially in the East, in Asia, and also in Germany. The marketing people would say, "Ah yes, the animals, okay, animals!" But not the British ... However, I didn't kill the animals in *The Last Cannibal World*. It was the producer that put them in the movie. I did not kill the animals, I finished the movie and this was later. So it is not my fault.'

TABOO BREAKERS

Whoever's decision it was, it is the scenes of explicit animal cruelty that led to *Cannibal Holocaust*'s subsequent ban and censorship by many nations. 'Now I know why it was banned, because of the animals,' concludes Deodato. 'But 25 years ago it was very different in the world. I will explain. I was born in Rome, and many times my family would go out to the country. The country people, the farmers, they would kill the pigs. They would turn them upside down and the blood … it was normal to see the pigs killed, the rabbit killed, the chickens … but now this is not normal. Now you do not see anything. Who killed your chicken? Now we don't know. But before, you saw the women in the village do it, so for me it was natural. When my father died, people would see the body, but now people don't want to see. For me, it was different. So when the Indios kill the monkey to eat, it was normal. Just like if people were to kill a cow for food. Now it has changed and I have changed too. My old girlfriend, we were in India and they had a turtle. It was to be sold for food, so I bought it because this upset her, and let it out to the sea … but when the man I bought it from saw this, he was very upset (*laughs*). I change too. Some years ago my pet dog was run over and it died. So I cried. I was very upset by this.'

Of course, the very nature of the movie was to push things as far as possible. 'In Milan they would call me and say, "It is a fantastic film but do more, go further … do something even stronger," states Deodato. 'One night I said, "Okay, tomorrow we will do the impaling." How? We invented it. In the morning I arrived on the set with a bicycle chair and some balsa wood. What happened for this famous scene is the woman sat on the seat with the balsa in her mouth …' After filming Deodato also had to make the footage look as if it had been recovered from months in the rainforest. 'After I finished I broke the film,' he smiles. 'I broke all the negatives after the production. The first side is all 35mm but the second is 16mm, but 16mm is okay – after it was scratched and exposed to light… the post production was more difficult than the shoot.'

Whereas Deodato's *Last Cannibal World* had been shot in the rainforest of Malaysia, *Cannibal Holocaust* was based in the Amazon. The result is certainly less scenic (the director's first jungle-adventure epic might be many things but badly made it is not, with some beautiful use of the natural locations) but the South America jungle setting was still full of potential. 'In Malaysia it was very difficult because it was so strange,' laughs the director. 'In Amazonia it was easier because the jungle is more open. It was also easier (to work) with the Indios because they have seen more of the outside world and the rivers are open to people. In Malaysia it was much more difficult because the jungle was really a jungle, it was also very far from the big city. I went with the film team, my group, in a canoe for seven hours, with all of the equipment, just to get to the location … But it is very nice in the jungle in Malaysia because they have delicious fruit. Massimo Foschi, the actor in *The Last Cannibal World*, was very strong, he would do everything, so he was fine in the jungle.'

Asked why he made such a brutal and explicit film with *Cannibal Holocaust* and Deodato maintains that his intentions were honourable. 'The reason – and I have explained this in the past – was because at the time, in Italy, we had a problem with terrorists and there were so many, many television reports that showed people killed. My son would cry every day and I was angry about that, and when I was shooting the movie I knew it was only going to be for people aged 18 years and older, but when something is on television it is free for everyone to watch. The part of the story where the journalists do everything they want … well sometimes when they film the scoop they are inventing the scoop. You see, I wanted this part of the movie to be very strong. I was making that for the journalists, not for me. The second part of that film is only for the journalists. It is different from *The Last Cannibal World* because that was just a normal story.'

One thing the critics and the fans of *Cannibal Holocaust* will both agree on is the musical score by Riz Ortolani. Frankly, it is one of the most memorable soundtracks of any Italian horror picture. 'I saw the films of Jacopetti, including *Mondo Cane* and I love the song *More*,' says Deodato. 'When I saw the film *Mondo Cane* I saw this incredibly violent scene but the song was amazing. When I shot *Cannibal Holocaust* and the violent scenes … if the music is violent then you are less surprised by things. I remembered *Mondo Cane* during the editing and I called Riz Ortolani and asked him if it was possible for him to score the movie. He came in and he watched it and told me it was a fantastic movie. He said, "I think you will become a very famous director and I will do the music." I said, "I want the music to be like *Mondo Cane*." But before that I showed Segio Leone the film and the first time he saw it he told me it was okay, but the second time he said it was fantastic. He told me, "you will have many problems."'

Talk about an understatement.

Carl Gabriel Yorke interview

As the leader of *Cannibal Holocaust*'s doomed search team, actor Carl Gabriel Yorke made an instant impression on Euro-trash viewers with his film debut. Loathsome, smug and hateful, Yorke's character of Alan Yates is shockingly believable, adding at least some air of professionalism to a movie that flounders under a bucket-load of cheap shock tactics. 'When you wake up in the morning, any morning, you have no idea what will happen that day,' states Yorke, who has come to embrace his role in the 1980 gore landmark. 'Sure, most days are just like the day before,' he continues, 'and sometimes what happens isn't so good. But once in a while, something comes out of the blue and if you just keep saying "yes" then you might just find yourself in the middle of a once-in-a-lifetime adventure. One Friday morning I got a call from a casting director I knew called Bill Williams, who asked if I was available and if I was willing to go to South America. Then he asked if I could get to his office immediately. I said yes to everything. I was cast that afternoon and flew from New York to Bogotá on Monday. There were only two planes a week from Bogotá to Leticia, the little town where the production was based, so I had to wait until Wednesday to fly down to the Amazon. Then, Wednesday night at dinner, I finally got to read the script.'

Yorke may have had second thoughts about his adventure if he'd known what was in store for him. 'I didn't have the luxury of reading the script before I got to the set,' admits the actor. 'They'd hired another actor who bowed out right before they went into principal photography, so I was an emergency replacement and I never had my own copy of the script. The day I arrived, they whisked me out to the set and put me in a shot before I had a chance to catch my breath. Like I mentioned, I read the script over dinner that night, which was a mistake. I don't remember how graphic the script was; all I remember is that part way through I lost my appetite and couldn't finish my dinner. There were many things in and out of the script that gave me great pause about being involved.' That said, Yorke did not view his character quite as negatively as most viewers have in the intervening years. 'I didn't see Alan as brutal or unpleasant at all,' he admits. 'He was smart and driven and ambitious, and so sure of himself that he was arrogant. That's how I saw him. It wasn't that hard to connect with those traits; people like that are around us all the time. In America at least, that sort of person is hailed as a hero, someone to model yourself after … I don't know how well I captured this guy. The circumstances were so bizarre; I had no prep time, no research time – all I could do was learn my lines and shoot.'

Then there were the trials and tribulations of filming out in the Amazon rainforest. 'The jungle is very beautiful, very mysterious and very dangerous,' admits Yorke. 'I didn't go wandering off by myself at all. I was living in New York when I did *Cannibal Holocaust*, and the first thing I felt when I got to the jungle was, "This place is more dangerous than Hell's Kitchen," because at least I knew where the bad neighbourhoods were in New York. In the jungle everything was unknown to me, but New York was good training because I had my sixth sense for danger working, and I was always on the lookout. After I settled in, I was fine and I was amazed at how life and death are happening all the time there, everywhere. Here's one example: You look up at the tops of the trees and it's a big, lush canopy of gigantic leaves full of monkeys and birds and insects. But you look at the base of the same tree and you see that it's rotting from the bottom up. Life at the top; rot at the bottom – just like New York!'

The actor also enjoyed a degree of harmony with director Ruggero Deodato. 'Looking back, I have to say that Ruggero knew how to work with actors,' says Yorke. 'He had that important sense of how to give you the ego stroke all actors need just to step in front of the camera, then just the right phrase or image to get the look or the emotion or the action he wanted. If that didn't work, he was not shy about kicking your ass!' Perhaps unsurprisingly, tempers flared between Deodato and his young star when the filmmaker expected his leading man to take part in the on-screen animal cruelty. 'I can't explain the animal stuff,' says Yorke. 'The only thing I can think is that Ruggero wanted to be as shocking as possible. I brought it up when they killed the monkey. I said, "This is a movie. You can fake it. That's what movies are all about." I said this to Salvatore Basile, the Assistant Director, who also starred in the picture as Felipe, but he just said, "That's the way it is." It came to a head over the pig. Ruggero called me a pussy when I wouldn't pull the trigger with live ammo in the rifle, and after that we all kept up a civil working relationship. I didn't feel like Ruggero and the crew respected me anymore, but that could be my imagination.'

Asked about how he felt about the movie's use of live animals and Yorke pulls no punches. 'I had a problem with the animal violence,' he says. 'However, Luca Barbareschi grew up on a farm and he didn't have any problem with it, so he did it, and the crew had that pig for dinner that night. Some of the stuff, like the killing of the turtle, happened before I got there. But I was on the set when they did the scene where the native eats the monkey brains. That was a turning point. That's when we all knew this wasn't a fun time and that it was going to be as grim on the set as it was in the script. I know that Perry Pirkanen, who played Jack, didn't seem that comfortable about it all, but we never really talked about it. Francesca Ciardi, who played my girlfriend in the movie, was very upset. In fact when they shot the monkey scene, I think she threw up. I know someone did.'

Despite the differences of opinion in regards to humanitarian decisions, Yorke still got along with his co-stars. 'We all got along fine. Luca is a great guy, but he didn't speak much English. Francesca was a handful. Perry was the only other American on the picture and we didn't really hang out. The way I understood it, the actor who had been cast in the role of Alan and quit was Perry's best friend. I may have that wrong. But when I showed up on the set I didn't get a particularly hearty welcome from Perry, and while we got along fine, we only saw each other once after the shooting was finished.' The performer also had to get personal with one of his fellow actors, Penelope Cruz look-alike Francesca Ciardi. 'The truth is I didn't want to do the love scene,' he sighs. 'Once we got going, it wasn't that much different from anything else you do as an actor except that it was more painful. That's because we were in a hut with a floor made of bamboo sticks that have pointy things on them and the floor wasn't level. We did five takes of the love scene, and I was in pain most of the time.'

After his role in *Cannibal Holocaust* came to a close, Yorke heard nothing about the movie for years and didn't even manage to see the picture for two decades! 'I did have a tangential, and entirely improbable, contact a year or two later,' he explains. 'I was walking down the hall at United Artists and I went past an office where a young guy suddenly started saying things like, "Oh, my God!" and, "Holy shit!" I didn't know the guy but I was right there so I stuck my head in to see what was up. He motioned me in saying, "You gotta see this – this is unbelievable." He was looking at production shots from *Cannibal Holocaust*. UA had a deal to distribute the picture and he was looking for publicity shots. I looked at the photos and couldn't believe what I was seeing. It was like an out of body experience. Out of the blue, there I was in all these photos on this stranger's desk. I told him that was me in the pictures, and I think it blew his mind. He said he would blow up any of the pictures I wanted and give them to me, but then the Italian censors seized the movie and the deal with UA fell apart. I never heard from him again. I didn't even see *Cannibal Holocaust* for twenty years. Rodman Flender, who's a great director and a friend of mine, sent me a copy.'

Now, nearly three decades later, Yorke looks back at his time in 'The Green Inferno' fondly. 'The whole damned thing was special,' he says. 'There was an excitement about that shoot that I haven't felt on any other picture or TV show. That probably sounds like we thought we were doing something historic or important, but it wasn't that at all. It was the rawness of the script, the exotic location, the uncertainty of jungle life, and the constant demand to push myself to do things I had never done, didn't want to do, or didn't think I could do. I learned a lot about myself and about human nature. The jungle is great for that. It brings out the beast in all animals. I'm surprised by the following that *Cannibal Holocaust* has today. I always knew it would be a good conversation piece, but I never thought a lot of people would still be talking about it.'

Robert Kerman interview

Although most famous for his leading role in *Cannibal Holocaust*, Robert Kerman rose to fame in adult cinema, starring in such porn titles as *Joy* (1977) and *Debbie Does Dallas* (1979). An actor in his college days, Kerman admits to acting in adult movies for the money. 'I was getting paid $100 a day,' he says, 'which was a lot of money in the early seventies. I ended up for ten years in that industry through laziness and stupidity and also through a desire to act.' However, when opportunity knocked in the shape of Italian B-films, the actor jumped at the chance to extend his talents. 'I played an Air Traffic Controller in a film called *The Concorde Affair*,' says Kerman of the disaster movie directed by Ruggero Deodato. 'I had about 18 minutes of screen time. I was talking to some old American actors on that movie and these were films with a $1 million budget, but I was just alone that day in this air traffic control room. Ruggero Deodato was directing and he really liked me, really took a shine to me – couldn't believe that I could remember the lines. I told him that I had done a lot of theatre and about six months, maybe even a year later, he called me himself from Italy. Giovanni Masini, the production manager, spoke because he had better English and he said, "How would you like to do the lead …," and I like that word, "… in an Italian movie, down in Italy, Colombia and New York?" I said, "I'd love it," and he said "We'll swap details in Rome. We are shooting in Colombia first."'

So began Kerman's involvement with one of the most controversial films ever made. 'They sent me a script,' he continues. 'Someone met me in New York and I bought some clothing, which all got lost, but I bought stuff for Doctor Monroe. They had a costume designer meet me in New York because they were shooting the stuff with the kids down in Colombia, they must have been in their twenties or thirties, they were down there shooting already and I was here in New York buying gear for what a jungle person would wear. Great stuff … big boots, expensive stuff … I loved it. Then I took a plane to Florida, Miami to Bogotá … let me tell you what Bogotá is like, because I stayed in Bogotá overnight. It is like the Wild West. I was told never to go out at night but I'm a bit of a piss-ant, I defy things (*laughs*). So I did, I was strolling around the streets like I was the toughest motherfucker in the world and I must have been out of my mind. I walked out and walked down the middle of the street and nobody bothered me. I think I was starting to live the part. In retrospect today I wouldn't have … but I had never been in a place like this. This was not New York.'

Upon arrival in Leticia, the area of South America where *Cannibal Holocaust* was filmed, there were yet more surprises for the New York native. 'My luggage didn't arrive' explains Kerman. 'All of my stuff was gone and I only had my carry-on bag. I went on a two hour flight over the Equator and arrived in the jungle but with no luggage. I remember this beautiful, long river, trees everywhere and no roads. Arriving by plane or by boat was the only way in. I was excited and nervous too because I didn't know anybody. I went to my hotel and went to see everybody. They were in their hotel and weren't shooting at that moment. The other people were ready to leave, either they were leaving the next day or that night.' The 'other people' were *Cannibal Holocaust*'s doomed film team. 'I saw them that day and they had finished their stuff,' recalls the actor. 'They looked like younger people to me, not much younger, and they seemed to be jovial. They looked the part, except the girl. I think the girl was Deodato's girlfriend but he got a new girlfriend after she left, so I had to get one of my own. So I did … I was younger then (*laughs*). I don't know if anybody knew that I was an adult star at that point, I didn't tell anyone because it wasn't important. They were upset about the costumes. They didn't know where the costumes were, they said the airlines had fucked it up and now they needed to get the costumes from somewhere else.'

Kerman also arrived just in time to see the film's most infamous image being put to celluloid. 'I was there the day that they impaled the woman on the stick,' he says. 'It was a great piece of make believe. The girl was wonderful, she was the makeup lady, she was very beautiful and I just wanted to get close because she was walking around with no clothes on and she didn't seem to mind so, hey … I didn't have anything to do. They were trying to work out how to do it, and it was genius. She was sitting on a bicycle seat with a piece of balsa wood coming out of her mouth because balsa wood is very light, and she was holding that with her teeth.'

However, as the movie began to unroll Kerman grew increasingly more upset with the nature of the picture. 'A big putz. That is what I used to call Deodato,' laughs the actor. 'In fact don't ask what else I use to call him. We had a love/hate relationship … There you are with killer fish around you, killer snakes and a killer director (*laughs*). I was wearing a real gun in that movie, with blanks, but I could have gotten bullets. The police wouldn't protest – they were the ones that gave it to me! They were amazed that a film crew was out there. Then the animal came along. I thought the scene we were filming was over. The script said that we were cooking something on some rocks and I thought we were going to be eating chicken. I didn't care what it was but all of a sudden this live animal comes being carried by a kid, and I'm thinking to myself, "Something is not right here."'

Indeed, Deodato was about to film the on-screen slaughter of the helpless creature, an aspect of *Cannibal Holocaust* that has secured its infamous reputation to this day. 'I asked, "What is going on here?" and Deodato says, "Don't you worry," and I said, "You're going to kill this animal aren't you?" And we never got a scene of me eating anything because Deodato wanted the killing on camera. I begged him, I did a plea, I said, "This is wrong, this is such a terrible thing to do, please don't do this," But Deodato was adamant and the young actor had no qualms. I think he would have killed me if Deodato had asked. You know what I mean? He didn't look as if he had a conscience or a soul. That's a terrible thing to say, who am I to judge? But it just didn't … it didn't look as if it would matter to him. You know, people are dying all over the world and here I am worrying about a chipmunk. But this isn't art. I don't know if what we were doing out there was art in the first place, but whatever this was, it wasn't good. I told him, I said, "I know how to do this. You take a prophylactic – I'm sure you can get a hold of a prophylactic – and you stick it to the animal and when the time comes, go to a close up, and stick it. The close up is the knife going in the prophylactic and blood will spurt out. The animal is going to scream like hell, not because you've hurt him but because he's had a fright." That would have been a better scene. You didn't need to kill the animal. He could have done it that way and got away with the sadistic necessity, but the idea of really killing it on film was a pleasure to him. I think it came from the film *Mondo Cane*, but that was like really watching people who were killing animals for a living, it wasn't for the camera, the camera is a detached spectator. It's like taking the camera to a slaughterhouse to see what has happened. But Deodato made it happen. In Hollywood the animal would have had his own dressing room with his own handler.'

Predictably, when it came to filming the scene of genuine animal slaughter, most of the crew had retired back to their hotel rooms. 'No, there weren't many people around during that scene. They all seemed to disappear,' reflects Kerman. 'The animal that the kid was carrying, I think they just found him. It wasn't hard to find animals, just put the word out to the locals. I wouldn't know how to find an animal but they found a crocodile and an anaconda so they must have paid someone. I'm sure the turtles were easy to find but basically it was 100% illegal. I'm sure there was a law against killing turtles even then because they were endangered.'

Thankfully, the actor was not around for the long, drawn out sequence in which Deodato's fictional film crew mutilates a live sea turtle. 'They did that before I arrived,' confirms Kerman. 'I only saw that in the finished film. I don't want to put anybody down but I didn't think I was dealing with a bunch of professional actors. I just didn't have that feeling. There is a certain walk … a certain kind of actor's walk. I remember they looked as if they had a lot of fun with that poor turtle. I thought it was horrible.'

Surprisingly, the actor reveals that some seriously sick acts never even made it to the final cut of *Cannibal Holocaust*. 'They also tried to get a crocodile and an anaconda to fight,' he sighs. 'They just never shot it. They are mortal enemies, an anaconda and a crocodile. They put them in a pen, I don't know how the hell they got them, I was walking around and I was disgusted by the whole thing. I was off getting drunk I think. I had a good time though. I met a girl … She was a tourist over from California. She asked what I was doing I said, "I'm an actor. I'm in this film." It always works (*laughs*). I was better looking back then. Ruggero had a girlfriend on the set too. We used to row these long, narrow boats up in the morning, they never had enough crew so I used to help out. I used to help lift boxes as well, but whether you're in the middle of Manhattan or the middle of the jungle it always looks like a film set. Chaos and boxes and these big white screens. So I would always help out in the morning, and his girlfriend used to always come along so I didn't even ask his permission. I said to my girl, "How would you like to come up to the set tomorrow as my guest?" I thought I had that right. I was the lead actor, I didn't have to ask permission. So she had breakfast with us and then on the ship she went. Deodato didn't mind, it was a very nice thing … you know, I got to sit in an actor's chair in the jungle. And somebody gave me a very small folded hammock that was good to lie on. It stops the insects and the snakes coming near you. The first thing I did when I got there was select my trees so I could relax when I wasn't shooting (*laughs*).'

Indeed, despite the hardship of the jungle, and witnessing some of the movie's more shocking scenarios being played out, Kerman admits that making *Cannibal Holocaust* had its fair share of highlights. 'I was having my good times because I love acting,' he smiles. 'My main concern was the young lady I was with but she was having a great time. Every day she was going up and down the river to different places where we were making the film. It was so funny, here we were in the middle of nowhere and if they left me there I'd have no chance of getting back. We were miles from anywhere.' The actor also has fond memories of the crew. 'I got along very well with the crew. It wasn't like an American film where the cast and crew don't hang out much but, then again, there wasn't much cast here. My guide in the film was a native of Colombia, I don't even know if he was an actor. The other kid, the younger one that killed the animal, I don't know where he was from.'

The challenges continued when the actor was asked to take a bite of some raw meat (which was substituting for human flesh). 'They actually had me eat that stuff,' groans Kerman. 'That ugly stuff … and it was originally a pig's liver but I told them I was kosher. So they had to tape scraps to the pork – so when I was taking a bite, I was taking a bite out of steak. It was a lot of fun.'

Kerman also had the chance to mingle with some of the natives who were, inevitably, dressed up as savage primitives on-screen but, apparently, could not have been further from this stereotypical view in the flesh. 'These people were not stupid, they were just locals that worked in Leticia,' says the actor. 'When I first met them they were wearing jeans and shirts – possibly hand me downs or something – and they lived in shacks about four feet off the ground. They seemed to be having a good old time. They may have known that they were being portrayed as the bad guys, but they were being paid $10 a day which was a lot of money for them. I got along well with these people. The crew would speak Italian to them and they would speak Spanish back but they used to understand each other.'

Despite being a non-SAG production, Kerman has no complaints about his deal on *Cannibal Holocaust*. 'It wasn't a lot of money, something like $10,000 and back then that's what you got for being non-union. Deodato came to me and said, "Listen, I've got a problem. I have to shoot a woman in New York, but she also has to be in the studio scenes in Rome. But I don't want to pay her. Do you have any ideas?" I said, "Yeah I do have an idea. I have a girlfriend." And in the movie she is the girl in the office, in the television studio, sitting next to me in the park ... that was my real girlfriend! I called her from a satellite phone and asked her how she'd like to go to Rome, be in the movie a little bit, and not get paid but get free air fare and hotel in Rome and basically be on vacation. She said, "Sure," and I wanted to go to Israel at the time, and we made a stop in Rome going and a stop in Rome coming back and it was almost the same price. Back then you could do that, but now you have to be more honest (*laughs*). So we managed to have a vacation. I think the scene of us feeding the pigeons was great, it was improvised, nobody paid the pigeons to come, they just did and I had some peanuts. That was in New York. I thought that scene was very good because it was improvised. It must have been October when we shot that, it was beautiful. Then we went to Rome and shot in the studios. They put us up in this lavish hotel and I was getting 100,000 lira a day.'

The actor spent three weeks shooting *Cannibal Holocaust* after which he lost touch with the director that he had come to despise. 'I didn't stay in touch with Deodato but I stayed in touch with Masini because he got me a part, almost immediately, in *Eaten Alive*, the Umberto Lenzi movie,' says Kerman. 'He got me cast before I went to Israel. I was three weeks in Italy doing *Cannibal Holocaust* and by the time I went to Israel it was nearly a foregone conclusion that I was going to be in Lenzi's film. I was in Israel for two weeks and then they had me signed up and measured me for things, Masini and I got along very well. I went to his house for dinner in Austria.' Consequently, for a brief period, things looked great for the actor. He had finally escaped from the shackles of adult moviemaking and was carving out a career for himself in Italian exploitation films. 'So I was going off to make *Eaten Alive*, and at this stage *Cannibal Holocaust* was still being edited,' remembers Kerman. 'The airplane film (*Concorde Affair*) was playing all over Rome at that time, and I had eighteen minutes screen time in that so I was a recognisable actor. I came back from Lenzi's film, where we were in Sri Lanka, New York and then back to Rome. I remember while we were wrapping up *Eaten Alive*, we had a big party in my apartment in New York. For the first film, *Cannibal Holocaust*, we had a big party in a restaurant in Rome and everybody was there. We had the whole restaurant for the night, and I was going to make another movie so I felt great, it was the best part of my life. But when I came back from Sri Lanka they had clamped down on Americans coming to Italy, which is why I never dubbed *Cannibal Holocaust*. I was supposed to go back to Italy and do the dubbing for all of the films. That was part of the deal that I had done. I didn't want anyone doing my voice. They got somebody very good for *Cannibal Holocaust*, but it wasn't me. I would have liked it to be my own voice.'

After that, despite having been to exotic world locations twice, and for two different Italian flesh-eating shockers, Kerman's liaison with the spaghetti splatter industry came to a sudden, and disappointing, end. 'I never went back to Italy even though I also did *Cannibal Ferox*,' he says. 'My scenes in that were done in New York, so my hopes of working over there were dashed. But a friend of mine was in Italy, he's a director of adult films but I forget his name, and he told me I was a star, that I was all over the papers, but *Cannibal Holocaust* went through hell. Deodato got himself indicted, and not just for animal cruelty but because they thought he might have killed the actors! But yes … he absolutely got into trouble for the animals. Although they weren't sure that he didn't kill that first batch of actors either (*laughs*). He had to bring them over from America, bring them to court and prove that they were alive! That is a real story. He almost went to jail for the animal stuff, but the production company got fined instead. It didn't play in a lot places but it made a fortune. It made a fortune in Germany, Italy and Japan but it hardly played in America. It didn't have any kind of big opening in the States, I remember it played in one sleazy theatre in 42nd Street. It was this grainy, lousy print. From what I was told they lost United Artists as a distributor because of the animal killings, Deodato really ended up fucking it all up.'

Moreover, when Kerman finally got to see *Cannibal Holocaust* he was mortified, and not just by the animal scenes. 'I thought the art direction was terrific but Deodato is such a shit,' says the actor. 'He played footage of real people being killed on a television screen that I was watching in the movie … In the narrative it was supposed to be fake. This fake film made by the team that got eaten by the cannibals. Only what Deodato used was actually real … real footage of wars and stuff. I think that is a complete sin to use real people's deaths like that. There is a lack of scruples there and it really spooked me, because I didn't know they were going to do that at the time. I cursed the film you know. I really cursed it.'

Now, thanks to Hollywood editor Bob Murawski – who also happens to a big fan of Italian horror flicks – Kerman is having something of a second lease of life on the big screen. Eagle-eyed fans will spot him as the tugboat captain who comes to the rescue of Kirsten Dunst in Sam Raimi's initial *Spider-Man* feature. It has also allowed him to face some of the demons from his past. 'I was at a convention a few years ago with Deodato. That is how I got involved with all of this again and ended up being in *Spider-Man*,' says Kerman. 'Deodato was older, but he looked the same. I ended up signing autographs at this convention and had no idea that I was going to be doing that. I don't know why *Cannibal Holocaust* is so popular. I would like to say that it is down to my great acting.'

To be fair, as repulsive as Deodato's gut-churner is, it is hard to deny that Kerman does put in a realistic, and frequently engrossing, performance. 'I'm also the voice of conscience in the film,' reasons the actor. 'The holocaust was really perpetrated on the cannibals. So when I went down I ended up making peace with the tribes. If I were directing it I would have had it that I ended up getting married to one of the tribe's people.' Now, Kerman has come to terms with his popularity among fans of Italian gore-fests, although he does recall a recent event where he took his girlfriend to see a Los Angeles-revival of *Cannibal Holocaust* on the big screen. 'She thought it was disgusting,' he admits. 'But I am glad it has a new following. When I did *Spider-Man* Sam Raimi told me he took a liking to me. He gave me a letter of recommendation. I was looking for an agent and Sam wrote that he really liked me and planned to use me again.' Presumably, then, the actor has some satisfaction about his current legacy as a popular cult personality. 'I not only have satisfaction,' answers Kerman, 'I have hope.'

MANIAC

Released: 1980
Directed by: William Lustig
Produced by: Andrew W Garroni, William Lustig
Written by: C A Rosenberg, Joe Spinell
Cast: Joe Spinell (Frank Zito), Caroline Munro (Anna), Gail Lawrence (Rita), Kelly Piper (Nurse), Tom Savini (Disco boy), Hyla Marrow (Disco girl), James Brewster (Beach boy), Linda Lee Walter (Beach girl), Tracie Evans (Hooker), Sharon Mitchell (Nurse No 2), Carol Henry (Deadbeat), Neila Bacmeister (Carmen Zito)

In a nutshell: Frank Zito was abused by his prostitute mother during childhood, and the cigarette burns on his body show the painful reality of his upbringing. Now a grown man, Zito stalks the streets of New York seeking random people to kill. He brings the bodies of dead women back to his apartment, scalps them and decorates the store mannequins that litter his rooms with the resulting, bloody hair pieces. In the meantime, a sense of normality enters his life when he begins to date a beautiful fashion photographer called Anna. However, their fling comes to an end when Zito attempts to strangle her during a visit to his late mother's gravestone. After fighting the murderer off, Anna flees to safety whilst Zito returns to his apartment, only for the mutilated bodies of his female victims to come alive and behead him. Nevertheless, a final twist reveals that this 'demise' may have all been a dream and, in fact, Zito is ready to stalk the streets of the Big Apple once again ...

Prologue: After the success of 1978's *Halloween* the floodgates began to open and a number of stalk and slash movies were hurried into production. Choice titles included *Terror Train*, *Prom Night* and, of course, *Friday the 13th* (all 1980). However, *Maniac* differs from these pictures through its deadpan seriousness, which owes as much to such true-life character studies as *The Boston Strangler* (1969) and *10 Rillington Place* (1971) as it does to *Halloween* and its ilk. Nevertheless, coming from a period where gore could result in good box office returns, *Maniac*'s hiring of FX supremo Tom Savini, and its ultra-bloody special effects, reflect the graphic splatter of *Deranged* and *Dawn of the Dead*, both of which the makeup maestro worked on. The movie's minimal use of music, and the camera's distant glare from the action, possibly indicates an attempt to duplicate the realism of *The Texas Chain Saw Massacre*, whilst Spinell's performance certainly owes at least some kind of nod of the head to Robert De Niro's Travis Bickle in *Taxi Driver* (1976). As if to draw attention to this, the script even has Spinell repeat De Niro's famous

'Are you talkin' to me?' line.

Prior to *Maniac*, Spinell was a jobbing character actor, best known for appearing in such mainstream, New York-set blockbusters as *The Godfather Part II* (1974), *Taxi Driver* and *Rocky* (1976). Co-star Caroline Munro, meanwhile, was most recognisable from her part as Naomi, the doomed Bond girl in *The Spy Who Loved Me* (1977) as well as being the poster girl for Lamb's Navy Rum. However, despite boasting a considerable presence in one of the most successful 007 capers, the role had only managed to launch Munro into the world of cut-rate Italian sci-fi (as seen with 1979's *Starcrash*, in which she first teamed up with Spinell). Other members of *Maniac*'s cast range from porn stars (Gail Lawrence, Sharon Mitchell) to obscure first-time actors and Savini himself, appearing in the movie's most spectacular death sequence.

Before embarking upon *Maniac*, Lustig had directed two adult movies, 1977's *Hot Honey* and the same year's *The Violation of Claudia*. He had also undertaken some uncredited work on Dario Argento's *Inferno* (1980), assisting with the Italian's horror director's night time shoots in New York (although the movie was based in the Big Apple, all the interior sequences were filmed in Rome).

About: *Halloween* started a trend within horror movies of either masking their killers (such as with *Terror Train* and 1981's *Graduation Day*) or keeping them off screen until a final, revelatory ending (as with *Friday the 13th*[80] and *Prom Night*). *Maniac*, however, belongs to a small subset of stalker flicks that never kept the audience in any doubt as to who was doing the dirty deeds (other examples include *Don't Answer the Phone* and *Don't go in the House*, both 1980, as well as *Nightmares in a Damaged Brain*, 1981's *The Burning* and 1984's *Silent Night, Deadly Night*). Perhaps more akin in tone to the two *Don't …* movies (both of which were similarly and not unreasonably tarred as being misogynistic at the time of their release), *Maniac* also has the habit of dwelling on a woman's figure or nudity before she is slaughtered. This is certainly not unique to Lustig's movie (all the women killed in *Don't Answer the Phone*, for example, are topless during their deaths) but, unlike these other films, *Maniac* features far more competency in building up suspense and in developing its title character's heinous personality. In other words, the movie could have been far more than just another exploitation flick.

To give an example, in one instance, erstwhile adult star Gail Lawrence takes a bath, with her nude body fully on show, before being kidnapped by Spinell and finally stabbed to death. There is a feeling that, whilst her death carries some sexual ramifications (Spinell mounts her and grinds against her as he begins to thrust in the knife) there is no need whatsoever to have the actress undress, in an irrelevant bath scene, before her demise. One can perhaps surmise that this scene-filler may stem from director Lustig's background in pornography, although it is strangely un-voyeuristic and presented in a very unsexy, matter-of-fact manner, almost as if the director just needed something, *anything*, to fill up a few more moments of screen time. Yet, despite being filmed with the same lack of passion, or interest, that most adult films reserve for their dialogue sequences, it is, nevertheless, rather sleazy to show a beautiful naked woman to

---

[80] The killer in the first *Friday the 13th* is not Jason Voorhees (as he is actually dead), but his mother. It was only in the sequels that Jason himself was resurrected and started slaughtering teens.

the (presumably masculine) audience and then slaughter her ... almost as if the filmmaker is inviting, and even encouraging, a link between sex and violence (or sexual violence). In another lengthy murder scene a prostitute poses for Spinell in a rundown hotel room before he strangles her to death and scalps her. During this sequence the link between the 'maniac's' building sexual frustration, and his eventual explosion into violence, makes more sense and is depicted with far more care, even if the gruesome pay-off feels a little bit too excessive, even for the genre.

Although *Maniac* undoubtedly comes from the stalk and slash era, as demonstrated by its various bloody set pieces, its horrors are not presented in the fun/white knuckle/rollercoaster ride spirit of either *Halloween* or its popular successor *Friday the 13th*[81]. As a result, Lustig's movie, both upon its release and over the subsequent decades since its debut, has met with a great deal of critical and fan hostility, almost always focused upon the film's alleged misogyny[82]. Indeed, Tom Savini himself explained in an interview for *Dreamwatch* magazine, that: 'I'd rather see the fantasy stuff and I'm serious when I say that. Jason doesn't exist, but the creeps that do exist are what bother me, like the character from *Maniac*. Even some of the movies you see today ... For example, I have no intention of seeing *Hostel*. The horror films today are just, "Hey watch how we can torture people." Yet, of course, I was the "King of Splatter" and killed many teenagers back when I was a kid (laughs). In saying that, though, it was always Jason doing it or a fantasy based character like that, except for in *Maniac*. The real stuff bothers me. You should have been at the meetings with the star of that movie, Joe Spinell, and heard the things that he wanted to do to the women in *Maniac*. "No Joe, we are not going to bite that off, I am not going to do that (laughs), I am not going to create that for you." I'm not surprised it's still cut in the UK though, because that was a film about a real creep.'

Certainly, *Maniac* is a problematic movie, largely because it attempts to deliver a serious character study of a serial killer yet, whilst doing this, the feature presents a series of exploitative, gory special effects, inviting the audience to revel in some incredibly staged death scenes. Perhaps what might strike first-time viewers as most distasteful is the manner in which some of the long, stalking sequences are concluded with a sudden, well orchestrated 'jump', as in *Friday the 13th*. Yet, because the killings in *Maniac* are perpetrated by a realistic creep it leaves a far nastier taste in the mouth. However, there is at least some attempt by Lustig to create a repulsive real life murderer rather than a Michael Myers-like, indestructible madman, and there can be little doubt that he presents Zito as a dislikeable, gruesome freak. Kudos, also, to Spinell for showcasing himself in such a vile manner because, unlike Hannibal Lector, Frank Zito is exactly what you might expect a serial killer to be: a sexually repressed, schizophrenic, sweaty slug of a man. The polar opposite of Anthony Hopkins in *The Silence of the Lambs* (1991) or Christian Bale in *American Psycho* (2000), there is nothing charming, funny or sexy about Spinell in *Maniac*, he plays exactly the type of figure you would cross the street to avoid.

Nevertheless, whilst Lustig and Spinell's attempts at realism are certainly admirable, it is

---

[81] 'Far too sordid to be any fun,' complains L A Morse in *Video Trash and Treasures*, perhaps missing the point. (HarperCollins, 1989)

[82] Even horror fans have been critical of the movie with James O'Neill noting that the 'underdeveloped characters ... exist solely to be slaughtered'. (Billboard Books, London, 1994)

when they push the film closer towards slasher/splatter territory that *Maniac* ultimately becomes almost too sleazy to watch. For instance, one of the movie's scariest moments is undoubtedly when Zito chases a nurse through a deserted New York underground station and into a toilet (which as an in-joke has 'Apocalypse Now' written on the wall). The nurse remains as silent as possible, even covering her mouth so as not to let out a whimper as her assailant stalks her. During this sequence our emotions become fully invested in this tearful, terrified young woman and we really want her to get out of harm's way successfully. As the tension becomes almost unbearable, Zito exits the bathroom and the hysterical female, believing that she is now safe, also starts to leave, stopping only to wet her face in the toilet's mirror. At this point, due to a predictable camera set-up, it is clear that Zito's grisly visage is about to appear in the reflection behind her, and this dilutes the suspense a great deal, but what the character then actually does to his female victim is simply revolting.

Accompanied by a jarring synthesizer buzz, Zito leaps into frame with a large machete in his hand and jams it through the woman's back and out of her stomach, a gruesome, unnecessarily explicit death scene for a very sympathetic character. Whilst the director's intended reaction is, presumably, one of shock and disgust, there is an inherent tastelessness in so heartlessly slaughtering someone with whom we have gone through hell with ... and it ultimately succeeds only in making you feel as if you are watching a 'maniac' director. In other words, the film becomes difficult to endure, it invites you to become attached to someone, no matter how mundane their character, and then has a big, hulking brute of a man come along and graphically destroy them. This is, undoubtedly, where *Maniac*'s perceived misogyny stems from: the picture sets up a series of faceless, walk-on female characters solely for the purpose of killing them in especially nasty, drawn out ways.

Of course, this is not to say that men don't meet with Zito's rage, they do, only their murders are less protracted and they are not subjected to long sequences of being stalked, as the nurse in the bathroom is. For instance, *Maniac*'s very first death belongs to a male, who is strangled to death on a beach, and, in the movie's most eye-opening gore scene, Tom Savini has his head blown apart by a shotgun whilst on a date with his lover. Coming straight from working on *Dawn of the Dead* and *Friday the 13th*, Savini obviously knew a thing or two about creating bloody on-screen deaths and here, in *Maniac*, he delivers a series of special effects that he would later admit were, 'the goriest I have ever created'[83]. Perhaps the last word on the splatter genre, the moment where Zito blows the unnamed Disco boy's head apart on-screen is one of the goriest deaths to appear theatrically during the 1980s and is a gob-smacking display of *Grand Guignol*. Yet, Lustig follows up this moment of messy mayhem (in which the desired effect is no doubt to make the audience say, 'Holy shit! How *did* they do that?') by terrorizing yet another woman, which, again, sits uneasily alongside the previous bout of carnage. Thus, on the one hand, *Maniac* jolts the viewer to life with some spectacular moments of excess but this explicit violence, which would be fine and perhaps even comical, in a *Friday the 13th* sequel, appears totally out of place in the context of Lustig's character study. Perhaps this is why 1986's *Henry: Portrait of a Serial Killer* swept up the acclaim that *Maniac* could well have achieved. In the case

---

[83] Savini, T, *Bizarro!*, Harmony Books, New York, 1983

of *Henry: Portrait of a Serial Killer* the murders are, wisely, kept largely off-screen, presumably because director John McNaughton realised that to add delirious levels of bloodletting to star Michael Rooker's murder spree would, ultimately, only sink his movie into the realms of sleazy exploitation.

Therefore, it is understandable why *Maniac* has upset so many people. On the one hand it has everything going for it: an excellent actor in Spinell, a fine director in Lustig and the benefit of location shooting in New York. Yet, even in spite of this initially gripping character study the director, and his star, appear to want to push things further and further … more gore and more close-ups of terrified women. After a while it becomes a little bit out of hand. Yet, in saying this, one cannot help but feel that *Maniac*'s misogyny does not belong to either Lustig or Spinell personally but rather to a fumbled attempt by both men to make a film about a man who hates women and has a serious Norman Bates complex. In defence of the movie, this aspect does come out from time to time, such as when a sobbing Zito mutters to the tied up Rita, 'Why did you need these other men? They didn't love you.' But it is too heavy handed to really hit home properly. Furthermore, even Spinell's bravura performance begins to get lost amongst all the nasty deaths (which, as the movie's theatrical poster suggests, includes the graphic scalping of two dead women).

As if *Maniac* is not polarised enough with its attempt to be a serious depiction of madness, and yet also showcasing a range of thrilling gore effects, it positively comes undone with the introduction of Caroline Munro's photographer character. It is simply impossible to believe that the beautiful brunette would even take a second glance at the overweight, greasy haired Zito let alone accept a date with him and this is one factor that really drags the viewer out of the movie. The twosome's relationship appears tagged-on (previous to this the film has been about little more than its main character stalking and slashing random people) and whilst Munro tries hard, Spinell is so deep 'in character' that it is impossible to accept that his new female friend would not see the warning signs a mile away. On the plus side, Munro's belated appearance blesses the film with a slightly more fleshed out female presence, even if she is not given a great deal to do except smile, look pretty and, finally, run and scream.

No discussion of *Maniac* can really be complete without discussing the film's ending, which is nothing less than confusing. First Zito, after a fight with Anna at his mother's gravestone, is attacked by his late parent when she dives out of her burial ground (in an attempt to mimic the closing 'jump' in *Carrie*). After this belated, and entirely unnecessary, introduction of the supernatural, Zito returns home only to be massacred by his female victims, who return to life to stab and behead him in a prolonged, gruesome act of violence. However, after the police reach his apartment and find nothing but the thought-dead 'maniac' (whom they confusingly opt not to report and instead leave the room) a close-up of Zito's face shows that he is still very much in the land of the living. It is also worth noting that his apartment is no longer populated with dead women, indicating, perhaps, that the entire film has been in his head and his gruesome deeds are yet to come. Interestingly, interpreted in this way (and it really is hard to imagine any other manner in which to accept *Maniac*, especially considering the dreamlike manner in which Zito is able to cart the bodies of his victims around New York without being caught) the film pre-dates the similarly inconclusive ending of the novel *American Psycho* by a decade.

Maniac is certainly not a perfect movie, but it is remarkably easy to become lost in Spinell's tawdry performance and to feel as if some kind of attempt at realistically depicting madness has been attempted by Lustig. The film's big problem still remains its mixing of fantastic acting and downtrodden New York locales, both very effective, with nasty gore and the compulsive terrorising of women; a recipe for exploitation that hurts what could have, and should have, been a tense, low budget character study. Nevertheless, if one does take the film's ending as representing Frank Zito awakening from a 'dream' then there is a strangely spooky feel as the end credits of *Maniac* roll. Without any closure, there is a definite feeling of 'he's still out there', a haunting finish to one of the few slasher movies that purposely tried to take the formula of sudden, violent, splatter-packed deaths and create something more realistic around it. Although it only partly succeeds, *Maniac* throws good taste out of the window and, even when viewed in today's world of *Saw* and *Hostel*, is a rare example of an eighties, American horror flick that still manages to shock.

What happened next? *Maniac* was released at a time when other women-in-peril flicks were making the rounds (for example De Palma's superior, but lambasted, *Dressed to Kill* (1980)[84]), and the horror genre was becoming bogged down in explicit misogyny. Choice examples include the aforementioned *Don't Answer the Phone* and *Don't Go in the House* (both 1980) and *Pieces*, all of which featured brutal scenes of man-on-woman violence. The worst would come in the shape of Lucio Fulci's despicable *The New York Ripper*, a clumsy, badly made film that so offended James Ferman, the then president of the British Board of Film Classification, that legend has it he had it specially deported out of the country. As if beamed from another time entirely, women-in-peril films such as *The New York Ripper* and the *Don't ...* titles are so politically incorrect that their cult reputation now seems perversely assured.

Although *Maniac* was badly received, it was a success, leading Lustig into an interesting directorial career that includes the enjoyable *Death Wish* rip-off *Vigilante* (1983), the not-bad slasher variant *Maniac Cop* (1988) and its two sequels (1990 and 1993 respectively) and the comical *Uncle Sam* (1997). The closest he got to repeating the tone of *Maniac* was with 1989's *Relentless*, starring *The Breakfast Club*'s Judd Nelson as a serial killer trying to outsmart the Los Angeles police force. It remains Lustig's finest achievement to date. Following 1997's *Uncle Sam*, however, the filmmaker would retire from directing to set up Blue Company and restore a number of grindhouse classics and forgotten obscurities onto DVD, complete with documentaries and audio commentaries. Choice releases include pristine editions of Dario Argento's *The Bird with the Crystal Plumage* (1971), George Romero's *The Crazies* (1973) and Gary Sherman's *Dead and Buried* (1981). As a result, Lustig has quickly become the cult film fan's best friend.

Maniac's Joe Spinell was so enamoured by his portrayal of Frank Zito that he attempted to get a sequel off the ground, even filming footage for a possible *Maniac 2: Mr Robbie* to show investors before his death in 1989 at the age of 52. The closest the world got to an actual *Maniac 2* was with 1982's *The Last Horror Film*, which paired Spinell up with Caroline Munro once

---

84 *Dressed to Kill* even picked up a Razzie nomination as worst picture of the year!

again, but this time in a far more comical vein. Sadly, the end result is merely dull. Prior to his death Spinell once again split his time between leading roles in low budget schlock (as with *Rapid Fire*, released in 1990) and small, supporting parts in more reputable, big budget fare such as *Married to the Mob* (1988).

Caroline Munro continued to act as a 'scream queen' for much of the decade, taking the lead role in *The Last Horror Film* and the trashy *Slaughter High* (1986), as well as acting in Jess Franco's mediocre *Faceless* (1988) and Luigi Cozzi's diabolical *The Black Cat* (1989). A popular face at conventions, Munro has starred in just enough cult classics to secure her a steady line of autograph seekers.

Maniac's biggest success would be Tom Savini, who, on the back of Lustig's movie and *Friday the 13th*, would be hired to oversee the cut-rate splatter in such low-rent offerings as *The Burning* and *The Prowler*. Finally, he would show what he could really do thanks to the opportunity of the bigger budgeted *Creepshow* and *Day of the Dead*. In 1990 Savini would be afforded the chance to direct, with his *Night of the Living Dead* remake, however the final result, whilst far from worthless, did not have enough identity of its own to really make a splash.

The influence of *Maniac* can most recently be seen in Alexandre Aja's surprise hit *Haute Tension* (2003, aka *Switchblade Romance*). Although Aja's picture fumbles, largely due to one of the worst 'twists' in film history, it does crib a lengthy scene from Lustig's movie, where the feature's overweight maniac 'stalks' the movie's heroine in a toilet. It is also easy to see *Maniac* as the unrecognised father of such later character studies as *Henry: Portrait of a Serial Killer*, and the more tastelessly exploitative likes of *Ted Bundy* (2002) and *The Hillside Strangler* (2004), which make Lustig's film look like an exercise in subtlety by comparison.

Bill Lustig interview

Maniac was an important picture for Bill Lustig. It was his attempt at making a legitimate 'breakout' feature film and, following the success of *Halloween*, horror was once again big box office. 'I guess you would call *Maniac* my first widely distributed film,' says the director. 'But, you know, all of the adult films that I made back then were released theatrically and played in Broadway theatres, so it was different back then than what it is today. We made the film with our own money. It was shot for $48,000 which encompassed $30,000 of my money, $12,000 of my co-producer Andy Garroni's money, and $6000 from Joe Spinell.'

Although *Maniac* had its share of gory special effects this element of the movie's success had nothing to do with the similarly explosive death scenes inherent in 1980's other slasher hit *Friday the 13th*. 'We only saw *Friday the 13th* when we were finishing *Maniac*,' says Lustig. 'We were invited to a screening by Tom Savini. We had actually hired Tom when he was working on *Friday the 13th* in New Jersey, but we shot the film just as *Friday the 13th* had wrapped shooting. However, *Halloween* was definitely on our minds ... (*Pauses*) I mean, there was nothing about *Maniac* that I felt was directly inspired by *Halloween*, although that was a film I loved and it had come out a year before *Maniac*. If any American horror film was, first and foremost, on my mind it was *The Texas Chain Saw Massacre*.'

However, *Maniac*'s actual storyline could not be further removed from the cannibalistic family-on-the-rampage theatrics of *The Texas Chain Saw Massacre*. 'Well we didn't copy it,' admits Lustig. 'But it was in the tone. We didn't pick scene for scene grabs or anything, although there is a shot in *Maniac* that I deliberately copied from *The Texas Chain Saw Massacre*, it is a portion of the scene where the woman is chased in the subway. She's running and then there is a dolly shot where the bars are between the camera and her. She's running, trying to find a way out and it was the shot that was inspired by the scene where the woman is running through the gas station in *The Texas Chain Saw Massacre*. Then eventually she bursts in the door only to find herself in more trouble, but in *Maniac* she bursts into a bathroom.'

Having obtained small, but notable, character parts in the likes of *The Godfather Part II* and *Taxi Driver*, actor Joe Spinell finally obtained a leading man role that he could throw himself into with *Maniac*. Indeed, even detractors of the picture would find it hard to deny that the actor is excellent in the film. 'I had been a production assistant on a movie called *The Seven Ups* where Joe was playing a small role,' says Lustig. 'He was the only actor who would really give me the time of day. He would talk with me and he had a great love of horror films and that led to a friendship because of this mutual love. He lived in Queens, New York and I was living in Manhattan and he would often stop by and visit and we would go to the movies together whenever a new horror film opened up. We had tried developing a screenplay for another horror project and that was in 1977, about three years before we actually made *Maniac*. We worked with a writer on a screenplay and at some point we abandoned it.'

In a notable in-joke, the name for Spinell's character came from another low budget terror director. 'The filmmaker Joe Zito is a dear friend of myself and Joe Spinell,' explains Lustig. 'We had this scene in the cemetery where he is going to the grave of his mother and, of course, we had to come up with a last name for the character. So we decided to call the character's last name Zito in honour of our friend Joe Zito. But it was one of those moments where we had to make a quick decision for the prop department (*laughs*).'

When asked to reflect upon Spinell's performance as Frank Zito, Lustig reveals that the actor was thoroughly committed to the part. 'He was involved with the film in a broader way than just being an actor but he truly loved the project and believed in it,' says Lustig. 'He was a tremendous supporter and I have got to tell you, for an actor who had worked with the greatest directors of that period, if not of all time, he treated me as the director of that film with the utmost respect. He would, of course, be a strong collaborator but at the end of the day he left it to me as to what we were going to do. He really supported my vision, which was also, to a great degree, his vision. From a creative standpoint I look back on it fondly.' Originally *Maniac* was scheduled to feature Italian scream queen Daria Nicolodi, the star of such Dario Argento shockers as *Deep Red* and *Tenebrae*. In the end, however, the role of Anna would be taken on by British actress Caroline Munro. 'What had happened is that Joe had starred with Caroline Munro in a movie called *Starcrash*,' reflects Lustig. 'While we were in New York shooting *Maniac* we had this role, it was a rather small-ish role, and I had worked with Dario Argento in New York on *Inferno* and met Dario's wife, Daria Nicolodi. I asked Daria if she would do the role and she agreed and when we got ready to do *Maniac* she was involved with an Italian television project or maybe she just changed her mind, I don't really know. So we were in New York, we were in the midst of shooting *Maniac*, and there was this *Fangoria* convention which Caroline was attending as a guest, and so was Tom Savini. So Joe went over there, saw Caroline, it was all hugs and kisses,

TABOO BREAKERS

"What are you doing?" and Joe comes up with an idea. He says, "We have a role available in this movie, do you want to be in it?" So she agreed and then what happened is that her husband was there and we said we had no money to pay anyone and everyone was working for free, and he said, "Well what if I go out and raise money for the movie?" It was in part to get Caroline some money and in part to make it a better vehicle for his wife. Sure enough, Judd Hamilton, much to our surprise, came up with some investors who put up around something like $70,000 which allowed us to get the rest of the film finished and ready for distribution.'

The other name involved with *Maniac* was Tom Savini. 'Because this movie was pre the release of *Friday the 13th* Tom Savini was not yet Tom Savini,' says Lustig. 'There wasn't, at that time, a great deal of attention being paid to special effects artists. It started later on. I remember the magazine *Fangoria* started around the time of *Dawn of the Dead* and so it was really *Fangoria* and its showcasing of the effects in horror movies that made celebrities out of the special effects makeup artists. So we were really on the cusp of Savini becoming famous. Anyway the motivating factor for Tom to do the movie, and this is no secret, is that he was in a relationship in Pittsburgh that had broken up. *Friday the 13th* was ending and he didn't want to go back to Pittsburgh so we offered him the opportunity to come to New York and, providing we got him an apartment for the month or so that he was in New York, he was happy to do it. He really cost us next to nothing, we just provided a place for him to live.'

At the time of *Maniac*'s release, Savini was quoted as saying that the movie was made by 'sleazy people', although he later denied saying this, noticeably on the film's DVD commentary track. Lustig, however, has nothing bitter to say about Savini. 'Well he probably wasn't misquoted,' admits the director. 'You know, I love Tom and I know we have a good relationship but I think there might have been a moment where he became swayed by what was popular opinion both in the mainstream and the horror press that *Maniac* had somehow perverted the genre. I think that he kind of found himself, I dunno, boarding that train for a period of a time. But I must tell you that one of my memories of Tom was after the very first screening of *Maniac*, he came up to me and literally planted a kiss on me thanking me for not cutting out his effects. He was so worried because here we are doing all of those state of the art gore effects and he thought that I would eventually chicken out and cut them out of the movie. But I think he went through a change of mind, or maybe he was just trying to be politically correct, but now he's come back the other way ...'

Certainly, Savini stages the movie's most gruesome special effect on himself, which is when he blows his own head off. 'Actually, Tom getting his head shot off was really a practical thing,' laughs the director. 'Tom had already made a fake head of himself and what we were doing was re-purposing a lot of the stuff that he already had in his workshop. Also, Tom wanted to be in the movie! He really had aspirations to be an actor, and later he was in *Knightriders*, and he had been in *Dawn of the Dead*, so it was really an accommodation to him wanting to do it and us working on a very tight budget and wanting to save money.'

When *Maniac* was released in America it was, by and large, greeted with a critical hammering. Lustig, as a young director, admits that he at least listened to his detractors. 'I had mixed feelings,' he says. 'Of course I never saw the film as being some kind of a catalyst for people to go out and kill people. That was never my intent and nor do I think that was the result. I guess I felt a little bit that the people who were the most vocal were probably a bunch of hypocrites. I looked at it in the same way as the people who denounce pornography. I'm put off by people that have these extremist views, that feel they have the right to come in and take away our freedoms because they have their own viewpoint. But I did accept some criticism and look at the movie today, from a storytelling standpoint, and think I could have done a better job. From a creative aspect I maybe could have done things better. But as far as *Maniac* being "the extreme of violence" and all that kind of stuff, from a political standpoint I don't buy into it … The truth is that we were just trying to make a scary movie. A very intensely scary film and it was kind of an idea to make something that was in the mould of *The Texas Chain Saw Massacre* but set in New York City, and which would take in a rough, uncompromising approach to its subject. We wanted to make it very unnerving, taking the audience on a journey that didn't have the slickness of a *Halloween* or *Friday the 13th* but almost had a semi-documentary feel to it. We didn't have any grander aspirations than that.'

Perhaps if Lustig had depicted more male victims, the criticism of *Maniac* would not have been quite so harsh, although the filmmaker thinks otherwise. 'I don't know,' he ponders. 'I just think that at the time we came out there were a lot of horror films out there and *Maniac*, with its advertising campaign, and the guy standing in a pool of blood, holding a head and a knife with an erection if you look closely … you know it's going to provoke controversy. Everything we did back then had to be provocative, so we got what we asked for. (*Laughs*) But now I have had the benefit of seeing *Maniac* with audiences around the world and I think you can equate that to a film like *Hostel*. *Hostel* is very much inspired by *Maniac* and I know that for a fact because I know Eli Roth and I know Quentin Tarantino and they have talked quite a bit about that. Yet people found entertainment value in *Hostel*, just as people found entertainment in *Maniac*. The DVD continues to sell extraordinarily well, the film is played at festivals constantly around the world and I think time has only proven that the film has a classic appeal to it. I think if people didn't enjoy watching it then they wouldn't. I also think at some point the gore becomes comical.'

Another New York-filmed study of psychosis, *Don't go in the House* (which was also released in 1980), has an ending almost identical to *Maniac* and a similarly sombre tone. Lustig, however, claims this is just a coincidence. 'You know, my recollection was that *Don't go in the House* came after our film,' he says. 'I hadn't seen it when I was making *Maniac* but I do remember seeing it afterwards because there was someone in the film, or someone creatively involved with it, who had somehow gotten our phone number and was sending us invites to come and see it when it opened. I can't remember his name now, but it was somebody connected with it. We didn't see it until it was in the cinemas though.'

A rumour surrounding *Maniac*'s troubled release was that Lustig himself had organised the feminist pickets surrounding the movie in New York in order to draw attention to his own film. The director, however, denies such self-publicity. 'Oh absolutely not,' he laughs. 'No it was not me, but it was welcomed and, ironically, there was a woman in California who was the head of an organisation called NOW and this is the postscript to all of that. She was in front of the theatre, I have news clips of her standing there denouncing the movie and then a year or so after that she was arrested for having been an accomplice in a murder. This had actually happened prior to her involvement with the NOW. The back story was that she was a prostitute and her then boyfriend had robbed one of her tricks and the john ended up getting killed. Her boyfriend was the one that actually did the killing but she had been involved in dumping the body. Well a year or so later she's in front of a theatre in California denouncing *Maniac* as being dangerous to women. I don't know but I think ketchup on people is a lot less dangerous than sticking them with knives (*laughs*).'

The director also admits that he was not really prepared for such demonstrations. 'I mean, how do you respond to something like that?' he asks. 'We didn't know! It was all new ground. Women's groups hadn't come out and protested at that time. We didn't know of any women's groups protesting movies. We had some issues ... like *The LA Times*. They refused to advertise the movie. They wouldn't even list the times or the name of the movie in the paper. That was the first, and only, time that ever happened. How do you know how to even respond to stuff like that? Here I am, a kid of 24 or 25 years old in New York and all of this shit is going on and people are angry, there are protesters, I'm being interviewed by Rona Barrett and I didn't know how to talk to the press. I was just hoping that we would make a few bucks in drive-ins and on the 42nd Street grindhouses (*laughs*).'

Nevertheless, it was not all doom and gloom during the picture's initial release. 'Because of Joe's relationship with people, and the love that people have for Joe Spinell, we would have celebrities show up to the movie because Joe was extremely proud of it,' recalls Lustig. 'We did have some genuinely enthusiastic responses to the film. One of them, in particular, was William Friedkin who said it was the scariest movie since *The Texas Chain Saw Massacre* and *Alien*. He was truly impressed with the film and I know it wasn't just lip service because he has continued to talk about it, even as recently as when he did the audio commentary for *The Guardian*, and he spoke about *Maniac* again and its impact on him. So we did have some people who really were enthusiastic about the film.'

Most importantly, of course, *Maniac* ended up doing stellar box office for such a low budget endeavour. 'The film actually opened quite wide,' says the director. 'We opened at 100 cinemas in the New York area, which was really big for that time. There were some theatres showing it at the same cinema on two screens. It immediately spread out to where we were at 400 cinemas and for a low budget horror film back then … sure, it pales in comparison to something like *Superman* but it was a pretty large release. As a result, it was supported by a lot of TV spots, radio spots and print ads. I think it gave us a very high profile, and I think that lit the fuse for those protesters. I know, of course, there are people with different opinions but I always thought that the overuse of gore has a way of diminishing some of the fright, but that is just me.'

In light of such success, it is a surprise that the movie never saw an official follow-up. 'Sequels weren't as automatic as you think back in that period,' claims Lustig. 'The sequelitis really started in the late eighties with the rise of home video. So when we made the film it wasn't in our thoughts to make a sequel. What Joe did instead, was that he went off with Caroline and Judd Hamilton and made a *Maniac* inspired horror picture called *The Last Horror Film*. Later in the late eighties we did a deal for the sequel. I wasn't going to direct it, but Joe very much wanted to do it. So, anyway, Joe shot a promo with Buddy Giovinazzo, the guy who did *Combat Shock*, and I didn't want to stand in the way because it was as much Joe's baby as mine so I stepped away and sold the sequel rights. Joe was about to start production, maybe he was about three or four weeks away, and then he died during the pre-production.'

Another reason that some might be surprised about the lack of an immediate sequel is that *Maniac* features a very open-ended conclusion. 'Yeah, I know, and I have to tell you that we shot several endings to the film,' reveals Lustig. 'For some reason I kind of liked the ending. I can't really justify it, it just seems like it had impact to it so I just went with the one that affected me the most. Again, it was not intended, it was not some master plan that his eye opens and ... "Ha-ha – now we're going to do a sequel." It was simply something to add an extra jolt. It could be that he imagined it all as well. That is another thing. It was a little bit of *Twilight Zone*. We even had a moment in there where the cops are coming into the apartment and there is a dolly shot that ended with a mannequin's hand in the foreground with some blood on it. Again, that was all very *Twilight Zone* and it was just me wanting to capture that feel. Just for no other reason than I thought it would be very cool.'

More recently, the idea of a *Maniac* remake has come to Lustig's attention. 'That is something that has actually been discussed,' he says. 'But there is a legal problem because we sold the sequel rights and when Joe died, which was never anticipated, we never focused on getting these rights back. So I hear there is someone working on untangling that but right now it is in limbo because it is with a company that is not in existence anymore and the principal of that company has died. And the other thing is ... how do you make *Maniac* without Joe Spinell? It's like saying you're going to do Freddy without Robert Englund. The fact of the matter is that *Maniac* and Joe Spinell are synonymous.'

Following *Maniac* another psycho-stalker study, *Henry: Portrait of a Serial Killer*, would go on to obtain critical respect. However, humble as ever, Lustig does not take any credit for being there first. 'I think that movies like *The Honeymoon Killers* pre-dated both *Maniac* and *Henry: Portrait of a Serial Killer*,' he replies. 'I consider that to be one of the best true life crime movies ever made. So when I think of *Henry: Portrait of a Serial Killer* I don't really think of *Maniac*, I think more of a movie like, as I said, *The Honeymoon Killers*. There have been other films of that kind but that is the title that comes to my mind right now and it is one of my favourites of all time.'

Even to this day *Maniac* remains cut in the UK, a fact that surprises Lustig. 'I am staunchly anti-censorship and I feel as though the BBFC has got to be corrupt,' smiles the director. 'How they view an independent film like *Maniac* is going to be different from how they view a big studio film. I think they have to be corruptible and, as such, shouldn't be positioned – and should not be in a position – to dictate what people should and should not see. Now you can tell me that children should be restricted from seeing a film and I would say that is totally appropriate. I wouldn't want children to see *Maniac* but don't treat me, as an adult, like a child and shield me from certain things. I think that, right now, what is cut is a close up of a switchblade going down a woman's chest.'

Looking back on his horror debut, Lustig admits that he is proud of *Maniac*, even in spite of its flaws. 'With every movie I have made I think it would be nice to go back and change it,' he says. 'I don't know of anybody that is satisfied with the final result of what they did, but I would say that, on the whole, I'm pretty satisfied. Given what we had to work with on *Maniac* it is a very effective film, Joe Spinell is brilliant in the movie and I wouldn't want to change that for anything. In the balance of it, *Maniac* is going to be on my tombstone.'

Caroline Munro interview

Having made her mark as leggy Bond villain Naomi in *The Spy Who Loved Me*, the gorgeous Caroline Munro went on to work with actor Joe Spinell in the Z-grade Italian *Star Wars* spin-off *Starcrash*. The two became good friends and, as a result, Munro found herself involved with *Maniac*, playing Anna, a fashion photographer who has one of the screen's least likely liaisons with sweaty, overweight serial slasher Frank Zito. 'Yes but I think that Anna has problems too,' laughs the actress. 'For a start, I don't think she was sure of her sexuality and that is what was lost on the cutting room floor. She was confused and it was meant to be more implied that she liked the girls and he was just a nice friend for her to be around. Bill couldn't believe that this stuff was lost when he went back to do the laserdisc. How it was lost I do not know but there were some scenes that explained us a lot better. It is sad.' Munro also mentions that she had no idea how controversial *Maniac* was going to be. 'I didn't at the time, and maybe that was naïve, but no. We were so into creating this film, and Joe was so into the character that, although you knew what he was doing, it was by the by. Plus, it was based on the Son of Sam, which was a true story.'

For Munro, *Maniac* arrived unexpectedly and the actress had to make a snap decision about whether or not to get involved. 'I met Bill Lustig through the lovely Joe Spinell. I remember Joe as this larger than life figure with black painted fingernails. We worked together on *Starcrash* and got on really, really well. I had been invited to a *Fangoria* show which was in New York and I hadn't seen Joe in a while. Well he was there with Bill and they were in production with *Maniac*, which they were telling me all about. They originally intended to have Daria Nicolodi in it but she hadn't arrived. Her schedule was overbooked I think and she was still working in Italy. So they were looking for a European and Italian-looking woman and Joe said, "It should be you! We start tomorrow morning though – can you do it?" I said, "Joe I can't. I have to go back to England. I have my stepchildren to look after." He said, "Please, we would love to have you." So I said, "Let me sleep on it." I literally did sleep on the script. I have a habit of doing that, which is a bit wacky, but I read it and then physically slept on it (*laughs*). Then I woke up and rang him at about 5am and said, "Okay Joe I'll do it." Then during the shooting, my husband and I decided to help them out financially. They wanted to add some more bits and pieces to make it seem more credible and so we gave him about $10 or $15,000.'

After agreeing to star in the film the actress got a quick lesson in the modern horror genre. 'That night Bill took me to see *Halloween*,' she laughs. 'I had never seen anything like it. That was like an entirely new genre to me. I was used to Hammer Horror and things like that (*laughs*). So this was something totally new. Bill told me, "This is the approach that we want." I recall that the first scene we did was very, very under-rehearsed – it was the restaurant scene. It was an interesting sequence and I feel it worked because we were both supposed to be quite hesitant. They took the first take, and kept all the pauses and everything, and that was the first day. A lot of what was on-screen was not necessarily what was in the script. But it did very well until the women's groups in Los Angeles got hold of it and said, "No, we don't like it." I was actually due to fly over there and I decided not to because I did not want to face that. I think Joe went instead because he could cope with it (*laughs*).'

Indeed, the actress admits that she opted to stay well clear of the controversy that surrounded *Maniac*. 'Maybe I should have defended it,' she muses. 'But I didn't have any defence really. I did it because it was an acting job and I got to be with my friends. They had quite a lot of footage already but they needed an actress and I happened to be quite cheap at the time (*laughs*). Then in Germany it was banned for years. Either the critics loved it and thought it was a piece of art or they thought it was the worst film they had ever seen. But now it is a new generation of young people who have discovered it although, in saying that, my two young girls saw it and they did not think it was very nice.'

Although Munro decided not to publicly defend the picture, she does admit that she never understood the idea that *Maniac* was misogynistic. 'Well it wasn't just women that he killed in the film, and there are also times when you think, "Is this all just in his imagination?" You don't know. But the scenes with Joe and the female mannequins were so disturbed. There wasn't a dry eye when we watched these parts. It was such a wonderful performance from Joe. It went through its period of controversy and it is now quite culty, don't you think? A lot of fans tell me that it is one of their favourite films and when you think about how small the budget was it looks great. It made a lot of money – and we put a lot of that in – and I think Bill Lustig was quite surprised when my husband went to him and said, "Can we have some money for it?"'

The actress also got to enjoy the movie's star-studded premiere. 'The opening night which was in New York, was the night the hostages were released in Iran,' she recalls. 'And when they came out they had their party in the same venue that we had the party for *Maniac*'s opening. Robert Duvall was there and a lot of Joe's friends were coming by and saying congratulations. They flew me out for that which was amazing, it received very good reviews at first and the people at the premiere all thought it was a fantastic film, very new for its time. I'm very surprised that it is still cut in the UK because of the amount of films that have come out after it which are far more, I suppose, gory. I mean, maybe, it was one of the leaders of that type, it followed *Halloween* … I think it was just after *Halloween*, so I suppose it was kind of new. The style of filmmaking was very raw … you know, it was all shot on the street, there was a lot of adlibbing and kind of a raw filmmaking which I think was great. If I go to a cinema, I don't personally like to go and see that sort of film but to be involved with such a good cast and such a fine director I felt I learned a lot.'

Being among *Maniac*'s gruesome special effects did not faze Munro either. In fact, she enjoyed watching Tom Savini work his magic. 'I liked Tom,' she smiles. 'He is a very good bloke. He tends not to talk about *Maniac* now but I think that he should be very proud of the special effects in the film. It was done way back when before CGI. I went along one day when they were filming, and I wasn't working. It was a night shoot. I was so mesmerised by watching Tom working that before I knew it the morning had arrived (*laughs*). He worked very quickly. I wasn't particularly aware of the amount of blood that they would show in the end result though …'

Following *Maniac*, Munro would go on to star alongside Lustig in *The Last Horror Film*, another slasher picture from the early 1980s. The end result was far more comical, and far less successful, than the twosome's first fear flick together. 'I loved working with Joe again. That was the final part in our trilogy together after *Starcrash* and *Maniac*,' recalls the actress. 'There was a scene in that which called for me to be chased down the red carpet at Cannes and, in order to do that, we had to tell nobody – we were guerrilla filmmakers before guerrilla filmmaking even existed (*laughs*). David Winters was our director and he was wonderful. He was the guy who had done *Linda Lovelace for President*. We shot it on the Croisette and we could only do it in one take. There was a camera in a car, and cameras placed around the crowd, and there was a red carpet. So the crowd were expecting a big actor to come out. Obviously we never told the police what we were going to do. I said to David, "What do you want me to do?" And I was told to hysterically run down the staircase and the red carpet chased by Joe. My hair was wet – because I was supposed to have just come out of the shower – and I had bits on underneath the towel, which turned out to be a good thing (*laughs*). So the camera crew was running along behind me and I got a lot of strange looks from the crowd. People's reactions were great, and this was all caught on film. I ran along until some man stepped out of the crowd and grabbed me by the waist and lifted me up. I was screaming, "Let me go," and security had to come and get him off me. That was one of the toughest things I have ever had to do.'

Following this Munro continued to carve out a niche in stalk 'n' slash flicks, including *Slaughter High*, an obscure *Friday the 13th* take-off that came at the end of the slasher boom. 'My husband directed that film,' says Munro. 'It was a bit silly that I was expected to play a teenager in high school, especially considering how old I was when it began filming. I didn't think that I was right for the part at all and I thought it just looked daft. I do have a lot of people tell me they like the film though. In fact, someone in Belgium just recently wanted to know if I had the rights to release it. It was originally called *April Fools Day* but then they had to change the name because of the American movie. I am not sure *April Fools Day* was the best title anyway … We ran out of money towards the end, even though we had quite a good budget for that kind of film. The dream ending that we have was not the original ending and it is something of a cop out.'

Before he died, Spinell was intending to complete *Maniac 2*, something that Munro admits she was hoping to come onboard for. 'Yes, he wanted to get the sequel off the ground,' she says. 'There was a lot of talk about it and I was interested but I always have *Maniac* itself. Bill was a good director, he has a very good eye, and I felt very comfortable with him. Bill doesn't direct anymore but he should and, of course, working with Joe was just fantastic.'

NIGHTMARES in a DAMAGED BRAIN

Released: 1981
Directed by: Romano Scavolini
Produced by: William Paul/John L Watkins
Written by: Romano Scavolini
Cast: Baird Stafford (George Tatum), Sharon Smith (Susan Temper), C J Cooke (C J Temper), Mik Cribben (Bob Rosen), Danny Ronan (Kathy), Tara Alexander (Sex Booth Performer), Randy Arieux (Police Officer), Ray Baker (Estate Agent), Tommy Bouvier (Joey), Craig Cain (Policeman), Carl Clifford (Hospital Attendant), Kathleen Ferguson (Barbara)

In a nutshell: George Tatum is a dangerous psychopath locked away in a hospital for the criminally insane. There, he is the subject of an experimentation programme, whereby it is hoped that the use of new drugs will explain the recurring nightmare that he has been experiencing and, eventually, rid him of all homicidal tendencies. Presently he continues to dream about a young boy breaking into the bedroom of two lovers and killing them with an axe. One evening George escapes from the hospital and begins to make his way from New York to Daytona Beach, Florida. Meanwhile, the film focuses on the Temper family, comprising of a single mother, Susan, and her young son C J. Things are not good at the

TABOO BREAKERS

Temper household as C J likes to play increasingly deranged pranks on his babysitter and also on his mother's lover, Bob. On his way to Florida George kills three people, whilst his psychiatrists try and trace his steps and catch him. Finally George makes it to the Temper household, where C J has been left with his babysitter, Kathy, and her boyfriend. George kills the two young lovers and focuses his attention on C J, who finds a handgun in his mother's bedroom and shoots the assailant. In a closing revelation we find out that George was the little boy in his nightmare, and he killed his parents at a young age. C J is his son and Susan Temper is his wife.

Prologue: The Italian language films made by Romano Scavolini prior to *Nightmares in a Damaged Brain* are suitably obscure, and his 1981 slasher shocker marks his first, and only, notable commercial feature. In light of *Nightmares in a Damaged Brain*'s focus on prolonged acts of gore and sadism, it is interesting to learn that Scavolini witnessed the real thing first hand as a freelance photographer in Vietnam. The cast and crew of *Nightmares in a Damaged Brain* is comprised of a horde of newcomers, almost all of them being 'one shot' deals, having quietly faded back into obscurity. With that said, the film does have its special effects work credited to Tom Savini. This, however, is also the subject of some controversy and, whilst photographic evidence shows that he was most certainly on the set of the movie, Savini allegedly threatened to file a lawsuit against the movie's producers for using his name on the theatrical poster. Whilst *Nightmares in a Damaged Brain*'s special effects are not on the level expected of Savini (the movie's much-celebrated gore is rather unconvincing and the blood is of a much richer colour than that which Savini typically uses) it is probably safe to assume that the artist may have offered some supervision to the FX crew.[85]

Prior to *Nightmares in a Damaged Brain*, the slasher genre had been catapulted into the public consciousness with the mega-hits *Halloween* and *Friday the 13th*. However, Scavolini's movie follows in the footsteps of such spin-offs as *The Burning* (1980) and *The Prowler*, which both hired Savini and attempted to outdo the other stalker clones by increasing the level of nudity and graphic violence. Whereas the more interesting of the *Halloween* variants, such as *The Boogeyman*, *The Slayer* (1981) and *Alone in the Dark* (1982), managed to at least achieve some degree of suspense and originality, *Nightmares in a Damaged Brain* aims squarely for the gut. Indeed, viewed in its original uncut form, the movie is almost certainly the most gruesome feature to emerge from the slasher boom's 'golden age'.

About: Although the controversy surrounding the use of Savini's name on the cinema poster gave *Nightmares in a Damaged Brain* some degree of free publicity and notoriety in the United States, the movie's real legacy lies in the United Kingdom. Re-titled in Britain from its original (less imposing) Stateside name of *Nightmare*, and with Scavolini's name given top billing for some inexplicable reason, the movie became one of the dreaded 'video nasties', a label given to a

---

[85] Indeed a picture of Savini on the set was published in the book *Spaghetti Nightmares*, but in the same book Savini comments, 'I didn't work on it ... I'd only had a brief chat on the phone in the early days of the project when it was known as *Dark Games*'. (Palmerini and Mistretta, Fantasma Books, Florida, 1996)

number of horror tapes that were deemed to be obscene during the early 1980s. In all, 39 titles were prosecuted under the British Obscene Publications Act, whilst another 35 were taken to court by the Director of Public Prosecutions but were, ultimately, not convicted of obscenity charges. In the fallout of the video nasties scare, extremely stringent regulation was introduced to the British market and even mainstream efforts such as *Straw Dogs* (1971) and *The Exorcist* (1973) would find themselves banned on home video. In all, the entire fiasco, which resulted in only 39 successful prosecutions let us not forget, would actually sweep hundreds of movies from the shelves of UK video stores. This sorry scenario would only be cleaned up in the late 1990s when the British Board of Film Classification finally moved with the times and granted legal video certificates to everything from *The Texas Chain Saw Massacre* to *Deep Throat*. There may still be some examples of excessive censorship (Ruggero Deodato's silly, but violent, opus *House on the Edge of the Park* had over 11 minutes removed from its recent DVD release) but these are few and far between.

This is, of course, digressing slightly, but *Nightmares in a Damaged Brain* is an example of a barely mediocre horror feature that soon became one of the most infamous genre movies of its time thanks entirely to the video nasty controversy. Along with Abel Ferrara's *The Driller Killer* (1978), the rape/revenge shocker *I Spit on Your Grave* (1978) and the more self-explanatory *SS Experiment Camp* (1976), Scavolini's slice and dicer would create an indelible mark on British culture by helping to kick-start an entire moral panic over the availability of violent films. Legend has it that it was an unsuspecting British journalist who, after viewing the movie's promotional campaign (which featured a 'guess the weight of the brain in the jar' contest) and scenes from the film, coined the phrase 'video nasty'. Furthermore, it would be because of his distribution of *Nightmares in a Damaged Brain* on videotape (in an uncertified, but still cut, version) that David Hamilton-Grant, the head honcho at an obscure British label called World of Video 2000, would end up spending six months in prison for selling material liable to 'deprave and corrupt'.[86] Looking back, it is unthinkable and shameful that someone should end up behind bars for something so innocuous as releasing a piece of make-believe on video tape but the 1980s was an increasingly more conservative time for the UK. Sadly, in the wake of his conviction video shop retailers panicked about facing a similar sentence for the distribution of uncertified material and horror titles were quickly removed from shelves across the nation. The video nasty had been well and truly born and, for years afterwards, titles such as *Nightmares in a Damaged Brain* would be bootlegged and sold at car boot sales or auctioned off in their original uncertified copies, often for three figure sums.

Strangely, of the 39 titles that were deemed 'obscene' back in 1984, *Nightmares in a Damaged Brain* is not even close to being the most gruesome or offensive. Films such as *Cannibal Ferox*, *Cannibal Holocaust*, *Faces of Death*, *The Gestapo's Last Orgy* and *I Spit on Your Grave* are far more likely to cause a viewer to be outraged and/or upset. Moreover, other listed horror efforts

---

86 'David Hamilton-Grant received an eighteen-month prison sentence of which twelve months were suspended. Two colleagues, Malcolm Fancey and Roger Morley, got between them a suspended sentence and fines,' explain Kerekes and Slater in *See No Evil* (Critical Vision, Manchester, 2001)

such as *Anthropophagous: The Beast, Cannibal Apocalypse, Island of Death* and the Bigfoot splatter offering *Night of the Demon* are umpteen times more gory and violent than *Nightmares in a Damaged Brain*. Nonetheless, as far as collectors of controversial splatter movies were concerned, Scavolini must have made one of the worst ... after all, someone had been sentenced to six months in prison for daring to bring *Nightmares in a Damaged Brain* to the general public. Just how bad could one film possibly be?

Alas, as many soon found out, there is actually nothing especially offensive about the film's content or tone (and in the post-video nasty era *Nightmares in a Damaged Brain* was typically imported by curious British fans from Holland, where an uncut Dutch VHS gave gore buffs all of the blood that was missing from the World of Video 2000 release). A slow-moving, badly acted slasher flick, *Nightmares in a Damaged Brain* may feature more blood spillage than your average *Friday the 13th* movie but close-ups of split latex spilling out crimson or a mannequin head being swiped off with an axe carry a certain joke shop feel to them. Therefore, whilst Scavolini tries hard to stage as many stomach churning set pieces, none of them are very effective and it is hard to really get lost in the film when the acting is so horribly amateurish.

The sole exception to this is Baird Stafford, who plays George Tatum, and who certainly puts some verve into his theatrics, which includes having a foaming-mouth fit at a strip booth and sobbing over a recently massacred carcass. Described by one critic as resembling 'a deranged Dick Van Dyke'[87], Stafford nevertheless gives the role his all and manages to build himself up as a formidable threat during the feature's running time. This is no small feat considering that C J Cooke, who plays his demented son, gives one of the worst child performances in history and Sharon Smith, playing the boy's hapless mother, is best described as totally useless in her flat, one-note delivery. When her role asks for her to break down into hysterics at the movie's (abysmal) 'twist' ending, it is akin to watching someone who has broken her nail just before a night out having a good old scream about it. 'That's my husband,' she screeches in all of her overacting glory, a sight that is likely to provoke amusement in the viewer rather than terror.

The most contentious of *Nightmares in a Damaged Brain*'s many gory moments is its climactic double axe murder, where a young George Tatum catches his mother and father engaging in a bout of sprightly sadomasochism. With his mother mounting his father, who is bound to the bedposts, the lady slaps the poor sap across the face and draws blood. The bewildered young lad promptly goes out to the garage, picks up an axe and beheads the woman, before burying the weapon in the face of his dad (the special effects highlight). As you do. Obviously carrying Freudian overtones, this scene is violent but it is also ridiculously nonsensical and as a 'surprise' ending it really isn't very impressive. Aside from the conservative nature of the set piece (boy exposed to sexual activity is confused and subsequently destroys his parents), it is also supposed to be the reason why Tatum has been incarcerated for so long. However, what is not explained is how he managed to grow into manhood, get married and reproduce without, apparently, embarking on a serial murder spree ... and if he hadn't killed anyone as an adult, and was a responsible husband and father, then just why did they lock him up? Questions such as this are not answered, or acknowledged, in the flimsy, threadbare logic that passes muster as *Nightmares*

---

[87] Critic James O'Neill is responsible for this apt observation (*Terror on Tape*, Billboard Books, London, 1994).

in a Damaged Brain's 'storyline'. Nor is it ever explained what Susan Temper does to provide her son with such a cosy middle class standard of living. Throughout the movie, her character does nothing except hire babysitters to look after him, and lounge around with her hippy boyfriend in his boat or by the beach. Hardly a responsible parent!

The plot also calls for characters to spout inane lines of dialogue simply in order to remind the viewer of the urgency of the situation. 'You lose a dangerously psychotic patient from a secret experimental drug programme and all you can say is, "I'm sorry"?' screams one of the psychiatrists. Another stuffed shirt claims that they intend to 'program' George 'for future government and private sector use'. It hardly takes a brain surgeon to ask why anyone would need the help of a psychopathic axe murderer for use in the private sector, but there you go … As you can probably tell *Nightmares in a Damaged Brain* really is a bit of a disaster. It is extremely silly, badly acted and painfully slow-moving (with some basic set ups, such as a car drive or Tatum walking from a phone booth back to his vehicle, taking forever to reach their conclusion). This, naturally, leads one to wonder why on earth it was singled out for obscenity charges when other, more offensive titles, barely scraped the radar of the Department of Public Prosecutions during the video nasty panic. The answer seems to be that the title's high profile, gimmicked release (with the aforementioned 'brain in the jar' contest) was tasteless enough to warrant media attention and the subsequent hysteria. The same can also be said of Ferrara's remarkably tame *The Driller Killer*, which has only one brutal slaying (shown on the cover of the video box) but it was this scene that resulted in a national outcry and the power tool massacre being blamed for so many of Britain's social evils. As with *Nightmares in a Damaged Brain*, *The Driller Killer* would also be banned and reach a huge audience over the years as a result, its 'contraband' status merely adding to the appeal, even if the actual film delivered few shocks and only minimal special effects.

Perhaps the best thing that can be said about *Nightmares in a Damaged Brain* is that, caught as it always will be in a time and place specific to its controversy, the movie is far from the worst of the video nasties. Indeed, in comparison to such stinkers as *Axe* (1977), *Bloody Moon* (1981), *Don't go in the Woods* (1982) and the aforementioned *SS Experiment Camp* (1976), Scavolini's flick looks like an unheralded masterpiece. The film also contains some slick camerawork and a sequence where Tatum prowls New York's 42nd Street is at least suitably atmospheric and sleazy (in the uncut version, Stafford views a stripper playing with a dildo, which is not hardcore but still seems totally out of place). Indeed, as a lasting testament to an era long gone, *Nightmares in a Damaged Brain* provides one of the best documents of 42nd Street in the early 1980s (the scene is shot from the window of a moving car with star Baird Stafford amusingly trying to keep a low profile in amongst the various gangs and homeless people). Ultimately, as silly as Scavolini's picture is, *Nightmares in a Damaged Brain* at least feels like a movie from another time and place. Its many plot holes and its focus on moving from one piece of gore to the next, with faceless 'walk on' characters quickly killed off, gives it a certain charm, predominantly because it is difficult to imagine how a movie of this quality ever managed to obtain a cinema release.

Although *Nightmares in a Damaged Brain* is nowhere near as accomplished as *Halloween* (and mentioning them both in the same sentence seems like heresy) or as skilfully set up as *Friday the 13th*, it does at least keep you watching, even in spite of the incompetence of its actors and plot. This is certainly more than can be said for such other slasher rip-offs as *Humungous* (1982), *The Mutilator* (1985) and *Prom Night* (1980) ... all of which are boring, banal movies that have nothing whatsoever to recommend them other than the occasional, inventive moment of bloody violence. Furthermore, it is doubtful that any other horror flick opens with an homage to *The Godfather* and for that reason alone, even whilst the days of video nasties are now long gone, *Nightmares in a Damaged Brain* might still be worth checking out for those interested in celluloid curiosities. It is also worth noting that, like many filmmakers of the day who hoped for a box office smash, Scavolini leaves his sole addition to the horror genre wide open for a sequel.

What happened next?
As one of the most notorious slasher films ever made, it is surprising that *Nightmares in a Damaged Brain* has yet to be released on DVD in North America (at the time of writing it was rumoured to finally be gearing up for release). Instead, fans continue to rely on bootlegged copies in order to see all the special effects in their full gory glory and, ironically, this has only added to the film's reputation as one of the scarcest, and thus most in-demand, video nasties. Outside of the UK, Scavolini's picture would meet only minimal success. Although released theatrically in North America, the movie would not be recognisable enough to stop its stateside video distributor from changing its title to *Blood Splash* in an effort to attract new custom. Nevertheless, the feature continues to attract a cult following in the United States, as shown by how frequently bootlegged copies sell on eBay and at film fairs. In Australia the film was put out on VHS in its full uncut form only to be banned at a later date.

Despite *Nightmares in a Damaged Brain*'s open ending Scavolini would never make a sequel and his next film would be the action feature *Dog Tags* (1985), which also stars Baird Stafford. He would then retire from filmmaking, becoming a lecturer, but would return to directing film in 2005 with *L'Apocalisse delle scimmie*, followed in 2007 by *Two Families*. As far as its influence goes, *Nightmares in a Damaged Brain* was not a movie that inspired any copycat features, but it remains a rare example of a commercial horror movie that goes to great lengths to create as sleazy an atmosphere as possible. Aside from Lucio Fulci's *The New York Ripper*, it is difficult to think of a theatrically released slasher feature of the time that featured quite such a heady mixture of sex and violence.

Romano Scavolini interview
Although Romano Scavolini is best known to horror buffs for his gore-shocker *Nightmares in a Damaged Brain*, the director actually began his career in the European underground, as he explains. 'It all started for me in Germany at the end of the fifties. I lived in Stuttgart. It took twelve months to do my first movie, *The Devastated One*, a full length 16mm black and white film. The story of my first movie is very entertaining ... I decided to shoot it using the type of film called reversal which means that you shoot and you develop the same raw stock which the lab then converts into positive film ready to screen. Shooting in reversal is very dangerous and I was too young to understand the risk, but if you lose or you destroy a portion of the film, then you don't have any negative to re-print the scenes you've lost, in fact you have only one original stock and that is it! This story I'm telling you is already a joke in the film industry! I gave the

only copy of my film to an American critic in Rome who asked to have it to show it in New York. This film was the expression of a 19 year old boy who did a full length movie. Writing, directing, acting, producing and editing without any kind of training! The copy, he said, was shown in New York with a certain kind of success. He then sent it back to Italy, mis-writing the address, and the Italian mail department then shipped it back to New York while the guy changed apartment! The film, the only physical copy, remained in the mail department of New York for two years, then it was sent to be destroyed with other uncollected items … After this I did nothing in films for various reasons, one of them is because I had to go to military service. I returned back to cinema making shorts, my first short *The Quiet Fever* won a series of awards and was acclaimed everywhere in Europe. In total I shot more than sixty shorts. Two of them, *Blind Fly* and *The Dress Rehearsal* are prohibited in Italy.'

However, it was in the fear film that Scavolini made his mark, producing a slasher picture that helped to blow up the whole 'video nasty' scandal in the United Kingdom. 'I thought that horror should be one hundred percent horrific, and all the movies that I saw were hypocritical and false,' says the director. 'Nobody had the guts to go all the way until the end of the horror film and I wanted to prove that horror is a reality that gets into our own bones and the minutest fibres of our body. Horror is a state of mind. Ask those who went to Vietnam, as I did as a French photographer, about horror … Horror in itself does not happen on the screen, it lies within the consciousness of the spectator and horror, as an altered state of consciousness, is inside all of is and this why we are so attracted to it, we fear being terrified by someone or something. However, human beings need a certain amount of horror in their lives in order to manage and face everyday life. All the time the question arises: "Why is *Nightmares in a Damaged Brain* so bloody? Why this? Why that?" In my opinion no one had offered a sincere look at the concept of horror until *Nightmares in a Damaged Brain* came along. The film industry does not know how to manage, or what to do with, this genre. They hide their face and their mind from horror movies, but *Nightmares in a Damaged Brain* has offered people something to think about, pointing the finger towards a different kind of experience, I believe, and this is my answer to the question.'

Having mentioned Vietnam, one feels obliged to ask Scavolini if bearing witness to the very real horrors of war influenced him in any way. 'Vietnam cannot influence any kind of cinema,' he replies. 'War films were always made, even before Vietnam, and that particular war couldn't really establish anything new in cinema. The Vietnam War has influenced my life, and I believed for a long time that it was almost impossible to do a movie based on my experiences.'

Nightmares in a Damaged Brain is perhaps most notorious for its final scene of slaughter in which a young, adolescent boy beheads his mother and then sinks an axe in the face of his father. The question has to be how Scavolini directed a child through such a horrible scene? 'This was the most incredible thing,' he exclaims. 'I had some personal concern to let a boy axe his mother and his father on-screen. So I called the boy's real mother and asked her to talk to him about the scene we were going to shoot, and the delicate aspect of it. The boy just listened to her, in silence, waiting until her sermon was over, and then he said that for him there was no problem at all since he always dreamed about killing his father! And this was the end of our concern about him! The boy and Tom Savini worked out the scene together. Tom showed him how to handle the axe and how to swing it and after a little while we were in business.'

As with many other slasher films, however, *Nightmares in a Damaged Brain* focuses largely on female victims, with two victims being killed during or after a sex scene. Questioned about this, Scavolini denies any misogynistic leanings in his picture. 'That is bullshit,' he maintains. 'Freud, blessed be his name, discovered some elements in his own unconscious hell, regarding his sexual attraction for a relative – daughter or sister I don't remember exactly – and from that moment on, humanity was forced to deal with one so-called "omni pervasive" system which controls our life – sex. The bottom line is that we are what we are because a female and a male had sex and procreated another being. If this pervasive reality permeates a film, it can probably be called misogyny or sexism, but I doubt it. If someone believes that horror only arises in the mind of someone sexually deranged … well it probably does, I am not the one saying it does not. My film has nothing to do with sexism in any way. But dear friend, let them say what they want … let them be happy bubbling concepts and spitting them in the void. Horror films sometimes help humanity in finding its own way towards intelligence and sometimes they even help humanity in finding its own stupidity! Horror films are good because, as a genre, they do not deserve anything. Either they are good or bad – no middle way. I was surprised when the weekly New York paper, *Village Voice*, said that this film was just "different."'

Unsure of how to end *Nightmares in a Damaged Brain*, Scavolini admits that he shot six different conclusions. 'We wanted to be sure that the message of the film came through and we imagined several different endings to the movie and then we tried to catch the best one,' he explains. 'Our final choice was the one where C J blinks at the camera – towards the audience.' Inevitably, the director remained aware of the films that were influencing the horror landscape during the making of his stalk and slash opus. 'I did watch *Halloween* and *Friday the 13th* but without any sort of anxiety,' he says. 'They were just two movies among many without any particular impact on me.' Surprisingly, Scavolini did not enjoy either picture. 'I hate horror movies without depth or significance and they haven't even a bit,' he says.

With such uncompromising, and sure-to-be controversial, opinions, it is no surprise when Scavolini takes some other famous filmmakers down a peg. 'I do not admire anybody and I don't follow anyone,' he insists. 'Yes, there are some directors I like, although I will not tell you their names. To be sincere. I actually consider *Nightmares in a Damaged Brain* to be the best movie of its genre, but not because it is better shot than other films, but because it goes where nobody else ever dared to go. The critic for *The New York Times*, she wrote two articles of hate against me at the time the movie was released, taking out her anger on me and accusing me of being some sort of demon! She could not believe that a movie, and a low budget film at that, could dare to revolt the audience's mind like this.' As an Italian director, Scavolini does not feel any lineage with his more famous colleagues either. 'Nobody can really be influenced by Fellini,' he says. 'Fellini's powerful cinema belongs to him and him alone and can be considered a genre in itself. As for a horror director like Dario Argento: I never liked his cinema except his first film (*The Bird With the Crystal Plumage*), and he is also peculiar, to the point that there aren't any directors around influenced by his cinema. Certainly not I …'

When *Nightmares in a Damaged Brain* was released in Britain, its distributor was sentenced to prison on account of releasing the movie without a BBFC certificate. 'All of the blame should go to Margaret Thatcher and the British Cabinet since they were the ones who voted against the film's release,' says Scavolini. 'It is a shame, but on the other hand I am proud to be the author of such a scandal. I am proud of being such a "nasty" director. Nothing makes me more proud than being considered a living scandal. We need to be more scandalous and upset the soft and sleepy mind of the living dead, to resurrect them from their own essence.'

Some controversy also greeted the film in the United States, when makeup effects legend Tom Savini became upset about his name being credited with the on-screen effects on the American video box. 'Tom wanted to be paid only,' maintains Scavolini. 'If the production would pay him, he would let his name be exploited. There were other people involved in the special effects and prosthetics, but Tom came along with all of them and he was paid. So at the end nobody really knows what changed his mind about being affiliated with the movie, it could be a little jealousy at the unexpected success of this little movie while he was fighting inside the industry to make himself a director. I don't know, but I don't care either – he was great and this is all I can say.'

Released in the United States as *Nightmare*, and later as *Blood Splash*, and undergoing its most famous metamorphosis into *Nightmares in a Damaged Brain*, Scavolini himself struggled to keep up with all of the title changes. 'You can change whatever you want, this movie went everywhere and that is because of its contents and not its title,' he shrugs. 'After *Nightmares in a Damaged Brain* everybody asked me to do another horror. But I refused. I didn't want to tie myself into Wes Craven's private hell. I believe that Wes is a good director, but is wasted by the industry and by himself, so I wrote (a film called) *Lost* and I got very near to doing it with Paramount. Then I wrote *The Wrath of God* and I got very near to doing it in England and Rome. Then I wrote *Twilight* and I got very near to doing it too! I spent two years in pre-production with *Twilight* in London, and suddenly I couldn't do it, the law on Tax Shelter collapsed … Somebody called me from Manila and asked me to fly over there because there were chances for me in that country. When I arrived in the Philippines, some events I experienced in Vietnam came to my mind and I wrote the screenplay to *Dog Tags*. Back in London I found the finances.'

Unreleased on DVD and genuinely tricky to find, *Dog Tags* was, according to Scavolini, a very different movie from *Nightmares in a Damaged Brain*. '*Dog Tags* is not so much a war movie,' he explains. 'It is a movie based on corruption and betrayal, which happened in Vietnam. In fact there is no action in *Dog Tags* … I don't really know why I did *Dog Tags* but certainly not as a personal reflection on the Vietnam War. A writer or director is always crossed by thoughts that are not really unique. A writer or director dreams what everybody else dreams. In certain moments in life we're hit by a war story, then by sex, then by memories … you don't know what you're doing next. And of course, there is also a market out there demanding certain kinds of stories. Not even Kubrick did films without pretending to do something that would be successful at the box office. Everybody wants the same – to make a hit, it doesn't matter about the plot – it matters only if you can have a hit at the box office.'

Baird Stafford interview

Baird Stafford may not have gone on to a grand screen career but anyone who has seen *Nightmares in a Damaged Brain* can attest that his portrayal of regretful mass murderer George Tatum is insanely entertaining. 'Oddly enough, I got the part in the movie through the classic "discovery" scenario,' recalls the actor. 'Romano was brought by a friend to a dress rehearsal of a production of *1776*, the musical about the writing and signing of the US Declaration of Independence, in which I played the role of John Dickinson, the villain of the piece. He apparently liked what he saw. Of course, I had not the slightest idea that I was being "discovered", I only knew that some dark-haired stranger with intense eyes stared at me during breaks in rehearsal …'

From there, Stafford was given the script for *Nightmares in a Damaged Brain* and recalls reading a shockingly violent story. 'The script I was handed was brutal, but otherwise had very little in common with the version that finally emerged from the cutting room,' he recalls. 'Many scenes which had originally appealed so deeply to me were cut from the release version. I recall one, in particular, in which the family discovered a discarded Halloween mask during a picnic on the beach that, when C J lifted it, revealed George grinning up at him. I remember that scene especially because it was so uncomfortable to film: the noon sun was directly in my eyes, and sand is awfully heavy even on an empty bladder! This was but one of several, similarly surreal, vignettes that never appeared in the release version of *Nightmares in a Damaged Brain*. Incidentally, the scenes in New York City were not included in the original script, but were added some months later as "background"'.'

Having to portray such a psychotic personality was, according to Stafford, easier than one might think, thanks largely to the amount of information that was becoming available about serial killers. 'What little research I did had already been provided by the popular press in the US,' he explains. 'The decade or so before the filming of *Nightmares in a Damaged Brain* had seen several serial killers apprehended, about some of whom whole books had been written. The subject fascinated me for a while so I read what I could. It was easy enough to use those templates to look for, and open, the dark closets in my own psyche.' Certainly, taking on such a violent role did not give the actor any pause for concern. 'No, I am an actor,' he says. 'I learned very early to keep "character" entirely separate from "self". I did not commit those crimes – George did. It did help, of course, that I got to watch the filming of the effects and so knew, emotionally, that none of this was real. Incidentally, I came away from both *Nightmares in a Damaged Brain* and *Dog Tags*, the second movie on which I worked with Romano, with the firm conviction that all FX people are actually 10 year old boys, no matter to what age category they may appear to belong.'

Although Scavolini denies being influenced by the likes of *Halloween* and *Friday the 13th*, Stafford reveals that these films were commonly referenced during the making of *Nightmares in a Damaged Brain*. 'It was a general topic of conversation, more than once, among the production staff,' says the actor. '*The Texas Chain Saw Massacre* was also mentioned prominently, mostly, as I recall, as a source of stylistic errors to avoid.' Much like its predecessors in the slasher genre, *Nightmares in a Damaged Brain* would also be singled out for accusations of misogyny. 'I think a good deal of that may lie in the eye of the beholder,' says the actor. 'My character, George, didn't only slaughter women after all. In fact his father was one of his two first victims! In any case, I don't see that *Nightmares in a Damaged Brain* should necessarily be singled out for that accusation from among all the other movies in the genre, some of which seem, to me, to display misogyny to an even more marked degree.'

With Scavolini having mentioned that he shot six different endings to the film, did Stafford recall much about this. 'I vividly remember shooting them, mainly because it was a long week's work,' he reflects. 'I don't recall what they all were. The only one that sticks in my memory is one in which George opened his eyes in the ambulance at the end. However, I don't think that was the ending that appeared in the original release version. However my video tape is so old that it's un-viewable at present and I can't check my memory. Five of the endings were not in the original script and, after consultation with his production crew, Romano was winging it on the others.'

Stafford also has clouded memories of Tom Savini's role in creating the movie's makeup effects. 'I know a dispute of some sort may have arisen about that,' says the actor. 'However, I think the problem may have been more between Savini and the producer than between Savini and Romano. Needless to say in this case I rely more on my memory of second-hand information than on first-hand observation and could be mistaken. I do know that some of the effects were re-shot later in New York.'

When he finally saw the movie, Stafford was also unmoved by the on-screen brutality. 'At that point I had been an actor for some fifteen years or so and had participated in my share of "violence" on stage,' he explains. 'As an actor you knew it was all make-believe, even though the character had to be convinced that it was absolutely real. One of the assistant directors was actually assigned to support me when I came off camera after every scene, and apparently no one envied her job! The other crew, when asked, muttered something to me about "your eyes".' The actor also feels that his first feature film stands up well. 'It has held up as well as anything else in its genre and perhaps better than some. Romano, being European and influenced by Fellini, brought a slightly different perspective to a genre that at that time was essentially American in inspiration. Some of his special touches, especially technical touches such as camera angles and lighting, made it through the editing and I think *Nightmares in a Damaged Brain* may, as a result, be a bit more interesting than the general run of splatter movies ...'

When questioned about his fondest memories of making the movie Stafford recalls, with delight, the time that he spent with Scavolini. 'Romano was a delight to work with. He knew exactly what he wanted, but allowed his actors to achieve his goals in their own ways. Coming, as I did, from a background on stage, the only thing I found a bit difficult was Romano's insistence on achieving the feeling of spontaneity through lack of rehearsal. I thought it didn't quite give me time to achieve some of the subtleties that might have been possible after even a couple of run-throughs. I did, however, develop a certain pride in the fact that my scenes generally went in the can after only one take instead of requiring several.'

Although *Nightmares in a Damaged Brain* was not a massive commercial success, and is now largely forgotten, Stafford recalls the picture's original American theatrical release. 'I do remember a night in my favourite local bar a week or so after the release. One of my friends came up to tell me she had just been talking to someone who was struck by my resemblance to a character in a movie he'd just seen. Then, with unholy glee, that she had been able to tell him, "I happen to know he *is* the actor". A friend in New York was kind enough to send me the pan of the movie in *The New York Times*, and the second one, the following week, hidden in a review of a different movie. Given the rather – uh – subdued critical reaction, I must say I'm somewhat surprised to discover that the film has lasted this long.' Stafford was also shocked to find out about the feature's fate in the UK. 'I actually learned about the British distributor's conviction and imprisonment much later,' he says. 'If I remember discussion during filming correctly, the possibility that the film wouldn't get past the Lord Chancellor was always recognised. The only surprise, therefore, was that someone would actually take the chance but prohibition didn't work in the US, either.'

Following his big screen debut Stafford would make only one other movie, *Dog Tags*, which was also directed by Scavolini. '*Dog Tags* is about the Vietnam War and was filmed in the Philippines,' says the actor. 'Vietnam and Cambodia were not safe places to take an English-speaking cast and crew at that time. My character in that one was nothing at all like George and thank goodness for that! One of George was enough! I did learn that using a makeshift crutch, instead of a real leg, to trek through jungles is no fun at all. The plot involves a couple of rangers sent to rescue captured personnel, one of whom is a member of their platoon. The promised helicopter does not arrive, however and the Rangers are instead sent to find and retrieve some boxes of "secret papers" from another helicopter that had been shot down – papers that turn out, in the end, to be gold ingots destined to fuel corruption somewhere. In its own way, given the connotations of the plot, *Dog Tags* is even darker than *Nightmares in a Damaged Brain*.'

Following this, Stafford moved away from acting and currently resides in Florida, where he is a local businessman. 'I spent some time as a day labourer and then as a grounds keeper,' he says. 'I am currently the president and CEO of a small consulting firm that deals with network computer security. I haven't acted in several years. The politics involved in finding roles when one has starred in two movies are even more cut-throat than those involved when one has only to answer cattle calls and I found I lack the taste for competition at that level.'

The PLAGUE DOGS

Released: 1982
Directed by: Martin Rosen
Produced by: Martin Rosen
Written by: Martin Rosen (from Richard Adams' novel)
Cast: John Hurt (Snitter), Christopher Benjamin (Rowf), James Bolam (Tod), Nigel Hawthorne (Dr Robert Boycott), Warren Mitchell (Tyson/Wag), Bernard Hepton (Stephen Powell), Brian Stirner (Laboratory Assistant), Penelope Lee (Lynn Driver), Geoffrey Mathews (Farmer), Barbara Leigh-Hunt (Farmer's Wife), John Bennett (Don), John Franklyn-Robbins (Williamson), Bill Maynard (Editor), Malcolm Terris (Robert), Judy Geeson (Pekinese), Philip Locke (1st Civil Servant), Brian Spink (2nd Civil Servant), Tony Church (3rd Civil Servant), Anthony Valentine (4th Civil Servant), William Lucas (5th Civil Servant), Dandy Nichols (Phyllis), Rosemary Leach (Vera), Patrick Stewart (Major), Percy Edwards (voice).

In a nutshell: Two laboratory animals, Rowf, a black labrador (voiced by Christopher Benjamin) and Snitter, a fox terrier (voiced by John Hurt), escape from a medical testing lab in the English Lake District. The scientists immediately come under scrutiny for allowing the two dogs to get free, especially after they begin to hunt and kill a local farmer's livestock. However, the biggest controversy arises when a journalist discovers that the science lab was researching the bubonic plague, resulting in the widespread public opinion that the dogs are carrying it. The resulting mess concludes when the armed forces are sent out on a search-and-destroy mission. Meanwhile, Rowf and Snitter befriend a wily fox called Tod (voiced by James Bolam), who acts as their guide around the Yorkshire moors and helps them out of trouble on more than one occasion …

Prologue: Prior to *The Plague Dogs* director Martin Rosen had overseen one of the finest animated films of all time with his debut feature *Watership Down* (1978), which was also adapted from a novel by Richard Adams. A supporter of animal rights, Adams would use his anthropomorphic characters to relate the abuse of wildlife (as in *Watership Down*) or laboratory guinea pigs (as is the case with *The Plague Dogs*) to a younger audience. However, with the grisly acts of vivisection graphically translated to the screen by director Rosen, *The Plague Dogs* makes for a very adult viewing experience and this, coupled with its uniquely political subject matter, makes it a true anomaly among animated features. Indeed, no other commercial, full length cartoon has taken such a hot topic (experimentation on live animals) and released it to a mass audience.

Vivisection had been touched upon before in motion pictures, albeit without the harsh, commercial setting of Rosen's picture. 1933's *Island of Lost Souls*, for example, based on H G Wells' *The Island of Dr Moreau*, addressed the issue of scientific irresponsibility, and a glossy remake appeared in 1977 (using the original *Dr Moreau* title). Otherwise the use of live animals in medical experiments was largely dealt with in fiction, as Wells had done with his novel back in 1898.[88]

By the time that Adams came to publish his novel in 1977, Australian philosopher Peter Singer had released his influential study *Animal Liberation*. As the title suggests, *Animal Liberation* called for a greater care towards nonhuman animals based on the notion that sentient beings with a central nervous system, human or otherwise, feel pain and, thus, their torture cannot be justified. Famously comparing the torture of sentient animals with that of mentally disabled people and/or infants (in that neither would be aware of their mortality or what was about to transpire and yet each would feel the same amount of pain) Singer made a controversial comparison.[89] He also drew attention towards the harsh realities of common vivisection procedures. Although the philosopher does not make an argument in favour of animal rights, Singer's book is, perhaps because of its blunt content, seen by many as the backbone of this modern movement.

In 1981 Channel Four in the UK financed and screened Victor Schonfeld's *The Animals Film*, a movie that focused, often unflinchingly, on the use of live guinea pigs in vivisection and radiation experiments. The use of a major star, Julie Christie, on narration no doubt cemented its appeal to the passive viewer. Also looking at the meat trade and fur farming, among other hot topics, *The Animals Film* imbedded itself in enough minds to be honoured with a belated "25th Anniversary" big screen re-release, where it played at such major cinemas as the Institute of Contemporary Arts in London and the Filmhouse in Edinburgh.

The Plague Dogs was animated using rotoscoping, a format that Ralph Bakshi had pioneered in his 1978 spectacle *Lord of the Rings*. Interestingly, Rosen was not subjected to the level of

---

[88] *The Island of Doctor Moreau* was released to great controversy in 1896 and led to the formation of the BUAV (British Union Against Vivisection)

[89] 'Experiments performed on nonhuman animals would cause less suffering since the animals would not have the anticipatory dread ... It should be noted, however, that this same argument gives us a reason for preferring to use human infants or severely retarded human beings for experiments ...' states Singer (*Animal Liberation*, Jonathan Cape, London, 1990)

criticism that greeted his predecessor.

About: *The Plague Dogs* is a difficult movie to watch, especially for those who are well aware of the use of animals for medical and toxicity experimentation and the number of pointless, but painful, tests that primates, dogs, cats and other creatures have had to endure under the guise of 'science'[90]. However, because minorities of people who stand opposed to animal experimentation have been involved in acts of gross misconduct it seems that no matter how much horrendous undercover footage is retrieved from laboratories the topic still dwindles under the media-happy focus on a handful of extremists. Nevertheless, even regardless of where one stands on the topic, it would be foolish to accept that all animal testing is necessary (it is likely that few would agree, for instance, that lethal toxins need to be force-fed to beagles over an agonising period of time in order to reveal the inevitable deadly results[91]) or that repeating tried and tested experiments in universities is an especially progressive practice for anyone. It is also impossible to deny that the use of nonhuman guinea pigs in the past has resulted in disastrous results. The best publicised of which would undoubtedly be Thalidomide, a drug that sailed through tests with primates but which proved dangerous to humans. Tragically, as a result of mothers using the drug during pregnancy, 4000 children were born with limb deformities over a two year period in Europe[92].

However, aside from the bad science argument, the most common anti-vivisection stance is linked to the element of ethics inherent in utilising a live animal for a painful, prolonged experiment. In short: this is really where the debate begins, with some arguing that, regardless of the agony involved, a sure-fire cure for cancer can one day be found with the use of animal models. Estimates have it, for example, that between one million and five million monkeys died in the race to find a cure for polio[93], many hunted, captured and imported from their wildlife habitat in such countries as India. Hence, the question remains: does the (possible) final solution to a human disease warrant the painful entrapment and slaughter of millions of animals? Rest assured that this is a controversial, delicate and very emotional subject and, for unfamiliar viewers, *The Plague Dogs* could well prove to be an unflinching and worthwhile introduction.

Of course, there is also the argument that animals have the right not to be caged in an

---

90 Regardless of where one stands on the debate, the fact that many experiments have been pointless is undeniable. 'A dog is crucified in order to study the duration of the agony of Christ,' writes Hans Ruesch. 'A pregnant bitch is disembowelled to observe the maternal instinct in the throes of pain.' (Ruesch, H, *Slaughter of the Innocent*, Slingshot, London, 2003) Meanwhile, Harry Harlow carried out pointless but grim maternal tests on monkeys: 'By putting females into isolation throughout infancy and then forcibly impregnating them, Harlow was able to create living evil mothers. The infants would come to cuddle. The mothers would slam them to the floor of the cage. Or kill them. One baby monkey starved to death; another was so badly battered that he was blinded and partially paralysed. In one case a mother crushed her baby's skull with her teeth ...' (Blum, D, *The Monkey Wars*, Oxford University Press, New York, 1994)

91 As seen in 1997's undercover television documentary *Countryside Uncovered: A Dog's Life.*

92 As documented in Blum, D, *The Monkey Wars*, Oxford University Press, New York, 1994)

93 As documented in Blum, D, *The Monkey Wars*, Oxford University Press, New York, 1994)

unnatural environment and violated in a torturous manner even regardless of the cause. This point of view is especially common in the case of primates, which even the famed vivisection practitioner Harry Harlow noted are 'much more mature intellectually than a human at birth'[94]. In light of this horrible revelation, Peter Singer's comparisons between nonhuman test subjects and the use of infants and the mentally disabled is not quite as far removed as many of us might want it to be. However, *The Plague Dogs* steers well clear of many of these issues (for instance, distressed primates are shown only twice in the entire movie) instead opting to present the viewer with two dogs who have been subjected to horrifying, yet outstandingly useless, experiments. Not once in the movie, for example, is the film's fictional contract research organisation ever seen to be dealing with a cure for any specific medical problem. Rather the organisation's tests are endurance-based, conducted for military purposes or, in the case of Snitter's brain tampering, just for the hell of it. Nevertheless, the movie becomes a far stronger experience if the viewer has at least some understanding of the central issues behind the modern day debate over animal testing. Certainly, coming to the film with some background knowledge means that even little symbolic touches suddenly make more sense (such as a dog urinating upon a petrol pump emblazoned with the Shell logo being a comment on that particular company's links with animal research).

The Plague Dogs begins with a slow-tempo rendition of a song playing over a black background. The softly sung words begin, 'I don't feel/no pain no more'. We hear the sound of splashing water. The lyrics of the music continue to indicate that something is deeply wrong ('I've left this cruel world behind/and I've found my peace of mind'). Then, suddenly, the melody is replaced by a sinister humming whilst the splashing water continues until … finally we are introduced to a small, but deep, water tank. A black Labrador (whom we come to know as Rowf) emerges from the depths whilst a laboratory worker very matter-of-factly states, 'I think he's starting to pack it in.' Sure enough the animal drowns. There follows some more chat among the workers. 'Two hours, 20 minutes, 10 and a half minutes longer than Wednesday's test and about 12 minutes longer than the one before that.' A response quickly arrives. 'It's remarkable how regular the increase appears to be isn't it? It will be interesting to see what happens when its expectation of removal is countered by its physical limits. Shouldn't be too much longer …' The most evident thing here is how the dog is referred to as an 'it' and how the animal's desperate struggle to stay alive is treated like a game. The tone of speech between the two doctors is also very cold. A live creature has just undergone a lengthy period of torture, and yet these human beings are incapable of relating towards it as a living, sentient being. Indeed, for all intents and purposes, they appear to have lost their humanity. Instead, discussion immediately turns to even more agonising tests, this time a 'sensory deprivation' test on a primate. 'We do have a monkey set aside for that?' asks one man as Rowf is spread upon an operating table and has a tube forced down his throat. 'Just waiting for the go-ahead,' is the reply. In the course of *The Plague Dogs* the doctors will come to be known simply as the 'white coats', each animal fearful

---

94 Nevertheless, Harlow still allegedly subjected his primates 'to surgical mutilations, traumatic, electric and psychological shocks, and other experiences that, if he did them on humans, would brand him as a monstrous criminal.' (Ruesch, H, *Slaughter of the Innocent*, Slingshot, London, 2003)

of them and equating them only with pain and sickness.

Few other movies, regardless of genre, open with such force and with this powerful introduction *The Plague Dogs* shocks its audience from the offset. The feature's realistic presentation of a cold, harsh animal testing laboratory is utterly gut wrenching and aptly sets the tone for the rest of the movie, dark, distressing and very difficult to turn away from.

After being resuscitated, Rowf is taken back to his small cage where he is situated in the next stall to Snitter, a fox terrier who has had his brain operated on. The result for the poor animal is the confusion between the subjective and the objective in his mind, often leading to bizarre hallucinations and powerful flashbacks. A former domestic animal, Snitter was confined to a laboratory after his master was run over (whilst trying to prevent his pet from being hit by a car) and his new trappings, coupled with the painful brain experiments, have left him a shell of his former self. Thankfully, Rosen's movie does not repeat the (highly unlikely) happy ending of Adams' book where Snitter is rescued by his thought-dead master at the last minute. Instead, *The Plague Dogs* is a bleak and morbid movie that contains no humour whatsoever and leaves the viewer with very little space to breathe. Of course, this does beg the question of exactly whom the picture is aimed at.

Although it is tempting to label *The Plague Dogs* as a propaganda movie (in that its central motive is to alert viewers to the horrors of vivisection) there is, at its core, a tremendously involving story about survival. As with *Thelma and Louise* (1990) or even *Butch Cassidy and the Sundance Kid* (1969) Rowf and Snitter become outlaws and our relationship with them is similar to our connection with the lead performers in the aforementioned films. In fact, the bulk of *The Plague Dogs*' middle section is a tale of two personalities trying to cope with an unfamiliar new terrain. As in *The Omega Man* (1971) Rowf and Snitter awake into a world where they are surrounded by enemies and have very little control over their fate. Mankind wants to destroy them, food is scarce and, to the eyes of the two dogs, the Lake District appears to be a barren wasteland. 'They've taken everything away,' bemoans Snitter when he reaches the outside world, 'the houses and roads, cars, pavement, the lot! How did they do it, Rowf?' This confusion turns into a difficult attempt to stay alive, something they manage by feeding on a local farmer's sheep, which they capture with the help of a friendly fox called Tod (brilliantly voiced by James Bolam), the only 'outsider' whom the two dogs come to befriend.

Thus, it could be argued that, outside of its political theme, *The Plague Dogs* is, at heart, an 'us against the world' story; yet that does not make its intended audience any easier to comprehend. For instance, despite its cartoon form, *The Plague Dogs* is far too disturbing for children. Certainly, the same could be said about Rosen's previous hit *Watership Down* but the horrors endured by the cute talking rabbits in that picture were, at least, inflicted by other wildlife and thus a tad more natural in execution. Furthermore, as a harsh introduction to life and death, *Watership Down* at least serves its purpose, although no doubt many parents, kept up with sleepless, teary-eyed children humming Art Garfunkel's 'Bright Eyes', wish they hadn't bothered. Yet *The Plague Dogs* is a different beast altogether. For a start, the opening scenes in the medical laboratory are hideous and feature everything from tortured dogs to shackled primates with electrodes attached to their brains. It is very difficult to endure for any animal lover or pet owner, and Snitter's worsening condition throughout the picture becomes genuinely harrowing to watch. Indeed, less than five minutes into the movie and we see the laboratory's feeder shovel a dead terrier out of his cage. 'What's this? Boy oh boy, too much for you, was it?' he says as the carcass is scooped up. As if the point hadn't been made before, Rosen makes it now: this is not a Disney movie.

Therefore, it is tempting to assume that *The Plague Dogs* was Rosen's attempt to take *Watership Down*'s grisly realism one step further and, in doing so, perhaps catch an adult or teenaged audience interested in the vivisection debate. That the movie was not a big success indicates that whereas a family trip to the cinema to watch talking rabbits was acceptable, a more adult audience was perhaps hesitant to embrace a picture that was, even regardless of its seriousness, presented in animated form. Even so, *The Plague Dogs* remains a rare example of a 'message movie' conceived with a paintbrush and, given the expense of undertaking such a commercially risky project again, its uniqueness is almost certainly guaranteed. Nevertheless, the finished film does warrant the question of 'what were they thinking?' Even back in 1982 vivisection was a touchy subject and a full length movie devoted to it, not to mention an entire animated feature, must have seemed like a huge gamble from the offset.

However, *The Plague Dogs* did have one thing going for it when it was released, namely that animal testing was headline news for the first time in history. In September 1981 police removed brutalised primates from The Institute of Behavioural Research in Silver Spring, Maryland, USA after an undercover operative had provided evidence of extreme animal abuse. The limbs of live monkeys (who were boxed alone in filthy cages as small as 18 by 18 inches) were documented as being, 'raw with bites ... chewed open, bloody, oozing with infection'[95]. That a public outcry resulted because people were finally allowed to see what happens behind the closed doors of an animal laboratory should have timed in well with *The Plague Dogs* release but, strangely, the movie's advertising relented from playing up its connection with vivisection. Indeed, the picture's tagline ('Man's best friend hunted by their greatest enemy') is so vague that it barely even touches upon what the film is about. To spend $5 million making a movie about animal experimentation and then to not fully exploit the subject matter in the subsequent marketing campaign is bizarre to say the least. Especially when one takes into account how prominent the topic was after the Silver Springs discovery. Indeed, it is not too far fetched to conclude that many potential viewers may not have any inkling as to what *The Plague Dogs* was even about, and its poster images of the two cartoon dogs running from a helicopter gives few clues to the uninitiated.

To call *The Plague Dogs* an anti-vivisection movie seems fair and yet director Rosen, whilst critical of painful experimentation and laboratory conditions, has stated that he is not totally opposed to the use of guinea pigs for medical research. This is an incredibly strange position to take considering how critical his movie is towards the cruelty enacted on live animals in the name of science, however, it could well be that Rosen was under pressure from writer Richard Adams to stay true to his beliefs and the political slant of his original book. Nevertheless, whether Rosen's post-*Plague Dogs* comments are simply tactical in nature is anyone's guess because his movie plays out as a fiercely graphic portrayal of mankind's injustices towards animals and it is

---

95 As documented in Blum, D, *The Monkey Wars*, Oxford University Press, New York, 1994)

THE PLAGUE DOGS

difficult to leave the movie without feeling angry and deeply upset. Yet, one thing that is notably absent from Rosen's movie is the name of the research organization (in Adams' book it is called the Animal Research and Scientific Establishment or ARSE as it becomes shortened to) which may well demonstrate his own uncertainty about where his movie was going. Nevertheless, there are too many rich ironies in the movie to view *The Plague Dogs* as anything but a staunchly anti-vivisection tale. From the journalist who offers the scientist a lift back to his workplace (despite being the owner of an especially pampered dog herself, indicating that what is out of sight is out of mind) to the mention from the head of the laboratory (anticipating a public backlash) that the government 'doesn't want to get involved, they know what kind of research we do here,' the film's message seems blatantly clear.

Certainly, the dialogue consistently hammers home the horrors of animal experimentation. 'Why do they do it, Snitter?' asks Rowf. 'I'm not a bad dog. There must be some reason, mustn't there?' he continues after escaping from his cell and spying rabbits entrapped and ready to undergo the notorious Draize test. 'It must do some good.' When the two become trapped in the laboratory's crematorium the imagery even mimics that of a Nazi gas chamber, 'Something's been burnt in there. It's a death place. Bones, hair ...' says Rowf. In *The Plague Dogs*' most perverse act (removed from some prints) the two starving canines feast on the body of a dead man who has fallen from a hill whilst trying to shoot them. It is the movie's ultimate irony: two dogs, the animal most considered to be 'man's best friend', have been transformed into wild beasts, losing any trace of trust in humanity.

The Plague Dogs also benefits from the first class voice talents of a number of familiar British thespians. John Hurt, who was also used in *Watership Down*, is faultless as Snitter, credibly bringing the animal's suffering to the big screen. However, praise must also be given to Christopher Benjamin and James Bolam, who both succeed in giving this animated feature a real air of maturity and intelligence. Another highlight of this underrated little gem is the opening and closing song 'Time and Tide' by Alan Price, a heart-wrenching, but never bombastic, melody that finally erupts into a cathartic, gospel clap-along: a strangely poignant moment as the end credits come to a close.

A beautifully animated, incredibly original and strangely unsentimental viewing experience, *The Plague Dogs* is a true, one-of-a-kind movie. The idea of a picture exploring such a taboo subject as vivisection in today's day and age of commercial ambition and big studio dominance is almost impossible to imagine. That this evocative, ambitious and truly original masterwork ever came to exist in the first place is nothing short of startling.

What happened next? *The Plague Dogs* did not lead to a boom in serious, adult-orientated animation. However, if its direct legacy can be linked to any movie then it is surely the British production of Raymond Briggs' *When the Wind Blows* (1986), a horrifying anti-war picture that details the effect of nuclear radiation on a kindly old couple. As with *The Plague Dogs* the end result is devastating and not for young children, however, similar to the fate of Rosen's movie, *When the Wind Blows* failed to find a large audience. Along with *Watership Down* and *The Plague Dogs*, *When the Wind Blows* completes a wholly unique trilogy of serious animated 'message' movies that were financed in the UK and appeared within just a few years of one

TABOO BREAKERS

another. One day someone is sure to write a thesis about the lack of faith in government and humanity that these pictures dictate, all during a period when British society was becoming increasingly more conservative.

Martin Rosen only directed one other picture after *The Plague Dogs*, the Sundance-nominated *Stacking*. Following this the director resurfaced to produce the *Watership Down* television series in 1999 before disappearing again. Writer Richard Adams, on the other hand, continued to be prolific throughout the decade and his 1980 book *Girl on a Swing* was adapted into a memorably erotic film starring Meg Tilly in 1988. Adams released his autobiography, *The Day Gone By*, in 1990.

Few films after *The Plague Dogs* dealt with vivisection. Perhaps the most promising opportunity was with John Frankenheimer's big budget remake of *The Island of Dr Moreau* (1996), however, the end product was a disappointing reworking of H G Wells' novel. Rather more effective was George Romero's horror opus *Day of the Dead* (1985), which addresses the topic via the graphic depiction of scientific experimentation on zombies (one of whom exhibits primate-like awareness of objects and his surrounding environment). Ultimately, *Day of the Dead* is crafted with far more care and intelligence than the 1996 version of *The Island of Dr Moreau* could ever hope for. Vivisection is also a central theme of the underrated New Zealand-shot slasher movie *Strange Behaviour* (1981), which was co-written by future Oscar winner Bill Condon.

As vivisection, and the debate for and against its use, continued, so too did some particularly effective documentaries. 1984's *An Unnecessary Fuss*, which documents 20 minutes worth of footage from a laboratory in the University of Pennsylvania, is especially well known because the cruelty (in this case towards baboons, who were inflicted with terminal head injuries) resulted in the doctor in charge being landed with a civil fine and having his funding removed. More notorious is the made-for-television exploration *A Dog's Life* (1997), which was an undercover investigation into England's Huntingdon Life Sciences. The resulting footage (which featured beagle puppies being violently abused by workers and injected with lethal toxins on a regular basis) resulted in the UK's only successful charge of animal cruelty against laboratory workers. Inevitably the debate rages on with heated opinions on both sides.

Martin Rosen interview

Director Martin Rosen may have begun his career as a producer on such live action pictures as *A Great Big Thing* (1968) and the notorious *Women in Love* (1969) but for his directorial debut he chose to adapt a classic children's book, *Watership Down*, into animated form. The result was a success with audiences, young and old, as well as critics. 'I first read *Watership Down* while I was on a location in northern India for a John Masters project that I was developing for Universal,' says Rosen. 'My production supervisor, later the producer of several of the Bond pictures, had a paperback edition of the book which he was raving about and there was not much to do in the foothills of the Himalayas except drink bad Sikkimese vodka (*laughs*). So I read Adams' book about rabbits. As soon as I returned to London, I rang Adams and bought the rights to the book, not having a clue as to how I was to make it. This was, I think, in 1975. After the quite phenomenal success of the book, the challenge was to see if I could bring it to a cinema audience and retain the wonder of the original.'

As it so happened another director, John Hubley, was actually let go from *Watership Down* – allowing Rosen to step in and take over the reins of the animated feature. 'John Hubley was a very distinguished animation director and he was contracted to direct the film,' explains Rosen. 'But when he found it necessary to spend over fifty percent of his time in New York, I was forced to dismiss him. I subsequently learned that he was making a Doonsbury animated special for ABC at the same time as making *Watership Down* which caused my London unit to be without its key creative force for long periods of time. In addition, Hubley was insistent on using felt tip pens as the main colouring technique for the film. I thought this was odd as we had agreed early on that we would employ classic trace and paint on the film. The jittery nature of felt tips might have been energising for a short film[96], but for a film of over 90 minutes in length, the technique caused serious headaches. Too much jitter, and inappropriate for this film ... I read a review of the film by Charles Solomon who commented that the only part of the film which remained of John Hubley's work was the aboriginal-like prologue. In fact, that entire sequence was designed by Luciana Arrighi, who had been the production designer for me on *Women in Love*.'

As well as directing, Rosen would also write the screenplays for both *The Plague Dogs* and *Watership Down*, something that presented an extra challenge. 'The screenplay for *Watership Down* demanded careful selection in terms of what was to be included in the film. Much was left behind, but for the film to be faithful to the book's construct, the cinema audience should not be aware of those story elements left behind. I had the picture I wanted to make in my mind, so when we had to start over, I wrote the screenplay in one go. As the animation process took place, and the more interesting actors emerged, I would tweak the screenplay to take advantage of whatever qualities the animators would discover in their characters. With *The Plague Dogs*, I made some radical changes to the book, not least of which was the ending. I never believed that Ron Lockley, the author of the book that inspired Adams, called *The Private Life of the Rabbit*, would just happen to be fishing in the Irish Sea and would be in a position to rescue the dogs. In retrospect, the ending I conceived was probably the biggest single reason that the film was not more successful. However, I still believe that it was exactly the right ending for the film. To have changed it would have made it a different film altogether. In my view, there really was no other place Rowf and Snitter could go ...'

That said, during the closing credits of *The Plague Dogs*, after Rowf and Snitter have apparently drowned, an island appears ... Thus, the question needs to be asked: Did Rosen show the audience this in order to give them a little bit of hope? 'Well what do you think?' Rosen answers ambiguously. 'I mean, the intention was to leave the audience with just that question. Was there really an island out there? And if so, could they reach it? The Alan Price song was intended to amplify that question. They were going to a place where they would "feel no pain no more". The fact that it was performed as a gospel piece was intended to suggest a sense of joyousness.' Inevitably, both *Watership Down* and *The Plague Dogs* were considerable undertakings for the filmmaker. '*Watership Down* took about two and a half years to make,' says Rosen. 'Now, approximately eleven months of work had to be discarded after the first director,

---

[96] The children's cartoon series *Roobarb* is created using felt pens and the resultant 'jittery' effect is very apparent.

John Hubley, was dismissed so that explains some of that. *The Plague Dogs*, however, took about the same time.'

Obviously *The Plague Dogs* came about following the success of *Watership Down* but, according to Rosen, concentrating on commercial plaudits has never been a part of his game plan. 'I have never been particularly interested in predicting the success or failure of a film. The major studios are committed to commercial success and are only able to succeed ten percent of the time, so for an independent to aspire to do as well or better was a conceit I couldn't think about or support. If a film I make recoups its production cost, there is a reasonable likelihood that I will be able to secure financing for my next project. Of course I was very pleased at *Watership Down*'s reception at all levels, notwithstanding early predictions that any success the film might enjoy would be limited to the Home Counties, that is the counties surrounding London. That judgment proved to be well short of the mark.' The filmmaker was also well aware of the harrowing images in *Watership Down* and, as he would have to do with *The Plague Dogs*, he insists he went out of his way to make sure parents were aware of the picture's content. 'I was careful to insist that the film's one-sheets showed an aspect of the film's intensity,' says Rosen. 'We settled on the very graphic painting of a distressed rabbit entrapped in a wire snare. If parents were unable to determine the suitability of *Watership Down* for their own children after seeing the artwork, I'm not sure what else I could do.'

When *The Plague Dogs* was released in 1983, it came on the heels of the beginning of the modern animal rights movement. 'I was very much aware of the anti-vivisection movement in the UK,' says the director. 'However, some of their aggressiveness was not helpful when the film was released, such as injecting turkeys with poison at Harrods and that sort of thing ... But I never thought much about it. It was only when I did the research on the film that I became aware of what was going on. The experiments shown in the film were ones to which I was witness, with the exception of the opening sequence, which was conducted with a rat, rather than a dog. My intention was to present a situation in which the dogs were subjected to terrible treatment by faceless scientists and technicians who were completely inured to the pain and fear they were inflicting on these animals.'

Since the release of *The Plague Dogs* there have been some especially disturbing exposés of vivisection labs – some of which have a shocking amount in common with the treatment of the dogs depicted in Rosen's film. 'I believe that subjecting animals to painful and frightening treatment is a terrible thing to do,' says the filmmaker. 'And if we are to be the stewards of animals, which I believe is our obligation, we have to value animals in a greater fashion than we do now. However, up until better methods have been devised, I think that animal testing can be a useful indication of the efficacy of new medical techniques. What I do object to is the lack of sensitivity towards the animals, and towards what is being done to them for our benefit.' Certainly, there is a lot of anti-vivisection symbolism in *The Plague Dogs*. For instance, in one satirical scene, the white coats of the lab workers are contrasted with the pale clothing of a butcher and, in another sequence, a dog urinates over a Shell Oil symbol. 'Well when an individual scene layout was completed, I would first determine if the set-up was one in which I felt the characters could act,' explains Rosen. 'After that, it was very much a collaborative effort and Colin White, the animation director, had a wicked sense of humour ... so it was his suggestions, along with those of other department heads, that informed a lot of the process.'

Nevertheless, it was not the movie's controversial subject matter that attracted Rosen to the project. Rather it was the quality of Richard Adams' original novel. 'I just thought that this book would make a terrific movie,' enthuses the director. 'It is as simple as that. But with both *The Plague Dogs* and *Watership Down* I learned that you can't do with animals in cinema what you can do with humans. Audiences find it too disturbing because animals in literature and films, have, in the most part, been loveable and, with the possible exception of *Animal Farm*, I can't think of another serious animated film up to that time.'

Rosen is still very pleased with his second animated feature and describes it as 'the film of which I am most proud'. However when asked to choose his favourite character, Rosen has trouble. 'I cannot separate them,' he says. 'The Tod is what he is: a wild canny animal and a real Geordie. Rowf has never known a good master, while Snitter has never forgotten better times. I tried to show a transformation of the two dogs in the last scene, when Snitter finally gives up, but Rowf "sees" Dog Island and leads Snitter to a better place. The gospel song at the end, "Time and Tide", with its lyrics of, "I don't feel no pain no more", says it all.' Considering that he made two of the finest animated pictures to grace cinema screens, one would think that Rosen might have continued on this road but he did not. However, the director does not rule out returning to the drawing board one day. 'I have one possible animation project on my schedule,' he admits. 'But my primary focus is on three new live action features which are in the funding process.'

The EVIL DEAD

Released: 1982
Directed by: Sam Raimi
Produced by: Robert G Tapert, Bruce Campbell, Sam Raimi
Written by: Sam Raimi
Cast: Bruce Campbell (Ash), Ellen Sandweiss (Cheryl), Hal Delrich[97] (Scott), Betsy Baker (Linda), Sarah York[98] (Shelly)

In a nutshell: Five youngsters (two couples and a single girl) arrive at an old cabin in the woods where they plan on spending a quiet weekend. However, as soon as they arrive it becomes clear that some kind of hidden, but very vocal, force is following them. In the cluttered basement of the cabin the two men (Ash and Scott) come across an old reel-to-reel tape recording and a book called *The Book of the Dead*, a tome penned in blood and bound in human flesh, which details a number of rituals designed to invoke evil spirits. The five kids play the tape recording, which is of a man reading the rituals aloud, until Shelly (Ash's sister and the singleton) forces them to stop. Later in the night Shelly asks to be driven home, but the bridge which connects the cabin back to the main road is destroyed. Later Shelly wanders outside after hearing voices and is attacked and violated by the branches of a tree, which somehow 'possesses' her with demonic characteristics. Upon returning to the cabin all hell breaks loose as Shelly's four friends battle to protect themselves against possession by the evil dead.

Prologue: Sam Raimi had surrounded himself with a group of film enthusiasts whilst at high school, including many of the people that would go on to work on *The Evil Dead*. This list included lead actors Bruce Campbell and Ellen Sandweiss, producer Robert Tapert and

---

[97] Pseudonym for Richard DeManincor
[98] Pseudonym for Theresa Tilly

THE EVIL DEAD

the likes of Scott Spiegel (who co-wrote *Evil Dead II*) and soundman Josh Becker. Prior to *The Evil Dead*, Raimi had filmed a fast-moving, half hour splatter effort entitled *Within the Woods*; an attempt to show potential investors what he could do with the proper financial resources. As with *The Evil Dead*, *Within the Woods* stars Campbell and Sandweiss and, although no legal copy has ever been made available, the full length feature continues to surface online.

Raimi's influences for *The Evil Dead* appear to be, at least partly, inspired by the explicit zombie-gore of 1978's *Dawn of the Dead*, whilst the movie's device of trapping its actors inside a cabin and summarily killing them is a similar scenario to Romero's original *Night of the Living Dead*. Colourfully lit mist covers the exterior shots, which may also indicate some inspiration from the gothic terror of Mario Bava. The tone of the picture, which is extremely unrelenting, can perhaps be best linked to *Suspiria* (1976) and 1977's *The Hills Have Eyes* (which the director pays homage to in *The Evil Dead* by having its theatrical poster plastered on the wall of the cabin's basement)[99]. However, Raimi's carefree, slapstick humour owes more to his much documented love of the Three Stooges than it does to the explicit nastiness of the seventies horror movie. *The Evil Dead*'s haunted house locale and the use of sudden, loud sounds (as well as the film's early hints towards an unseen, supernatural force) certainly brings to mind the terrifying subtleties of *The Haunting* (1963) whilst the overall premise of attractive teens being brutally slaughtered is reflective of the time it was made and the success of films like *Halloween* and *Friday the 13th*. The voice of the transformed female demons also mimics the sound effects of the possessed Linda Blair in *The Exorcist*. *The Necronomicon*, the 'Book of the Dead', which is central to the movie's mayhem comes from the works of H P Lovecraft, who first wrote about it in his 1924 story *The Hound*.

Despite being rooted firmly with inspiration, direct or otherwise, from a wide variety of film and literary sources, *The Evil Dead* still manages to gain distinction for brutally victimising a male during a time when independently produced, low budget horror movies such as *Maniac*, *Don't Go In The House* and *The Prowler* were reserving their nastiest on-screen demises for shapely female characters. It should also be noted that the plot of *The Evil Dead* has long been linked to a story entitled *House of Evil*, which appeared in the American horror comic *Eerie* back in 1966.

About: With its vast array of perfectly timed jumps and non-stop barrage of blood and guts *The Evil Dead* is justly revered as a classic of the modern horror movie, whilst some critics even go so far as to label Raimi's debut feature as his 'best and most striking work'[100]. In the wake of the director's commercial success with *The Gift* (2000) and, especially, *Spider-Man* (2002), and its two sequels, this may seem to be a positively cult/fan-boy reaction but it is true that the filmmaker's later Hollywood films lack the renegade oomph and skid-row style that makes *The*

---

99 This torn up poster may also signify things that lie ahead, as has been pointed out by Kerekes and Slater: 'In *The Hills Have Eyes* a torn poster for *Jaws* can be seen on the wall, as if to signify that however scary that particular film was things here are scarier.' (*See No Evil* Critical Vision, Manchester, 2001)

100 *See No Evil*, Critical Vision, Manchester, 2001

TABOO BREAKERS

Evil Dead so easy to love. Without the overblown CGI of a *Spider-Man* picture it is comparatively charming to watch *The Evil Dead* today and to discover that, for all of its cheap and nasty blood and gore, the feature never stops after the central 'plot' starts to fall into place. Whilst this breathless array of one set piece after another would not work quite as well in the director's later work (such as 1985's disappointing *Crimewave* and 1995's ambitious Western *The Quick and the Dead*, whose bombastic, slam-bang style has much in common with *The Evil Dead* pictures) it serves his zombie-horror calling card well. Pivotal to the picture's success, of course, is leading man Bruce Campbell whose priceless facial expressions, and willingness to play the fool, rightly led to a fanatical fan following that is almost unrivalled among contemporary genre stars. Whilst the actor's baby-faced performance shows that he has yet to obtain the confidence that would inform 1992's *Army of Darkness* (which, alongside 2002's *Bubba Ho-tep*, remains Campbell's standout role) he still has more than enough charisma to carry the needed heroics and to get the audience on his side.

Considering that *The Evil Dead* came about at a time when low budget horror was largely associated with the endless stream of slasher movie spin-offs that followed in the wake of *Halloween* and *Friday the 13th*, it is interesting to see how the feature avoids becoming just another teen-kill flick. From the moment Raimi's camera glides through a misty lakeland setting, the film evokes a wonderful atmosphere (despite the movie's low budget the director simulates the movements of an expensive steadicam with remarkable ease) and the cinematography never remains still for anything more than a few seconds at a time. Instead, almost every shot shows remarkable imagination, with the action shot from a distance, from above, from far away, in fierce close-up and in a number of forced and disjointed angles. However, far from being just a 'gimmick' the result is that each shot tells its own story, just like a comic book, and the picture achieves a remarkable artistry. Showing a fine knowledge of horror, Raimi even cribs shots from Mario Bava's *Blood and Black Lace* (whose opening image of a sign thumping across the screen in the wind is repeated here with a swing-chair outside of the ominous forest cabin) and *The Texas Chain Saw Massacre* (whose lengthy woodland chase sequence is also reflected here).

This is a far cry, of course, from the monotonous, static happenings of the grungy, badly-lit slice and dice movies that were *The Evil Dead*'s contemporaries[101]. All the same, the feature still reveals some linkage with the more extreme end of the grindhouse horror tradition and, for all of its comical bile-spewing zombies, the fact remains that *The Evil Dead* also features a particularly unpleasant rape sequence. Looking back at the horror films of the 1970s (*The Evil Dead* began shooting in 1979) one can see that sexual assault was a prominent plot point for many low budget shockers. Whilst 1972's *Last House on the Left* uses a graphic rape scene to harrowing and powerful effect (and, in doing so, manages to hint at an America which has lost its innocence in the wake of the Vietnam War) most of the movies that followed in its footsteps

---

101 Perhaps summing up best how shocking it was that *The Evil Dead* got caught up in the UK's 'video nasty' fiasco (thus reducing it to the likes of *Cannibal Ferox*, *Faces of Death* and *I Spit on your Grave*) author Tom Dewe Matthews says, 'Any cinematic difference between fast-moving, innovative examples of the horror genre like *The Evil Dead* and the static dismemberment of women or animals which distinguished other "nasties" was lost in the hot-house atmosphere of a government party conference ...' (*Censored*, Chatto, London, 1994)

utilised sexual violence as little more than a way to appeal to extreme filmgoers and/or to court controversy.

As the British film critic Kim Newman has noted in regards to *I Spit on Your Grave*, 'It is easier to fake a gang rape than a convincing death-by-power boat propeller,'[102] and it would appear that many horror directors began to see rape as an alternative (read: cheaper) 'exploitable' content to gore and violence. Thus, alongside *I Spit on Your Grave* the decade also saw the likes of *The Candy Snatchers* (1973), *The Toolbox Murders* (1978) and *Mother's Day* (1980) as well as such European shockers as *Thriller: A Cruel Picture* (1974) and *Night Train Murders* (1975). These low budget movies generally forego explicit splatter effects (perhaps lacking the resources to create such trickery) and instead rely on sexual abuse to create their on-screen tension and horror. Whilst none of these pictures are as nasty (or monotonous) as *I Spit on Your Grave* they do reveal that the depiction of rape was becoming more common in the genre and, as a result, it is possible that Raimi saw nothing 'out of the ordinary' about creating such a moment in *The Evil Dead*. Nevertheless, despite the actual attack being committed by a tree, the sight of actress Ellen Sandweiss being forcibly pinned down (with one of her breasts exposed) and her legs spread apart is quite difficult to watch. Furthermore, although the idea of tree-rape is obviously ridiculous, the culmination of the scene, which features a branch penetrating the helpless woman, still manages to feel mean-spirited and sleazy. Considering that *The Evil Dead* is at its best when throwing buckets of blood around or punishing its leading man with ridiculous levels of tongue-in-cheek brutality, it does seem out of place to have any sort of sexual horror in the plot. Nevertheless, the film can at least claim to be the first, and most probably the last, motion picture to include a rape-by-tree.

For British fans *The Evil Dead* became notorious after it was caught up in the quagmire of the video nasties scandal. Whilst it now seems ludicrous to compare what is little more than a cinematic penny dreadful (albeit with plenty of spurting blood) with the more serious sexual horrors of *I Spit on Your Grave* or the genuine animal slaughter of *Cannibal Ferox* and *Cannibal Holocaust* it was with these very titles that *The Evil Dead* was suddenly associated. In fact, dubbed 'the number one nasty', tax payer's money was spent trying to prosecute the movie (unsuccessfully) as obscene, a tag that would result in the feature being cut to ribbons in re-release after re-release up until its eventual, uncut DVD debut in 2001[103]. Perversely, and showing how times have changed, *The Evil Dead* would then be broadcast, unedited, on UK national television, a far cry from the days when Brits could be charged by the police with importing the uncensored VHS tape from abroad. However, as the number one rental tape in Britain for 1983, *The Evil Dead* demonstrated that a low budget shocker could, effectively, out-gross its Hollywood rivals on an even playing field such as home video, a format which, at the time, could give even the most obscure slice of schlock the same shelf space as the latest Spielberg hit.

---

102 Kim Newman, as quoted in *Screen Violence*, Bloomsbury, 1996

103 One judge at the time of *The Evil Dead* attempted prosecution in the UK stated, 'I regard it as quite lamentable that in relation to a single film there should have been over forty separate pieces of litigation up and down the country.' (Kerekes and Slater, *See No Evil* Critical Vision, Manchester, 2001)

TABOO BREAKERS

Considering *The Evil Dead*'s dark humour, ambitious special effects and knowing play on traditional genre clichés (during the film's finale Raimi even has time reverse itself so that there is, literally, no escape for Campbell from the cabin nightmare he is trapped in) the film's closest contemporary is probably Frank Henenlotter's 1982 gem *Basket Case*. Although *Basket Case* did not obtain the same level of success as *The Evil Dead*, the two pictures are notably distinct from other independently made shockers of the early 1980s, mainly because neither has the desire to victimise females as its top priority and both have ambitions that are well above their budget levels. Each film, for example, comes to a close with lengthy displays of stop-motion animation effects which, whilst a tad jerky, are difficult not to admire considering the cash limitations. Whilst Raimi's film is undeniably better made than *Basket Case*, Henenlotter's pitch black comedy is every bit as well realised and the pace of his film never lapses. Telling the story of a man who carries his mutant, razor-toothed twin-brother in a wicker basket (and only letting him out when the time comes to massacre the doctors who separated them), *Basket Case* stands alongside *The Evil Dead* as an example of quirky, independent genre fare in a decade famous for cash-driven repetition. Certainly, comparing either film to your average 1980s *Friday the 13th* sequel (or rip-off) shows how much of a breath of fresh air these two pictures really were.

Where *The Evil Dead*, and also *Basket Case*, really stand out is with their intentional comic-horror, which, with the exception of *An American Werewolf in London*, was still relatively rare within the genre back when both films were released. Although the laughs in Raimi's flick are not as blatant as in his later *Evil Dead II* and *Army of Darkness*, there are still plenty of chuckles to be had, especially in the seemingly endless torture of Campbell's Ash, who is tormented, beaten across the head with an iron girder and sprayed with geysers of blood. As the film progresses and Campbell's ordeal becomes increasingly more excessive (and, by extension, daft), it is true that the scares take a backseat to the sheer, hilarious spectacle of the leading man's attempt to stay alive. However, the two styles rarely jar (the aforementioned rape sequence is the sole moment where the narrative seems ill at ease) and it is refreshing to find out that even James Ferman, the chief British film censor, was prone to 'howls of laughter' whilst watching the picture.

Sadly, it would appear that not everyone was confident in the success of *The Evil Dead*. Indeed, as odd as it might seem given the movie's contemporary classic status at least two of the cast are billed under pseudonyms (Theresa Tilly is billed as Sarah York, whilst male co-star Richard DeManincor is credited as Hal Delrich). This does give at least some indication as to the general consensus that must have surfaced during the making of the picture, where, one presumes, the idea of Raimi striking it big with his debut effort must have seemed ludicrous to some of the cast. In a sense, one can perhaps comprehend that the actors, having been asked to vomit bile, bite flesh and die in spectacularly gory fashion, would only have seen a cheap and violent chiller and something likely to disgust the majority of moviegoers. When one considers that pseudonyms are usually only reserved for pornographic actors it is quite a feat, and somewhat amusing, that two of the actors apparently could not bear to have their real names attached to the final product.

Although Campbell stands out as especially watchable, the rest of the cast are perfectly acceptable in their roles. Whilst there can be little denying that no one is likely to remember the movie for containing outstanding acting, the three leading ladies do a good job of physically depicting their transformation into hell-spawn demons, complete with arched backs, pained grimaces and outstretched arms. The performances may well appear quite amateurish at times but, given that none of the cast are seasoned thespians, no one has anything to be ashamed of and the scares and laughs never miss their mark, which is a sure-fire testament to the on-screen action. Sandweiss, in particular, is a minor miracle considering the hell that her character goes through.

Considering its surrealism, which would probably even do Salvador Dali proud (perhaps most evident in the sequence where time literally reverses itself as Ash begins to break down) *The Evil Dead* indicates a creativity behind the camera that is difficult to miss and easy to appreciate. However, in many ways, Raimi's little backwoods opus inadvertently paved the way for the horror genre in the 1980s and the eventual MTV-crossover appeal of films like Wes Craven's *A Nightmare on Elm Street*. For, without the inherent misogyny of so many teen-kill movies, Raimi's picture has an appeal that is not limited to a male audience (in 2001's *Donnie Darko*, *The Evil Dead* is even used as an example of a date film) and, moreover, the director makes it okay to laugh along with the on-screen happenings. Whilst this renders the controversy that *The Evil Dead* kicked up in the 1980s even more puzzling, it has secured the film an almost legendary reputation and it feels trivial to pick at any of this low budget wonder's few shortcomings. In short, the horror movie has rarely been as purely entertaining as *The Evil Dead*.

What happened next? Considering that Raimi never made a movie as violent as *The Evil Dead* again it was up to others to match the film's excess. Rising to the challenge was New Zealand's Peter Jackson, who unleashed *Bad Taste* in 1987, an ultra-low budget alien-invasion feature that took Raimi's splatter-comedy one step further by simply throwing restraint to the wind. Vomit drinking, a man consistently scooping his own brains back into an open head wound and a gruesome chainsaw finale make *Bad Taste* a genuinely stomach churning experience. Before winning critical acclaim (and a Best Director Oscar in 2003) for his *Lord of the Rings* trilogy, Jackson followed up *Bad Taste* with 1993's *Braindead* (aka *Dead Alive*), which is pretty much the last word on making a graphically violent horror-comedy. The end result is not to be watched during lunch and it is easy to see why Jackson never felt the need to try and top himself, instead moving on to more commercial fare beginning with 1995's *Heavenly Creatures*, the breakout movie for a young Kate Winslet.

In the wake of Raimi's super-paced popcorn shocker other horror flicks hit the cinema screens with their tongues firmly implanted in their cheeks. Better examples of the trend include *Return of the Living Dead*, *Re-Animator* (both 1985) and the spoof sequel *The Texas Chainsaw Massacre 2*. Less successful was the so-so 8mm effort *The Dead Next Door* (1988, which Raimi produced under a pseudonym), *Return of the Living Dead Part II* (1988), *Neon Maniacs* (1986) and *The Video Dead* (1987).

Although *The Evil Dead* was a hit in the UK it fared rather less well in North America, however it gained a cult following on videotape. This led Raimi to embark on *Evil Dead II*, a bigger budgeted remake of the first feature with Bruce Campbell returning as Ash. Lacking the jumps and the hyper-violence of the original, *Evil Dead II* is played for humour and generally succeeds with some laugh-out-loud moments. 1992's *Army of Darkness* (the last in *The Evil Dead* series to date) met with a mixed reaction from critics and fans alike, although its comedy is a lot more successful than its predecessor. In its own way, *Army of Darkness* could well be the finest project that Raimi has ever sunk his talents into and its current reputation as a cult classic *par excellence* is well deserved. Outside of his *Evil Dead* trilogy, Raimi's directorial career has been varied. There are moments of brilliance in *The Quick and the Dead* (1995) and *A Simple Plan* (1998) but neither of them really begs for a repeat viewing. 2000's *The Gift* is a fine little tale of terror, although it seems to have been largely forgotten in the wake of the success of *Spider-Man*, which is a difficult film to appreciate outside of its comic book origins. Nevertheless, 2007's *Spider-Man 3* was the year's biggest grossing film.

Actor Bruce Campbell took some time to translate his *Evil Dead* success into a functioning film career, even taking on a job as a security guard whilst looking for acting work. His role in *Evil Dead II* shows that he can perform physical comedy with the best of them but his follow-up roles were in largely mediocre horror flicks such as *Maniac Cop* (1988), the inevitable *Maniac Cop 2*, *Mindwarp* (both 1990) and *Sundown: The Vampire in Retreat* (1991). After his phenomenal turn in *Army of Darkness*, Campbell played the lead in *The Adventures of Brisco County Jnr* television show (which ran from 1993 to 1994) before being wasted in forgettable bit parts in the likes of *Escape From LA*, *From Dusk Til Dawn 2* (1999) and *The Majestic* (2001). His lead role in the independent breakout *Bubba Ho-tep* (2002) really should have won the actor the respect he deserves but, instead, it led to more sub-par parts in independent horror flicks, including Lucky McKee's *The Woods* (2006). Campbell enjoyed a recurring role in the *Xena: Warrior Princess* television series and has released two autobiographical books: *If Chins Could Kill: Confessions of a B Movie Actor* (2002) and *Make Love! The Bruce Campbell Way* (2005).

Meanwhile, producer Rob Tapert would set up Renaissance Pictures with Raimi and produce such winners as *Hercules: The Legendary Journeys* (1995 – 1999) and *Xena: Warrior Princess* (1995 – 2001) television shows as well as the blockbuster films *The Grudge* (2004), *Boogeyman* (2005) and the superior *30 Days of Night* (2007). Another *Evil Dead* success story is Scott Spiegel, who is listed as a 'fake shemp' in the film's credits (Raimi-talk for a production assistant). Spiegel would go on to co-write *Evil Dead II* and direct the top notch slasher flick *Intruder* (1988) and *From Dusk Til Dawn 2* before finding his biggest success as the producer of *Hostel* (2006) and *Hostel: Part II* (2007).

Tom Sullivan interview

Having worked on *Within the Woods*, Tom Sullivan was the natural choice to oversee the special effects in *The Evil Dead*. Indeed, the artist's relationship with Sam Raimi goes back some way. 'Back in 1978 my wife was going to Michigan State University and I was taking this drawing class there,' recalls Sullivan. 'However, even back then I knew what I wanted to do with my life and I read in the school paper about the Michigan State University Creative Filmmaking Society and that was something that Sam Raimi and his brother Ivan worked on. Basically, college students who lived on campus could rent auditoriums for a very low price and Sam would show his super-8 comedies on a Friday night, charging a dollar or two. That is how we met. I showed up, thinking they were filmmakers and wanting to meet them and what he made were not the most ambitious films production-wise but they had lots of story and Three Stooges-like plots and gags. Sam was making a feature length Super-8 comedy at the time called *It's Murder* and I ended up doing some sound effects on it and did some posters for them. At that time Sam was also working on the idea for *The Evil Dead*, which was known as *Book of the Dead*, and he was in a class dealing with mythology or something and they talked about the Egyptian *Book of the Dead*, which Sam thought was a great title for a movie. Of course, he had only made goofy comedies but Sam came up with an idea for this half hour project called *Within the Woods*, which we all contributed to and which was shot over a weekend. I did the makeup and special effects and by this time we were a close-knit group of filmmakers. It's interesting because Sam had about seven or eight friends growing up who were seriously interested in making films but I was not one of them, I was stuck out in a little town called Marshall. I was all alone out there so I couldn't drag anyone into filmmaking and so I began experimenting with my own stop-motion animation. So, anyway, when we met up I had a good portfolio of things and a reel or two that I could show them and which would give them an idea of what I was capable of.'

Sullivan remembers Raimi being easy-going back in high school and someone who was already developing his talent for visual comedy. 'Sam had such ease even back then. Comedy is very difficult to do, much less when you are 13 or 14, but his stuff was pretty amusing and he had a style, he was telling stories with different relationships and completing everything with a "moral", you know, a proper finish. It was rudimentary but also pretty sophisticated. It is amazing to watch the *Spider-Man* films and to see how much of that is actually still in there. Peter Parker is the perfect Sam Raimi character because he's the Joe Blow on the street who falls into being a hero. I think Sam made them into pretty personal films and if you look at his work, then that is the recurring theme, the geek, the goofball, the outcast guy who gets his moment.'

The author Bill Warren wrote in his *Evil Dead Companion* book that Sullivan was only on the set for three days, something that the artist wishes to clear up. 'Yeah, that is completely wrong. I was on the film for seven weeks but the author never got to interview me. They never gave him my address, although I get Christmas cards from those guys every year they never passed my phone number onto him *(laughs)*. But he is confusing me with Bart Pierce who visited the set for three days and who went on to complete the stop-motion animation with me, we partnered up for the finale. But I was there for seven weeks and I went through the hell with everybody else. The thing was that we all had jobs, we were all college students, and I had taken seven weeks off from work, but I had to get back or I was going to find myself without a job. That was the same case for everybody, we had six or seven weeks off and we all agreed to complete the film the following year.'

One of Sullivan's most iconic creations was, of course, the *Necronomicon*, the film's ghoulish book. 'In the script it was described as a book with some form of animal skin for the cover and with a few letters from some ancient alphabet on it,' remembers the artist. 'To me it sounded like a high school album book and I said, "Sam this book is supposed to be evil, so in my mind you should look at it and not even want to pick it up." Now, the most evil thing that I had ever heard of my fellow human beings doing, and there is so much to compete with *(laughs)*, came from a person called Ilse Koch. During World War 2 she was the wife of a concentration camp commandant and she would have prisoners skinned, and then bind books and lampshades with their flesh. So that was pretty disgusting and I felt that the *Necronomicon* would come from a culture like that. I made a cast of Scotty Spiegel's face, or it might have been Hal Delrich, and that was the cover.'

The Evil Dead was released just as *Fangoria* magazine was beginning to make celebrities out of special effects artists like Rick Baker and Tom Savini, and Sullivan himself admits that he had some special effects icons to draw inspiration from. 'I kept an eye on all of that,' he admits. 'I was aware of William Tuttle, Dick Smith, Jack Pierce and all of those great guys who had done the *Planet of the Apes* stuff, which was highly influential. At around the same time there was also a magazine called *Cinemagic*, which was published by Don Dohler. This magazine was a how-to for Super-8 filmmakers and it was an outstanding digest. Each issue would cover makeup and stop-motion animation and creature building and stuff like that. I can only imagine that magazine was at least as influential as something like *King Kong* in inspiring artists to get into the trade. They made things available to people, special effects were no longer this mystical trick that only people in Los Angeles could do *(laughs)*.'

The artist also got to ad lib some effects of his own. 'The script did indicate certain things, such as hands being cut off and burning faces,' says Sullivan. 'But there is this thing in show business, and this was certainly my intention, which is that you want to get as much of your work on camera as possible so I kept bringing little extra ideas I had to the set. So, for example, when Shelly is stabbed with the dagger, the hilt of the weapon has a little skull on it and the skull pukes blood. That was an improvisation of mine, where I drilled a hole through the mouth of the thing and I told Sam, "Hey, when Shelley gets stabbed, why not have somebody blow some stuff through it and we can get a close up of the skull puking blood?" And here's another scoop. The scene when Ash is going crazy at the end of the film and looks in the mirror, and then the mirror turns into water … well that was my idea. It was some goofy little thing and I had seen the Jean Cocteau films, *Orpheus* and *Beauty and the Beast*, where he employed tricks like that. I told Sam to get a little children's tub, paint it black, take the frame out of the glass, lower the wall and everything and then hang Bruce at an angle, turn the camera 90 degrees and film it.'

During the making of *The Evil Dead* Sullivan also admits to paying attention to the other horror films that were being released at the time. 'That was a very active subject. Sam had the idea that we should go to drive-ins and watch horror films and then talk about them because you learn more from bad movies than you do from good ones. There is stuff in the good ones that you can steal but then everyone says, "Oh, you got that from Hitchcock," or whatever but with the bad ones you can at least think, "Well they tried this but they blew it because they didn't have this production value or they had bad lighting or editing." Then you have something that you can build on and call your own, but I remember seeing *The Toolbox Murders* and *Motel Hell*, all these dreadful things. Thank God for marijuana *(laughs)*. But at the drive-in you can dissect the film as you watch it and everyone would be making mental notes. We were talking about *The Evil Dead*, which Sam had locked down, and he didn't even send me the script until three weeks before shooting, which, for a special effects guy, is barely enough time to think about what you want to make and to buy the supplies for it. So everything from my part was pretty much created the night before we filmed it. Usually that would be a disaster for a film production but fortunately I am a genius and it worked out just fine *(laughs)*.'

The artist also remembers that Raimi was more influenced by George Romero than he was by slasher flicks. 'I think that Sam was mostly inspired by *Night of the Living Dead*. The idea was that with *Night of the Living Dead* you could take this small group of people, stick them in a house and it harkens back to a Western almost, that simple conflict. Then with *The Evil Dead* it was us saying, "Well we can't afford all those extra zombies so we'll just get these five characters and turn them into monsters only you can switch them on and off, like a light switch." So they terrorise you and everything but then when you are about to kill them they return back to normal and you hug and then of course they turn back into monsters, so what we were doing was torturing the audience and that was definitely one of Sam's goals. He spelled it out to us, "We have to torture the audience, give them these expectations, because they'll be familiar with the genre and know that when that creaky door opens by itself you shouldn't go through it and end up screaming at the screen." Now I've seen *The Evil Dead* in a theatre and I've never seen an audience react to any movie like that, they scream "idiot" at Bruce and everything (*laughs*).'

Sullivan also faced some challenges from working with an amateur cast. 'It turned out that all three of the ladies were, and I guess still are, very claustrophobic,' he laughs. 'However, they were incredible troupers and it is their performances that give my makeup such impact, they really got into it and it just worked really well. It is almost iconic when I watch the film now, I'm very proud of what I did.' The artist also remembers that many of *The Evil Dead*'s crew had no visions of greatness. 'It's funny because when Sam was developing the idea for *The Evil Dead*, Rob Tapert, who was Ivan Raimi's roommate in college, had a plan to go into wildlife and game management and he told me he wanted to count fish for a career,' laughs Sullivan. 'Sadly, that dream was vanquished and he had to settle for being a multi-millionaire film and television producer, marrying a Warrior Princess and making babies in New Zealand.'

The Evil Dead would originally hit US cinemas without an MPAA rating. It was not, however, an instant hit. 'I think they lost money on it at first,' says Sullivan. 'They didn't submit it to the ratings board, largely because we all knew it would get an X, which would have made it look like a porno film. So they went out unrated and as far as getting television airtime or commercials in newspapers, well, there was little chance of that. They put "not rated" on the poster and it was basically limited to show-times and you wouldn't know what it was unless you read *Fangoria* or something. From what I read, the first theatrical run through America made $2 million and I can't imagine that covering the advertising budget or the prints but, at the same time, it made $26 million in Europe, and in Japan they went fanatical over it. I was invited to Japan and it was almost like being a Beatle, except that people found you creepy (*laughs*). I remember hosting a showing of it in Japan and as I left the theatre there was a sea of people and they just parted, they were terrified of the guy who did the special effects on this movie.'

The movie also shocked enough people in the UK to end up being banned as a 'video nasty'. 'Back in 1983 Sam Raimi and I were invited to England,' recalls Sullivan. 'Stephen Woolley of Palace Pictures had the rights and, of course, it was termed a "video nasty" and when we got there and were exposed to the press we were asked questions like, "Are you worried that you might be arrested?" We arrived just a day or two before an armed raid on a video store to get *The Evil Dead* and one or two other films. Now, the thing is that in England it's a big deal for a police officer to have a gun, and here he had one to go into a video store and get a copy of a VHS tape (*laughs*). Holy cow! That is extraordinary but you can't buy that kind of publicity. And, you know, after it was banned I heard from a friend who owned a video store in England and he told me that *The Evil Dead* was the most stolen videotape because for a long time it was so difficult to find over there. That is just great isn't it?'

As *The Evil Dead*'s cult following grew a sequel seemed like a safe bet and Sullivan hopped on board for the follow-up. 'I think *Evil Dead II* is a terrific film,' he says. 'There is that thing where you can look back at how these franchises developed. The first one has a hard edge and then they turn more and more comedic, to the point that by the third one it is almost like a Three Stooges movie, there isn't really a scare in the entire film. It couldn't be more different from the first film and what we got on-screen was only a fraction of what we wanted to do. There were a number of sequences that got cut from *Evil Dead II* and the one that really breaks my heart is the flying Deadite at the end. That is three months of my life going by when you watch that little two and a half minute sequence. Ash ends up in 1300AD and this big thing with flying red wings appears but that was actually meant to be an entire sequence with Bruce and the Knights battling this monster. To me it was like a Harryhausen fight, with this thing knocking the Knights off their horses and all of this stuff. There is this woman running with a child from the creature and then that is when Ash shows up and blows its head off. Sam had ignored all of our technical advice and how to shoot the background plates and I believe it is the most expensive sequence in the film, it had 30 or 40 Knights in full armour on horseback which is no small logistics problem. They blew this dust up into the air, but back in 1986, pre-digital you couldn't put things behind dust. It would look like a superexposition. So that all got scrapped, the thing shows up, gets shot and that is it, and that was the reason I wanted to do the movie! To be the next Ray Harryhausen (*laughs*).'

Looking back on the success of *The Evil Dead* now, Sullivan admits that the film's popularity is a strange blessing. 'It is very odd,' he laughs. 'A couple of weeks ago I had the honour to be invited to New York to see *The Evil Dead: The Musical* and it was strange to be sitting just a few blocks from Times Square and watching people portraying your friends doing lines from this movie … what an amazingly bizarre experience to see a part of your life fictionalised like that (*laughs*). But it is an amazing play and, by all means, everyone should see it and I hope they travel all around the world with it because it is so much fun. But, yeah, there is that shock of, "Wow we worked on something that really made an impact on people." The great thing is that I get invited as a guest to horror conventions all around America and inescapably someone will walk up to me at least once every show and tell me they are an artist, do special makeup effects and started in the profession after seeing my stuff in *The Evil Dead*. Now I never expected that, I got the same thing when I saw *King Kong*, the original Willis O'Brien masterpiece, which I first saw when I was five years old. I remember that I asked my mum, "Was that made in America?" And when I found out it was I knew I wanted to do that. So I set up my own little workshop area and drew, made dinosaurs and learned as much as I could about filmmaking.'

Ellen Sandweiss interview

Before *The Evil Dead* splattered its way across the world's cinema screens, actress Ellen Sandweiss was toiling it out in some Michigan woods with Bruce Campbell and Sam Raimi on their 8mm promo-film *Within the Woods*. By day, however, the three were more concerned about passing their exams. 'I went to high school with Sam, Bruce and a lot of other guys who are now very successful in the film industry,' recalls Sandweiss. 'We have never been able to figure out what it was at that time period and at that particular high school that spawned all these filmmakers (*laughs*). But, anyway, there were a bunch of them and they had all been making movies since they were about 12 or 13 years old and we were all in plays together during high school. I had been in a couple of their old films so when it came time for them to make *Within the Woods* it was just natural that they would ask me because I was one of the gang. The big difference between that and *The Evil Dead* is that the roles are reversed between me and Bruce. First of all, Bruce and I are boyfriend and girlfriend in *Within the Woods* whereas in *The Evil Dead* we are sister and brother, which a lot of people don't know. So in *Within the Woods* I'm Bruce's girlfriend and the role reversal came in that he was the one who turned into the awful monster and I was the one defending myself, killing everybody off and ending up as the lone survivor at the end of the movie.'

Within the Woods has yet to appear on one of *The Evil Dead*'s many DVD incarnations. 'I would like to see it on DVD but there is a little bit of history about it,' explains Sandweiss. 'It was supposed to be on the most recent DVD and they were all set to do it but there were some problems as far as Sam and the Renaissance Pictures guys were concerned. Basically they just wouldn't allow them to do it. So, you know, I don't think it will be ever seen except for all of the bootleg copies that are floating around (*laughs*).'

After high school Sandweiss moved on to further education, but, nevertheless, was called upon to take on the leading lady role in *The Evil Dead*. 'I was in college at the time studying theatre and they said, "We're going to make our first feature film and we want you to play this part,"' recalls the actress. 'They showed me the script, which wasn't much, it was just mostly people running around and screaming without much dialogue (*laughs*). It did change an awful lot, they added bits and pieces, but when you are 20 years old and somebody says, "Let's go make a feature film," well sure … but to be honest I didn't think anybody was ever going to see the movie (*laughs*).'

Had Sandweiss known the success that *The Evil Dead* was going to achieve she may well have declined filming one of the movie's most controversial moments. 'I had lots of problems with my rape scene,' she recalls. 'People have asked me in other interviews, "When you read that in the script what did you think?" My reply is always, "That is not how it was described in the script." In the script it said that I was attacked by trees, the sexual aspect of it really evolved as we were shooting and I guess I just didn't really realise what it was going to look like on the screen. It was dark, and there was a lot of fake fog, and I didn't think that it was going to look as graphic as it did. I also didn't know they were going to add all the extra sound effects and I was absolutely shocked and mortified when I finally saw it. Actually, I was just beside myself (*laughs*). However, although it was mortifying when I finally saw it at the premiere with my mother and father (*laughs*), I still kind of thought, "Well it will be okay because no one else will ever see it. After the premiere it will just kind of quietly disappear." Then years later I couldn't hide it anymore because my kid's friends were renting it at the video store and watching it so I had to own up to it and get a sense of humour about it.'

Amongst all of the comical, slapstick blood and gore, the film's rape seems especially out of place, something that the actress concedes. 'Well that is very true. I've never heard it put that way but that is very true. It is kind of weird and out of place but then a lot of people say that the reason *The Evil Dead* is so well known is that it is just so over the top. That scene is nothing if not over the top.' Also over the top are the moments where Sandweiss has to vomit fake grue out of her mouth and nose. 'Spewing stuff out of our mouths, the contact lenses … it was all very uncomfortable and at times painful. Look, like I said, I'm not a big lover of horror movies so it is not anything that I would intentionally go and see but I didn't have a problem from any moral or ethical standpoint. It was just so over the top it was ridiculous.'

Moreover, by consistently terrorising one of the male characters instead of one of the women, *The Evil Dead* was at least doing something different from what was going on at the time in the horror genre, when it was usually screaming women on the end of a madman's knife. 'I didn't really think of that, I have to say,' replies Sandweiss. 'I wasn't a big film connoisseur at the time. I liked movies as much as anybody else but I didn't have the ability at that time to look at *The Evil Dead* and to really see the inventiveness of Sam Raimi and the unusual camera techniques or all the other things that I can see now and which are so creative and unique about it. All I could see was that I was doing things on screen that I was really embarrassed about and I actually thought it was stupid and funny. What I kept seeing was how fake everything looked. You know, I would see the rubber fingers jiggling when the hand got slammed in the door and I thought it was so fake that it wouldn't scare anybody. So I think that the important thing here is that you need to know something about horror films to come to that conclusion and both then and now I just haven't watched enough of them to know that what Sam was doing was in any way groundbreaking. Now, I guess, especially in the last few years since I've been going to horror conventions and becoming a sort of spokesperson, I know a little bit about them and know it was groundbreaking in its own way. To me we were just making a low budget movie and that was all I knew …'

Despite having to be caked with lots of painstaking, and painful, prosthetic makeup, Sandweiss admits that she got along very well with Tom Sullivan. 'Oh he is just a darling, a very nice guy and he still is,' enthuses Sandweiss. 'I see him quite a bit because we end up at a lot of the same conventions and we just worked on another movie together called *The Dread*, Tom plays a role in that and did a few special effects, I think he designed the monster but he is just a sweet guy and obviously very, very creative. He was just learning on that film as all of us were because, you know, he had done a lot of special effects and artwork but he had not done a lot of makeup. So he was just learning and he was delightful to work with.' Another good sport, according to the actress, was Bruce Campbell. 'I had been in plays and stuff with Bruce previous to *The Evil Dead* and, you know, our relationship was that he would try and make me laugh and I would,' remembers Sandweiss. 'In fact, I would laugh hysterically. Both he and Sam, they were clowns, they were and are such funny, entertaining, smart people and I was always their best audience. But when it came to making *The Evil Dead* those guys were serious. They were bound into making this movie and it wasn't fun and games anymore. You know, they would still do their shtick once in a while but they were serious about making this movie. They both had quite a work ethic and would do anything for this film. Bruce is still a real gentleman, a genuinely nice guy and at the time he was really shy, especially with girls (*laughs*).'

THE EVIL DEAD

The Evil Dead stopped filming a few times due to lack of money but, according to Sandweiss, she never had any doubts that it would be finished. 'Yes, they kept running out of money but they were so driven,' she maintains. 'I guess I always knew that, come hell or high water, somehow, some way they were going to finish it. But there were certainly times where it seemed quite hopeless.' Then came the US cinema release where, sadly, the movie failed to rack up big box office numbers. 'It was not an overnight success here, in fact it took a long time to take off,' she says. 'I wasn't really in touch with it during those years but a lot of what I have learned about its evolution, by reading Bruce's book and other books too, I wasn't aware of. I wasn't in touch with any of that at all, I didn't even know it had a cult following.'

Indeed, where *The Evil Dead* really began to pick up steam was in the UK where its publicity as a 'video nasty' helped it to top the VHS rental charts. 'I did hear about that at the time,' laughs Sandweiss. 'But I couldn't really understand the controversy because, to me, the movie is, in so many ways, ridiculous. It is almost like comic book violence so I thought it was pretty silly. But I did hear that Sam was going to go to court to defend the movie or something like that but I was just happily raising my children. I was working in arts administration and I had no idea. I was so out of touch with this I didn't even know they were making *Evil Dead II* until well after it had already been made and released. '

Sandweiss has managed to catch up with the sequels to her original horror hit. 'I recently watched *Army of Darkness* again but I only saw *Evil Dead II* once and that was ten years ago,' she says. 'I just read in the papers this morning that they are showing *Evil Dead II* in a nearby theatre later this week so I might go along and see it.' Alas, after *The Evil Dead* began to pick up its huge cult following, Sandweiss did not receive any further acting offers. 'Absolutely nothing happened,' she says. 'But then a lot of that was by choice. After we finished the movie I went back and completed my college degree. I made a decision that I didn't want to push my acting and that is why I went back to graduate school and got a Masters in arts administration, basically dealing with the business end of the performing arts. So I didn't pursue it but, also, nobody pursued me (*laughs*). Things were not so big back then and I was not living in LA or New York or any of the hot spots for that and, you know, it wasn't the same kind of situation as it would be now where if a film is popular it plays everywhere. But had I put some effort into it and tried to make myself more visible, well, who knows? I have no idea what would have happened. But the good news is that now I'm having a bit of a renaissance and that is great. *The Evil Dead* has at least got me that ...'

Currently the actress does autograph signings as part of The Ladies of The Evil Dead, where she joins her two female co-stars at conventions worldwide. 'In 2002 I believe there was a showing of *The Evil Dead* in LA, which is where Theresa and Betsy both live,' she says. 'It was advertised that the cast and crew would be there and they were both friends, they had kept in touch with each other, and they said, "Do you know anything about this?" So they showed up, saw Rob Tapert there and that gave them their first inkling of how big *The Evil Dead* had gotten. At the same time, here in Detroit, I started seeing *Evil Dead* t-shirts and my kid's friends were talking about it, also the company that distributed it, Anchor Bay, is based here. So the three of us thought, "You know, *The Evil Dead* seems to be really popular and everybody is benefiting from it except us." So they called me, they somehow found me, and we decided at that time to go out there and see what it was all about. We formed The Ladies of the Evil Dead, got a web site and started going to conventions and it has been great. It's been a lot of fun, we've made a little bit of money and it's opened up doors for more horror movies, which has been great.' The actress has also been able to catch up with Sam Raimi. 'I've seen him a few times. The last time I saw him I went to the premiere of his movie *The Grudge*. We had contact mainly because, in order to do The Ladies of the Evil Dead, we had to have permission and make sure everything was okay and legal. I see Bruce a lot.'

Most recently, the actress appeared in the independent horror movie *Satan's Playground* directed by Dante Tomaselli. Her return to horror was, by her own admission, a welcome one. 'Dante is a huge *Evil Dead* fan and he told me that when he was a kid he had a poster of me over his bed, all made up like a monster and in the cellar, of course,' laughs Sandweiss. 'But his father made him take it down. So Dante and I were featured in the same edition of *Rue Morgue* magazine around 2003. So he emailed me, said he was working on this movie and asked if I wanted to do a role in it. Now I am not a big horror genre fan so I cannot say that I knew who Dante was, but I did a little bit of research, found out that he has legitimately made some movies and the rest is history. Of course, once I met him we really hit it off. But *Satan's Playground* was really different from *The Evil Dead*. When we made *The Evil Dead*, Sam was 20 years old and we had this miniscule, skeletal crew and very little money. Everyone knew how to make movies in regards to the technical aspects and so on but they didn't really know the ins and outs of movie production such as organising shots and actors and so on. Sam was really driven and just knew exactly how he wanted a shot to look but he didn't work so much with the actors on their performances but, then again, in *The Evil Dead* there really wasn't much acting. With Dante, he's more mature and well schooled at this point in his life than we were when we did *The Evil Dead*. I would say he knows how to work with actors a little better and how to get them to emote.'

HOUSE of 1000 CORPSES

Released: 2003
Directed by: Rob Zombie
Produced by: Andy Gould
Written by: Rob Zombie
Cast: Sid Haig (Captain Spaulding), Bill Moseley (Otis Driftwood), Sherri Moon (Baby Firefly), Karen Black (Mother Firefly), Chris Hardwick (Jerry), Erin Daniels (Denise), Jennifer Jostyn (Mary), Ranin Wilson (Bill), Walton Goggins (Deputy Naish), Tom Towles (Lieutenant George Wydell), Matthew McGrory (Tiny Firefly), Robert Allen Mukes (Rufus Firefly)

In a nutshell: On 30 October 1977, four teenagers stop by an off-road haunted house ride/fried chicken restaurant in Texas. The attraction is run by Captain Spaulding who, in the film's prologue, shoots a couple of would-be burglars dead. One of the teens, Jerry, is writing a book on strange, off-road tourist attractions and he persuades his girlfriend, and their two travelling companions, to hop on Spaulding's ghost train ride which takes them on a trip through a history of North American serial killers. Featuring such familiar faces as Ed Gein, the ride culminates with 'Doctor Satan', supposedly the worst of them all, whose death was at the hands of some vengeful locals, although the medical murderer's body remains missing to this day.

When the ride comes to a close, Jerry asks about the tree where Doctor Satan was supposedly hanged and, on a night of hellish weather, he opts to try and find it, picking up an attractive female hitchhiker on the way called Baby. The teen's car is shot at by an unknown assailant and Baby offers to take them back to her house, where they can get her brother and go and retrieve the vehicle. However, once at the house the foursome is introduced to a bizarre, psychopathic family led by a long-haired thug called Otis. As Halloween dawns, the four teenagers are killed, one by one, whilst the local police, investigating the disappearance of the teens and also five local cheerleaders, are likewise slaughtered. Who will survive? And what will be left of them? Sound familiar?

Prologue: *House of 1000 Corpses* would mark heavy metal musician Rob Zombie's directorial debut, a low budget horror offering produced by Universal Pictures. However, the studio dropped the movie after its completion in 2000, reportedly because they were outraged by the final product and its excessive level of gore and violence. Following this, MGM were due to take over the picture's distribution but they too would back out, which opened the door for Lion's Gate to take on the US release of Zombie's first feature. *House of 1000 Corpses* finally opened in 2003.

For B-movie buffs the most exciting thing about the film would be the return to the screen of perennial supporting player Sid Haig, fondly remembered for his turns in such drive-in classics as *Spider Baby*, *The Big Doll House*, *Black Mama, White Mama* and the television series *Jason of Star Command* (1979). Zombie also cast Bill Moseley, something of a fan favourite after his turn as Chop Top in *The Texas Chainsaw Massacre 2* in the dominant part of Otis and brought Karen Black, well remembered from the likes of *Easy Rider* (1969) and *Five Easy Pieces* (1970), into the fold as Mother Firefly. The casting of cult faces did not stop there, with *Henry: Portrait of a Serial Killer*'s Tom Towles winning a prominent role as the feature's doomed police lieutenant. *House of 1000 Corpses*' sexy leading lady, Baby, was played by Zombie's real-life wife, Sherri Moon. The giant Matthew McGrory, most well known from his role in Tim Burton's *Big Fish* (2004), would also make a memorable on-screen presence in the shape of the ironically named Tiny.

In terms of where *House of 1000 Corpses*' plot comes from, its feel and lineage really dates back to the likes of *Spider Baby*, *The Texas Chain Saw Massacre* and *Tourist Trap*: in other words, films where hapless travellers are captured by a family of marauding psychopaths. However, Zombie tries to echo the grungy, 'take no prisoners' feel of such seventies grindhouse staples as *Last House on the Left*, *Bloodsucking Freaks*, *Last House on Dead End Street* and *The Toolbox Murders*, titles whose escalating levels of graphic violence won them enormous controversy and a built-in audience of curious thrill-seekers. In its closing moments, *House of 1000 Corpses*' degeneration into senseless, drawn out slaughter echoes a more supernatural, less blatantly sexual take on Pasolini's *Salo* whilst Zombie's colourful lighting and absurd sets are no doubt inspired by Dario Argento's *Suspiria* and 1975's film version of *The Rocky Horror Picture Show*. However, his underground maze, revealed at the film's close, resembles that which Tobe Hooper depicted in *The Texas Chainsaw Massacre 2*.

HOUSE OF 1000 CORPSES

About: On a purely superficial level it is easy to understand why *House of 1000 Corpses* became the most controversial horror movie of the new millennium. The film typifies everything that critics of the genre have long complained about - namely, the lining up of a group of young, virtually indistinguishable victims who are then subsequently killed in long, protracted ways: a 'fuck the world' kind of hostility that director Zombie perhaps feels his fan base wants to wallow in. Yet this cynical viewpoint is almost guaranteed to alienate those whose teenage angst has long since departed. Certainly, the director's wife is dolled up as the ultimate Goth-chic vamp from hell in the flick and the murdered youngsters include beautiful cheerleaders and attractive young teens, figures of a typically wholesome, Beaver Cleaver America. Whether or not this is the filmmaker's on-screen revenge towards the personalities that aggravated him as a youngster is anyone's guess, but the final result is not pretty. It is an ugly movie about ugly people and, yet, *House of 1000 Corpses* also has an ace up its sleeve ...

In short, Zombie's cast is wonderfully inspired. For any lover of obscure drive-in cinema or seventies B-movies it is difficult not to be impressed by the director's funky homage to the period via his wonderful actors, a hodgepodge of yesterday's grindhouse heroes, finally reunited for a bloody, merciless horror flick.

For example, Sid Haig, who opens the movie, is a larger-than-life figure in the role of Captain Spaulding, a scene chewing, rotund maniac plastered in clown makeup (*á lá* John Wayne Gacy), and the long-time supporting actor is finally presented with a chance to show his skills after years of languishing in B-list fare. For the first 18 minutes of Zombie's picture, Haig is given ample screen time and makes the most of it; portraying a deceptively cheerful character but one who is nevertheless ready to turn nasty at any second. Indeed, it is to Zombie's credit that he refrains from turning Spaulding into an outright sadist from the get-go, yet gives us just enough insight into his mindset (in the prologue he kills two potential robbers, and this is where his real spirit comes alive – he positively *celebrates* in the spilt blood) that we know something is just not right about his little roadside business. Whilst Spaulding's real personality, and relation to the larger Firefly story, would not become clear until Zombie's superior 2005 sequel *The Devil's Rejects* (a film that is better than *House of 1000 Corpses* in every single way), Haig plays an unforgettable role here, managing to be funny, terrifying and likeable. To give the actor further plaudits, he is able to switch from one emotion to the next with such fluency that it never feels forced, or false, and Zombie pulls an A-plus performance out of him.

Bill Moseley is, perhaps, the movie's curveball. Most famous for playing the comical Chop-Top in *The Texas Chainsaw Massacre 2*, although he portrayed a lesser mad psycho role in the redundant *Silent Night, Deadly Night III* (1989), fans would have every right to expect Zombie to draw upon the persona for which the actor is best known and loved. Instead, he avoids this temptation and presents the audience with a new face of Moseley, one that demonstrates what a fine actor he actually is. A true horror movie 'heavy', in the tradition of David Hess in *Last House on the Left* or Michael Rooker in *Henry: Portrait of a Serial Killer*, Moseley is nothing to laugh about as Otis, the Firefly family's foremost maniac. 'Maybe it's just not a good idea to be prancing around where you don't belong,' he sneers at one victim, and what makes Otis so genuinely horrifying is the manner in which he is so blasé towards torture and murder. His victims can beg for mercy all they want, but the character has no humanity whatsoever, his view of the world begins and ends with his family and the belief that anyone who comes near his property is fair game to be cut to ribbons. Whilst even Rooker and Hess were permitted to give their serial slashers some fleeting glimpses of humanity, Moseley permeates Otis with an icy cold glare and a heartless centre. He is threatening and dislikeable in a way that even the similarly sadistic John Jaratt doesn't manage in 2005's *Wolf Creek*. Whereas a character such as Jaratt's Mick Taylor is little more than a smirking sadist, straight from the build-your-own-psycho mould, Moseley's Otis is a lot more layered, we are drawn to watch the actor and allowed to hate him, as opposed to being encouraged to laugh along with his horrors as for example in *Wolf Creek*. Thankfully, Zombie resists the temptation to give Otis any one-liners or humorous motivations and it makes for a far better lead villain.

Also along for the ride is Karen Black, an actress who, at the time of 1970's *Five Easy Pieces*, and her subsequent Academy Award nomination, appeared to be on the brink of stardom. Yet, by the end of the decade, even in spite of acclaimed turns in *The Great Gatsby* (1974) and Hitchcock's *Family Plot* (1976), the actress was reduced to such continental B-level schlock as 1978's Italian crime bomb *The Squeeze* and the following year's *Piranha* rip-off *Killer Fish*. For Black, the eighties and nineties would be spent as a journeyman actress, taking on roles in whatever seemed to pay the rent. Thankfully, Zombie understands the kitsch appeal in both the 'where are they now' sections of entertainment magazines and the car crash fascination of watching a down-on-their-luck performer acting in the sort of exploitation that they, more than likely, would have turned their nose up to at the height of their fame. As a result, seeing Black, decked out in ludicrously colourful attire, in the role of Mother Firefly is a joy to behold and, perhaps unexpectedly, the actress puts in one of her best performances of recent memory. Never quite overacting, but nonetheless, grasping her character's obscene level of absurdity, Black is forthcoming enough in the part to be quite threatening (although, once again to Zombie's credit, this is largely because he allows her to be a sexually overt, seductive, *mature woman,* quite a rare thing in contemporary American cinema!) and yet jovial enough to laugh along with.

Sadly, the real problem with *House of 1000 Corpses* begins when Black and Haig exit the picture and Moseley and Moon are given free rein to take over. Whilst both prove themselves to be strong, believable performers, more than capable of handling a major theatrical feature (again, one has to mention the far better *The Devil's Rejects*, where the twosome are positively pitch-perfect throughout), neither has a character interesting enough to carry the storyline to the end credits. Thus, Zombie's feature degenerates into an orgy of torture and death, with violent murders and ridiculously prolonged nastiness (much of it aimed towards women) taking the place of the Technicolor carnival ride that he initially promised us. It is a horribly frustrating change of pace because, for its first reel, *House of 1000 Corpses* really is enjoyable, creepy enough to get under the viewer's skin and gradually building up an ominous feel of impending nastiness. Yet, when that nastiness finally happens it isn't scary or especially pivotal to understanding the motivations of the Firefly family. Rather it is just unpleasant, and it is at this point that many viewers may feel the need to turn off.

Of course, this could be seen as a back-handed compliment and, indeed, it should be pointed out that Zombie executes his murderous set pieces with horrifically real gusto. Most unforgettable is the sequence where Baby chases one of the captive females, who is clad in a humiliating bunny outfit (a possible attempt to chastise the gender exploitation of Hugh Hefner's *Playboy* empire perhaps?), and stabs her repeatedly to death. Although the director can be seen to avoid accusations of wallowing in this thanks to his decision to leave the actual stabbing of a helpless, screaming female off screen, there is still something excessively nasty about this moment. Some of it, no doubt, has to do with the fact that Zombie's screen blood looks shockingly real, but there is also an uncomfortably voyeuristic feel to this on-screen bout of brutality, a pseudo-snuff scene that leaves you feeling dirty for even having watched it. Again, this is probably the point, and it certainly echoes the 'anything goes' sadism from the worst 'video nasty', but the problem still remains with Zombie's inability to transfer this sheer visceral splatter into something frightening or interesting. Rather, it is just disgusting, arguably the easiest emotion of all to extract from your audience. Furthermore, without human victims to really associate with it is hard to get the emotional gut-punch that such a horrific slice of sadism should incur in the viewer.

Another major fault with *House of 1000 Corpses* is with its frustrating habit of inserting clips from old black and white movies, or music video type interludes, into the action. Just as likely to draw the viewer out of the 'real' action of the movie (something Uwe Boll's much maligned 2003 dud *House of the Dead* also succeeded in doing with its use of on-screen video game footage), this ploy simply doesn't pay off as anything but an annoying gimmick. Again, this may be one of the reasons that Zombie's subsequent *The Devil's Rejects* works so much better: it takes itself seriously from the start and, thus, does not come across nearly as schizophrenic.

Finally, *House of 1000 Corpses* comes undone with its belated introduction of the supernatural. An underground maze finally leads the movie's last two survivors (by this point in the film they have become indistinguishable from their dead friends, but then this is perhaps best viewed as a flick about the maniacs) into the lair of Doctor Satan, the mass murderer thought dead after being hanged by some locals many decades ago. This, in turn, gives way to a macabre operating theatre, which features strange slave-men appearing from the walls. Ultimately, Zombie's decision to tack on a bizarre, fantastical ending to his feature turns his debut into an incredible mess, something that doesn't really know what it is or where it is going. Moreover, whereas the shocking finale of *Night of the Living Dead* or *Easy Rider* worked because, in neither case, did we expect the lead characters to die, here it is obvious that no one is getting out alive. No good horror movie can really make predictability work to its benefit, and *House of 1000 Corpses* is no different. When the chaos starts and you realise that it isn't going to end until the final screaming teen is flayed alive, there is nothing to really do except nod in distant disapproval as each on-screen victim is slaughtered.

Still, in spite of all this, *House of 1000 Corpses* is a passable homage to times past and an admirable attempt to bring real horror back to the multiplex. Taken alongside 2003's *Texas Chain Saw Massacre* remake and the similarly unrelenting *Wrong Turn*, the movie was an attempt to make a scary movie into exactly that: something nasty, sweat inducing and downright disturbing. Although Zombie doesn't quite manage to do this, the fact that he created enough offence to upset two studios and the American censor board is quite admirable at a time when PG13 shockers seemed poised to take over. Sure, the director never broke any *new* taboos, but, by learning from the past, he created a cauldron of carnage just unpleasant enough to outrage the establishment. Plus, he showed that yesterday's B-movie mavericks could still whip up a storm on-screen. Respect, indeed!

What happened next? Zombie's next film, *The Devil's Rejects*, is not perfect but it is a far more focused effort than *House of 1000 Corpses*, giving the protagonists much more personality and playing out as an especially nasty road movie. Sadly, it is hindered by a preposterous ending that suggests actual sympathy with the Firefly psychopaths. Naturally, it doesn't work *at all*. However, with a cast that includes yet more B-names showing their talents, including Ken Foree, Michael Berryman and William Forsyth, *The Devil's Rejects* is one of the most fascinating theatrical releases of recent years. Zombie would return for an ill-advised remake/re-imagining of John Carpenter's classic *Halloween* in 2007. The result was a sadistic mess.

House of 1000 Corpses was released before Eli Roth's *Cabin Fever* and its positive box office may well have encouraged Lion's Gate to give the latter movie the sort of wide release that it did. Since the release of *House of 1000 Corpses*, the studio has turned its attention to developing a number of nasty, unrelenting shockers, namely the *Saw* series (which began in 2004), the disturbing *Open Water* (2004), *The Toolbox Murders* (2005), *Hostel* (2006) and the inevitable *Hostel: Part II* (2007). Sadly, the success of *House of 1000 Corpses* led to less talented filmmakers getting in on the gore game and trying to 'shock'. Say what you want about Zombie, but his stylish seventies throwback is not even comparable to the misogyny of something such as *Murder Set Pieces* (2006), a movie without one unique quality, other than, perhaps, the director's worrying inability to make his female characters come over as anything other than pieces of meat.

The stars of both *House of 1000 Corpses* and *The Devil's Rejects* never quite graduated onto bigger things after the success of both. However, Haig did enjoy a second coming as a leading man in such B-fare as *House of the Dead 2* (2005), *A Dead Calling, Night of the Living Dead 3D* (both 2006) and *Brotherhood of Blood* (2007). Moseley joined Haig in the shot-on-digital dud *A Dead Calling* and also turned up in the theatrically released thriller *Thr3e* (2006) and *Repo! The Genetic Opera* (2008). Zombie, meanwhile, would cast Moon in his *Halloween* remake, although she also turned up (against-type as a victim) in Tobe Hooper's creepy rehash of *The Toolbox Murders*.

Rob Zombie interview

For Rob Zombie the biggest challenge of *House of 1000 Corpses* was not completing the film but, rather, finding someone to put it out in American cinemas. 'It was taking so long that it was just getting crazy,' laughs the director. 'It was amazing when it came out, you know, it got to a point where my only goal in life was to get the movie into theatres, so you can imagine how happy I was when it was released, and financially it was a big success. So, yeah, it was fucking awesome to get it out there.' The film's initial problems began when Universal Studios decided that, in spite of bankrolling the picture, they didn't want anything to do with the final product. 'That was what was so weird about everything, because they had already seen the film several times while I had been making it, and they all loved it,' exclaims Zombie. 'I mean they sunk money into it and they were all behind it from the start. Then when I finished it only one person at Universal had yet to see it and that was the Chairperson, you know the big cheese, and she saw it and just flipped out. So that was the end of that.'

Perhaps surprisingly Zombie was pleased when the film was held back by Universal. Indeed, there could have been an even worse scenario. 'At first I was kind of relieved because originally I thought they would want to re-edit it and take out all the violence and gore and I was totally against that. So I was relieved when they finally just let it go ... and then I realised that there was going to be this long process to get it released by someone else. However, it was the theatrical cut that went out to every country and that was based on it costing too much to go back and do an uncut version for other markets, and strike new prints. The distributors, Lions Gate, can't really afford to be doing that for the movie and I've actually still to prepare an uncut version, which I imagine would have a lot more violence (*laughs*).'

One thing that does stand out, right from the start, about *House of 1000 Corpses* is how garish and beautifully filmed this little B-movie actually is. Suffice to say, this is something that makes its director very proud. 'Yeah it is a really colourful movie,' says Zombie. 'I was pretty much one hundred percent in control of all that, the hair, the makeup, the costumes, the sets and everything else stuck pretty closely to my original design.' Yet, despite paying homage to such similarly colourful fear flicks from yesteryear as *Suspiria* and *Halloween*, Zombie's movie does not have any hero or heroine and, arguably, it is all the worse for it. 'To me there was still something unrealistic about those films,' says the director. 'I mean, I'm a fan of them ... and I know this is going to sound weird ... but you know when Manson's gang went to Polanski's house and killed Sharon Tate? There were no heroes with that, it just happened. That was what I wanted to do, show that these guys in the film were professional killers and the victims weren't going to suddenly escape or anything. If these guys get you, you're fucking screwed. I mean that's the way it is in real life. If you are caught by a serial killer then basically you're fucked. And it is nihilistic, and I think that's what most upset the Chairperson at Universal.'

All the same, looking back at the film, Zombie admits that there are a few changes that he would make. 'In a way I would probably do one million things differently actually,' he laughs. 'It is all a blur in my mind now, because after all I went through getting it released it seems so long ago. I did whatever I could do at the time of shooting the movie, and yeah I think some shots are maybe not as good as I would have liked, but that was because I was running out of time, or running out of sunlight or moonlight. Also, I didn't have enough money to re-shoot. So there's a ton of stuff I'd probably change, I'd like to have had more time for one, we only had twenty five days ...' That said, Zombie admits that the low budget did not stop him getting the cast that he wanted. 'For movies like this you don't really think about big stars,' he says. 'I got all my first choices for the roles anyway, and I always wanted to work with Sid Haig, but sure there are some actors I'd still like to work with. Pam Grier is one, Bill Smith, all those seventies exploitation names and the good thing about the sequel (*The Devil's Rejects*) is that you can start filling in the blanks a bit more and telling the audience a bit more about who's who in the movie.'

House of 1000 Corpses also captures a delirious carnival atmosphere, something that is totally understandable when one learns that Zombie grew up under the big top. 'Yeah, my family's business was as a travelling circus and side-show and as a kid it seemed really normal.

But looking back on it with adult eyes you can see how it was fucking weird. And as a kid, surrounded by all these freaks, you learned a few things …'

Zombie is also happy to reveal some of the films which have influenced him. 'Horror is my favourite genre, but I love Westerns too. I'm as big a fan of John Wayne and Clint Eastwood as I am Bela Lugosi and Boris Karloff. In fact, *The Devil's Rejects* has a real Western storyline to it and it has a lot more in common with Westerns than you might think. As for some of my favourite films – let me think (*pauses*). There's *Taxi Driver*, *Dawn of the Dead*, *A Clockwork Orange*, I've seen all of those several times. As for directors I'm a huge fan of Martin Scorsese and Stanley Kubrick.' And has anything ever offended the director of *House of 1000 Corpses*? 'Well not really,' replies Zombie. 'I guess there's only one that's made me stop and think that it went too far and that was *Cannibal Holocaust* … As far as showing gore and showing rape or whatever I don't have a problem with that but when real things get involved, I mean, I'll show all sorts of violence but I'd never hack up a turtle on screen. That crosses the line. I first saw that movie at 42nd Street in New York, back in the eighties, at an old grindhouse theatre, this was before they cleaned the area up. It was really sleazy and disgusting and also kind of fun (*laughs*).'

Sid Haig interview

A cult B-movie actor from the seventies, Sid Haig returned to the big screen and made an instant splash with his turn as Captain Spaulding in *House of 1000 Corpses*. For those who never forgot his turns in such low budget classics as *The Big Bird Cage* and *Coffy*, the actor's prolonged leap to stardom was well worth celebrating. 'Rob probably cast me because he was a fan of these old films,' admits Haig. 'He and I have never really talked about it but at his wedding reception I was standing there talking to his brother. His brother said to me, "This is really weird, having you here and talking to you." Of course I replied, "Well why do you say that?" He said, "Because when we were kids, Rob and I would get up every Saturday morning and watch you on *Jason of Star Command* and you scared the crap out of us." So putting that together with the way in which I got the film, which was that my agent called me and said, "I'm going to send you over a letter of non-disclosure and a script, read the script and if you like it then the part is yours." So that indicated to me that Rob knew my work and he was basically giving me the film based on what I had done previously. I remember when I first read the *House of 1000 Corpses* script and I said to myself, "I could have so much fun with this guy." The reason I stopped acting was because the roles I was being offered were so stereotypical. That's why I backed out, Hollywood just didn't get it, and I couldn't play the roles they were offering me anymore. So I think Rob is taking on the simplicity of these so-called grindhouse films, even down to the music. I think he basically saw the effect that these films can have but he made it clearer.'

Haig also admits that he was not prepared for the success that his turn as Captain Spaulding would bring him. 'Absolutely not, not in the slightest, I mean I only have four scenes in *House of 1000 Corpses*,' he says. 'I was completely taken by surprise. I always knew it was going to be a good film but I didn't know it was going to have the impact that it did. I have a certain amount of pride in what I did with the character and what Rob gave me to work with is a huge part of that. I would have absolutely no qualms about having a quote from *House of 1000 Corpses* on my gravestone. Something lyrical like "shit the dead" and I don't even know where the hell I came up with that *(laughs)*.'

This 'impact' included Captain Spaulding Halloween costumes and action figures. 'The character was so out there and bizarre and he was a totally new icon for horror,' laughs Haig. 'Now his image appears at conventions whether I'm there or not *(laughs)*. The action figures were a total trip, and I love how that took off, you have the 8 inch, the 19 inch, the bobble head doll, the lunch box … these are all so much fun. I also have my own line of candy and coffee, but it's not Captain Spaulding's because the legal department kept dragging their feet. I tell you, I was waiting at an airport to go to a convention and I was tired of waiting around so I called Rob and said, "Let's make it happen, Captain Spaulding candy and coffee." Rob wanted to do it, but the lawyer was having trouble with it. So I was tired with fooling around and I called the sweet company and offered them the idea for this new candy and coffee using the *Spider Baby* logo. They said, "That would be great because it's such a huge cult film, but we'll get in legal trouble for using that." So I said, "Don't move, I'll be back in just a few minutes." I called Jack Hill and he gave me the go ahead. So now we have *Spider Baby* coffee and it's a great product and completely addictive, it's this orange flavoured dark chocolate covered espresso bean. I put some out on my table at conventions and the fans might take one and then they get about three steps away before they return and ask me how much they are. They are seriously addictive. I ask fans if they would be surprised if we put cocaine in there …'

Another thing that surprised Haig was the problems that the movie encountered and the three year process that it took to get *House of 1000 Corpses* into the cinemas. 'I thought it was the most stupid thing I had ever seen in my life,' he says of the fiasco. 'I have said this before but Universal had their own producer on the set every day watching the dailies and they were going over the survey cards at the screenings. So I went to one of these screenings and at the end of the screening the Chairperson from Universal, she was sobbing and shaking in the lobby and the next day the film was axed. I just thought that was a little strange. You know? That is all I can say about that *(laughs)*. But I always knew it was going to get a release. I kept propping everyone up. I had so much faith it would do well and it did. The only problem was that they gave it a limited release in about 600 theatres, but *The Devil's Rejects* was the biggest release that Lion's Gate had ever done. It (went out in) between 2500 and 3000 theatres … *The New York Times* did an article on Lion's Gate two or three weeks ago and the basic thrust of the article was that while everyone else is thinking about Academy Awards, Lion's Gate is making all of the money. They have a very smart business strategy, they never invest more than $8 million, they never will, and they get tremendous results.'

However, that said, the actor at least maintains that he can see why some people were shocked by Zombie's horror film debut. 'I kind of had a feeling that it was going to be nihilistic,' he laughs. 'Maybe not to the extent that it was, because that was the proverbial watching a train wreck situation, but you were compelled to watch. To say, "Oh my God I cannot believe what I am seeing." However, you couldn't turn away from what was going on, and I think that is the earmark of a great film. The movie starts off quite light and then it turns very nasty. I am reminded of the saying, "This is all fun and game until somebody gets hurt." And in *House of 1000 Corpses* somebody does get hurt. A lot *(laughs)*.' Haig was also never concerned that someone from a more conservative part of the United States, and perhaps unprepared for the guts and gore of Zombie's horrifying opus, might kick up a stink about the movie's contents. 'I think that the American mid west probably doesn't know that we exist, which is a good thing,' laughs the actor. 'So, oh well (*laughs*), they would probably never go onto a site where they could see that. But our fans, the fans of the genre, will find us no matter where we are. I can remember a friend of mine telling me that his grandson, who lived in Northern California, wanted to see the film but the city council banned *House of 1000 Corpses*, and what happened was that all of the kids from the local high school just piled in their cars and went to the next town and watched it over there. So they'll find us no matter where we are.'

Haig maintains that part of what made his job on *House of 1000 Corpses* and *The Devil's Rejects* so much easier was a genuine connection with his director. 'Rob reminds me so much of my son,' enthuses the actor. 'So it was hard not to get that feeling, that connection, he impresses me with everything that he does. I am a fan of the man, okay? And what he has created is just the icing on the cake. As a person he is a great guy.'

Moreover, having made an early splash in Jack Hill's twisted masterwork *Spider Baby*, Haig admits that he is a long time horror movie fan. 'Yeah I always liked these types of films. It wasn't a question of finding a home in horror movies, but as a kid I saw every one of them that hit the screen. Then I got disillusioned, if you will, with all these formula horror films. Who needs a part five or six when it's clear they should not have gone past part one? All they're going to do is slaughter six more kids every time! The one thing that makes me really happy, and I really respect Rob's decision on this, is that he won't do a Part Three. After *The Devil's Rejects* you wonder where we can go anyway.'

Currently, if you happen to be a film studies student at Catawba Valley Community College in Hickory, North Carolina there is actually the opportunity to do an entire semester-long class on the work of Sid Haig. This, above all else, perhaps certifies the actor's current beloved status among fans of horror cinema. 'I am extremely flattered by that,' admits Haig. 'There was a part of me that was totally shocked and another part that thought, "Actually, with the amount of work I've done you probably could do a class on it." I don't know, maybe I should stay in touch with that more.'

Bill Moseley interview

Although actor Bill Moseley rose to fame as Chop Top in *The Texas Chainsaw Massacre 2*, he had actually began to carve (no pun intended) out his acting career in the early 1980s, whereupon he was moonlighting as a journalist. 'I got a job on a Miller's Beer commercial back in 1981 and I had already gotten into the Screen Actor's Guild,' reflects Moseley. 'Back then I was the editor in chief of *CB Bible Magazine*, a publication dedicated to the senior side of Citizen's Band radio. My personal crusade, at this time, was to find out more about the mysterious cattle mutilations plaguing some states in the mid-seventies and that is, strangely enough, how I got my SAG card. You see, I saw page six of *The New York Post*, and it was about Carolyn Pfeiffer doing a movie directed by Alan Rudolph called *Endangered Species*, which was originally titled *Cows* and which was about mysterious cattle mutilations. So I contacted them and said, "I have real pictures," and they said, "Well can you give them to us? We don't have any money we can give you but we'd love to have them." So I said, "Well you know what, I'd love to get into the Screen Actor's Guild." So we swapped, I gave them the pictures of mutilated cattle and they gave me a role as the cab driver in a scene with Robert Urich and I had a couple of lines like, "That will be four fifty," "Well here's five," "Oh thanks bud," and I remember being really excited about doing that and getting into the SAG. And then I went to a screening and I was mortified because they had dubbed my fucking line. They dubbed it with a Brooklyn accent! I remember thinking, while still in shock, "Well maybe they didn't dub my second line." Of course, it came seconds later and it was dubbed by the same guy.'

However, it was the actor's unforgettable turn as Chop Top that really turned Moseley into a modern horror icon. In the same breath, though, it also typecast the actor into the genre and left him trapped in direct-to-video hell until *House of 1000 Corpses* rolled around. 'I remember at the premiere screening of *The Devil's Rejects*, Sid Haig, Sherri Moon and Ken Foree were all there and they actually look like their characters,' says Moseley. 'And yet I don't. You know, I have short hair and no beard and I felt like I had to keep saying to people, "Hi, I played Otis." So I still have my private life ... I mean, once in a while I get recognised. Someone comes up to me and says, "Are you ...?" I always say, "Who?" Then they say, "John Walton?" "No, now get away from me." (*Laughs*). But I was thinking about this just last night while I was in the local laundromat, putting my load into the dryer (*laughs*). I'm happy to be unrecognised and be able to access that once in a while when it is fun.'

The actor also admits that he pays close attention to his own work. 'I saw *House of 1000 Corpses* probably about eight times in the theatre,' he laughs, before relating how he got involved with the movie. 'It probably started back when I got a call from a friend of mine who is the publicity director for Universal City Walk. This was back when Universal did a Haunted City walk every weekend in the run-up to Halloween and they would put up spider webs and have a bunch of monsters walking around. They had a little awards ceremony called The Igor Awards which was basically an in-house awards ceremony so they would honour old Universal monsters and just whatever was good for Universal. So they were looking for an MC and my friend knew that I was "a monster" and called me up to see if I would MC the show and I said, "Sure, would you like me to come as Chop Top because I have a friend who can do the makeup?" There was some concern because I wasn't a Universal character but it was okay because I had been in *Army of Darkness* and so I had a Universal connection and it was deemed "okay". So I showed up as Chop Top and wore a tuxedo, and did my MC stint as Chop Top. This would have been in '99, and one of the award recipients was Rob Zombie. Rob said later that he thought it was just someone doing a decent impersonation of Chop Top (*laughs*). Anyway we got talking in the green room after the show and a month later his producer/manager called and said, "Rob's got this script green-lighted, would you like to be in it?" and I said, "Well fuck yeah!"'

Moseley's character of Otis in *House of 1000 Corpses* was a far cry from the more darkly comical persona of Chop Top. 'At first I thought that Rob wanted another Chop Top-type of part and he was very helpful at guiding me through Otis,' explains Moseley. 'Originally, when we were filming *House of 1000 Corpses*, I would even try and talk like Chop Top. The transition happened after I decided that I needed to get the body movements between the two characters different. Chop Top was all in the shoulders, whilst Otis is all in the watch (*Bill glares across the table*), he is just like, "Hey, fuck you." When I got that down, that started to help me ... And the funny character in *House of 1000 Corpses* is Captain Spaulding, but Otis' job is to walk into every scene and suck the air out of it. When I finally understood that, I was excited about being chosen to do it. Previous to that I was the clown, but Rob already had his clown, so to be really bad was kind of cool.'

The character evolved even further in *The Devil's Rejects*. 'I got to do a lot of cool stuff in the sequel,' exclaims Moseley. 'It's funny because it just tells me that Rob is a really smart guy because I don't think he ever wanted to do a sequel. He has said that most horror sequels suck because it is the same story re-told in an attempt to milk a few more dollars out of the few suckers in the seats and I think Rob wanted to avoid that at all costs. So what he ended up doing was changing genres, there is a storyline that carries over and characters that carry over but we all look different. Otis is not an albino; in *The Devil's Rejects* I have a beard and blue eyes this time as opposed to pale skin, white hair and lenses. Tiny has ears, don't ask me how that happened. Captain Spaulding for the most part doesn't have clown makeup and Baby doesn't laugh. So there are some glaring differences, and it goes from horror to more of an action/adventure type of movie. It's really realistic, not as theatrical, it is just fucking brutal, gritty and real and these are just some of the words I've heard used to describe it.'

One person who was absent from *The Devil's Rejects* was Karen Black (she was replaced by *Police Academy* star Leslie Easterbrook), although Moseley has some insight into this. 'The actors in the first one all worked for what is known as scale plus ten, which is basically minimum wage plus ten for your agent,' he claims. 'So I think there was also the understanding, or at least the expectation, that somehow the second one, since we all shared the risk of the first movie we would somehow share in the reward, so sometimes these expectations lead you to expect things that are not going to come.'

Nevertheless, the actor had such a good time on *The Devil's Rejects* that he feels that a third film would not be out of the question if he was asked. 'Would I do a third one?' he ponders. 'It would be kind of hard but, sure, money is thicker than blood (*laughs*).'

OLDBOY

Released: 2003
Directed by: Park Chan-wook
Produced by: Lim Seung-yong
Written by: Hwang Jo-yun, Lim Chun-hyeong, Lim Joon-hyung, Park Chan-wook
Cast: Choi Min-sik (Dae-su), Yu Ji-tae (Woo-jin), Kang Hye-jeong (Mi-do), Ji Dae-han (Joo-hwan), Kim Byeong-ok (Cheol-woong), Lee Seung-Shin (Mr Han/Hyung-ja), Yun Jin-seo (Soo-ah), Lee Dae-yeon (Beggar), Oh Kwang-rok (Suicidal Man), Oh Tae-kyung (Young Dae-su), Ahn Yeon-suk (Young Joo-hwan)

In a nutshell: Dae-su literally vanishes from the streets of Seoul on a rainy evening in 1988. He wakes up in a fully furnished apartment where he is held captive without any explanation as to where he is or why this happened. He is fed well during his imprisonment and gassed at regular intervals so that the room can be cleaned, his hair cut and his clothes changed. However, he has no contact with the outside world except for a solitary television set in his room. Whilst imprisoned he learns that his wife has been murdered and he is the prime suspect. After 15 years he is suddenly let free, without explanation, and provided with money and a mobile phone. Almost immediately he stumbles into a fast food restaurant and eats a live octopus before waking up in the apartment of the young, attractive waitress (called Mi-do) who served him. The twosome begin to bond and together they begin to investigate what has taken place over the past decade and a half and who is responsible, with Dae-su eventually tracing the plot to a mysterious individual by the name of Lee Woo-jin. Just as he is about to kill Woo-jin, however, he is told that a much deeper secret lies behind the imprisonment. Woo-jin has a pacemaker and threatens to shut his own heart down. Dae-su is given five days to find out why he was taken from the streets in the first place. If Dae-su can achieve this goal then Woo-jin says that he will kill himself. If he cannot then Woo-jin warns that the consequences for Mi-do will be terrible …

Prologue: Even prior to the international success of *Oldboy*, director Park Chan-wook was widely seen as the leading voice in modern Korean cinema. His hard-hitting thriller *Joint Security Area* (2000) was a huge success in its native country and Park Chan-wook attracted worldwide acclaim with his outstanding 2002 effort *Sympathy for Mr Vengeance*, the first of what is now viewed as an unrelated trilogy of films focusing on the theme of revenge. *Oldboy* would be the second instalment in this series.

TABOO BREAKERS

Cast in the part of Dae-su in *Oldboy* is actor Choi Min-sik, who had earlier played the lead roles in the largely unknown *Painted Fire* (2002) and the far more widely seen *Shiri* (1999). His *Oldboy* co-star Yu Ji-tae had appeared in the tremendous Korean *Blade Runner* spin-off *Natural City* (2003) and the underwhelming horror shocker *Nightmare* (2000). The gorgeous Kang Hye-jeong was a relative newcomer to the screen at the time of *Oldboy*, although Park Chan-wook has since cast her in his subsequent productions.

Oldboy came at a time when Korean cinema was beginning to pick up steam on the international stage. Possessing a relatively new film industry, South Korean cinema certainly had some indigenous hits in its post-war period (including 1960's *A Stray Bullet* and 1961's *Chunhyang*) but these titles failed to travel to international territories and remain unfamiliar to all but the most dedicated Asian film scholar. However, the aforementioned *Shiri*, *Joint Security Area* and *Sympathy for Mr Vengeance* had become known in the West via import DVD (as well as eventual domestic releases in Europe and North America) and film festival screenings. As a result, by the time the new millennium came into force, Korean cinema was ready to make its mark on the international stage. Indeed, 2001 brought the sleeper smash *My Sassy Girl* and the exciting gangster opus *My Wife is a Gangster*, which spawned two sequels, the first arriving in 2003, whilst *A Tale of Two Sisters* (2003) became a sensation with horror fans, becoming alerted to the Asian ghost story genre following 1998's *Ringu*, with Dreamworks immediately buying the rights for a Hollywood remake. *A Tale of Two Sisters'* director Kim Ji-woon can perhaps best be viewed as Park Chan-wook's most impressive contemporary, with his best work maintaining a quality comparable to that of his better known colleague. Also helping the cause was the more serious Kim Ki-duk, whose studied and often marauding work (which includes 2000's *The Isle* and 2002's *The Coast Guard*) has gained its fair share of acclaim. Currently, Korea's cinema makes up almost fifty per cent of its home market's box office – a not inconsiderable feat.

As with many recent Asian blockbusters (such as 2001's *Ichi the Killer*, 2006's Hong Kong hit *Dragon Tiger Gate* and the same year's odd little fantasy *Mushishi*) *Oldboy* was adapted from the pages of a comic book. In this case a popular Japanese manga.

About: 'I said I want to tell you my story ...'

Oldboy is a masterpiece of contemporary cinema. The film is an incredibly stylish modern noir/thriller and, when viewed for the first time, leaves an overbearing air of disgust and depression. However, if you have only seen it once then take another look, because it is also easy, especially in retrospect, to approach *Oldboy* as a decidedly sick, not to mention ludicrous, black comedy. Indeed, it is to Park Chan-wook's credit that the various ridiculous twists that inform his film's plot only become evident after repeat screenings, and subsequent to the viewer's awareness of where the storyline's all important 'mystery' is heading. For instance, Woo-jin's skill at tracking Dae-su, even without a bug, is hard to fathom (not to mention his ability to commit bloody murder in a conveniently empty internet café) as is his knack for making every single little detail of his plan work in accordance to what has been set out. Ultimately, Woo-jin can be seen as a more sexually devious, less ambitious version of Lex Luthor or any other comic book super-villain, a larger than life figure whose scurrilous plan can only really exist in the realms of a fantastical plot. Meanwhile, Dae-su's superhuman ability to take on an entire gang of heavies is so overdone that it ultimately inspires laughter rather than shock, as does the entire possibility of having a complex, manned, secret underground operation where paintings can leak sleeping gas and a group of 24/7 workers cater to prisoners with food, clothes and haircuts. Even little aspects of the story (such as the briefly seen suicidal man who jumps to his death, presumably after suffering his own horrific revelation in regards to his captivity) become downright comical during subsequent viewings.

Nevertheless, the nasty surprise at *Oldboy*'s end is so repulsive and difficult to shake off that it is understandable why the picture became instantly notorious. Moreover, there are elements of *Oldboy* that one simply does not see in contemporary Hollywood cinema (and in some cases that might be for the best!). The most notable is undoubtedly the sequence where leading man Choi Min-sik, in a piece of character acting that even Robert De Niro might shy away from, eats a live octopus. That viewing the death of the cephalopod is far less messy (and, let's face it, more difficult to empathise with) than the skinning alive of a turtle in *Cannibal Holocaust* goes without saying, but this is still a singularly unnecessary set piece and is utterly disgusting to watch. Park Chan-wook's decision to film the scene from afar helps only slightly and the unforgettable sight of Choi Min-sik with the creature's still-moving tentacles dangling from his mouth is nothing less than sickening. Then, of course, there is the element of incest which only becomes apparent at the end of the movie. Despite continuing rumours about an American remake of *Oldboy*, it would be difficult to imagine many A-list stars wishing to indulge in such on-screen deviance.

Yet, even putting the incest and octopus-consumption aside for a moment, *Oldboy* also features a great number of gritty, violent sequences. From Choi Min-sik's dental torture of one of his captors ('each tooth I yank out will make you age for one year') to the brutal slaying of an entire gang of Mafiosi, Park Chan-wook has crafted an undeniably bloody story of vengeance. Curiously, the rise in popularity of Korean cinema ties in with a level of split heads and erupting squibs that cannot be doing much for the country's tourist board. It is a strange phenomenon indeed, with the director's 'vengeance trilogy' leading the way but with other filmmakers crafting a series of disturbing gangster and horror pictures.

For instance, when Kim Ki-duk unleashed his gruesome shocker *The Isle*, some viewers were taken aback by the real life gutting, electrocution and beheading of fish, all of which serve little purpose to the plot[104]. The director's later film, *Address Unknown* (2001), features some rough handling of dogs (also highlighted in *The Isle*). Of course, this should not indicate that Korean cinema is some kind of safe-haven for animal abuse, no, far from it, rather it points to the fact that the country's films which are having a huge impact abroad (be it at film festivals[105], on DVD or even in a wide theatrical release) transgress the boundaries of Hollywood acceptance and are often surprisingly vicious. The explosion in popularity for violent Korean cinema is perhaps

---

104 These scenes got *The Isle* into hot water in the UK. According to the BBFC web site: 'Four compulsory cuts were required to the sight of animal cruelty in accordance with the Cinematograph (Animals) Act 1937.' http://www.bbfc.co.uk/website/Classified.nsf/0/6556CF030A28126E80256D200041C931?OpenDocument

105 It is perhaps worth pointing out here that *The Isle*, shown uncut, was a Sundance Film Festival choice.

only rivalled by the glut of 'heroic bloodshed' epics which found their way from Hong Kong to the West in the mid-1980s after the success of John Woo's classic *A Better Tomorrow* (1986). However, whilst these, often spectacular, pictures have been taken to task for glamorising Hong Kong's shady crime syndicates ('Never before had the underworld of the triads been so lovingly rendered' exclaimed one reviewer of *A Better Tomorrow*[106]) the fierce immorality of the Korean equivalent has gone largely undocumented.

Certainly, if *Oldboy* has a contemporary, outside of Park Chan-wook's own *Sympathy for Mr Vengeance* and his later *Sympathy for Lady Vengeance* (2005), then it is Kim Ji-woon's *A Bittersweet Life* (2005) which is also dark, violent and painfully nihilistic. As with *Oldboy*, the picture deals with Seoul's colourful underworld, albeit with the same comic book abandon and excessive bloodletting that Chan-wook shares with the Hong Kong 'heroic bloodshed' genre. These titles, along with the comical gore of the monster movie *The Host* (2006), represent the most popular of the country's exported cinema, perhaps because, unlike their Hollywood counterparts, Korea's genre pictures are not afraid to get down and dirty.

It is surely no coincidence that when audiences discovered Chow Yun Fat and the relentless brutality of movies like *A Better Tomorrow*, *Hard Boiled* (1992) and *Full Contact* (1992) it was during a time of cynical, formulaic big studio action franchises such as *Die Hard* (1988) and *Lethal Weapon* (1987). However, just as the 'heroic bloodshed' genre eventually burned out (as any screen fad does), there was something else to pick up the slack. In the case of Hong Kong cinema it has been a return to the lavish, costume kung-fu epics of yesteryear (once popularised by the Shaw Brothers) with such outstanding works as *Crouching Tiger, Hidden Dragon* (2000), *Hero* (2002) and *House of Flying Daggers* (2004), each one of which was a hit in English-speaking territories. Meanwhile, a bizarre underbelly of excess began to surface in Japan courtesy of Takashi Miike, creator of such gory excess as *Audition* (1999) and *Ichi the Killer* and Ryuhei Kitamura (who helmed 2000's *Versus* and 2003's *Azumi*). The popularity of such violent features in the West has surprised even veteran actor Hiroyuki Sanada, who explained that 'in Japan (these) are what I would describe as cult films. There is not any wide appeal, sometimes people elsewhere in the world love that kind of film even more than Japanese audiences ... I still have to ask why? Where is the appeal?'[107]

Certainly, the bloody theatrics of Miike and Kitamura, alongside the superior work of Park Chan-wook and Kim Ji-woon, began to attract a new tag, that of 'Asia Extreme'[108]. It can be argued that the close proximity between Japan and South Korea has resulted in a notable exchange of ideas (the Korean horror films *Cello*, *The Ghost* and *The Wig* are all blatant spin-offs from *Ringu*, whilst Miike and Park Chan-wook both collaborated on 2004's *Three Extremes*). However, at a time when a handful of major studios dominate Hollywood cinema it is perhaps not too shocking that, as with the popularity for *A Better Tomorrow* and its ilk, thrill-seeking viewers are looking to foreign shores for challenging, and genuinely 'alternative', cinema. That the likes

---

106 As stated in Hammond, S & Wilkins, M, *Sex and Zen & A Bullet in the Head*, Titan Books, London, 1997

107 As told to the author of this book for *Impact* magazine (Issue 170, February 2006)

108 'Asia Extreme' is now the name of Tartan's DVD label dedicated to violent Eastern cinema. Meanwhile, in 2005 the writer of this book took over the long-running monthly section in *Impact* magazine entitled, you guessed it, 'Asia Extreme'.

of *Audition*, *A Bittersweet Life* and *Oldboy* grab the viewer by the throat and feature storylines that twist and turn their way to an uncertain outcome certainly makes them comparable to the aforementioned 'heroic bloodshed' genre. Indeed, the vengeful plots, downtrodden characters, pulp visuals and ferocious violence of *Sympathy for Mr Vengeance*, *Oldboy* and *A Bittersweet Life* indicate that the influence from such Hong Kong maestros of mayhem as John Woo and Tsui Hark cannot be understated.

Talk of *Oldboy* cannot ignore the presence of actor Choi Min-sik. Aside from making a convincing transition from a drunken street lout to a near-insane captive of 15 years and, eventually, to a revenge-seeking tough-nut, there is an innate poetry to his dramatic ordeal. Given the task of having to relate an emotional journey to the viewer (and this is within the first 20 minutes) Choi Min-sik steps up to the challenge by convincingly expressing a series of emotions during a montage that details his imprisonment in a murky, windowless apartment. We share his sexual frustration and see him lose hope, attempt to slit his wrists and then, finally, inflict self-harm on himself and begin to train for an eventual showdown with his tormentors (the sole scenario that appears to keep his mind alive). The loss of his humanity, not to mention his dignity, is completed when he attempts to rape Mi-do shortly after waking up in her apartment (and while she is on the toilet, no less, an uncomfortable and yet shamefully comical scene). Remaining cold and distant throughout the movie, Choi Min-sik only really recovers his soul when he learns that the woman he has fallen in love with is his daughter. The following scene, where he breaks down and begs Woo-jin not to tell her the truth, is horrendous to watch but does give *Oldboy* a sophisticated Shakespearian twist and the resonance of a truly important work of art. It is, in this day and age of overriding predictability, refreshing when a film can wrap up all of its loose ends in such a satisfactory manner, leaving the viewer gob-smacked and well aware that they have just sat through an all too rare instance of a modern classic.

Oldboy's final moments take place in a dreamlike landscape, with Dae-su being hypnotised in the midst of the beautiful snow covered mountains of New Zealand (although the location is never made explicit). Mi-do sits nearby, unaware of the horrific secret that her partner is trying to eliminate from his mind, and an argument could be made that she is the film's biggest victim precisely for this reason. When father and daughter are together as lovers at the movie's end it is difficult to approve or to protest the decision because, having gone through hell with Dae-su, the viewer has come to accept him as a deeply unfortunate character. Someone who was once a husband and a father has been transformed into a monster and, finally, a fragile mess of a man. Left without even a tongue to speak with (he cuts it out in front of Woo-jin when his relationship to Mi-do is made clear), the 'Oldboy' of the film's title is in a sorry state as the story concludes.

Whilst no one gets out of *Oldboy* in one piece (except maybe for the blissfully ignorant Mi-do), and some scenes are difficult to endure, there is a strange melancholy to the film's final moments and, for all the spilled blood, the movie remains exciting enough to encourage repeat viewings. The most difficult thing, when it comes to Park Chan-wook's masterwork, is really placing it within any single genre. Part-thriller, part-splatter movie, part-noir and part-mystery, the film is as unique as *Sympathy for Mr Vengeance* before it and *Sympathy for Lady Vengeance* after it. Yet, as the title most synonymous with 'Asia Extreme', *Oldboy*, like Chan-wook's other work, exists almost within a stratosphere of its own making: representing a new kind of cinema from a country whose film industry is only starting to boom. With its unpredictable, often tasteless, plot twists and characterisations, *Oldboy* breaks down the barriers of genre acceptance that *Hard Boiled* and its ilk brought to the action film before it. If 'heroic bloodshed' classics such as *A Better Tomorrow* and *The Killer* (1989) showed that the 'hero' did not necessarily have to see the end credits alive then the likes of *Oldboy* and *A Bittersweet Life* represent a tradition of unpredictability that is purely Eastern in nature. It also indicates that some of the most shocking, non-linear examples of 'taboo breaking' are still emanating from the Orient, and long may they continue to do so.

What happened next? Park Chan-wook's career highlight to date is undoubtedly *Oldboy*, although his follow-up film *Sympathy for Lady Vengeance* (2005) comes close. The final part of his 'vengeance trilogy', this stunning, and inevitably violent, story focuses on child abuse and a woman scorned (brilliantly played by Lee Yeong-ae). The end result is, like its predecessor, essential viewing and extremely hard-hitting. Between movies Park Chan-wook directed a stellar segment of the *Three Extremes* horror anthology alongside Takashi Miike and Hong Kong's Fruit Chan (whose macabre *Dumplings* was the highlight of the three efforts). The filmmaker's latest effort is also his weakest to date; the lightweight fantasy *I'm a Cyborg, But That's OK* (2007). This bizarre film is set in a mental institution and zips between the real world and the imagination of a young girl convinced she is a destructive terminatrix.

Following his outstanding performance in *Oldboy*, actor Choi Min-sik went on to impress in follow-up films such as *Brotherhood* (2004), *Crying Fist* (2005) and *Sympathy for Lady Vengeance*. All three movies could not come more highly recommended. Co-star Yu Ji-tae also returned in *Sympathy for Lady Vengeance* although his post-*Oldboy* best is in *Antarctic Journal* (2005), written by Bong Joon-ho.

Indeed, alongside Park Chan-wook, writer/director Bong Joon-ho is one of the shining lights of the 'new' Korean cinema. His best work is 2006's superior creature feature *The Host* although he first began to attract positive word of mouth with 2003's exceptional thriller *Memories of Murder*. As already mentioned, Kim Ji-woon's 2005 gangster shocker *A Bittersweet Life* is one of the best films of recent memory and of a quality that rivals even *Oldboy* itself, any reader of this chapter who has yet to see it should do so immediately. Other, post-*Oldboy*, examples of recommended 'Korea Extreme' include *Natural City* and *R-Point* (2004), whilst gritty noir thrillers, made before Chan-wook, include the nonsensical but fun *Tell Me Something* (1999), the less impressive *H* and *Yesterday* (both 2002) and the ambitious *2009: Lost Memories* (2002).

Although Korean cinema, as a global attraction, is still in its infancy, the speed of its growth is mind boggling. Whilst fans of Eastern cinema probably still look to Hong Kong and Japan to fulfil the majority of their diet it may be only a matter of time before their output is dwarfed by the quality and quantity of films emerging from this exciting area of the world.

Park Chan-wook interview

In person, director Park Chan-wook is a likeable and good humoured individual and not, it should be said, the sort of personality that one connects with octopus-eating, incest-related storylines and split skulls. But, as the director maintains, it was not the violence inherent in *Oldboy*'s plot that attracted him to the film, rather it was the story's pivotal use of a modern invention which very few of us live our lives without. 'I have not watched TV since my childhood and I only watch it for about 10 minutes a year, unless I am in a restaurant or somewhere where a TV is on,' says Park Chan-wook. 'In that case I might watch it for a short while. So what was definitely interesting for me, in the original manga story, was that TV was the only outside contact for the person that is imprisoned in this cell. I thought that in such a case it would be possible for a television to be a good friend … I also thought that it was convenient to adapt from a manga comic because not only would the story be there but the storyboards (*laughs*).'

Oldboy was a success in its native South Korea and garnered a theatrical release in several Western nations. However, one scene in particular caused upset. 'In comparison to my other films I have noticed that *Oldboy* has a general appeal,' smiles the director. 'So the reaction from audiences in various countries was not all that different apart from the one scene where he (Choi Min-sik) eats an octopus alive … Now, obviously that is not something to be tried by the viewer (*laughs*). But different countries have different cultures and I have to respect that.' Indeed, the filmmaker insists that there was never any debate about shooting this particularly gross sequence. 'No, there was no problem,' he shrugs. 'But the incest theme, of course, was problematic in Korea … I think that people reacted to that rather than the octopus scene. The violence has caused some complaints but I express the violence in my film through how much pain the character played by Choi Min-sik has to suffer. For example, in an erotic film the sex scene has to arouse the audience sexually, in the same way that in my film the violence has to keep the audience suffering. Those who ask me about why I did not make a film that was easier to watch, and less violent, I tell them that if they want a nice time they should just visit a spa instead (*laughs*).'

Considering that there is an American remake of *Oldboy* currently under consideration, it will be interesting to see how Hollywood handles this particular bout of taboo breaking. 'I have heard that it will be very difficult for them to keep this element,' admits Park Chan-wook. 'I am very curious as to how they are going to make the film without it but I have heard that the theme of incest just will not go down well with the American public (*laughs*). What kind of film will they make if they take this away? I think that looking at the case of *Insomnia*, Hollywood got great actors and a great director to remake the original, but it is unavoidable that the original is better. The American public is not even aware that *Insomnia* is a remake of a French film so I just hope that when *Oldboy* is remade they will know about the original. I also hope that the remake will not be better than mine, of course …'

Park Chan-wook also maintains that his leading man had no qualms about devouring a live octopus on screen. 'Eating a live octopus did not play a big part in his decision to do the movie,' laughs the director. 'In fact this is nothing for Korean actors because they will do a lot worse, they will probably even allow themselves to be eaten alive by an octopus (*laughs*). For an actor in Korea it is the criteria of whether they like the director and the script. My actor (Choi Min-sik) is in fact a Buddhist so it was especially difficult for him. He would offer an apology to the octopus and pray before every take and he didn't actually eat the animal, he just chewed the flesh! I don't know how much consolation it is to kill something but not eat it though (*laughs*). In Korea the actors will do anything that a director asks for the film, they don't protest if something is against their personal beliefs.'

Despite being an extremely violent film *Oldboy* also happens to be very beautiful and stylish, something that Park Chan-wook is very proud of. 'If you look at our emotions they are never simplistic,' says the director. 'Something can be brutal yet beautiful at the same time, or sadness can become humorous or comical and that is just life. Virginia Woolf once said that a beautiful landscape painting conjured up horror for her because the more beautiful something is the more fearful it becomes. The reason why I use such beautiful scenery is because it remains present after me, my family, my friends and all of humankind has gone, our stories do not affect it.'

Looking to create the most aesthetically pleasing finale to *Oldboy* as he could, the filmmaker opted to shoot the movie's poetic climax in the snow covered mountains of New Zealand. 'New Zealand was perfect for different reasons,' mentions Park Chan-wook. 'I wanted to have this epilogue which emphasised the ambiguity between time and space. There is no explanation offered as to why the end takes place in the middle of a snowfield or why it is snowing, it is dreamy. So it is not even clear if the epilogue is real or not. It is only the ending if you want it to be. I wanted to use a time which was ambiguous so you could not pinpoint where, when or why. We shot this part of the film in the winter in the Northern Hemisphere, although it could just as easily have been a part of South Korea ... the audience never knows.'

On the surface at least *Oldboy* appears to be, largely, about the futility and hopelessness of revenge, something that the director agrees with. 'Well that is the nature of active revenge and that was exactly my intention,' replies Park Chan-wook. 'There is the question about whether or not the war started by the Americans in the wake of 9/11 can bring satisfaction to them. I raise an identical question about revenge in the film. I don't know if the tragedy of the war can make revenge satisfying but revenge is everywhere. I would not say that it is particularly relevant to the West, although maybe the West can learn more from such a thing. Revenge is the most difficult part for someone, they must give up everything else in their life to chase it and it takes energy and passion. But, like *Sympathy for Mr Vengeance*, I would say that *Oldboy* is a film noir, but in a broad sense.'

One particularly gruelling sequence in *Oldboy* depicts a graphic tongue-chopping, something that might remind fans of Takashi Miike's equally controversial gore-fest *Ichi the Killer*. 'I only remembered that scene just now,' answers Park Chan-wook defensively. 'No, I didn't think of this during *Oldboy* because the cutting out of the tongue in my film came from Oedipus cutting out his eye.' That said, the director does have his own cinematic influences. 'When I started out it was actually Hitchcock who was my greatest influence,' he says. 'I am also influenced by Kurosawa, I love *Rashomon*, and by a lot of Hollywood B-movie directors, but far too many to mention. I like Takashi Miike a lot and, of course, I have worked with him but I am not sure I see the connection ...'

Asked if he is satisfied with *Oldboy* and Park Chan-wook is surprisingly quite self-deprecating. 'The degree of satisfaction and the degree of embarrassment are similar,' he smiles. '*Sympathy for Mr Vengeance* was less commercially successful than *Oldboy* but I think I like it better.' Whilst many fans of the director's work are likely to disagree with this comment, the filmmaker admits that he likes to surprise people. 'Well, we all have pre-assumptions on certain filmmakers but I consider the director to be an artist and I think that it is my job to surprise people and work with different stories. I think it is like a musician who is only famous for playing gloomy music. They should still be able to play something a bit cheerier once in a while, you know? So it is good to change direction. For example, *I'm A Cyborg But That's OK* is my favourite film so far.'

Park Chan-wook is also very pleased that his country's indigenous cinema is attracting such worldwide acclaim. 'Yeah I am very proud of my fellow Korean directors,' he beams. 'If I was alone making Korean films it would be very lonely so I am glad that others are having success. I am friends with many of the other Korean directors and sometimes I send them my scripts to look at and give me some feedback on. That is a great help for me. So as a whole I would say that things are going rather well but some of the films that are commercially successful are perhaps too successful, whilst other films are not making any money. So the gap is widening …' The filmmaker does, however, say that going to Hollywood is not really top of his 'to do' list. 'In only two cases would I ever contemplate going there,' he says. 'The first is that the script is so good I can sacrifice this right to a final cut! Many Hollywood people come to me to propose co-working and they ask me, "What is your favourite made by an Western director?" I tell them that it is *The Ice Storm* and they say, "Okay, well I've got an important meeting to run to" (*laughs*).'

One thing that Park Chan-wook wishes to point out is that *Oldboy* is not something that carries a lot of social commentary. 'The only time I have put social commentary in a movie was with my segment in *Three Extremes*,' he claims. 'My idea for that was that people only really become nice after they have enough money to live a good life. I think that the way we behave is all down to money, but if you are poor then you have no time to be nice and you can very easily turn nasty. For me, this was a very important point, and that was why I made that movie.' And as for what shocks the director of so many disturbing cinematic efforts? 'I actually had this conversation with someone else earlier and I said that a truly shocking image can happen anywhere and to any person,' replies Park Chan-wook. 'Honestly, I have never really tried to shock anyone. I just make stories where certain things are relevant to the plot (*laughs*). But I can't think of any film that has shocked me yet!'

HOSTEL

Released: 2006
Directed by: Eli Roth
Produced by: Chris Briggs/Mike Fleiss/Eli Roth
Written by: Eli Roth
Cast: Jay Hernandez (Paxton), Derek Richardson (Josh), Eythor Gudjonsson (Oli), Barbara Nedeljakova (Natalya), Jan Vlasak (The Dutch Businessman), Jana Kaderabkova (Svetlana), Jennifer Lim (Kana), Keiko Seiko (Yuki), Lubomir Bukovy (Alex), Jana Havlickova (Vala), Rick Hoffman (The American Client), Petr Janis (German Surgeon)

In a nutshell: Two young American males (Paxton and Josh) and an Icelandic friend (Oli) are backpacking across Europe. The trio reaches Holland and waste no time in visiting a brothel, flirting with the locals, drinking copiously and smoking weed. Finally they meet a young Dutch man who tells them to head to Slovakia, the best place for parties and easy women. On the train to the former communist realm, Josh is accosted by a homosexual man, much to the amusement of his two friends. Once in Slovakia, the threesome book into a hostel and are introduced to two beautiful women who have little hesitation in stripping off and sleeping with the Americans. Oli, the Icelandic native, hooks up with an attractive woman later that night and disappears shortly thereafter. The next morning, in a cold, dilapidated building, Oli has been decapitated and his one night stand is in the process of being tortured by a mysterious figure. Unable to find their friend, the two Americans decide to spend one more night in Slovakia before taking off elsewhere. However, after another night of hard partying, Paxton wakes up to discover that Josh is nowhere to be seen. Back at the run-down building, Josh is being slowly murdered by the same man who tried to hit on him during the train trip to Slovakia. Sensing something is amiss, Paxton goes in search of some answers, revealing the truth about a hideous, underground business that centres upon the torture and killing of kidnapped travellers.

Prologue: After the box office success of *The Ring* (2002) and *The Grudge* (2004) the general consensus among the Hollywood studios was that PG13 horror was the sure-fire way to gain a large audience. As a result, Wes Craven saw his werewolf opus *Cursed* (2005) re-shot twice, plagued with further post-production issues in regards to its ending and, finally, slashed down to a PG13 rating[109]. The result was both artistically and commercially redundant. Nevertheless, although *Cursed* failed at the box office, other PG13 rated, 2005 genre releases such as *The Boogeyman*, *The Ring 2* and *The Exorcism of Emily Rose* raked in money, and even the pitiful remake of John Carpenter's classic *The Fog* did respectable business. However, as the year drew on a new wave of horror releases began to haunt the cinemas, nastier, nihilistic and featuring ridiculous levels of bloodshed, titles such as *The Devil's Rejects* and *Saw II* pushed the limits of the R rating and, on small budgets, attracted huge crowds. Without CGI, name stars or the benefit of huge production values many a Hollywood suit was, no doubt, baffled by the popularity of these movies.

As the first terror release of 2006, *Hostel* (which was made for a paltry $4 million) would score high and cemented *Cabin Fever* director Eli Roth as the latest 'Master of Horror'. Undoubtedly, the 'Quentin Tarantino Presents' label helped *Hostel*'s commercial fortunes no end, whilst the 'based on true events' tag that accompanied its release was no doubt cribbed from such exploitation hits of the past as *Mark of the Devil* and *The Texas Chain Saw Massacre*. Proving that audiences are as susceptible now as they were back in the seventies, few actually questioned Roth's insistence that *Hostel* was based on a genuine website offering real life game hunting ... albeit one that only the investigative brilliance of the director and web critic Harry Knowles could actually find.

Suffice to say, William Castle would be proud.

About: On the one hand *Hostel* is a brilliantly realised, relentlessly terrifying and extremely well acted dose of old fashioned, gory grindhouse terror. Yet, on the other hand, its youth-orientated, travelogue plot opens itself up to allegations of sexism, homophobia and xenophobia that are impossible to ignore. So ... where do we start?

First of all, considering that such recent efforts as *Wolf Creek*, *H: Diary of a Serial Killer* (2006) and *The Lost* (also '06) appear to revel in their explicit violence against women, Roth should be applauded for victimising men in his film and asking audiences to believe in, and accept, the sight of crying, terrified, vomiting males. Make no mistake about it, this is extremely unusual for a horror movie, with even such 'smart' post-modern efforts as *Scream* (1996) and *Halloween: H20* (1998) falling back on the basic premise of a masked killer terrorising a screaming female. Indeed, even when males have been the focal point of a horror release (such as with *Jaws* or John Carpenter's *The Thing*) it has usually been within the atmosphere of spunky male bonding and lots of macho chit-chat. There have, of course, been exceptions to this, the British shocker *The Wicker Man* (1973), *The Evil Dead*, Kathryn Bigelow's *Near Dark* (1987) and 1986's *The Hitcher* all show that terrorised men can weep, plead and bleed as well as any female can and, more to the point, can grab the audience's attention and sympathy. Recently, the most impressive examples of the male victim have come from the Far East, namely Takashi Miike's *Audition* and *Oldboy*. Although Miike has not been oblivious to accusations of misogyny in his own right, *Audition* can be read as a fascinating feminist parable about the male expectancy of women and

---

[109] States Craven: 'You can smell it in the studios just now, there is this whole thing about doing PG13 horror films because they figure that because *The Grudge* and *The Ring* were both so big that this is the way to go. There is even this theory that if you go out with a PG13 rating then you will get between $14 to $15 million more in your box office take, guaranteed (*laughs*). Seriously, that is what they are saying just now, but you can't expect that when you shoot an R rated film and then cut it down to a PG13.' (As explained to the writer of this book for *Dreamwatch* magazine, Issue 132, September 2005)

the masculine desire to obtain a 'trophy' girlfriend irrespective of the female's feelings or needs. *Audition*'s final depiction of a man violently dominated by a beautiful young woman, with the underlying air of sadomasochism, is truly shocking and reveals that the horror film works best when it can single out fears that are not gender specific.

Therefore, whilst it is hard to imagine many women wishing to sit down and watch a scene of near-pornographic violence, and the repulsive likes of *Murder Set Pieces* appear to exist purely to exploit this sort of thing, it is not too hard to see why both sexes flocked to something such as *Scream*. For, in spite of its central motive of a male killer chasing a beautiful, busty leading lady (Neve Campbell), *Scream* at least featured hunky actors (for the women) and strong-willed, intelligent female characters, as well as a notable lack of scream queen nudity, a factor that should not be ignored. After all, how many straight men would wish to look at scene after scene of males undressing in the way that, say, your average eighties slasher flick focuses on shower room sequences and bare breasts? Typically, the post-*Scream* horror movie has stayed clear of presenting female nudity as a 'draw', perhaps indicating that studio suits have wised up to the genre's potential beyond a core audience of pimply, virginal teenagers (or beer-bellied middle aged men). The most recent exception to this, however, is Roth's previous *Cabin Fever*, a crude, but stylish, body-horror opus whose nastiest death sequences are saved for the two central female characters and which does not shy away from recording star Cerina Vincent's nude physique in salivating close up. As such, *Cabin Fever* feels very much like a 'lad's' horror movie, a tits 'n' gore splatter flick for *Loaded* readers that never, during its running time, gives anything but the impression that it is shot through with a male's point of view. Perhaps not surprising, then, *Hostel* begins in much the same way ...

After a chilling opening, where a lone, whistling figure cleans up an obvious scene of death, *Hostel* suddenly fills the screen with bright, neon colours and takes a completely different turn from its macabre prologue. The viewer is placed onto the streets of Amsterdam where our trio of travellers are presented in all of their obnoxious glory. The initial feeling that one has towards *Hostel* is that, like *Cabin Fever*, this is very much a guy's movie. For instance, women are introduced through close-up shots of their bottoms and every female cast member is alarmingly beautiful ... indicating that either Roth believes that Amsterdam is populated with only *Playboy* Playmate contenders or simply wanted lots of attractive female actors on his set. It is worth noting, in fact, that even the walk-on parts required for a nightclub scene are given to model-like beauties. Nevertheless, there is one exception to this rule, a briefly glimpsed, overweight prostitute who is degraded by Jay Hernandez's Paxton as being 'a fucking hog', although this does lead the characters into some discourse about the nature of paying for sex. 'Paying to go into a room to do whatever you want to do to someone is not exactly a turn on,' says Josh, the more refined of the two American men. This, obviously, draws some interesting parallels between the movie's revelation of an underground torture trade.

Consequently, *Hostel* wastes little time in baring some female skin, with porn star Paula Wild stripping out of her lingerie and the backpackers being told, by one hostel inhabitant, to head to Slovakia whilst a gratuitous scene of a couple having sex plays out in the background. This, accompanied by comments such as 'that bitch had the best fucking tits in Amsterdam' makes one compelled to argue that *Hostel* is the epitome of sexism, an argument that is hardly squashed when the storyline reaches Slovakia. Indeed, our first view of the city's natives is (sigh) a beautiful female clerk at the hostel registration desk. This is followed by the introduction of two extremely attractive women who meet the film's three travellers and instantly invite them down to the establishment's sauna room. There, the girls strip (whilst other nude women walk around) and proceed to screw the two Americans. By this stage, Roth has allowed us to believe that the copious nakedness and casual sex is simply part and parcel of the plot. In turn, we become convinced that he is creating a male-orientated fantasy, a tits and ass adventure for the men who miss the days of *Slumber Party Massacre* (1983) and who want their fix of female skin in our more PC modern day environment. Yet, intentional or not, *Hostel* makes the audience question their own acceptance of 'easy women' and 'no strings attached sex' as soon as the real motivation behind the two Slovakian girls is revealed (they are used to seduce and then drug travellers, finally selling them into an underground death network). Natalya's kiss-off line to her horrified ex-lover, Paxton, says it all: 'I get a lot of money for you, and that makes you *my* bitch.'

Perhaps because of such teen comedies as *Euro Trip* (2004) and *Road Trip* (2000) viewers now rarely question the idea that beautiful screen females are 'easy' and 'loose', and, having begun much like these films, *Hostel* lures its audience into a similar acceptance. Yet, the two Slovakian women are anything but easy, instead they are poor (in reality, Slovakia has one of the highest unemployment rates in Europe), and hired to be part of a real-death cult, ruthlessly exploiting their own beauty as part of something much more sinister. This revelation is all the more shocking because, up until this point, we do not actually doubt the high sex drive of the two girls - instead it is easy to believe that Roth is simply making a typical Hollywood 'teen' adventure. In a sense, then, *Hostel* does at least reveal the somewhat odd representation of female sexuality that those American 'teen' comedies, post-*American Pie*, showcase (to give but one example, in *Road Trip*, the character portrayed by Amy Smart has sex on her first date with a guy she has spent literally minutes getting to know). Roth may follow this pattern initially, but both the viewer and his male characters are played for fools by accepting such character traits at face value. In doing this, Roth proves himself to be a far smarter, and savvier, filmmaker than many have given him credit for.

Nevertheless, it is possible to see a prevalent misogyny in *Hostel* during the sequence where Kana has her right eye blow-torched out by a raving American madman. Although the scene in question does not display any sort of violent transgression towards femininity, Kana's subsequent leap in front of a speeding train when she glimpses her massacred facial features suggests that, without her beauty, she may as well be dead. Obviously this is hardly the most positive comment on womankind, although, again, it depends on how one wants to read the scene. Is it that Kana, without her model good looks, is worthless? Or is she representative of what society indicates we should judge a woman by? Going by Paxton's earlier, sexist rundowns of the working girls in Amsterdam, it could well be the latter option.

This said, *Hostel*'s biggest misstep is probably down to its choice of location, because the film portrays Slovakia as one the most barbaric places on earth. It is puzzling why the director chose this country, in particular, to be the site of juvenile hooligan gangs (who hold up travellers for bubble gum), drug abuse, prostitutes galore and police who have little qualms at being part of a mass murder ring. It could be that *Hostel*'s worldview is that of its two American leads and perhaps a mirror for the current war in Iraq. Using Slovakia as a metaphor for the 'war on terror' serves to express a chilling point of view, whereby Westerners believe that they can waltz into a country foreign to them and effectively colonise it (as reflected by Paxton and Josh and their cold, hard bedding of two women they only just met).

The other issue that has to be addressed with *Hostel* is whether or not it is homophobic, a claim that Roth denies. Characters use the word 'fag' and throwaway lines such as, 'Roommates huh? That's gay.' Of course, no one wants to be overly politically correct, but these lines come from characters that we are supposed to empathise with, yet they are introduced to us as being the most horrific human beings imaginable[110]. Misogynistic, homophobic, foul-mouthed, drugged up – none of *Hostel*'s central male characters are in any way likeable and when they finally are under threat we only really feel for them because of the sheer, painful brutality of their torture. However, in spite of this, it is difficult to conclude that *Hostel* shows any real, pointed hatred towards gay men. The characters *may* be homophobic, and Vlasak certainly portrays a sadistic man with homosexual tendencies, but his torture of Josh does not contain any sexual abuse. Moreover, when Josh actually takes the time to sit down for a drink with the Dutch Businessman (prior to finding out his true personality), his character is somewhat distanced from his on-screen friends and their loutish behaviour. Thus, it is interesting that Paxton is the film's hero as he is probably the most dislikeable leading man in recent memory, and whether or not sacrificing *Hostel*'s predictability in favour of such an obnoxious 'good guy' was a good idea is certainly up to debate.

In spite of *Hostel*'s on-screen sexism and xenophobia, and its glorification of laddish behaviour, one cannot help but be impressed by the film's ability to scare the living hell out of the viewers. An obvious horror connoisseur (*Hostel* features a Takashi Miike cameo and the use of 'Willow's Theme' from *The Wicker Man*) Roth controls the movie's suspense expertly, with Josh's escape from the terror palace being absolutely frantic and wonderfully set up. In fact, it is so damn edge-of-your-seat thrilling that it deserves to be listed amongst the finest fear set pieces ever put to celluloid. The actual scenes of torture are quickly passed over and never lingered upon, yet the effect of the run-down building where the murders take place, the clever use of sound and enough quick-snippets of limbs being chopped off make *Hostel*'s horrors nearly impossible to forget.

Compared to something as dull as the aforementioned *Wolf Creek* (with its 'kill the bimbos' mentality) *Hostel* positively shines, although it goes without saying that a more positive female character would have been welcome. As it stands, the film is open to several readings, including the more liberal one expressed here, but, in spite of where one may stand, one thing is for certain: after the comparable slap-stick of *Cabin Fever*, its director has proven that he is more than able to calculate a nicely timed scare or two. The next 'Master of Horror'? Roth could well be the guy.

---

110 Roth answered the criticism of homophobia directly in the pages of *Fangoria* magazine claiming that 'fag' should no longer be seen as an insult directly aimed at homosexuality and that the gay studio execs who viewed *Hostel* loved the movie. (See issues 253, 255 for the letter page kerfuffle that resulted.)

HOSTEL

What happened next? *Hostel: Part II* of course! After the overwhelming popularity of his original, a franchise was born and Roth, along with producers Spiegel and Tarantino, quickly released a sequel in mid-2007 which started from where the first film concluded. After quickly slaughtering the original movie's survivor Paxton (in a plot twist that seems as random as it is unwelcome), *Hostel: Part II* focuses its attention on the slaughter of females. There is something distinctly unpleasant when the genders are reversed and the sight of a naked girl being hung upside down and having her throat cut, or another getting her head sliced with a bandsaw, leaves a bad taste in the mouth. Seemingly aware of its own misogyny (right down to its climax wherein the sole surviving woman becomes a literal *femme castratice*) the sequel feels like a ninety minute attempt to offend. That said - despite his reputation as the innovator of 'torture porn', Roth is well served at his knack at building suspense and this, rather than out-and-out gore, is something that one hopes to see more of in the future.

Meanwhile, Tarantino himself revisited the drive-in exploitation days that he holds so nostalgically with the three hour flop *Grindhouse* (2007), which he co-directed with Robert Rodriguez (Roth also came onboard to cameo in *Death Proof*). Although one applauds Tarantino's tireless ambition to bring low budget, largely forgotten, trash cinema to the masses, the man who gave the world such instant classics as *Reservoir Dogs*, *Pulp Fiction* and *Jackie Brown* now seems less and less likely to produce the type of serious, gritty thrillers that made his name. Suffice to say, however, that he remains one of the most interesting filmmakers working in the Hollywood studio system. Interestingly, the real highlight of *Grindhouse* is its trailer segments and Roth's *Thanksgiving*, in particular, is a work of genius.

Hostel immediately spawned a number of copycat productions including the superior *Turistas* (2006), which was renamed *Paradise Lost* in the UK. Relocating *Hostel*'s East European torture chambers to Brazil, *Turistas* is a fine nail-biter, something which cannot be said for Roland Joffe's controversial *Captivity* (2007). Written by Larry Cohen, *Captivity* sees a teen star played by Elisha Cuthbert (from the likes of *24* and *Old School*) drugged and captured by a mysterious rotund psychopath who forces her to drink a concoction made from whisked human remains and to endure her fingernails being pulled out. The end result is as a boring as it is stupid. None other than Lindsay Lohan ended up being mutilated and kidnapped in 2007's well made, but redundant, *I Know Who Killed Me*, a movie now almost synonymous with Razzie Awards. The 'torture porn' trend continued in 2008 with the release of *The Girl Next Door*, based on a novel by Jack Ketchum, which takes all of 45 minutes to start stripping, bludgeoning and raping its leading lady (who is supposed to be only 14 years old). The movie's nadir comes when her clitoris is blowtorched off, a scene that it is hard to imagine many people wanting to see. In comparison, the oft-criticised *Saw* series seems like child's play. Although *Saw II* (2005) took its level of torture to new levels of explicitness it was done with a certain comic book relish. The same can be said for 2006's mediocre *Saw III* and the following year's *Saw IV*, which showed a franchise quickly running out of ideas ...

Certainly, when future critics look back at the first decade of the new millennium, the horror genre will, for better or for worse, be represented by the sort of low budget, brutal, gruesome thrills that *Hostel* and the *Saw* series gave audiences during a time of war, real life torture and global uncertainty.

TABOO BREAKERS

Eli Roth interview
(Conducted before Hostel's *theatrical release)*

After making an immediate splash with *Cabin Fever*, director Eli Roth knew his sophomore project had to be something special. Thankfully, he spent his time waiting for the right idea, and *Hostel* was just that. 'I'm really, really happy with *Hostel*. After *Cabin Fever* I had offers to do all kinds of studio movies and I thought that the scripts were just terrible … I was sent lots of non-horror movies too, including comedies and action films. I just felt the scripts sucked. They would say, "Well put your own spin on it," but you really can't polish a turd, so why not make your own turd? (*Laughs*) No, seriously, I just didn't want to do any big studio movies because your second film either makes you or breaks you. You are either a one hit wonder or a real director. So I sat down and I was speaking about this with Quentin Tarantino. I said, "What do you think I should do? I've got these different projects that are at different stages and with different studios and I kinda don't know what to do next." I told him about this one idea, the idea for *Hostel*, and he said, "Oh my God, you have got to fucking do that, it is the best idea I have ever heard. You have got to fucking do that." We were in his pool talking about it and I ran home and just started writing and writing and writing. I burned out the draft really quickly and went back to him. The idea actually came from years ago when I saw this web site in Thailand. Harry Knowles from *Ain't it Cool News* had shown me this site where you could sign up, pay $10,000, to walk into a room and shoot somebody in the head. Just to see what it felt like. Harry had found this and he told me, "This is the most disturbing thing that I have ever found on the internet." That idea, that there is someone out there who is so numb to drugs and hookers that they didn't get off on it anymore, really, really disturbed me. We keep looking at the site and it looked legitimate and I thought, "Well even if this is fake, someone still thought about this. Somebody still created it." It just really disturbed me, and then I was talking to Mike Fleiss, who produced the remake of *The Texas Chain Saw Massacre*, and his friend Chris Briggs and they were saying, "We want to do a movie called *Hostel* but we don't know what it is about." Then it struck me, it's about exploitation and the things people can do to each other. That is why I wanted to set it in Amsterdam and make it about these guys who are looking for hookers, looking to be able to go in a room and do whatever they want to someone, but then they wind up as the hookers in a weird way.'

Hostel came along at a time when torture began to become newsworthy again following the execution of Daniel Pearl and the events at Abu Ghraib and Guantanamo Bay, something that Roth acknowledges. 'I think it is just coincidence but I think the fear, right now, is that Americans are definitely afraid of foreigners and of terrorism,' he says. 'There was something really, really disturbing about, and how should I say this … well, everyone knows about the Al Qaeda movies that were released on the internet. Well I made the mistake of watching one. I thought, "Jesus, what if you were in a room and some guy was going to come in and kill you and nothing you could say, no combination of sentences, no amount of money you could offer were going to make a difference?" Now what about if you took away the political elements of that, and someone was doing it as a sexual act, then there is nothing, nothing you could do or say, someone was going to end your life and you are just in the wrong place at the wrong time? So I think that, right now with that girl disappearing in Aruba, it has definitely been in the air, people travelling and disappearing and Americans thinking they are invincible and protected and, yet, they are not. When you are in another country anything can happen to you. But wouldn't it be great if the people doing this were other Westernised nations? Americans, Japanese, Germans … that is what I found fascinating. This web site in Thailand was targeted towards Americans, so the people doing this were from your own country. It just seems sick on so many levels but this is where I think things are headed. I see things moving in that direction.'

Roth insists that the web site which he and internet critic Harry Knowles discovered is genuine and also becomes quite defensive when asked why, if this was the case, he never alerted the police to the URL. 'Well, I mean … what the fuck are the police going to do?' he asks. 'Everyone thinks, "I'll just go to the police," but wake up. The Russian mafia runs Brighton Beach, you know Little Odessa, everyone knows that, but just because they do doesn't mean anyone can stop it. They are too powerful. It is irrelevant. Everybody wants to believe that this organisation "the police" are there but there is an article that I read in The New York Times about human sex traffic, you know white slavery was the number one black market trade … bigger than drugs, bigger than anything. They get these girls from Odessa, the Ukraine and ship them over to Tel Aviv to these brothels and if the girls complain, if they go to the police, then they are killed, they are publicly decapitated, thrown off buildings in the middle of the town square."

There are no big name actors in the cast of *Hostel*; something that Roth insists was always his intention. 'I don't cast by that,' he says. 'I go for the best cast I can. I try and get the best people that I believe are the best actors for the role. We had a lot of stars and name actors that came in and wanted to be in the film, but they weren't right and I wasn't going to cast them. Jay Hernandez is great, he is in a new movie by Oliver Stone, *Twin Towers*, and he also recently did a movie called *Crazy, Beautiful*. He's got a great reputation and he has a following, and although he's not a big star he's touted to become a big star in the future. Another actor we used is Derek Richardson, and he is one of these guys that came in and gave a great audition and, yet, since he had the lead role in *Dumb and Dumberer: When Harry Met Lloyd* he hasn't worked, and Derek is kind of a genius, he is so funny, his drama is incredible and he is an amazing actor. For the rest of the actors I wrote roles that we could cast in Eastern Europe, in Prague, and they could have an accent but they wouldn't have to pretend they were American and we wouldn't have to loop them. A lot of these actors will be in movies that have been shot in Prague and then they will get looped or they will appear as "Waiter Number Two" with one line or something. But here, I found an incredible actress called Barbara Nedeljakova who plays Natalya and she is a brilliant actor, I think she is on the level of someone like Monica Bellucci, Maria Schneider, she has this stunning Eastern European beauty about her. She is from Slovakia. She is like Emmanuelle Beart, one of these girls where you think, "Oh my God she should be an international movie star." For me it is really great to find people like that, who are the best people for the roles. There is definitely an advantage when you don't recognise somebody in a role, when you don't know who they are and they kind of become that character but, first and foremost, just get the best person for the role and everything else will fall into place.'

Asked to compare *Hostel* to some other horror movies and, perhaps surprisingly, Roth does not opt for some of his favourite gore flicks such as *Cannibal Holocaust* and *Pieces* but instead mentions some artier genre fare. 'This is like *The Vanishing* or *Audition*,' he says. 'I set out to make a movie like those or even *The Wicker Man*. This is not a grindhouse movie, this is not a drive-in movie, this is not like an eighties splatter movie. This is the movie that I wanted to make, that would be violent on those levels but smarter and more intelligent. Just a better made film. It does not look like a cheap horror movie, I wanted to make something that would be profoundly disturbing. Quentin Tarantino, having him involved, he would not have put his name on it if he didn't feel so strongly about it, and he came in at the script stage.'

The director was also pleased that *Hostel* could hit cinemas with an R-rating during a time when PG13 horror was already starting to wear out its welcome. '*Saw II* really killed the PG13' he laughs. '*The Exorcism of Emily Rose* made $75 million on an $18 million budget and *Saw II* passed that figure on a $4 million budget, and the advertisements were, "Oh yes, there will be blood." *The Exorcism of Emily Rose* brought the PG13 back but *Saw II* just ended it. Any idea that people want PG13 is out of the fucking window now. We had a *Masters of Horror* dinner, where all the horror directors got together, and I invited *Saw* director James Wan, Darren Lynn Bousman, who did the sequel, and I also brought Quentin and we all raised a glass and toasted Darren and James for *Saw II* and killing the PG13 (*laughs*). But with *Hostel* we actually sailed by the ratings board with almost nothing, hardly any changes, just 12 frames out of the movie. I think that the ratings board has really come around to horror movies. They know that, with *Saw II* ... they kind of get it now. They know that if it is a horror movie people are kind of expecting certain things and they have to meet these expectations. My whole point was that if you have a movie with my name and with Quentin Tarantino's name, no parent is going to send their kids to that movie thinking that there is no blood in there. Everybody is going to know what they are in for and there are certain expectations that our fans have that need to be met. We said, "Look we are selling this as a bloody horror movie from the guys that did *Cabin Fever* and *Kill Bill* so no one is going to be surprised when there is carnage and blood." They got it, no problem. There were scenes that I was certain were going to get cut and they never touched them.'

It was *Saw II* that also resulted in *Hostel*'s release date being bumped until early January 2006. 'The original date was 21 September 2005, and then it got bumped to January 2006,' says Roth. 'The reason was *Saw II*. Basically, *Saw II* was going to open the same day. We have two studios, Sony and Lion's Gate, and when these studios are releasing movies they don't want their own movies competing against each other. So we had to find a date where there wasn't a Lion's Gate or a Sony movie opening. Originally we were going to open against *Fun with Dick and Jane* and that is a Jim Carrey, $125 million comedy, as well as a Sony movie, so they figured, "Well *Hostel* is so different. These are two different things." Well *Saw II* changed all that, *Saw II* made double what *The Legend of Zorro* did and suddenly everyone realised, "Okay well wait a minute. Maybe everybody is going to see horror movies now and not just some hardcore geeks." So they said to us, "You gotta move the date."'

Roth admits more surprise at how lucky he has been in the UK: *Cabin Fever* received a 15 certificate whilst *Hostel* went out in cinemas without a single cut (and this in the country that took until the year 2000 to give a video certificate to *The Texas Chain Saw Massacre*!). 'I think that the 15 for *Cabin Fever* helped us, we were a huge hit in the UK,' he admits. 'If *Hostel* had gotten a 12 certificate I'd be happy too ... Start them young, you know what I mean? But this is not funny the way *Cabin Fever* is, I think it is the humour that got *Cabin Fever* a 15. If people can go, "Yeah this is scary but also funny," somehow that makes it less hardcore. With the first 15 to 20 minutes of *Hostel* it is funny, it is guys having fun and getting into trouble. Like when you see guys going to Europe to get laid, you want to see if they are going to get laid, but then lots of horrible things happen to them. The last 30 minutes are so violent, and so realistically intensely violent, that I just didn't know if we would ever get away with it.'

Back in the eighties the directors were the stars of the horror movie, names like John Carpenter, David Cronenberg, Wes Craven and Clive Barker drew the crowds but the biggest name to have emerged since that heyday has been Peter Jackson, director of *The Lord of the Rings*. But more recently things seem to be developing again with names like Guillermo Del Toro, Neil Marshall and now Eli Roth moving to the forefront of terror cinema. 'I don't know if that is a function of the films I make or if that is a function of the fact that nobody else really wanted that,' Roth says. 'Horror has been a dirty word for the past 15 years and I thought, "Well this is bullshit. I miss horror movies," and I'm proud to call myself a horror director. People forget that guys like Sam Raimi and Peter Jackson moved on to making these huge, massive, incredible genre movies. A lot of people are terrified of being pegged as a horror director but I think that if you are a good director ... I mean, honestly, I don't think of myself of a horror director, I just think of myself as a director. I love horror movies and this is what I am making now, but I don't think that there is anybody who wanted that title, whose whole life's ambition was to be on the cover of *Fangoria* magazine. I got that with my first film, you know? When I was a kid that was all that I ever dreamed of, and I made a film that came out in theatres and it really turned around on how R-rated, low budget horror movies can be commercially viable. It is nice. It is weird because I don't think of myself as that guy, I just think of myself as part of a wave of guys that are making horror movies, you know, James Wan, Rob Zombie ... guys that love these movies and that want to make interesting genre projects.'

Scott Spiegel interview

As an executive producer on *Hostel* and *Hostel: Part II*, Scott Spiegel, most famous for scripting *Evil Dead II* and directing the cult classic slasher picture *Intruder*, found a new genre franchise to sink his creative teeth into. 'Well Boaz Yakin and I were talking about doing a horror company with Green Street films and through them we met Eli Roth,' begins Spiegel, reflecting upon how he got involved with *Hostel*. '*Cabin Fever* was all very brand new and everything and I had been following it in the trades and thinking, "Who's this guy Eli? He sounds cool." Then before we knew it Eli, Boaz and I met, we hit it off, we formed Raw Nerve and *2001 Maniacs* was our first production. I thought that if we do a $1 million movie and have Robert Englund in it then that is a pretty good deal. It seemed like a good opportunity and the perfect project to get the bugs worked out, so we came up with the title Raw Nerve, the guys liked that, and it was an attempt to do edgier horror films and stuff. It just seemed really cool, and working on *2001 Maniacs* was tough because we had to work it around Robert Englund's schedule so everything became super-rushed and it was a $1 million movie so there were challenges there for everyone. But it turned out really cool and somewhere along the line Eli mentioned that Chris Biggs and Mike Fleiss had this idea about a hostel and they were kicking some ideas around together. So Eli took the bull by the horns and really went with it. We were developing some other projects around that time but, as the story goes, Eli and Quentin were hanging out and Eli ran *Hostel* past him and when Quentin gave it the thumbs up the next thing I knew we were in pre-production. It all came together really fast but I'm glad it did because it forced us, as a company, to really keep our focus, and having producers that are also writers is a really cool thing too because, between Boaz and me, in the early stages of *Hostel*, and I don't want to take any credit because it's Eli's show basically, but it was really cool because we were able to talk and work on the same page and add things to the film.'

Perhaps the most effective moment in *Hostel* is actually the opening credits sequence which depicts a stranger whistling whilst he is cleaning blood off pure white walls. For a movie renowned for its graphic gristle, this is one of the creepiest cinematic moments of the new millennium and it makes its impact without actually revealing too much … 'Yeah that was Eli,' says Spiegel. 'It was a great opening, just great. I didn't know if we should do that, I was going for the old school … very gross and graphic (*laughs*). I had a subplot with the Japanese girl's dead brother, she knows that there is something up with this hostel and she ends up becoming a victim herself, and in the beginning you saw this Japanese guy being tormented. A little more vague and done with flash cuts, you would hear moaning and stuff like that, but those guys didn't go into that. I always thought it was kind of cool when you thought that somebody was just an innocent victim and then you find out, like with Vera Miles in *Psycho*, that she is trying to track down what happened to Marion Crane, you know? But, still, I have to give Eli credit there, what he came up with is simple, not too complicated and perfect to creep you out. You end up thinking, "Well what is this place? It could be a slaughterhouse for animals but, God forbid, is it for people? I don't know."'

After the popularity of *Hostel*, *The Devil's Rejects*, and the critical, if not commercial, success of the Tarantino/Rodriguez collaboration *Grindhouse* it might be safe to assume that a whole new generation is finding out about 42nd Street and exploitation cinema. True? 'Yeah, that's a great question, but who the hell knows?' laughs Spiegel. 'I hope so but, on the other hand, there are only so many people that know how to do that sort of thing. Obviously Quentin, Robert Rodriguez, Eli, I would definitely throw myself into that ring, so to that extent I hope so, it would be so freaking cool if this was true because I grew up in that era of grindhouse. I did not make it to 42nd Street but we had our own Detroit version of that. It was more of a suburban, low budget area and a theatre called The Northgate and they would have double bills. This was between 1978 and 1984 and they had everything … double features for $2.50. I remember Sam Raimi, Bruce Campbell and I going to see one of the *Blind Dead* films and they had re-titled it. This was back in the late seventies and they had the most ridiculous titles, it was called *Revenge from Planet Ape*. And we were laughing because the last *Planet of the Apes* film came out theatrically in 1973 or 1974 and so we were thinking, "Do they expect you to think this is real? This is some cheesy dubbed Spanish horror film." (*laughs*). This was back in the day when they could just barely get away with it, but that was our version of 42nd Street. I did get to see a movie near there, not exactly on 42nd Street, but I saw *Excalibur* in 1981 when I went to see Bruce and Sam in New York when they were editing *The Evil Dead* and I was stunned to find out that you could smoke in these movie theatres. I was freaked out, I was a smoker back then and I still didn't think it was a good idea. You couldn't see anything, people were stubbing out cigarettes on the seats, you could start a fire that way, you know? But it was an experience unlike anything I had ever had because it was a cool, old school movie palace, run down, but I guess we weren't brave enough to go to the real grindhouse theatres. When I came out to California I went to a theatre called the Cameo and I had to watch the movie like Bazooka Joe, with my shirt over my nose and mouth. It was just a wino hangout (*laughs*). We saw *Zone Troopers* and, oh my God, it must have been a second run film by that time but they kept having those cheesy Charlie Band 1980s optical effects, you know what I mean? Well some drunken African-American guy, whenever one of those cheesy effects happened I would hear, "Hollywood!"' (*laughs*). I told that to Eli and now, when we're watching a movie and something like that happens, I hear, "Hollywood." But I loved this guy, he must have been some wino in the back and he had this great street-speak.'

Certainly, *Hostel* can be seen to pay homage to such unrelenting seventies shockers as *Last House on the Left* and *The Texas Chain Saw Massacre* by never really letting the viewer feel safe and by gradually, and even subtly, increasing the sense of dread as the plot moves along. This is something that Spiegel agrees with. 'Oh yeah, and it does that in a classy way,' he says. 'You've got to throw in the *Saw* movies too because they do that well. I think that Eli really hits it over the park in *Hostel: Part II*. The whole *Last House on the Left* thing, because that movie wasn't so well made, and I'm a huge fan of Wes and Sean don't get me wrong, and it was their first film, but *Last House on the Left* was so brutal and so raw, but it was one of those landmark horror films. Look, no matter what you want to say, a chick running from terror, whether it's Leatherface or the Alien, is always far more scary in my opinion than a guy being terrified. You know, Richard Matheson is probably the only writer who has disproved my theory. I am so sympathetic for when Dennis Weaver is being chased by that big truck in the movie *Duel* and I also like what Matheson did with *The Incredible Shrinking Man*. But that grindhouse seventies feel, not quite *I Spit on your Grave* ... but I know what you're talking about ... Right now, I am just fascinated with what you can and cannot get away with in regards to the ratings out here but I'm not going to push that issue (*laughs*). I am very, very thankful for how lenient they were with *Hostel* and I think Quentin's name on it gave it a big air of credibility because he's an Academy Award winner, he's his own institution and that obviously helped us in a big way. I couldn't believe they let in as much as they did gore-wise. I mean, when you look at the first *Friday the 13th* you think, "My God, talk about liberal ratings policy," and then, over the years, you match the first *Friday the 13th* against the later ones, the first is hardcore and brutal and later it's very "Hollywood" (*laughs*). Of course I understand that with *Freddy Vs Jason* you want to get in the ten year olds and stuff but I just think it's great that everything came together on *Hostel* in every conceivable way. What a great, great way to all come together. I'm very proud to have been a part of that.'

Of course *Hostel* also received some criticism for its perceived misogyny. For instance, the women in Slovakia are portrayed as sluts who lure men to their death, every woman is beautiful and wants to have sex with the lead guys and the male characters treat their bed partners with total disrespect. So is this criticism warranted? 'Well, what are you going to do, you know?' laughs Spiegel. 'It is what it is. At the end of the day, a lot of people, including quite a few women, like to see naked chicks (*laughs*). If you're going to do a sauna scene then you want to see the women naked.'

Although when Jennifer Lim, who plays the beautiful Japanese girl in *Hostel*, kills herself it does feel as if a silent voice from behind the camera is stating that a woman without her beauty is useless … 'I actually liked that scene,' replies Spiegel. 'In fact it reminded me of Savannah, the famous porn star, who back in the nineties got in a car accident or something and then ended up killing herself in a suicide. I haven't thought about it in over a decade but I just thought that poor girl … for me, and maybe I'm reading too much into it, but I thought that not only was her face fucked up but her brain was fucked up. Like, "I'm so fucked up I can't ever see myself overcoming this but I may as well try and save this guy who tried to save me." One of my close friends thought that was a very poignant scene, he didn't think it was misogynistic at all, but if you are clued in that way I can see how you might think that. But I just thought she was so hopelessly scarred inside and out but I don't know …'

Spiegel also claims that there is, as has been speculated, a deliberate link between *Hostel* and the hellhole prisons of Abu Ghraib and Guantanamo Bay. 'Yeah I think it does reflect that,' he says. 'Regardless of what anyone thinks about the war in Iraq or Guantanamo Bay I am sure there are some innocent people in there and I'm sure there are also some bad ones too. But it is so in the news, so in your face, but it goes into more than that, it goes into Al Queda and Daniel Pearl and the beheading of these journalists and the kidnappings and everything else. So, hell yeah, it's a great question, if America hadn't gone into Iraq and if Saddam was still in there I'm wondering about the success of *Hostel* in a weird way. So thank God for George Bush! No I'm kidding (*laughs*). I really, really didn't mean that.'

Spiegel is credited, alongside Tarantino and Boaz Yakin, as a producer on *Hostel*, but he insists that three was not a crowd and that everyone worked closely, and fluently, together. 'We were onboard from formulating the script, which was written by Eli,' says Spiegel. 'What happened is that Eli would do a draft and then Boaz and I would mark it up with our notes and so would Mike Fleiss and Chris Briggs and then we would have a meeting. After that Eli would do the next draft and we were pretty active participants from the concept of the idea to the execution. Also, with the editing process, during the production of *Hostel*, Quentin and I would be hanging around at Eli's place and talking about the film. I remember Quentin said, "Jay should have his whole arm cut off," and I said, "No he could not survive that, we should just cut a few off his fingers off." Quentin would say, "Wait we gotta call Eli up," and I'd tell him to hang on, "How about if he grabs his fingers, puts them in his pocket, then they fall out and the guy in the torture chamber scoops them up and puts them into the fire?" So we would call Eli up at Prague, it's two in the morning, and yeah it was pretty wacky. It was that kind of thing. Eli emailed me and said, "I need a Scotty Spiegel cutaway," which I thought was so cool. So when the wire cutters come down on the Asian girl's toe you cut to the other Asian girl doing her nail varnish, you know? That worked great. It was really cool, the stuff with the script, coming up with a lot of the gags and right through to the editing room, it was an incredible process that I will always cherish. I always thought of myself as a creative producer and it was really cool working with him, Boaz, Quentin, all of those guys.'

The *Saw* series, *Wolf Creek* and *Hostel* also attracted a new label, that of 'torture porn' … 'I think you have to ask, once again, what is the context?' comments Spiegel. '*Psycho* is one of the all time great horror movies ever made and yet it is also quite depraved. This guy thinks he is his mother and he's slicing women up in the shower. It still has potency today! The idea of killing someone when they are naked in the shower, let alone a beautiful young woman in her twenties, it is the context! It has nothing to do with torture porn! What I didn't like about *Wolf Creek*, and I thought it was a well made film, is that nobody was acting like a human being. The killer sounded like Steve Irwin, which I didn't find scary, but I enjoyed the last 20 minutes when that guy ended up surviving. You thought, "Well how did that happen?" But what drove me nuts was that nobody asked, "Is this guy fucking with us? Did he fuck up our car?" Then they are drinking his coffee and not one of them thought they should stay awake, then you realise the guy is looking at the coffee cup and wants to wake one of the girls but he crashes because he's been drugged. Then she goes back and looks at his videotapes, "You're in his torture chamber! Take the chainsaw and cut off his head after you've shot his body 100 times." That sort of stuff drives me nuts, like in the first *Saw* movie where the guy is holding the mother and the kid hostage and she gets the gun and says, "Freeze," and right away you think, "Blow his head off because you're endangering your child." Then he gets the gun from her and you think, "I'm not rooting for you anymore because you are too stupid." That is my main issue. So to answer your question, it is all in the context. I have seen enough horror films to think, "Oh please," but this stuff happens out there to whatever extent and there are those people out there.'

One thing impressive about *Hostel* is that it remains logical throughout, regardless of how garish or downright bizarre the whole concept surrounding the movie might be. For instance, in one sequence the film's hero, Paxton, goes back to save Kana, who has been captured and is about to be tortured. In this scene Roth really allows the viewer to put themslves in Paxton's shoes and think about what they would do … 'Right, yeah I agree,' says Spiegel. 'And we tried hard to "pump up that Japanese girl screaming in there Eli, let's pump that up more" (*laughs*). That was one of the problems that I had. Originally Eli had him get the hell out of there, although I think he still saved the girl. I said, "Dude you're missing all of the cool stuff of having him hide underneath bodies, don't have it so easy for him to get out because that is where all the suspense and the horror is." Like in *Coma* with all the hanging bodies and stuff, I love that movie, and what a great ending, it has some contrivances in it but I love it. Anyway, I said, "Eli let's make it not so easy for Jay to get out," and he seized on that and went insane with it. The other issue that I had was with Takashi Miike's cameo, "You can spend all your money in there." Well originally he just drove up and went in there. So I thought, "Well I'm the audience coalition, I'm Jay and I'm *not* fucking going in there," (*laughs*), so I thought there should maybe be a normal-looking businessman standing outside. Of course, Eli gets Takashi to play him and he looks scary even in the movie (*laughs*). But at least it's some guy, at least there's other people coming out, but the way it was written originally it was like taking someone and dropping them off outside the Bates Motel at one in the morning. "Sure, I'll go and rent a room in there," so, to me, I try and find that stuff because it just bugs me … what's that gag? "People won't believe implausibility but they will believe that *Star Wars* could happen," you know what I mean? It's like that thing in *Wolf Creek* where no one seems to be thinking what I'm thinking, that this guy is a crazy son of a bitch and he might just be fucking with us. You have three people, somebody would have thought that and if the audience is thinking about that and your actors aren't then that's tormenting …'

But how about the idea that *Hostel* was so successful because audiences thought Quentin

Tarantino had made it? 'God, you know, I have heard that more and more over the past couple of months,' says Spiegel. 'Quentin was incredible promoting it but it was a 50/50 proposition because around the same time he produced *Daltry Calhoun* and that certainly didn't hit the $100 million mark. Now I liked *Daltry Calhoun*, but I guess if you mix Quentin's name with a cool horror title and a good horror director like Eli … you know what I mean? Quentin is my mentor, my man, the godfather, there ain't no negative things to say about him, so does that make sense to you? I mean, it still said, "A film by Eli Roth," and Eli's name was pretty big. Quentin's name was certainly bigger but, yeah, he's the rock star of this franchise and that's that. But what's great now is that Quentin still "presents" *Hostel: Part II* but it's still Eli Roth's *Hostel*. Quentin did a terrific thing by doing that and solidifying Eli as a first rate horror director. It is great see the growth from the first *Hostel* to the second one, the filmmaking quality, the gore, everything … "Eli you're not going there are you? Oh man, you can't! You are not going to show *that* are you?"'

Spiegel also claims that he always envisaged a series of sequels to *Hostel*. 'Yeah, absolutely, sequels and a television series and the whole nine yards,' he laughs. 'It has one of those great one word titles and you wonder why no one ever used it before and what is interesting is that the concept is tied in exactly to the audience's age group because everyone who goes to see this movie has been to a youth hostel. Somehow, some way, somewhere, the person who buys a ticket to go see *Hostel* has stayed at a youth hostel some time in their lives. The people paying to see the film are the same age as the people in the film, it's really kind of awesome in that way, and to use that cliché: it had franchise written all over it. *Hostel* cost $8 million to make and took over $100 million worldwide, so I'm happy (*laughs*). I'm part of this whole thing and I can't wait to see the third film, that's the honest to God truth. Look at how successful *Saw* is, and I'm really happy to maintain the same level of quality and to keep you interested.'

ABOUT the AUTHOR

Born and raised in Fife, Scotland, Calum Waddell made the silly mistake of believing his schoolteachers who told him that further education actually counts for something in the post-Thatcherism/New Labour UK. As such he wasted five years in further education, gaining a BA (Hons) degree in English and a Masters in Broadcast and Film Studies, qualifications that he begrudgingly describes as 'useless pieces of paper'.

When neither 'award' got him anywhere except the unemployment line at his local Job Centre, he turned to freelance journalism and, after a long hard slog, has managed to contribute towards a number of the world's leading entertainment magazines including *360 Gamer*, *Bizarre*, *The Dark Side*, *Dazed and Confused*, *Death Ray*, *Dreamwatch*, *DVD Review*, *DVD World*, *Fangoria*, *Filmfax*, *Geek*, *HD Review*, *Rue Morgue*, *Sci-Fi Now*, *SFX*, *Shivers*, *Shock Cinema*, *Total Film* and *Videoscope*. In addition, Waddell currently edits the Asian Film Reviews section for *NEO* magazine and has a monthly 'Asian Extreme' section in *Impact*, Britain's 'action entertainment' publication. Waddell's film credits include 2003's *The Collingswood Story* (as Associate Producer) and 2007's *Brotherhood of Blood* (also as Associate Producer). In addition, the author has written the film notes for the UK DVDs of *Aragami*, *Dumplings*, *Intruder*, *Strange Behaviour* and *Three Extremes*, appears as an interviewer on the British DVD release of *2001 Maniacs* and contributes a commentary track to the US and UK DVDs of Tobe Hooper's *The Toolbox Murders*. Waddell has also helped to programme such film festivals as the Fearless Tales event in San Francisco and Manchester's annual Festival of Fantastic Films.

Waddell's book *Minds of Fear* (Midnight Marquee, 2005) was given a personal recommendation by Tony Timpone, the editor of *Fangoria*, in issue 249 of the magazine. It also achieved two award nominations: Independent Publisher Book Awards: Arts Category (2006) and Rondo Awards (2006).

Outside of writing, Waddell's interests include politics, classic Disney movies, indie music and travelling. He remains in love with Los Angeles.

WITHOUT WHOM

Books do not happen without the encouragement, help and support of several people. First up, of course, are Stephen James Walker and David J Howe at Telos Publishing. They have been incredibly patient with this book, especially in extending my deadline as new interview subjects became possible. I really cannot thank these two wonderful people enough for their confidence in this project. Special thanks also has to go to Marc Morris at Nucleus Films and Joe Venegas at Creative Talent Communications.

I also cannot express enough gratitude towards the following people who all assisted in 'taboo breaking' in their own little way: Chris Alexander, Ralph Bakshi's delightful daughter Victoria (please visit www.pervertthemovie.com), Angelica and Michael Davidson, Don Edmonds, Jenny Erwood, Del at Dark Delicacies (please visit www.darkdel.com), Paul Gaita, David Gregory, David Hess, Craig Jex, Andy Lalino, Heidi Martinuzzi, Floyd McCrory, Steve Puchalski, Paul Smith and Virginia Todd at Tartan Films, the music of Belle and Sebastian, Iain Robert Smith, John Squires, Tim Sullivan, David Szulkin at Grindhouse releasing, Tony Timpone, Dante Tomaselli, Richard York at Media Blasters and the ever helpful Tal Zimerman. MAJOR thanks to all the editors who publish my work, without them I wouldn't be writing this.

XX

This book is dedicated to my ever supportive mother Helen, who was extremely ill during much of its production but who pulled herself into better health with the love and support of a dedicated family.

BIBLIOGRAPHY

Blum, D, *The Monkey Wars*, Oxford University Press, New York, 1994
Bogle, Donald, *Toms, Coons, Mulattoes, Mammies & Bucks*, Continuum, New York, 1992
Boulenger, G, *John Carpenter: The Prince of Darkness*, Silman-James Press, California, 1993
Briggs, Joe Bob, *Profoundly Disturbing*, Plexus Publishing, London, 2003
Clover, C, *Men Women and Chainsaws*, BFI, London, 1996
Curry, Christopher Wayne, *A Taste of Blood*, Headpress, London, 1998
Fenton, Castoldi and Grainger, *Cannibal Holocaust and the Savage Cinema of Ruggero Deodato*, FAB Press, Surrey, 1999
French, Karl (ed), *Screen Violence*, Bloomsbury, London, 1996
Friedman, David, *A Youth in Babylon*, Prometheus Books, New York, 1990
Grahame-Smith, Seth, *The Big Book of Porn*, Quirk, Philadelphia, 2005
Halliwell, Leslie, *The Dead That Walk*, Grafton, London, 1986
Hammond, S & Wilkins, M, *Sex and Zen & A Bullet in the Head*, Titan Books, London, 1997
Hardy, Phil (ed), *The Aurum Film Encyclopaedia: Horror*, Aurum Press, London, 1993
Kane, Joe, *The Phantom of the Movies: Videoscope*, Three Rivers Press, New York, 2000
Kerekes and Slater, *Killing for Culture*, Creation Books, London, 1994
Kerekes and Slater, *See No Evil*, Critical Vision, Manchester, 2001
King, Stephen, *Danse Macabre*, Warner Books, New York, 1981
Koven, M, *Blaxploitation Films*, Pocket Essentials, London, 2001
Krogh and McCarty, *The Amazing Herschell Gordon Lewis*, Fantaco, 1983
Landis, B and Clifford, M, *Sleazoid Express*, Fireside Books, New York, 2002
Lewis. J, *Hollywood v. Hard Core*, New York University Press, New York, 2000
Maltin, Leonard, *Of Mice and Magic*, Plume, New York, 1987
Maltin, L, *The Disney Films*, Disney, New York, 2000
Matthews, Tom D, *Censored*, Chatto, London, 1994
McCarty, John, *Splatter Movies: Breaking the Last Taboo of the Screen*, St. Martin's Press, New York, 1984
McCumber, David, *X-Rated*, Pinnacle Books, New York, 2000
McDonagh, Maitland, *Broken Mirrors/Broken Minds*, Sun Tavern, London, 1991
McNeil, L & Osborne, J, *The Other Hollywood*, HarperCollins, New York, 2005
Morse, L.A, *Video Trash and Treasures*, HarperCollins, 1989
Muller, E and Faris, D *Grindhouse: The Forbidden World of 'Adults Only' Cinema*, St Martin's Press, New York, 1996
Newman, Kim, *Nightmare Movies*, Bloomsbury, London, 1988
O'Neill, James, *Terror on Tape*, Billboard Books, London, 1994

TABOO BREAKERS

Palmerini, Luca M and Mistretta, Gaetano, *Spaghetti Nightmares*, Fantasma Books, Florida, 1996
Puchalski, Steve, *Slimetime*, Critical Vision, London, 1996
Ruesch, Hans, *Slaughter of the Innocent*, Slingshot, London, 2003
Ross, Jonathan, *The Incredibly Strange Film Book*, Simon & Schuster, London, 1993
Savini, Tom, *Bizarro!*, Harmony Books, New York, 1983
Sims, Yvonne D, *Women of Blaxploitation*, McFarland, North Carolina, 2006
Singer, Peter, *Animal Liberation*, Jonathan Cape, London, 1990
Thomas, Bob, *Walt Disney: An American Original*, Pocket Books, New York, 1980
Thrower, Stephen, *The Eyeball Compendium*, FAB Press, Surrey, 2003
Waddell, Calum, *Minds of Fear*, Midnight Marquee, Maryland, 2005
Zalcock, Bev, *Renegade Sisters*, Headpress Publishing, London 1998

CAST/CREW INDEX

Numbers in *italics* indicate appearance in cast/crew lists

Adams, Richard *205,* 206, 209, 210, 211, 212, 213, 215
Ahn Yeon-suk *243*
Aja, Alexandre 184
Akkad, Moustapha *144,* 144, 150
Alexander, Tara *193*
Allen, Nancy 152
Anderson, Pamela 16
Andress, Ursula 158
Andrews, Brian *144*
Antonioni, Michelangelo 161
Arbus, Allan *78,* 82
Argento, Dario 31, 34, 68, 145, 156, 179, 183, 185, 200, 232
Arieux, Randy *193*
Arkoff, Samuel Z *78*
Arnold, Mal *10,* 14
Arquette, Rosanna 154
Arrighi, Luciana 213
Ayers, Roy 84
Babb, Kroger 18
Bacmeister, Neila *178*
Bacon, Kevin 149
Baker, Betsy *216,* 229
Baker, Ray *193*
Baker, Rick 224
Bakshi, Ralph *54,* 54-59, 59-66, 206
Bale, Christian 180
Barbareschi, Luca *157,* 165, 167, 170, 171
Barker, Clive 261
Basile, Salvatore *157,* 170
Bauer, Michelle 104
Bava, Mario 13 (footnote), 30, 94, 217, 218
Becker, Josh 217
Bell, Jeannie 84
Benjamin, Christopher *205,* 211
Bennet, John *205*
Berry, Halle 85
Berryman, Michael 164, 236
Bertram, Barbara *67*
Bigelow, Kathryn 253
Billitteri, Salvatore *78*
Black, Karen 164, *231,* 232, 234, 242
Blair, Linda 150, 217
Blum, Deborah 207 (footnote), 210 (footnote)
Bogle, Donald 79 (footnote)
Bolam, James *205,* 209, 211
Boll, Uwe 236

271

Bolla, Robert – pseudonym for Robert Kerman 158
Bologna, Ray 18
Bolton, Lyn *10*
Bong Joon-ho 248
Boorman, John 91
Bottin, Rob 14
Boulenger, Gilles 144 (footnote), 147 (footnote)
Bourbon, Barbara *107,* 112
Bousman, Darren Lynn 260
Bouvier, Tommy *193*
Bowen, John 93 (footnote)
Bradford, Mike *41*
Bradshaw, Booker *78,* 82
Bragaglia, Carlo Ludovico 166
Breillat, Catherine 49
Brewster, James *178*
Briggs, Chris *252,* 258, 261, 264
Briggs, Joe Bob 13 (footnote), 15 (footnote), 93 (footnote), 121 (footnote), 125 (footnote)
Briggs, Marilyn (maiden name) – see Chambers, Marilyn
Briggs, Raymond 211
Browning, Tod 16
Brudo, Joann *107*
Bukovy, Lubomir *252*
Burns, Marilyn *89,* 91, 92, 94, 100, 101, 102
Burns, Robert 91, 95, 104-106
Burr, Jeff 96, 98, 104
Burton, Tim 232
Cahill, Barry *78*
Cain, Craig *193*
Calvert, Toni *10*
Campbell, Bruce *216,* 216, 217, 218, 220, 221, 222, 224, 225, 226, 227, 228, 229, 230, 262
Campbell, Neve 254
Canby, Vincent 68 (footnote), 71 (footnote), 135-136
Carpenter, John 15, 16, 31, 85, 138, *144,* 144-151, 152, 153, 154-156, 236, 253, 261
Carradine, David 72
Carstensen, Margit *67,* 68, 69
Castle, Nick *144,* 151
Castle, William 253
Castoldi, Luca 162 (footnote)
Castro, Joe 24
Caven, Ingrid *67*
Chambers, Marilyn *41,* 42, 43, 44, 45, 46, 47, 48, 49-53
Chan, Fruit 248
Chan, Jackie 49
Choi Min-sik *243,* 244, 245, 247, 248, 249
Chow Yun Fat 246
Christie, Julie 162, 206
Church, Tony *205*
Ciardi, Francesca *157,* 170, 171
Cimber, Matt *107,* 108-113, 113-118, 145
Clark, Bob 145
Clerici, Gianfranco *157*
Clifford, Carl *193*
Clifford, Michelle 109 (footnote), 123 (footnote), 125 (footnote), 158 (footnote), 164 (footnote)
Clover, Carol 146 (footnote)
Cocteau, Jean 224
Cohen, Larry 108, 109, 111, 257
Condon, Bill 212
Conway, Tim 138
Cooke, C J *193,* 196, 200, 202
Coppola, Francis Ford 79
Corbucci, Sergio 165, 166
Corday, Mara 11
Corman, Roger 53, 59, 79, 84, 85, 122
Corrina, Anna 76
Courtier, Gene *10*
Courtin, Robert 89
Cozzi, Luigi 184
Craig, Charles 25
Craven, Wes 19, 49, 50, 90, 91, 146, 150, 153, 201, 221, 252, 253 (footnote), 261, 263

CAST/CREW INDEX

Creamer, William 89
Cresse, Bob 127
Cribben, Mik 193
Cronenberg, David 48, 53, 126, 150, 261
Crumb, Robert 54, 58, 59, 61
Cundy, Dean 136, 137, 145, 149, 150-151
Cunningham, Kevin 49, 50
Cunningham, Noel 50
Cunningham, Sean 42, 49, 50, 149, 263
Curci, Loris 161 (footnote)
Curry, Christopher Wayne 14 (footnote)
Curtis, Jamie Lee *144*, 145, 146, 149, 150, 151, 153, 155
Curtis, Tony 72
Cuthbert, Elisha 257
Cyphers Charles *144*, 149
D'Amato, Joe 158, 159
Dallesandro, Joe 68
Damiano, Gerard 42, 44, 48
Daniels, Erin *231*
Daniels, Godfrey 48
Daniels, John *107*, 108, 110, 111, 114
Dante, Joe 96, 106
Danzinger, Allen 89
Davis, Ossie 79, 109
Davis, Phyllis 125 (footnote), 132
Davis Jr, Sammy 117
de Broux, Lee 78
De Niro, Robert 46, 178
De Palma, Brian 145, 151, 152, 183
Del Toro, Guillermo 261
Delrich, Hal (Pseudonym for Richard DeManincor) *216*, 220, 224
DeManincor, Richard 220
Demme, Jonathan 121, 122
Deodato, Ruggero *157*, 158-165, 165-169, 170, 172, 173, 174, 175, 176, 195
Deville, Jo Jo *119*
Di Nunzio, Franco *157*
Di Savoia, Lionello Pio *157*
Dietrich, Erwin C 141
Disney, Walt 54, 55, 58

Doak, Frank 25
Dobson, Tamara 79 (footnote), 80, 82, 84, 87
Dohler, Don 224
DoQui, Robert *78*, 82
Dowd, Tom 19
Downe, Allison Louise *10*
Dreyer, Carl 68
Dugan, John *89*, 94, 103
Dullea, Keir 72
Dunning, John 127, 130, 134
Duvall, Robert 191
Dworkin, Andrea 43
Easterbrook, Leslie 242
Eastman, Marilyn *25*, 39, 36
Edmonds, Don 108, *119*, 120-126, 127, 129-138, 139, 140, 141, 142
Edwards, Percy *205*
Eleniak, Erika 16
Elliot, William *78*, 81
Engles, Judy 54
Englund, Robert 48, 261
Estevez, Emilio 48, 52
Evans, Tracie *178*
Falana, Lola 117
Faris, Daniel 43 (footnote)
Farmer, Marva *107*
Farringer, Lisa *78*
Fassbinder, Rainer Werner *67*, 67, 68, 71, 73, 74
Fellini, Federico 200, 203
Fengler, Michael *67*, 68
Fenton, Harvey 162 (footnote)
Ferguson, Kathleen *193*
Ferman, James 91, 126 (footnote), 183, 220
Ferrara, Abel 195, 197
Findley, Roberta 128
Finnell, Mike 106
Fleiss, Heidi 141
Fleiss, Mike *252*, 258, 261, 264
Flender, Rodman 171
Flower, George 'Buck' *107*, 108, 117, *119*,

137
Foree, Ken 236, 241
Forsyth, William 236
Foschi, Massimo 158, 168
Franco, Jess 120, 122, 126, 141, 143, 159, 184
Frankenheimer, John 212
Franklyn-Robbins, John 205
Freda, Riccardo 165, 166
Friedkin, William 188
Friedman, Carol 21
Friedman, David 10, 11, 12, 13, 14, 16, 17, 18-22, 23, 24, 119, 120, 126, 127-129, 132
Fuentes, Ricardo 157
Fulci, Lucio 32, 35, 183, 198
Fuller, Dana 41
Gacy, John Wayne 233
Garfunkel, Art 209
Garroni, Andrew W 178, 184
Geeson, Judy 205
Gein, Ed 91, 97, 231
Gemser, Laura 159
Giger, H R 102
Gilliam, Terry 150
Giovinazzo, Buddy 188
Giskes, Heinrich 67
Goff, John F 119
Goggins, Walton 231
Gordon, Larry 78, 85, 86, 88
Gordon, Stuart 32, 106
Gould, Andy 231
Graham, John Michael 144
Grahame-Smith, Seth 43
Grainger, Julian 162
Grant, Lisa 41
Grau, Jorge 32
Greene, Joe 114
Gregory, David 95
Grier, Pam 78, 79, 80, 81, 82, 83, 84, 85, 86, 87, 108, 111, 117, 237
Gross, Jerry 61
Gudjonsson, Eythor 252

Haarmann, Fritz 68, 71, 72, 73
Haig, Sid 32, 78, 79, 83, 85, 231, 232, 233, 234, 236, 237, 238-240, 241
Haines, Eli 107
Hall, Scott H 10
Halliwell, Leslie 15, 29 (footnote)
Hamilton, Judd 186, 188, 191, 192
Hamilton-Grant, David 195
Hammond, Stefan 246 (footnote)
Haneke, Michael 72
Hankerson, Tom 107, 110
Hansen, Gunnar 89, 92, 94, 95, 99, 101, 102-104
Hardman, Karl 25, 36
Hardwick, Chris 231
Hardy, Phil 69 (footnote)
Harlow, Harry 207 (footnote), 208
Harris, Ed 31, 33, 154
Harryhausen, Ray 35, 226
Havlickova, Jana 252
Hawthorne, Nigel 205
Hayes, Isaac 80
Haynes, Linda 78
Hefner, Hugh 20, 235
Hell, Richard 72
Henenlotter, Frank 220
Henkel, Kim 89, 90, 93, 96, 96-99, 104
Henley, Elmer Wayne 97
Henry, Carol 178
Hepton, Bernard 205
Hernandez, Jay 252, 254, 259
Hess, David 90, 233, 234
Hill, Debra 137-138, 144, 147, 150, 153
Hill, Jack 78, 79-85, 85-88, 109, 111, 112, 120, 121, 122, 239, 240
Hinnant, Skip 54, 59
Hinzman, Bill 25
Hitchcock, Alfred 11, 12, 22, 30, 72, 91, 155, 224, 234, 250
Hoffman, Rick 252
Holliday, Billie 60, 64
Hooper, Tobe 31, 89, 90-99, 101, 103, 104,

CAST/CREW INDEX

105, 146, 232, 236
Hopkins, Anthony 180
Hubley, John 213, 214
Hurd, Gale Anne 165
Hurt, John 205, 211
Hutson, Tracy 52
Hwang Jo-yun 243
Irving, Amy 152
Jackson, Peter 221, 261
Jackson, Samuel L 113, 114
Jacopetti, Gualtiero 161, 162, 169
Jagger, Mick 68
Jameson, Jenna 48
Janis, Petr 252
Jaratt, John 234
Jeremy, Ron 48
Ji Dae-han 243
Joffe, Roland 160, 257
Jones, Duane 25, 26, 28, 29, 33, 37, 38
Joseph, Irwin 18
Jostyn, Jennifer 231
Jürgen, Kurt 77
Jürges, Jürgen 73, 75
Kaderabkova, Jana 252
Kaltheuner, Walter 67
Kamp, Louise 10
Kane, Joe 82 (footnote)
Kang Hye-jeong 243, 244
Keach, Stacy 158
Keeler, Rodina 119
Kelly, Roz 50
Kennedy, Jackie 76
Kennedy, Richard 107 (footnote), 108, *119*, 125, 137
Kerekes, David 158 (footnote), 162 (footnote), 217 (footnote), 219 (footnote)
Kerman, Robert *157*, 158, 160, 162, 164-165, 167, 171-177
Kerwin, William 14, 16
Ketchum, Jack 257
Keyes, Johnny *41*, 47
Keyes, Nancy 144, 149, 151

Kim Byeong-ok *243*
Kim Ji-woon 244, 246, 248
Kim Ki-duk 244, 245
King, Stephen 31, 35-36, 95
King, Tracy *107*
Kitamura, Ryuhei 246
Knoph, Gregory *119*, 123
Knowles, Harry 253, 258, 259
Koch, Ilse 125, 135, 141, 223
Koch, Karl 125
Kosana, George *25*
Koven, Mikel 79 (footnote)
Krantz, Steve *54*, 54, 61
Krogh, Daniel 11 (footnote)
Kubrick, Stanley 49, 201, 238
Kurosawa, Akira 250
Kurten, Peter 71
Lake, Andre 127
Landis, Bill 109 (footnote), 123 (footnote), 125 (footnote), 158 (footnote), 164 (footnote)
Landis, John 151
Landon, Laurene 112
Lang, Fritz 68, 71, 75
Larroquette, John 89
Lawrence, Gail *178*, 179
Lawson, Carol *78*
Le Fluer, David 143
Leach, Rosemary 205
Lee Dae-yeon *243*
Lee Seung-Shin *243*
Lee Yeong-ae 248
Lee, Penelope 205
Leigh, Janet 12, 147
Leigh-Hunt, Barbara 205
LeNoire, Rosetta *54*
Lenzi, Umberto 35, 157, 158, 159, 161 (footnote), 165, 175
Leone, Sergio 169
Levine, Yank *41*, 45
Lewis, Herschell Gordon *10*, 11-21, 22-24, 26, 30, 120

TABOO BREAKERS

Lewis, Jon 43
Lieberman, Jeff 95
Liebesman, Jonathan 96
Lim Chun-hyeong *243*
Lim Joon-hyung *243*
Lim Seung-yong *243*
Lim, Jennifer *252*, 264
Locke, Philip *205*
Lockley, Ron 213
Loder, Kathryn 122
Lohan, Lindsay 257
Lommel, Ulli *67*, 68-72, 73-77
Lorre, Peter 68
Lovecraft, H P 217
Lovelace, Linda 42, 43, 44
Lucas, William *205*
Lustig, William *178*, 179-183, 184-190, 190, 191
Lynch, Paul 149
MacDonald, George S *41*, 45
MacKinnon, Catharine 43
Malcolm, Derek 43
Malet, Arthur *144*
Maltin, Leonard 15, 58 (footnote), 59 (footnote)
Manners, Missy 49
Mansfield, Jayne 108, 113
Manson, Charles 237
Margheriti, Antonio 165, 166
Marrow, Hyla *178*
Marshall, Lance *119*
Marshall, Neil 261
Martin, Ashlyn 10
Martin, John 13 (footnote)
Martin, Strother 101
Martino, Sergio 158
Marx, Maria *119*
Masini, Giovanni 172, 175
Mason, Connie *10*, 11, 13, 14, 16-18, 20
Matheson, Richard 26, 263
Mathews, Geoffrey *205*
Mattei, Bruno 35

Matthews, Tom Dewe 91 (footnote), 126 (footnote), 218 (footnote)
Maurer, Howard 142-143
Maynard, Bill *205*
McCambridge, Mercedes 122
McCarty, John 11 (footnote), 12 (footnote)
McConaughey, Matthew 98, 101
McCumber, David 42 (footnote), 47
McCurry, John *54*
McDonagh, Maitland 26 (footnote)
McDonald, Meri *107*
McGrory, Matthew *231*, 232
McKee, Lucky 222
McMinn, Teri *89*
McNaughton, John 182
McNeil, Legs 45 (footnote)
Meade, Dale *41*
Metzger, Radley 43, 48, 129
Meyer, Russ 14, 18, 86, 87, 125 (footnote), 134
Miike, Takashi 246, 248, 250, 253, 256, 265
Mikels, Ted V 15
Miles, Vera 72, 262
Miller, Marvin 43
Milligan, Andy 15
Miner, Steve 32
Minor, Bob 83-84, 87
Mira, Brigitte *67*
Mistretta, Gaetano 194 (footnote)
Mitchell, Adrienne *41*
Mitchell, Artie *41*, 42-50, 52
Mitchell, Jim *41*, 42-50, 52
Mitchell, Sharon *178*, 179
Mitchell, Warren *205*
Moon, Sherri *231*, 232, 234, 236, 241
Moreno, Ruben *78*
Morgan, Jacky 22, 24
Morris, Mercury 114
Morrissey, Paul 68
Morse, L A 149 (footnote), 180 (footnote)
Moseley, Bill 93, 101, *231*, 232, 233, 236, 240-242

CAST/CREW INDEX

Mukes, Robert Allen 231
Muller, Eddie 43 (footnote)
Mumolo, Tony 119
Munro, Caroline 178, 179, 182, 183, 184, 186, 188, 190-192
Murawski, Bob 164, 176
Murnau, F W 68
Murphy, Eddie 85
Neal, Edwin 89, 91, 92, 94, 95, 99-102, 103
Nedeljakova, Barbara 252, 259
Nelson, Judd 183
Newman, Kim 12 (footnote), 26 (footnote), 149 (footnote), 159 (footnote), 219
Nichols, Dandy 205
Nicolodi, Daria 185, 190
Nutman, Philip 90
O'Brien, Willis 226
O'Dea, Judith 25, 30, 33, 34, 36-40
O'Neal, Ron 80
O'Neill, James 180 (footnote), 196 (footnote)
Oh Kwang-rok 243
Oh Tae-kyung 243
Olson, Astrid 10
Ortolani, Riz 163, 169
Osborne, Jennifer 45 (footnote)
Paglia, Camille 43
Palaggi, Franco 157
Palance, Jack 72
Palmerini, Luca M 194 (footnote)
Paoloni, Paolo 157
Papazian, Robert 78
Paris, Henry (pseudonym) – see Metzger, Radley
Park Chan-wook 243, 243-248, 248-251
Parks, Gordon 80, 109
Partain, Paul A 89, 94
Pasolini, Pier Paolo 121, 126, 232
Paul, William 193
Pearl, Daniel 258, 264
Pearl, Daniel C 91, 95
Pearl, Dorothy 95

Peckinpah, Sam 15, 118
Perkins, Millie 112
Pfeiffer, Carolyn 240
Pierce, Bart 223
Pierce, Jack 224
Piper, Kelly 178
Pirkanen Perry 157, 167, 170, 171
Pitt, Brad 59
Pleasence, Donald 72, 144, 145, 149, 150, 151, 152, 153, 164
Poitier, Sidney 28
Polanski, Roman 28
Powell, Michael 11
Praetorius, Friedrich Karl 67
Price, Alan 211, 213
Prochnow, Jürgen 72, 73-74
Puchalski, Steve 109 (footnote)
Quaid, Dennis 154
Quinn, Anthony 33
Raab, Kurt 67, 68, 70, 71, 72, 75
Raben, Per 68
Raimi, Ivan 222, 225
Raimi, Sam 176, 177, 216, 216-222, 223, 223, 225, 226, 227, 228, 229, 230, 261, 262
Rassimov, Ivan 158
Redford, Robert 68
Reitman, Ivan 119, 121, 126, 127, 134
Rich, Hal 10
Richards, Kyle 144
Richardson, Derek 252, 259
Richardson, Sallye 90
Richman, Sandy 119
Riddell, Nicolle 119
Ridley, Judith 25, 31
Rigg, Diana 80
Riva, Michael 136, 137
Rocchi, Luigina 157
Roden, Jeff 67
Rodriguez, Robert 257, 262
Roehm, Edward (pseudonym for Richard Kennedy) 107, 108
Romero, George A 12, 15, 19, 25, 26-31, 32-

36, 37, 38, 90, 183, 212, 217, 224
Ronan, Danny *193*
Rooker, Michael 182, 233, 234
Roundtree, Richard 80
Rosen, Martin *205,* 205, 209-212, 212-215, 214
Rosenberg, C A *178*
Rosenthal, Rick 150
Ross, Jonathan 13 (footnote), 28 (footnote)
Rossellini, Roberto 158, 165, 166
Roth, Eli 187, 236, *252,* 253-257, 258-261, 262, 263, 264, 265, 266
Royale, Tony *41*
Rubinstein, Richard 35
Rudolph, Alan 240
Ruesch, Hans 207 (footnote)
Russo, John 25, 32, 36, 39
Sanada, Hiroyuki 246
Sandweiss, Ellen *216,* 216, 217, 219, 221, 226-230
Savannah 264
Savini, Tom 14, 30, 32, 33, 35, 38, 39, 94, *178,* 178, 179, 180, 181, 184, 185, 186, 191, 194, 199, 201, 203, 224
Scapperotti, Dan 78 (footnote)
Scavolini, Romano *193,* 194-198, 198-201, 202, 203
Schlesinger, John 68
Schneck, Wolfgang *67*
Schon, Kyra *25*
Schonfeld, Victor 206
Schow, David 96
Scorsese, Martin 46, 238
Scott, Tony 129
Seiko, Keiko *252*
Seuling, Phil *54*
Shackleton, Alan 128
Shaw Brothers 122, 246
Sheen, Charlie 48, 52
Shepherd, Cybil 46
Sherman, Gary 183
Siedow, Jim *89,* 90, 92, 93, 94, 100, 103

Simon, Adam 106
Sims, Yvonne D 79 (footnote), 82 (footnote), 84 (footnote), 109 (footnote)
Sinclair, Sandra *10*
Singer, Peter 206, 208
Sirabello, John 22
Slater, David 158 (footnote), 162 (footnote), 217 (footnote), 219 (footnote)
Smart, Amy 255
Smith, Bill 237
Smith, Dick 224
Smith, Iain Robert 104
Smith, Sharon *193,* 196
Smoke 112, 117
Soles, P J *144,* 145, 149, 151-154
Solomon, Charles 213
Spelvin, Georgina 44
Spiegel, Scott 217, 222, 224, 257, 261-266
Spielberg, Steven 94, 96
Spinell, Joe *178,* 178, 179, 180, 182, 183, 184, 185, 188, 189, 190, 191, 192
Spink, Brian *205*
Stafford, Baird *193,* 196, 197, 198, 201-204
Stark, Ray 50
Stephens, Nancy *144*
Stevens, Stella 16
Stewart, Patrick *205*
Stirner, Brian *205*
Streiner, Russell *25,* 34, 39
Sullivan, Tim 16
Sullivan, Tom 222-226, 228
Swires, Steve 125 (footnote)
Tallman, Patricia 30
Tapert, Robert G *216,* 216, 222, 225, 229
Tarantino, Quentin 85, 113, 133-134, 187, 253, 257, 258, 260, 262, 263, 264, 266
Tate, Sharon 237
Taylor, Renée 18
Taylor, Robert 59
Terris, Malcolm *205*
Theakos, George *107,* 108, 109, 112, 117
Thomas, Bob 55 (footnote)

CAST/CREW INDEX

Thorne, Dyanne *119,* 120, 124-125, 126, 127, 128, 132, 134, 136, 137, 138-142, 143
Thrower, Stephen 70 (footnote)
Tilly, Theresa 220, 229
Tomaselli, Dante 230
Tompkins, Ptolemy 30
Towles, Tom *231,* 232
Traeger, Herman (pseudonym for David Friedman) *119*
Travolta, John 152
Traynor, Chuck 44
Tsui Hark 247
Tuttle, William 224
Urich, Robert 241
Vail, William *89*
Valentine, Anthony *205*
Vickers, Yvette 11
Vincent, Cerina 254
Vlasak, Jan *252*
Van Peebles, Melvin 79, 80
van Trier, Lars 49
von Liebezeit, Karl *67*
Waddell, Calum 145 (footnote)
Walter, Linda Lee *178*
Wan, James 260, 261
Warhol, Andy 68 (footnote), 72, 76, 77
Warren, Bill 223
Washington, Gene 113, 114
Waters, John 15, 16
Watkins, John L *193*
Wayne, Keith *25*
Weaver, Dennis 263
Welles, Orson 113
Wells, H G 206, 212
Whale, James 156

White, Barry 117
White, Colin 214
Whitehouse, Mary 97
Wild, Paula 254
Wiene, Robert 68
Wilkins, Mike 246 (footnote)
Williams, Bill 169
Williams, Linda 43
Williamson, Fred 80, 84, 111
Wilson, Ranin *231*
Winslet, Kate 221
Winterbottom, Michael 43
Winters, David 192
Winters, Shelley 80, 85
Woo, John 246, 247
Wood, Thomas *10,* 14
Woods, Bambi 48
Woolf, Virginia 250
Woolley, Stephen 225
Yablans, Irwin *144,* 150, 154-156
Yakin, Boaz 261, 262, 264
York, Michael 164
York, Sarah (pseudonym for Theresa Tilly) *216,* 220
Yorke, Carl Gabriel *157,* 165, 169-171
Yu Ji-tae *243,* 244, 248
Yun Jin-seo *243*
Yuzna, Brian 32, 105, 106
Zalcock, Bev 122 (footnote)
Zellweger, Renée 98
Zemeckis, Robert 96
Zito, Joe 185
Zombie, Rob 133, 150, 155, *231,* 232-236, 236-238, 239, 240, 241, 242, 261

TITLE INDEX

Titles in *italics* are alternative titles, or proposed films that were not made.

9 Songs 43, 49
10 Rillington Place 178
30 Days of Night 222
99 Women 120, 122
2001 Maniacs 16, 261
Action Jackson 85
Across 110th Street 109, 117
Address Unknown 245
Adolf and Marlene 76
Adventures of Lucky Pierre, The 11, 14
Adventures of Pluto Mars, The 85
Aeon Flux 165
Africa Addio 162
Africa, Blood and Guts 162
Alice in Wonderland 48
Alien 188
Alone in the Dark 194
Amanda by Night 164
American Nightmare, The 106
American Pie 255
American Pop 59, 60
American Psycho 180
American Werewolf in London, An 220
Anatomy of Hell 49
Angel of H.E.A.T. 48
Anima nera 166
Animal Farm 215
Animals Film, The 162, 206
Antarctic Journal 248
Anthropophagous: The Beast 196
Antibodies 72
Apollo 13 137, 151, 165
April Fool's Day 150
April Fool's Day 192
Armageddon 165
Army of Darkness 218, 220, 221-222, 229, 241
Assault on Precinct 13 144, 145, 147, 156
Audition 246, 247, 253, 254, 260
Autobiography of a Flea, The 47
Axe 197
Azumi 246
Babylon Pink 46
Back to the Future 137
Bad Taste 221
Bamboo House of Dolls 122
Barbara Broadcast 46

TITLE INDEX

Barbarians, The 164
Barbed Wire Dolls 126
Bambi 162
Bare Knuckles 113, 126, 129, 136, 138
Basket Case 16, 220
Battle Royale 156
Beast in Heat, The 126
Beauty and the Beast 224
Behind the Green Door 41-53, 123
Bell, Bare and Beautiful 11
Better Tomorrow, A 246, 248
Beverly Hills Cop II 72
Beyond, The 32
Beyond the Valley of the Dolls 84, 86, 125 (footnote)
Big Bang, The 59
Big Bird Cage, The 79, 86, 238
Big Doll House, The 79, 86, 120, 122, 232
Big Fish 232
Big Trouble in Little China 150
Bird with the Crystal Plumage, The 145, 183, 200
Bitter Tears of Petra von Kant, The 68
Bittersweet Life, A 246, 248
Black Caesar 80, 108, 111
Black Cat, The 184
Black Christmas 145, 149
Black Mama, White Mama 79, 232
Black Shampoo 113
Black Six, The 108, 113, 114, 115
Black Sunday 13 (footnote)
Blair Witch Project, The 148, 165, 167
Blank Generation 72, 76
Blind Fly 199
Blood and Black Lace 94, 218
Blood Feast 10-24, 26, 120, 127
Blood Feast 2: All U Can Eat 16, 24
Blood Sabbath 139
Blood Splash 198, 201
Bloodsucking Freaks 13, 16, 232
Bloody Moon 197
Body Count 164

Boin-n-g 11
Bone 108
Boogeyman, The 68, 72, 76, 77, 194, 222, 252
Boogeyman 2 72
Boogeyman 3 72
Boogie Nights 49
Book of the Dead 223
Boston Strangler, The 178
Boy Who Could Fly, The 151
Braindead 221
Bride of Frankenstein, The 156
Bring Me the Head of Alfredo Garcia 118
Brotherhood 248
Brotherhood of Blood 85, 236
Bruiser 31
Brutes and Savages 162
Bubba Ho-tep 218, 222
Burn Coffy Burn 88
Burning, The 15, 179, 184, 194
Butch Cassidy and the Sundance Kid 209
Butcher of Hanover, The 75
Butterfly 112
Cabin Fever 148, 236, 253, 254, 256, 258, 260, 261
Cabinet of Dr Caligari, The 68
Café Flesh 48
Caged 122
Caged Heat 122
Candy Snatchers, The 219
Candy Tangerine Man 107-118
Cannibal Apocalypse 196
Cannibal Ferox 159, 161 (footnote), 164, 165, 176, 195, 218 (footnote), 219
Cannibal Girls 126
Cannibal Holocaust 157-177, 195, 219, 238, 245, 259
Cannibal Holocaust 2 165
Cannibal Metropolitana 164
Cannibal Terror 161
Cannibals 159
Cannonball Run, The 49

Captivity 257
Carrie 145, 151, 152, 153, 154, 182
Cat o' Nine Tails 68
Cello 246
Christine 150
Chunhyang 244
City of the Living Dead 32
Cleopatra Jones 78, 79 (footnote), 80, 85, 86, 117
Cleopatra Jones and the Casino of Gold 108
Clockwork Orange, A 97, 238
Coastguard, The 244
Cocaine Cowboys 72, 76
Coffy 78-88, 108, 109, 112, 115, 117, 238
Color Me Blood Red 16, 19, 21
Coma 265
Combat Shock 188
Concorde Affair, The 158, 167, 172, 175
Cool World 59
Coonskin 57, 58, 65, 66
Corpse Grinders, The 16
Cotton Comes to Harlem 79
Cows 240
Crazies, The 29, 31, 183
Creepshow 31, 33, 184
Crimewave 218
Crocodile 96, 101
Crouching Tiger, Hidden Dragon 246
Crying Fist 248
Curse of Frankenstein, The 10, 12
Cursed 252
Cut and Run 164, 165
Daltry Calhoun 266
Dark Half, The 31
Dark Star 144
Das Boot 72
Daughter of the Sun 11
Dawn of the Dead 16, 26, 31, 32, 34, 35, 178, 181, 186, 217, 238
Day of the Dead 26, 29, 31, 32, 33, 34, 35, 184, 212
Dead Alive 221

Dead and Buried 183
Dead Calling, A 236
Dead Next Door, The 221
Dead Zone, The 150
Death Line 145
Death Proof 257
Death Trap 95
Debbie Does Dallas 47 (footnote), 48, 158, 171
Deep Red 145, 156, 185
Deep River Savages 157
Deep Throat 42, 43, 44, 45, 46, 47, 52, 108, 195
Defiant Ones, The 28
Defilers, The 19
Deliverance 91, 99
Demon Lover, The 104
Dennis the Menace 151
Deranged 178
Detroit 9000 111
Devastated One, The 198
Devil in Miss Jones, The 43, 44, 46, 47 (footnote), 48
Devil's Rejects, The 16, 85, 233, 234, 235, 236, 237, 238, 239, 240, 241, 242, 253, 262
Devonsville Terror, The 72, 77
Diary of the Dead 26, 31, 33, 35
Die Hard 246
Dirty Duck 59
Disco Godfather 113
Dog Tags 198, 201, 202, 204
Dog's Life, A 212
Don't Answer the Phone 179, 183
Don't Go in the House 179, 183, 187, 217
Don't Go in the Woods 197
Donnie Darko 221
Dracula, Prince of Darkness 145
Dragon Tiger Gate 244
Dread, The 228
Dress Rehearsal, The 199
Dressed to Kill 183
Driller Killer, The 195, 197

TITLE INDEX

Duel 263
Dumplings 248
Easy Rider 30, 55, 232, 235
Eaten Alive 95, 164, 165, 175
Eggshells 90, 96
Elvis 156
Emmanuelle and the Last Cannibals 158, 159
Endangered Species 240
Era notte a Roma 165
Erotic Adventures of Pinocchio, The 120, 139
Erotic Adventures of Zorro, The 16, 127
Escape from LA 150, 222
Escape from New York 147, 150, 151, 156
Euro Trip 255
Evil Dead, The 15, 16, 216-230, 253, 262
Evil Dead II 217, 220, 221, 222, 226, 229, 261
Excalibur 262
Exorcism of Emily Rose, The 252, 260
Exorcist, The 91, 195, 217
Eyes Wide Shut 49
Faceless 184
Faces of Death 195, 218 (footnote)
Fade to Black 150
Family Plot 234
Fantasia 55
Fatal Attraction 145
Female Prisoner #701: Scorpion 122
Fire and Ice 59
Fish Called Wanda, A 151
Fisher King, The 150
Five Easy Pieces 232, 234
Flesh Factory 42
Flesh Gordon 42
Fog, The 149, 150, 253
Four Flies on Grey Velvet 68
Foxy Brown 81, 84, 85, 88, 108, 109, 111, 112, 117
Frankenstein 156
Freaks 16

Freddy Vs Jason 263
Friday Foster 84
Friday the 13th 15, 19, 42, 145, 149, 150, 178, 179, 180, 181, 184, 186, 187, 194, 196, 197, 200, 202, 217, 218, 220, 263
Fritz the Cat 54-66
From Beyond the Grave 145
From Dusk Till Dawn 2 222
Full Contact 246
Full Moon High 95
Funhouse, The 96
Funny Games 72
Future Kill 102
Gestapo's Last Orgy, The 195
Ghost, The 246
Ghostbusters 126, 127
Ghosts of Mars 85
Gidget Goes Hawaiian 120, 135
Gift, The 217, 222
Girl Next Door, The 257
Girl on a Swing 212
Glory 83
Godfather, The 79, 83, 198
Godfather Part II, The 179, 185
Goldilocks and the Three Bares 11
Gone With the Wind 13
Gore Gore Girls, The 15, 16, 23
Graduation Day 179
Great Big Thing, A 212
Great Gatsby, The 234
Great Waldo Pepper, The 104
Green Inferno, The 165
Greta, the Mad Butcher 126, 140, 141, 143
Grim Prairie Tales 24
Grindhouse 133, 257, 262
Grudge, The 222, 230, 252, 253 (footnote)
Gruesome Twosome, The 21
Guardian, The 188
Guess Who's Coming to Dinner 28
H 248
H: Diary of a Serial Killer 253
Halloween 15, 16, 19, 31, 72, 138, 144-156,

283

178, 179, 180, 184, 187, 190, 191, 194, 197, 200, 202, 217, 218, 236, 237
Halloween II   147, (footnote) 148, 149, 151
Halloween III: Season of the Witch   150
Halloween 4: The Return of Michael Myers   150
Halloween 5: The Revenge of Michael Myers   150
Halloween Resurrection   150
Halloween: H20   150, 253
Halloween: The Curse of Michael Myers   150
Hand That Rocks the Cradle, The   145
Hard Boiled   246, 248
Hatchet Murders, The   146
Haunting, The   145, 217
Haute Tension   184
Haytabo   68
He and She   108
Heavenly Creatures   221
Heavy Traffic   58, 62, 64, 65, 66
Hell Night   150
Hell up in Harlem   108
Henry: Portrait of a Serial Killer   181-182, 184, 189, 232, 233
Hero   246
Hey Good Lookin'   62
Hills Have Eyes, The   95, 104, 217
Hillside Strangler, The   184
Hitcher, The   253
Hollywood Chainsaw Hookers   95, 102, 104
Honeymoon Killers, The   189
Host, The   85, 246, 248
Hostel   16, 91, 180, 183, 187, 222, 236, 252-266
Hostel: Part II   222, 236, 257, 263, 266
Hot Box, The   122
Hot Honey   179
House of 1000 Corpses   85, 231-242
House of Flying Daggers   246
House of the Dead   235
House of the Dead 2   85, 236
House of Wax, The   37
House on the Edge of the Park   164, 195
Howling, The   95, 106
Hulk   165
Human Tornado, The   113
Humungous   198
Hundra   112
I Am Legend   32
I Drink Your Blood   32, 61
I Know What You Did Last Summer   150
I Know Who Killed Me   257
I Spit on Your Grave   148, 195, 218 (footnote), 219, 263
I Walked with a Zombie   26
I'm a Cyborg, But That's OK   248, 251
I'm Gonna Git You Sucka   85
Ice Storm, The   251
Ichi the Killer   244, 246, 250
Idiots, The   49
Idle Hands   165
Il Generale della Rovere   165
Ilana   138
Ilsa Meets Bruce Lee in the Devil's Triangle   126, 137
Ilsa, Harem Keeper of the Oil Sheiks   126, 129, 136, 137, 141, 142
Ilsa, She Wolf of the SS   16, 119-143
Ilsa, The Tigress of Siberia   126, 137, 140, 143
Ilsa, The Wicked Warden   126, 137, 141
Immoral Mr Teas, The   14, 18
In a Year of 13 Moons   68
In the Heat of the Night   28
Incredible Shrinking Man, The   263
Incredible Torture Show, The   13 (footnote)
Inferno   179, 185
Insatiable   47 (footnote), 48
Inside Daisy Clover   68
Inside Deep Throat   49
Insomnia   249
Interns, The   120
Intimacy   49
Intruder   222, 261

TITLE INDEX

Invaders from Mars 96
Invasion of the Blood Farmers 16
Invisible Man, The 156
Ironweed 95
Island of Death 196
Island of Dr Moreau, The 206, 212
Island of Lost Souls 206
Isle, The 244, 245
It's Murder 223
Jack's Wife 31, 33
Jackie Brown 85, 257
Jason Takes Manhattan 15
Jason X 155
Jaws 94, 145, 217 (footnote), 253
Jimmy the Boy Wonder 16
Johnny Firecloud 127
Joint Security Area 243, 244
Joy 158, 171
Judge Dredd 72
Jungle Holocaust 158
Jurassic Park 151
Just Before Dawn 95
Keep, The 72
Kill Bill 260
Killer, The 248
Killer Fish 234
King Kong 224, 226
Klansman, The 111
Knightriders 31, 186
L'Apocalisse delle scimmie 198
La Dolce Vita 55
Lady Cocoa 112, 113, 117
Land of the Dead 26, 31, 33, 34, 35
Last Cannibal World, The 158, 159, 162, 164, 165, 166, 168, 169
Last Feelings 158
Last Horror Film, The 183, 184, 188, 191
Last House on Dead End Street, The 13, 232
Last House on the Left 49, 90, 91, 134, 146, 218, 232, 233, 263
Last Starfighter, The 151
Leatherface: Texas Chainsaw Massacre Part III 96, 98
Legend of Nigger Charley, The 84
Lethal Weapon 246
Lifeforce 96
Linda Lovelace for President 192
Living Dead at the Manchester Morgue, The 32
Living Venus 11
Lord of the Flies, The 156
Lord of the Rings 58, 59, 65-66, 206, 221
Lost 201
Lost, The 253
Lost Memories 248
Love Camp 7 120, 122, 127, 130
Love is Colder than Death 67, 68, 73
M 68, 71, 72, 75
Mack, The 108, 109, 112
Mad Ghoul, The 34
Magic of Mother Goose, The 16
Majestic, The 222
Make Them Die Slowly 127
Man and Wife 108
Man Bites Dog 72
Man from Deep River, The 157, 158, 159, 161 (footnote), 165
Maniac 178-192, 217
Maniac 2: Mr Robbie 183, 192
Maniac Cop 183, 222
Maniac Cop 2 222
Mark of the Devil 253
Married to the Mob 184
Martin 31
Mask of Satan 13 (footnote)
Massacre in Dinosaur Valley 165
Matinee Idol 128
Meatballs 126
Memories of Murder 248
Microwave Massacre 106
Midnight Cowboy 68
Midnight Crossing 126
Mindwarp 222
Miriam 112-113

285

TABOO BREAKERS

Miss Congeniality 95
Mission, The 160
Mona 42
Mondo Cane 158, 161, 169, 173
Monkey Shines 31
Moonshine Mountain 21
Mortuary 96
Mosquito 95
Motel Hell 95, 224
Mother's Day 95, 219
Mountain of the Cannibal God 158
Multiple Maniacs 16
Murder Set Pieces 236, 254
Mushishi 244
Mutilator, The 150, 198
My Bloody Valentine 150
My Girl 151
My Sassy Girl 244
My Wife is a Gangster 244
Nail Gun Massacre 94
National Treasure 83, 95
Natural City 244, 248
Nature's Playmates 11
Near Dark 253
Neon Maniacs 221
Never a Tender Moment 48
New York Ripper, The 112, 183, 198
Night of the Anubis 36
Night of the Demon 196
Night of the Flesh-Eaters 32
Night of the Living Dead 12, 25-40, 90, 94, 184, 217, 225, 235
Night of the Living Dead 3D 32, 85, 236
Night Porter, The 120, 122
Night Terrors 96
Night Train Murders 219
Nightmare 244
Nightmare 194, 201
Nightmare City 32, 35
Nightmare on Elm Street, A 221
Nightmares in a Damaged Brain 179, 193-204

Nine Lives of Fritz the Cat, The 59, 65
Nosferatu 68
Ocean's Eleven 83
Olivia 72
Old School 127, 257
Oldboy 243-251, 253
Olga 122
Omega Man, The 209
Omen, The 145
Once Upon a Girl 59
Open Water 236
Opening of Misty Beethoven, The 43, 44
Ordeal 44
Original Gangstas 85
Orpheus 224
Owl and the Pussycat, The 42, 50
Painted Fire 244
Paradise Lost 257
Passenger, The 161
Peeping Tom 11
Performance 68
Phantom of Death 164
Philadelphia 70
Phonebooth 108
Pieces 95, 150, 183, 259
Pinocchio 55
Pit Stop 85
Plague Dogs, The 59, 205-215
Plague of the Zombies, The 26
Planet of the Apes 224, 262
Platoon 93
Point of Terror 139
Poltergeist 96, 101
Prince of Darkness 151
Prime Time, The 11
Prisoner of the Cannibal God 158, 165
Private Benjamin 151, 154
Prom Night 145, 149, 178, 179, 198
Prowler, The 15, 150, 184, 194, 217
Psycho 11, 12, 13, 22, 30, 91, 94, 147, 151, 155, 262, 264-265
Pulp Fiction 114, 257

TITLE INDEX

Querelle 69
Quick and the Dead, The 218, 222
Quiet Fever, The 199
R-Point 248
Rabid 48, 53, 126
Rampaging Nurses 42
Rapid Fire 184
Rashomon 250
Rated X 48, 52
Raven, The 72
Re-Animator 32, 95, 105, 106, 221
Reform School Girl 122
Relentless
Repo! The Genetic Opera 236
Repulsion 28
Reservoir Dogs 257
Resurrection of Bronco Billy, The 144
Resurrection of Eve, The 47, 52
Return of the Living Dead 32, 221
Return of the Living Dead III 32
Return of the Living Dead Part II 221
Return of the Texas Chainsaw Massacre 96, 98
Revenge from Planet Ape 262
Revenge of the Stolen Stars 72
Revenge of the Zombies 26
Ring, The 252, 253 (footnote)
Ring 2, The 252
Ringu 244, 246
Road Trip 127, 255
Rob Roy 95
Rock and Roll High School 153, 154
Rocky 179
Rocky Horror Picture Show, The 20, 232
Roommates 46
Sadomania 126
Salem's Lot 96
Salo 121, 126, 232
Salon Kitty 126
Satan's Playground 95, 230
Savage Man, Savage Beast 162
Savage Terror 158

Savannah's Ghost 72
Saw 15, 183, 236, 257, 263, 264, 265, 266
Saw II 253, 257, 260
Saw III 257
Saw IV 257
Scary Movie 150
Scream 153, 253, 254
Scum of the Earth 11, 120
Season of the Witch 31
Second Spring, The 77
Seven Ups, The 185
Scream 150
Shaft 57, 78, 79-80, 85, 86, 109, 110, 115, 116, 117
Shaft in Africa 80, 108
Shaft's Big Score 80, 108
She Devils on Wheels 23-24
She Freak 16
Sheba, Baby 84
Shiri 244
Shivers 126
Silence of the Lambs, The 15, 180
Silent Night, Deadly Night 150, 179
Silent Night, Deadly Night III 233
Simple Plan, A 222
Slaughter 80
Slaughter High 184, 192
Slayer, The 194
Slumber Party Massacre 255
Snow White 55 (footnote)
Sodom & Gormorrah 47
Sometime Sweet Susan 46
Song of the South 58
Sorceress 85
Southern Double Cross 138
Spider Baby 79, 85, 232, 239, 240
Spider-Man 164, 176, 177, 217, 218, 222, 224
Spider-Man 3 222
Spontaneous Combustion 96, 101
Spy Who Loved Me, The 179, 190
Squeeze, The 234

287

SS Experiment Camp 126, 195, 197
Stacking 212
Starcrash 179, 185, 190, 191
Starman 156
Still Insatiable 48
Story of Joanna, The 48
Strange Behaviour 212
Straw Dogs 97, 195
Stray Bullet, A 244
Stripes 126, 151, 154
Student Bodies 147 (footnote)
Sunday Bloody Sunday 68
Sundown: The Vampire in Retreat 222
Superfly 78, 80, 81, 86, 87, 108, 109, 110, 111, 112, 115, 117
Superfly TNT 108
Suspiria 145, 156, 217, 232, 237
Sweet Dreams 154
Sweet Sweetback's Baadasssss Song 61, 78, 79, 109, 111
Swinging Barmaids, The 139
Swinging Cheerleaders, The 85
Switchblade Romance 184
Switchblade Sisters 85
Sympathy for Mr Vengeance 243, 244, 246, 247, 250
Sympathy for Lady Vengeance 246, 247, 248
T.N.T. Jackson 84
Tale of Two Sisters, A 244
Tales from the Hood 85
Taste of Blood, A 21
Taxi Driver 46, 178, 179, 185, 238
Ted Bundy 184
Tell Me Something 248
Tender Loving Care 108, 120
Tenderness of Wolves, The 67-77
Tenebrae 185
Terror Train 155, 178, 179
Texas Chain Saw Massacre, The 19, 31, 89-106, 134, 146, 149, 178, 184, 185, 187, 188, 195, 202, 218, 232, 253, 260, 263
Texas Chainsaw Massacre, The 96, 235, 258
Texas Chainsaw Massacre 2, The 93, 94, 96, 101, 103, 104, 221, 232, 233, 240
Texas Chainsaw Massacre: The Beginning, The 96
Texas Chainsaw Massacre: The Next Generation, The 96
Texas Chainsaw Massacre: The Shocking Truth, The 103
Thanksgiving 257
Thelma and Louise 209
There's Always Vanilla 31, 33
Thing, The 147, 149, 150, 156, 253
Thr3e 236
Three Extremes 246, 248, 251
Thriller: A Cruel Picture 219
Together 42, 49, 50
Tombs of the Blind Dead 32, 262
Toolbox Murders, The 94, 95, 96, 148, 219, 224, 236
Tourist Trap 95, 150, 232
Towering Inferno, The 145
Trading Places 151
Trash 68
Truck Turner 109
True Lies 151
True Romance 126, 129, 133
Turistas 257
Twilight 201
Two Evil Eyes 31
Two Families 198
Two Thousand Maniacs 14, 16, 17, 18, 19, 20, 23, 127
Uncle Sam 183
Undertaker and his Pals, The 16
Unnecessary Fuss, An 212
Untamed Youth 122
Urban Legend 150
Vampyr 68
Vanishing, The 260
Versus 246
Video Dead, The 221
Vigilante 183

TITLE INDEX

Violation of Claudia, The 179
Viva L'Italia 165
Watermelon Man, The 79
Watership Down 205, 209, 210, 211, 212, 213, 214, 215
Welcome to the Jungle 165
Werewolf Women of the SS 133
Wham Bam Thank You Spaceman 120
When the Wind Blows 59, 211
White Zombie 26
Who Framed Roger Rabbit 150
Wicker Man, The 253, 256, 260
Wig, The 246
Wild Bunch, The 101, 118
Wild Eye, The 158
Wild Honey 120
Wild Man of the Navidad, The 99
Windsplitter, The 90
Winner, The 79
Witch Who Came from the Sea, The 112, 117, 118, 145
Within the Woods 217, 222, 223, 226, 227

Wizard of Gore, The 15, 16, 21, 23
Wizards 59
Wolf Creek 91, 234, 253, 256, 264, 265
Women in Cages 122
Women in Love 212, 213
Women's Camp 119 126
Wonderland 49
Woods, The 222
Wrath of God, The 201
Wrong Turn 95, 235
Yellow Hair and the Fortress of Gold 112
Yesterday 248
Zodiac Killer, The 72
Zombi 32
Zombi 2 32
Zombi 3 32
Zombi Holocaust 161
Zombie Creeping Flesh 32, 35
Zombie Flesh-Eaters 32
Zombie Nation 72
Zombie Strippers 48
Zone Troopers 263

TABOO BREAKERS

Index to Colour Section

Page 1
Marilyn Chambers poses in her porno-chic days.
Original theatrical poster for *Blood Feast*.
Original theatrical poster for *Candy Tangerine Man*.
Bruce Campbell as Ash in *Evil Dead II*.

Page 2
Fritz the Cat with admiring groupies.
Michael Myers (Nick Castle) in the original *Halloween*.
Actress Jennifer Lim loses an eye in *Hostel*.

Page 3
Captain Spaulding (Sid Haig) invites people to his show in *House of 1000 Corpses*.
Ilsa (Dyanne Thorne) tries to seduce Wolfe (Gregory Knoph) in *Ilsa, She Wolf of the SS*.

Page 4
Joe Spinell stars as the title killer in Bill Lustig's *Maniac*.
Salvatore Basile and Robert Kerman in *Cannibal Holocaust*.

Page 5
UK video poster for *Nightmares in a Damaged Brain*.
UK DVD art for *Night of the Living Dead*.
Coffy (Pam Grier) and King George (Robert DoQui) from *Coffy*.

Page 6
Choi Min-sik is a broken man (spot the symbolism!) in *Oldboy*.
Choi Min-sik and Kang Hye-jeong on the trail of trouble in *Oldboy*.

Page 7
Snitter (left) and Rowf (right) swim for their lives in the shocking conclusion of *The Plague Dogs*.
From left to right: Rowf, The Tod and Snitter on the run in *The Plague Dogs*.

Page 8
The disfunctional family from *The Texas Chain Saw Massacre*. L to R: Hitchhiker (Edwin Neal), The Cook (Jim Siedow), Grandpa (John Dugan) and Leatherface (Gunnar Hansen).
Sally (Marilyn Burns) in *The Texas Chain Saw Massacre*.
Original American theatrical poster for *The Texas Chain Saw Massacre*.

Other Telos Titles Available

TIME HUNTER
A range of high-quality, original paperback and limited edition hardback novellas featuring the adventures in time of Honoré Lechasseur. Part mystery, part detective story, part dark fantasy, part science fiction ... these books are guaranteed to enthral fans of good fiction everywhere, and are in the spirit of our acclaimed range of *Doctor Who* Novellas.

THE WINNING SIDE by LANCE PARKIN
Emily is dead! Killed by an unknown assailant. Honoré and Emily find themselves caught up in a plot reaching from the future to their past, and with their very existence, not to mention the future of the entire world, at stake, can they unravel the mystery before it is too late?
An adventure in time and space.
£7.99 (+ £1.50 UK p&p) Standard p/b
ISBN: 1-903889-35-9

THE TUNNEL AT THE END OF THE LIGHT by STEFAN PETRUCHA
In the heart of post-war London, a bomb is discovered lodged at a disused station between Green Park and Hyde Park Corner. The bomb detonates, and as the dust clears, it becomes apparent that *something* has been awakened. Strange half-human creatures attack the workers at the site, hungrily searching for anything containing sugar ...
Meanwhile, Honoré and Emily are contacted by eccentric poet Randolph Crest, who believes himself to be the target of these subterranean creatures. The ensuing investigation brings Honoré and Emily up against a terrifying force from deep beneath the earth, and one which even with their combined powers, they may have trouble stopping.
An adventure in time and space.
£7.99 (+ £1.50 UK p&p) Standard p/b
ISBN: 1-903889-37-5
£25.00 (+ £1.50 UK p&p) Deluxe signed and numbered h/b ISBN: 1-903889-38-3

THE CLOCKWORK WOMAN by CLAIRE BOTT
Honoré and Emily find themselves imprisoned in the 19th Century by a celebrated inventor ... but help comes from an unexpected source – a humanoid automaton created to give pleasure to its owner. As the trio escape to London, they are unprepared for what awaits them, and at every turn it seems impossible to avert what fate may have in store for the Clockwork Woman.
An adventure in time and space.
£7.99 (+ £1.50 UK p&p) Standard p/b
ISBN: 1-903889-39-1
£25.00 (+ £1.50 UK p&p) Deluxe signed and numbered h/b ISBN: 1-903889-40-5

KITSUNE by JOHN PAUL CATTON
In the year 2020, Honoré and Emily find themselves thrown into a mystery, as an ice spirit – *Yuki-Onna* – wreaks havoc during the Kyoto Festival, and a haunted funhouse proves to contain more than just paper lanterns and wax dummies. But what does all this have to do with the elegant owner of the Hide and Chic fashion chain ... and the legendary Chinese fox-spirits, the Kitsune?
An adventure in time and space.
£7.99 (+ £1.50 UK p&p) Standard p/b
ISBN: 1-903889-41-3
£25.00 (+ £1.50 UK p&p) Deluxe signed and numbered h/b ISBN: 1-903889-42-1

THE SEVERED MAN by GEORGE MANN
What links a clutch of sinister murders in Victorian London, an angel appearing in a Staffordshire village in the 1920s and a small boy running loose around the capital in 1950? When Honoré and Emily encounter a man who appears to have been cut out of time, they think they have the answer. But soon enough they discover that the mystery is only just beginning and that nightmares can turn into reality.
An adventure in time and space.
£7.99 (+ £1.50 UK p&p) Standard p/b
ISBN: 1-903889-43-X
£25.00 (+ £1.50 UK p&p) Deluxe signed and numbered h/b ISBN: 1-903889-44-8

ECHOES by IAIN MCLAUGHLIN & CLAIRE BARTLETT
Echoes of the past ... echoes of the future. Honoré Lechasseur can see the threads that bind the two together, however when he and Emily Blandish find themselves outside the imposing tower-block headquarters of Dragon Industry, both can sense something is wrong. There are ghosts in the building, and images and echoes of all times pervade the structure. But what is behind this massive contradiction in time, and can Honoré and Emily figure it out before they become trapped themselves ... ?
An adventure in time and space.
£7.99 (+ £1.50 UK p&p) Standard p/b
ISBN: 1-903889-45-6
£25.00 (+ £1.50 UK p&p) Deluxe signed and numbered h/b ISBN: 1-903889-46-4

PECULIAR LIVES by PHILIP PURSER-HALLARD
Once a celebrated author of 'scientific romances', Erik Clevedon is an old man now. But his fiction conceals a dangerous truth, as Honoré Lechasseur and Emily Blandish discover after a chance encounter with a strangely gifted young pickpocket. Born between the Wars, the superhuman children known as 'the Peculiar' are reaching adulthood – and they believe that humanity is making a poor job of looking after the world they plan to inherit …
An adventure in time and space.
£7.99 (+ £1.50 UK p&p) Standard p/b
ISBN: 1-903889-47-2
£25.00 (+ £1.50 UK p&p) Deluxe signed and numbered h/b ISBN: 1-903889-48-0

DEUS LE VOLT by JON DE BURGH MILLER
'Deus Le Volt!'…'God Wills It!' The cry of the first Crusade in 1098, despatched by Pope Urban to free Jerusalem from the Turks. Honoré and Emily are plunged into the middle of the conflict on the trail of what appears to be a time travelling knight. As the siege of Antioch draws to a close, so death haunts the blood-soaked streets … and the Fendahl – a creature that feeds on life itself – is summoned. Honoré and Emily find themselves facing angels and demons in a battle to survive their latest adventure.
An adventure in time and space.
£7.99 (+ £1.50 UK p&p) Standard p/b
ISBN: 1-903889-49-9
£25.00 (+ £1.50 UK p&p) Deluxe signed and numbered h/b ISBN: 1-903889-97-9

THE ALBINO'S DANCER by DALE SMITH
'Goodbye, little Emily.'
April 1938, and a shadowy figure attends an impromptu burial in Shoreditch, London. His name is Honoré Lechasseur. After a chance encounter with the mysterious Catherine Howkins, he's had advance warning that his friend Emily Blandish was going to die. But is forewarned necessarily forearmed? And just how far is he willing to go to save Emily's life?
Because Honoré isn't the only person taking an interest in Emily Blandish – she's come to the attention of the Albino, one of the new breed of gangsters surfacing in post-rationing London. And the only life he cares about is his own.
An adventure in time and space.
£7.99 (+ £1.50 UK p&p) Standard p/b
ISBN: 1-84583-100-4
£25.00 (+ £1.50 UK p&p) Deluxe signed and numbered h/b ISBN: 1-84583-101-2

THE SIDEWAYS DOOR by R J CARTER & TROY RISER
Honoré and Emily find themselves in a parallel timestream where their alternate selves think nothing of changing history to improve the quality of life – especially their own. Honoré has been recently haunted by the death of his mother, an event which happened in his childhood, but now there seems to be a way to reverse that event … but at what cost?
When faced with two of the most dangerous people they have ever encountered, Honoré and Emily must make some decisions with far-reaching consequences.
An adventure in time and space.
£7.99 (+ £1.50 UK p&p) Standard p/b
ISBN: 1-84583-102-0
£25.00 (+ £1.50 UK p&p) Deluxe signed and numbered h/b ISBN: 1-84583-103-9

CHILD OF TIME by GEORGE MANN
When Honoré and Emily investigate the bones of a child in the ruins of a collapsed house, they are thrown into a thrilling adventure that takes them from London in 1951 to Venice in 1586 and then forward a thousand years, to the terrifying, devasted London of 2586, ruled over by the sinister Sodality. What is the terrible truth about Emily's forgotten past? What demonic power are the Sodality plotting to reawaken? And who is the mysterious Dr Smith?
All is revealed in the stunning conclusion to the acclaimed *Time Hunter* series.
An adventure in time and space.
£7.99 (+ £1.50 UK p&p) Standard p/b
ISBN: 978-1-84583-104-2
£25.00 (+ £1.50 UK p&p) Deluxe signed and numbered h/b ISBN: 978-1-84583-105-9

TIME HUNTER FILM

DAEMOS RISING by DAVID J HOWE,
DIRECTED BY KEITH BARNFATHER
Daemos Rising is a sequel to both the *Doctor Who* adventure *The Daemons* and to *Downtime*, an earlier drama featuring the Yeti. It is also a prequel of sorts to Telos Publishing's *Time Hunter* series. It stars Miles Richardson as ex-UNIT operative Douglas Cavendish, and Beverley Cressman as Brigadier Lethbridge-Stewart's daughter Kate. Trapped in an isolated cottage, Cavendish thinks he is seeing ghosts. The only person who might understand and help is Kate Lethbridge-Stewart … but when she arrives, she realises that Cavendish is key in a plot to summon the Daemons back to the Earth. With time running out,

Kate discovers that sometimes even the familiar can turn out to be your worst nightmare. Also starring Andrew Wisher, and featuring Ian Richardson as the Narrator.
An adventure in time and space.
£14.00 (+ £2.50 UK p&p) PAL format R4 DVD
Order direct from Reeltime Pictures, PO Box 23435, London SE26 5WU

HORROR/FANTASY

URBAN GOTHIC: LACUNA AND OTHER TRIPS edited by DAVID J HOWE
Tales of horror from and inspired by the *Urban Gothic* televison series. Contributors: Graham Masterton, Christopher Fowler, Simon Clark, Steve Lockley & Paul Lewis, Paul Finch and Debbie Bennett.
£8.00 (+ £1.50 UK p&p) Standard p/b
ISBN: 1-903889-00-6

CAPE WRATH by PAUL FINCH
Death and horror on a deserted Scottish island as an ancient Viking warrior chief returns to life.
£8.00 (+ £1.50 UK p&p) Standard p/b
ISBN: 1-903889-60-X

KING OF ALL THE DEAD by STEVE LOCKLEY & PAUL LEWIS
The king of all the dead will have what is his.
£8.00 (+ £1.50 UK p&p) Standard p/b
ISBN: 1-903889-61-8

ASPECTS OF A PSYCHOPATH by ALASTAIR LANGSTON
The twisted diary of a serial killer.
£8.00 (+ £1.50 UK p&p) Standard p/b
ISBN: 1-903889-63-4

GUARDIAN ANGEL by STEPHANIE BEDWELL-GRIME
Devilish fun as Guardian Angel Porsche Winter loses a soul to the devil …
£9.99 (+ £2.50 UK p&p) Standard p/b
ISBN: 1-903889-62-6

FALLEN ANGEL by STEPHANIE BEDWELL-GRIME
Porsche Winter battles She-Devils on Earth …
£9.99 (+ £2.50 UK p&p) Standard p/b
ISBN: 1-903889-69-3

THE HUMAN ABSTRACT by GEORGE MANN
A future tale of private detectives, AIs, Nanobots, love and death.
£7.99 (+ £1.50 UK p&p) Standard p/b
ISBN: 1-903889-65-0

BREATHE by CHRISTOPHER FOWLER
The Office meets *Night of the Living Dead*.
£7.99 (+ £1.50 UK p&p) Standard p/b
ISBN: 1-903889-67-7
£25.00 (+ £1.50 UK p&p) Deluxe signed and numbered h/b ISBN: 1-903889-68-5

HOUDINI'S LAST ILLUSION by STEVE SAVILE
Can the master illusionist Harry Houdini outwit the dead shades of his past?
£7.99 (+ £1.50 UK p&p) Standard p/b
ISBN: 1-903889-66-9

ALICE'S JOURNEY BEYOND THE MOON by R J CARTER
A sequel to the classic Lewis Carroll tales.
£6.99 (+ £1.50 UK p&p) Standard p/b
ISBN: 1-903889-76-6
£30.00 (+ £1.50 UK p&p) Deluxe signed and numbered h/b ISBN: 1-903889-77-4

APPROACHING OMEGA by ERIC BROWN
A colonisation mission to Earth runs into problems.
£7.99 (+ £1.50 UK p&p) Standard p/b
ISBN: 1-903889-98-7
£30.00 (+ £1.50 UK p&p) Deluxe signed and numbered h/b ISBN: 1-903889-99-5

VALLEY OF LIGHTS by STEPHEN GALLAGHER
A cop comes up against a body-hopping murderer.
£9.99 (+ £2.50 UK p&p) Standard p/b
ISBN: 1-903889-74-X
£30.00 (+ £2.50 UK p&p) Deluxe signed and numbered h/b ISBN: 1-903889-75-8

PARISH DAMNED by LEE THOMAS
Vampires attack an American fishing town.
£7.99 (+ £1.50 UK p&p) Standard p/b
ISBN: 1-84583-040-7

MORE THAN LIFE ITSELF by JOE NASSISE
What would you do to save the life of someone you love?
£7.99 (+ £1.50 UK p&p) Standard p/b
ISBN: 1-84583-042-3

PRETTY YOUNG THINGS by DOMINIC MCDONAGH
A nest of lesbian rave bunny vampires is at large in Manchester. When Chelsey's ex-boyfriend is taken as food, Chelsey has to get out fast.
£7.99 (+ £1.50 UK p&p) Standard p/b
ISBN: 1-84583-045-8

A MANHATTAN GHOST STORY by T M WRIGHT
Do you see ghosts? A classic tale of love and the supernatural.
£9.99 (+ £2.50 UK p&p) Standard p/b
ISBN: 1-84583-048-2

SHROUDED BY DARKNESS: TALES OF TERROR edited by ALISON L R DAVIES
An anthology of tales guaranteed to bring a chill to the spine. This collection has been published to raise money for DebRA, a national charity working on behalf of people with the genetic skin blistering condition, Epidermolysis Bullosa (EB). Featuring stories by: Debbie Bennett, Poppy Z Brite, Simon Clark, Storm Constantine, Peter Crowther, Alison L R Davies, Paul Finch, Christopher Fowler, Neil Gaiman, Gary Greenwood, David J Howe, Dawn Knox, Tim Lebbon, Charles de Lint, Steven Lockley & Paul Lewis, James Lovegrove, Graham Masterton, Richard Christian Matheson, Justina Robson, Mark Samuels, Darren Shan and Michael Marshall Smith. With a frontispiece by Clive Barker and a foreword by Stephen Jones. Deluxe hardback cover by Simon Marsden.
£12.99 (+ £2.50 UK p&p) Standard p/b
ISBN: 1-84583-046-6
£50.00 (+ £2.50 UK p&p) Deluxe signed and numbered h/b ISBN: 978-1-84583-047-2

BLACK TIDE by DEL STONE JR
A college professor and his students find themselves trapped by an encroaching horde of zombies following a waste spillage.
£7.99 (+ £1.50 UK p&p) Standard p/b
ISBN: 978-1-84583-043-4

FORCE MAJEURE by DANIEL O'MAHONY
An incredible fantasy novel. Kay finds herself trapped in a strange city in the Andes … a place where dreams can become reality, and where dragons may reside.
£7.99 (+ £1.50 UK p&p) Standard p/b
ISBN: 978-1-84583-050-2

TV/FILM GUIDES

DOCTOR WHO

THE TELEVISION COMPANION: THE UNOFFICIAL AND UNAUTHORISED GUIDE TO DOCTOR WHO by DAVID J HOWE & STEPHEN JAMES WALKER
Complete episode guide (1963 – 1996) to the popular TV show.
£14.99 (+ £4.75 UK p&p) Standard p/b
ISBN: 1-903889-51-0

THE HANDBOOK: THE UNOFFICIAL AND UNAUTHORISED GUIDE TO THE PRODUCTION OF DOCTOR WHO by DAVID J HOWE, STEPHEN JAMES WALKER and MARK STAMMERS
Complete guide to the making of Doctor Who (1963 – 1996).
£14.99 (+ £4.75 UK p&p) Standard p/b
ISBN: 1-903889-59-6
£30.00 (+ £4.75 UK p&p) Deluxe signed and numbered h/b ISBN: 1-903889-96-0

BACK TO THE VORTEX: THE UNOFFICIAL AND UNAUTHORISED GUIDE TO DOCTOR WHO 2005 by J SHAUN LYON
Complete guide to the 2005 series of Doctor Who starring Christopher Eccleston as the Doctor
£12.99 (+ £2.50 UK p&p) Standard p/b
ISBN: 1-903889-78-2
£30.00 (+ £2.50 UK p&p) Deluxe signed and numbered h/b ISBN: 1-903889-79-0

SECOND FLIGHT: THE UNOFFICIAL AND UNAUTHORISED GUIDE TO DOCTOR WHO 2006 by J SHAUN LYON
Complete guide to the 2006 series of Doctor Who, starring David Tennant as the Doctor
£12.99 (+ £2.50 UK p&p) Standard p/b
ISBN: 1-84583-008-3
£30.00 (+ £2.50 UK p&p) Deluxe signed and numbered h/b ISBN: 1-84583-009-1

THIRD DIMENSION: THE UNOFFICIAL AND UNAUTHORISED GUIDE TO DOCTOR WHO 2007 by STEPHEN JAMES WALKER
Complete guide to the 2007 series of Doctor Who, starring David Tennant as the Doctor
£12.99 (+ £2.50 UK p&p) Standard p/b
ISBN: 978-1-84583-016-8
£30.00 (+ £2.50 UK p&p) Deluxe signed and numbered h/b ISBN: 978-1-84583-017-5

MONSTERS INSIDE: THE UNOFFICIAL AND UNAUTHORISED GUIDE TO DOCTOR WHO 2008 by STEPHEN JAMES WALKER
Complete guide to the 2008 series of *Doctor Who*, starring David Tennant as the Doctor. PUBLISHED DECEMBER 2008
£12.99 (+ £2.50 UK p&p) Standard p/b
ISBN: 978-1-84583-027-4
£30.00 (+ £2.50 UK p&p) Deluxe signed and numbered h/b ISBN: 978-1-84583-028-1

WHOGRAPHS: THEMED AUTOGRAPH BOOK
80 page autograph book with an SF theme
£4.50 (+ £1.50 UK p&p) Standard p/b
ISBN: 1-84583-110-1

TALKBACK: THE UNOFFICIAL AND UNAUTHORISED DOCTOR WHO INTERVIEW BOOK: VOLUME 1: THE SIXTIES edited by STEPHEN JAMES WALKER
Interviews with cast and behind the scenes crew who worked on *Doctor Who* in the sixties
£12.99 (+ £2.50 UK p&p) Standard p/b
ISBN: 1-84583-006-7
£30.00 (+ £2.50 UK p&p) Deluxe signed and numbered h/b ISBN: 1-84583-007-5

TALKBACK: THE UNOFFICIAL AND UNAUTHORISED DOCTOR WHO INTERVIEW BOOK: VOLUME 2: THE SEVENTIES edited by STEPHEN JAMES WALKER
Interviews with cast and behind the scenes crew who worked on *Doctor Who* in the seventies
£12.99 (+ £2.50 UK p&p) Standard p/b
ISBN: 1-84583-010-5
£30.00 (+ £2.50 UK p&p) Deluxe signed and numbered h/b ISBN: 1-84583-011-3

TALKBACK: THE UNOFFICIAL AND UNAUTHORISED DOCTOR WHO INTERVIEW BOOK: VOLUME 3: THE EIGHTIES edited by STEPHEN JAMES WALKER
Interviews with cast and behind the scenes crew who worked on *Doctor Who* in the eighties
£12.99 (+ £2.50 UK p&p) Standard p/b
ISBN: 978-1-84583-014-4
£30.00 (+ £2.50 UK p&p) Deluxe signed and numbered h/b ISBN: 978-1-84583-015-1

HOWE'S TRANSCENDENTAL TOYBOX: SECOND EDITION by DAVID J HOWE & ARNOLD T BLUMBERG
Complete guide to *Doctor Who* Merchandise 1963-2002.
£25.00 (+ £4.75 UK p&p) Standard p/b
ISBN: 1-903889-56-1

HOWE'S TRANSCENDENTAL TOYBOX: UPDATE No 1: 2003 by DAVID J HOWE & ARNOLD T BLUMBERG
Complete guide to *Doctor Who* Merchandise released in 2003.
£7.99 (+ £1.50 UK p&p) Standard p/b
ISBN: 1-903889-57-X

HOWE'S TRANSCENDENTAL TOYBOX: UPDATE No 2: 2004-2005 by DAVID J HOWE & ARNOLD T BLUMBERG
Complete guide to *Doctor Who* Merchandise released in 2004 and 2005. Now in full colour.
£12.99 (+ £1.50 UK p&p) Standard p/b
ISBN: 1-84583-012-1

THE TARGET BOOK by DAVID J HOWE with TIM NEAL
A fully illustrated, large format, full colour history of the Target *Doctor Who* books.
£19.99 (+ £4.75 UK p&p) Large Format p/b
ISBN: 978-1-84583-021-2

TORCHWOOD

INSIDE THE HUB: THE UNOFFICIAL AND UNAUTHORISED GUIDE TO TORCHWOOD SERIES ONE by STEPHEN JAMES WALKER
Complete guide to the 2006 series of *Torchwood*, starring John Barrowman as Captain Jack Harkness
£12.99 (+ £2.50 UK p&p) Standard p/b
ISBN: 978-1-84583-013-7

SOMETHING IN THE DARKNESS: THE UNOFFICIAL AND UNAUTHORISED GUIDE TO TORCHWOOD SERIES TWO by STEPHEN JAMES WALKER
Complete guide to the 2008 series of *Torchwood*, starring John Barrowman as Captain Jack Harkness
£12.99 (+ £2.50 UK p&p) Standard p/b
ISBN: 978-1-84583-024-3
£25.00 (+ £2.50 UK p&p) Deluxe signed and numbered h/b ISBN: 978-1-84583-025-0

BLAKE'S 7

LIBERATION: THE UNOFFICIAL AND UNAUTHORISED GUIDE TO BLAKE'S 7 by ALAN STEVENS & FIONA MOORE
Complete episode guide to the popular TV show. Featuring a foreword by David Maloney
£9.99 (+ £2.50 UK p&p) Standard p/b
ISBN: 1-903889-54-5

SURVIVORS

THE END OF THE WORLD?: THE UNOFFICIAL AND UNAUTHORISED GUIDE TO SURVIVORS by ANDY PRIESTNER & RICH CROSS
Complete guide to Terry Nation's *Survivors*
£12.99 (+ £2.50 UK p&p) Standard p/b
ISBN: 1-84583-001-6

CHARMED

TRIQUETRA: THE UNOFFICIAL AND UNAUTHORISED GUIDE TO CHARMED by KEITH TOPPING
Complete guide to the first seven series of *Charmed*
£12.99 (+ £2.50 UK p&p) Standard p/b
ISBN: 1-84583-002-4

24

A DAY IN THE LIFE: THE UNOFFICIAL AND UNAUTHORISED GUIDE TO 24 by KEITH TOPPING
Complete episode guide to the first season of the popular TV show.
£9.99 (+ £2.50 p&p) Standard p/b
ISBN: 1-903889-53-7

TILL DEATH US DO PART

A FAMILY AT WAR: THE UNOFFICIAL AND UNAUTHORISED GUIDE TO TILL DEATH US DO PART by MARK WARD
Complete guide to the popular TV show. PUBLISHED SEPTEMBER 2008
£12.99 (+ £2.50 p&p) Standard p/b
ISBN: 978-1-84583-031-1

FILMS

A VAULT OF HORROR by KEITH TOPPING
A guide to 80 classic (and not so classic) British Horror Films.
£12.99 (+ £4.75 UK p&p) Standard p/b
ISBN: 1-903889-58-8

BEAUTIFUL MONSTERS: THE UNOFFICIAL AND UNAUTHORISED GUIDE TO THE ALIEN AND PREDATOR FILMS by DAVID McINTEE
A guide to the Alien and Predator Films.
£9.99 (+ £2.50 UK p&p) Standard p/b
ISBN: 1-903889-94-4

ZOMBIEMANIA: 80 MOVIES TO DIE FOR by DR ARNOLD T BLUMBERG & ANDREW HERSHBERGER
A guide to 80 classic zombie films, along with an extensive filmography of over 500 additional titles
£12.99 (+ £4.75 UK p&p) Standard p/b
ISBN: 1-84583-003-2

SILVER SCREAM: VOLUME 1: 40 CLASSIC HORROR MOVIES by STEVEN WARREN HILL
A guide to 40 classic horror films from 1920 to 1941. PUBLISHED OCTOBER 2008.
£12.99 (+ £2.50 UK p&p) Standard p/b
ISBN: 978-1-84583-026-7

SILVER SCREAM: VOLUME 2: 40 CLASSIC HORROR MOVIES by STEVEN WARREN HILL
A guide to 40 classic horror films from 1941 to 1951. PUBLISHED OCTOBER 2008.
£12.99 (+ £2.50 UK p&p) Standard p/b
ISBN: 978-1-84583-029-8

TABOO BREAKERS: 18 INDEPENDENT FILMS THAT COURTED CONTROVERSY AND CREATED A LEGEND by CALUM WADDELL
A guide to 18 films which pushed boundries and broke taboos. PUBLISHED SEPTEMBER 2008.
£12.99 (+ £2.50 UK p&p) Standard p/b
ISBN: 978-1-84583-030-4

IT LIVES AGAIN! HORROR MOVIES IN THE NEW MILLENNIUM by AXELLE CAROLYN
A guide to modern horror films. Large format, full colour throughout. PUBLISHED OCTOBER 2008.
£14.99 (+ £4.75 UK p&p) h/b
ISBN: 978-1-84583-020-5

CRIME

THE LONG, BIG KISS GOODBYE by SCOTT MONTGOMERY
Hardboiled thrills as Jack Sharp gets involved with a dame called Kitty.
£7.99 (+ £1.50 UK p&p) Standard p/b
ISBN: 978-1-84583-109-7

MIKE RIPLEY

Titles in Mike Ripley's acclaimed 'Angel' series of comic crime novels.

JUST ANOTHER ANGEL by MIKE RIPLEY
£9.99 (+ £1.50 UK p&p) Standard p/b
ISBN: 1-84583-106-3
ANGEL TOUCH by MIKE RIPLEY
£9.99 (+ £1.50 UK p&p) Standard p/b
ISBN: 1-84583-107-1
ANGEL HUNT by MIKE RIPLEY
£9.99 (+ £1.50 UK p&p) Standard p/b
ISBN: 1-84583-108-X
ANGEL ON THE INSIDE by MIKE RIPLEY
£12.99 (+ £1.50 UK p&p) Standard p/b
ISBN: 978-1-84583-043-4

HANK JANSON

Classic pulp crime thrillers from the 1940s and 1950s.

TORMENT by HANK JANSON
£5.00 (+ £1.50 UK p&p) Standard p/b
ISBN: 1-903889-80-4
WOMEN HATE TILL DEATH by HANK JANSON
£5.00 (+ £1.50 UK p&p) Standard p/b
ISBN: 1-903889-81-2
SOME LOOK BETTER DEAD by HANK JANSON
£5.00 (+ £1.50 UK p&p) Standard p/b
ISBN: 1-903889-82-0
SKIRTS BRING ME SORROW by HANK JANSON
£5.00 (+ £1.50 UK p&p) Standard p/b
ISBN: 1-903889-83-9
WHEN DAMES GET TOUGH by HANK JANSON
£5.00 (+ £1.50 UK p&p) Standard p/b
ISBN: 1-903889-85-5
ACCUSED by HANK JANSON
£5.00 (+ £1.50 UK p&p) Standard p/b
ISBN: 1-903889-86-3
KILLER by HANK JANSON
£5.00 (+ £1.50 UK p&p) Standard p/b
ISBN: 1-903889-87-1
FRAILS CAN BE SO TOUGH by HANK JANSON
£5.00 (+ £1.50 UK p&p) Standard p/b
ISBN: 1-903889-88-X
BROADS DON'T SCARE EASY by HANK JANSON
£5.00 (+ £1.50 UK p&p) Standard p/b
ISBN: 1-903889-89-8
KILL HER IF YOU CAN by HANK JANSON
£5.00 (+ £1.50 UK p&p) Standard p/b
ISBN: 1-903889-90-1
LILIES FOR MY LOVELY by HANK JANSON
£5.00 (+ £1.50 UK p&p) Standard p/b
ISBN: 1-903889-91-X
BLONDE ON THE SPOT by HANK JANSON
£5.00 (+ £1.50 UK p&p) Standard p/b
ISBN: 1-903889-92-8

Non-fiction
THE TRIALS OF HANK JANSON by STEVE HOLLAND
£5.00 (+ £2.50 UK p&p) Standard p/b
ISBN: 1-903889-84-7

The prices shown are correct at time of going to press. However, the publishers reserve the right to increase prices from those previously advertised without prior notice.

TELOS PUBLISHING
c/o Beech House, Chapel Lane, Moulton, Cheshire, CW9 8PQ, England
Email: orders@telos.co.uk
Web: www.telos.co.uk

To order copies of any Telos books, please visit our website where there are full details of all titles and facilities for worldwide credit card online ordering, as well as occasional special offers, or send a cheque or postal order (UK only) for the appropriate amount (including postage and packing – note that four or more titles are post free in the UK), together with details of the book(s) you require, plus your name and address to the above address. Overseas readers please send two international reply coupons for details of prices and postage rates.